Caesar Triumphant
by R.W. Peake

Also by R.W Peake

Marching with Caesar-Conquest of Gaul
Marching with Caesar-Civil War
Marching with Caesar-Antony and Cleopatra, Parts I & II
Coming in August, 2013:
Marching With Caesar-Rise of Augustus

Critical praise for the Marching with Caesar series:

"Fans of the author will be delighted that Peake's writing has gone from strength to strength in this, the second volume...Peake manages to portray Pullus and all his fellow soldiers with a marvelous feeling of reality quite apart from the star historical name... There's history here, and character, and action enough for three novels, and all of it can be enjoyed even if readers haven't seen the first volume yet. Very highly recommended."

~The Historical Novel Society

"The hinge of history pivoted on the career of Julius Caesar, as Rome's Republic became an Empire, but the muscle to swing that gateway came from soldiers like Titus Pullus. What an amazing story from a student now become the master of historical fiction at its best."

~Professor Frank Holt, University of Houston

Caesar Triumphant
R.W. Peake

Printed in the United States of America
First Printing, 2013

Foreword

While Caesar Triumphant contains characters with whom readers of the “Marching with Caesar” series will be familiar, in its genesis it couldn't be more different than the story I tell of Titus Pullus and his friends. One thing that as an author I strive very hard to achieve is a fidelity to the historical record; when I make deviations, it's usually for a particular reason, and I like to explain why I have changed my narrative in a way that shows it's for a good reason. At least, that's my hope; of the many, many things I have learned in what has been one of the wildest and most enjoyable periods of my life, it's that there is still a burning passion for Rome in the hearts of many people, and some of those have come to the conclusion that they are the most appropriate keepers of the flame. This trait is admirable, but it also comes with a bedrock belief in their version of the thousands upon thousands of events in Roman history, teaching me that it doesn't really matter which version you choose, there are going to be people who insist you got it wrong! My goal has been to keep those "mistakes" to a minimum, and as I said, explain those of which I'm aware because I have made them on purpose.

But this? A story of Julius Caesar invading Japan? In what universe does that happen? It's a fair question, and the only answer I can provide is, "In my universe."

It stems from a deceptively simple question: If the Legions of Rome met the samurai on the battlefield, who would prevail? And while there's actually a show on the cable network channel named Spike, titled "Top Warrior" and one which I enjoy watching, not only did it not pair up their Roman Centurion with a samurai, their show is more focused on a one-on-one matchup. One thing that the more than four years (actually it's continuous) of research into the Roman army I conducted, in order to have Marching With Caesar meet my own standards, has revealed is that, one on one, a Roman Legionary wasn't the most formidable warrior of his age. Nor would he be, I'm very confident, in any age. However, to leave it at that is, at least to me, a supremely unsatisfying conclusion, if only because it doesn't provide anything like what could be called a reasonably accurate guess. What made the Legions of Rome the finest military machine of the ancient world was that they in fact were NOT warriors. Instead, they were cogs in a great and terrible machine that rarely tasted defeat.

That meant that a show like "Top Warrior" wasn't going to suffice for my purposes. No, in order for my mental wanderings to give me any sort of satisfaction, it had to be on a much larger scale, army against army. However, although I was willing to stretch the boundaries of credulity, I do have limits, and there was no circumstance that I could dream up whereby the men of Caesar's Legions faced the samurai of the classical era of Japan, namely the Tokugawa Shogunate, without using the convention of time travel. And that, dear reader, I simply couldn't bring myself to do.

Which got me thinking, and like many of my thoughts, what resulted has turned into this book. What we know of Caesar includes his fascination with Alexander; the scene where he weeps at the foot of Alexander's statue was a powerful one in my mind. We also know that Caesar was to embark on his conquest of Parthia, some sources cite the day after his assassination, so March 16th, to avenge the death of his friend and former Triumvir, Marcus Crassus. But what would he have done if he had achieved his goal? I understand that there's no indication in anything we've found in the form of primary sources he entertained any idea of continuing eastward, but frankly I don't think it takes a huge stretch of the imagination to think that he might indeed have pushed onwards, with the goal of at least matching the record of Alexander. After all, comparatively speaking, by this point Rome was more powerful and had more resources than Alexander had, even with his Hellenic League.

Besides, if Caesar hadn't kept going, then he wouldn't have reached the spot where Caesar Triumphant opens, on the Korean Peninsula, staring across the water.

Which brings us to the other huge problem in such a narrative, and this is another area where I beg the indulgence of the reader. In order to bridge the huge gap in time and technology between Caesar's time and when Tokugawa Ieyasu ruled Japan, my answer was to endow the inhabitants of the islands with the characteristics that I believe were exemplified by the code of *bushido* and the society from which the code sprang. Hopefully I will be forgiven for giving my Wa the appellation of "proto-samurai". My Wa have the unflinching courage and obedience to authority, and the phenomenal skills which have made the samurai justly famous, but otherwise I realize I have been more vague in my descriptions and underlying context than readers have come to expect in Marching With Caesar.

Part of this vagueness is intentional, but I must also add that, comparatively speaking, the historical record that is available for the same stretch of time that is so abundant for Rome of the Late Republic is correspondingly scarce when it comes to Japan. Granted, I didn't delve nearly as deeply and with as much rigor as I did when it came to the research I did for Marching With Caesar, but what I have tried to do is be somewhat accurate in my descriptions of the lives of the people. That being said, I am prepared for the probability that there will be some readers who are more familiar with this period of Japanese history to let me know that I've gotten it wrong, and for this I offer a preemptive apology. All I can say is that it came from a good place.

Ultimately, my goal for Caesar Triumphant is simple; I wanted to write something that posed an interesting "What if" while providing a reader with something that would at the very least entertain them. If it gets you thinking along the same lines that sent me down this road, then that's all that I can ask.

Finally, I want to take this time to thank someone who has become not only one of my biggest fans and supporters, but a great friend, Ute St. Clair. We began communicating through my blog that forms the basis for this book, and not only was she extremely enthusiastic in her enjoyment of Caesar Triumphant, she is the person responsible for turning this from a series of slightly disjointed blog posts, into the polished, hopefully seamless story that you are about to read. She volunteered for this role, and one of the best parts of our collaboration is that she is extremely conversant with Rome in general, and Caesar in particular. In fact, over the process of editing this project, we enjoyed many a spirited debate over a number of areas when it came to Gaius Julius Caesar, and I am extremely grateful, even when we didn't agree. She made this story better than it was when she first stumbled onto it on the Internet, and in the process has actually taught this grammar savant a number of things, including the proper use of the subjunctive!

So Ute, thank you. And to the readers, I hope you enjoy Caesar Triumphant as much as I enjoyed telling the story.

Table of Contents

Prologue

Even for a man of the prodigious energy of Gaius Julius Caesar, this day promised to be one of the busiest in a career filled with sleepless nights and long days. It didn't help that he was roused even earlier than he planned, because of the restless thrashing about of Calpurnia. By his estimate, he had barely been asleep a full watch when he was awakened, although he wasn't sure whether it was from the movement of their bed as she waved her arms, or the tortured moans that escaped her lips. Rousing himself, he looked over at her with concern and was forced to dodge one of her arms as they flailed wildly about in a clear attempt to ward off whatever demons were assaulting her in the recesses of her subconscious. If this had been the first time, Caesar would have been extremely alarmed, but it had become an unfortunately regular occurrence, and what made it more disturbing—at least for his wife—is that this dream was always the same. He knew from bitter experience that waking her, when she was like this, was the worst thing he could do, so, heaving a sigh, he decided that since the chances of more sleep was practically non-existent, he might as well get started on what was going to be a challenging day. So much to do, he thought, here on these Ides of March, the day before he was to leave to meet his army for the Parthian campaign. Perhaps Calpurnia had done him a favor, although there was a part of him that was honest with himself: leaving before Calpurnia was awake would allow him to avoid a scene that had become quite tiresome, as his wife begged him essentially to retire from public life. And all because of some silly dreams! No! He was Caesar, and Caesar wasn't subject to such superstitious nonsense. Still, if it had been just Calpurnia's dreams, they would have been relatively easy to dismiss, even if it caused his wife distress. He couldn't say he loved her, exactly, but he did hold her in very high regard, and he did have affection for her. But it wasn't just Calpurnia's dreams, Caesar was forced to acknowledge, however grudgingly, and only to himself. No, there were many other signs, rumors, and whispers of plots by the jealous mediocrities who were, unfortunately, members of his own class, at least by birth. Still, Caesar refused to show that he feared any man, or any group of men; to do so would be unthinkable, especially for a man who had walked into the maelstrom of missiles at Munda and emerged completely unscathed. Nevertheless, the knowledge that there were plots was there, even if he forced it into the recesses of his mind.

Before he could leave his villa—the official residence of the Pontifex Maximus that he had occupied for many years by this point—like all members of his class, it was customary for Caesar to meet with some of his clients, who always gathered at the crack of dawn to press their petitions with their patron. It may have been customary, but no Roman of his time—and or of the past for that matter—had as many clients as Gaius Julius Caesar. That meant that the vestibule of his residence was always jammed full of men, most of them waving scrolls that contained the details of their particular woes or requests, all of them shouting his name. It was always chaotic, but it was even more than usually so on this day, as every man there knew that the Dictator For Life was leaving for the wastes of Parthia. Consequently, there was a din that Caesar was sure would rouse his wife, so while it made him angry to do so, he made the decision to conduct his daily audience as he walked to what was going to be the most important part of his day and probably one of the more crucial days of his time as Dictator. The fact that the Senate wasn't meeting in the Curia—it had burned down and had yet to be rebuilt—forced the body of men who ostensibly ruled Rome to meet in the only building large enough to hold their newly inflated numbers, Pompey's Theater—and the delicious irony of that location wasn't lost on Caesar. In all honesty,, he had what men like Cicero would call a perverse streak that colored his sense of humor, and perhaps it *was* perverse to exercise his role as First Man in Rome at the very feet of the Roman he had defeated for that title. But Caesar was also practical, and there simply was no better place to hold a meeting that would undoubtedly be attended by every Senator currently in Rome.

With his lictors clearing the way, shoving the mass of men who were still arriving to present their cases to the Dictator, Caesar walked slowly from his residence in the heart of the Roman Forum, surrounded by his petitioners. His pace was leisurely, but this was not his norm; the combination of the early start and the sheer number of men with requests to be heard meant that he couldn't move with his usual speed. Using his lictors, Caesar would signal to them to allow one man at a time to approach him and walk at his side, where he would have a very short time to make his case. Although almost all of the supplicants had come bearing scrolls containing the particulars of their grievances or pleas, Caesar rarely looked at any of them, preferring instead to listen briefly, then ask one or two questions that always demonstrated that he had, indeed, been paying attention. Some of the cases were straightforward, so Caesar was able to adjudicate them with a quick aside to one of the half-dozen secretaries trailing in his wake—each of them responsible for a particular area of their master's concerns—whereupon the scribe would hastily jot down the notes Caesar dictated. Other matters, however, did require more of his attention, so with these, Caesar slowed even further, giving him time to ask more questions and, in one or two cases, actually deigning to look very quickly at the proffered scroll, ignoring the hopeful look on the petitioner's face as he took this to be a positive sign of his patron's interest. It was in this manner that what was a crowd totaling some two hundred — exclusively male—Romans made their way along the Via Sacra, the main thoroughfare that passed through the Forum, heading in a roughly northerly direction towards the base of the Capitoline Hill, the most sacred of the seven hills of Rome.

Just before Caesar and his entourage reached the foot of the Capitoline, the crowd—growing in number, as the ranks of the petitioners swelled with the early risers of the city, drawn to the sight of the most powerful man in Rome—now numbered several hundred. It was always this way with Caesar: as reviled as he was by some members of his own class, he was adored and revered by that teeming mass of people that their betters sneeringly referred to as the Head Count, when they weren't just calling them "the mob". Many among the crowd called out his name, which only added to the commotion and din, all of them hoping that he would at least look in their direction, or better yet, acknowledge their hail with a wave, giving them something to tell their children and grandchildren about: the day that the greatest man in Rome actually acknowledged their existence. And Caesar, knowing as he did that the source of his power rested on the twin pillars of these nameless, faceless people and the Legions, whose ranks were filled by men of the same class, took more of his time in acknowledging these shouts and waves than he did with his petitioners, even stopping from time to time to share a quick word with a butcher or a tanner. And some of them, much to their astonishment and delight, he actually knew by name! The fact that his recall of them was just another way for Caesar to demonstrate his most formidable and useful gift, the astonishing memory that never forgot a fact, face or name, didn't matter to them at all. That he remembered them was all they cared about. Yet, even as Caesar did this, there was a part of him that was untouched by this tumult, and was devoting only a portion of that gifted intellect to the activity around him. It was always this way, he thought, when they reached this part of the Forum, because to the right, at the corner of the Vicus Iugarius and Via Sacra, was the partially completed Basilica he had commissioned to honor his daughter Julia, now dead for almost a decade. Even now, after so much time, he felt a familiar tightness in his chest at the loss of his firstborn child, because as fond as he may have been of Caesarion, his child by Cleopatra, Julia was not only pure Roman, she had also been a beautiful, captivating child that had grown into a woman with even more wonderful qualities about her. While her marriage to Pompey Magnus had been arranged for strictly political considerations—as all marriages of the upper classes were—Caesar had been both relieved and happy to see that she had been genuinely happy in her marriage. Although Caesar would never say it, he had personally never really understood how his beautiful daughter had been able to look at Pompey—who had long since passed into the land of the middle-aged man, with the receding hair, jowls and thickening waist, something that Caesar himself hadn't suffered from—and seen something to love in him. It was just another example of how silly women could be about such things, he mused. Shaking himself from his thoughts, inwardly at least, he stopped at the corner of the two streets. However, this was prearranged, and was his signal to his lictors that his audience was now over. This was always the most irritating part of his day, because some men refused to take the hint and disperse on their own, forcing the lictors to muscle them away from their charge. It was one of the times, when Caesar was acutely aware of appearances, understanding that his enemies pointed to this simple exercise of extricating himself as an example of haughtiness and as a sign that he believed himself to be above the rest of them. The fact that, to one degree or another, every one of Caesar's rivals did essentially the same thing—albeit with a much smaller crowd and in the privacy of their own villas—was something his enemies universally ignored. Dispersing the crowd took some doing, more than normally, and although Caesar understood why this was the case, it was still trying his patience. He needed at least a few moments of solitude, as he made his way around the base of the Capitoline to the Campus Martius, where Pompey's Theater was located so that he could marshal his thoughts.

Once the way was cleared, Caesar resumed walking, but as much as he had on his mind, when he spotted a lone figure, squatting in his accustomed spot—where there was a small street off the Vicus Iugarius that led to the Velabrum—he couldn't resist the urge to have a little fun. Somewhat unusually, Caesar didn't know the man's name, but that was because, as far as he knew, nobody knew it. He was just referred to as The Seer, because of the way he made his living, soliciting passersby with offers to tell their future. For some time now, The Seer had called out to Caesar, every single time he saw him, the same prediction he had first made several months earlier. And since today was the day about which Caesar had been warned by The Seer, and since the day had dawned bright and clear, Caesar decided it was time to take The Seer down a notch.

"Good morning, Seer," Caesar called out genially, raising his voice, so that not just his entourage, but also anyone within earshot could hear, knowing that what he was about to say would be known through every precinct of Rome by sunset. "You said that the Ides of March would see my doom, but here I am! The Ides have come, and," he made a point to peer down at himself, affecting surprise before he returned his gaze back to the squatting man, giving him a grin, "I'm all in one piece!"

As he expected, this brought a hearty round of laughter, not just from his lictors and scribes, but from the dozens of men nearby. For his part, The Seer didn't seem to be in the least bit embarrassed, and, in fact, smiled back at Caesar, although he said nothing, at least at first. Caesar had already turned away and was resuming his walk, when The Seer called out, "Yes, Caesar. You're right, the Ides have come. But they're not finished yet."

Although he heard The Seer's response, Caesar didn't turn back around, not wanting to prolong the exchange. And yet, despite continuing on his way, something was...wrong. Shaking his head, Caesar chided himself for allowing the superstition of a beggar in the Forum to burrow its way into his own brain, so to show that he had dismissed the thought, he lengthened his stride.

Then, without knowing how, Caesar found himself coming to a stop. Turning around, he could still view The Seer watching him calmly, his face expressionless. And Caesar would wonder for the rest of his days how it happened, but he began walking again. This time, however, it was back towards the Forum, away from Pompey's Theater, and away from his death.

Chapter 1

Gaius Julius Caesar sat astride his horse, staring across the expanse of water at the dark line of land on the horizon, feeling every one of his 65 years. He supposed it was natural that he would be reflective at this moment, staring at what he was told was the end of the world. The people in this part of the world called what he was staring at the Land of Wa, supposedly populated with a race even more fierce and martial than the armies Caesar and his men had faced to this point. Of course, he thought wryly, he had heard that refrain more than once in his career: it always seemed that the next land over the horizon contained the fiercest and most bloodthirsty warriors. Sometimes, he admitted to himself, it was even true. But now, there was just this last obstacle, this last land to see and to give the people in it a taste of what Rome was about.

Rome. Just the name gave him a harsh stab of longing in his heart, the homeland he hadn't seen and in whose name he had endured and done so much. No, be honest with yourself, Gaius—if not with anyone else, at least with yourself. All that you've done has been to glorify YOUR name, not that of Rome's. But if he hadn't been born a Roman, he mused, would he even be here at this point in time, in this place, making history? So, Rome would share in the glory just as much as he and those who shared his name. That thought brought another twinge, albeit of a different type and for different reasons. Despite trying to keep his mind focused on the moment, the thought forced its way into his consciousness, a glimmer of a face, a name—but that was all, before he ruthlessly pushed it back into the recesses of his mind. Caesarion, his son by Cleopatra, now almost 14 years old and, as far as he knew back in Alexandria with his mother, after accompanying Caesar and his army for a few months, before events became too dangerous for Caesar to be comfortable with allowing him to stay. Oh, how he missed that boy! But he had done the right thing; he knew it in his bones, and it did free him of one worry.

Then there were his other sons, or those that remained, for that is how he thought of the men of his army. Even if some of them are almost as old as I, he laughed to himself. Because, no matter what their age in years, in so many ways the men of the Legions were like children, needing the firm hand of a loving, but harsh, father to make sure they behaved themselves. Not that there were many men left of those who started with him so many years before! He turned in his saddle to look back at the mass of men behind him, most of them stretched out in the spot, where they had halted. All of them were brown as nuts, although by this point a good number of them came by that color naturally and did not need the sun to do the work for them. In fact, a substantial number of these had the yellowish cast and almond eyes of the people of Han. Supposedly the people across the water looked similar to the Han , but only time would tell, if that was the truth. Yes, he acknowledged sadly, there were precious few proud Roman noses in that mass of flesh behind him, but those that were there belonged to the fighting core of his army, and he wouldn't have given up one of these men for 100 of the fiercest fighters he had come across on this campaign. Even so, he was thankful that the Roman contingent seemed to have settled down and accepted their lot; it had been almost a year since the last attempted mutiny, and that had been quelled only when Caesar had pointed out to them that their chances of making it back to their homes without the protection of the larger army was nonexistent. No, they were all in this together, and whether they were grasping each other's hands in a bond of friendship and sense of duty, or because they were chained together like galley slaves really did not matter at this point. They would either succeed together, or perish together.

Now he would be calling on these sons for one last effort, although he knew better than to describe it as such, since he had used that reason too many times. But it seemed that there was always one last river to cross, or gulf, or inland sea. Caesar had learned more about what it took to transport an army by water than he ever thought possible; and secretly, he was as sick of ocean voyages as the men, even when they were better than the alternatives. For perhaps the thousandth time, he thanked the gods for the contents of Ptolemy's library in Alexandria and those diaries, charts, and maps he had managed to locate and take out of the great library, before that regrettable incident, when he had been under siege and the fire had gotten out of hand, consuming a treasure trove of knowledge. It was only with the vital pieces of information found in the rescued library that he had been able to avoid the mistakes of Alexander, bypassing the harsh mountains of the Hindu Kush for the more southerly, albeit longer route to this shore. Yes, the men had endured great hardships crossing the vast deserts, the privation almost overwhelming even Caesar's prodigious capacity for planning. He had to bring hundreds, no, thousands of camels, their only cargo nothing but precious skins of water. Still, it had been a close-run thing, and was the first major crisis of Caesar's grand campaign. To this day, deep down in his bones, he believed that he, and by extension the army, had survived only because his famous luck had held. That luck, Caesar's luck, had become as much of a talisman against misfortune to the men as any of the gods they prayed to, even those they had adopted, worshiped by the inhabitants encountered during their passage across the vast lands lying to the west behind them.

Even now, he had to laugh at his own hubris, to decide on an act so audacious that tongues were wagging about it years later. Instead of moving his massive army, ensconced aboard the largest fleet ever assembled, by hugging the coast all the way around to Alexandria, he had gambled it all by ordering the fleet to take the most direct route, straight across Our Sea. Individual ships and small fleets had braved the open sea before, but never before had a flotilla of more than a thousand ships done so, and done it with a loss of only ten ships. Ten! That passage had planted the seed, a seed that had been nurtured by Caesar and watered by more examples of the gods' favor for him and his cause, until it was now blossomed into a full-blown faith. In fact, Caesar was aware that some of the men had surreptitiously set up shrines with clay figurines made in his likeness, worshiping him as a god. But he had learned from Alexander's mistakes, and not only discouraged such practice, but actually executed a half-dozen men caught worshiping him, as an example that he was sincere in his statement that he was not a god, but a man. However, that was a couple years before, and he had been walking on an ever-narrowing razor's edge between mortality and divinity, knowing that the men obeyed so readily, because in their heart they believed him a god. He would need that faith in him now more than ever, if he were to be successful, because Caesar was going to sail across this narrow passage, and he was going to see this Land of Wa for himself. And more importantly, they were going to see him. And his army.

Titus Pullus and Sextus Scribonius, Centurions of Caesar's 10th Legion, sat in Pullus' tent, discussing the orders they had just received from Caesar.

"The men aren't going to like it much," Sextus commented, as he sipped at the cup of beverage Titus had provided. He knew that it wasn't the fault of his Primus Pilus that it was this disgustingly tepid and weak drink the Han called "chai", but, oh, how he longed for some Falernian. Even some of that abominable rice wine the Han drank would be better than this, he reflected, almost missing Pullus' reply.

"They don't have to like it, they just have to do it," his Primus Pilus said, staring moodily into his own cup, his thoughts of both the larger question Scribonius raised and the smaller issue of beverage choice running along almost identical lines as those of his Secundus Pilus Prior and best friend.

"And I haven't heard them doing much more than complaining so far, have you?"

Scribonius shook his head. "So far all they've been doing is moaning. I haven't heard a whisper of anything more serious." He looked up and gave his commander a pointed stare, making sure he looked Pullus in the eyes, as he finished, "But that doesn't mean it won't happen. Especially, the longer we wait here in this place."

That was the nub of the problem, really, mused Titus. The men had become so accustomed to Caesar's decisions always working out, as long as they weren't given a lot of time to think. As he thought about it, he realized that almost every attempted mutiny or uprising had come about, after the army had stayed in place for more than a couple of weeks, at least if it was not winter camp. Now they were stuck here waiting for the fleet that had transported them to the western side of this large peninsula, while they marched across it, as the fleet made its way down the coast and back up to the eastern side to meet the army. This fleet, now a mishmash of vessels, much like the composition of the Legions, was the only way to get to the island nation the Han called the Land of Wa. As far as Titus was concerned, he didn't care, why it was so important to Caesar to make this passage and possibly to face another fight against people defending their land. Because Caesar wished it—that was enough for him, and was a prime reason Titus Pullus had risen through the ranks and been named Primus Pilus at a relatively young age. That, and the fact that by an accident of birth, he was born larger and stronger than almost any man, not just in the armies of Rome, but in all the nations they had met. He couldn't help being born that way and, in fact, it had caused quite a bit of anguish in his life, since his large size had essentially killed his mother when she bore him, an event his father never let him forget about. Their hatred for each other had led to Titus' enlistment in the army a year earlier than at the minimum age of 17, aided by his large size and his father's eagerness to be rid of his only son. Titus had found a home in the army, and had been recognized by Caesar very early on, in the first campaign the then-Praetor had conducted in Lusitania some 27 years before. The reality was that Titus Pullus was one of Caesar's men through and through, and he made no apologies for it. This didn't mean there weren't times that being Caesar's man wasn't a trial, and this was one of them.

But while Titus appreciated Sextus' words of caution, he wasn't particularly worried about the possibility of trouble. In his opinion, the men had resigned themselves to their fates, and had more faith in Caesar's luck and—more importantly—they absolutely believed in their general's divinity in a way the men of Alexander never had. Even so, he admitted, if only to himself, following a god could be exceedingly difficult. So he took his best friend's words of caution with a measure of seriousness and resolved to himself that he would keep his eyes and ears open. However, his biggest concern right now was the more practical problems posed by the composition of his Legion, and it was this subject he wanted to discuss with the commander of his Second Cohort. Setting down his cup, Titus asked Scribonius the real question he was worried about:

"How's the new dilectus coming?"

Scribonius made a face, causing Pullus to laugh.

"About like one would expect, I suppose," Scribonius finally said, the grimace still on his lined face. "As usual, it's the language that's the biggest problem, but I have to admit that these Han bastards that Yuan gave us learn languages faster than anyone I've ever run into. They've been helping with this last bunch. The Gayans are some backwards bastards, but they can fight."

"I'm more worried about how they integrate with the rest of the Legion and how quickly they learn our commands," Pullus replied. "We both know that Caesar isn't going to wait any longer than he absolutely has to. My gut tells me the fleet will be here in less than a week, and I don't see him waiting more than a day, before he loads us up and heads over there to face those Wa barbarians."

And that was the challenge facing Titus Pullus and all the other Centurions of Caesar's armies. Every Legion in Caesar's command was a Roman Legion in name only. In the 10th, for example, less than a quarter of its ranks was filled by Roman citizens, and more than half of that number consisted of men raised in a second dilectus drawn from the African provinces early in this campaign. The men of Titus' and Sextus' own enlistment, those men who enlisted in Scallabis back when then-Praetor Gaius Caesar had formed the Legion, numbered barely 10 percent of the remaining Legion. But as much as Caesar valued these men, he did not value them nearly as much as Titus and Sextus did, so it was this core they relied on very heavily to accomplish the tasks that had become almost second nature. For despite the Legions being a polyglot mass of nations and races, their identity, and most importantly, their command structure and training, were thoroughly Roman, grounded in the traditions and practices a man like Cincinnatus would recognize even now. The men were still organized in tent sections, and Titus, along with the other Primi Pili, took great pains to ensure that every tent section contained at least one Roman. However, there was another lesson that had been learned, at great cost, barely more than 3 years into this great trek, and this was that restricting the officer ranks to only Romans was a recipe for insurrection. And, as always, Caesar was quick to learn from his mistakes, so that there were now Tribunes, Centurions, Optios and tent section Sergeants who would have caused a respectable Roman matron to run screaming for her life, sure that there was a barbarian horde who had slaughtered a Roman Legion and stolen their uniforms! If, Pullus thought, any of us ever live long enough to see Rome again and march in a triumph. But what a triumph it would be! Titus knew that it was this thought that kept the Roman contingent going, believing that Caesar's godly powers would protect them long enough to survive what would surely go down, not just in Roman history, but in human history, as the greatest exploit of any type ever known. And, he reflected, it had actually been several months since the last Roman had died, but Titus suspected that this had more to do with the Han physicians that Caesar had persuaded to join the army than Caesar's divine protection. Like all Romans, he had been profoundly skeptical about anyone claiming knowledge of the healing arts, but these

Han doctors had made not just the Greeks, but also the medicine men from the Indus appear as charlatans and half-wits. As well-off as they were in that respect, and as skilled as they were, Titus Pullus suspected that their skills would be challenged more than ever with this last expedition.

Pushing that thought out of his mind, Titus returned to the topic he and Sextus were discussing.

"Do you think that Mardonius is ready to be Optio?" Pullus asked, referring to one of the non-Roman additions to the Legion, a Parthian who had joined, albeit reluctantly, but who had proven to be a superb Legionary, picking up the customs and language of his conqueror.

Scribonius considered for a moment, then replied, "I think he is. His Latin has improved, and there's no questioning his courage. He's a solid man, and I think he'll rise to the challenge of leading such a motley group of misfits and craven bastards that's ever marched under the standard."

Pullus grunted, which Scribonius knew was a sign that he agreed with the assessment. It was amazing, to both of them, if the truth were known, how well the integration of so many different people into the Legions had gone, but it served as proof that fighting men were essentially the same, no matter the color of their skin. Of course, there were cultural differences that had to be accounted for: Titus found it impossible to keep track of the deities his men worshiped, but when boiled down to its essence, warrior culture seemed to be always the same. Fighting men want to be led by a general who brings them victory, and in Caesar they had such a general. Through thousands of skirmishes, and probably in excess of 200 battles, Titus couldn't remember the last time they had tasted defeat, and even their defeats proved to be temporary. Gergovia, which had seemed so devastating a loss, was now a distant memory and barely registered as a defeat now, Titus mused. Now, here he and Sextus sat, in a tent, many thousands of miles away and some 20 years after that fight, and they were talking about essentially the same thing: the men. Always the men. For it was their strong right arms on which success or failure rode, on their ability to impose Caesar's will on this last race, the people of Wa. And Titus Pullus, as he always had, would do everything to ensure that his general could rely on the 10th Legion, whether they were Romans or not.

Chapter 2

Of course it would be pissing rain, Titus Pullus thought sourly, as he watched the tedious boarding process taking place in the darkness of the watch before midnight. The men were fully kitted, the rain making them gleam in the light of the sputtering torches, as errant rays bounced off helmets and armor. Over the sound of the waves lapping against the sides of the ships and posts of the pier from which they were loading was the underlying hum of men talking. None of them, Titus included, liked sea voyages, no matter how many such excursions the veterans of Caesar's army had made to that point. How many was it, he wondered idly, as his ears tried to filter out the gibberish of the Gayan, Han, Pandyan, Parthian and the gods knew what other languages, in order to listen to the commands of his Centurions who were supervising the loading process. Despite the requirement that every non-Roman in Caesar's army learn all the basic commands and words needed for their duties in Latin, there was no such restriction on their speech, when they were gathered together in moments like these. It might have made the men more comfortable, but it made it much more difficult to understand what was going on, Titus was sure, and there were always mishaps, when embarking men on board transport vessels. Someone was bound to lose his balance going up the gangway or get too close to the edge of the pier, and a friend would accidentally bump them, and into the water they would go. Sometimes, it wasn't an accident; Titus was well aware that this was a favored way some men chose to settle scores, so to forestall such an event happening in his Legion, he had ordered the Optios from each Century to maintain a vigil at the edge of the pier, where their men were boarding. Despite these precautions, Titus knew that at some point it was extremely likely there would be a splash that sounded over and above the noise the waves produced, followed quickly by a shout alerting those nearby that a man had gone into the water. From that moment, it was critical that he be fished out, the rescuers using a long pole with a sort of hoop attached at the end that the man could grab onto, when it was thrust down into the spot, where he was last seen. Even so, there was an even chance that he would drown, rather than have the presence of mind to reach out in the murky water around him to find the pole he knew would be coming. It was only the experience of dozens of these types of operations that had taught the men of Caesar's army what needed to be done, if there was going to be any chance of rescuing a fallen man. Exactly how many voyages have we made, Titus wondered?

"They always clump together, don't they?" Scribonius' question jerked Titus from his reverie, and he turned to see the dark outline of his friend, his helmet gleaming from the combination of torchlight and rain.

Titus knew what Scribonius meant, without asking, because as usual, his friend was right. The new men from the last dilectus were, indeed, huddled together, seeking the solace of the familiar in an extremely alien and unfamiliar situation. Some of the Gayan in this draft had been fishermen, Titus knew, but an equal number had been poor farmers, and he imagined that the farmers were now seeking out the counsel of countrymen more familiar with the world of ships than they themselves were.

"One or two fights will sort them out," was Titus' only comment, and in this he was also correct.

Before these Gayan men were blooded, it was only natural that they cling to each other. But once the man next to you, who was more likely to be a Han, Pandya, or even a Roman, saved your bacon, barriers like language and culture wouldn't seem so important. This was something Caesar had known, despite the downright refusal of his Legates, men like Hirtius, Pollio, and even old Ventidius, formidable men in their own right, to accept this idea. It had been one of the first crises of many, Titus remembered, when it had become apparent that the only way to achieve Caesar's ambitious goals was by replacing the men lost in the ranks. By the time this was obvious to everyone, which even Titus acknowledged was much, much later than Caesar's recognition of this fact, they were well into the Parthian empire. It had been the last battle against Pharnaces that had precipitated the decision, and a whole winter was spent dealing with this new reality. But Hirtius and the rest of the Legates—and Tribunes and Centurions, if the truth were known—had insisted that the only way integration would work was by requiring the men to essentially forget their former ways, down to their language and customs. They must become Romans in everything but blood, almost every officer argued, or they will fracture the army. But Caesar was undeterred, and he was proven right. Now, all they needed to cement the bonds so essential to an army was a good, bloody fight.

In the briefing conducted by Caesar, they were told that the crossing would take more than a day, and judging from the chop, Titus thought that was optimistic. What nobody could tell any of the Centurions was the kind of reception they would receive. Pullus could only hope that it wouldn't be like Britannia, or any of the half-dozen opposed landings the army had made to that point. In some ways, heavy seas were something of a blessing, because they kept the men occupied by being miserable and not dwelling on what awaited them. Titus was past being seasick, but he abhorred the idea of being cooped up on a ship, at the mercy of strange men and even stranger gods that controlled matters on the water in this neck of the world. Perhaps the worst part was once the Legion was loaded and they had to wait for the rest of the army out in the harbor that served as the embarkation point: then they would be sitting out in the water, bobbing about, but making no headway toward their landing site, so it would not be long before the first man would vomit, which invariably created a chain reaction of retching that could be heard on shore.

"Which Cohorts are loaded?" Titus asked his scribe, standing next to him and almost swallowed up by the regulation sagum he was wearing to ward off the rain. Even without the cloak, they would have made a ludicrous sight, because Diocles, Titus Pullus' scribe, body slave, and chief clerk of the Legion, stood more than a foot shorter than his master and was very slight in build. But what Diocles lacked in bulk and height, he more than made up for in intellect and ability to keep track of all the thousand details involved in running the Legion. And while it wasn't something that either Titus or Diocles spoke about to anyone else, their relationship had long since passed from master and slave to that of friends. But as much as Titus trusted Scribonius and confided in him, there were still things only Diocles knew.

"The Fourth through the Tenth," Diocles answered immediately, not having to consult the wax tablet he carried everywhere with him. "The Third is loading now and should be finished in less than a sixth of a watch."

Titus merely grunted in reply, understanding that it was time for him to rouse his Century, and for the other Centurions to do the same with the rest of the First Cohort. Turning back to Scribonius, he gave his Second Cohort commander the order to make ready to embark. Before Scribonius left, he offered Titus his hand, which the Primus Pilus accepted.

"See you onshore," Sextus said with a smile.

"The gods and the Wa people willing," Titus smiled back.

"They're not going to stop us," Scribonius laughed, as he walked away, prompting Titus to call after him.

"Who's not going to stop us? The gods or the Wa?"

Scribonius stopped and, despite the dim light, Titus saw the same smile on his friend's face.

"Why, the Wa of course. The gods wouldn't dare turn on one of their own, would they?"

Scribonius spoke these words loudly enough for the men immediately nearby to hear, and they let out a cheer of agreement, so despite being irritated at his friend, Titus had to laugh. Both of them were secretly amused at the men's belief that their general was a god, but they also knew how deadly serious it was to express anything resembling disbelief or mockery of that idea in front of the rankers. Only Titus knew that Scribonius was being facetious, but it still made him nervous, when his friend uttered such things outside the privacy of either of their tents.

Giving Scribonius a wave of dismissal, Titus returned his attention to the dark bulk of the men of his Century, all of them sitting huddled in groups under their cloaks, rigged as makeshift shelters, so they could continue their dice games uninterrupted by the weather.

"All right, you lazy *cunni*," Titus roared. "Get your thumbs out of your asses and get on your feet. Our turn to board is coming up, and I'll flay the man who makes the rest of the army wait. That might be fine for other Legions, but not for the 10th!"

Titus was pleased to see the reaction of the men, as they scrambled to pack up their dice and wine flasks and climb to their feet. Even after all these years, Titus thought, they're still scared of me. And that's a good thing.

In a manner that had become accepted as normal by most of the army, the crossing to the Land of Wa went smoothly, with only minor discomfort from seas heavy enough to make the weaker stomachs rebel, but not threaten to swamp any of the transports. The landing went even better, the only opposition coming in the form of a handful of frightened natives who, at least at first, could only openly gawk at the sight of men leaping over the sides of ships rowed ashore onto the beach. First ashore were, of course, the *signiferi,* followed by the Optios and Centurions, who moved into their pre-assigned spots to present a front prepared for any reception the natives might care to give them. Fortunately for the Wa fishermen—for that is what the natives were—with no martial ability or inclination, the sight of such quick organization was more than enough to deter them from attacking and committing suicide. Instead, as soon as they had at least a basic sense of what was happening, that these strange figures coming from the sea were clearly warriors of some type, they turned tail and fled as fast as their feet would carry them, back to the small village, less than a mile away, from which they had come.

"They run faster than rabbits," Publius Vellusius, *Gregarius* of the last section of the First Century, Second Cohort, laughed at the sight of the heels of the barely clad natives running in terror.

"Wouldn't you run, if you saw us coming?" Scribonius asked, although he was as amused at the sight as Vellusius, and hoped it boded well for this operation. Normally, a ranker wouldn't have felt free to banter with his Centurion, particularly a Pilus Prior, the leader of the entire Cohort, but Vellusius was a special case. He, Scribonius, and Titus Pullus had enlisted in the *dilectus* that had birthed the 10th Legion, and had, in fact, been in the same tent for the first parts of their respective careers. While Pullus' rise had been dizzying in its height and rapidity and Scribonius had displayed the characteristics needed to qualify as a Centurion in Caesar's army, Vellusius had neither the ability nor the aspiration to such lofty heights. He was perfectly content with his lot, and was one of the steady, reliable men who form the backbone of any fighting unit worth anything. The very fact of his survival, ten years into this campaign and 27 years under the standard, was a tribute to his fighting ability, and he was one of the most-respected rankers, not just in the Second Cohort, but the entire Legion, even among the non-Romans.

Pullus was ashore, as well, bellowing at the Centurions of not just his Cohort but of the rest of the Legion to hurry the men into their spots. In Pullus' case, this was less a worry about a possible attack—since he had seen the same thing that Scribonius and Vellusius had—as it was a matter of winning a wager with the two other Primi Pili in the first wave about whose Legion would be the first to fully form up and be ready to march off the beach. There would be a total of four waves, and Pullus had learned from bitter experience the importance of the first wave's getting off the beach as quickly as possible. Otherwise, you would have what happened, when they had landed on the beach of the Pandya, whose warriors came dangerously close to pushing the landing back into the sea! That, Pullus thought, had been worse than the first landing in Britannia, something he wouldn't have thought possible. This time, however, things were going smoothly, and it looked very much as though he would be collecting from Torquatus and Balbinus, the Primi Pili of the 25th and 12th, respectively.

The first three Legions formed up quickly, and began marching inland, up a narrow valley through which a river flowed, as it emptied into the sea. Caesar's *exploratores*, led by the Legate Volusenus, who had been the officer responsible for picking landing sites, since all the way back to Britannia, had chosen a narrow inlet at the far southern tip of the island. This was far from ideal, because it would require the army to move northward through what Pullus and the rest of the army could see was extremely mountainous and rugged terrain, and the landing site itself was extremely small for an army of this size. But as bad as it was, according to Volusenus, it was the best available, and it was no better or worse than any other of a half-dozen Pullus could think of. Still, he was thankful that there was no immediate opposition to add to the difficulty. Marching at the head of the 10th, leading the way as always, in a line of Cohorts, with only one Century ranging ahead as an advance party, Pullus and the first wave moved barely a half-mile, before the valley had narrowed so much that it could barely support two Centuries in open formation, side by side, so he ordered a halt, while sending a runner back. Caesar was arriving in the second wave, which was unloading already, and Pullus wasn't willing to go any farther, until Caesar saw for himself what was facing them. Because, while Volusenus had picked a landing site that worked, he clearly hadn't gone very far inland, if he had landed at all. What faced Pullus right now was a steep ridge, perhaps a thousand feet high that, from the look of it, was going to be too steep to climb by the most direct route. Instead, he was sure that they would have to wind their way up, in order to make the grade gradual enough for the men to ascend. The men were one thing; Pullus was sure that the only way the wagons, artillery and all the other baggage needed to support such a huge army would be able to cross that ridge was by the legionaries building a road that would have to be cut out of the hillside. Although the hills were covered with green vegetation, Pullus could clearly see ribs of rock sticking out between the thick shrubs. He wasn't an engineer, by any means, but he was experienced enough to know that what he was looking at was a massive amount of work.

Caesar saw the same thing, and made one of his instant decisions.

"We're not going to unload any more of the fleet," he told the assembled officers and staff. "In fact, whatever artillery or baggage that's been unloaded will have to go back aboard!" He ignored the stifled groans, his eyes still on the ridge. "The Legions that are ashore will head north, over the ridge, while the fleet will continue to sail to the eastern side of the island and look for a better place."

"I thought Volusenus said this was the best spot," Aulus Hirtius, one of Caesar's Legates spoke up, voicing the question of the others.

"On the western side it is," Caesar replied calmly. "But I didn't like the idea of setting up a base from which to assault the Wa's islands without clearing this island first, and the best way to do that is to march across it, since it's not very wide."

For a moment, Titus Pullus was unsure that he had heard correctly, and a quick glance at most of the others confirmed that he was not the only one feeling this way. In fact, only Hirtius and Pollio of the perhaps 20 senior commanders seemed to be the only ones unsurprised. Caesar continued issuing instructions, until he paused for a moment; then Balbinus, the Primus Pilus of the 12th spoke up:

"Caesar, I'm confused. You said we were setting up a base to assault the islands of the Wa?"

If Caesar knew what was coming, his face betrayed nothing, although he knew very well what was on Balbinus' mind.

"Yes, Balbinus, that's exactly what I said."

Caesar could have continued, but he refused to do so, choosing to force Balbinus to articulate exactly what was on his mind. Pullus knew that this was a favored tactic of his general, and had,in fact, been subjected to it himself, but that didn't mean he liked it any more than Balbinus.

Seeing that Caesar wasn't going to be forthcoming, Balbinus continued, "I thought this was the Land of the Wa's or Was, or whatever they're called."

"It's one of the islands of their land," Caesar agreed, "but it's a minor one. In fact, there are several islands, but the main island is where we're headed next."

"So, we have to make another crossing?" this question came from Aulus Flaminius, the Primus Pilus of the 30th Legion, and now Caesar for the first time looked uncomfortable.

"Yes, that's what it means, when there's another island, Flaminius," he said dryly. "I would have hoped that one of my Primi Pili would be aware that being on one island and having to get to another means they would have to get back aboard ship."

There were a few muffled snickers, and Flaminius reddened, but kept his tone even, as he asked, "And how far away is this other island?"

Now there was no mistaking Caesar's discomfort.

"We don't know exactly. In fact, that's what Volusenus is off doing right now. He and the two thirty's," Caesar was referring to the two triremes, galleys with three banks of oars, and the only two vessels of that type to have survived this long into the campaign, "and they're scouting the island and a good landing site."

"I hope it's better than this one," Pullus muttered under his breath to Torquatus, standing next to him, who grunted in agreement.

Despite Caesar's matter-of-fact tone, he was as discomfited as the men around him, if for slightly different reasons, and he hoped that none of the men would raise the obvious question. Which, of course, they did.

"Why didn't you tell us this before, Caesar?"

The only surprise Caesar felt was not at the question, but who had asked it. Titus Pullus was usually the last man to question him on any of his decisions or orders, and the fact that it was he who uttered the question told Caesar how deeply he had misjudged the men's acquiescence. With any other of his Centurions, or Tribunes, and Legates, for that matter, Caesar would have tried to finesse the answer, dissembling, if need be, but not with Pullus. Of all his Centurions, Pullus occupied a soft spot in Caesar's heart for the man, remembering the large, powerfully bumptious boy in a man's body, who covered up his insecurity with boasting and with a desire for greatness second only to Caesar's. No, he would tell Titus Pullus the truth. He owed the man that much.

"Because if I had told you, and by extension the men that there were actually several islands that compose the Land of Wa, how many of you would have gotten aboard the ships?"

Pullus wasn't surprised by the answer, but he was disappointed, and he returned his general's candor with his own, saying, "Probably not all of us would have. But this is not going to make the men any happier to know they still have to get back on board a boat and risk drowning."

"I know that," Caesar admitted, "but I'll deal with that, when it comes. Right now, we have preparations to make to get us in a position to take the next voyage. And that starts with getting the baggage and artillery back on the ships and sending the already landed Legions up and over that ridge. Then we'll have a better idea of what's facing us."

Looking around, Caesar finished by asking, "Are there any more questions?"

There weren't, and so the men turned back to their respective Legions and tasks, lost in their own thoughts. Like the other Primi Pili, Titus Pullus hoped that Caesar hadn't reached into his bag of tricks one too many times and come up empty, or he would have his hands full with a very angry Legion. Somehow, he thought, we have to find a way to convince them to keep going, that there are still more lands to conquer. He had been in this Land of Wa only a short amount of time, but he already didn't like it much.

Just as Pullus had feared, the climb up the ridge had been brutal. Despite the fact that he was fit, he was also in his 40's, and he felt every foot of the climb up the ridge. The only reward was a spectacular view, but it was a disheartening one, because lying before him was an apparently unending series of ridges of a similar height and steepness, with just a glimpse of the ocean beyond. The scouts had ridden ahead, looking for more signs of habitation, and, most importantly, resistance. With the 10th leading the way, the army was ascending the ridge, the men grunting and panting from the effort, the sounds plainly heard at the top, as Titus Pullus caught his breath. Standing next to him was Quintus Balbus, the Pilus Posterior of Titus' Second Century, First Cohort, and next to

Scribonius, Titus' closest friend in the army. Where Scribonius was cerebral, with a diffident nature, Balbus was a brawler, with a horribly scarred visage, the right side of his face disfigured from a slicing Gallic sword during that earlier campaign, along with a missing right ear. But as different as Balbus and Scribonius were, they were almost as close friends to each other as they were to Titus. Now, standing on the top of the ridge, the two Centurions talked about what they were both looking at.

"Does anyone know if the big island has as many fucking hills as this one?" Balbus asked Pullus. "Because if it does, we're going to be old men before we conquer it."

"We're already old," Pullus reminded him, bringing on a snort Pullus knew passed for Balbus' laugh.

"Speak for yourself," Balbus retorted. "I can still fuck today like I did when I was twenty."

"Which means you haven't improved as a lover. At least, that's what I heard."

Both men turned to see that Scribonius, along with his Cohort, had made the top, and that he was the one who made the barbed jest. As close as they were, both Balbus and Scribonius covered their affection for each other with the rough-edged, cruelty-tinged humor that is so abundant in the ranks of fighting men of every age.

"Well, you heard wrong," Balbus retorted. "I'm the best lover in the Legion. Just ask any of the whores."

"You also pay them better than the other men," Titus observed wryly. "That might have something to do with it."

"*Gerrae!*" Balbus scoffed. "I don't know what you're talking about."

Turning his attention back to the serried landscape in front of them, he asked his Primus Pilus what their orders were. Pullus shrugged in response.

"As far as I know, we keep going. And we're not getting any younger standing here."

Without waiting for an answer, the Primus Pilus of the 10th Legion began following the men of his Century who, now that they had recovered, were making their way tentatively down the slope. The men were following what appeared to be a game trail, but it was so narrow, it made them walk in single file. At this rate, we're going to have to stop at the base of this ridge to make camp, Titus thought dismally. By the time the rest of the army that had landed made their way to the other side, it would be so close to dark that trying to ascend the next ridge would be downright dangerous, not to mention difficult. Pullus estimated that the ocean he could see was perhaps five miles away, but it would take them not only this day, but also most of the rest of the next day to reach it. And as dismissive as he was of Balbus' question, he had his own reservations about the terrain they would be facing, so ultimately he agreed with Balbus that the conquest of an island that according to Caesar was much, much larger than this one could very well take years. It all depended on how much of a fight the people of Wa put up.

By the time the 10th was together at the base of the ridge and ready to ascend the next one, Pullus had not only received orders to make camp, but the scouts had also returned with news that there was what appeared to be a fishing village, composed of about 100 buildings, made of thatch and little else. Also, the only defense of any note, according to the scouts, was a ditch surrounding the village, but they insisted there was no wall. If they were right, and there was no reason to think otherwise, Pullus estimated it wouldn't take much time at all to take the village; in fact, he doubted they would even need any artillery, which was a good thing, since it was loaded aboard the ships of the fleet that even now were making their way around to the eastern side of the island. Making matters even more miserable was the fact that there was barely space to make a proper camp at the foot of the first ridge, and only then, if it was configured in more of a rectangle than the perfect square layout of most Roman camps. Otherwise, a good portion of the army would be pitching tents on the side of the slope they had to ascend the next day. More important than the men's comfort was the problem that trying to defend a camp, where there was a height immediately overlooking it was a practical impossibility. Despite the scouts' assurance that there was no sight of a force large or organized enough in that fishing village to do anything more than cause some nervous sentries a scare, they had no idea if there was a larger town or even a city further north on the island. While the Romans had seen no signs of such habitations, as they approached from the west, Caesar couldn't discount the possibility that, tucked away out of sight of the fleet, was a force large enough to cause this operation to be put in difficulty, before it ever got started.

Speaking of Caesar, the overall commander of the army was peeved, to put it mildly. Sitting astride his horse—not the mount that had become as famous as his owner by the point Caesar left for Parthia, but one of his offspring—the general looked down icily at the Han interpreter that had just given him even more bad news.

"Three days? It will take three days to sail to the large island? Did I hear that correctly?"

Even as Caesar asked this, he knew he was wasting his time. One of the biggest problems in this campaign, as unsurprising in hindsight as it was impossible to plan for, was the language barrier. By the time Caesar and the army had reached the Pandya kingdom, Caesar was acutely aware of the problem, and, true to his prodigious nature, had devoted a substantial portion of his time and attention to the matter. Despite his best efforts, the best he could come up with was a complex, three-way system, whereby he ordered a Parthian who spoke the tongue of the Pandya to relay his general's statements or questions to a Pandyan interpreter, who spoke the tongue of the Han, and who, finally, told the Han representative provided by the Chinese emperor Yuan. The fact that this man was here at all was a testament to how widely Caesar's fame had spread and how it had preceded him into a kingdom that would, under other circumstances, have arrayed an army to meet him with the intent to do what so many other armies had failed to do: destroy Caesar and his men. Caesar's cause was helped by the fact that Yuan had his hands full with infighting between his possible successors, factionalism in the imperial government, and military action against Zhizhi Chanyu, of whom Caesar knew very little, but knew that he wanted to take at least part of Yuan's empire. Or Yuan wanted to take it from Zhizhi, Caesar hadn't been able to tell. All that mattered, as far as he was concerned, was that Yuan had been more than welcoming, even offering to feed Caesar's men, although it was with that abominable food they called "rice". Like his fellow Romans, Caesar missed bread and olive oil terribly, and would find himself thinking wistfully of a warm loaf, straight from the *panera,* still steaming and drenched in olive oil—always at odd moments. Like this one, he thought, as he shook himself back to the present, just in time to hear the answer so laboriously translated and given to him by the Parthian, a man named Achaemenes.

"That's because of the winds at this time of year. If they are favorable, then it will only be two days. But he says that often there are things called tai-funs this time of year that make it hard to cross," Achaemenes' Latin was almost flawless by this time; thank the gods, thought Caesar. Of course, he had had almost 8 years to practice it, so perhaps there was hope yet. As far as the problem at hand was concerned, Caesar nodded his understanding to the Han who had given the information, as he wondered for perhaps the thousandth time, if the emperor Yuan had planted an agent with orders to give information that would ultimately lead to the destruction of his Roman army. So far, all of Caesar's knowledge of the Land of Wa was given to him by the Han, and wouldn't it make sense for Yuan, as stretched and depleted as his resources were, to send Caesar and his army to their doom at the hands of the people whose lands they were about to invade?

These and a thousand other thoughts were crowding in Caesar's brain, just another detail that had to be attended to, another problem solved, another challenge overcome, if he were to succeed in his ambition. Even the knowledge that he had far surpassed Alexander didn't seem to be enough to quell his restless spirit, the hunger for....whatever it was that drove him, and by extension the army, to see worlds never even imagined by Rome. Rome knew of the Han, although most of what was known was shrouded in mystery, half-fact, and outright nonsense, as Caesar had learned. But never before had there been a whisper in the Forum about the Land of Wa, and it was this fact that he knew, deep down in his bones, drove him to push the men of his army. Now he, and the army, were poised on the brink of discovering just what the Land of Wa was all about and what their men were made of. But first, he had to convince the men to make this next voyage. After they had taken this miserably small and obviously poor village, of course, and as he looked down on it from the height of the ridge, he could only hope that the rest of the Land of Wa wasn't this impoverished; because if it was, even Caesar would have his hands full.

Chapter 3

Julius Caesar stood in the prow of the one and only remaining quinquereme, the largest, most powerful ship remaining of the original fleet of Roman ships that departed for the expedition against the Parthians, making it the obvious and only choice for flagship. Straining his eyes and ignoring the spray lashing his face, he peered ahead for the first sighting of the large island that marked the Island of Wa. Arrayed behind his craft were more than 300 other vessels, and to a casual observer, in fact to any observer, they would appear to be the most ramshackle, motley collection of craft that ever graced the waters of any sea, anywhere. Sailing side by side were the remaining transports, of the design originated by Caesar for his second invasion of Britannia, and powered by both sail and oar. These ships carried the bulk of the Legions, although they had been so reduced in numbers that a substantial number of men were spread among the other types of craft; dhows from the Arabian peninsula with their triangular sails, and a smattering of ships taken from the waters of the Pandya. But the predominant transport ship in use was what the Han called a "chuan", with high prow and stern, powered by sail and steered by means of a long oar. Leading all of these were the warships, though Zhang, the Han interpreter, had assured Caesar that they would meet no resistance on the water. However, as much as Caesar relied on his luck, he also believed in taking proper precautions—hence the vanguard of warships.

Caesar's mood wasn't helped when a lookout excitedly shouted that land was finally sighted, and even after several moments he still couldn't see it. He had long been accustomed to having perhaps the keenest vision of anyone he knew, but over the last few years he had noticed that it was failing him. Despite being in excellent health overall, it seemed that even Caesar was not immune to the ravages of time, a fact that privately peeved him to no end. It wasn't until almost a full watch later that he finally got his first glimpse of Wa. Despite seeing so many such sights before, he still felt a quickening of his heart at this last obstacle, still nothing more than a dark, greenish line on the horizon. Turning to Achaemenes, Caesar began the laborious process of extracting information from Zhang, his suspicion for the Han envoy growing deeper by the day.

"It appears that Zhang was correct about resistance from the Wa on the water, but he still hasn't satisfied me about what we can expect, when we land."

Caesar waited for the process to finish by studying Zhang closely, but as usual, he couldn't detect any flicker of emotion. These Han, he thought, almost have faces that are built to guard their emotions, at least for us. It's impossible to tell with any of them what they're thinking. The same for the Gayan, and according to everything I've heard, the Wa will look very similar to the Han, at least to us.

Achaemenes, after a short conversation, turned to Caesar and said, "Zhang assures us that where he's taking us to land is lightly defended, because it's a remote part of the island. However, he insists that there is ample space to build a camp that can be easily defended."

Caesar grunted noncommittally, not willing to trust that assurance, until he saw with his own eyes that it was true. As far as he knew, there could be an army of thousands of Wa waiting for him and his army, but at the moment, there was nothing else to be done, but wait for the land to grow slowly larger.

Shortly before nightfall, the fleet drew near enough to see that while the landing site was large enough and the beach was suitable for landing the entire army, it would not be unopposed. As the sun sank behind them, the light created by thousands of fires dotted the land immediately surrounding the beach. Well, Caesar thought, it was a bit much to expect to keep a fleet of 300 ships secret. Of course, there was no question of landing now, with darkness almost here; in fact, he was faced with a choice he didn't care to make: whether to land in the face of opposition, or sail farther north along the coast and look for a spot, where they could avoid fighting their way off the beach. Whatever the case, this was a time to confer with the commanders of his army, so Caesar ordered the flags run up the mast to signal for his officers to meet at the flagship. They'd be thankful for the calm seas; he knew that pitching about in one of the small boats was hard on the strongest stomach, and his Romans, in particular, had long since made it clear that they abhorred anything to do with the sea. That will just make them all the more eager to get off these boats and onto land, he thought with grim amusement, even if they have to fight their way off this beach to do it!

While he waited, he scanned the beach, straining his eyes to pick out any possible details of the army they were about to face, but it was simply too far and too dark to make out anything other than a mass of men lining the shore staring out at his fleet. Some of them appeared to wear armor of some sort, but it was impossible to tell, if it was similar in style to that worn by the Han, which Caesar was sure would be as susceptible to the short, stabbing Spanish sword as anything else they had run into.

Titus Pullus fought the urge to vomit, attributing it to the combination of rough surf and what he knew was about to happen. No matter how secure his hold over the 10th, and no matter his reputation in the army, he couldn't allow himself to show such weakness in front of others, so he ruthlessly forced himself to appear as calm and placid as circumstances allowed. If his color was a little green, well, that was something he couldn't help, but he'd be damned if he was going to act as if this was his first time to jump over the side of a ship.

It had been a long and contentious meeting, with men like Pollio and Hirtius shouting themselves hoarse by the time a decision was made. Pullus wondered briefly, if the men on the ships nearest to the flagship might have heard the row that took most of the night, and if they had, what their frame of mind was. Whatever it was, he thought, it doesn't matter. Because Caesar had decided to throw the dice and hoped they came up Venus, just as they had all those years ago, when he crossed that muddy creek, the Rubicon. In fact, he had used the same phrase that he uttered, when marching on Rome, "alea iacta est"—the die is cast! Well, he always did have a flair for the dramatic, Titus mused, his external eyes still riveted to the sight of the approaching shore. He knew from experience that while it would seem they weren't moving at all, suddenly the boat would be ramming itself onto the beach, almost always surprising everyone aboard. Pullus was determined that it wouldn't happen this time. Helping to focus his concentration were the ranks of men waiting for the leading transports to disgorge their load. Titus Pullus couldn't say he was surprised that Caesar had chosen to go ahead with the landing, but for the first time since he could remember, the Primus Pilus of the 10th was forced to recognize that the knot in his stomach threatening to eject all occupants was more than the normal pre-assault jitters. It wasn't just the numbers of men; they had faced a similar host during their first invasion of Britannia and when landing in the territory of the Pandya. But for a reason he could no more define than ignore, there was something different about this time as far as Pullus was concerned. It's probably because it's the last one, he thought: the last beach, the last group of people to face the Legions of Rome and know defeat. But even as he told himself this, he knew there was more to it than that. The instinct honed over hundreds of battles and thousands of skirmishes was screaming at him that this time was different for reasons he couldn't fathom.

Just a couple of ships away, Julius Caesar again stood in the prow, oblivious to the surging spray produced by the definitely higher chop of this morning. Like Titus Pullus, his stomach was churning, and if they were standing side by side, perhaps one of them would mention it and discover that their anxiety stemmed from the same place, which was that nagging spot called the unknown. Because, like Pullus, Caesar couldn't define what felt different about this day. But whatever it was, he would see it through, and even as unfamiliar as he may have been with the feeling, he wouldn't have called it doubt. Never that! Caesar didn't experience doubt or fear. Still, it was hard to dismiss the gnawing feeling in his gut, as he stared at the ranks of men, as unmoving as any Roman Legion.

Sextus Scribonius, Pilus Prior of the Second Cohort and Titus Pullus' best friend was too busy to worry about what was coming, as he checked the men of his Century, hoping that his other Centurions were doing the same. These transports fit only two Centuries apiece, but in the case of each First Century of each Cohort, save the First, instead of the Second Century, there was a contingent of missile troops. Accompanying Scribonius and his Century were the last of the slingers from the Balearic Isles, a hardened group of men who still wore their traditional tunics, although the original material had long since been replaced, and who disdained the lamellar cuirasses made of leather most of the other missile troops had taken to wearing, once they were introduced to them by the Han. They also insisted on stubbornly conversing in their own tongue whenever a Roman Centurion was about, Scribonius noted sourly, but he knew they would fight like the Furies, and his inspection would yield nothing with which he could find fault. Scribonius made his usual small talk with his men; unlike Pullus, whose very size and bulk made him so formidable and, coupled with his reputation, made him respected out of fear as much as from devotion, Scribonius was genuinely loved by his men. He could be a harsh disciplinarian, but he was scrupulously fair and did whatever he could to make the lives of his men easier. Now he was making bad jokes and complimenting his men for their efforts to make themselves presentable under the circumstances. But these men were veterans of Caesar's army, and it had always been their practice to go into battle wearing their decorations and horsehair plume, so today was no exception. When Scribonius stepped in front of Publius Vellusius, he spent more time than with the other men, as the two shared a quiet word, their bond even stronger, because many years before, they both had been scared, wide-eyed teenagers, sharing the same tent. Even now, that bond transcended the normal gulf that existed between Centurion and ranker, and both were glad that the other was there to face the coming battle.

Pullus and the First Cohort were naturally in the first wave, the men of the first two Centuries now standing from a point amidships to the rear of the transport, in order to raise the prow in preparation for the moment when the ship would ram itself onto the beach. As he did every other time, Pullus wished there were a better way to accomplish an amphibious landing than just rowing a boat onto the shore and jumping over the side into water that could be anywhere from waist-high to deep enough to drown most of the men. That was never a problem for Pullus personally, but it was still a worry, nonetheless—just one of the thousand things that crowded the mind of a Primus Pilus going into battle. Like Caesar, Pullus was the only man standing in the prow of his ship, eyes riveted to the beach that was now rapidly approaching.

"If they've got missile troops, we're coming into range right about...now," he muttered to himself, and as if he had summoned it by his words, the sky suddenly darkened with the slivers that he knew were arrows, originating from the rear ranks of the waiting Wa. Before he himself could bellow the words, a few of the men, peering over the side at the beach, shouted the warning, as men's shield arms automatically lifted. Normally, this would have been a move executed with precision but because of the cramped conditions on the deck, most of the men ended up jostling those immediately in front of them, forming what looked somewhat like a shuddering beast trying to shake itself. The delay caused more than just a superficial problem, because there were gaps in the normally impenetrable testudo, gaps through which those missiles shot, seeking a fleshy target to land with the wet, thudding sound that signaled a strike. The air immediately filled with sounds of men in pain, some howling, some cursing, but others only seemed to utter a soft sigh before partially slumping to the deck, held upright only by the pressure of their tightly packed comrades on either side. Even before Pullus could react and more rapidly than he had ever before seen even against the Parthian archers, another volley came slicing towards him and his men, just as thick as the first. *Thank the gods I decided to grab a shield from stores, instead of waiting for one!* The thought flashed through his mind even as he felt the shield he was trying to shelter behind shudder from one, two, then three solid strikes from the feathered shafts. Still at a range where the barbed points barely poked all the way through, Pullus knew that by the time they were on the beach itself, the enemy's arrows would carry enough force to protrude several inches through the layers of wood and glue that comprised his shield. The only thing working in the Romans' favor at that point that Pullus could see was that the Wa infantry was deployed almost to the water's edge, making it impossible for their missile troops to continue this murderous fire, once he and his men went over the side. Looking behind him, he could see that the second volley had mostly been blocked, but already the first several ranks of men had multiple arrows sticking out of their shields. Even as he took this all in, yet a third volley came slamming down into the packed ranks, while the open deck between where Pullus was standing and where the Century was amidships was literally studded with arrows. *It looks like a pincushion*, he thought absentmindedly, as he felt the scraping, grating jolt of the prow of the transport coming into contact with the sand of the beach, almost throwing him off his feet because his attention was focused elsewhere. Fortunately, his men were better prepared, some of them only stumbling slightly; but a couple of men, further hampered by the body of a wounded or dead comrade lying at their feet, lost their balance to fall clumsily onto the deck.

The transport now grounded, this was normally the time when speed was vital, that the faster the men unloaded and stormed the beach, the more quickly the transport could pull away from the beach and another could take its place. After conducting almost a dozen such operations, Pullus, along with every veteran of the army, officer and men alike, knew that the key to such an assault was normally to get as many men on the beach as quickly as possible. Yet this time, the men didn't move. It was almost like Caesar's first invasion of Britannia, when nobody got off the boats, until the Legion *aquilifer*, carrying the sacred eagle standard of the Legion, leaped into the water. But despite that similarity, this time was very, very different, because on this occasion, it was by design: Caesar, seeing the packed ranks of the Wa warriors and their proximity to the surf line, had signaled shortly before reaching missile range for the men to remain aboard. His reason for waiting was to enable his warships, along with a squadron of specially designed and armed *chuan,* to maneuver themselves into a position parallel to the beach, but arrayed so that the bulk of each craft was in the gaps between transports. Caesar's purpose was made clear in a matter of moments, when the first salvo of artillery fire, a combination of scorpion bolts and the smooth, one pound rocks from the ballistae bolted to the deck of the warships sliced into the ranks of the Wa, tearing bloody holes into the tightly packed mass. For the first time, Pullus could hear the screams of the Wa, the first real sounds they had made, but even as he watched with a sense of unease, those holes were immediately filled in a disciplined manner with which no Primus Pilus could find fault.

Unfortunately, the men on the beached transports were still on the receiving end of what was appearing to be an endless supply of arrows, and very quickly Pullus realized that even if his casualties were minimal, it was extremely likely that a substantial number of his men would have their shields rendered useless, because they would be so weakened from being riddled with arrows. While knocking the shafts off would help restore the balance to the shield, with a dozen or more arrows in it, it was probable that a shield would be cracked, making it vulnerable to splitting apart at the first strike from a bladed weapon or spear. But there was nothing that could be done about it, and was just one of those things that might tip a battle in either direction, depending on how the men responded to fighting without that protection. For

Centurions and Optios, it was not as much of a challenge, but there were only two of those per Century. Still, the punishment was no longer one-way, and as Titus crouched behind his shield, between dodging arrows, he took great satisfaction in watching the bodies of the Wa warriors being transfixed or mangled, depending on what hit them. The scorpions, in particular, were great for producing mass casualties, particularly at this relatively close range of perhaps 150 paces from the surf line, with one iron bolt usually passing through at least two and sometimes three men. Even as Titus watched, one bolt, aimed a little higher than the rest, struck a Wa warrior right in the nose, causing his head to explode in a spray of red mist, as what Pullus assumed was the top half of his skull went spinning off to the right, trailing bits of gore behind it. As many times as he had seen such things, it still made him shudder and thank the gods that he wasn't on the receiving end.

Despite soaking up this punishment, the Wa continued to shift their ranks rapidly to fill the gaps opened by the carnage wreaked by the vicious bombardment. And there seemed to be no end to the supply of men willing to step into the front ranks, despite knowing the fate that awaited them; it was this sight more than anything that fueled Titus Pullus' growing sense of unease. However, he would still be the first over the side to wade ashore and into the mass of waiting men. Suddenly, the barrage stopped, and there was the blast of a horn coming from Caesar's flagship, the call quickly picked up by the *cornici* on the other ships.

Without hesitation, Titus Pullus stood and strode to the starboard side of the transport, and, without looking back to see if he was being followed, he bellowed, "Over the side you, *cunni*! It's time to earn our pay!"

And then with a splash, he disappeared over the side.

While Sextus Scribonius wasn't in a position to see his Primus Pilus go over the side, he clearly heard the blast of the *cornu*, the heavy, curved horn that was used in battle, because its sound carried so far. But like his best friend, he was the first over the side as well, creating a huge splash as he struggled to keep the shield he had drawn from stores above his head, so that it wouldn't get wet. Pullus had ordered the men to keep the leather covers on their shields to protect them from the inevitable splashing about, because if the shield was completely immersed, nothing could keep it from becoming waterlogged, and a shield in that condition was worse than useless. Even so, either because of where his craft had landed, or because Scribonius was just unlucky enough to land in an underwater hole, he went completely under, almost losing himself in panic as his feet scrabbled to find purchase on the bottom, which seemed to be mostly sand, with precious few rocks to provide traction. Finally his head burst above the surface, water streaming from the transverse crest and his helmet and still obscuring his vision as he spluttered and gasped for breath. Shaking his head and blinking to clear his vision, he caught in glimpses the fact that his men hadn't hesitated in following him over the side, and that they were now churning through the surf to make their way onto the beach.

Even as he took this in, he heard a huge roar, issued from the throats of the thousands of Wa warriors who leaped forward to come sprinting the short distance from their spot on the beach to the very edge of the surf. Indeed, he saw dozens of them charging forward, wearing helmets similar in style to those worn by the Han, and carrying as their primary weapon a long shafted weapon with a teardrop-shaped blade at the end. Otherwise they carried no shields, apparently counting on the length of the spear to keep the enemy from getting close enough to do any damage. Their armor was the lamellar style also used by the Han, but the overlapping plates were of leather, at least for these men. All of these details Scribonius took in as he waded ashore, his shield now up in what was called the first position. Because of his stumble, a number of his men had reached the beach first, and he thought with equal parts regret and relief, no *corona litus* for me, referring to the crown, devised by Caesar, that was an addition to the various *coronae* in use in the Roman army for centuries as decorations for bravery. As he watched, the Wa warriors slashed into the leading elements of his men, who were unable to do anything more than form a partial single line, although more men were making their way either alongside or behind their comrades already on the beach. Therefore, Scribonius wasn't too worried when he saw a couple of his men stumbling backward from the potent jabs and thrusts of the Wa, knowing that once the Romans got into formation, they would be able to support each other. And Scribonius, like Pullus, had been in so many battles, and had been victorious so often that his mind didn't even register the possibility of defeat.

Titus Pullus was lucky, both because of his height and because of his landing in water that was barely above his waist. Naturally it meant that he made more of a target, but this was something to which he'd long been accustomed, and, frankly, he was thankful that his shield, already weakened by arrows, didn't have to withstand any more of those missiles. Instead, just like in Scribonius' area, the Wa weren't content to wait to let the invaders come to them, but the Wa found in the Roman fighters opponents with as much battle fervor as they possessed. Seeing a small number of Wa, carrying the same weapon that faced Scribonius and his men, dashing towards him, Pullus tried to generate as much momentum as he could by surging through the water, his thighs pumping in a futile attempt to gain speed. Just as the first Wa warrior, eyes almost invisible as his face contorted in a primal scream of anger and hatred, thrust his long weapon at Pullus' midsection, Pullus took the blow on his shield, surprised by the strength behind it for such a small man, but using his blade, put all his strength into a slicing downward blow, cutting through the shaft of the spear as if it were a twig.

The blade Pullus was wielding was one he had paid to have made for him more than 20 years earlier, in Gaul, and despite his searching through all the lands he had traveled through, there was still no weapon that he had found that matched it. Even more than Scribonius, this blade was his oldest and best friend, and it didn't let him down now, as he saw the Wa's eyes widen in shock at what this giant was able to do. In fact, he was still in shock when Pullus made his next move, bashing the boss of his shield into the gaping face of the Wa, hearing the bone crunch above the din of surf and battle. The Wa collapsed in a heap, as if the bones in his body suddenly disintegrated, but even before he did, Pullus was moving toward the next Wa. Titus Pullus was a very quick man for his size, and up until that instant, he had never met anyone quicker than his boyhood friend and first comrade in the Legions, Vibius Domitius; but he had never seen a single man, let alone so many, move with such blinding speed as he did. Before his mind could register, his shield arm had moved to block another blow from a second Wa, and he felt the shuddering jar of the blow all the way up his arm. Even worse, he heard a distinctive crack that warned him that his shield was weakening. For an instant, the teardrop-shaped blade lodged in the wood of his shield, which wouldn't have been such a problem, except that a third Wa came at him—but this time with a high, downward sweeping blow designed to cleave Pullus' helmet and skull, and Pullus was unable to use his shield. Instead, raising his blade above his head, a tiny shower of sparks was created when the sword and the head of the spear clashed together, except that instead of bouncing off as normally happened, Pullus immediately saw the purpose in the two tines angling from the head of the spear, when his blade was caught between the head and one of the tines. The Wa warrior gave a ferocious jerk, and it was only because of the grip taught to him almost 30 years before by his first weapons instructor, Aulus Vinicius, that it wasn't yanked from his hand. Instead, the Wa was thrown off balance, as Pullus twisted the blade to free it from the spear, then made a sweeping cut that slashed across the throat of his adversary. By this point, the second Wa of the original three—with two now dead—had freed his spear for another attack, but before he could renew it Pullus' men had arrived, and suddenly Pullus found himself shoved not so gently to the side, as his men rushed to engage the enemy.

All along the surf line, similar struggles were taking place, as the men of Wa met the Legions of Rome, men who up to this point had never laid eyes on each other, and of whom only one side knew anything about the other—and that was only muttered whisperings of superstition and myth, hint and legend. Now these men were trying to kill each other for reasons the two sides could no more fathom than they could articulate, but that didn't stop them from doing their best to slaughter each other. From his vantage point, Caesar watched the fighting, and nothing he saw soothed his earlier sense of unease. He had never seen a foe that committed itself so early to the attack in any previous amphibious assault, and he could only watch as his men struggled to make headway onto the beach, most of them still standing in water that was at least knee-deep. Like Pullus, he did appreciate that in their fervor to engage, the Wa had deprived their missile troops of continuing their onslaught, but even without the archers adding to the carnage, the men of Wa were giving his men all they could handle and then some.

For the first time in many, many years, Caesar had the presentiment of defeat, that perhaps this landing wouldn't be successful. Ignoring the twisting in his gut, he coolly ordered the shipboard artillery to continue firing, but to elevate their aim, so that the missiles slashed into the rear ranks of the Wa, who were still packed together as each pushed the man to his front towards the beach, each of them clearly eager to get at the Romans. Bloody swaths were torn through the Wa ranks, and the detached part of Caesar's mind was pleased and interested to see that the *chuan* converted to serve as floating artillery platforms seemed to be most effective. He had thought this would be the case, because of their high prow and stern that served as a broad and relatively stable platform, and it made him happy to see his intuition was right. The men serving the weapons were working furiously, feeding their respective weapons as though they were ravenous beasts, feverishly working the torsion ropes of the ballistae or cranking furiously to cock the scorpions, taking aim just long enough to ensure that their missiles didn't land short and inflict casualties on their own comrades. However, the rocking motion of the boats from the surf meant that sometimes their aim was off, and Caesar grimaced when he saw an errant scorpion bolt skewer two of his men from behind. Even knowing this inevitability, it didn't help ease the anguish of seeing his own men cut down by a comrade, no matter how accidental it was. Turning his attention back to the fighting, he estimated that a sixth part of a watch had passed, but none of the first wave had made any significant headway off the beach. The transports had finished disgorging their occupants, and were backrowing off the beach to make way for the second of the four waves. But Caesar could see that unless something happened, and happened quickly, there would be nowhere for the men of the second wave to unload. The landing was in serious jeopardy of failure.

Sextus Scribonius was unable to form the men of his Century into their standard 8-man front; instead it was closer to 6 men across, but even that changed so rapidly it was impossible for him to keep track. He could see his *signifer*, directly in the middle of what was the most disorganized melee Scribonius had ever been a part of, instead of his normal spot at the far right end, anchoring the front rank. Normally, this would have been cause for at least a tongue-lashing by Scribonius, but he could see that there was nothing his *signifer,* a Parthian named Artabanus, could have done to get into the right spot. The Wa were unrelenting in their pressure, a mass of small yet fierce men, wielding the long spears with a savage skill, slashing and thrusting into the ranks of Scribonius' men. It was not all one-sided, however; as Scribonius glanced to his left, he saw one of his men step inside the thrust of one of the Wa's and unleash one of his own, perfectly aimed thrusts that punched into the Wa's gut, cutting through the lamellar leather patches as if they weren't there.

However, even as the Wa fell another took his place, and before Scribonius could do anything more than shout in rage and grief, he saw his man take a blow from the long weapon that sliced down in between the Legionary's neck and shoulder, the blade almost cleaving him in two. Without thinking, Scribonius let out a roar and completely forgetting his role in directing his men, rushed forward, shield up and sword held out to the side, ready to plunge it into the Wa, who, seeing the Centurion approaching, was working frantically to free his blade. Before he could do so, Scribonius was on him, bashing him with his shield, staggering the man long enough for the Roman to come from under the shield in a sweeping thrust that plunged into the Wa's groin. Letting out a shriek, the man let go of his blade and fell immediately to the ground, clutching his crotch as blood spurted between his fingers from the severed artery. But as before, the spot was vacant for just an instant before another Wa came hurtling at Scribonius, this one whirling his spear in an overhand fashion that Scribonius had never seen before, causing Pullus' friend to hold his shield higher than normal. All around him men were engaged, the pace of the fighting at a frenzied level normally seen only at the very beginning or at a moment when one side sensed that one great effort would cause their opponent to crack. These warriors didn't seem to tire, and without knowing it, Scribonius' thoughts were echoing those of both Caesar and his friend at that moment, as the idea of defeat seemed to be a real possibility.

The First Cohort was doing better, but only marginally. By virtue of his size and strength, Pullus had managed to push the Wa in his immediate area back from the surf line, while the men immediately on either side had taken advantage of this pocket and pushed inland themselves. It wasn't much, but even as Pullus was finishing off another Wa with a slashing blow to the throat, Caesar, from his spot on the flagship, deemed it to be enough to signal for the transport immediately behind the First to row to the beach to unload. Caesar was pleased at the damage his artillery was inflicting, but even so, there seemed to be no end to the Wa. As he watched, his eye picked up movement on the plain immediately behind the beach, and to his dismay he saw what looked like at least another 2,000 or 3,000 more Wa heading toward the battle. Meanwhile, on the beach, Pullus had managed to move next to his *aquilifer,* Valerius, and began bellowing at the top of his lungs.

"First Century, form on me! Wedge formation! On me!"

While unorthodox, to say the least, Pullus' plan was one that could work only with a Century and Cohort as experienced as the 10th. While the 10th, like the other Legions was composed of just a little more than a quarter Romans in their ranks, Pullus and the other Primi Pili had gone to great lengths to ensure that the First Cohort was more heavily loaded with Romans than the other Cohorts, since they traditionally were the first in battle. And of the First Cohort, the First Century, in particular, had more than its share of Romans. It was these men that Pullus was counting on to make their way to his side, understanding that there was neither the time nor the space for men to fall into their normal spots. A few, a very, very few, had been with Pullus as a lowly Gregarius when Caesar's army had been ambushed by the Nervii at the Sabis River and they had been in a similar situation, without the time to get into their proper spots. These men had regaled all the newcomers to the Legion over the years about that day and others like it, as they sat around the fires at night, much to the chagrin and dismay of those who were forced to listen for what they were sure was the hundredth time. However, all those tales paid off, as every man of the First Century responded quickly, disengaging while one of his comrades from the Second Century, who had been standing in the surf behind him, stepped in to take his place. Despite the unrelenting pressure from the Wa, the men of the First Century moved into the formation Pullus had ordered, with Pullus as the point of the wedge. As the men were getting ready, Pullus, between thrusts with his Gallic blade and swinging blows with his shield to keep the Wa at bay, looked over for his Pilus Posterior, who as usual was in the middle of the action.

"Balbus!" Pullus had to shout several times, before the scarred face of his second-in-command turned to look in his direction. Once he had Balbus' attention, Pullus pointed to a spot farther down the beach.

"Move your men further down that way, so the Third Century can move into your spot," he roared, then repeated it twice before Balbus signaled that he understood.

The Second immediately began pushing their way to the left, meaning that it was essential for the Third to wade ashore. Telling Valerius—who was using the standard as a weapon, swinging it in a wide arc to keep the Wa at bay for a moment—to watch his back, Pullus turned quickly and pointed to the nearest man, one of the Roman veterans.

"Go tell Camillus to bring the Third up now!"

Without waiting to see if his command was obeyed, Pullus turned just in time for a warning shout from Valerius, as a Wa warrior managed to get inside the swinging standard. Unlike the others, this man carried a sword, but still disdained a shield, although he was wearing lamellar armor, except Pullus could see that instead of leather patches, this man's lamellae were made of iron plates. The armor didn't seem to hamper his movement at all, as he made a lunge, low and hard, at the Primus Pilus. Although Pullus blocked the blow relatively easily, he wasn't prepared for the Wa's rapid recovery, as the smaller man violated one of the primary rules of combat by turning his back on his opponent. Spinning around and pivoting on his right foot, moving himself to Pullus' left, before Pullus thought it possible for a human being to move so quickly, he had recovered and made a slashing blow, this one again aimed low, only Pullus' greave saving his leg. Even so, the force of the blow was terrific, much harder than Pullus thought possible, and despite himself, an explosive hiss of pain escaped his lips. Because of the Wa's position, the shield was the only weapon he could bring to bear, and Pullus lashed out with it, but the Wa was too quick for it to be a solid blow. Nevertheless, even a glancing blow from Titus Pullus felled most men, and this one was no different, the Wa flying off his feet, but before Pullus could take advantage, he leaped upright and renewed his attack. This time aiming high, he began raining slicing blows, which Pullus managed to catch, but on the fourth one, Pullus' shield, already weakened from the rain of arrows, split in half. At the worst possible time, Pullus was left with a jagged half of a shield!

Farther down the beach, where the men of the 28th Legion were part of the first wave, their situation was even more precarious. The first Centuries to land were still standing in the water and, despite their best efforts to keep their shields from getting soaked, too many of the men were now carrying waterlogged shields. Although wet shields were still useful for protection, facing men like the Wa, who were so damnably quick, they were much too heavy to wield effectively. As a result, the casualties were heavy, the surf rolling onto the beach foaming pink from all the blood spilled. Because of their armor, fallen men quickly dropped below the water's surface, so that if they were wounded and if they were unable to pull themselves erect, they were dead men. Worse still, their bodies became obstacles and hazards underfoot for the men still fighting. In short, the landing was failing, and Gnaeus Cartufenus, the Primus Pilus of the 28th Legion, knew he and his men were in danger of being annihilated. Cartufenus didn't have the same idea as Pullus, but he knew he needed to do something quickly, or his men would be faced with the choice of death in battle or by drowning. Desperately looking about, Cartufenus saw that there were perhaps 20 men who were not engaged. Every Legion has its share of shirkers, and these men were the cream of the crop; those too stupid, too slow, or too unskilled in battle had long since been winnowed out. Normally, Cartufenus would never rely on such men as these, but there was nobody left, at least out of these two Centuries.

Blowing a blast on his whistle to get their attention, he bellowed, "You! That's right, you," he pointed his sword at the nearest of the shirkers who, at the sound of the whistle, had tried to wade to a spot out of sight of the Primus Pilus. "You and that bunch get over here, NOW!"

For a moment Cartufenus thought the men wouldn't obey, but after they took a look around, they saw the obvious: there was nowhere else for them to hide.

Once they were by his side, without waiting for any doubt or hesitation to surface, he shouted, "Follow me! We've got to get off this beach, and the only chance of doing it alive is that way." Cartufenus pointed at the mass of men and began, as Pullus had, to churn through the water, desperately trying to pick up speed. Although he didn't look back, he could hear from the splashing that the other men were following. Aiming for a spot where his men had been so worn down that there was only a single thin line of Legionaries, Cartufenus began bellowing, "Caesar!" over and over, his small group of men picking up the cry as they followed him to slam into the Wa.

With only half a shield, Titus Pullus was in a desperate position, and both he and the Wa facing him knew it. The Wa made another lunge, aiming this time for a spot toward the ragged edge of Pullus' shield, knowing that the Roman would have to move the ruined shield farther than normal to block the blow. Since it was the left half of the shield now lying on the ground, this meant that Pullus had to move the remnant of the shield away from his torso, opening him up to the next blow, and the Wa wasted no time in making a second thrust. Fortunately for Pullus, he had been in innumerable such moments, courtesy of hundreds of battles and skirmishes, so he was prepared to meet the Wa's blade with his own, deflecting it upward with a sweeping parry. He was only partially successful, as the point of his enemy's blade still managed a glancing blow just below the left collarbone. Because Pullus blocked the Wa's blade, most of the force behind the blow was absorbed, but there was enough to break several links and for the point to penetrate, not deeply, just enough to draw blood. Pullus let out a half-curse, half-snarl of pain and, using the jagged edge of the shield, whipped it horizontally across the face of the Wa warrior, the splintered wood tearing the enemy's forehead. Blood spurted and, most importantly, streamed into the Wa's eyes, temporarily blinding him, and he desperately tried to clear his vision with one hand while swinging his sword wildly in front of him to ward off any attack. It wasn't enough! Pullus easily knocked the Wa's blade aside as he stepped inside the arc of his swing, then made a high, hard thrust right at the base of the Wa's throat. Between the sharpness of the point and the strength of the blow, Pullus' blade exited the back of the Wa's neck, but even before he could fall, Pullus had withdrawn his Gallic sword and jumped back. Even so, he narrowly avoided being decapitated by a sweeping blow from a Wa tear-drop spear, yet before the man wielding it could follow up with another blow, one of Pullus' Legionaries leaped in front of his Primus Pilus, protecting his leader with his own, undamaged shield. Given a brief respite, Pullus took the time to grab a new shield off the beach, then quickly took his place at the head of the wedge, which was still holding together, but just barely. Camillus' Third Century had come into the gap between Balbus' Second and the First, but now they had their hands full. Compounding matters were the bodies piled on the beach, creating both an obstacle and a makeshift barrier for the Romans to use. The problem was that it gave the men an easier option than actually advancing. With the men facing the toughest fight any of them had been in, this was doubly tempting and Pullus knew, as Cartufenus did, hundreds of yards away, that to stay on this beach was to die. Without waiting any longer, Pullus took a step forward, using his new shield to punch at the Wa directly across from him, his blow knocking the Wa backward and enabling Pullus to deal with the man to his right with a slashing blow that landed on the side of the Wa's helmet, knocking him senseless. Before the second man could recover, the Legionary directly behind Pullus to his right, thrust downward into the man's face. The first Wa, now back on the attack, came back at Pullus, weaving his spear in an elliptical pattern to draw Pullus' attention to it, instead of the eyes and face of his enemy, in an effort to deceive the Roman about his intentions. Pullus was much too experienced for such a maneuver, his eyes never leaving the face of the Wa who, as Pullus was expecting, grit his teeth when he launched his real attack. It was a backhanded slash, that Pullus blocked with his blade, knocking the spear aside while punching at the Wa with his shield, using the raised boss as a cudgel. Though it was only a glancing blow, it was just enough to allow Pullus to step inside the arc of the spear. Undeterred, the Wa whipped the butt end of the weapon at Pullus' head, but again Pullus' experience stood him in good stead, having seen that move before, and he was able to block the blow. In the instant after blocking the blow, Pullus suddenly went into a squat, sweeping his blade in a wide arc that brought the blade into a position just behind the Wa's left leg. Pulling back towards him with all his considerable strength, he sliced the sharp blade into the Wa's leg at the kneecap, sending a shower of blood in a fan-shaped spray that spattered the already blood-soaked sand. It was only because of Pullus' massive strength that he was able to completely sever the Wa's lower leg from the rest of him. Letting out a shriek that rose above the already incredible din, the Wa collapsed in a heap, and Pullus didn't even bother to finish him, intent on taking advantage of the momentary gap. Stepping forward, he came into immediate contact with more Wa waiting to kill him, but he was a step farther onto the beach.

Gnaeus Cartufenus, with 20-odd men, most of them found lingering towards the back of the mass of men, now went charging into the continuing melée. While he hadn't ordered a wedge formation as such, the men following him had aligned themselves more or less in the same manner as Pullus' First Cohort, although this was due more to Cartufenus' men's unwillingness to be at the head of their body of Romans. Nevertheless, they followed their Primus Pilus as he threw himself into the fight, picking a spot where his men were distributed at their thinnest. Knocking one of his own men aside, Cartufenus smashed into the Wa, but he didn't have Pullus' advantage of size and strength. Still, he somehow managed to knock one Wa backward, while slightly staggering the man next to him, and before either could recover, Cartufenus made a downward thrust that hit the first Wa squarely in the groin. The second man was finished by one of the bolder of Cartufenus' men, who followed his leader close behind. This was all the forward momentum they could manage, however, as the Wa immediately closed around the Primus Pilus and his men, all of them slashing and hacking at the invaders.

Sextus Scribonius had managed to defend against the unorthodox attack of the Wa warrior, but he was given no time to celebrate his victory, as the spot was immediately filled by another man, this one also wielding a sword. This was the first Wa swordsman Scribonius faced, and like Pullus, he couldn't help feeling unsettled by the obvious speed and grace of his opponent. Everything the Roman method of warfare counted on: teamwork, relentless training, sometimes bone-crushing discipline—none of these seemed to matter against the Wa, each of whom seemed to be an endless fount of energy and skill. Regardless, Scribonius and his men fought on, having pushed their way a few paces farther up from the surf line, stepping over the bodies of the fallen, Wa and Roman. None of the *medici* had landed yet, so the wounded were forced to look out for themselves the best they could, hoping they survived long enough to receive treatment. Some of them managed to draw themselves up under their shields, and there were a number of these, looking a bit like turtles who have drawn in their feet and head, scattered about the beach among the corpses or those wounded unable to do even that to protect themselves. Behind him, Scribonius heard another blast of the *cornu*, sounding the signal to advance, and he wondered if it was meant for the transports carrying the rest of his Cohorts. Because he had just landed with his Century and the Balearic slingers, his men were hard-pressed: the slingers were at this point almost useless, because the range was too close, so they were huddled together, standing knee-deep in the surf and occasionally sending a missile into the packed mass of Wa whenever an opportunity arose. It would have been better if they had stayed on the ship and used the height advantage to fire over our heads, Scribonius thought, immediately after killing the sword-wielding Wa with a backhanded slash to the neck. From Scribonius' quick assessment, he was dismayed to see that almost half his men were down, leaving fewer than 40 packed together, still fighting. To his immediate right, the men of the Third Cohort of the 10th were faring little better, although they seemed to have suffered slightly lighter casualties.

"Either we get reinforced, or we get back on the boat," Scribonius muttered to himself, but even as he glanced over his shoulder, he saw that the ship from which he unloaded had already pulled off the beach and was rowing away. Stifling a curse, he turned back around, his only hope that another ship had answered the *cornu* command and was rowing up to replace it.

Caesar was watching all of this from his flagship, and somehow, without making a conscious decision, he began the process of determining what needed to be done in order to extract that part of his army on the beach. Although a relatively small part of his overall numbers was trapped there, it represented the fighting heart of his army, and to lose those men would be a catastrophe from which not even Caesar's luck could save him, and he knew it. Still, it was almost impossible to bring himself to give the order to send in the transports that had pulled away from the beach back in to retrieve the men. Part of this hesitance was because of his deep-seated belief in himself and his men, but just as much of it was due to the fact that neither he nor any of his officers had ever discussed the best means to conduct such a withdrawal. The last time it might have been necessary was the first invasion of Britannia, and that was so long ago, and so many more landings had been effected that withdrawal didn't seem to be worthy of contemplation. But here Caesar was, watching his men die just for a few paces of sandy beach, desperately struggling to keep from being thrown into the pounding surf. With a start,

Caesar realized that the swells had been steadily increasing, the waves crashing onto the beach growing ever higher, only compounding his headaches. If they got any stronger, he thought, they will be enough to knock some of the men off their feet, and then they'll be done for. With growing dismay, he knew that his time to decide was running out faster than even his prodigious mind could compensate for, and he turned to his personal *cornicen.*

"Be prepared for my command," he told the wide-eyed man calmly, the steadiness of his voice belying the turmoil he was feeling inside, as he prepared to give an order he hadn't given once during this entire 10 year campaign.

Titus Pullus heard the blast of the *cornu* once, twice, then a third time, before his mind finally registered the meaning.

Retreat? he thought. Could that possibly be what he had heard? His wedge formation had finally made its way several paces inland, the men in it fighting savagely to secure this tiny foothold of beach. Now, after losing the gods knew how many men, he was supposed to give it up? Never before had Pullus' loyalty to Caesar and instant obedience to orders been so severely tested, not even at Pharsalus, as it was at this moment. His men, and he himself, had fought like Achilles this day to gain territory, however little it may have been, and Titus Pullus wasn't the type of man to surrender ground won at such cost willingly. In fact, he continued fighting, counting on his example to keep the men around him inspired to do the same.

Caesar watched as the transports of the first wave that had unloaded their cargo then left the beach now try to maneuver their way back. The increasingly heavy surf compounded matters, causing two of the transports to collide heavily against each other, snapping off at least a half-dozen oars from both craft. Caesar couldn't help a curse escaping his lips; it was very rare that he lost his composure, at least in public, but this was one of those occasions. Giving his *cornicen* a sidelong glance, he saw that the man was much too occupied with the sight before him to give any indication that he noticed his general muttering about men whose mothers may have been prostitutes. Turning his gaze back to the beach, he could only watch as the two damaged transports tried to disengage from each other, with limited success. Meanwhile, he saw that Pullus and his Century had managed to use their wedge formation to gain more of a foothold on the beach, causing him a pang of anxiety. For an instant, he experienced a sense of doubt, a very foreign feeling to Caesar, as he wondered if he had been premature in sounding the retreat. Then he looked down the length of the beach, and seeing the majority of his men still standing on the fringe of the beach or in the surf, his resolve returned. If Pullus and his men were able to fight their way onto the beach, they were able to fight their way off it!

For Sextus Scribonius, the call to retreat was something of a relief, and in fact, he had been half-hoping for that signal. Turning his mind to the immediate problem, he called over his shoulder to his own *cornicen*.

"Give the signal for fighting withdrawal," he shouted.

Almost instantly the deep, bass notes issued from the large curved horn, and Scribonius immediately took note that the faces of the men around him showed nothing but relief. Indeed, the command seemed to infuse the men with more energy as they began the process of shuffling backward. Now, Scribonius thought, all we need is a boat to get aboard. As his Legionaries began the process of withdrawing, Scribonius disentangled himself from the crush of men, shoving his way to the rear. It was only because of the respect and regard in which his men held him that none of them thought for an instant that he was positioning himself to be the first aboard; they knew him too well. Instead, he was making his way to Andros, the commander of the slingers, who had provided very little support to that point.

"I need you to form up there," Scribonius shouted, while pointing to a spot where the surf was perhaps knee-deep. "You're going to fire over our heads and keep these *cunni* at bay, while we get back on the boat."

Andros stared at Scribonius in disbelief.

"Are you mad?" he gasped. "Being this close means some of your men will be hit. My men are good, but they're not that good."

"I know that," Scribonius replied grimly, "but that's the only way to get any breathing room." Grabbing Andros by the arm, he finished urgently, "If you don't do this, we're all going to die on this beach."

Gulping, Andros only nodded in answer.

Farther down the beach, Gnaeus Cartufenus and his group of 20 men had just gone smashing into the Wa ranks when the signal to withdraw sounded, but neither he nor his men heard it over the din of clashing metal and shouting men. Oblivious to anything but the Wa across from him, Cartufenus was a snarling, spitting mass of malevolent energy and focused violence, thrusting and bashing with his shield, fighting desperately to gain a purchase of more sandy beach. Infected by the example of their leader, men who normally would have never found themselves in the thick of fighting were standing next to him, matching Cartufenus in his fury. For the first time there was a wavering in the Wa line, as they absorbed the impact of this small group of Romans, hacking their way into the midst of the Wa ranks. Knocking spears aside, the Romans demonstrated a level of teamwork and controlled ferocity that countless enemies before them had been forced to endure, and like those enemies, the Wa found themselves taking a step backward, tentative and halting, but definitely backward. The bulk of Cartufenus' men, however, heard the signal, and his Optio, a man named Spurius Lentulus, seeing his Primus Pilus isolated and either ignoring or not hearing the command, did his duty and took control. Like Scribonius, Lentulus ordered the *cornicen* to sound the call to make a fighting withdrawal. Only then did Cartufenus take notice, his head whipping around at the sound, but by this point the Wa on his flanks had enfolded his group so that they were completely isolated. The only way for Cartufenus and his men to join the rest of his men would be to fight their way out.

The empty transports finally made their way back up to the beach. Caesar, who had ordered the bombardment of his artillery to cease, in order to conserve ammunition, now commanded the galleys to re-commence firing to provide covering fire. For those Centuries that had not made headway onto the beach, withdrawing was more straightforward, although there was substantial difficulty in extracting wounded men. Those wounded who could, staggered and waded through the now-heavy surf, some of them covered in blood, seemingly from a wound to their upper body, and were dragged aboard by crewmen. Ironically, these were the lucky men, because those still able-bodied enough to fight had the extra pressure of keeping the Wa across from them at bay, as they backed up through the surf. Fortunately, the Wa were now showing their first signs of fatigue and were not as eager as they had been just moments before. Much of it had to do with the bodies piled on the fringe of the beach, the sand and surf on either side of the line almost completely red. Not only was it demoralizing to see so many casualties, they served as a barrier to keep the Wa somewhat at bay. Even so, there were quite a few Wa who clambered over and around the bodies to keep up the pressure. Unlike those Wa who were in the first few ranks, these men were almost exclusively armed with swords, which they wielded in a manner unlike any the Romans had encountered before. Like the Gauls, the Wa slashed with their weapons, but unlike the swords of the warriors of that now-faraway land, the Wa blades were more slender and the men wielding them seemed adept at attacking from any angle. Unlike the Gauls, who attempted to decapitate their opponents with their long swords, the Wa seemed content to land a damaging blow wherever they found an opening, clearly counting on their conditioning and endurance to outlast their opponents. From his ship, Caesar could see the flashing blades of those Wa who came pushing against his men, as they shuffled backward, shields up. He was pleased to see that the Romans were scoring hits, as Wa warriors were bested by the short, thrusting sword they all still carried. Even now, Caesar mused, as skilled as some of the warriors of the lands I have conquered have been, when it comes to a weapon, nothing has been superior to the Spanish sword. Until now, he thought grimly, although this was only half-formed, something worthy of further contemplation, but not until he had extricated the rest of his army.

Pullus' sword arm was soaked up to the elbow with blood, and it ached like never before from all the work he had done. Still, he was proud of his men, because they had now actually managed to crack the Wa lines. But now he was supposed to give all this up? Despite the fatigue, despite the loss of so many men, Pullus still couldn't really fathom the idea of retreat. So, out of all the Centurions on the beach, Pullus alone refused to give the order to withdraw, choosing to ignore the command. And save for a couple of glances over their shoulders, his men didn't hesitate to continue following their Primus Pilus. Not only were they conditioned to obey their Centurion, but they also had ultimate faith in him; he was a legend, not just in the 10th Legion, but in all of Caesar's army. And if he still believed that victory was possible, then they did as well. Consequently, they continued trying to move forward, confident that their Primus Pilus knew best. For his part, Pullus continued surging forward, always applying pressure on whoever stood opposite him, slaying each of them in turn. Besides his wound in his upper shoulder, he had a gash on his shield arm and a cut just above his left greave, so while most of the blood on him was not his, not all of it was that of his enemies. None of those wounds deterred him; his body was already covered in scars by this time. In fact, Scribonius often joked that it was harder to find a spot on Pullus that didn't have a scar than the opposite. All of these Pullus bore proudly: they were the proof of his accomplishments even more than the phalarae, torqs, and crowns that he had won. It was because of these scars that men followed him so readily and so steadfastly, and that bond was in evidence now, as Pullus continued fighting.

A short distance away, Scribonius was backing up, slowly, across the small expanse of beach his men had claimed, trying to avoid the bodies. The Balearic slingers had begun whirling their arms above their heads, loosing their lead missiles—much deadlier than the smooth rocks they had used previously—sending them whizzing just inches above the heads of the Romans. Despite their best efforts, there would be a stray shot, smashing into the unprotected back of one of the Romans, followed by either a grunt or shrill scream. One of the stricken man's comrades would grab him by the harness, dragging him backward to deposit him unceremoniously on the sand, or as the withdrawal continued, in the shallow surf. Those men unlucky enough to be unconscious ended up face down in the surf, either by the action of the waves or because the men dropping them there had other things on their minds. Only because slingers who, between loosing shots, were grabbing those men and turning them over, were they saved, since no *medici* had landed. There was still the problem of loading not just the unfortunates felled by the slingers, but also those wounded earlier in the action who were unable to help themselves. Realizing this, Scribonius reluctantly gave the command for half the slingers to cease fire and begin loading these men onto the boats, an order they obeyed with alacrity. No man was willing to leave a wounded comrade behind, if only because, if it ever happened to them, they didn't want to suffer the same fate. Whatever the reason, there was no hesitation on the part of the slingers as they either carried or dragged the unconscious men back toward the waiting transport. Very slowly and methodically, the men of the Second Cohort disengaged and made their way toward the waiting transport.

By this time Caesar wasn't bothering to hide his agitation, but this time it was aimed at the Primus Pilus of his 10th Legion, his favorite and best Legion. Seeing that Pullus had made no attempt to withdraw either himself or his men, Caesar pounded the rail in frustration. Of all the men he could afford to lose, Pullus and by extension, the First and Second Century of the First Cohort of the 10th were last on the list. His judgment was not entirely based on just the practical; he vividly remembered the first time he had decorated the tall, broad man now on the beach as a raw youth of 17, and over the years they had become as close as it was possible for men in their respective positions to be. In fact, Caesar was now faced with a choice he had no desire to make, but this time he didn't hesitate.

"Send the rest of the First Cohort onto the beach," he snapped at one of his aides. "Their orders are to help Pullus get his insubordinate *ass* back aboard their ship," he roared the last few words. "So I can *crucify* him myself."

Responding to the commands, the transports carrying the rest of the First Cohort came riding the heavy surf up onto the beach. Their task was made more difficult, because the transport originally carrying the first two Centuries had responded to Caesar's command and was pulling back onto the beach. The other two transports had to aim on either side of the beached vessel, but both captains managed to do just that, and before the transports came to a halt, the men aboard were jumping into the seething water. The Princeps Prior, commander of the Fourth Century of the First Cohort, Servius Arrianus, was the first over the side, followed close behind by the rest of his men, each of them eager to save their friends in the other Centuries. Thanks to the incursion made by Pullus and the men of the First Century, there was sufficient room to form up before plunging into the Wa ranks. The Wa, seeing the arrival of fresh men, realized that, at the least, this meant that their time to annihilate the wedge formation of the First Century was growing shorter, and as a result picked up the fury of their assault on the compact group. Balbus and Camillus had also managed to push the Wa back a bit, if only to maintain contact with the First on their right, now several dozen paces up the beach. Arrianus had one simple task: get to Pullus and make sure he understood that Caesar had ordered a withdrawal. Despite the seemingly straightforward nature of his task, Arrianus was not looking forward to delivering the message. As much as he admired and respected Titus Pullus, there was a healthy dose of fear there as well, so between facing these Wa barbarians or Pullus, to Arrianus it wasn't that different. Nevertheless, he was at the head of his men as they left the water behind and stepped over the piles of bodies on the beach, some of whom were reaching out and calling for help from friends they recognized and who were charging past. Nobody had time for these unfortunates at that moment, save for a sympathetic glance as they went by. Pushing his way through the packed rear ranks, where in each row the legionary was holding the harness of the man ahead of him, Arrianus forced his way forward between the files, snarling at men when they wouldn't immediately give way. Finally reaching just a couple rows behind his giant Primus Pilus, who was still thrusting and slashing at the Wa in front of him, Arrianus was at a loss what to do. Shouting might distract Pullus, although for the first time the Wa immediately surrounding the front of the wedge formation were no longer pressing as closely as they had. In fact, there seemed to be a pocket of space just outside the radius of the reach of Pullus and the front ranks of the formation, and even Arrianus was troubled with the thought, should we really be retreating? Nevertheless, those were the orders he was to relay, so he finally reached out and tapped Valerianus, the *aquilifer* of the Legion standing immediately behind Pullus. Whipping his head about so quickly it almost dislodged the wolfskin headdress that everyone in his position wore, Valerianus' eyes widened in surprise at the unexpected sight of the Fourth Century Centurion.

"I bring orders from Caesar," Arrianus shouted, surprising the *aquilifer* even further.

Arrianus proceeded to relay them to Valerianus, who visibly blanched before turning about. Tapping his Primus Pilus on the hip, a move they had obviously used before, because instead of turning around, Pullus merely leaned back so he could hear what Valerianus had to say. Arrianus saw Pullus stiffen, and even over the din of battle he heard the string of oaths from his commanding officer. For several moments, Pullus continued his slow and steady shuffle forward, lashing out first with his shield, following up with his blade, as if he hadn't heard a word. It looked very much to Arrianus that Pullus wasn't going to obey.

Meanwhile, Cartufenus and his small group of men had become totally isolated, as the remnants of the First and Second Century obeyed the command to withdraw. Moving backwards in good order, the First, under the command of the Optio, maintained their cohesion as they edged back into the surf, abandoning the toehold of beach they had fought so hard to attain. Those who were able dragged wounded comrades back with them, but too many were being left behind, some of them begging their friends to take them along, others beyond caring, knowing they would be dead soon, one way or another. Cartufenus, glancing about, seeing and understanding what was happening, knew that he and the rest of the men with him were doomed, and a part of him was grimly amused that it would be these men, the shirkers, who would buy with their lives enough time for the rest of his men to clamber back aboard the transport.

"All right you *cunni*," he snarled to the dozen men still standing, "we're all fucked. But we're going to show these slant-eyed bastards how a Roman dies!"

It was hard to say who was more surprised at the hearty roar that issued from the throats of every single man as they signaled their assent: Cartufenus or the men themselves, but none of them hesitated as they renewed the fury of their attack, moving deeper into the ranks of the Wa pressing about them, their blades flashing in the air.

Scribonius was the last man of his Century off the beach, backing up slowly, his shield, riddled with arrows and scarred from several spear and sword strikes, but still intact, still in the first position. The slingers, after loading the wounded, had clambered back aboard, immediately moving to the foredeck of the transport, and were now sending a hail of missiles into the massed ranks of the Wa. This was all the protection that Scribonius had, as he continued backing through the surf, trying to steady himself against the waves and praying he didn't step into the same hole that he landed in when he had jumped into the water just—what, he thought with some surprise—about two thirds of a watch before, if that? Helping keep Scribonius safe were some of his Legionaries who, scrounging up unused javelins, were launching them at any Wa who gave them a target by getting too close. However, for the most part, they seemed content to stop just out of missile range and stand there, jeering at the retreating Romans. Despite having no idea what was being said, Scribonius and his men burned with shame and indignation, needing no translator to understand the scorn being heaped on them. Somehow, Scribonius managed to make it to the side of the transport, where several helping hands reached down and unceremoniously hauled him aboard, where he lay gasping on the deck from the exertion, still shaking from all that had transpired. Finally clambering to his feet, he took a quick glance around, dismayed at the sight of the carnage on the deck, as the *medici* attached to his Century, all two of them, hurried about, trying to assess those casualties that had a chance of being saved. Very quickly, Scribonius realized that there was little, if anything, that could be done for these men, since any treatment they would receive should be given by the more skilled Han physicians, or even the Pandyan, or the Greeks. But Caesar had planned only on success, counting on having space on dry land, after being successful, so he hadn't thought to disperse the physicians among all the transports. Any chance Scribonius' seriously wounded had now rested in the hands of these two *medici*, and it didn't take an expert to see that they were completely overwhelmed, since it appeared that at least half of the remaining members of his Century were wounded to one degree or another.

After what seemed to be another full watch, Titus Pullus snapped an order over his shoulder, never turning his head away from the enemy, and his *cornicen*, standing next to Valerianus, lifted the horn and blew the same notes that had sounded from Caesar's own man earlier. Automatically, and without any hesitation, the men in the rear ranks of the wedge formation, helped by the members of the Fourth Century on one side and the Fifth Century on the other, pushed outwards against those Wa still trying to apply pressure on the flanks of the formation. Bashing with their shields, the fresher men of the relieving Centuries very quickly made a space for the men of the First to extract themselves, and now all the watches of training for a maneuver that the Centurions and men alike scoffed at as something they would never do paid off. Closing the distance back to the surf line much more quickly than they had moved forward, the Romans rapidly began the process of loading back onto the transports. The Sixth Century had landed next to the Second, who had been anchoring the far left of the First Cohort's sector, and Balbus followed his men off the beach under the fresh javelins of the Sixth, who followed immediately after. However, there was no real pursuit; as in the case with Scribonius, heavy missile fire kept the Wa at bay, although this came from the heavier artillery of the offshore warships, instead of from slingers. Still, it was more than that, because the Wa showed no inclination towards pressing their victory, instead standing there amid the piles of bodies, many of those moving, but most lying still in the sand, panting heavily and unable to speak. Titus Pullus, surveying the beach, saw the Wa and with a brief flash of excitement understood that this was the moment to press the attack again, sure as he had ever been that victory was still in the Romans' grasp. He was about to turn his head and give the command to unload the ships and renew the assault when, out of the corner of his eye, he caught a glimpse of a tall, spare figure standing on the deck of the flagship. Even from this distance, he could see Caesar glaring at him, causing the flare of savage jubilation to fizzle out immediately, and he hissed in frustration at what he was sure was an opportunity lost. Still, he obediently continued backing up, until he reached the side of the ship. Unlike Scribonius, he spurned the offers of help, but before he clambered aboard he turned back to face the new enemy, the only one who had ever made him retreat.

"I am Titus Pullus," he roared at the top of his lungs, lungs conditioned by decades of bellowing orders across vast expanses, so he knew the Wa would hear, even over the pounding waves and moaning men. "I am the Primus Pilus of Caesar's 10th Legion, and I swear by my gods Mars, Bellona, Shiva, and Mithras that we will be back! And I will have vengeance!"

Climbing aboard, he heard the jeering catcalls of the Wa, and like Scribonius and his men, he needed no translator to understand them.

Gnaeus Cartufenus had only a half-dozen of the original twenty men around him, and he had never been more exhausted than he was at that moment. He was barely able to hold his shield in the first position; this was the third shield, the others having been splintered, and his sword arm ached so badly that he couldn't hold his arm out upright, even though his life depended on it. Panting for breath, it felt as if he were inhaling pure fire, and every part of his body shook, as if he had the ague. His men were in the same situation, and they were now hemmed in on all sides by spear- and sword-wielding Wa, their weapons all pointing at the beleaguered group of Romans. Still, they didn't finish them off, and Cartufenus dimly wondered why, although it didn't seem to matter all that much. At that moment the idea of death was a relief, and after several moments, where nobody moved, Cartufenus finally had enough.

"Come on you savages," he gasped, waving his sword feebly in the direction of himself and his men, "come get us! Let's get this over with and we'll show you how Romans die!"

There was still no movement, until the ranks immediately opposite the Romans suddenly opened up and a Wa warrior stepped forward. This man wore the lamellar iron armor, along with a helmet adorned with what Cartufenus assumed was some sort of bird. A crane, perhaps, he thought dully? Whatever, it didn't matter. The man was, like the rest of the Wa, short but compactly built, and without knowing a thing about him, Cartufenus and his men immediately understood that this was what passed for a nobleman of these people, his air of command and authority the same as if he were standing in the Forum of Rome. When the Wa spoke, it was in a guttural language that sounded nothing like the singsong pattern of the Han, but more like the language of the Gayan, those people of the peninsula the army had crossed just before coming here. Cartufenus had a few Gayan in his ranks, but none of them were here now, and even so, it wasn't likely that they could understand that much, either. But that didn't deter the Wa commander, who, as he talked, kept gesturing with the point of his sword. Once he was finished, he stood looking expectantly at Cartufenus and his survivors, telling the Primus Pilus that something was expected of him, although he had no idea what. Finally, Cartufenus spat onto the sand of the beach, then threw down his sword.

"Drop the weapons, boys," he told the rest of the men. "We might as well see what the gods have in store for us. Who knows," he said with grim and heavy humor, "maybe they'll be so impressed with us that they'll let us go."

Individually, none of Cartufenus' men, all veterans and all born survivors, would have believed their Centurion, but something happens when men group together, and a collective consciousness seems to take over, and along with it, the will to survive increases dramatically. Perhaps it's because the idea that one won't be alone when facing the unknown gives some men courage, but whatever the cause, Cartufenus' men followed suit, throwing down their swords. They were now captives of the Wa, and only the gods knew exactly what their fate would be.

Still standing at the rail, Caesar could only watch as the remnants of the first wave of his army boarded the transports, then slowly pulled away from the beach. Left behind was carnage on a level that Caesar couldn't recall seeing since Alesia, and while he took grim satisfaction in the sight of the majority of those lying strewn in the sand being Wa, he knew that his army had been badly hurt. Good men, really good men, were being left behind, and even as this thought crossed his mind, he heard a shout that alerted him to a sight farther down the beach. He could barely make out a small knot of what looked like Wa warriors, but they were clearly surrounding a smaller group, and with a sinking feeling in his stomach, he recognized that some of his men were prisoners. Hopefully it won't be a Centurion, he thought, not knowing that his worst fears were being realized. Unfortunately, there were even bigger problems, and Caesar began preparing himself mentally for the reality to sink in: the Wa had repulsed the landing. Caesar had been defeated.

Chapter 4

It was a somber group of men crammed into Caesar's stateroom aboard the flagship. None of them was accustomed to defeat, and there was no way for any of them to pretend this was anything but a defeat, and a resounding one at that. Standing and bracing himself against the rolling ship, Caesar surveyed the faces of the men around him, his expression matching theirs. Now is not the time to grieve, he admonished himself, recognizing that as they had done so many times before, this group of men, leaders of his army, were looking to him to set the tone and to provide a solution to their dilemma.

"Before I say anything else, I would like to offer a prayer to the gods for Cartufenus and his men, and request not only their blessing on him and his men, but a curse onto the Wa for what they did."

Although the men all bowed their heads and held their arms out in supplication, as Caesar intoned the words, the sense of anger and frustration was palpable in the small room. Titus Pullus, in particular, felt a surge of rage and guilt— Cartufenus having been more than a colleague but also a friend—as Caesar's voice droned the ritual blessing. Had this been his fault, he wondered? Had his stubborn refusal to withdraw from the beach helped to spur the Wa into the act of barbarity they were all forced to witness in helpless anger, as they stood at the rail of their respective ships? Shaking his head, trying to dispel such thoughts, he was singularly unsuccessful in banishing the memory of Cartufenus and his men, kneeling, with their hands bound, being systematically decapitated. The roars of rage and helplessness clearly carried across the entire fleet, as a Wa warrior—probably the leader judging by the adornment of his helmet and quality of his armor— walked from one Legionary to the next. There would be the flash of a blade as it slashed down in a graceful arc, and the detached part of Pullus' mind found itself in grudging envy of the fluidity and obvious force behind each blow. The sight of a head rolling in the sand, spattering gore as it tumbled a couple of paces, jerked him from that admiration, and as hardened a soldier as he was, he felt a clenching in his stomach that signaled the possibility of its expelling whatever contents were left in it.

Now, standing shoulder to shoulder with the other Primi Pili, Tribunes, and Legates, Pullus looked to Caesar, his prayer finished, to issue the orders that would begin the process of avenging the death of not just Cartufenus, but all of those left behind on the beach. All of the assembled men understood that if the Wa had executed those able-bodied men left behind, their stranded wounded suffered the same fate, making their anger a palpable force. Conscious of it, Caesar was careful in his speech.

"There is no question that we must avenge the death of those men who were left behind," he began, but seeing the faces of the Centurions, most notably Pullus, darken, he hastily added, "through no man's fault but my own." Seeing a slight relaxing in their posture, Caesar continued, "But we cannot afford another setback like today's."

That's one way to put it, Pullus thought, but he knew how hard it was for a man like Caesar to utter the word "defeat".

"To that end, I've sent Volusenus farther up the coast to find a landing site that's unlikely to be contested. Barring that, he has orders to look for another island that is either uninhabited or lightly defended, so that we can land there and recover."

The men digested this, saying nothing, unsettling Caesar a bit. Normally there would be questions, or at the least some comments, but nobody said a word.

Silence stretched out for several heartbeats, prompting Caesar to ask, somewhat irritably, "Are there any questions?"

None were forthcoming, so nonplussed, Caesar dismissed the men to return to their respective ships, each man buried deep in his own thoughts.

Volusenus' ship returned to the fleet three days later, meeting up as the main group continued to beat north into the teeth of a steadily growing wind. After rowing to the flagship, Volusenus reported the presence of what appeared to be an uninhabited island another two days farther north, but Volusenus was adamant that there wasn't a single beach or anchorage sufficient for the fleet. The only other option was the much larger island they had seen to the south during their passage to the main island, but even from a distance, it had looked as forbidding a place to land as the island Volusenus had found. Additionally, Caesar reasoned that the larger island was in all likelihood inhabited, and despite taking the first island east of the Gayan peninsula with ease, even the man renowned for his luck and daring was shaken.

Turning cold eyes to Zhang, he addressed his question to Achaemenes, "Does he know whether the island to the south is inhabited? And if so, in what numbers and, more importantly, are there any of those abominable savages there?"

As he waited for the translation, Caesar pondered all that Volusenus had told him. He knew very well that every day at sea that passed, more of his men who still might be saved would die, but he couldn't suffer another setback like the one that had occurred a few days before. NOT a setback, Gaius, he chided himself. Even if you don't utter the word aloud, you must not lie to yourself. We, no, I was trounced, defeated, beaten. Suddenly and savagely, the word NO screamed unbidden in his mind, almost making him utter the word aloud, but only with the discipline of Caesar did he avoid making such a blunder. I may have been defeated, but I am NOT BEATEN, he raged at himself, all the while maintaining the same, calm demeanor his men knew so well. For that was the power of being Caesar: never, ever, did he betray what he was really thinking at any time, and this time, more than others, this was important, because any sign of self-doubt would fuel what he knew were already mutterings among the men, that Caesar's luck had finally run out. One such defeat he could master, but two? No, not even Caesar could overcome that, hence the importance of his next decision.

Achaemenes finally turned to Caesar and reported, "Zhang says that the island to the south, while it's uninhabited, doesn't have an anchorage of a sufficient size for the fleet."

Despite his best attempt, Caesar hissed in frustration, turning back to Volusenus, who looked extremely uncomfortable being the sole focus of his commander's attention.

Nevertheless, his gaze never wavered as he spoke, "By my calculations, Caesar, there are only two anchorages on the island I found. It's clearly uninhabited, save for one lone shack. But the island itself is very small; I would estimate it being no more than a mile across and 2 miles long. There is one anchorage on the southern end and one slightly larger one on the eastern side."

"How many ships could fit in each?" Caesar asked, arms crossed.

Volusenus sucked through his teeth as he thought about it before answering, "Perhaps 50 in the smallest anchorage and more than 100 in the other. But," he admonished, "they would be very cramped. Meaning that......."

"....If a storm came, they would damage each other, just like in Britannia," Caesar finished for him, his tone peevish, although he knew that it wasn't Volusenus' fault.

Clearly frustrated, Caesar began pacing, head down as he stared at the deck, pondering what to do. If he went south to the larger island, there would be more room, perhaps, but Zhang had been frustratingly vague about the conditions needed for a safe harbor for his ships. And, more than anything, Caesar knew from long and bitter experience that the men viewed the fleet as their lifeline back to any semblance of security. He was disturbed from his thinking by the sound of a clearing throat, and he looked up irritably to see that, judging from the reactions of the men around him, it had been Zhang who had made the noise.

"Yes?" Caesar asked, masking his annoyance, both at the situation and at Zhang, whom he was beginning to consider as an agent for the Han court and who had no intention of aiding Caesar and his men. When Zhang spoke, Caesar almost gasped in shock, while the men around him were not so circumspect, making the rest of what Zhang said very hard to understand. The reason for the surprise was that Zhang was speaking in Latin! Slow, halting, but clearly understandable Latin!

"Caesar," he had begun, and despite the surprise, Caesar was forced to stifle a smile at the awkward pronunciation of his name. "Forgive my poor Latin, but I know that this ..." for perhaps the first time Zhang showed emotion, screwing up his face as he searched for the right word, "*...process* of translation has been..." For a moment he couldn't continue, causing Caesar to prompt gently with the word, "frustrating, I believe is the word you are looking for."

Zhang's face cleared, as he inclined his head in what could have been gratitude for the help.

"Yes, that is the word. However, I have not wanted to speak in your tongue, until I had a better hold of it."

You mean "grasp," Caesar thought, but said nothing. No, you didn't let us know because you wanted to gather as much information as possible, before you let us know that you held a throw of Venus in your hand. Regardless, Caesar was at least thankful that there would be a bit less time wasted, and listened intently as Zhang continued.

"Since we are, how do you say, searching? Yes, searching for a spot where your army can rest, I know of perhaps a place."

The attention of every man in the room was riveted on him, but the eyes staring at Zhang were anything but friendly. If he were aware or shaken by the scrutiny he didn't show it as he described what he knew, and undoubtedly had known all along.

"There is a passage that will lead you to what the Wa call their Inland Sea," he explained. "Once there, you will find not only many spots to anchor, but there is also a region that is almost completely empty of people."

Caesar's jaw tightened, while the others' shoulders slumped as the tension released from them, disappointed at the Han's words.

"Yes, I know that there are better anchorages, but we would have to reverse our course and go around the southern end of the island," Caesar said patiently. "Or, we can continue north, but you have said yourself, you're not sure how far the northern end is. We don't have that long, Zhang."

Zhang immediately shook his head, in the style that Latins were accustomed to, and not in the circular motion used by the Han.

"No, this is not one large island," he told Caesar. Then, for the first time, his face showed a bit of alarm at the sight of Caesar's face darkening, as blood rushed to it, which he had learned didn't bode well. "It appears to be, but I know there is a very, very narrow strait that is very hard to find. In fact, judging from the landmarks, we are not that far from it. We could be in those straits by the end of the day."

"And why didn't you see fit to tell us of this strait before?" Caesar asked in a deceptively mild voice his officers knowing this was even more dangerous than his rage.

Men disappeared from around their fires whenever Caesar spoke in this manner, but nobody looked at Zhang with any sympathy. In fact, if it had been up to almost all of them, particularly the Primi Pili, like Pullus, Torquatus and Balbinus, Zhang would have been pitched overboard long before. For the first time, Zhang seemed to become aware that there was a danger present, and Caesar was gratified to see tiny beads of sweat appear on the Han's brow.

"I did not speak of it before because I have only heard of it. I have not been through the strait myself. And it is supposed to be very dangerous to navigate. There are many rocks and the water is, how do you call it," at this Zhang for the first time turned to Achaemenes for help with the word, uttering what he was looking for in Han.

Achaemenes thought for a moment and said, "Shallow."

"Yes," Zhang nodded. "The water is very shallow, and I do not know whether all of your ships can pass through. I have been told that this strait fills up with dirt washed from the rains and this makes it very likely that some of your ships will become stranded. Also, I do not know about the," again he turned to Achaemenes, who supplied the word, "tides in this strait."

All of what Zhang said made sense, and Caesar relaxed just a little bit. He still didn't trust Zhang, but he supposed that it would be understandable that Zhang wouldn't be forthcoming with this information, if it meant there was a chance the ship he was on was the most likely to be stranded, or worse.

Whatever the case, Caesar immediately recognized that this was his only real choice, to trust Zhang to provide the information needed to guide them through these straits. Turning to Volusenus, he gave him his orders.

"Take Zhang onto your Liburnian," referring to the lone remaining scout ship, still the fastest of any that Caesar had encountered, "and follow his directions looking for this strait. We'll follow on your heading. When you find it, come back and guide us."

Volusenus saluted and turned immediately to go, but before he did, Caesar grabbed his elbow and whispered a few words to his exploring officer. Volusenus listened, then gave a grim nod, before leading Zhang out of the stateroom.

Once they had left and Caesar was sure they were no longer within earshot, he told the rest of the officers calmly, "I told Volusenus that if Zhang lied, he's to tie him to the prow of the ship, cut his hamstrings, and let the sharks eat him."

With grim smiles, the officers of Caesar's army left the flagship to return to their men and inform them of what was coming.

Whether or not Zhang was planning any treachery, Caesar didn't know, but he was thankful that he apparently didn't have anything malevolent in store for the passage through the straits. As Zhang had predicted, traversing the strait was a nightmare, made all the more urgent and vivid by the knowledge that every watch spent at sea meant more of his wounded were likely to die. Nevertheless, they made it, although as they rowed their way through the strait, they were forced to hug one shore, because of the narrowness of the passageway, and because the opposite shore was lined with Wa archers who were waiting for any ship to come within range. Thank the gods these Wa didn't have any artillery, or Greek fire, for that matter, Caesar mused. If they had, it was highly likely that most of his fleet would have been damaged or destroyed. As it was, his own flagship had suffered damage when it had come close to foundering on the built-up silt and had to be hauled into deeper water. There hadn't been just mud in that strait, as the buckled timbers of the quinquereme attested, but fortunately they were now safely ashore, a camp was built, and repairs could be made. Once through the strait, Volusenus, with Zhang's help, had guided them due north to where a river flowed into the Inland Sea, with a smaller stream entering the inlet from the western side. The ground wasn't perfect; there were some heights to the west less than a mile from the edge of the camp, but judging from what Caesar had seen of this island so far, he suspected that level ground was going to be hard to come by. Regardless, the men had worked hard and well, erecting a strongly fortified camp with their usual speed and efficiency, and if they ended up staying longer than a week, Caesar would have them improve the defenses even more. Nothing gave men better sleep than knowing they were safe, and Caesar was no different in that regard. Sighing, he rose from behind his desk in the *praetorium*, straightening his tunic before he had his slave lower his cuirass over his head, then hand him the eagle-headed handle of his sheathed sword. He was about to go to the hospital tent to make one of his twice daily visits to the wounded, knowing that the sight of their general seemed to help them heal more quickly than any potion.

Titus Pullus and Sextus Scribonius sat in Titus' tent, the remains of their evening meal still sitting in front of them before it would be cleared away by one of the slaves. It had been almost a week since the aborted landing, but Pullus was still sore, just another sign to him that he was getting too old for this kind of nonsense. This didn't help his mood any; like the rest of the army, there had been a pall hanging over his head resulting from the recent defeat. For a couple of days, the Primus Pilus of the 10th had been more in a state of shock than anything else, not quite believing what he knew to be true: that for the first time in this campaign, now 10 years old, Caesar's army had been beaten. Once that new reality sank in, it had plunged him into a depression, the likes of which he had never experienced before. It hadn't been as acute as his grief over the loss of some of his comrades who were close friends, but, while not quite as painful as those personal losses, this one was more profound in ways he couldn't describe, even if he were so inclined. Which he wasn't, thanking the gods for how well his friend Scribonius knew him and recognized that trying to cheer him up wouldn't help. Besides, Scribonius had his own grief to deal with; after all, he had been on the beach as well, and while not as overt about it, he was just as proud as Titus. Still, there were matters to discuss that couldn't be avoided forever.

Finally breaking the silence, Scribonius asked, "Have you given any more thought to what we talked about?"

A flash of irritation showed on Titus' face, but it disappeared as he heaved a weary sigh, knowing that Scribonius was right to bring it up and that it couldn't be avoided any longer.

"Yes," he finally answered, if a bit grudgingly. "But I still haven't made up my mind."

Now it was Scribonius' turn to be irritated, but they had been friends much too long for him to be cowed by either Pullus' rank or reputation. "Pluto's thorny cock, Titus," he snapped. "You can't put this off forever. I don't remember ever going this long without an Optio, and I didn't argue with you when you took mine to put in your Cohort. And Mardonius is the logical choice to be my Optio."

Instead of getting angry, Pullus rubbed his face, a habit of his whenever he was thinking or distracted.

"I know that," he finally replied, his tone as tired as his face looked. "But we both know that this isn't as straightforward as it looks. We *are* talking about the Second Cohort."

Now it was Scribonius' turn to sigh, because he knew Pullus was just as right as Scribonius himself was, and that this was the reason no decision had been made. The nub of the problem was that Mardonius was a Parthian, and while he was Tesseraurius in one of Scribonius' upper Centuries, there had been a string of Parthians promoted in the last few months, and some of the men—and not just Romans—were muttering about it. Compounding matters was that Mardonius would be the Optio of the First Century of the Second Cohort, leapfrogging other men who were at the least more senior, if not more qualified. Normally, this was little more than a headache, but the situation was made more difficult because of the overall mood of the army. Too many men rescued from the beach had gone on to die of their wounds from being laid out on the pitching deck or crammed into the holds of ships, because there had been no place to land. Suffering the defeat was bad enough, but the combination of all these things meant that Pullus' hold on the 10th was more tenuous than it had been since the dark days immediately after Pharsalus, when he had stood with Caesar against not just his comrades, but also his longest and dearest friend, Vibius Domitius. In fact, Titus had come dangerously close to striking Vibius down, a memory that had stayed with the giant Primus Pilus to this day. However, he wasn't alone; aside from the promotion issue, the other Primi Pili were in similar straits, none of them sleeping well at night, even with the security of the camp walls around them. The threat was from within, and for any leader, this is the most difficult challenge he will face, no matter what his circumstances.

"Well, as bad as it may be," Scribonius broke the silence between them, "at least we're not the 28th."

"Who are you telling?" Pullus asked, with grim humor. "If we were, I wouldn't be sitting here right now."

And with that thought, they toasted each other with the rancid rice wine Diocles had managed to scrounge up.

Scribonius was correct; the men of the 28th were devastated, both at the loss of their Primus Pilus Gnaeus Cartufenus and at the manner of his death. It was a situation of which Caesar was acutely aware, but he had not yet replaced the Primus Pilus, nor had he addressed the men of the 28th or the rest of the army for that matter. This was another thing troubling the men of the ranks, but it troubled the officers even more: to men like Pullus, who had followed Caesar for 27 years, it was very uncharacteristic. Normally, when there had been a setback, Caesar never hesitated to not only face trouble head-on, but in cases where the army appeared in danger or faced a huge threat, he often exaggerated the danger, as he did in the case of Ariovistus, or when the army faced elephants for the first time at Thapsus. Yet for reasons Pullus and the other Centurions could only guess, Caesar had chosen to remain silent to this point. Pullus, who knew Caesar better than almost any other man from the ranks, suspected that his general was in what passed for him as a state of shock. Oh, he had conducted his daily briefings, but they had been extremely short, and before anyone could raise a question, he would end the meeting and stride out of the large partitioned area that served as the Generals' and staff's mess, when it wasn't used for meetings. Pullus had been tempted to seek an audience with Caesar to speak to him in private, both to try and plumb the depths of Caesar's despair, and also to remind him gently that he needed to be more of his old self and address the army. Yet something held him back; as much as he loved and respected Caesar, there was still a healthy dose of fear there. Over the years he had seen men suddenly disappear, and had even been peripherally involved in an incident, where a Centurion who struck down one of his own men during the time when Caesar was besieged in Alexandria was killed in action under suspicious circumstances. Although Pullus knew that in almost every case, the disappeared men had been troublemakers, it still instilled in him a healthy caution around Caesar. Instead of talking with Caesar, like his general, Pullus made regular visits to the hospital, and he was relieved to see that all but a few men were on the road to recovery; those whom the gods had fated to die for the most part had done so.

Finally on the fifth day after they landed, two things happened. The first was that Charon's Boat, the separate section of the hospital tent , where those destined to die were taken, was finally empty—the first concrete sign that there would be no more deaths. The second came when Diocles burst into Pullus' private quarters, where his master and friend was resting after conducting a morning's worth of weapons training. Titus Pullus' first post in the Legions had been as a weapons instructor, and even now he still prided himself on his prowess with a sword. Sensing Diocles' presence, he looked over from his cot, instantly understanding that something momentous was taking place, so he swung his feet to the ground, then stood as he reached for his *vitus*, the twisted vine cane that was symbol of his rank.

His instinct was correct: Diocles said excitedly, "I just heard from Apollodorus," naming one of Caesar's secretaries. "Caesar is calling an assembly of the army."

"When?" Pullus asked, his mind automatically running through the things that needed to be done, whenever Caesar ordered the parade of the entire army.

"At the beginning of the next watch," Diocles answered, causing Pullus to swear.

"That's less than a third of a watch to go," Pullus protested, but even as he was doing so, he began donning his mail shirt and strapping on his harness. "But maybe we'll find out what his plan is."

Diocles was already on his way out to begin his own set of tasks required to summon the Legion, but he clearly heard Pullus mutter, "Gods help us if he doesn't have one."

"Comrades," Caesar began his speech in his usual manner, accustomed to the longer delay required for the interpreters to translate his words into the almost dozen tongues his soldiers now spoke. "We have suffered a loss," he raised his hands at what he knew would be the inevitable howls of protest, "*not* a defeat! It would only be a defeat if we were to load up on our ships and return home," even as he uttered the last word, Caesar felt a pang of...what? Regret? Remorse? Could it be homesickness? He knew that as acutely as he felt it, his men would suffer from that longing even more, so he hurried on. "But we are not going to do that!"

Immediately a hush filled the forum of the camp, the men needing no translation of his tone, if not his words, to understand what he was saying. Without realizing it, almost every man was leaning forward from their position of *intente*, focusing on what Caesar was about to say.

"We will not let this defeat us! No, my comrades, we have come too far, suffered too much, seen too many of our friends die to lose heart now! We must AVENGE those comrades we lost on the beach! And for the men of the 28th Legion," Caesar turned in their direction, his hand upraised, "there is a special debt that must be repaid in blood! You have lost your leader, the great Gnaeus Cartufenus, your Primus Pilus and a man who has served me well, going back to the difficult days when I was in Alexandria, besieged by Ptolemy!"

Caesar's reference to those days struck Titus Pullus like a blow; he had been the *de facto* Primus Pilus of the 2 Cohorts of the

6th Legion Caesar had brought to Alexandria in pursuit of Pompey, only to be trapped there for better than 7 months. During those days, Titus had become good friends with Cartufenus, and he remembered the trials they had both endured, when the 28th, then a green Legion, had almost mutinied because of a lack of water. Cartufenus had been steadfast then; in fact, Titus remembered, it had been Cartufenus who, leading 2 Cohorts of the 28th, had scaled the heights above the Egyptian camp during the battle that saw the final defeat and drowning of Ptolemy, breaking what had been to that point a bloody stalemate, with the day still very much in doubt.

"Even as I speak, I have sent ships scouting further along the coast of this wretched Island of Wa. Now that we are in their Inland Sea, I have it on good authority that there are large stretches of coast that are uninhabited. We are going to land again, but not until after we have regained our strength. Also, now that I have seen how these Wa fight, we are going to train differently. I will teach you the best way to defeat these savages, and show them that of all the soldiers in the world, those who march for Rome, no matter where they are from originally, are the greatest in the world!"

Once his words were translated, the ground shook with the roars of the men, as Pullus thought, he's done it again. I don't know how, but he's managed to make the men forget how badly we were beaten just a week ago.

Later that day, Pullus and the other Primi Pili were summoned to a briefing in the *praetorium*, and as Pullus, Torquatus and Balbinus walked together to the headquarters tent, they discussed what they had heard earlier.

"Any idea what this new tactic is?" Balbinus asked, not really aiming the question at anyone, but Torquatus understood that it had been aimed at Pullus, both men believing, with good reason, that of all the Primi Pili, Pullus was the one closest to Caesar.

"No," Pullus answered, "and trust me, I had Diocles work his network of spies under the tentpole working overtime trying to find out. But Caesar's been playing this one very, very tightly."

"Figures," Torquatus grunted, "gods know he's been withdrawn the last week."

The other two Centurions agreed this was the case, but any more conversation was cut short by their arrival. Entering past the guards, they were waved immediately to the conference room, where about half of the other Centurions and staff had already gathered. Very quickly the rest arrived, and not more than a dozen heartbeats later, Caesar strode in, followed by Hirtius, Pollio, and the rest of his staff. Waving his audience to their seats, Caesar began immediately by pulling the cloth off the tent wall that, as the others saw immediately, had been covering a surprisingly detailed map of the Island of Wa, with most of the detail concentrated on the vicinity of the Inland Sea. Despite themselves, most of the men made small sounds of amazement and surprise, showing how impressed they were that Caesar had been able to amass so much information in such a small amount of time.

"As you can see, Volusenus and his staff have been very busy, with no small thanks going to Zhang," Caesar nodded in the direction of the Han emissary, seated in the first row, whose face as usual betrayed no emotion whatsoever, save for a small nod of the head in acknowledgement.

Uppity bastard, Pullus thought to himself, acting like he's the one in charge. I'd love to gut that slanty-eyed bastard myself. Turning his attention back to his general, Pullus listened, as Caesar continued.

"As you can see, about a day's sailing west of here start a number of islands, as the coast swings to the south. Zhang has told us, and Volusenus has confirmed," Caesar's emphasis on this last part stopped the muttering of the assembled men, "that there is one very large island, then a very large bay, with perhaps two dozen more islands of varying size. However, there is one," as he talked Caesar pointed to a crudely drawn mass of land south of the main island that to Pullus looked a bit like the letter V, although the right arm of it had a protuberance that almost closed off the top, "that has a very protected harbor. It is uninhabited, but as you can also see, it is not far from the main island. And directly north of that island is a large settlement, with what looks like a fair-sized garrison of troops. That, gentlemen," he finished, "will be our target."

The plan, as Caesar outlined it, like most of his plans, was simple. While there were a number of small craft in the area of this city, none of them were warships, at least of a sufficient size or number to stop Caesar's fleet from investing the island to the south.

This island would be the base of all operations from this point forward, he told them, and the harbor would be heavily fortified. The entrance into this protected bay, because of the knot of land that Pullus had noticed, narrowed it down to less than a half-mile, and with artillery emplacements on either shore, there would be no way for any hostile force to enter without being raked by fire. The land in the pocket of the V was flat enough for a camp that would hold the entire army, and according to Volusenus, who had landed on the island, there was wild game and plentiful fresh water. Caesar made it clear that after establishing a defensible position on the island, the first target was the city across the bay where, he told his officers with a wolfish smile, the Legions would be turned loose to exact revenge in a way the Wa would never forget.

All that remained was this new tactic that Caesar had promised, but he had refused to enlighten his Centurions about what he had in store, saying only that once things were settled in their new position, he would make his plans known. But, he assured them, neither they nor the men would be disappointed.

Chapter 5

The move to the new island went smoothly, with only one minor skirmish between a small group of Wa warships, very small craft, poorly armed and crewed, all of them quickly sent to the bottom of the bay. As Caesar's massive fleet cruised by the mainland, heading for the protected harbor of the island, the men lined the rails to watch the activity on the shore, which was a swirl of movement as thousands of Wa stood watching the foreign invaders sailing by.

"How many do you suppose there are?" Sextus Scribonius asked Titus Pullus, the two standing side-by-side on one of the transports.

"I don't know, but there's a lot of 'em," Pullus grunted. "But I don't worry about the civilians. I worry about those bastards," he pointed to a large group of Wa warriors, standing separately from the others.

"I don't know," Scribonius said doubtfully. "If the civilians are even half as fierce as their warriors, we're going to have our hands full."

Pullus laughed and slapped his friend on the back. "What, did you want to live forever? Besides, didn't Caesar tell us he's got a plan to defeat them?"

"Actually, I did plan on living forever," Scribonius retorted, "or at least longer than you. But speaking of Caesar's plan: still no idea what it is?"

Pullus answered with a frustrated grimace and shake of his head. "No, not a clue. And I'm beginning to wonder..." before he finished, he lowered his voice and took a furtive glance about to see, if anyone was listening. "...if he really has a plan, or he's just telling us that he does."

Scribonius couldn't hide his shock; never before had he heard his best friend express this level of doubt in their commanding officer. With those words ringing in his ears, Scribonius turned his attention back to the sight on shore, both men lost in their own thoughts.

As usual in Caesar's army, everything moved with absolute efficiency and speed, so that within two watches of the first ships pulling into the protected harbor, the camp was completed. By the next morning, the northern edge of the island facing the bay was dotted with small forts, each one with a complement of artillery in the form of scorpions and ballistae. Just outside the camp, Caesar ordered a large area cleared of all underbrush and trees, and on the second night he called a meeting of all Primi Pili and Pili Priores, to be held outside the camp walls, out of earshot of the men.

Without preamble, he told them, in the high-pitched tone he used when addressing large groups, "I know that you have been waiting to hear about the new plan I have for defeating these barbarians, now that we know how they fight." He waited a moment for the inevitable buzz, as men muttered to their friends, and only those standing close enough could see the twitch of his mouth, as he continued, "And I know that some of you have doubted whether or not I actually had a plan, or if I was just saying it to appease the men."

Although Pullus was standing closely enough to see the shadow of a smile on his general's face, he still experienced a shiver of dread, wondering if this was just a shrewd guess on Caesar's part, or if he had spies in even more places than Pullus thought. Whatever the case, Caesar's words served to focus the minds of the assembled Centurions in a most effective way, and all murmuring and shifting about stopped as they listened intently.

"As you all saw, these barbarians are extremely aggressive," Caesar continued, "and the reason we were repulsed had nothing to do with the bravery of our men. The reality is that the method we use in making a beach assault, while it has been successful thus far, is not suited for the type of resistance we saw a week ago. Therefore, after giving it much thought, I have come up with what I believe will give us the best chance of making a successful landing."

Caesar paused for a moment, and despite themselves, the men found that they were leaning forward, waiting for him to continue. Their general knew this, and accordingly didn't say a word for several moments, drawing out the tension and anticipation of the Centurions, until he could tell they were on the verge of shouting at him to continue.

"You all know that I set great store in the use of artillery, but I realize my mistake with this landing was that I didn't use the artillery nearly as much as I should have. Therefore, I am doubling our artillery, and I am converting even more ships into floating artillery platforms. Before we send in the first landing craft, we are going to pound those barbarians into jellied meat and teach them what the true might of Rome is all about!"

The last part of his statement was drowned out by the roars of his Centurions, as they thrust their fists into the air, shouting their approval and defiance. All of the anger and frustration came roiling out of these hard-bitten men, and Caesar was content to let them continue for several moments, before finally raising his hand for silence. Finally, once it was quiet again, he continued.

"But that's not all. We are going to have to get onto the beach more quickly than we have in the past. To that end, I am also ordering a number of transports to be broken down, and their timbers will be used to make smaller craft, holding no more than a Century, so that we can unload more quickly, and these ships can go back to the larger transports and load up with another Century. We are going to practice that maneuver here in this inner harbor, where the Wa cannot see us, until I'm satisfied that it can't be done any more quickly."

Caesar paused again, letting his Centurions absorb this plan and this time they were silent, more thoughtful, as they considered it. All of them knew that this meant their men would be worked until they dropped, then worked some more, for Caesar was nothing if not a hard taskmaster. But if it meant that fewer of them would perish on some foreign beach, far from home, then none of them begrudged the work that was to come. There were a few more details Caesar wanted to go over, then he dismissed the Centurions to go prepare their men for their upcoming ordeal.

And Caesar was good to his word: the very next morning work began, as ships were dragged onto the beach and torn apart, their timbers used to build both the artillery platforms and smaller transports. While this was taking place, those Legionaries who were not *immunes* involved in the work on the ships were sent out to the stakes to work on their sword work, or to the range, where they worked on hurling their javelins. Everywhere was a scene of nonstop activity, and every man retired to his tent at the end of the day sore and tired, the Centurions included. But despite the pace and harshness of the regimen, no man complained, all of them knowing that it was time to avenge their earlier defeat, and that the harder they worked now, the greater was their chance of not only seeing another sunrise, but also avenging the loss of friends and comrades. Caesar's army was determined that they would not be turned back a second time.

It had been a long time since Caesar had worked the men of his army so hard. But day after day, he had them loading and unloading from the smaller ships that he had ordered built, working them relentlessly on leaping over the low sides of the craft, then sprinting to shore in order to form up as quickly as possible. The fact that they had to do so in waist-deep water made no difference. Caesar judged them as if they were running across open ground, consequently every night the men staggered to their tents, barely able to consume their evening meal, engaging in only the most desultory conversation. Despite this, there was no complaining, because every man knew, after what had happened barely two weeks before, that this training was their best chance for not only performing, but also surviving the next landing.

As all this was taking place, Caesar was just as relentless in working the crews of the shipborne artillery, not sparing any expense in using live ammunition, aiming at a series of targets on shore, knowing that the rocks for the ballistae could be reused, while the bolts for the scorpions would be repaired by the *immunes* responsible for such matters. Over and over the crews drilled, until they were sending their respective missiles faster and more accurately than anyone in the army had seen, including Caesar.

"There's no way those Wa will be able to stand up to this," Quintus Balbus said, as he and Pullus stood watching the crews work, as they waited for their men to slog back aboard the transports in order to be rowed back out into the harbor to repeat the process of landing.

"I certainly hope not," Pullus agreed, "I just wonder how much longer we're going to be practicing, before we get on with it."

"Why?" Balbus asked. "It can only help us, the more we train."

"I suppose so," Pullus said doubtfully, but while he had reservations, he was unable to articulate the reason for his worry, because he knew that what Balbus said was true.

Still, he couldn't shake the feeling that with every day that passed, the Wa weren't just sitting idly by, themselves, and he worried what they had in store.

Another reason for Caesar's delay was to allow as many men to heal as possible, knowing that they were the most experienced in his army, and that even with his new approach, he would need every one of them to accomplish his goal. Like Pullus, Caesar worried, but as was fitting for the overall commander of the army, his concern extended beyond this next landing to the rest of the campaign. Of all the officers, he knew better than anyone that neither he nor the army could afford to take the kind of casualties they had suffered in the first assault, not if they had any hope of conquering the entire island. Not, that is, unless they stayed on this gods-forsaken island for two or three years and managed to recruit men from here—a prospect that he didn't hold in particularly high regard as being likely. So despite his nature, he forced himself to be patient, checking with the *medici* every day for progress reports, doing his best to hide his disappointment when they couldn't tell him what he wanted to hear: that all the men in the tent had recovered and would be ready to march the next day.

Finally, a couple of days more than three weeks after the repulse on the beach, the last man limped out of the hospital tent to return to his own tent section. Although none of the last dozen men were truly fit for duty, Caesar could wait no longer, and knowing their general and still willing to give every last ounce of their energy and life to him, they struggled to convince him that they were fit enough to march with their comrades. And Caesar was a receptive audience, so an assembly was called that night, the faces of the men lit by the flickering torches surrounding the forum.

"Comrades," Caesar called out, his voice ringing and strong. "Tomorrow, we begin our task of avenging the comrades we lost!"

If there was more to this statement, it was drowned out by the roar of the assembled men, even those whose native tongue wasn't Latin not needing any translation. Caesar was content to let this demonstration continue for several moments, before holding his hands up for silence. Finally the men quieted down enough for him to continue.

"We'll load the first wave in the watch before dawn. Because it's such a short distance, we won't need more time than that. As the first wave is loading, the artillery ships will be making their way across the bay to get into position. Comrades," he raised his voice even louder, his tone taking on the quality of icy anger that his long-time officers knew so well, "this is one time we don't want to surprise our foe. No, this time we want them to see us coming and to prepare for the assault. If all goes according to plan, they will be as eager to stop us on the beach as the last time. And when they come running to the edge of the shore, they will be mown down like wheat before the scythe!"

This time Caesar didn't bother trying to stop the men cheering.

The ships bearing the artillery had one other refinement of Caesar's design. As a further way to entice the Wa into crowding the beach, he ordered the sides of the artillery craft raised, with pivoting sides that hid the artillery pieces and disguised the ships as transports. Each captain was under orders to wait until the last possible moment before swinging the sides down to expose the artillery pieces. It was dark when the artillery ships left their moorings and began making their way out of the protected harbor. As they did so, Titus Pullus and the men of the 10th designated for the first wave sat quietly on the shore, waiting for the orders to begin their own loading process. Of all the new parts of this operation, Pullus thought, probably the trickiest was going to be loading into the new transports. In order to enable the quickest unloading possible, the sides of the transports were mere inches above the water, making these craft completely unsuitable for any type of voyage longer than what was facing them and in any seas, other than the inland bay they would be crossing. But what made it dangerous for the men was that, in order to increase speed, the beams of the vessels had been narrowed substantially as well, so that as the men loaded, they had to do it in roughly equal proportions from each side, or there was a very real danger of swamping their transport. Of course, the transport consequently had to be exited in the same manner, but that was what Caesar had trained them so hard to do, with each tent section assigned a specific side of the craft to exit. Still, as Pullus and the rest of the men well knew, what went smoothly in training rarely translated the same way in combat, but it was in the gods' hands now.

As the men of the first wave of the 10th waited, Pullus walked among the men, sharing a joke here, chiding another man there for some past transgression, although it was all done with good humor. He had long since learned that there was a time for the harsh discipline that was a staple of Legion life, but that the moments just before a man faced his possible end were not among those times. As was his usual habit, Pullus lingered with the few remaining veterans of his own tenure, men like Publius Vellusius, each man drawing comfort from the presence of the other. Finally, the *cornu* sounded the call to begin the boarding process, and in the time it took for the last note to echo across the inner bay, Pullus was once again the Primus Pilus, the hardest man of the Legion.

"All right you lazy *cunni,*" he roared, shoving men he considered to be moving too slowly, "get aboard your ships and by the gods, if any of you forget what side you're boarding and you capsize one of these buckets, I'll flay you and use your shriveled ball sac as a coin purse!"

And, as usual, his men obeyed, quickly and without mistake, each transport loading up, then moving out into the harbor to allow another transport to take on its own complement. Less than a third of a watch after the *cornu* had sounded, the entire first wave was loaded up and moving to the entrance of the harbor, headed for the Wa beach. It was almost time to exact retribution.

The slaughter resulting from the pre-landing artillery barrage was so total and so devastating that the biggest challenge for the men unloading in the first wave was keeping their footing amid the bodies and pieces of bodies bobbing and rolling in the red surf. Adding to the eeriness and unfamiliarity of the scene was that it was also the quietest landing in which any man of Caesar's army had participated. It wasn't truly quiet, but the only sound competing with the rumbling waves was a— low-pitched moan that seemed to ebb and flow with each crash of water onto the beach. There was occasional punctuation to the generally continuous sound in the form of shouted commands from the Centurions and Optios, yet what was conspicuously missing, besides the sounds of battle, were the calls and curses of the rankers.

No, Titus Pullus thought, he had never experienced anything like this, and neither had anyone else. It wasn't until Pullus was on the beach, standing amidst carnage the likes of which he had never seen in his 27 years, not at Alesia, not at Alexandria, not at Persepolis, not at Bargosa—that he realized what was so strange. The volume and style of the sound he was hearing was what one heard after a battle was over, not when the landing was just moments old. Right now should be a frenzy of action, a riot of noise, so many things going on before one's eyes that the brain can't comprehend it all: the colors and smells, all of it threatening to be overwhelmed by the fear and rage of battle. But nothing like that was happening, and it was clear to Pullus that he wasn't alone in his feelings as he watched his men trying to form up, although this was next to impossible, because of the bodies packing the beach.

Just as Caesar had predicted, at the first sight of the Roman warships appearing through a low-hanging mist that allowed them to creep to within 200 paces, the Wa had stormed right up to the edge of the beach in their tightly-packed but ordered ranks. And just like the first landing, there was a minimum of the kinds of demonstrations made by the warriors of other nations. The Wa seemed content to wait for the Romans to land, but Caesar and the entire army knew what kind of ferocity the Wa were capable of, so none of them were swayed by the lack of activity. In fact, their close formation fit into Caesar's plans quite well, and his one hope was that they didn't break ranks, making them harder to hit. Within a tenth part of a watch, the floating artillery batteries had moved into their positions, each one turning broadside to the beach, while the Wa contented themselves with shouting in their tongue as they watched the ships maneuver.

Perhaps they don't know what's about to happen, Caesar mused, standing at the flagship rail, his ship positioned roughly in the middle of the spread of warships. He restrained himself from looking over his shoulder in the opposite direction of the beach, knowing how futile it would be trying to spot the assault force rowing towards the beach, because of the mist. No, he thought, I'll have to count on my generals to make sure all is going as planned. His attention was brought back to the beach by the sharp cracking sound that was the signature of the ballistae, arms crashing against crossbars, when they shot to the vertical position and launched their respective cargos of death. Caesar was unable to track the flight of the first missiles from his ship, but there was no missing the result, as the first one-pound stones slammed into the front rows of Wa. No matter how many times he saw it, he was still somewhat surprised at the amount of damage a relatively small rock could inflict, not just to one man, but to several in a row, especially at closer range. Only one missile fell short in the first volley, so that almost immediately bloody gaps were torn into the front Wa ranks; but just as last time, those holes were closed almost immediately. Again, this was something Caesar was counting on, and in this he wasn't disappointed.

What he was unprepared for, however, was that the Wa would stand there and soak up this punishment, without withdrawing from the surf line. Instead, they stood there, first shouting their anger, then screaming out in fear and pain, as rocks and scorpion bolts savaged them without letup. Part of the original plan had called for a brief respite, planned by Caesar to give him the opportunity to assess the situation, and, if necessary, to allow his floating batteries to reposition closer to shore in anticipation that the Wa would have to remove themselves from the surf line. However, they never moved; yet, Caesar nonetheless ordered those of his ships that carried a higher complement of scorpions to move closer inshore, staying just out of range of the Wa archers, who fired a few volleys of fire arrows to no avail. With the range closer, the scorpion bolts were particularly lethal, punching through the lamellar leather armor and torso of the first and usually second Wa, before burying itself in the bowels of its last victim.

The slaughter recommenced, with the Wa giving no sign whatsoever that they were inclined to retreat out of range. In fact, from where Caesar was standing, although his eyesight wasn't what it had been, he could clearly see that there were no officers or cavalry behind the rear ranks forcing men forward. No, he realized with a shock, these Wa were moving forward without prompting, despite the fact that they had to know what awaited them. As disciplined as these men were, and Caesar was certain that they would be more than a match for the warriors of Sparta, not even the most hardened of men could keep from shrieking in agony from the kind of damage done by the artillery, and the air was filled with such noise. Even more than the noise, Caesar knew, the sights of their comrades being eviscerated, having a limb torn off or even being decapitated had to be extremely daunting, yet no Wa that he could see hesitated in stepping into the next spot, even when it was stepping over the mangled body of a comrade. Even when their numbers were reduced to perhaps a quarter of their original strength, the Wa never wavered, and, in fact, Caesar was sure that the ships would run out of ammunition. Some of the vessels did, particularly those carrying the scorpions, but in the end, there was enough.

This time the landing of Caesar's army was totally successful, and in sharp contrast to the first attempt, there were no serious injuries. In fact, there was only one death, a Legionary who had been leaning over the side watching the slaughter on the beach and who had lost his balance, falling into the sea and disappearing from sight, before anyone could grab him. The Wa, on the other hand, had lost what Caesar believed was the bulk of their army, at least 20,000 men, or so he hoped, anyway. He couldn't imagine wasting his soldiers in such a profligate manner, so there was something deeply troubling about the Wa, something he had first felt during the previous assault that he couldn't identify and had put down to stemming from his first defeat in many years. But now here he was, standing on the beach as its master, yet being just as troubled as he had been the time before. Try as he might, he couldn't come to grips with the feeling, and while to everyone around him he was his same, efficient self, inwardly he was in turmoil. The first inkling of what it might be came when Aulus Hirtius, one of his top lieutenant generals came to give his report on the task Caesar had set for him. Even before Hirtius spoke, Caesar could see the answer on his general's face.

"I'm sorry Caesar," Hirtius said uncomfortably, only after rendering a proper salute, of course, "but we have no prisoners."

Even knowing the answer by Hirtius' expression, Caesar was flabbergasted, so shocked that for several moments he couldn't speak, a fact that Hirtius took as a rebuke. His face colored, and like every member of Caesar's army, Hirtius felt great shame at having failed his general.

"I'm sorry, Caesar," Hirtius repeated, his tone so miserable that it snapped Caesar out of his shocked state.

Caesar shook his head, putting a hand on Hirtius' shoulder, admonishing him, "It's not your doing, Hirtius. I don't blame you. It's just hard to understand how out of this many men on the beach, we couldn't find any wounded lightly enough to take prisoner to interrogate." Something in Hirtius' eyes prompted Caesar to ask, "What am I missing?"

"It's hard to describe, Caesar," Hirtius responded. "Even after I saw it happen, I can't really understand it. But," he continued after Caesar's prompting, "we did as you said, looking for those men whose wounds weren't mortal and finishing off those whose were. But every time we found such a man, we couldn't get close to him. It was like they were...possessed by some *numen*, screeching in that language of theirs, I can't understand a *word* of that gibberish, and I've already picked up a fair amount of the Han dialect...where was I? Ah, yes, when we got anywhere near these men, they would put up so much of a fight that we had no choice but to kill them."

"That's to be expected," Caesar interjected, his mind still working on the larger problems, "but surely not all of them."

In every battle he had ever fought, across the entire known world, Caesar had never seen it fail that there were a group of men who chose life as a possible slave, rather than death, at least when it was this large a group.

"That's what I thought as well," Hirtius said with what Caesar suspected was respect bordering on awe, something Caesar didn't like a bit. "Until I saw these Wa. Every one of them who was able took a blade, an arrow, whatever was at hand, and ended himself. To a man."

For several moments, neither said a word, their thoughts running along very similar channels. Finally, and appropriately, it was Caesar who broke the silence.

"If we're fighting a race where even men in the ranks would rather die than submit, how can we defeat these people?"

Once it was determined that all Wa on the beach were dead, Caesar had the men of the entire army, once landed, form up in his now-famous *acies triplex*, the three line formation that had seen the defeat of armies from Hispania to Pandya. It was somewhat difficult, given the problem of so many heaped bodies, but the moment they were formed up, with the orientation that he wanted, Caesar sounded the order to advance. Their objective was not an army, but the large town that lay to the east of the landing beach. The 10th was in their usual spot, anchoring the right of the line, meaning that Titus Pullus, the Primus Pilus, was the last remaining Roman on the right, or unprotected side. It had been this way for so long and so often—save for a couple of times, one being Africa during the civil war—that if Caesar had ordered the Legion somewhere else, Pullus wasn't quite sure how it would have reacted. Caesar's army moved quickly into position, and the march began towards the town, which was only protected by a low wall, barely more than a man's height. More importantly, there were only a handful of Wa warriors on the wall, although they were too far away to make out their features. When they were within 200 paces, Caesar ordered a halt, followed by the command for all Primi Pili to join him.

Once they were all gathered, he told them, "It doesn't look like there will be much resistance, so I don't foresee this taking very long. However," his gaze turned to the assembled Centurions, "we have to decide what to do about this town. It looks large, so there should be a substantial amount of loot. I doubt we'll find many civilians to sell as slaves, but whatever we find will be rounded up and Zhang's man can see to it."

Caesar was referring to a member of Zhang's personal retinue who had acted as broker to sell the slaves that had been rounded up when crossing the Gayan Peninsula. However, his announcement was met with silence, and some furtive glances between some of the Primi Pili. Instantly picking up on them, Caesar pressed his Centurions, and all eyes turned to the giant Primus Pilus of the 10th.

Seeing that there was no avoiding it, Pullus, face reddened as he said, "It's just that the men want vengeance for the first assault."

Caesar's first instinct was to argue, but he caught himself. While it had been weeks since that first assault was bloodily repulsed, and they had just slaughtered close to 20,000 Wa, he knew that watching men die from a distance, from artillery, wasn't the same as plunging your own sword into the guts of the man across from you, acting in vengeance for the loss of a comrade. In addition, Caesar recognized that his control over the army had been badly shaken by the setback, and this victory, while it helped, hadn't done enough to restore matters back to what he considered normal.

Instead, he simply asked, "What do the men want?"

"That the town be given to them, to do with as they will," Pullus answered instantly, causing Caesar's eyes to narrow in suspicion, understanding that this had been planned.

While he didn't fault them for being prepared, he still wasn't happy that he was unaware this was coming. I'm going to have to talk to my network of spies in the army, he reminded himself.

Nevertheless, he gave his assent to this, his only admonishment being, "Don't let the men start fires. You know I hate that."

Assuring him that they would control the men who exhibited this proclivity, the Primi Pili quickly returned to spread the news. As each Legion was informed, they gave a rousing cheer, causing a rolling wall of noise that lasted for several moments. What effect it had on the Wa on the wall, waiting for what came next, was impossible to tell, because not one of them moved a muscle.

The assault on the town, as Caesar and the rest of the officers suspected, didn't take long. Those Wa who stayed on the wall, and most of them did, died fighting, though not with the same spirit and resolution of their comrades on the first beach.

"These were probably the sick, lame, and lazy," Balbus remarked to Pullus, using the term Romans used for malingerers, as they watched their men pull down the low wooden wall.

Very quickly several gaps were torn in the barrier, allowing the men to stream through, those who participated in the first assault being given the honor of leading the rest. More importantly, it gave them the first pickings of whatever loot was in the town. But almost immediately, the flow of men stopped, those still outside the wall forced to stand, shouting and cursing their frustration at their predecessors who seemed to have stopped everything.

"What in Pluto's thorny cock is the holdup?" Pullus growled, then pushed his way through the waiting men, bashing those too slow to jump out of the way with his *vitus*, and he was followed closely by Balbus.

Finally getting through the gap and elbowing his way into the front ranks, his snarled command died in his throat, as mystified as the rest of the men. It was Publius Vellusius, the old *Gregarius* and long-time comrade of both Pullus and Scribonius who sidled over to his Primus Pilus and broke the silence.

"What are they doing? Sir?" Vellusius amended hastily, but if Pullus took offense he gave no sign.

"They're kneeling," Pullus replied in a whisper, although he had no idea why he was doing so.

"But why?"

"How should I know?" Pullus snapped, instantly regretting it; it was a valid question, and one that Pullus was wondering himself. Then, with an idea, he said, "I suppose they're throwing themselves on our mercy."

"They're not going to get any from me," Vellusius replied fiercely, remembering his friend Ganusius, gutted on the beach those weeks ago.

For that is the sight that greeted the first Romans through the wall; not a deserted town like they expected, which they could now see was very close to being a city, but the lines and rows of people, obviously the townspeople, kneeling, with heads touching the ground, filling the square and streets of the town. Every open inch of ground was covered by a person or group of people. Just in front of the first row was a smaller group, perhaps ten villagers, all male, but they were in the same kneeling position, and none of them raised his head or looked up. Whatever the Legionaries were expecting, this wasn't it! The normal scene of the sacking of a town was one of chaos, with people running in any direction they thought gave them the best chance for escape, the screams of women filling the air, either trying to evade being captured and raped, or having been caught and ravished.. Just not this...silence. It unnerved Pullus, and he could see he wasn't the only one so affected, that none of the men seemed as eager to go about the business of rape and slaughter as they had been just moments before. It was silly, Pullus observed, since this would make rounding them up easier, but that wasn't how he felt.

Turning to Balbus, just behind him and as silent as everyone else, he said, "Go get Caesar."

By the time Caesar arrived, Pullus and the other Primi Pili had managed to get most of the men inside the walls of the town and had them formed up, their backs to the wall, in a long single line of Centuries, curving around the contour of the wall and out of sight. A quick check had confirmed that all the streets ringing the wall, or perpendicular to it, were empty. Everyone, it seemed, was gathered in one place. Even Caesar, normally so unruffled, was taken aback, and ,unbidden, the same thought he had just a short time before came back. Can we beat these people? Like Pullus, he chided himself for precisely the same reason. Here they were, all lined up, waiting for whatever their fate may be, but this was so unlike anything he had experienced, it gave him a deep sense of unease. It was one thing to kill running men and women as part of the bloodlust following a battle or siege, or to execute one or more kneeling men who had been captured after a fight. But this, to walk up and down the rows, systematically beheading each person, turned even his stomach. Of course, there was no guarantee that these Wa would sit passively and silently accept their fate, but some instinct, deep inside, told him they would. This, more than anything else, was what troubled him. Like most Romans, he had always accepted as fact that his people were the most disciplined and obedient to higher authority in the world, and none of his conquests had shown him any differently. But he knew that no Roman would be so stoic, so resigned to his fate without considerable weeping and gnashing of teeth, at least. Not these people.

"Well, Caesar? What are your orders?" Pullus asked his general.

Caesar turned troubled eyes to Pullus and said, "I don't know."

As it turned out, only the town elders, the group that had been kneeling in front of the rest of the townspeople were executed, before the men of Caesar's army were sufficiently unsettled by the sight of a few thousand supine victims, passively awaiting their fate. As much as they wanted vengeance, exacting it in this manner was extremely disturbing, when the only sounds were a chorus of muffled sobs, punctuated by the sodden thud of a blade meeting a neck. On a couple of occasions, there was a choked scream from one of the townspeople as an elder was decapitated, there presumably being some connection between the victim and the afflicted person. Once the dozen elders were executed, their heads and bodies separated from each other, save for a pool of blood connecting the two, the men who originally eagerly volunteered for the duty looked at Caesar expectantly, and it didn't take an experienced leader to see they were silently pleading for it to stop. Glancing at the assembled Primi Pili, along with the higher-ranking officers of the army, Caesar could plainly read by their faces and body language that they were ready for this business to end as well.

Raising his hand in a command to stop, Caesar said hoarsely, "I believe we've made our point. The rest of these people will be taken as slaves. Zhang's man will see to the details."

Not finished, Caesar turned to address the ranks of the men drawn up against the wall of the town, who were standing mutely watching all that had taken place.

"But as a reward for your valor, I give you the proceeds from the sale of these prisoners, the first of many Wa to fall under the yoke of Rome!"

If he said anything else, it was drowned out by the roaring approval of the men in the ranks, and once his words were translated for those who still didn't understand Latin, the din only increased in volume. Realizing the futility of anything further, Caesar gave a half-smile, half-grimace in surrender as he waved his subordinates to come closer so that they could hear his orders.

"As soon as the prisoners are out of the way, turn the men loose on the town to do with it as they will. Looting and burning should appease them, since they've lost their taste for blood vengeance."

Pullus and the other Centurions exchanged somewhat alarmed glances, thinking there was a rebuke there about their troops' unwillingness to shed blood.

Caesar caught the looks, raising a hand in a dismissive wave as he said, "Oh no, I don't blame them. In fact, I was worried that they would want to go through with it. But I'm glad to see that we're of a like mind; it appears that none of us finds much pleasure in beheading people who don't seem to care."

Prompted by his general's bringing it up, Pullus blurted out, "Why do you suppose they behaved that way, Caesar? I've never seen anything like that before. And," his brow furrowed, as he frowned, which Caesar knew was Pullus' sign that he was worried, "what does it mean? I mean, for the rest of the campaign?"

"I wish I knew," Caesar replied honestly, "because I've never seen this before, either. Put that together with the way those Wa on the beach seemed content to be slaughtered, we can deduce that at the very least, they don't fear death in any way. Which," he added, superfluously, as far as the Centurions were concerned, "makes them very dangerous, indeed. Perhaps not tactically, they don't seem to be generaled very well, if at all. But if they have enough numbers, and are willing to throw them away in such a profligate manner, tactics may not matter."

With that worrying admonition in their ears, Caesar briskly turned back to other topics.

"This town isn't big enough for the whole army to fall upon, which is one reason I'm giving the slaves to the army. That should help quell any discontent for what I'm about to order now." This time he ignored the looks of concern of his assembled officers, as he continued, "I want two Cohorts from each Legion to be given a section of town to loot. The rest will work on cleaning this place up. We can't have all these bodies stinking up the place and bringing disease. I don't know how long we'll be here, but you know I like a tidy battlefield."

Indeed his Centurions did; it was one of Caesar's peculiarities that kept the men and the Centurions, as well, talking around the fires, speculating on where it came from. To most of them, a tidy battlefield was a misnomer, but after the countless battles, it was something they accepted as the cost of marching with the greatest general of all time.

It turned out that the sacking of this town didn't provide the bounty of loot for which the men had hoped. Despite the look of overall tidiness and prosperity, what the men discovered as they entered the individual houses—ridiculously easily, because they appeared to be made of nothing more than flimsy wooden frames over which some sort of thin tissue was stretched—was that these people didn't seem to have many possessions. Oh, there was some silk to be found in some of the homes, and there was a fair bit of jade, but after marching through the lands of the Han, the men had become inured to the value of this semi-precious stone. If they ever made it back home, they had a fortune, but most of them had resigned themselves to the idea that they would never set foot on Italian or Spanish soil again. For Pullus, as for so many of the men, the army had been his real home for so many years that he could barely remember what his farm outside of Astigi, in the province of Hispania even looked like. Watching his men tear through these houses—in most cases literally, as soon as the men discovered that the wooden frames were made in such a way that they could be lifted out with relative ease—Pullus was lost in thought, worrying about what he had brought up to Caesar. He didn't know why, but the sight of the Wa kneeling there disturbed him more than the sight of their warriors waiting to be slaughtered on the beach.

"I don't think these savages lock anything away," Pullus was torn from his reflection by the sound of Balbus' voice, and with a start he turned to see his second-in-command standing next to him, the side of his face that was horribly scarred and missing an ear the sight that greeted Pullus.

However, he had long since become accustomed to the gruesome visage of his Pilus Posterior, and, in fact, rarely noticed him in this way.

"Doesn't look like it," Pullus agreed.

Both men stood for a moment as some of the men began whooping with delight from inside one of the houses. A moment later, a Legionary emerged from a nearby home, not bothering with the door, but instead kicking one of the flimsy walls down. Staggering a bit under his burden, the two Centurions quickly understood why he was so happy: they saw a pair of feet kicking, as what turned out to be a young girl struggled in a futile attempt to free herself, all the while screeching at the top of her lungs in her language.

"Pluto's cock, we don't need this," Balbus groaned. "It's one of the Pandya. What's his name? Shrinam?"

Pullus thought for a moment, then said, "Shrinar. His name's Shrinar. He's in the third section of your Century, isn't he?"

"I know who he belongs to," Balbus snapped, irritated as much at the tone of his Primus Pilus as he was by the sight of one of his men carrying off what was, in effect, contraband.

Over the years, Caesar's army had developed a set of simple rules that his men learned, sometimes in a very harsh manner, had to be obeyed without question. One of those concerned the treatment of women. After learning from bitter experience early on in the campaign, when there had been a near-riot after the sacking of a Parthian town and where Caesar's orders were somewhat vague, the general gave very explicit instructions that whenever the occupants of a town were destined for slavery, it included every single person, whether they were part of the original group of captives or not. If they lived in that town and everyone else was being sold into slavery, they were off-limits from being used by the men for their enjoyment. Of all of Caesar's orders, it was one of the most unpopular, because of cases like this, which were inevitable. Terrified parents would try to hide their children—almost always daughters, and almost always the most beautiful daughter in the family—creating the situation that was facing the two Centurions now.

"Shrinar," Balbus bellowed, and for a moment it looked like the dark-skinned, lithe Legionary was going to pretend he didn't hear and keep walking. "By the gods, I'll skin your black ass and use it for a mourning tunic if you don't get over here!"

With visible reluctance, the Legionary turned and trudged over to the two Centurions. Meanwhile, the girl's struggles continued unabated, and when she gave a sudden twist of her body, she managed to escape from Shrinar's grasp, thudding heavily onto the ground. Quickly trying to scramble to her feet, she was too slow for Shrinar, who had too much experience in such matters to be easily thwarted. Because she struggled, her hair—long, black, and very straight—covered her features, and her head whipped about as she tried to pull her arm out of Shrinar's grasp. Finally, in exasperation, Shrinar gave her a cuff on the head, stunning her enough to stop her struggling, but she managed to remain on her feet. Half-carrying, half-dragging the girl with him, Shrinar finally reached Pullus and Balbus, sullenly coming to *intente*, or at least as much as possible, while still holding onto the girl.

"What by Pluto's cock do you think......" Balbus got no further, letting out an audible gasp, which was only drowned out by the same sound from his Primus Pilus.

Before he could finish, the girl's head had come up, and with her free hand she pulled the hair blocking her face out of the way. She was, Pullus was sure, the most beautiful girl he had ever seen. Balbus was no less sure of the same thing, as both men stared at the girl, who, seeing their eyes on her, quickly looked down at the ground. Her skin was the color of honey, and while she had the almond-shaped eyes of all of the people in this part of the world, they were slightly larger. Most interesting was her nose, not the normal stub with no bridge between the eyes so common among the people of the East,, but pronounced enough that, while not Roman, it made her distinguishably different from anyone else. Gazing at her oval face, high, pronounced cheekbones and a full set of lips that both men immediately longed to caress with their own, both of them understood Shrinar's reluctance. In fact, unbeknownst to each other, both Balbus and Pullus experienced a flash of sympathy for the Legionary, while at the same time being aware of a strong desire to make this girl their own. And at the same time, they both knew that this was impossible.

"You know the rules, Shrinar," Balbus finally spoke. "You can't keep her."

Shrinar said nothing, deciding that his best and only hope was to pretend he didn't understand, but Balbus wasn't fooled in the slightest.

"I know you understand me, you *cunnus,*" the Pilus Prior growled. "Remember I come around the fires at night and I hear you and Galba chattering like magpies in our tongue. So," he thrust his free hand out toward the Legionary, while in the other hand his *vitus* hovered menacingly, "hand her over."

Shrinar's shoulders slumped, not bothering to hide his bitterness, and while neither Centurion would normally be disposed to let such insolence pass, they were, at the very least, sympathetic to his loss. Taking the girl by each arm, Pullus and Balbus carried her, her struggles now having subsided into a whimpering fear, as her feet barely touched the ground. Neither man spoke, but both were incredibly aware of the girl's scent and the feel of her lithe body bumping against them. They headed for the line of Wa townspeople who, with bowed heads, were being shackled together. Standing nearby, Caesar and his staff were discussing whatever it was that officers discussed at times like this, but at the approach of two of his Centurions, Caesar called out to them.

"*Eho* Pullus, Balbus! What do you have there?"

"Just someone trying to hide, Caesar," Pullus replied, counting the moments before his general stopped them. He didn't get past ten.

"Hold there! Bring the girl over here," Caesar ordered.

Both men shot sidelong glances at each other, but, of course they obeyed, stopping in front of their general. Caesar gave neither of them as much as a glance, taking a gentle hand and lifting the chin of the girl to see her face. Just as his Centurions had shortly before, he let out a gasp at the sight before him.

"By the *gods*," he managed at last. "I think she's the most beautiful creature I've ever seen."

"Normally, I don't like your taste in women, Caesar," Hirtius, standing behind his general said genially, thinking of Cleopatra, "but in this case I have to agree with you."

The girl, for reasons only she could know, hadn't shrunk from Caesar's touch, and, in fact, looked up at him shyly, through lowered lashes, studying him as much as he was studying her. She was an ignorant girl from a town whose name nobody knew, but she instinctively understood that this was a powerful man, despite his hideously pale skin and eyes that looked like the water of the bay on which she lived. She also understood that the next few heartbeats were the most important of her life, that wherever her family and friends were being taken, it wasn't going to be a place where there would be any joy or happiness. So, despite her fear, she favored Caesar with a shy smile, not showing any teeth, of course, but a smile, nonetheless. Thinking the moment over, the two Centurions started to take her away, and her eyes widened in fear, fixed on Caesar.

"Wait," he said softly, but it was no less a command than anything he might bellow in battle, so both Centurions halted immediately. For another moment nobody spoke or moved. Then, seeming to come to a decision, Caesar said, "Take her to my tent. She'll be staying here, with me."

The town, because of the construction of its houses, didn't take nearly as long to loot as a town its size normally would in other parts of the world, it being relatively easy to rip them apart for hiding places. By the time the men were through, the town was a shambles of shattered wooden screens and piles of what passed for furniture lying scattered about. It took even less time to burn, the thin tissue serving as the walls of the structures catching instantly. In fact, it turned so quickly into a conflagration that two men were trapped within the town, barred from escape by blazing houses and the piled debris, burning to death. These were the only two casualties of the landing, and Caesar ordered the sacrifice of a bull in thanksgiving to the gods for such good fortune. But neither he, nor any of the officers, believed it would last. Sooner or later, they knew, they would meet a real army, led by a real general. Then matters would be different.

Chapter 6

The ruins of the town smoldered for two days, days in which Caesar kept his scouts very busy while the men recovered from their exertions, such as they were, in taking the town. Their biggest problem came from their massive headaches from the stores of rice wine they had found, as they also discovered that it was much more potent than what they were accustomed to in the land of the Han. As the men lounged about outside their tents, playing the inevitable games of dice, along with some games that were imported by the polyglot of nations comprising the Legions, Caesar's mounted scouts were ranging far and wide, scouting the terrain and looking for signs of a concentration of the enemy. It wasn't until the third day that the first of them returned, and while they didn't report any sightings of an enemy force, the news wasn't good, as far as the terrain facing the army was concerned. Neither was there good news about the possibility of food being available, because the land was too mountainous for the growing of rice, at least in any quantity sufficient to feed an army. There were small, terraced farms, but they were designed to feed very small villages of fewer than a hundred villagers, and there were precious few of those. This forced Caesar to make a decision.

"After receiving the reports from the patrols I've sent out, it's clear that we won't find enough rice to feed the men. In addition, the terrain to the east is very mountainous. We'd do well to make 20 miles a day, if that."

Caesar was addressing an assembly of the officers of the army, including the Primi Pili, who had gathered in the *praetorium* to hear what their general had to say.

"But I'm neither blind nor deaf to the complaints of the men about getting back aboard the ships to travel," he continued. He paused, letting his officers digest what he said before he pressed forward. "However, I'm not willing to sacrifice the speed that we would gain by moving by sea, so we're going to be boarding the ships to continue moving eastward. According to Zhang, the farther east we go, the more populated we'll find the island. He also says that what passes for their capital is still several days' sailing away, and the closer we get, the more likely we'll be to meet resistance from a much larger army than the one we've faced to date. Once we defeat that army, the island will essentially be ours."

Once more, he paused and waited for the men to digest this, and, while he wasn't surprised, he was somewhat disappointed at the looks of doubt and uncertainty some of the men had on their faces, and those looks weren't confined to the Centurions. Hirtius, Pollio, and the less senior Legates also looked distinctly uncomfortable, but since Caesar had made up his mind, he didn't give them the opportunity to raise whatever objections they may have had, dismissing his officers immediately. A couple of them, notably Pullus and Hirtius, stood there, not moving for several moments, both of them looking at each other, waiting for the other to speak. But using their hesitation, Caesar turned on his heel and left the meeting room, leaving the two of them open-mouthed.

"I thought you were going to say something," Hirtius fumed, but Pullus was unapologetic, though as irritated as Hirtius.

"It seems to me that rank has precedence in a situation like this," the Primus Pilus shot back, to which Hirtius had no real reply, recognizing that Pullus was right in this instance.

Both men left discontented, but Pullus had the more immediate problem of passing the word to the men of the 10th Legion, and he, better than anyone, knew that they weren't going to be happy. Before he summoned them, he met with the Pili Priores to let them know what Caesar had decreed. Almost in unison, the Pili Priores sucked in a breath, each of them immediately thinking about the reaction of their respective Cohorts, and none of them felt sanguine about how the men would take this latest order.

"We'll be getting the loading order later today," Pullus informed them, and, like Caesar, he wasn't in the mood for questions.

Unlike Caesar, however, he had nowhere to go, since they were all crammed into his tent.

"And what do we do, if they don't get on the ships?"

This question came from the Pilus Prior of the Fifth Cohort, Gnaeus Macrianus, whom Pullus considered to be a candidate for his own post at some point in the future, although Pullus was nowhere near ready to step down. If it had come from someone other than Macrianus—perhaps Scribonius—Pullus wouldn't have entertained the question, but with them he felt compelled to answer.

"We stripe as many backs as we need to," he answered harshly. "But I'm counting on each of you to keep that from happening."

"How, exactly?"

This time it was Scribonius who asked the question, and he refused to flinch at Pullus' angry glare, not cowed in the slightest by his friend's bluster. Expelling a harsh sigh, Pullus was forced to think for a moment.

"You need to convince them that staying here isn't possible, and that if they want to spend all day scrabbling up mountains and making 20 miles a day, that's what's in store for them if they don't get aboard the ships. Also," he added, suddenly inspired, "let them know that there's no food in the area, and we have to find more food than the surrounding countryside offers."

He paused to let this sink in, somewhat pleased to see that the Pili Priores seemed to accept this reasoning, mulling it over and not rejecting it out of hand.

Finally, Scribonius spoke, "I think we can make that work with them, although I can't guarantee it. But none of them want to go hungry."

"Or climb these fucking mountains," Metellus, the Pilus Prior of the Third Cohort, added.

"Well, go do what you need to in order to make sure they're ready to board in the morning."

Pullus, and if truth were known, Caesar and the rest of the Legates, were vastly relieved to see that in the morning, the men fell to their tasks of breaking down the camp and readying to board with only a bit more grumbling and discontent than was normal. Because of so much practice, the men were ready well within the time Caesar expected, and the boarding process commenced without delay. By the middle of the day, the fleet began moving out of the harbor, sailing west first, in order to clear the large island to the south that was their original anchorage. Once past this land mass, they turned south, making good time, clearing the southern tip of the island in less than a full watch, before turning east. Although most of the army was aboard, Caesar had taken a gamble, leaving almost his entire mounted force ashore to move eastward overland. Their orders were specific: keep close to the coast, staying within visual sight of the fleet whenever possible; Caesar had informed them he would send the Liburnian scout ship ashore twice a day to pick up any reports they made. In this manner, Caesar hoped to be informed of the presence of either larger areas of arable land that could be plundered for their harvest of rice, or of a large armed force.

Caesar's plan, like all of his plans, was both simple, but sweeping in scope. Sure that there had been some survivors of the assault on the town who escaped, his hope was that they would spread the alarm, and give the Wa sufficient time to muster a force that represented the bulk of their army. The real reason Caesar chose the sea route was that, given the success the Romans experienced with the last beach assault, he hoped that word of his fleet would reach the Wa commander, whoever he may be, and that the Wa army would choose the same tactic as the previous two times: to meet the Romans on the beach. To that end, Caesar had ordered that all usable bolts possible be salvaged from the site of the last fight, along with the rocks, but he had also had his men scrounge up as much in raw materials as they could in the time allowed. As the fleet sailed eastward, his *immunes* were hard at work, repairing the scorpion bolts and making new ones, along with shaping the hundreds of rocks that had been gathered. Caesar was counting on the idea that, moving with the speed for which he was famous, his army would appear at a place that was strategically important, before the Wa had a chance to reflect on what changes needed to be made in their tactics. If he could have his artillery do the brunt of the work as they had during the previous encounter, , Caesar was sure his army could vanquish any foe before them.

Caesar and his army, heading east, were bringing Rome deep into the land of the Wa, still seeking to conquer one last land and one last people.

It was a little more than a month after the Romans launched their invasion of Wa that there was the first appearance of trouble, of a sort that threatened not just the campaign, but the army itself.

"We haven't located nearly as much rice as we thought we would," was how Caesar put it to his assembled Primi Pili. "However, we still expect to be resupplied from the stockpile we have on the first island."

Caesar was referring to the lightly populated island they assaulted when they crossed from the Gayan Peninsula. Dubbed "Fortuna" by the men, Caesar had established a forward base on this island, directing that the Legate he left in charge, an older man who had been in charge of the vast herd of livestock needed to transport the army, put his energies into ferrying supplies from the Gayan Peninsula to the island. This man, Publius Ventidius Bassus by name and known throughout the army as Ventidius, the Muleteer, was a superb hand at the grindingly mundane, but crucially important, art of logistics. Caesar trusted Ventidius implicitly; therefore, he wasn't particularly worried at the dearth of consumables on the large island they were on now. According to Zhang, who was his only source of information about not only the size of the island, but also about practically everything else, they had barely covered a quarter of this island, so Caesar still harbored hopes of stumbling onto a settled area with the requisite foodstuffs his army needed. However, in the meantime, he had total confidence in his older Legate to provide the needed supplies. Caesar kept the base on Fortuna apprised of his latest position and intentions, using his Liburnians, still the fastest sailing craft he had at his disposal. Yet, the farther east along the coast they traveled, the longer the supply line stretched. It was a concern for the general, but not yet a worry.

The progress of the army was slowed by the fact that Caesar insisted that the fleet halt every third day for the army to go ashore and make a proper camp. From this camp, they would spend a day, alternately resting and scouting, looking for signs of large settlements or arable land that showed signs of cultivation. Sometimes they would camp on one of the hundreds of islands that dotted this inland sea, but usually they tried to find campsites on the main island from which they could launch their forays. This was made difficult by the terrain: not since Greece had Caesar seen such a mountainous country, and it was no wonder his men had trouble finding large areas of cultivation. But, Caesar mused, as he sat in his stateroom one night thinking about the problem, it may also be that we're not going far enough inland. However, Zhang insists that the farther east we go, that's when we'll find fields of a substantial size to support my army. Until then, we'll have to count on Ventidius.

It was just another sign of the gods' blessings that the day the dreaded storm Zhang called the *tai-fun* came, the army was actually ashore in their camp. Even so, the storm was horrific, wreaking terrible damage to the fleet and ripping a large number of the men's tents to shreds. Even with the damage, it could have been worse—much worse—a fact the Centurions wasted no time in impressing on the men. It was little short of a miracle that none of the ships, all of them riding at anchor in a bay barely large enough to fit all of them, had sunk; instead, the damage they sustained came almost exclusively from their bashing into each other.

"How long to repair the damage?" Caesar asked the Roman he had put in charge of all matters regarding the navy.

Claudius Nero consulted the wax tablet he was holding, considering for a moment, before answering, "At least a week, and that's if we use all the *immunes* who have experience with this kind of work."

Caesar sucked in a breath through his teeth, grimacing despite suspecting the answer, before it was given.

"Well," he said after a moment's reflection, "perhaps we can make this work for us. While we're working, I'll send out at least 2 of the Legions and have them head north, into the interior, to see what they can find in the way of food. Or an army," he added, almost as an afterthought. "In the meantime, we'll wait for Ventidius' fleet to catch up with us. Yes," he finished briskly, once again the Caesar who was never put on the back foot for more than a moment, "we can actually make this work for us."

And it would have worked, if the gods, as suddenly as they favored Caesar, hadn't taken that favor away; although it wasn't until almost the full week had passed before he and the army learned of the misfortune that had befallen them, without their being aware of it. Until, that is, three heavily damaged transport ships, all that were left of the fleet of 30 that had left Fortuna, came limping into the small bay. As soon as they anchored, the senior captain, a Greek *navarch* who had been with the fleet since the beginning of the campaign and who was one of the most experienced sailors left, rowed ashore. He was quickly led to the *praetorium*, which was still standing, although a panel from the roof had been blown out and a patch applied, the darker leather showing starkly against the faded panels of the rest of the headquarters tent. Immediately allowed into the tent, the *navarch* Lysandros saw Caesar standing with two of his scribes, dictating something to one, while discussing a totally different topic with the other. Seeing Lysandros and recognizing him, Caesar stopped immediately and beckoned him to approach, his eyes taking in the Greek's haggard appearance and instantly understanding that it boded ill. His instinct was confirmed a moment later, when after exchanging salutes, Lysander gave his report.

"General, I regret to inform you that all but my ship and two others were destroyed by that cursed wind the Han call the *tai-fun*," Lysandros' voice shook with a combination of emotion and exhaustion. "We tried running before the wind, but between the waves and rain, all the boats became swamped or foundered."

Caesar stood there motionless for several moments, not saying a word, and all other activity in the tent ceased as well.

Finally, he managed to ask, in a strangled voice, "All but three? Are you sure? Did you search for any other ships?"

Lysandros nodded as he said sadly, "Yes, Caesar. We spent two days after the storm on one of the islands that gave us the chance to make repairs and watch for any survivors or ships that made it through as well. All we saw were corpses and flotsam," he finished bitterly.

After a few more questions that convinced Caesar that there was no hope of a miracle, Lysandros was sent to see to his crew's needs and to his own. As if that wasn't enough, there was a stir at the entrance to the headquarters not long after Lysandros left, this time it was caused by a messenger, a cavalrymen assigned to one of the Legions Caesar had sent out on patrol. The only thing Caesar didn't know was which of the two Legions it was, but that was immediately answered when the cavalryman reported.

"General, I've been sent by Primus Pilus Pullus. He reports that his Legion has found a large town that appears to be well supplied with food." Before Caesar could digest this however, the messenger continued, "But the Legion was forced to make camp in the face of the enemy because a large, armed force of those savages appeared out of nowhere!"

"How large?" Caesar asked instantly.

"Primus Pullus estimates at least 15,000," the cavalryman replied.

Caesar let out a string of curses and snapped out an order to one of his aides to have the call sounded summoning all Primi Pili and officers. Turning back to the messenger, he asked several questions, trying to ascertain an exact location, all while consulting the crude map of the surrounding area. Once finished, he dismissed the messenger who, instead of departing at once, seemed to hesitate.

"Well?" Caesar forced himself to be calm, knowing that snapping at this man wouldn't help anyone. "Is there something else?"

"Yes sir," the man stammered, "I mean, I don't really know sir. It's just that as I topped the last ridge before the 10th was out of sight, I stopped to make sure I wasn't being followed. And when I did, I naturally just looked back over my trail looking......"

"Yes, yes, just tell me what you saw," Caesar snapped, his patience finally fraying.

"Well sir, I could see the camp. It's in a good position, like I said, but those Wa bastards already have it surrounded. And," he swallowed hard, "they were already beginning to attack the camp. I don't know if they'll be able to hold long enough for us to save them."

Smiling grimly, Caesar simply put his hand on the man's shoulder, giving it a comforting squeeze.

"Then I guess we'd better hurry then, shouldn't we?"

And with that, he dismissed the messenger and began issuing orders.

"I really wish we had brought siege spears," Pilus Posterior Balbus called to his Primus Pilus, Titus Pullus, over the raging din created by the wave of Wa warriors throwing themselves at the earthen rampart of the fortified camp holding the 10th Legion.

"Me too," agreed Pullus, standing just behind a line of his men jabbing down at the clawing warriors trying desperately to reach up and drag the wooden palisade down, the first step toward breaching a Roman camp. "But hopefully Andros got through and Caesar will be here soon."

"He better be," Balbus shouted grimly, as he shoved a Legionary—who had just taken a spear thrust through the shoulder from one of the teardrop-shaped weapons used by the Wa—out of the way and grabbed his relief man to throw him into the gap, before it could be exploited.

All around the perimeter of the camp, similar scenes were being played out, as the Wa, having brought with them bundles of sticks to throw into the ditch, were streaming across to tear at the earthen rampart. There was a steady roar of noise, punctuated by shouts and screams, the tenor and frequency telling Pullus' experienced ears that his camp was in mortal danger of being overrun. Taking a moment to step away from his own Century and Cohort, the Primus Pilus of Caesar's most famous and feared Legion paused to look around the entire perimeter of the camp, taking in the scene before him. Unlike the normal army camp, this one was much smaller, since it had to protect just one Legion, and Pullus was thankful that he had been given enough time to erect one in a strong position. Yet its smaller size was both a blessing and a curse: while it allowed for his reserve—consisting of just one Cohort—to move more quickly to a trouble spot, there was also less space to maneuver, if and when the walls were breached. As Pullus watched, he began the mental process of deciding at what point he would sound the call for the *orbis*, the formation of last resort for the Roman Legion, and where the best location for it would be in the camp. As it was, the 10th was already in something of an *orbis,* because there wasn't one side of the camp that wasn't under assault. Making a decision, Pullus shouted at Balbus to take over command of this sector of the wall, which Balbus acknowledged with a sketched salute with his sword, whereupon Pullus ran down the ramp into the camp, heading for a spot on the wall that looked harder-pressed.

That part of the wall was under the control of the Quintus Pilus Prior, commander of the Fifth Cohort, Gnaeus Macrianus, a veteran of the second *dilectus* of the 10th, making him more than a decade younger than his Primus Pilus. Blood was streaming down the Macrianus' cheek, but he looked otherwise unhurt, as he swiftly made a short hop into a suddenly opened gap, and from Pullus' position down on the ground, he could only see a pair of hands reaching out to grasp the wooden stakes of the palisade directly in front of Macrianus. Even as Pullus watched, he saw Macrianus' blade draw back, seem to hover for an instant, before plunging down quickly and brutally, presumably into the face of the Wa reaching for the stake. The set of hands immediately disappeared, but just as quickly, first one, then another set of hands appeared to replace the first. Seeing this, Pullus began sprinting up the ramp, reaching Macrianus' side just in time to see the contorted faces of the two Wa warriors, trying to wrench the stakes out of the ground, their eyes in such tiny slits that the detached part of Pullus' brain marveled at how they could see at all. Even as this thought flitted through his mind, his hand was moving, gripping his sword in the manner in which his first weapons instructor had taught him: with his thumb wrapped on the inside of his fingers instead of the outside. With a quick and economical, but extremely powerful thrust, his Gallic blade punched down into one of the helmeted faces, the point entering the open mouth and slicing through the back of the man's throat, not only killing the Wa instantly, but also severing the nerves, so that his hands dropped limply to his sides, his spirit fleeing before the body hit the ground. Meanwhile, Macrianus did the same to his man, but even so, there was no respite. Despite himself, Pullus let out a gasp at the sight of the seething mass of warriors, men practically trampling each other in their frenzied haste, as they boiled up out of the ditch and, using the bodies of those already fallen, threw ladders up and climbed the side of the earthen wall.

"There's thousands of these bastards," he muttered, catching himself too late, but relieved that he hadn't said it any more loudly, and that Macrianus alone seemed to have heard, and he only gave a grunt in answer.

On the opposite side of the camp, Sextus Scribonius and his Second Cohort were faring better, but not by much. To this point, his men had been able to keep the Wa contained in the ditch by using their javelins, both as missiles, and as spears to stab downward at any men who ventured too near. But for the same reason Balbus wished for siege spears, Scribonius was afraid that it wouldn't be much longer before there were no more usable javelins left. The Roman javelin was designed to be thrown and more importantly, was engineered in such a way that it couldn't be thrown back, with a softer metal shaft and a wooden pin designed to shear off on impact. This meant that when used as a stabbing weapon, sooner or later the shaft would bend or the pin would break, hence the need for the broad-leafed, heavier siege spears. Scribonius could see that there were perhaps a dozen intact javelins left for the men of the front rank guarding the palisade, giving him just moments before those men would have to draw swords, as well. His casualties had been relatively light, which was a blessing from the gods, but he also knew that this couldn't last, once the Wa were able to close with his men and get inside the reach of their swords. Even as he thought this, he heard a choked cry to his left and whirled about just in time to see one of his men disappear over the rampart, hands clutching at his Legionary's armor pulling him down into the teeming mass. He had the briefest glimpse of a pair of legs straight up in the air before they disappeared, followed by a scream that made the hair on the back of his neck stand up. Fortunately, it was short-lived, the man going immediately silent, as his life undoubtedly was quickly snuffed out. But to his horror, Scribonius saw in that next instant that nobody had moved in to plug the gap opened by the loss, and it took a moment for his brain to comprehend that it was because there was nobody left near that spot. Even as this registered, he saw that while he could pull a couple of men from a spot farther down the wall, he was nearest, so of their own volition, his legs began propelling him quickly towards the gap, yet not before a helmeted head appeared at the empty spot in the palisade, arms hands grasping and pulling the stakes.

Pullus and Macrianus, standing side by side, were all that kept the Wa from swarming over that section of the wall, as one more time the giant Primus Pilus showed why he was one of the most famous men with a sword in the army. Using a shield he had taken from a man who no longer needed it, his sword arm was bloody to the elbow, as he thrust, chopped, and hacked down at the scrambling Wa, none of whom had managed to gain purchase on the rampart, at least in Pullus' immediate area. But the Primus Pilus was desperately tired, barely able to keep his shield in the first position—the most basic defensive position and, unsurprisingly the first one taught to all Legionaries. His sword arm was little better, and he could feel the tremors in his biceps that signaled that unless he got some relief, he wouldn't be able to defend his part of the wall much longer. At the very edge of his vision, he saw a flurry of movement telling him that some Wa had at last managed to make it up to the rampart, and there was a struggle for control of the packed earthen platform. However, Pullus couldn't pay attention to this, having to count on the Legionaries in that spot to do their duty to protect their comrades, because climbing out of the ditch and scrambling up the ladder that had been thrown against the wall came another Wa, this one with the curved sword they favored. Normally the contest would be tilted heavily in favor of Pullus, as the Wa had to concentrate on climbing the ladder, whereas Pullus only needed to wait for him to come within reach. But between Pullus' fatigue and the fact that not three paces away from him he saw Macrianus take a thrust from a long spear that knocked him backward with such force that he went tumbling down the ramp to land in a heap on the camp floor, the Primus Pullus was distracted enough, so that the Wa managed to scramble up quickly, slipping under Pullus' poorly aimed thrust to stand on the rampart. Immediately, the Wa launched a furious attack, catching Pullus on the wrong foot and forcing him to take an involuntary step backward. The Wa warrior, this one wearing the lamellar iron armor and flared helmet that marked him as one of the elite of the Wa army, kept up the fury of his assault, the blade of his sword a blur as it flashed about the edges of Pullus' defenses. First blocking with the shield, then barely parrying with the sword, Pullus tried to ignore the screaming fire shooting down his arms and to concentrate his energy and attention on the Wa's attack, looking desperately for an opening. Just as he had experienced in the previous battle, these Wa didn't seem to tire out, but kept up the same pace in the middle of the battle as they did at the beginning and end, something that no man in the army had encountered before. Still, Pullus hadn't lived this long on just luck, and summoning his rapidly draining reserves, he lashed out with his shield immediately after the point of the Wa's blade skipped off the boss when he had attempted a straight lunge. The blow was completely unexpected, catching the Wa square in the chest and knocking him flat, but before Pullus could leap astride his body to finish him with a sword thrust, in a move Pullus had never seen before, the Wa raised his legs up by drawing his knees to his chest, then quickly thrusting them out, levered himself back upright from his supine position. Pullus was so astonished that he stood motionless for a moment, his jaw hanging slack, and barely got his shield up in time to block the next sword thrust, this one a vicious sweeping blow aimed to disembowel him.

It had often been said that the gods smiled on Titus Pullus, not as brilliantly and often as they did at Caesar perhaps, but he had been shown their favor on numerous occasions, and this was one of them. The Wa had put all of his power behind this attack, hoping to capitalize on the hesitation caused by Pullus' astonishment, but Pullus blocked the sword with his shield. The blade of the Wa's sword cut deeply into the edge of the shield, normally the type of blow that would render shield or sword useless, either splitting the shield or breaking the blade. But this time, not only did the sword not shatter, its razor sharp edge enabled it to cut so deeply into the shield that the only thing that stopped it was the metal boss. Pullus felt a searing pain along the edge of his hand, but the Wa's sword was now trapped, caught by the friction caused by the two pieces of the shield. Taking advantage of this, Pullus twisted the shield, using his superior strength to push the sword down and away from him, but instead of employing the point of his blade, which would have taken more time to hit its mark, he gave a straight punch into the Wa's face with the pommel of his sword, catching the man flush between the flaps of the helmet and in his face. Once, twice, three times Pullus punched the man with all his strength, and though it may have been waning, he was still extremely strong. The Wa's head jerked back with each impact, going limp with the third punch, before Pullus dropped the shield and thus his hold on the warrior, who dropped to the ground in a heap. The huge Roman wasted no time thrusting his blade into the throat of the Wa, whose wrecked face twitched, as his life ended and he gurgled blood with his last breath.

Only then was Pullus able to turn his attention to the larger situation, and his heart almost stopped when he surveyed the walls of the camp. In more than a dozen places, the perimeter had been breached, and in at least three spots that he could see; his men had been pushed down onto the camp floor, where there was savage fighting going on. Suddenly, all pain and fatigue were forgotten as he realized that it was getting perilously close to the time, when he would have to order the *cornicen* to sound the order to form *orbis*. He began looking for the nearest one, having left his Cohort *cornicen* with Balbus. He spotted the Fifth's man, one of the old veterans, standing next to the Quintus Pilus Posterior, Vibius Pacius. But just as he was about to call him over, very faintly, over the sounds of the fighting, Pullus heard something he could not quite bring himself to believe hearing. In fact, he had just convinced himself that his mind was playing tricks with him and had opened his mouth, when it happened again, and this time he wasn't the only one to react. Several heads turned at the sound, all of them Roman, and quickly a new sound was added to the din.

It was the sound of cheering, because what the Romans heard was a horn, but it wasn't Pullus' signal to form *orbis*. The pattern of notes signaled that another army approached, a friendly army.

Caesar had come to the rescue! Now Pullus had to hope that it was in time to save the 10th.

Chapter 7

Caesar had arrived in time...barely. Although Titus Pullus never ordered the *orbis*, it had been a close-run thing, and his Legion was badly hurt. A little more than a quarter of his men were unwounded; of the rest, there was almost a Cohort's worth of men seriously wounded enough that they would be immobilized for days, if not weeks. The rest of Caesar's army had suffered relatively light casualties; he had moved with his customary speed, so the Wa were completely unprepared for the swift savagery of a Caesarian attack. The men of the relief force had been ordered to drop their packs and move from column into line, a maneuver that was practiced over and over during the winters, and that drill paid off, as the Legions of Caesar slammed into the undefended Wa rear. Just a handful of the Wa had become aware of the threat from behind, but they were too few in number and were brushed aside as the Legions roared their battle cry. The attack devastated the Wa, the slaughter of the rear ranks immense, forcing the Wa army to reel backward from the walls of the 10th's camp. Those Wa who had made it into the camp itself through one of the several breaches were surrounded and quickly overwhelmed, since no support or reinforcements came through the breaches. In fact, for the first time, more than just one or two Wa warriors were captured alive, although they had yet to talk. But Caesar was grimly determined that they would, counting on the experience and imagination of the men of his torture detachment, which had swelled in number and the techniques picked up in his march across Asia. From Parthia came a couple of men well versed in their unique methods; another man from the Pandya, and from the Han an even half-dozen men whom Zhang had recommended. Caesar wasn't a cruel man—although this last 10 years had hardened him even more than either Gaul or the civil war with Pompey had—but he also understood a commander's need for good intelligence and would stop at nothing to get it, no matter how much flesh had to be stripped from a man, or blood spilled.

Now, Caesar faced a dilemma. There was no way he could move for the next several days; too many men—good, hard veterans all—would die if they were disturbed in their recovery. Fortunately, the Wa army besieging the camp did not try defending the town located just two or three miles from the 10th's camp, allowing Caesar's army to fall on it. This time, most of the citizens had managed to flee, and the few left behind were too old or sick to be of any value and were put to the sword. More important than the slaves was the cache of food and supplies the town yielded, although when compared with the vast amount his army ate, it was enough for perhaps a week, at most. Still, that was a week of food he didn't have before. What concerned him was that his lack of mobility meant that the Wa army besieging Pullus' camp could retreat without being harried, and, even worse, could meet up with more Wa. More than anything, not knowing what he was facing ate at Caesar and kept him awake at night. But it couldn't be helped; giving orders that the 10th's camp be enlarged to accommodate the rest of the army, he settled down to let his wounded men recover enough to resume the march.

However, the other facet of the situation he found himself in that worried him was whether or not he would have the army return to the fleet to resume their sea voyage. In the first days after the battle with the 10th, his answer to that was an absolute affirmative, but a week after the battle, and just two or three days before they were to pack up and march back to the sea and the fleet, some of Caesar's scouts had returned with news. As was his usual custom in territory he didn't know, Caesar sent his scouts into every direction, both to get a better idea of the land through which they were marching, but also to avoid stumbling into another army. But the news the scouts he sent to the south brought had upset his plans of marching back to the fleet, because they informed him that his army was encamped in the middle of the neck of a peninsula that extended an approximate 70 miles to the south from their position.

That was bad enough, but the scouts he had sent to the east also returned, and from their information he was able to piece together a fairly solid idea that this peninsula was more than 50 miles wide, as well. Calling on Lysandros, now the ranking *navarch*, Caesar was informed that to march the 15 miles back to the fleet, board, and then sail around the peninsula, would take more than a week. Or he could march overland across the neck of the peninsula and rejoin the fleet on the other side. This is what he and the army had done on the Gayan Peninsula, although it had been much wider and longer than this one, making it a month-long journey without contact with the fleet. The difference, of course, was that no resistance was met on the Gayan Peninsula. It didn't take Caesar long to make the decision.

"We're marching overland from here, because I've been informed that we're located at the top of a large peninsula," Caesar announced to the assembled officers. "According to our best calculations, it would take us more than a week to cover the same distance that we can make in two hard days."

There wasn't much comment at this; as usual, the clerks in the *praetorium* had told their friends among the Legion clerks, who in turn had told their respective Centurions, meaning every man there had already had time to learn and absorb this. The only question came from a Centurion.

"When do we break camp?" Titus Pullus asked, thinking of the men who would be consigned to the jolting, bouncing wagons.

None of the original wagons that started the campaign into Parthia ten years ago now, had survived. In their place was, like in the naval fleet, a mishmash assortment of carts and wagons, many of them covered only with tarpaulins stretched over wooden frames, a trick picked up along the way. Unlike the wooden structures on wheels that were the original Roman wagons, these, while not as durable, were lighter overall, meaning they could carry more cargo. However, the wagons designated for medical transport were the sturdiest of the bunch. However, another refinement was that the men were actually slung from vertical poles within each wagon, which reduced the jarring impact a great deal, although not completely.

Pullus knew from bitter experience that about ten percent of the men that survived the first two crucial days would end up dying on the way, their final resting place an unmarked grave on the side of the trail. The only blessing, Pullus thought, was that so few Romans were left that this was no longer the huge problem it had been early on, as in Parthia, and the Roman belief that anyone buried underground was destined to walk the world as a shade was no longer as prevalent in the ranks as it had been.

"Two days from now," was Caesar's answer. "Those men who were fated to die will have done so by then, and those fated to recover will be strong enough to endure the march."

With that, the officers were dismissed to pass the word on to their men.

Just as Caesar had promised, two days later the army left behind the smoldering ruin of the camp, joining the still-smoldering ruins of the town to send smoke into the sky. Marching in the *agmentum quadratum*, the baggage train protected in the middle, guaranteed that the army would move more slowly than normally, but it also provided greater security. But what bothered Caesar more than any other challenge facing his army was the disappearance of the Wa army. His scouts had followed their trail, as the Wa moved eastward as well; but after crossing a river, the tracks seemed to disperse in every direction, leaving too many different trails to follow. Caesar knew in his bones that this was a ruse, and that the separate parts of the enemy army would recombine at some point. His hope was that it didn't also join up with yet another Wa force, before he could come to grips with it.

The men were exceptionally alert; their experience with the Wa so far had been singularly unsatisfying, resulting in far more casualties and less loot than they had experienced in some time. At the same time, they were extremely morose and sullen, the normal bantering on the march completely absent. Caesar was acutely aware of this, too, and he knew that unless he was able to provide them with something substantial in terms of a city or a fortified position held by a Wa nobleman, and a substantial one at that, he would face the biggest challenge of the campaign.

For the first time, Titus Pullus was really questioning Caesar's decision to continue the march. He wasn't willing to talk about it with Scribonius or Balbus yet, but he was close to the point where he wouldn't be able to keep his reservations inside. And Pullus knew that if he himself felt this way, the men were simmering with resentment. Caesar had always come up with something before, but this occasion was more important than ever. There either had to be a decisive battle, or they had to come across a city with enough loot to appease the men. Little did Pullus know that Caesar's and his thoughts were on parallel tracks, and neither knew what the future held.

The gods hadn't forgotten their favorite son, however. It was on the first night on the march that a member of the torture detachment, a grizzled former gladiator named Prixus, reported to the *praetorium*. He was allowed in immediately, Caesar giving orders to that effect, and in moments he was standing in before his general.

"We need your man Zhang," Prixus told Caesar, after the formalities were observed. Caesar noticed, but didn't comment on, Prixus' swollen and battered hands, despite the fact that Caesar knew these men always wore linen wrappings on their hands when they did their work. "We have two of these bastards ready to talk."

Caesar leapt up from behind his desk, but even as he was moving, Prixus added a warning, "He needs to hurry. I don't know how long either of them is going to last."

Fortunately, they lasted long enough to tell Caesar more about the island of Wa than he had learned in all of the time he had been on the island. For the first time, Caesar knew the general shape and size of the island and, more importantly, the location of the largest cities. But, most crucial of all, he discovered that in the capital city, still weeks away to the east, the alarm had been sounded, and that a huge army was being formed to repel the invaders. One tidbit Caesar found grimly amusing: one of the Wa continually used a word Caesar had never heard before. When he asked Zhang, the Han was reluctant to translate it, and then when he finally did, it meant nothing—until it had gone through the laborious process of traversing the Pandya-Parthian-Greek connection. All of the translators were shocked when Caesar threw back his head and roared with laughter. When Hirtius and Pollio heard the long unheard sound of their general laughing, they quite naturally came running.

"You know what the word the Wa use to describe us means?" Caesar asked between gasps for air. Without waiting for an answer, he finished, "Barbarians! They call US barbarians! The same thing we call them!"

Once over his bout of mirth, he told the two, "Sound the assembly. I want to let the men know exactly where we're going and exactly what we can expect to find when we get there."

The march was a hard one, and, as Titus Pullus had feared, a number of the wounded who had survived the critical two days after the assault on the 10th's camp succumbed from the rough ride in the wagons.

"At this rate, we're going to be lucky to field a Cohort before we get off this island," was how Balbus put it on the third night after they broke camp, sitting in Pullus' tent with his Primus Pilus and Secundus Pilus Prior Scribonius, eating their evening meal.

Pullus' only reaction was a grunt, but Scribonius added, "That's if we get off at all."

Normally, this was talk that Pullus would have quashed, even if his heart wasn't in it, but now he saw no point, because he was in the same frame of mind as his friends. Educated they were not, but between the three of them were decades of fighting experience, and all three of them saw how dire the situation was. During their march across the lands of the Parthians, the Pandya, the Gayan and the Han had tacitly accepted the presence of Caesar's Legions-once they had demonstrated their military might and smashed whatever armies they faced, and this was especially true with the Han. Once they determined that not only was Caesar not overly interested in conquest, and that subduing his army would have been an extraordinarily costly endeavor, there had been a quiet word sent out that their Emperor would have no objections if men sought to enlist in this foreign army. Caesar instantly understood this as a shrewd move on the part of the Han: the Emperor had his hands full already with the various rebellions, and allowing men to enlist in the exotic armed force removed these men from the rolls of the rebels at one stroke. Moreover, there was a strong allure to joining Caesar's army; as strange and foreign as they may have appeared, it was clearly apparent to any Han warrior that the Romans could fight, and once their origins were known, the fact that they had marched across the vast expanse of Asia marked them as favored by every god imaginable.

But none of that seemed to matter to the Wa. Those Wa that Caesar's army had encountered either fled or fought to the death. Those that chose to fight did not show any interest in doing anything other than kill the men of the barbarian army, and it had also become clear that they viewed their lives as cheap, especially when compared to the chance of repelling these foreign invaders. Simply put, Caesar was running out of men and they were no longer being replaced. In fact, it wasn't just the Centurions who were aware of this. Around every fire there were faces missing, particularly in the 10th, where the loss was even greater. While it was true that many of those faces would return, once they recovered, there were still too many gaps for anyone not to notice, even if most of the missing faces weren't Roman, but brown or yellow. What it took to be accepted at a tent section's fire was one simple requirement: a man had to be able to fight proficiently enough to be considered a member of Caesar's army, an army that each man now knew was famous throughout the entire known world. This notoriety was a source of huge pride and had as much to do with a section's cohesiveness, and their willingness to endure far beyond anything their predecessors in Alexander's army had, and was as powerful as the lure of loot and women. But now even this wasn't enough to keep men from complaining, and, more importantly, worrying.

Caesar was well aware of all that was taking place in his army: the muttered conversations, the small acts of defiance that men in the ranks would perform to let their Centurions and Optios know they were unhappy. The problem was, he didn't know what to do about it. The idea of turning back now was unthinkable to him, not after all that had been endured for the last 10 years. Didn't the men realize that they were now so close to their goal? The idea that he had already surpassed Alexander no longer brought Caesar any satisfaction. No, his soul still ached for more, more conquest, more new sights, more distinction. In fact, he was worried about the moment when they had traversed the length of this island and put down the last sparks of armed rebellion. What would they do then? As much as the men thought him a god, he knew he was mortal; in fact, he was aware that he was starting to fail. Caesar knew in his bones he would never see Rome again, that the only knowledge his countrymen would have of his exploits would come from those few, those very few men who might make it back. Oh, he knew that word of some of what he had done had undoubtedly reached the ears of those little men in the Senate. How bitter they would be, he thought with some satisfaction, whenever a merchant arrived from the East, bringing word of all that Imperator Caesar had accomplished. If only Cato had survived Thapsus to see this! And what of Cicero, he wondered? Was he still alive, carping about what Caesar was doing, all from the comfort of his luxurious villa in the Roman countryside? Turning his mind back to the matter at hand, he concentrated his prodigious intelligence planning his next step. Finally, he came to a conclusion: he would do nothing! At least, nothing overt. Despite its going against every fiber of his being, Caesar made the decision that his only and best chance was to fight a defensive battle. If the two Wa warriors who had talked were to be believed, and Prixus assured him that they were telling the truth, there was a huge Wa army headed their way. If he could shatter that army, then the island would be his to do with, as he willed. More importantly, he could turn it over to his men and let them wreak their vengeance. Just as he had at Pharsalus, he would lure the enemy army into thinking him weak and ready to crack. Then? Well, then he would show these Wa what Caesar was capable of, and the matter would be decided once and for all.

The Wa capital, according to what the prisoners had yielded up, was almost due north, barely a hard day's march away, and yet the scouts still hadn't reported sight of more than small groups of armed Wa— too large for the scouts to engage, but too small to be anything worthwhile pursuing with the entire army. Without knowing where the Wa army was, it was very hard for Caesar to choose the ground on which to make a stand, but he finally found the spot he was looking for: a ridge that was oriented on a north/south axis. It ran for more than 14 miles, which was a longer distance than he would have liked, but it was part of an almost unbroken line of ridges that almost cut the island in two on a northwest/southeast axis, the southern part of the ridge projecting deep into the peninsula they had just crossed. He would have the fleet behind him, to the east, since the capital city was to the west, meaning his line of supply would be secure. But even if the Wa army were somewhere else, to the east of Caesar's current location, for example, Caesar would be between the Wa army and the capital. The ridge itself was extremely rugged, and Caesar knew it would be a hard job to fortify it properly, but he was also thankful that there were only two places to cross the ridge, at least without climbing hand over hand: one at the northern end and one at the southern end. After doing a thorough reconnaissance, Caesar deemed it impossible for the Wa to ascend the ridge anywhere along its length in any numbers sufficient to cause more than some mischief. That meant he could put a strong, fortified camp at one end and one at another, while his engineers would carve out a road traversing the length of the ridge to enable his troops to rush to any trouble spots.

"No, this will do very nicely," was Caesar's comment to Pollio, who was sitting his horse next to his commander. It had been a hard climb for the horses; but, Pollio thought, as always, Caesar knew what he was about. The view was tremendous; any army could be seen coming from any direction for miles.

"Give the order to make camp at the base of the ridge, on the eastern side, so we're near the bay. The fleet's not here yet, but it will be in the next day or two. This," Caesar extended his arm to encompass the ridge, "is where we crush these Wa once and for all."

As disgruntled as Caesar's men were, they nevertheless dug. And dug. Thousands of shovels threw mounds of dirt up to form the basis for the rampart of what would be a line of fortifications extending almost 16 miles along the ridge. The northern end overlooked the one northernmost passage from the interior out to the huge bay behind them, where the fleet was going to be anchored, with the southern end overlooking a similar pass in that direction. Although Caesar didn't have enough men to cover the entire length, he had his men construct a series of fortified camps, each one holding at least a Legion, while the two camps anchoring both ends contained two. Linking each camp, Caesar ordered a road hacked out along the top of the ridge, wide enough for each Legion to march in a column formation, in order to move men to wherever they were needed. Even as experienced as his army was at constructing fortifications, this was a massive project and would take more than a week before Caesar felt that the bare minimum would be accomplished.

Meanwhile, his scouts continued to range about the countryside, concentrating their efforts to the northwest and northeast, looking for the Wa army, and on the third day after Caesar's army started working, they found what they were looking for. Unfortunately, the small group of scouts that came into contact with the outriders of the Wa army were ineptly led, so the entire force was wiped out in an ambush. Consequently, Caesar was unaware of the Wa army's existence for two more days, until they had moved southward along the shores of the great lake to Caesar's west, barely 20 miles away.

"We've finally found the bastards," Primus Pilus Pullus informed his Centurions, gathered in the forum of the camp that was designated for the 10th's use, the northernmost camp, where Caesar deemed it the most likely that the Wa would make some sort of attempt to outflank his army. Pullus' news was met with the predictable stir, a buzz of low-toned conversation crackling through the ranks of the 60 Centurions, as they murmured to each other about the import of this news.

"*Silete*!" Pullus snapped, his nerves betrayed by the harshness of his command. "You're as bad as the rankers! This isn't the first time we've faced this, so stop acting like it!" Chastened, the men immediately fell silent to listen to their Primus Pilus, who took a deep breath before he continued. "We don't know all that much, but there's a lot of them, and they're camped on the shores of that big lake we heard about. So far, though, they haven't budged for the last couple days."

"What are our orders, Primus Pilus?" Scribonius, the commander of the Second Cohort asked, and, in fact, this was prearranged between the two of them, because Pullus had predicted that this news would unsettle his Centurions, a judgment proven correct by their reaction.

"We're going to do what we did at Alesia, and at Ecbatana," Pullus said, naming the Parthian city that was the site of a siege and battle rivaling that of Alesia, for which Caesar had won everlasting fame. "Caesar wants the ground in front of the rampart filled with his lilies, the stakes, and all the other little surprises he loves so much."

There was an appreciative chuckle from the men at this, each of them thinking back to the two times such extensive traps had been laid. Alesia had been particularly brutal; some of these Centurions, having been in the ranks back then, still smarted over the money they had lost from wagers placed on how long Gauls who were hooked on the lilies—the barbed iron points skewering their calves and keeping them in place—could survive being the targets of their javelin practice. Some of those Gauls had looked like blood-soaked porcupines by the time the Legionaries were through, and there were some rueful memories, as these Centurions stood listening to Pullus. Well, more than one of them thought, this might give them a chance to recoup some of the money they had lost back then.

This was the start of a grim race against time, all the men of Caesar's army knowing that every Wa they could disable or kill with a well-placed stake, or a sharpened iron hook, was one less screaming, sword- or spear-waving Wa they would have to face trying to clamber up the rampart to skewer them. Now that the Wa army was located, Caesar demanded reports several times a watch, so that men were seen constantly galloping back and forth across the valley floor, the lake barely a glint of blue on the horizon. The Wa army wasn't visible from the ridge, although every once in a while one of the men would shout at a cloud of dust rising in the air, although that always turned out to be one of Caesar's scouts coming or going, the premature alert drawing the jeers and curses of his comrades down onto the head of the unfortunate who raised the warning. But for reasons neither the men nor their commander could fathom, the Wa seemed content to stay in their spot on the shore of the lake, despite the fact that Caesar knew without any doubt that the Wa were aware of the location of the Roman army. Just as Caesar's scouts were busy, the Wa scouts had been seen on their small ponies in the vicinity, and, in fact, a couple of them had been captured, although they never yielded any useful information before they succumbed to the questioning by Prixus. Whatever the reason for their lethargy, Caesar was thankful for it, pushing the men relentlessly to bring the fortifications up to a level that met with his approval.

While some men were occupied constructing the traps, others were just as busy, a number of them entering the several running streams, searching their banks and beds for stones to pull from the water and making them perfectly round to serve as ammunition for the artillery. There were forests of new-growth trees along the slopes as well, and from the suitable branches of these trees, more scorpion bolts were made. Unfortunately, there was no seasoned timber of a sufficient quantity or size to make more artillery pieces, which Caesar was unhappy about, but he hoped that he and the men would have all they required to repulse the Wa. As it was, Caesar's legions marched with more artillery than any other army of Rome to date, but it was never enough as far as he was concerned. One of the secrets to his success was his use of artillery to inflict as many casualties on his enemy as possible, even before they came to grips with his Legionaries, so that they were already demoralized from the casualties they suffered, as they marched to close within sword length of the Romans.

The men worked through the watches, but on the sixth day they were heartened by the news that the fleet, taking the long way around this huge peninsula, had just been spotted rowing northwest along the shore, around the headland that jutted out at the bottom of the bay.

"They should be here by second watch tomorrow," Caesar announced to his officers and Primi Pili, all of whom to one degree or another let out a sigh of relief. None of them liked being out of sight of their fleet, especially on this accursed island, so the days spent waiting for them had been tense ones, exacerbated by the knowledge of the Wa army just a day's march away.

"Once they're in position, we'll begin transferring every kernel of rice, every pig, and every chicken up to the camps," he continued. "Minus what the men of the fleet need, of course. But I want our position to be as self-sufficient as possible, just in the event that the Wa do manage to force either of the passes, get behind us and cut us off."

What he didn't say, for there was no need, was that if that happened, Caesar would have to force battle, because once they were out of the food that the ships were carrying, there would be no resupply. That knowledge filled his Centurions, particularly Pullus, with a determination that the Wa would be stopped from negotiating the pass.

To help Pullus in his goal, the next day, when Caesar, Pollio, Hirtius, and the rest of his staff went out for a ride to inspect progress to that point, the commander of the army saw that there was still one weakness to his position. The pass to the north was actually relatively wide; Caesar estimated that the width was almost 3 miles, which meant that the Wa could hug the far slope, avoiding the array of Roman artillery to swing around behind his position. However, the Wa couldn't simply march down the middle of the pass either, because of a river and a mass of swampy ground that extended from the banks on either side for perhaps almost a mile.

"I want a fortified redoubt of at least 5 Cohorts' strength over on that far slope," Caesar pointed across the floor of the pass, "and I want it by the end of the day."

"Caesar, do we have any idea how deep that river is? Or how soft the ground is? I can tell from here that it's a swamp, but have any of our scouts surveyed the ground?" Pollio asked.

"Yes," Caesar replied, not perturbed in the slightest to be questioned. "They say it will support men, but only if they're spread out; and the river is shallow, with a rocky bottom."

"So how are they going to get any artillery across?" this came from Hirtius.

"They're going to carry the scorpions, and that's all, but I'm going to give them a Legion's worth of scorpions and extra ammunition. All we want to do is to keep the Wa from moving along the far side of the river, because that's the only firm ground they can use to negotiate the pass to get behind us. With the muck down there, they're likely to keep close to this slope, but only if we have someone on the other side making sure they don't go on the other side of the river."

His orders issued, Caesar turned away to resume his inspection of the rest of the position. The 5 Cohorts were on the move in less than a watch later, accompanied by a cavalry escort, and as they discovered, the ground they had to cross to get to the far ridge was very soggy; the horses plunged almost to their stomachs in the worst spots, while the men went knee-deep. They arrived at the slope opposite from where Pullus and the 10th were still improving their camp filthy and tired, but they were men hardened from years of such toil, and they knew the stakes for which they were playing, so they paused just long enough to catch their breath, before they began work. Siting the position as low on the opposite slope as was practical, the Centurion in charge, Vibius Pacuvius, from the 15th Legion and one of Caesar's Gallic veterans, knew that the farther down the slope he put his camp, the greater the reach of the scorpions. Even so, he detached a Century of men to go down onto the floor of the pass, as close to the edge of the mire as possible, to serve as a forward post, their orders being to buy as much time as possible in case the Wa tried to dislodge the main body. What not just the Centurion on the far slope, but Caesar and, by extension the rest of his army, were counting on was that the Wa commander would be unwilling to turn his attention to the smaller force, because it would expose the rear of his army to the 10th.

Unfortunately, the only way they would know if this position would be effective was at the point when the Wa army actually began its move. It was two days short of 2 weeks after the fortified line was begun that a group of scouts came galloping across the floor of the plain, trailing dust that hung in the still air, and thus pointing like an arrow back to the northwest from where they had come. Balbus had the duty, and he sent a man to fetch his Primus Pilus, who arrived in time to see the scouts begin laboring up the slope of the ridge, following what had become a well-worn path up to the position 3 miles to the south of the 10th's camp, where Caesar had located his headquarters.

"They look like Cerberus was after them," Pullus commented to his friend, who grunted in agreement.

"Probably means those slant-eyed barbarians are on the move," was Balbus' only comment, as Pullus turned away to go back to his tent and don his armor.

Because of the distance, Caesar had decreed that his senior Centurions had to ride at a quick trot, whenever they were summoned to the *praetorium*, something Pullus hated to do. His size and weight meant he always had to have a large horse, but all that was available for him was one of the island ponies, so that his feet were bare inches off the ground, making him feel ridiculous. Fortunately for everyone, the men knew better than to laugh at the sight, except that it still didn't help his frame of mind. He was on his pony and already a mile down the road that ran along the top of the ridge, made as smooth and level as possible to Caesar's exacting standards, when he met the mounted courier galloping in his direction. Seeing the large Primus Pilus, the courier curbed his horse, spraying dirt and rocks everywhere, and in his excitement forgot to render his salute.

Pullus was about to reprimand him, but before he could speak, the courier shouted to him, voice straining with excitement, "Caesar summons you immediately, Primus Pilus. The Wa are marching and are expected to be here by nightfall!"

"How many, do you figure?" Sextus Scribonius asked Titus Pullus, as they both stood on the rampart of the northernmost camp along the ridgeline. Spread out on the valley before them was a rolling mass of humanity, still too distant to distinguish individuals, but the leading edge was moving inexorably in the direction of the Roman lines.

"Hard to say," Pullus replied, squinting as he tried to peer through the dust cloud raised by the feet of the men in the front of the Wa army. "But that dust goes back as far as I can see."

"That's because you're old," Scribonius joked, although, in fact, he was a few years older, and his vision was no better than that of his Primus Pilus.

Pullus laughed, but his eyes never wavered from the sight before him, and for several moments neither spoke.

"I don't know exactly, but I would guess at a minimum there's at least 80,000 down there," he finally broke the silence.

Scribonius' only response was a faint nod, because that was his estimate as well.

"I don't know whether they're going to settle in and make camp first, or go straight to the attack, but I'm going to play it safe and have the men ready," Pullus decided. Clapping his friend on the shoulder, he finished by saying, "Go get your men up on the ramparts. I want them, my Cohort, and the Third ready at the walls. The rest of the Legion I'll have on alert."

And with that, they both left the rampart to perform their respective tasks.

As it turned out, there was no need for alarm, at least that first day, as the Wa army moved into position. For the next two watches, the men on the ramparts stood observing, as the Wa moved into what was essentially a series of camps, spread evenly along the valley floor. Because the northern end of the ridge curled slightly to the west, it formed a bit of a pocket, where the valley floor extended a little farther east and was, in effect, surrounded on three sides by the ridge. Caesar had hoped that whoever was commanding the Wa would make the mistake of putting some of his army in this pocket, because it did allow the Wa some flexibility as to which way they could assault the ridge. To counteract that, the camp that held the 10th was not in its normal square, but in a slightly curved, rectangular shape, so that the slopes within the pocket were covered, as well as the northern tip, which overlooked the pass. Along with the 10th in this camp was the 12th, and probably most importantly, roughly half of the artillery the army possessed. This was why Caesar wanted the Wa to move all the way to the foot of the slope, because although the main camp was several hundred paces up the ridge and near the top, there were carefully prepared and camouflaged positions farther down the slope, within artillery range of any Wa camp. At each position was a supply of combustible ammunition: small jars of pitch, stoppered and stuffed with rags to serve as wicks, ready to be set alight and rain flaming death down onto the heads of the Wa. However, their commander, whoever he was, was either too canny or had luck of his own that kept him from placing his men there.

Pity, Pullus thought, as he continued watching the Wa move into position. He now saw that his estimate was woefully low, as the dust cloud continued to hover above the enemy army, obscuring the trailing elements, until they would suddenly appear out of the dust as if by magic. . And they kept coming, and coming, and coming, Pullus saw, his mood growing more dismal. What he couldn't see was the composition, other than how many men were mounted, and very, very few were. What he was more worried about was the proportion between archers and infantry, and of the infantry, how many would be carrying the long spears. Those would be the Wa's most effective weapons in the event of a straightforward assault, because of their reach; yet even knowing this, Pullus feared the men with the swords the most, something that he would never, ever admit to anyone but himself. However, for the first time in his career in the army, Titus Pullus had seen men handle a sword as skillfully as he did, albeit in a completely different way. What was most unsettling was that the controlled frenzy these warriors possessed, combined with such a skill level meant that they were formidable, indeed. Well, he thought grimly, we just have to make sure those slanty-eyed little *cunni* don't manage to get up on the rampart. For that, Pullus was convinced, would be the key to avoid being overwhelmed. What remained to be seen was where the focal point of the Wa attack would be, but Pullus felt deep down in his bones that it would be the 10th that would either add to the laurels of their standards, or become another forgotten Legion, because it would be wiped out to the last man, with nobody left to tell their story.

For his part, Caesar also watched, from the camp roughly in the middle of the ridge. This meant that the leading edge of the Wa first appeared several miles farther away than it did for Pullus, but he was kept informed by a steady stream of couriers galloping along the rough road and carrying messages from Hirtius, whom he had put in command of the northern camp. Then, gradually, as the Wa continued moving south to fill the valley with their horde, Caesar began to understand what was facing his army. Standing next to him, Asinius Pollio, Tiberius Nero, and the Primus Pilus of the 25th Legion, Torquatus, talked softly to each other, but all of them were of a like mind. None of them had faced an army of the size that the Wa army appeared it would be, and, as one man, they looked to Caesar who alone appeared unperturbed.

Turning to Pollio at last, Caesar's tone was calm. "I estimate more than 100,000 men are down there, Pollio. Do you agree?"

Pollio, doing his best to match his general's demeanor, if not his voice, replied, "Yes, Caesar, and then some. It wouldn't surprise me if it turns out to be 120,000 barbarians down there."

Caesar considered for a moment, then nodded. "I think you're right." Giving the others a wry smile, he admitted, "I thought that was about right in the first place, but I was afraid to say it aloud."

This brought a nervous but appreciative chuckle from the others, but Caesar's confident manner reappeared immediately.

"Well," he rubbed his hands together, "that just means the glory will be all the greater. Now, let's see what our opponent has planned, shall we?"

It turned out that the Wa were content to spend the rest of that day, then the next one as well, getting settled into their camps. Caesar was interested to see that their commander placed the largest number of his men in the camp nearest to the northern Roman camp, with the southernmost Wa position holding the second largest number, but he was not particularly alarmed. If I were their commander, he reflected, I would do the same thing. If my main focus was going to be on the northern camp, then I would want my troops to travel the shortest distance. However, if I was going to attack somewhere else along the line, and I had 120,000 troops, I would still put a larger number at the ends, to pin as many of my numerically inferior enemy's troops down. That would allow me to choose my spot, and, because I am on the flat valley floor, I can move men more quickly. Of course, Caesar continued his thought, the Wa commander can't see that we have a road running along the top of the ridge, so that I can move almost as quickly as he can. And that, Caesar thought with grim amusement, is just one trick up my sleeve. As much as he had seen, as many new nations and their warriors Caesar had faced, he still believed down to the core of his being that when all facets of warfare were considered, he and his Romans had no equal. He had been forced to acknowledge, however grudgingly and only to himself, that in martial ardor and pure fighting skill, the Wa were more than a match for his men. But there is more to warfare than fighting, something that no other general in history understood better than Caesar, and as confident as he was, he also knew that this battle, what he somehow instinctively understood would be his last great battle, one way or another, would require every ounce of skill, every particle of luck that the gods still owed him, and would be the greatest test of his career. Nevertheless, he was ready; he just hoped the rest of the army was, as well.

On the second day, once it became apparent the Wa were still preparing for whatever they had planned, Caesar made the decision to send all of his noncombatants—other than the *medici* of course—down the opposite slope to the security of the fleet. He did the same for the cavalry and, after careful consideration, his auxiliary forces, save for the remaining men of his missile troops. His reasoning was slightly different for each group, but ultimately, there was one common thought; this fight was for the Legions, Caesar's hard men of iron. As useful as the extra bodies of the auxiliaries might be, Caesar also understood that none of his Legionaries held them in much regard. The cavalry was a simpler matter, and while he knew some of them were nearly as skilled with their weapons on foot as they were on horseback, their style of fighting wouldn't be a good fit for the defense of the camps. The tent section slaves whose tasks were to lead the sections' mules and other duties, would all just be in the way. Only those who had been trained as *medici,* and a handful per camp to act as stretcher bearers, would be left behind. Finally, Legion clerks without dual training were also sent to the ships. This included Diocles, over his strong objections, but Pullus' will prevailed, and the diminutive Greek marched down the slope, muttering all the way to the fleet. Caesar had done everything he could think to do to prepare his army for the coming trial.

In the pre-dawn morning, on the third day after the Wa army appeared, Titus Pullus was awakened by the shouted alarm of the sentry nearest his tent. Normally, what followed was the sound of rustling that told him Diocles, in the outer portion of the Primus Pilus' tent that served as the Legion office, had sprung from his pallet; but it took Pullus a moment to remember that Diocles was now with the fleet. A brief instant later, he heard someone call his name, and without wasting time pulling on his armor first, Pullus strode to the entrance of his tent to see a man, standing at *intente*, waiting.

"Report," Pullus snapped, and the Legionary, drilled in this as with everything, began speaking.

Because of the gloom, only then did Pullus realize that it was Mardonius, the Parthian who had been seconded to Scribonius as his new Optio some weeks before. Fortunately, although

Mardonius' Latin still carried the heavy accent of his native tongue, he was clearly understandable.

"Pilus Prior Scribonius has sent me to report that the Wa army has begun leaving the northern camp and appears to be forming up by torchlight," the swarthy Parthian snapped out.

Even having known before he went to sleep the night before that this was the most likely day for the confrontation, Pullus nonetheless felt the lurch in his stomach, but his demeanor remained unchanged, as he nodded to Mardonius.

"Very well. Thank you, Optio. You can report to Scribonius and tell him that I'll rouse the rest of the Legion and he's to keep me informed if anything unusual happens. I imagine," Pullus finished casually, as if he were talking about nothing more momentous than the day's duties, "that with that big an army, it'll take them the better part of a full watch to form up."

"On your way back, rouse Valerius," he told Mardonius, speaking of the *cornicen* for the First Cohort, and, by extension, the whole Legion; Valerius' tent was right next to that of the Primus Pilus, a tent shared with the *Tesseraurius*, the *signifer,* and the First Cohort's *aquilifer,* the bearer of the sacred Eagle standard of the Legion. "Tell him to sound assembly, entire Legion. It's time to get the boys up and ready."

Barely a sixth part of a watch later, both the 10th and the 12th Legion, the two most veteran Legions in Caesar's army, were fully formed, with the bulk of both Legions assembled and in the Forum of the camp, minus the Cohorts currently manning the ramparts. It was still dark, but there was a pinking of the eastern sky that hinted at the coming day, and not lost on any man of either army was the possibility that this would be the last dawn they would see. Such knowledge makes these moments all the more precious, particularly for that group of men, part of the second *dilectus* held in Africa and Syria, who worshiped the sun god Baal, and nothing was said when these men, as they did every dawn, prostrated themselves in the direction of the rising sun. In fact, more men than usual followed suit, dropping to their knees, and, while not trying to mouth the prayers, stayed silent as the others finished. The Forum, packed with Legionaries, generated a quiet hum, a throaty sound of men whispering to each other, speculating on what was to come, making the same stale jokes or wagers as before every battle. While Pullus had been rousing his Legion, Hirtius had sent one of the dispatch riders galloping along the ridge top road to Caesar, although he was sure Caesar would be aware by the time the rider arrived. Very quickly, all that was left was to wait, wait to see what the Wa were going to do, and, more importantly, where they were going to do it. Despite the fact that neither Pullus nor Hirtius had confided in each other, their thoughts ran along identical lines, both of them sure that it would be their position that would come under the heaviest assault. From what they had seen, just the contents of the northernmost Wa camp gave the enemy a 5 to 1 advantage, or thereabouts. But despite this, neither Hirtius nor Pullus was particularly worried by that alone, because the artillery was just waiting to rip bloody gaps in the Wa ranks as they struggled up a steep slope. What *did* worry both of them, and had kept them up the night before, was what else the Wa had in store for them: what surprise of their own they had in store for the army of Caesar. But the only way to know was to face it.

The sun was just fully above the horizon to the east when the *bucina* of the guard Cohort—the Second Cohort—blasted out the signal that the enemy was moving, and Pullus, Hirtius, and Balbinus all went trotting from the Forum to the rampart to see what the day held in store for them. Mounting the parapet, all three officers came to an abrupt halt, staring down at the sight before them, and for several moments, none of them could find any words.

Finally, it was Pullus, who managed to say, his voice suddenly hoarse, "Well, we're going to earn our pay today."

Chapter 8

Just as Pullus had predicted, it took the Wa almost a full watch before they were in what was apparently their battle formation, and at first, it appeared that the Wa commander was going to behave precisely as Caesar had expected him to. There hadn't been any real shift in terms of the numbers, so that the same size Wa force was now aligned roughly even with the base of the northernmost camp, giving every indication that they would make a straightforward assault. Elsewhere, smaller groups of Wa, but still in contingents that looked to be about 10,000 men in strength, lined themselves up across from each of the five Roman camps. What Caesar couldn't see was beyond the camp to his left, namely the rest of the southernmost positions that ended in an almost identical situation at the southern end of the ridge with the camp commanded by Pollio. While he could just make out the Wa camps that were roughly aligned exactly like the others, he could tell there was movement only because of the large clouds of dust from the closest camp and because the mounted couriers were galloping back and forth. However, even with the road that Caesar had the men cut along the top of the ridge, it would be at least a sixth part of a watch before he could expect to be informed by a courier, and that was only if he rode hard and the horse didn't founder. Consequently, as soon as the Wa began making their own camps, he had sent Asinius Pollio to the southernmost camp. He needed a man he could trust, even though he felt certain that there would be no major attack on that position. He also had a group of couriers stationed along the ridge road at each camp, where they would act as relay riders, each passing the message to the next waiting rider, so that he would be informed as quickly as possible, in the event he was wrong in his prediction.

His reasoning was simple; the northern pass was closest to where he had been told the capital lay to the northwest, and he didn't think that any commander would risk concentrating his forces in such a way that if his opponent stole a march, the capital lay undefended. And he was sure that by this point, the one thing the Wa knew about this "barbarian" was that he and his army were capable of moving very swiftly, indeed. No, he was sure that the north would be where the action was going to be. What was still unclear to him was the Wa commander's intent. Since the Wa possessed no navy to speak of—and what they did have was certainly not strong enough to be of any threat to his own fleet, now riding at anchor just on the other side of this ridge—it didn't really make sense for the Wa to try to force a passage through that northern pass to get to the bay. The only thing their infantry could do in that event was shake their fists at the ships; in fact, some of the ship-borne artillery still hadn't been stripped from the vessels, so if they got too close to the shore, the navy would punish them for that. Furthermore, forcing the pass would effectively put the Roman army at their backs, with the bay on the other side. Despite their numerical superiority, they would be in a tactically inferior position, and the Romans could move down the slope to within artillery range, putting the Wa in a vice. No, Caesar mused, I don't think that's it. That left only one other option, the one that makes the most sense on a number of levels: the Wa commander's intent was to come up this ridge and destroy this army once and for all, in a decisive battle.

The only question was, how? Caesar had spent a sleepless night turning that over in his mind. He had long since learned that while it was of some value to think about what he himself would do in an enemy commander's place, his adversary didn't always make the same decisions as he. In fact, he rarely did, so Caesar turned his prodigious mind to trying to divine what the Wa commander would do. What made this so damnably difficult was Caesar's unfamiliarity with his opponent, both in a general sense, as far as understanding the Wa mind, and in a specific sense, with this particular general. He assumed he had never faced this man, and while there had now been a few engagements with the Wa, they had acted in such unexpected ways that Caesar was very reluctant to draw any firm conclusion. Hence, a lot of tossing and turning. Would the Wa commander just send that large body of men scrambling up the slope, ready to absorb whatever punishment his men must endure, in order to close with the Romans, while using the smaller forces to keep the other Roman camps occupied so that no reinforcements from them could be sent to help the northern camp? On its surface, that would certainly seem the most likely approach, but Caesar had spent enough time in this strange land to understand one very important thing: the people of this entire part of the world didn't think at all like those from the West. It was this thought gnawing at his brain that finally prompted him to summon Zhang. The Han emissary came very quickly, and it was clear he hadn't been sleeping, either.

"It's nice to know I'm not the only one losing sleep," Caesar said in Latin, more as a test than anything else.

"Tomorrow is...important day," Zhang replied haltingly, in Caesar's tongue.

One thing that Caesar was famous for, and if the truth were known, was one of the things of which he was proudest, was his facility for languages. However, this Han had demonstrated to be his clear superior in that regard, as his Latin, just in the weeks since he had first surprised them, was markedly improved. It irritated Caesar quite a bit, in fact; when you have always been considered the best at something, it's always a rude shock to find out you're not. This was something Caesar tried very hard not to show, keeping his countenance and demeanor as close to normal as possible. Achaemenes had been summoned as well, and Caesar turned to him now.

"I want you to stay here, but Zhang and I are going to carry on this conversation. Only step in when it's clear that either of us is having difficulty, is that clear?

After being assured that it was, Caesar turned to Zhang.

"I need to ask you a question, and it's a very, very important one. The reason it's important is that it affects your future, just as much as it does mine and that of this army. So I need you to be completely honest with me. Do you understand?"

Zhang didn't answer immediately, his flat features giving nothing away, but after what seemed to Caesar to be a very long moment, he finally nodded.

"Yes, I understand, and I will be as honest as it is possible to be."

"That's a courtier's answer," Caesar snapped, but Zhang didn't understand the word 'courtier', so there was a pause as he and Achaemenes talked in Zhang's native tongue. After a moment, Zhang made a small noise that Caesar took to mean he now understood.

"Forgive me, Caesar," Zhang bowed his head toward the Roman. "That was a poor choice of words. Yes, I will be completely honest with you."

Not completely satisfied, but understanding he would get nothing better, Caesar then posed his question.

Now, as Caesar watched matters unfolding, his mind went back to that conversation with Zhang, and despite himself, he clenched a fist in frustration. It had been singularly unsatisfying; the people of this part of the world were worse than Greeks, speaking in riddles that, to a Roman, smacked of sophistry and duplicity. If Zhang didn't know, how hard would it have been to say that? Still, his mind chewed on what little grist the Han had provided, and as he saw the neat, serried ranks of the northernmost Wa force begin to move, he slowly relaxed. They were heading directly for the slope, and gave every indication that they were going to try to overwhelm Pullus and Balbinus' Legions with sheer brute force. His attention was pulled away by the sound of a *bucina* in his own camp, and he turned to see that the smaller Wa force that had arrayed itself at the foot of the slope below his camp had also begun to move.

Turning to Torquatus, whose Legion was one of the two that held this camp, Caesar said, "Remember what we discussed Torquatus. I want you to wait longer than normal for the Wa to get into range. I want to let them get really close, before we commence firing."

Titus Pullus had seen the same thing as Caesar and had much the same reaction. Standing next to him was Balbus, and Pullus could clearly see that his friend was just as troubled.

"The Legion stores are going to be drained dry of shields by the time we're through," Balbus said, his tone calm, despite the scene before him.

Both of these men were vastly experienced in the art of leading men and knew that the rankers hung on every word uttered by their Centurions and Optios, no matter how hard they tried to look as though they weren't listening, as the men near the pair were doing now. It was essential that the Centurions sound unconcerned, especially at moments like this, Pullus reflected, happy that Balbus was as aware as he was that his tone would do much to keep the men as calm as possible.

"You're right, Balbus, but you know what? I'm not going to let the army cheat my boys just because these Wa bastards are going to poke some holes in their shields. I'll pay for every ruined shield out of my own purse!"

Just as he had hoped, the men within earshot let out a happy shout; the upcoming threat and the fact that it was likely a good number of them wouldn't live through the day was temporarily forgotten, as they rejoiced at the idea that the rankers would put one over on the army. It never failed to amuse Pullus that the entity known as "the army" was universally loathed by the men and that any chance at foiling what they considered the army's never-ending plot to rob them of their hard-earned pay at every turn was a cause for celebration. The Legion, on the other hand? Well, these men would fight and die for the Legion, as they would fight and die for the friends immediately to their left and right, never stopping to think that it was the amalgam of Legions, filled with men just like them, with the exact same viewpoint, that comprised the hated "army". The other thing Pullus knew was that the word of his largesse would fly down the length of the rampart from where he was standing, as the men passed the word to those comrades who wanted to know what the cheering was about. In fact, even as he and Balbus stood there, he could hear the ripple of shouts making its way down the rampart, where it abruptly stopped, when the last man of the 10th turned to pass the word and saw that it was, in fact, a man from the 12th standing next to him. Although they were not quite as loud, Pullus could hear the groans from the 12th, as they heard of the bounty their comrades in the 10th had been given, cursing the luck that came from being in the wrong Legion. Out of the corner of his eye, Pullus saw Balbus' scarred face grimace in what he knew was his friend's version of a grin, made sinister-looking by the severed nerves that made his lip permanently droop.

"Balbinus isn't going to thank you for that," he laughed. "Now he's going to have to match you or his men will curse his name every day from here on."

Pullus grinned back at Balbus, giving a shrug. "Not really my problem, is it? And he can always refuse. He's a cheap bastard; he still owes me 50 sesterces from our last dice game. Although," the Primus Pilus finished with a laugh, "I don't know why I care. It's not like I can spend it anywhere."

"It's the principle," Balbus immediately replied, without thinking, and cursed himself as he saw Pullus wince. "Sorry," Balbus said awkwardly, "I didn't mean....."

Pullus waved him off. "I know. Don't worry about it. Well," he abruptly changed the subject, "let's check to make sure every man has his siege spear ready." Without waiting for a reply, Pullus turned toward his own Century, bawling out, "You *cunni* better have those siege spears ready! I want to see nothing but points sticking out over the wall!"

Balbus, before he turned to his own men, stared at the back of his retreating friend. "When are you going to learn to keep your mouth shut?" he asked, only of himself, since the men around him within earshot wouldn't dare respond. Not if they didn't want to suffer a fate that scared them more than the sight of the Wa marching up the slope.

What Balbus had said that disrupted the moment suddenly transported Titus Pullus back to the scene of another battle, one from years before this campaign started, on a dusty plain outside a town called Pharsalus. It was there that Titus Pullus and his longest and best friend ,Vibius Domitius, had found themselves on the opposite side, a moment that had severed for all time a friendship that had started when they were 10 years old. In the immediate aftermath of the battle, when Caesar had called on his exhausted men to accompany him in his pursuit of Pompey—who had escaped the battle with barely a Century's worth of men—the 10th, Caesar's favorite and most loyal Legion to that moment, had refused. It had been a huge shock to Caesar, and it was only less of a shock to Pullus, who was the Secundus Pilus Prior, commander of the Second Cohort, because he had gotten a few moments' warning just before it happened. Vibius had been his Optio then, and in the heat of the moment, as he and Vibius stood there, face to face, Pullus had come perilously close to drawing his sword and striking down his best friend. Ironically, that act had done Pullus' career an enormous amount of good, despite the personal pain it caused him, because Caesar had seen it happen, as well.

Knowing in that moment that Pullus' loyalty to his general was unflinching and recognizing that the rankers of the 10th were not likely to forgive the giant Centurion, at least at that moment, Caesar had appointed him as the *de facto* Primus Pilus of the two Cohorts of the 6th Legion that had been on the field in the ranks of Pompey just a watch earlier. In the resulting rout, these two

Cohorts, the 7th and 10th, had been stranded on the wrong side of the river, as the rest of the Legion made its escape, "joining" Caesar's forces somewhat involuntarily, after being made to choose Caesar or death by Marcus Antonius, the commander of that portion of the field. However, these two Cohorts of the 6th had then served Caesar steadfastly and well, no matter how their service started, accompanying him to Alexandria. They were also the part of Caesar's force that had soundly defeated the dreaded Pontic chariots at Zela, the battle that prompted the "I came, I saw, I conquered" dispatch from Caesar that was in many ways more famous than the battle itself.

By the time Caesar and Pullus had returned, a year after Pharsalus, matters had settled and passions had cooled to the point where Pullus had been appointed the official Primus Pilus of the 10th Legion, while Vibius continued to serve out his enlistment as the Optio of what became Scribonius' Century and Cohort. Neither man spoke to the other after that, and when the original men of the 10th saw their enlistment expire, Vibius chose not to re-enlist, instead going home to finally marry his childhood sweetheart Juno. She had once jilted him to marry another man during the Gallic campaign, and he had since had the good grace to die and leave her a widow. It was only through Scribonius, who had managed to maintain his friendship with both men, that Titus learned that the son Juno had borne Vibius was named Titus, just as Titus' dead son had been named Vibius, back when they had been friends and sure that nothing would ever sever that bond.

As Pullus went through the motions of doing a last-minute inspection of the men, his mind was elsewhere, thinking about all that he had lost in his life, balanced against all that he had gained. The words that Balbus had uttered surprised Pullus, because of how much they still hurt to hear them. "It's the principle" had been one of Vibius' favorite phrases when he had found himself in an intractable position. One time it had been over what was essentially just a spoonful of vinegar that he became convinced Vellusius had filched from his flask, until Scribonius had found the small hole near the bottom that allowed the remaining fluid to leak out. Even faced with such evidence, while Vibius had grudgingly apologized to Vellusius, he had insisted that "it was the principle" about which he was arguing, and in that principle he maintained that he was vindicated in his condemnation of Vellusius. It was the kind of incident that was infuriating to all involved in the moment; indeed, Pullus had seen Legionaries kill each other for similar reasons over the years, but years later they provided some of the loudest, longest laughs around the fire at night. And here, on this hill in Wa, with thousands of armed men marching to try to end not just Pullus' life, but the very existence of the 10th and the army in general, this was what occupied Pullus' mind.

Pullus' mind might have been elsewhere, but his body was very much standing on the rampart of the northernmost camp, and the sheer size and bulk of his presence heartened his men more than even Pullus realized. The post of Primus Pilus was almost always filled with only the most exemplary of Centurions, but even among the Primi Pili, Titus Pullus was a legend. He had long since shown that there was more to his prowess in battle than his size and strength; from the age of 12, an outsize 12, it was true, he and Vibius had begun training for the Legions, at the hands of a veteran of Sertorius' Spanish Legions who was Titus' brother-in-law. And from that first day, it was very rare that Pullus didn't spend at least a third of a watch every day working on his skills with the sword. Early on, he had been lulled into a sense of invincibility by the constant praise of his Pilus Prior, the famous Gaius Crastinus, his weapons instructor Aulus Vinicius, and most of his comrades, but in his first campaign he had learned that as talented as he may have been, he could be bested. From that first close call to this day, he never took his skills for granted. His subsequent exploits had built one upon another, until his men held him in an awe that was just slightly below their awe of Caesar, who they were convinced was a god. If Caesar was god, they were sure their Primus Pilus was a demigod, and just having him standing there next to them, waiting for what was to come, gave them enormous comfort and instilled in them a belief that despite the odds, they would be victorious once again.

Only dimly aware of this, Pullus continued walking among the men, putting a hand on the shoulder on one, while sharing a joke with another about some past exploit or error, but his mind still ranged back over the years of his life. He supposed that this was understandable, because although he didn't have the same visceral feeling that Caesar was experiencing, he was aware that this would in all likelihood be the toughest battle he and the 10th had ever faced, and that made the chances very good that he wouldn't live to see another day. After all, he reasoned, everyone's string plays out, and I've had more luck than anyone, other than Caesar. Even as this thought, the last of his reverie, ran through his mind, there was a shouted warning that the Wa had halted their progress. Turning to face them, Pullus was just in time to see a rippling movement in the rear ranks, as the massed archers tilted their bows upward with impressive precision—considering their large numbers—each man pulling his other arm backwards, drawing the string up to his cheek, where the taut string was held for an instant, before the short, sharp blast of some sort of horn sounded.

"Shields up!" Pullus' roar mingled with that of the other Centurions and Optios, but he continued, in the same bellowing volume, "Remember boys! I'm paying for the shields!"

Any cheers that came from the men was wiped out by the sudden hollow clatter of arrows striking the wood of shields, punctuated by a number of clanging rings, as some missiles hit metal bosses and, even worse, joined by shouts and cries of men who were struck down. Over the din, Pullus heard the *cornu* blow the command that told the ballistae, all of which had been positioned off of the rampart about 40 paces from the walls, where their arcing fire would clear the men on the ramparts, to open fire. They would be essentially firing blind, but with their ammunition of rocks, precision wasn't as important as with the scorpions. Those scorpions were arrayed on the walls, and no order had been given to them at this point, although the leading Wa were well within range. Still, this was part of Caesar's plan for each of the forts, to maximize the casualties they inflicted, because he had a real fear that they would run out of bolts well before they ran out of Wa, so every shot had to count. To protect them from the Wa arrow fire, fascines—large wicker baskets filled with dirt—had been placed side by side, with just enough of an opening for each scorpion to have an arc of fire of perhaps 10 degrees; but there were enough of them, so that their fields of fire interlocked, leaving no spot where the Wa would be safe. While Pullus understood and accepted Caesar's reasoning, it was still hard for him to crouch in place without hearing the distinctive twanging report from Caesar's favorite weapon when he knew the Wa were well within scorpion range. But he at least had the comfort of the crashing sound, as the arm of the ballista hit the crossbar, stopping it abruptly while sending the contents of its basket into the ranks of the Wa. Unfortunately, the hail of arrows was too thick to risk peeking out to see what kind of damage was being done. Just as had happened on the beach—and to a lesser extent when their makeshift camp was attacked when the 10th had been out on patrol—the rain of arrows was practically nonstop, the air so thick with feathered missiles that it indeed appeared possible they would blot out the sun. Within the span of perhaps 100 heartbeats, the barrage was so intense that as Pullus looked to each side—still holding the shield he had drawn from stores in front and slightly above his body—he saw that there wasn't a man who didn't already have at least 3 or 4 arrows protruding from his shield, while the ground all around was studded with shafts, some of them still quivering from their impact. Realizing that if this continued, every man's shield would be useless, Pullus made a quick decision.

"I need a section of volunteers from each Century to stay with me on the rampart to keep an eye on these *cunni*! The rest of you I want down off the rampart out of range to save your shields! Pass the word!"

Pullus bellowed this order first to his right, then repeated it to his left, counting on his Centurions and Optios to divine his purpose immediately and react accordingly. To his relief, there was only a slight delay, as Centurions either asked or in some cases, ordered certain men to stay behind, and so those who didn't volunteer or weren't asked, as the case may have been, began backing down the slope of the rampart, their shields still up. Inevitably, some men were still struck down, although it was a blessed few, but the shields suffered more damage.

"Plautus, you bastard! I've had you on report for a month now but I've been too busy, so you're one of the volunteers," was how it was expressed by Marcus Glaxus, the Primus Princeps Prior, or commander of the Third Century of the First Cohort, to a veteran of Gaul, one of the few remaining in the army.

Although it was ostensibly true that Plautus was on report, Glaxus also knew that of all the men in his Century, Plautus was one of the toughest and wasn't likely to crack under what was shaping up to be the most intense barrage they had ever endured.

As he watched his orders being carried out, it took Pullus a moment to become aware that someone had made his way through the men moving all around him to stand beside him. Finally turning, he saw Balbus, holding up his own shield, which was now studded with more than a half dozen arrows. Immediately understanding his friend's intent, Pullus shook his head emphatically.

"No, you get back to the rear as well. I need you to be ready to take over the Legion in case I don't duck quickly enough."

Despite the circumstances, Balbus still gave his version of a grin at the attempted humor, appreciating the effort, if not the wit, but he made no move to go. Pullus' voice hardened.

"I mean it, get out of here!"

Just as he finished the sentence, there was a loud clanging crack, and Balbus' shield was almost jerked from his hand by an arrow that had struck the boss.

Grimacing, he nevertheless gave his superior and friend a curt nod, but before he turned away, he said as quietly as possible under the circumstances, "All right, but promise me you won't stand there like a statue. Nobody is going to think less of you if the great Titus Pullus actually acts like the rest of us and tries to avoid getting hit by one of these damned things."

At first Pullus didn't answer, but seeing that Balbus wasn't going to budge, he snapped, "Fine. I promise. Now get out of here!"

Balbus then began backing up, careful of his footing as he moved backward down the packed dirt slope that led to the rampart and that allowed Roman Legionaries to get to their spots on the wall more quickly than any other army who used ladders. Satisfied that Balbus was leaving, Pullus turned his attention back to the remainder of his men, the volunteers staying behind to watch the Wa, who at this point were content to have halted for a time, obviously to allow their archers to soften up the Roman defenses. We'll be softened all right, Pullus thought grimly, as a man—one of the Pandyans, by the look of him—who had stayed behind suddenly let out a strangled, gurgling cry, then staggered backward to fall tumbling down the ramp with an arrow in the throat. His attention resting on the stricken man for just a heartbeat, Pullus turned back to the front just in time to sense, more than see, a Wa arrow streaking down from the sky, almost vertically above him. The angle was such that it would skim over the top of his shield before he could move it, and displaying reflexes honed through years of battles, Pullus merely twisted his body a fraction, far enough for the arrow to miss, but close enough that he could hear the whistling and feel the slap of the wind against his cheek as it shot past to bury itself in the ground just behind him. Despite the gravity of the situation, Titus Pullus burst out laughing in relief, glad that he had actually heeded Balbus' advice. Even so, there was a small part of his mind that chided him that what he had done could look like cowardice, a feeling that hearkened back to very early in his career, before he was a legend.

Titus Pullus was only in his 20's when he was promoted from his post as Optio of the First Century, Second Cohort, by Caesar, immediately after Alesia. This, in and of itself, was not unusual; he had been Optio for almost 4 years, but what *was* unusual was that instead of assigning Pullus to one of the most junior Cohorts—traditionally it would have been as the Decimus Hastatus Posterior, the most junior Centurion in a Legion—Caesar had named him Secundus Pilus Prior, the most senior Centurion of the Second Cohort and its commander on detached operations, this being one of the most senior positions in the Legion. It had been an extremely bold, and controversial, decision by Caesar, who was never bound by tradition if it served as an impediment to what he viewed as the most effective or efficient way to run the army. The promotion thrust Pullus into a position that, although in his secret heart he had coveted, he never thought he would actually have to face, commanding Centurions more experienced and older than he was.

One of them, in particular, that unsurprisingly gave him the most trouble had been Gnaeus Celer, the Pilus Posterior and the customary choice to move up when the previous Pilus Prior—who had been sarcastically known as Pulcher, "The Handsome," because of the leering scar he bore on his face—was killed. From that moment and for the next few years, Celer had done whatever he could to undermine Pullus: subtly mocking his age and trying to engineer events so that he could appear to the men as the sympathetic figure when Pullus was deemed to be harsh. Between Celer's actions and his own youth, Pullus was acutely aware that the eyes of all the men of the Cohort were on him, judging him, measuring him, so that he developed a habit of displaying a disdain for moments such as this that bordered on the foolhardy. Yet, somehow he had survived, despite what seemed at times to be his best attempt to do otherwise. Now, under the constant rain of arrows, Pullus, if he was forced to admit it, was more than happy to risk his reputation for bravery as he held his shield above him, peering under the rim as the arrows first came into sight, and relying on his innate instinct to tell him what to do. He had long since learned that the worst thing to do when under intense missile fire was to try to think rationally about what to do in order to avoid being skewered; you were much better off letting your body take over, so he spent the next few moments hopping first one way, then making a quick step forward, before leaning to the side, all to avoid being hit. Nevertheless, as well as he was able to dodge the odd arrow, more missiles were caught by the shield, and while at first they had lodged so that their points were barely half-way embedded in the wood, Pullus began noticing that now the barbed heads were protruding all the way through. That could only mean one thing, he realized; the Wa had resumed their advance, and were still releasing arrows as they closed the distance.

Understanding that the only way he could see whether they were close enough for the scorpions to commence firing was by moving the few feet closer to the wall of palisade stakes and taking a look, despite the danger; he muttered a curse as he shuffled forward, shoulders hunched and ready to receive a blow. The footing had become treacherous, simply from all the shafts of arrows sticking out of the earthen rampart, but he tried to kick as many away as he could, knowing that his men would have to do the same. All around him, the Legionaries who had remained behind were in similar postures, in a half-crouch, their bodies pinched up in an attempt to avoid overlapping the edge of the shield with a body part that they cherished, their faces screwed up with the tension and fear of the moment. Fortunately, only a handful of these men had been struck, and of those that had, it looked to Pullus that perhaps only a half dozen were permanently out of action. Even so, he didn't like losing any men to the Wa arrows, because he felt sure he would need every strong right arm. Reaching the wooden stakes that made up the wall, despite two more strikes to his shield—one of which started a slight crack that Pullus could see went all the way through to the back—he took a deep breath. Leaning over to the side, he peered around the edge of the shield, his gaze directed to where he estimated the Wa to be. He let out an explosive gasp, as it took him just a fraction of a heartbeat for his mind to register what his eyes were telling him:

that he had looked in the wrong place, too far down the slope, although what he saw was useful in its own way. The Wa were barely more than 150 paces away, and the only thing that was saving the Romans from the enemy's closing the remaining distance by bursting forth in a run was the severity of the slope.

"Scorpions begin firing! Open fire! Hurry you bastards!" Pullus began shouting over and over, prompting the men who crewed the weapons and were at the back edge of the rampart, sheltering themselves with their shields, to scurry forward to man their weapons.

Even as they did so, Pullus thought that it would be too late to do any good. Almost the entire assault force would be scaling these walls, bringing death to the 10th Legion.

Caesar's redoubt was under a similar assault, although it was nowhere near the severity as the attack the northern camp was enduring. In fact, he had yet to be informed that the Wa had begun their missile attack there, the courier bringing that news still galloping along the undulating road on the ridgetop. Consequently, he was able to risk a glance at the Wa, who had stopped down the slope to allow their archers to begin their work, and making a quick decision, gave his orders for both the ballistae and scorpions to begin firing back. Immediately, the reports of both types of weapons began, followed a few moments later by thin cries that could barely be heard above the storm of noise caused by the arrows hitting shields or men. Despite the distance, Caesar could tell that the first volley had drawn blood, giving him a savage satisfaction. For all of his faults, Gaius Julius Caesar did love his men, so seeing them suffer was one of the few things that brought him genuine grief, and there was nothing worse than seeing them suffer without being able to strike back. Now we'll see how they like it, he thought grimly, his ears tuned for more sounds signaling that the Roman missiles were finding fleshy targets, even as he gave orders to one of his Tribunes, a young Parthian nobleman who was related to the king, Pacorus, and who had chosen the side of the victors after seeing what destruction Caesar and his army could wreak. That had been when it was still an all-Roman army, a massive and deadly magnificent machine of chaos and destruction, relentlessly and ruthlessly grinding up and spitting out all who stood in its path.

Caesar's current army was no less deadly. In many ways, it was more so, as Caesar picked up other methods of warfare and modified them to suit his style, but Caesar knew that this was going to be the severest test these men had ever faced, and all of his faculties, every bit of his experience and resolve, were going to be needed to survive the day. Finishing his orders, he made the Parthian Tribune—Bodroges was his name—repeat everything back to him, before he was dismissed to go fulfill his task. The moment he left, Caesar turned to another Tribune, this one a Pandyan, and, like Bodroges, a member of his people's nobility who had started out as a hostage, but after exposure to Caesar now desired nothing more than to be considered Roman himself. He had even gone so far as to have a toga made, although it was made out of silk and was the source of much amusement on the part of the true Romans among the officers, who had tried to persuade him that only a woman would drape herself in such material, no matter how it was cut. But he would not be dissuaded, and, for all his affectations, he had the makings of a good Legate one day. Caesar, his voice raised because of the racket, gave this man another set of orders, listened to him repeat them back; then, as with the Parthian, he was sent on his way. Turning back to the matter at hand, Caesar unknowingly mimicked Titus Pullus, shuffling forward a bit to get a better look at the Wa before his walls. He hadn't seen the need to send the bulk of the men away from the walls, so there was no chance of his being surprised as Pullus had been, but he was still concerned to see the Wa closing the distance at a steady, if not altogether swift climb. As he watched, something that he couldn't immediately identify puzzled him, until he finally realized that he hadn't seen any ladders among the Wa troops in the front ranks. It was only when he happened to be watching, as a rock from a ballistae bounced just in front of the leading edge of the Wa before punching a bloody hole through the first two or three ranks, that he saw why. Immediately after the men fell, he could see more deeply into the Wa formation, and that is when he saw that they were, in fact, carrying ladders, but farther back in the ranks than he had ever seen before. It was customary for the men who would reach the wall first to carry scaling ladders, and Caesar wondered what the meaning of this was, or if there was any at all. Even as he watched, another disturbing thing happened. When the Wa immediately behind the two men of the first two ranks that fell stepped forward to move to the front, Caesar spotted one end of a ladder the Wa was carrying. However, rather than carry it with him, Caesar saw him hand his end back to the man immediately behind him, who in turn did the same, as he moved forward to take the second spot.

"Why on Gaia's earth are they doing that, I wonder?" Caesar asked aloud, something extremely unusual for him, but this for some reason was unsettling him.

That is when he noticed something else with the dawning of a realization. Another thing that was missing were the hurdles, the big bundles of sticks thrown into a ditch in front of a wall that allowed the attackers to cross relatively swiftly and without having to scramble up the side of the ditch. The Wa weren't carrying any, so how were they planning on getting across? Could it be they weren't planning on crossing? Surely they wouldn't just stand there, absorbing punishment from the artillery! As Caesar thought about it, suddenly still, despite all the din and action around him, he again tried to put himself into the mind of the Wa commander. Even now, he was sure that this engagement wasn't the main focus of the Wa assault, and that his enemy's goal was merely to keep the Romans in this camp tied down, so that they couldn't go to the aid of the men in the northern camp. Thus, it made some sort of sense that the Wa would be willing to halt short of the ditch, or even go through the laborious process of crossing the ditch, despite its being laced with all of Caesar's refinements, some of which the Wa could see, once they got close enough and looked down, though they could not see most of the obstacles, because they were concealed. But why subject your men to that kind of wholesale slaughter? Wasn't there a better way to use your men?

"What if *they* are the hurdles?" he suddenly asked, again aloud, and as soon as he said it, a sort of leaden ball materialized in his stomach.

He knew that feeling: it was the one he got when he had arrived at an answer to a problem that was a horrible answer, one that he would rather not know. That was it, he was suddenly sure: the Wa commander was going to march his men up to the ditch allow them to be mown down like stalks of wheat, and use their bodies to fill the ditch. After all, look at what they did at the beach, when we first used our artillery on them, he thought, this time silently. A strange feeling came over Caesar, one that he had never experienced before, a strange combination of revulsion and...admiration? Could that be it? Yes, he acknowledged, yes, admiration. Suddenly Caesar understood the mind of the Wa commander better than he had before. He knew that he had met a man as ruthless as he himself, , maybe even more ruthless, because Caesar couldn't fathom ordering Pullus and the 10th to do such a thing. But this Wa, whoever he was, was willing to do whatever was necessary to win, even if it meant slaughtering his own men. Despite the fact that it was promising to be a warm day, the sun now a full hand's width above the eastern hills, Caesar felt a chill run through his body. Was this how a premonition of defeat felt?

As the scorpions opened fire along the parapet of the northern camp, Pullus bellowed the command to his *cornicen* to blow the notes that commanded the men of the 10th waiting out of range to rush to the rampart. With a huge shout, his Legion responded, although the men took care to keep their shields raised above their heads as they scrambled up the slope and into position. Inevitably, some men fell, despite the protection of their shields, and Pullus could see that because of the closer range, the arrows that found their mark were buried more deeply in whatever body part of the unfortunate it struck, so much so that in some men just the feathered end of the arrow protruded out of their bodies as they fell. Some of these men fell without a sound, while others let out a shout or a shriek, but all of those struck were either mortally wounded or at least out of action. The only satisfaction Pullus felt was that the noise emanating from the Wa ranks, in the form of groans, pained shouts, and what Pullus assumed were oaths of some sort in their gibberish, was much louder. Risking another peek, Pullus got a glimpse just as a scorpion bolt hit a Wa in the front rank in the middle of his torso, and then, trailing a spray of red mist, passed through this first man, then through the man behind him to lodge with half its length showing in the chest of yet a third man. Letting out a shout of savage exultation, the Primus Pilus shook his free fist in the direction of the Wa, now just a matter of a few paces on the other side of the ditch.

"How do you like that, you sorry, slanty-eyed bastards?" he shouted, lips pulled back in a fierce grin.

"Probably not very much," Pullus was too experienced to do more than turn his head, still keeping tucked safely behind his shield—although it was about to become useless—to see that Balbus was back by his side.

He would never utter it aloud, but Pullus was thankful to have a friend with him right now, and he laughed at the jest.

"No, probably not," he agreed, then turned serious. "But I'm afraid I left it too late. I doubt the scorpions are going to be enough to stop them."

"I don't think they would have been, no matter when you gave the order," Balbus told him, and while normally Pullus expected, and in fact demanded, brutal honesty from his subordinates and friends alike, this was one time he thought that if Balbus was lying, he would forgive him.

Without replying, Pullus turned his attention back to the Wa, and it was at this point that he noticed what Caesar had some time before, although neither had any way of knowing it.

"They don't have any ladders or hurdles," was how the Primus Pilus put it, but, unlike Caesar, he didn't comprehend the purpose.

In fact, it was Pullus' other friend, the Secundus Pilus Prior, Sextus Scribonius, who sent a messenger scurrying behind the men now standing on the rampart, the rank nearest the wall resting their shields on top, while their comrades behind them held theirs above the heads of the first rank and themselves, with the other ranks behind them doing the same. Even as wide as the rampart was, there wasn't enough room for the normal depth of a Century formation, forcing the last few ranks of men to stand behind the rampart, a pace away from the slope. Scribonius' messenger, none other than the old tentmate of both Pullus and Scribonius, Publius Vellusius, had to weave in and out among men, including those lying on the dirt who had yet to be dragged off, one and usually more arrows sticking from them. Reaching the Primus Pilus, Vellusius took a moment to regain his breath, before blurting out what Scribonius had sent him to tell his commander.

"Pilus Prior Scribonius says that he thinks the Wa are planning on letting the poor bastards in the front ranks fill up the ditch! That's how they're going to get across!"

Exchanging disbelieving glances, both Pullus and Balbus took another look, this time braving the volley of arrows, which was just beginning to slacken, to study their enemy.

"By the gods, he's right," it was Balbus who broke the silence. "I knew that big brain of his would come in handy sometime."

Pullus was torn; although he didn't want to believe that any man was so merciless and cruel as to send his men to die in such a manner, in his gut he recognized that both his friends were right. This left only one question; what to do about it?

At the southernmost camp, the Wa had yet to begin their assault in earnest, and were, in fact, just then marching up the base of the slope. Standing next to Asinius Pollio was the Primus Pilus of the 5th Alaudae, a grizzled veteran originally from Pompey's 1st Legion named Vibius Batius, who was one of the oldest Centurions in Caesar's Legions, - actually being less than 5 years younger than Caesar himself. He was as brown, scarred, and tough as old boot leather, but while Titus Pullus stood more than 3 inches over 6 feet, Batius was a foot shorter. However, where the gods take away in one area, they give in another, and Vibius Batius possessed the ferocity and sheer determination that many men of smaller stature have; coupled with a first-rate brain and a toughness second only to his counterpart in the 10th—though he would never concede that—Batius was a good choice to stand next to Pollio. While there was another Roman of Legate rank there, the pecking order in Caesar's army had long been established, so nobody questioned that if Pollio should fall, it would be Batius who would conduct the defense of this camp. To assist him, he had the 28th Legion, who had lost their Primus Pilus, Gnaeus Cartufenus, on the beach those weeks ago. The new Primus Pilus was the former Pilus Posterior, moving up one Century, but he was too junior and too new to even think of contesting Batius for leadership, and he, in fact deferred to Batius. Because of Caesar's conviction that the most serious threat was to the northern camp, Pollio and Batius had at their disposal a much smaller complement of artillery, but to compensate, Caesar had given them the majority of the Balearic slingers. Unfortunately, as they were about to find out, the lightly armored slingers were easy targets for the Wa archers, numbering about a thousand in this force, more than enough to inflict real damage. Although whoever was commanding the Wa force was moving more slowly than his other countrymen, he was using the same tactics: once within range, the archers began sending sheaves of arrows into the sky, each making a graceful arc in the air as it soared skyward before pausing for the barest fraction of a heartbeat, then plunging down to earth. As missiles rained down, Batius' men sheltered under their shields just like the Romans in the other camps, and just like them, men began to fall, most of them writhing in pain and cursing their luck, while some simply collapsed.

"Batius, I think we should answer back with the artillery now," Pollio's voice sounded eerily calm, but Batius could hear the strain underneath the words.

"But Caesar said we needed to wait until they got closer," Batius reminded Pollio, but this didn't change the general's mind.

"Yes, but he also thought our slingers would be able to make a dent in their numbers before they got close, and that's not going to happen."

Even if he had been disposed to argue further, Batius saw the sense in what Pollio was saying, and he snapped the order to his *cornicen*, who blatted out the series of notes that gave the signal for both ballistae and scorpions, few as they were, to open fire. The men, hearing the horn and knowing the command it sounded, managed to let out a cheer that, for just a brief moment, drowned out the racket caused by the raining death.

Both men gave each other a grim smile, and Pollio said, "Sounds like the men are ready to get stuck in."

"My boys are always ready, general," Batius boasted. "These *cunni* will wish they had never crawled out from between their mothers' legs by the time we're through!"

Gods, I hope so, Pollio thought, but said nothing, turning his attention back to the sight of the Wa, now moving steadily up the slope, their archers firing as they went.

Caesar, now that he understood the intent of the Wa commander, realized that he was essentially doing what the Wa wanted by slaughtering the leading edge of the attacking force, and instantly understood that while he couldn't completely forestall the tactic, he could make it harder to employ. He gave the order for the artillery to shift their aim slightly, to a point farther back and deeper in the Wa ranks, and he quickly found that this had the added benefit of slackening the archers' fire, now that they were suffering casualties. Even so, when he checked, he saw that the ditch was already a quarter full of men who had been struck down, for its entire length. Although most of these unfortunates had been killed—either pierced through with a scorpion bolt or eviscerated and mangled with a rock from a ballista, there were enough who had yet to die to make it seem as if the bloody mound in the ditch was moving in juddering, spastic jerks and twitches, as those still alive either suffered through their death throes or tried in vain to claw their way to the top of the pile. The sight of the carnage left Caesar speechless, not so much for the numbers of men, but because of what their purpose was intended to be.

The front ranks of the Wa, arrayed just on the other side of the ditch, were close enough for Caesar to see men's faces, and for them to see his, and he supposed that both their thoughts were running along much similar lines: here are the men who want to kill me. In Caesar's case, this was less a general representation and more of an actual goal of each of the Wa warriors; unbeknownst to Caesar or anyone else in the Roman army, these warriors had been offered a huge reward for the head of the barbarian general who led a force of men who looked like the kind of white, pale grubworms that were dug out of the ground in the garden and crushed. That's what would happen to these grubworms, even if they did stand upright and look somewhat like men. And there wasn't a man in the Wa ranks in a position to be able to see Caesar who didn't know that he was the barbarian general, the commander of this foul horde who had come to their land unbidden, bringing invasion and destruction.

But first, they had to cross that ditch, and to do that, the men in the front ranks knew their duty, and were, in fact, keenly disappointed when the savage fire from the barbarian machines—machines that they had never seen before but had come to fear—stopped concentrating on them and instead were now laying waste to their comrades behind them. The shouting they were doing wasn't enough to drown out the screams of men who suddenly had half their faces torn away by rocks flying so quickly that they were impossible to duck, or silence a man's gurgling call to a dear friend in the ranks, as one of those large, iron-tipped arrows struck deep into his chest, filling his lungs with blood. Hearing all this behind them and knowing that they had to fulfill their purpose, without any command being given, some of the men in the front Wa ranks began throwing themselves down into the ditch, calling their comrades behind them to follow suit and pile on top. Those first men who did this knew that eventually they would be crushed, the wind driven from their lungs by the weight of more armored men following their lead, yet they didn't hesitate. Caesar stood aghast at the sight, and it so unnerved the men serving the weapons that, for a moment, they could only stare in disbelief. Perhaps strangely, or perhaps not, the sight also filled the Romans with fear, despite knowing that these were men who wouldn't be clambering up the ladder and over the wall to come kill them. What kind of men were these? It was a question that had become as common a refrain around the fires at night as the complaints about eating rice and the lack of wine, but seeing the answer in front of their eyes didn't bring them any comfort.

Pullus' problem was more immediate: the ditch below him was already half-filled with Wa, and he hadn't made the connection between the fact that his artillery was wreaking havoc in the front ranks, but that this was exactly what the Wa commander had intended. To Pullus, it was simply a matter of mathematics: the more Wa he killed, even if they did fill the ditch, the fewer Wa his men had to face. Whose tactic was the correct one would be played out only over the next watch, although neither Pullus nor Caesar had any idea what the other was doing to counter this threat. So Pullus never ordered his artillery to shift aim, and, in fact, he had called on the men safely out of range to pass their javelins forward, so that their comrades could hurl them down into the packed mass of men just on the other side of the ditch. They did this with a bitter and savage relish, every fiber of their being pumping up their throws, so that the javelins carried even more velocity than normal. Aided by their higher position on the rampart, some men's javelins traveled completely through one of the enemy to lodge deep in the next man's body.

While this made the Romans feel better, it also helped the Wa by dropping more men into the ditch, until in three or four spots, whoever was in charge of the attackers in that area deemed the ditch to be filled enough to give the command to cross. Not surprisingly, one of those spots was directly in front of the area where Pullus and the First Cohort were positioned, so at the sight of able-bodied warriors taking the short hop down into the ditch—heedless of the shrieks of pain from their comrades who had yet to expire—Pullus roared the order for all men to return to the rampart with their siege spears. The arrow fire was still intense, and Pullus understood that he was going to lose men as they moved into position, no matter how careful they tried to be, but he couldn't afford to wait any longer. As the Legionaries scrambled up the slope, Pullus continued to watch the Wa clambering over the packed meat that was still quivering in spots, causing many of the enemy to stumble and fall on top of the bodies. When this happened, those of Pullus' men who still had javelins didn't hesitate and hurled their missiles down, usually into the backs of the unfortunate Wa who would be trying to regain their footing. Every Wa struck down in this manner brought a cheer from those who saw it happen, but as many Wa as were being slaughtered there, Pullus could see that he and the men were still outnumbered.

All around him he could sense his men moving into position, and he glanced to either side to make sure that the men with the siege spears would be those on the parapet, and that each one had a comrade along with a relatively intact shield. The job of each such comrade would be to provide as much shelter to the man wielding the spear as possible, and each man had a replacement immediately behind him, ready to step in, should he himself fall. The faces of his men mirrored the expression of their Primus Pilus: a look of grim determination as they readied themselves for the coming onslaught. Down in the ditch, those Wa carrying the ladders had just begun to cross, drawing a curse from Pullus, as he realized that he had been too hasty with the order to loose javelins, because there were none left to eliminate these men. Not that it really mattered in the long run; even if they killed every Wa holding a ladder, there were more than enough ready to step in and pick it up—but it was a matter of principle, and Pullus chided himself for his lack of professionalism.

It was as he was engaged in dressing himself down that he became aware of a change in the sounds of the fight. To be precise, it was the lack of a sound that alerted him that something was amiss, but before he could make the mental shift necessary to determine what it was, he was alerted by a shout, and again turning only his head and not his body while keeping his shield up, he saw one of the *Immunes* who was the de facto commander of the men manning the scorpions make his way toward Pullus in a crouching run along the rampart. Before the man could even reach him, Pullus knew what he was going to be told, because the sight of the *Immunes* had served to tell him what that missing sound was.

Therefore, he wasn't surprised when the man reached him, saluted, then gasped out, "We're out of scorpion bolts!"

Aulus Flaminius, Primus Pilus of the 30th Legion was in the camp immediately to the south of Caesar's, and up to that moment, he and his men were faring better than any of the other positions, mainly because the Wa commander had sent the smallest contingent of archers to this spot. Still, the Wa were at the ditch, and because of the fact that Flaminius had been given only 2 scorpions and 3 ballistae, he had been unable to stem the advance. Ironically, this posed a problem for the Wa in charge of this assault, who had been given the same orders as all the others: to sacrifice the leading ranks of men to fill the ditch. But they hadn't suffered enough casualties to do so; instead the Wa began leaping down into the ditch, whereupon they learned firsthand of Caesar's genius for diabolical traps, cunningly disguised. Although the Wa could plainly see the sharpened stakes imbedded in the opposite wall of the ditch, what they discovered only the hard way were the rows of Caesar's lilies, the iron hooks in blocks of wood, buried in pits, then first covered with a loosely woven mat of rice leaves, and finally covered with dirt. Over and above the din came the shrieks of pain, as men were hooked through the calf, immobilizing them and making them easy targets for Roman javelins. Those few who weren't dispatched in this manner were faced with a horrible choice of either waiting until one of the barbarians with the javelins noticed them and finished them off, or enduring the agony that came from pulling themselves off the hook, inevitably tearing through the calf muscle and crippling them for life, if they survived.

Even so, the Wa continued to tumble into the ditch, moving across the bottom to stumble into the next row of lilies, then the next. Yet, they still came, but in their haste and ardor to get their ladders up, the men following behind pushed the leading Wa, screaming in alarm and then in agony, onto the points of the stakes, where the crushing weight of their own comrades served to pin them, the bloody points protruding from their backs. It was only when some of the Wa wearing the iron lamellar armor and carrying swords began striking at their own men, pushing them back, that the slaughter was stopped. Very quickly, Flaminius' men had expended their supply of javelins and now stood with their siege spears, the points sticking out from between the stakes of the rampart and shields, waiting for the next phase of the assault to begin. Ladders, again carried by the enemy several ranks back, were now passed down into the ditch, and the Wa, for the first time free from any javelin or artillery fire, as desultory as it had been, paused, as their officers began trying to organize the next phase of the operation.

"Get ready boys," Flaminius—who was able to peer down into the ditch with only moderate risk from the archers, and determined they were also too dispersed to concentrate fire on one point—saw what was happening, understanding that his camp was about to come under assault. "Let's give these *cunni* a taste of Roman iron! What do you say?"

His answer was a roar from the throats of his Legion, accompanied by the clattering sound of swords beating against the metal rim of shields, a sound that had struck fear into more enemies than that of any other army in history. No matter who these yellow men were, Flaminius and the 30th Legion were ready to face them.

By this point in time, back at Pullus' camp, the ditch had become sufficiently filled for the Wa holding the ladders to begin moving down into the ditch. As the Wa clambered over the grisly human flooring filling the ditch, the Romans, having expended all of their javelins, could only watch as the ladders were carried forward.

"Get ready boys!" someone shouted and was answered with a low growl.

The men holding the siege spears made last-moment adjustments, most of them wiping their sweaty palms on their tunics, despite it not doing much good, because most of them had already soaked through the fabric. No man on that rampart was under any illusion that after all the battles and all the bleeding that had hardened the 10th Legion into what it was this day, today would be the sternest test any of them had ever faced, even the hoariest veterans, like Vellusius. No, they knew individually and collectively that today would see either the destruction of the 10th or the most glorious victory in its storied history. Titus Pullus stood among them and, sharing that knowledge with his men, he felt a sudden surge of affection that threatened to overwhelm him, filling his heart until he was sure it would burst. And with no little surprise he realized that, as much as he wanted to see another day, just like any of his men, there was still no place he would rather be than at this spot, in this moment. What finer thing could there be, he wondered, than to make history, no matter how the day turned out? After all, what happened today would live forever in the annals of warfare, even if the 10th was exterminated along with the rest of Caesar's army. Pullus was then struck with a thought. If the unthinkable happened and the Romans were defeated, how would anyone back in Rome know of all that had been accomplished?

As suddenly as they had come, the feelings of pride and affection were replaced by a leaden ball of doubt, not about the outcome as much as about the aftermath. Who would be left to return to Rome and tell the Roman people, he wondered? Suddenly, his train of thought was interrupted by a number of shouting curses, so jerking his mind back to the moment, he turned to see the very tips of the ladders peeking up above the palisade stakes, even as the men holding the shields reached out with their free hands to push the ladders away from the stakes. Pullus knew that only a few men were strong enough to do that with one hand, and because he happened to be one of them, he leapt forward from his spot, heading to the nearest ladder. Despite the fact that there were Wa warriors now scrambling up the ladders, some of their archers continued to fire, their feathered missiles streaking just inches above the heads of their comrades. While not of the same intensity as their earlier barrage, this fusillade was still sufficiently dangerous so that as Pullus moved forward, he saw one of his men who was holding a shield lean too far outside the edge of it and take an arrow in the eye. Killed instantly, the man's suddenly nerveless fingers released their hold on the shield and' before the Legionary behind him could lunge to recover it, it fell forward and down into the Wa, leaving a gaping hole that made the otherwise unbroken line look like a mouth suddenly missing a front tooth.

Into that momentary gap came the first Wa who, in one fluid and incredibly quick movement, pushed off from the ladder to leap over the palisade, seemingly hovering there in midair for the briefest instant, before landing squarely on the back of the fallen Roman. Even as Pullus' mind tried to register what his eyes were seeing, the Wa's sword was swinging in what Pullus recognized from brutal experience as a deceptively smooth arc that nonetheless packed an incredible amount of force. Before anyone could react, the Wa's blade sliced cleanly through the neck of the Roman standing next to the fallen shield bearer, and in one of those strange moments of clarity, what was burned into Pullus' memory for the rest of his time on earth was the expression of open-mouthed surprise and astonishment, as his Legionary's head went spinning into the air, the helmet still attached, leaving a briefly upright corpse still spurting bright, arterial blood provided by a pumping heart that had not received the message that it was no longer needed. In the instant after this act, the body of the second Roman collapsed, slumping forward over the palisade, still spraying blood over the helmeted head of the second Wa on the ladder, drenching him so thoroughly that when his head appeared over the palisade, he appeared to be solid red. Scrambling to join his comrade, the second Wa took the more conventional approach, but that only served to emphasize his appearance as some sort of demon sent from the underworld, waving a sword and eager to take as many Romans as possible back down with him.

Now the gap was even larger, and although Pullus had been heading for the man closest to him, he suddenly veered to meet this larger threat without thought and without hesitation, his sword out and his shield up and ready. In the bare fraction of time that it took to close the distance, Pullus noticed that, with the second Wa now standing atop the body of the second Roman like his comrade, both of them disdained the use of shields and were armed only with their swords, the same slightly curving blades Pullus had seen before. Before the attack on his camp, when the 10th had almost been overwhelmed, Pullus would have sneered at the idea of any warrior with the hubris to fight without a shield. But not anymore; he had seen firsthand the skill with which the Wa employed their weapon and knew that they didn't use shields because they didn't need them. Nevertheless, he went charging forward with his shield out before him, still confident enough in his own abilities, experience, and strength that the idea of facing two Wa, no matter how skilled, gave him no pause whatsoever.

Caesar had still kept his own sword sheathed, choosing to continue to direct the action from his spot just a few paces behind the palisade of his camp. Unlike the main assault force at Pullus' camp, the Wa assaulting Caesar's position had yet to fill the ditch completely, and the ladders were still a few rows behind the front ranks. However, as each rank of the enemy moved up and became the rank closest to the ditch, there was still no hesitation on any of their parts, as one by one they threw themselves on top of their unfortunate comrades. The Wa that were the first to do this had since had the life crushed out of them, but the top two or three layers still contained writhing, gasping men. If anything, Caesar could see that his own men were becoming increasingly more unnerved, now that their supply of javelins had been expended , and they could only watch in horror, as they took an occasional peek around their shields.

Since the ladders had not gone up yet, the archers in the rear ranks were still firing volley after endless volley of arrows, and just within Caesar's range of vision, he saw that the majority of his men now had shields studded with at least a dozen arrows apiece, some with more, some with fewer. That meant their shields were dangerously weakened and unlikely to survive the first few moments of action. While there were spares, Caesar knew that not only were there not enough of those, but there was also no way to get them distributed in time. His men would have to fight without what was not only a defensive weapon to the Roman Legionary, but also a potent part of his offensive arsenal. However, a good commander knows when there is no point in worrying about what cannot be changed, so as quickly as this realization was formed, he put it out of his mind, returning his attention to what could be controlled.

"Caesar!"

Like Pullus, Caesar was too experienced to do more than turn his head, staying behind the protection of his own shield, although in the case of the commanding general, there were three Legionaries detailed to provide an umbrella of protection for him. Looking back toward the interior of the camp, he saw the Tribune Bodroges hurrying toward him. He was so intent on reaching his general's side that he seemed oblivious to the fact that he was entering within the range of the Wa missiles, the line clearly marked by the serried ranks of arrows protruding from the ground in uneven rows. Just as he was about to enter the beaten zone, a lean, grizzled Optio—another of the few remaining Romans of the army—unceremoniously grabbed the Tribune by the arm. Caesar couldn't hear what the Optio said, but no matter how sharply he may have spoken to a man who was technically his superior, he would have received no censure from Caesar, who understood completely what the Roman was doing, and that was saving Bodroges from possible harm. Caesar saw the swarthy features of his Parthian Tribune flush darker, but he meekly took the proffered shield, one of the few that were undamaged, before he resumed making his way to Caesar. Dashing through the hail of missiles that, while not falling as thickly as they were moments before, still posed a huge hazard to anyone without protection, Bodroges reached Caesar's side, huffing and puffing. Instinctively coming to *intente* and about to render a salute, Bodroges froze, as he mentally tried to work out how to do that, while keeping his shield raised in its protective posture. The expression on the Tribune's face caused Caesar to burst out laughing in one of those strangely humorous moments that occur in even the most hazardous of situations.

"This is one time I think the formalities can be forgotten, Bodroges," Caesar said, his tone light, despite pitching his voice loudly enough to be heard over the racket of arrows striking wood and the shouting of men. Turning serious, he asked, "What's your report?"

"The first of the couriers have arrived, Caesar," Bodroges replied, trying to match the calm demeanor and tone of his general, as if they were standing in the forum watching the men drill, instead of fighting for their very survival. "The northern camp is under attack by a force of at least 15,000 infantry and almost 2,000 archers, according to General Hirtius. He also reports that he's already out of ammunition for the artillery. His casualties are light at this point, but...."

"But that won't be the case for long. Yes, I know," Caesar interrupted grimly.

While nothing he was being told was unexpected, although the number of archers was higher than his estimate, he was troubled by the news that his most trusted general had already expended his stock of ammunition. Had Pullus and Balbinus been too profligate? Had they not obeyed Caesar's explicit instructions, or were the numbers they were facing just so overwhelming that it was inevitable that they were going to run out quickly, no matter what the orders? Bodroges began to speak again, jerking Caesar from his musings; this would be something to discuss with Pullus later and see what went wrong. If they survived, he amended, but only to himself.

"General Pollio's courier hadn't arrived, but the courier from Generals Ventidius and Primus Pilus Flaminius has arrived, as well. He reports that, as expected, the forces facing his Legions number only about 8,000, and fewer than 1,000 of those are archers. He still has artillery ammunition, and when he dispatched the rider the Wa hadn't made it to the ditch, so he had yet to open fire with it. Although I imagine that by now that's happened."

"Don't speculate, Bodroges," Caesar admonished, although it was more of an automatic gesture, since his mind was still processing all that he knew to this point in time. "Tell me only what you've been told. Your job is to relay only what the couriers have told you. Trying to decide what it means is my job." Seeing Bodroges' face fall at this gentle rebuke, Caesar added, "However, you're undoubtedly right."

Finally, Bodroges finished with the fifth and final camp, in between Flaminius and Pollio's southernmost camp. It was the only one not occupied with a man of Legate rank, the two Legions in it, 11th and the 8th, commanded by the senior Primus Pilus, Quintus Ausonius Felix, and while Titus Pullus was the most feared and respected fighter, Felix was considered the luckiest man in the army, because despite exhibiting a bravery that Caesar required of all his Primi Pili, he had never been seriously wounded, never needing more than a few stitches to close up the odd slash wound. Now, his camp was under an assault of what appeared to be about the same intensity as that the camp of Ventidius and Flaminius was weathering, with similar numbers of enemy combatants.

"Now," his expression hardened a bit and his tone turned severe, "Is there a reason that you chose not to wait for General Pollio's courier, as I instructed?"

Bodroges swallowed hard, but his tone was even, as he replied, "I judged that the information from Primus Pilus Pullus was more important and couldn't wait, so I decided to come immediately."

For a moment Caesar said nothing, then rewarded Bodroges with a smile and a nod.

"You made the right decision, Bodroges. That information is definitely more important. Now," he continued, ignoring the visible sag in Bodroges' body, as he went limp with relief that he had guessed correctly. "I need you to go back and give this," Caesar was scribbling in a wax tablet handed to him by a shaking secretary who had been crouched at his feet, the sheer terror at being exposed to fire etched on his features, "to a courier, to go to General Hirtius."

Snapping the tablet shut, he handed it to Bodroges who, remembering the folly of saluting, simply began backing away, holding the shield above his head with a clearly shaking arm, the other clutching the tablet. Before Caesar could turn to resume watching the situation in front, an alarmed shout came from the palisade. It took him a moment to find the source among the line of men, but he quickly picked out the figure of a Centurion standing just behind the Legionaries directly next to the palisade in the first line of defense. Assuming that this shout signaled that at last the Wa were in the ditch and throwing up their ladders, Caesar was quickly disabused of this by the Centurion, who called his name, while pointing at a spot farther out into the valley.

"Caesar, come quickly!"

The tone, if not the words, was enough to spur Caesar to push quickly past the Legionaries designated as his protectors, disdaining their cries of alarm that he needed to stay behind the shields and they would escort him to the Centurion's side. Even now, at 65 years of age, Caesar was a man unaccustomed to fear and was at least as reckless as Titus Pullus in exposing himself to danger in order to set an example for his men, if not more so. Now he strode quickly forward, bareheaded, his scarlet *paludamentum* swirling behind him as he moved.

Reaching the Centurion's side, he demanded, "What is it?"

In answer, the Centurion, the Secundus Hastatus Posterior, pointed again, but not down to his immediate front, but out toward the floor of the valley, in the direction of the Wa encampment.

"The bastards have tricked us! Look there, Caesar!"

And Caesar did look, and when he did, he felt his heart seize so violently that for a fleeting moment he thought he was having an apoplectic fit and would drop dead on the spot. But, seeing the scene before him, immediately following was the thought that perhaps dropping dead right now would be a blessing, because the Centurion was right. They had been tricked, well and truly fooled. And in being fooled, that premonition of defeat Caesar had felt earlier only strengthened. For, streaming out of the Wa camp was still another force, and while not as large as the body of men assaulting Caesar's camp at this moment, it was perilously close to the same size. Even as he watched the Wa, now out of the camp and moving quickly across the valley floor, Caesar tried to determine how they had done it, and all he could surmise was that, somehow, in the night, the Wa commander had managed to shift men from one camp to another and doubled up the number of occupants of the Wa tents. This second group of men had remained behind, hidden from view, until the action had begun in earnest, before springing from their hiding place. And now they were moving; but instead of moving to reinforce the men assaulting Caesar's camp, they were angling across the valley floor, clearly headed for that site where the ridge made the pocket he had worried about earlier. In effect, they were going to slice into the Roman lines at a spot where they could fall on Pullus' camp from the rear, completely enveloping the 10th and 12th. As he watched in growing horror, Caesar was forced to silently salute his counterpart, because unless he could think of something, and think of it fast, his northernmost position would be overrun, and he would have a large enemy force sitting on his right flank. Moreover, as the Wa that were now throwing the ladders up against the rampart of his camp kept the men in this camp occupied, that force could then essentially repeat what they had just done to Pullus' camp, thereby rolling up the entire Roman position like a carpet.

"They're at the walls!"

This shout tore Caesar's attention away, and he turned to see, not more than a dozen paces away, the top of the first ladder being thrown against the rampart. His army, his men, his life, were in all likelihood in the last watches of their collective existence; because, for once, a feat in itself, Caesar had no idea what to do.

Just before reaching the two Wa, Titus Pullus skidded to a halt, stopping so suddenly that both Wa, anticipating that he would careen headlong into their waiting swords, swung their blades at the spot where they thought the giant Roman would be. And while the Wa were the fastest men Pullus, or any Roman for that matter, had ever seen, Titus Pullus himself was one of the fastest moving big men of his time, and it was with that speed that he struck now. Lashing out with his shield at the Wa to his left, he simultaneously launched a hard, low thrust with his Gallic blade, the point aimed at a spot well below where the Wa's blade was still hovering in midair, in the bare instant before he recovered. While both Wa managed to react, neither of them was completely successful in blocking his respective attack. The boss of Pullus' shield, which he had aimed directly for the first Wa's face, was partially blocked, but it was at the Wa's shoulder, as he twisted to the side. Pullus felt the jolting blow all the way up his arm, the Wa grunting in pain but managing to hold onto his sword, as he staggered a step back. In doing so, he came within range of the Roman next to the two dead men, one of the Legionaries armed with a siege spear; but the long spear was so unwieldy that by the time he moved the pointed end from its spot protruding over the rampart, the first Wa had moved to close with Pullus again. Even if he continued with his movement and stabbed the Wa in the back, the Roman was now faced with an enemy warrior, who was just two rungs from the top of the ladder to his left and coming in range.

Understanding the greater threat, the Legionary also had utmost faith in his Primus Pilus, so he returned his attention back to the ascending Wa, stabbing down at the man the moment he came within reach. Pullus' sword thrust, meanwhile, was also partially blocked, the second Wa desperately sweeping his blade in a downward arc that managed to keep Pullus' blade from plunging deep into his gut. Instead, the point of Pullus' finely honed Gallic blade, one that he had been carrying for more than 20 years, buried itself into the meat of the Wa's left thigh. Despite how excruciatingly painful the thrust was, the Wa only let out a hissing sound through tightly-clenched teeth, and before Pullus could twist the blade and do further damage, the Wa lashed out with his own blade in a wild swing that swept at an upward angle. Now it was Pullus' turn to twist aside in desperation, and in doing so, he withdrew his blade, leaving behind a relatively clean gash in the Wa's leg that, instead of spurting arterial blood, flowed a dark red. The Wa's blade struck Pullus a glancing blow right at the junction of the right shoulder, where his mail protected him from further damage, as several links broke instead. Even so, the force from the blow jolted Pullus, so it was his turn to let out a gasp of pain and he felt his arm go instantly numb, the only thing saving his grasp of the sword being the grip taught to him by Aulus Vinicius when he was a *tiro*.

All three men had taken some damage in the first exchange, making them content to take a step backward to gather themselves; despite the damage Pullus had inflicted, he was in essentially the same position, outnumbered two-to-one. Everywhere around him he heard the shouts and screams of men, and he knew that there were Wa now on the rampart, meaning that the men immediately around him were occupied. Now he had to rely on men in relief, waiting just paces away, but this was a moment when Titus Pullus was a victim of his own legend. Too many times he had waved other Legionaries away from a private battle, his pride and never-ending drive for acclaim and glory having the result that those who had intervened in the past hadn't earned anything other than a tongue-lashing, or worse. Consequently, his men just stood there, watching and unwilling to risk his wrath, sure in the knowledge that their Primus Pilus couldn't possibly fall to barbarians. Knowing this, Pullus was spurred on by their faith in him and was determined that even if his life was coming to an end this day, it wouldn't be at the hands of these two Wa.

Consequently, he was the first to break the slight lull, lunging again. This time, instead of placing himself roughly equidistant between the two Wa as he did in his first attack, he moved directly to his right, putting himself to the extreme left of the second Wa, and effectively putting this warrior in the path of the first Wa. It was a move that would buy him only a fraction of a moment, but he was counting on the wound this Wa carried to slow him down sufficiently, and it worked. As the second Wa pivoted to face Pullus squarely, he was forced to shift his weight onto his right leg, and while it didn't buckle altogether, it did cause him to stagger for an instant. That was all the time Pullus needed, this time delivering a high, overhand thrust, aimed at the base of the Wa's throat. Despite the speed with which the blow was delivered, the Wa's reflexes were still quick enough that he was able to twist slightly, so that instead of hitting him in the throat, Pullus' thrust struck home high in the Wa's left shoulder, the point of his sword punching through the iron lamellar armor as if it weren't there. Pullus had struck with such force that the blade, entering just below the Wa's collarbone, punched all the way through the warrior to protrude by half a foot through his back. This time the Wa wasn't so controlled, letting out a shrill cry of pain that only increased in volume, because this time Pullus was sure to twist the blade savagely, wrenching it back and forth before he yanked it free. Paralyzed by the pain, the Wa was standing motionless, allowing Pullus the time to lift one of his feet and give the Wa a good kick, sending him flying backward and out of sight over the rampart with a long scream, until it was cut short with a gurgling cry. Fortunately for Pullus, his training and instincts had kept his shield up in what the Romans called the first position, the elbow braced against the hip and the forearm parallel to the ground. Even as he turned his attention back to the first Wa, there was a splintering, cracking sound when the Wa struck with a thrust of his own, delivered with savage force, and, to Pullus' surprise and discomfort, he saw the point of the Wa sword punch through his shield just inches above his arm.

Already weakened by all the arrow strikes, Pullus noticed with horror the large, longitudinal crack running almost the entire length of the shield, where a sliver of daylight came streaming through. As the Wa yanked his blade free, almost tugging the shield out of Pullus' grasp, the crack grew even wider, and Pullus knew that it would last at most two, or perhaps three, more blows, if that many. His arm still tingling from the blow of the Wa he had just dispatched, Pullus nonetheless lashed out with his sword, but not before the Wa managed to extricate his own, which he used to parry Pullus' strike. The blades clashed together in a small shower of sparks, and this time the greater brute strength of the Primus Pilus of the 10th showed, as the Wa's blade recoiled backward from the force of the Pullus' blow, leaving his body temporarily vulnerable and unprotected by nothing more than his other arm. Without hesitating, Pullus stepped forward using his shield to pin the Wa against the rampart at his back to keep him from escaping, and pushed him hard, applying his massive weight behind his shield with every ounce of his strength As he did so, he heard the wood protesting with a shrieking crack, but he continued to press. No matter how strong the Wa was in his own right, he was no match for Titus Pullus, and he thus found himself completely pinned as the breath was crushed from his lungs. Lashing out desperately with his blade, his movement was restricted by the pressure of the shield, but even so, Pullus used his own sword across the top of his shield to knock the Wa's blade aside contemptuously.

"Thought you would do for me, huh you *cunnus*?" Pullus snarled into the Wa's face, several inches below his own, the saliva spraying into his enemy's face, which was turning purple, as the Wa vainly tried to draw breath into his lungs.

Suddenly, the Wa brought one knee up in a savage blow, aimed at Pullus' groin, but the Roman was much too experienced and had been expecting such a move, turning his hips to the side, so that the knee struck him in the meat of the thigh. It was painful, but by this point Pullus' battle fury was fully aroused and he barely felt the blow, being only dimly aware that if he survived this day, he would awaken the next morning with a huge bruise and try to recall the circumstances around how he had gotten it. Yet in that moment, as he watched the life drain from his opponent's body, the only thing Pullus felt was the savage exultation that comes from besting your enemy, in seeing him vanquished. And as weary as Titus Pullus may have grown of so much of army life, this was a feeling of which he never grew tired. In fact, it was what kept him marching and fighting. Finally, the Wa gave a rattling sigh that Pullus knew from long experience was the signal that the Wa's spirit had fled his body; Still, he continued the pressure for a moment longer, before finally stepping back. The Wa immediately collapsed, as if all his bones had suddenly been removed, and Pullus stood there for a moment, chest heaving, staring down at the dead man. Then, completely unmindful of everything else going on around him, the Primus Pullus of the 10th Legion suddenly hopped up onto the body of his enemy, so that he could stand higher than the rampart. Showing total disdain for the furious fighting, the arrows still flying into the camp, and all the maelstrom of battle, Titus Pullus filled his lungs.

"I am Titus Pullus, Primus Pilus and hero of Caesar's 10th Legion! I piss on you savages! I will fuck your mothers and your daughters, but not until I've waded in your guts! DO ANY OF YOU *CUNNI* THINK YOU CAN DEFEAT ME? THEN COME ON!"

As he roared his challenge, bellowing with a volume that came only from decades of shouting commands in battle, he held his arms out wide, ruined shield in one hand, sword in the other, beckoning to the Wa down in the ditch. For just the briefest instant, the action immediately around the large Roman stopped, as men openly gaped, the Wa astonished, and, if the truth were known, a little afraid at the apparition before them. Conversely, Pullus' men took savage pride at the sight of their Primus Pilus. Here they were, in the fight of their lives, and their Centurion was mocking the enemy, daring them to do their best! How could they lose with men like Pullus leading them? In response, without any order, a low-pitched, savage growl began emanating from the Roman lines along the rampart. Without any prompting from their Centurions or Optios, the Legionaries of Rome, no matter where they came from, suddenly increased the fury of their fighting, thrusting and stabbing into the enemy, as the Wa, with equal fervor and not a little desperation, scrabbled to gain a solid foothold on the rampart of the barbarian camp. Never before, and perhaps never since, had any army of Rome fought with such savage intensity, but never before had they been so evenly matched in their fury, as they were against the Wa.

At the far southern outpost, Asinius Pollio and Primus Pilus Batius still stood side by side a short distance from the rampart, watching the men before them meet the attacking Wa who were throwing their ladders against the turf wall and starting their ascent. Unlike Pullus' camp, the archery barrage had done minimal damage, both in casualties and in damage to the shields of the defenders. There were no gaps in the row of men lining the ramparts, and for the most part their shields were sufficiently undamaged, so that they were able to withstand the first wave of Wa attackers that attempted to breach the defenses. While the fighting was fierce, it wasn't of nearly the same intensity as what Pullus and Balbinus were facing, though neither man had any way of knowing that.

Over the noise of the fighting, Asinius turned to Batius and asked in as close to a conversational tone as possible, "Do you think it would be a good idea to have the reserve Cohorts give their javelins to the front line men? If we need the men of the reserve, it will probably be too late for them to use their javelins."

"True," Batius agreed, "they'll probably need to go straight to the sword. That's a good idea, sir, I'll make sure it's done."

With a salute, Batius turned to go give the orders. Before he could, however, a lone arrow—actually loosed by a Wa in his death throes, after being pierced by one of the last javelins of the last volley, the trajectory of the missile describing an arc high in the air—came hurtling down to earth, picking up even more speed than normal. Batius was just turning, so the arrow pierced his neck, the barbed tip slashing tissue as it buried itself deep in the Primus Pilus' body. Taking one halting step, he uttered a gurgled, choking cry before collapsing, dead before he hit the ground. It took Pollio a moment, before the import of what happened hit him, and he instinctively moved to kneel by Batius' body. Then he stopped himself, understanding that it was too late, knowing from experience when a man was killed instantly. His lips moved in a silent prayer as he interceded on behalf of Batius, asking the gods to transport him not to Charon, but Elysium, the home of all the bravest warriors. When he was finished, he called to the nearest

Centurion standing with his Century as part of the reserve. The Centurion's attention had been on the action going on before him while Pollio and Batius had stood off to his left front.

"Centurion! Centurion!" Pollio bellowed, the man turning in surprise at the sound of his general. Pollio pointed down at Batius' body, and said in his command voice, "Your Primus Pilus has fallen! Who will carry him from the field with the honor he deserves?"

As it had been with Pollio, it took a moment for the general's words and what they meant to register, but once they had sunk in, he was deathly afraid his legs would collapse from under him. While Batius' status wasn't quite as legendary and covered in glory as that of Titus Pullus, he was still a formidable Legionary with a sterling record, and, more importantly, he was the only Primus Pilus the Centurion had ever known. In fact, this was true for the vast majority of the men, other than a very small handful of no more than thirty men whose time in the Legions equaled his. Standing unmoving, Pollio had to repeat himself before the Centurion shook his head, and turned to call some of the men from his Century. In a small group, while the fight for the rampart continued, they marched to where Batius lay, then with a gentleness that was close to reverence and using a shield, they lowered him onto it. Then, with a man at each corner, they lifted the shield on their shoulders, and with the Centurion leading the way, marched into the center of the camp, where the Primus Pilus would be laid in the forum, to await the bodies of his comrades to join him on his next journey. As they did so, Pollio tore his attention away, forcing his mind back to the scene before him, where more fighting and dying was taking place.

Caesar had never experienced the emotions that threatened to take over his whole body as he did at that moment, watching the surprise attack of the Wa unfolding. Streaming across the valley floor, they were moving with a rapidity he wouldn't have believed possible of such a large body of men, if he wasn't watching as it happened. Frozen in his spot, he stared, unblinking, unmoving, his mind reeling in shock, before racing through every possibility he could think of that would salvage the situation. There was one shred of hope—or at least so he thought for a few moments—until the leading Wa hordes flowed around the bulge of the ridge and into the pocket, crossing the short expanse of open ground and hitting the base of the slope, still at a dead run. This was the maximum range for the three small outposts that had been emplaced roughly halfway up the slope, and as Caesar had commanded, they immediately began releasing their missiles. Each outpost was armed with two scorpions and one ballistae apiece, and manned with a Century, but despite several of the Wa in the leading ranks being struck down, Caesar saw with sickening clarity how this effort was much too little to slow down the Wa assault, let alone stop it. In fact, the outposts would in all likelihood simply be bypassed; even combined, three Centuries attacking from the rear of such a large force would be akin to a fly hoping to take down an elephant. Even before it happened, Caesar recognized this eventuality, destroying his last shred of hope that he could at the very least buy the time to get a warning to Pullus. As it was, riding even the swiftest horse, there was no way a courier would be able to slip past that surprise force, because at the rate they were climbing the slope, they would be at the ridgetop road before the courier.

Making matters even worse were the orders he had given for Bodroges to give to the courier riding to the northern camp, understanding that it was under enormous pressure. These orders authorized Hirtius to use his reserve as he saw fit, now that he was out of artillery ammunition.. Caesar, as he did in every battle, retained the control of all reserve forces, so it would require an order on his part to release them, although he knew that, if absolutely necessary, Hirtius would order his reserves into battle, before orders arrived and then ask forgiveness later—which of course Caesar would grant. Going further, Caesar also trusted his giant Primus Pilus more than any other of the Primi Pili and second only to his generals Pollio and Hirtius. Even with all that, knowing that it was probably futile, Caesar realized he had to try, so he called for the Pandyan Tribune, since Bodroges had yet to return. Shaking himself from his malaise with a supreme effort of will, Caesar composed himself mentally, his face still the same calm, composed mask that gave nothing away, and snapped an order for the secretary to hand him another wax tablet.

When none was forthcoming, he turned his head in irritation, ready to reprimand the man, one of his minor secretaries, but then saw why he hadn't answered. The man had taken an arrow through the soft spot at the base of the throat, right above the chest and was lying there in a slowly growing pool of blood, eyes wide and staring up. It had obviously just happened, but Caesar had been so shaken and absorbed in his own thoughts and fears that he hadn't even noticed, and it was this fact that disturbed him more than the man's death. Still, to an outside observer he looked like his normal, composed self, as he bent down—,careful to stay sheltered behind the shields as he reached to pluck a tablet from the dead secretary's hand. However, when he took hold of the tablet, the dead man's hand closed tightly around it, giving Caesar a start. He had been looking back up toward the Pandyan Tribune when grabbing the tablet, but now his eyes turned back to the fallen secretary, and when they did his heart suddenly jumped, as the man's eyes blinked once, twice, then three times. The secretary wasn't dead, yet! His wound was definitely mortal, but whatever is in each of us that clings to life, that keeps our heart beating, even when it should have stopped, was strong within the spirit of the secretary, so he stared up at Caesar with desperate, pleading eyes, unable to talk because of the blood that pooled in his mouth and flowed out of its corners onto the ground. That didn't stop him from trying, though, and his jaw moved attempted to form the words, and Caesar, shaken to his very core, strained to understand what the dying man was saying.

"Please...kill...me," the man made no sound, but Caesar could read lips better than most people, although it took the man repeating it three times, before he understood.

Without hesitation, Caesar gave him a nod, and despite the fact the secretary was a slave, told him, "I will say prayers myself and have a sacrifice made, so the gods accept you into the afterlife."

Truthfully, this being a minor secretary who had been captured during the Parthian portion of the campaign, Caesar was unsure what gods the man prayed to, but he silently vowed that if he lived through the day, he would find out. It was the least he could do. Caesar placed his free hand gently on the man's forehead, while he temporarily relinquished his hold of the tablet, drawing his *pugio*—the Legionary's dagger—with the other. As he did so, his hand moved from the secretary's forehead down over the man's eyes to shield them from what Caesar was about to do. With the practiced skill of an augur, Caesar made a quick, but strong, slash across the man's throat, the blade of the dagger cutting deeply just above where the shaft of the arrow protruded. Wiping the blade on the secretary's tunic, Caesar closed the man's eyes, then took the tablet from the now-lifeless hand, standing erect and reaching for his stylus in one motion.

The Pandyan, who was given a shield as Bodroges was, had reached Caesar's side and waited for the general to write his orders, orders that the general knew had almost no chance of reaching the intended recipient. Nonetheless, that didn't stop him from handing the tablet to the Pandyan, with curt instructions, whereupon the Pandyan moved as quickly as he dared, shield still held aloft. Only when Caesar saw the Tribune safely away did he turn his attention back to the fighting. Immediately he saw a spot where there were several bodies, roughly equally divided between Romans and Wa, but, more importantly and dangerously, a small group of Wa had formed a pocket, their backs to the rampart and facing the Legionaries in a slight bulge, with just enough space left, so that more Wa could climb the ladder located there and join these men. Caesar was, like Titus Pullus at heart a warrior, as well as a general, so seeing that every other Roman was occupied, and that he was the closest, he drew his sword.

As he did so, he called to the three Legionaries protecting him, "It's time to earn our pay, boys. Follow me!"

And without waiting for their answer, Caesar strode toward the waiting Wa, sword in hand.

Prompted by Pullus' challenge, the Wa increased the fury of their assault, something that no one in Caesar's army would have believed possible, until they saw it happen. If they had had the time, they probably would have muttered under their breath about how it was their Primus Pilus and his defiance that had created this situation, but every man on the rampart was either engaged or holding the leather harness of the man ahead of them, who was thrusting, blocking, and slashing in a desperate attempt to stem the threatening flood of Wa warriors. And while Pullus had stopped the immediate danger posed by the first two Wa over the wall, there were even more such trouble spots boiling up all along the 10th's sector.

Immediately after dispatching the two Wa, Pullus occupied himself with running from one spot to another, but very quickly recognized that there was so much going on in so many different places, he was better off doing his primary job in directing the Legion, rather than following his instincts and training to fight in the front line. Backing away from the fighting, he paused to catch his breath, then began walking down the rampart, behind the short lines of the men standing in support of those doing the fighting. Each Century was fighting on a front of 10 men and was theoretically 10 deep, but by this point it was more commonly only six deep, and even less in some Centuries, particularly those of the senior Cohorts of the First, Second, Third and Fourth. These were the Cohorts almost always in the front line of every battle, consequently suffering the most casualties. This day, each Cohort was aligned in a three-Century front, with another Century immediately behind, arrayed several paces away from the raised portion of the rampart.

The dimensions of Caesar's camps had long since become standard in the Roman army, even before he and his men essentially disappeared from the view of Rome on this historic campaign; accordingly, every rampart was wide enough so that it could accommodate a Century of men at the current strength levels, each man holding the harness of the man in front of him, except of course for the first man and the last. Every Centurion was equipped with a bone whistle, which he blew at intervals to signal that the man in front was to bash his opponent with his shield, knocking the opponent backward to give the Legionary the time to step aside quickly to let the man behind him take his place, before the first man moved back into the space between the files to become the last, resting while supporting the Legionaries in front by bracing them, as he had been braced.

Fighting in this accustomed manner was now less a case of pushing the opponent away, as the Centurion judged the best moment when there was a momentary lull, because the Wa at the top of the ladder was either sent plunging to his death or sufficiently staggered. This relief system was the first thing Pullus watched, as he moved along the rampart, judging the men’s fatigue level, and, most importantly, the casualties the leading Centuries had suffered, a number telling him that a Century needed to be pulled out in relief. Much to his dismay, he saw that, even this early in the actual assault on the wall, several Centuries had suffered heavy casualties, as evidenced by the bodies that had been dragged off the rampart to lie in neat rows. While the number of dead wasn't extremely high, Pullus knew from experience that for every body he saw, it was likely that there were at least two wounded men who had been carried off by the Legion's clerks—

and the slaves kept behind as stretcher bearers—and taken to the hospital tent, which Pullus was sure was already overflowing, as the *medici* worked to save those men they could.

Stopping at a number of Centuries, he ordered that the supporting Century relieve the one currently on the rampart. To achieve this, the relieving Century was marched directly behind the one they were replacing, grabbing hold of the leathers of the last men of the Century on the rampart. Much like a normal relief within a Century, this was how the Romans had perfected the act of switching out fatigued troops with fresh ones, as the Centurion of the fighting Century continued blowing his whistle. Each time, the Legionaries in front would do whatever they needed to disengage and then move backward; however, in this dire situation, they moved all the way off the rampart, where they would collapse, panting and exhausted from the frantic combat going on just paces away.

By the time Pullus reached the point along the rampart where the Seventh Cohort was standing next to the First Cohort of the 12th, roughly half the Centuries had been swapped out for fresh ones, but Pullus knew that, barely a sixth of a watch since the first Wa ladders had touched the rampart walls, the 10th and, of course the 12th, were in serious trouble. Stopping to talk to Balbinus, the Primus Pilus of the 12th, Pullus quickly determined that the 12th was in much the same condition as the 10th.

With his inspection done and his conversation with Balbinus finished, Pullus was turning away when above the noise came the blast of a *cornu*, causing both Primi Pili to exchange an alarmed glance before they looked in the direction of the call.

It had come from the farthermost end of the camp, in the 12th's sector, and after a moment's hesitation, Balbinus told Pullus, "I'll go check."

With that, he trotted off, while Pullus decided to stay put for the time being. Even with the chaotic fighting taking place just twenty paces away and up the slope of the rampart, Pullus' attention was focused on the spot where Balbinus was heading. Because of the slight curve of the camp, which followed the contour of the hill, he couldn't make out anything more than the sight of the men of the 12th, fighting with as much fury as his own. Despite his natural urge to at least move back in the direction of the men of his own Cohort, Pullus stayed where he was, occasionally shouting an order to the Centurion in command of the Third Century, Seventh Cohort of his Legion, which was nearest to him, then reminding the man, Vibius Pacuvius to shorten his relief intervals. Without turning his head, Pacuvius raised his *vitus* in acknowledgement, immediately blowing his whistle for his men to shift places. Watching briefly and satisfied that Pacuvius was obeying his instructions, Pullus returned his attention to the direction that Balbinus had headed, spotting him coming around the slight curve at a trot. When he drew within fifty paces, Pullus could see by the grim set of his mouth that the news would not be good.

"Hirtius is down," Balbinus confirmed Pullus' suspicions, both men alerted by the *cornu* call that signaled a senior officer had fallen. "But he's not dead. At least," Balbinus added grimly, "not yet."

"What happened?" Pullus asked, although it didn't really matter.

He was in command of this camp now.

"He took an arrow through the neck," Balbinus replied. "But he had the gods favor because the arrow didn't sever any of the big vessels." He gave a bitter chuckle. "In fact, it looks kind of funny. The arrow is just sticking through his neck, the point sticking out over one shoulder, and the feather end out the other. They're not moving him any more than they have to, but he's been carried off to the *praetorium*."

Balbinus gave a salute to Pullus that was both slightly mocking, and conveyed his sense of sympathy for his counterpart now that he was in charge.

"Well, commander," he said, "if you don't mind, I have a Legion to attend to."

Pullus, understanding the sentiment behind the gesture, gave a bitter laugh, but returned it nonetheless.

"Very well, Primus Pilus," he said formally, "carry on."

With that, the two returned to their respective Legions.

When it came to the two Primi Pili, Caesar had been explicit in putting Pullus in charge; although Pullus was technically senior to Balbinus Caesar had made it clear to remind Balbinus that he was to obey Pullus as if the order came from Caesar himself, as it well might. As reluctant as Pullus was to do it, not only because of what it meant in a tactical sense, but also knowing how the men would interpret it, he recognized that he at least had to order the reserve Cohorts of the Eighth, Ninth, and Tenth of both Legions to come closer to the rampart. Just the sight of them standing there would be meaningful to the men currently engaged, but there was no denying that he would have to do it at some point. Deciding to be prudent, he turned to his *cornicen*, who followed him wherever he went except into the thick of the fighting, Pullus told the man to be ready to sound the signal that the reserves were to move forward. Heading back toward his Cohort, he stopped long enough to confer with Scribonius, who was standing at the edge of the slope, watching men of his Century surround a group of a half-dozen Wa who had managed to get a foothold on the rampart. There were already several bodies, most of them Wa, but Pullus saw among the tangle of limbs—some of them moving, some twitching and some lying still—that there were Romans as well. The Wa were standing back-to-back, all of them armed with swords and using them so skillfully that it was clear that the Legionaries engaging with them were more than a little intimidated. As Pullus approached, Scribonius suddenly saw an opening, and with commendable speed crossed the short distance, sword held high and slightly out from the body, with the point angled down, in what the Romans called the second position. His target, a Wa warrior who Pullus could see was extremely muscular and stocky, in stark contrast to the smaller, leaner builds of most of the Wa, was engaged with one of Scribonius' men and, in doing so, had turned slightly. Since he was the man on the outside, there was no other Wa to protect him, a fact that Scribonius took full advantage of with a hard, brutal thrust downward. The point of his blade cut deeply into the Wa at the base of the neck, half the blade disappearing into his body cavity. Dropping immediately, he landed on top of another Wa body, opening up a space that Scribonius' men immediately filled to press in on the Wa who was next to the now dead warrior. This was the only advantage needed, and even before Pullus had ascended the slope up to the rampart, the immediate threat was over. Working quickly, the Romans pitched the bodies over the palisade, doing their best to drop them down on the heads of the next Wa ascending the ladder. Sensing movement out of the corner of his eye, Scribonius turned his head just enough to see out of his peripheral vision that it was his

Primus Pilus, and with his eyes still fixed on the fighting in front of him, slowly backed up to meet his friend. Once he was out of the immediate area, only then did Scribonius turn to face Pullus, and for the first time Pullus could remember, Scribonius didn't start the conversation with a light remark or some attempt at a joke.

"We're in trouble," the Secundus Pilus Prior said, lips thinned down in a grimace at the thought. "I think we might not survive today, Titus."

Essentially behind and to the left of Titus and Scribonius, outside the camp and down the slope, the leading edge of the surprise Wa force was scrambling around the perimeter of the Roman position placed closest to the point where the bump of the ridge turned from its east/west orientation to the north/south direction of the rest of the ridge. Like water flowing around a rock, the Wa made no attempt to attack the position, virtually ignoring it, despite the Century of Legionaries felling dozens of Wa with their javelins and the scorpions and ballista drawing blood as well. Caesar had moved to a spot where he could watch this Wa advance, and although he was grimly pleased at the sight of a good number of bodies strewn all around the Roman position, he also understood the brutal arithmetic of it. Perhaps, if the Wa had to run a gauntlet of a dozen more such positions, they wouldn't pose such a huge threat, but of course that wasn't the case. Once past this site, the main body continued ascending the steep slope of the ridge, and Caesar could tell that at last the Wa were showing signs of fatigue, as the mad dash had slowed to more of a steady climb. He felt confident that once at the top, whoever was commanding this contingent would give his men the opportunity to catch their breath and regroup in whatever organizational structure they used. In fact, Caesar thought bitterly, they would probably use the very road he had ordered cut along the length of the ridge as an impromptu forum, the width of the road giving just enough of a clear space where at least the center of the Wa formation could gather.

A few feet above the first of the Wa, Caesar could just make out a thin veil of dust still hanging in the air, and he understood the meaning of it. That would be the dust trail left by the first courier, carrying Caesar's orders to release the reserve to Hirtius' control, which, if Hirtius hadn't already taken it he would once those orders arrived. That meant that there would be no men on the walls on that side to meet the assault from the direction the Wa were coming from, except for the sentries, and their only impediment would be pulling down the turf wall and palisade stakes. Caesar could see the scene in his mind: the horde of barbarian warriors, showing the same controlled frenzy they displayed in their ascent up the ridge, making short work of the ditch, which didn't have any of the traps embedded in the bottom of the other side. The only hazards lining that part of the ditch were the sharpened stakes, but they would slow the Wa down for only a matter of moments.

In fact, it wouldn't surprise Caesar at this point if some Wa merely leaped into the ditch to impale themselves to give their comrades an easier path. Why would that be any different than what was happening right in front of his eyes? Once the ditch was crossed, the turf wall torn down, and a breach effected in the walls of the camp, the Wa would pour through it like water, roiling and angry, destroying everything and everyone in their path. They would reach the forum of the camp first, since that was always in the middle of the camp, next to the *praetorium*. Caesar knew that in all likelihood the forum was now packed with casualties, as the *medici* tried to administer to those men that could be saved. If he were the commander, he wouldn't waste time with the wounded, instead continuing the sweep through to fall on the unprotected rear of his men. If the reserve Cohorts were still being held back, they would be at the edge of the forum, and at least those men would have a hint of the danger—not that it would ultimately make any difference. There were just too many Wa, and Pullus' camp was about to be caught between two crushing jaws, he and his men annihilated between them.

"Primus Pilus! A courier's arrived!"

Pullus took several paces backward, before turning to see the Optio left in charge of the section of sentries at the Porta Praetoria—the main gate of the camp—dashing in his direction, waving a wax tablet in his hand. Snatching the tablet, Pullus ignored the man's gasping report, for once unconcerned with the formalities required of all junior officers reporting to a senior. Although it was the message he was more or less expecting, reading the words Caesar had incised into the wax—as always using his dot above the last word of each sentence—still sent a chill up the giant Centurion's spine. Pullus hadn't had time to send more than one report, but Caesar had seen what was happening and obviously understood the import and gravity of the situation at the northern camp. Even as his mind raced with the implications, there was a stray flash of relief: now Pullus was off the hook for doing what he was about to do on his own. Snapping the tablet shut, Pullus turned to his *cornicen*, opened his mouth to give the order that Caesar had now authorized...and nothing came out.

For the rest of his time on earth, Titus Pullus would never be able to articulate what stopped him, or why it did, for that matter. He stood there motionless, much as Caesar was at that same moment, seemingly oblivious to all that was happening around him. Barely a couple of dozen paces away was a thin line of Wa who had managed to gain a foothold, and in several spots, in fact, were now two deep, the second rank providing the same kind of support to their comrades in front of them as the Romans in their line did. Those Romans currently engaged were hampered by the bodies of their friends and enemies, some of whom were trying to drag themselves through and around the legs of the men still fighting. Like wounded animals who seek a quiet place to die, these Legionaries were single-minded in their purpose of getting away from what had hurt them in the first place.

Everywhere one looked along the rampart, the ground the men were fighting for was soaked wine-dark with the blood of friend and foe, as each side did its utmost to bring on the destruction of the other. Shouts, screams, splintering wood, and the ringing sounds of iron hitting iron so filled the air that for anyone unaccustomed to it, this cacophony would banish any vestige of sanity from them as surely as the rising sun drives away the darkness. Even for men long hardened to the sounds of battle, these were by far the loudest conditions they had ever fought in, and that would seem to make it impossible for anyone to think. However, Pullus stood there, completely immobile, face expressionless, almost as if were in a morning formation and he and the men were waiting for the Legate or one of the Tribunes with the duty that morning. His only movement was to open the tablet again, staring down at the writing with a frown, before giving a minute shake of his head, while snapping it shut again. Thrusting the tablet into his belt, Pullus turned back to the Optio.

"On your way back to your post, go find Pilus Prior Tetarfenus," Pullus commanded, naming the Centurion commanding the Eighth Cohort of the 10th. "Tell him I want him and the other Cohorts of the 10th to move to the far side of the forum."

If the Optio was surprised, he didn't show it; junior officers of the Legion were so accustomed to obedience that it actually never occurred to the man to question his Primus Pilus. He was turning to leave, but, good Optio that he was, he thought of something.

"What about the 12th, Primus Pilus? What do you want them to do?"

Pullus thought for a moment.

"Have them stay on this side of the forum, but move a street closer," he commanded, and with that, the Optio dashed off to carry out his orders.

Titus Pullus didn't know it yet, but he had just made one of the most important decisions of not just this day, but of his entire life.

Gnaeus Tetarfenus, the Pilus Prior of the Eighth Cohort of Caesar's 10th Legion, had been standing with Titus Nasica, his Pilus Posterior, speculating on what they were both sure would be the command to move up. Tetarfenus had been sending men across the forum to check on the fighting on the rampart, so he knew the situation was growing desperate, and when he saw the duty Optio returning, he was sure he knew what the orders would be. In fact, when they were the exact opposite of what he was expecting, Tetarfenus made the Optio repeat himself twice more before, with a shake of his head, he called the Centurions of the reserve.

"The Primus Pilus has ordered us to move in the direction of the Porta Praetoria," he announced, to the obvious surprise of the assembled officers. Still, surprised or not, they didn't hesitate when they moved back to their respective Centuries, where their men were crouched and waiting. As they shuffled themselves into position, the duty Optio hurried over to the reserve of the 12th, and they in turn began their own process of moving closer to the action. With his duty discharged, the Optio proceeded to his post, where his men were standing on the rampart. As he drew closer, the Optio saw that his men's eyes weren't facing outward, but back into the camp, towards the forum.

While understandable, this was a clear breach of regulations, and the moment he was close enough to them, the Optio roared, "You there! Prixus! You bastard! Don't think I don't see where you're looking! By the gods, I'll stripe you good!"

Before the Optio's words were out of his mouth, Prixus, along with his comrades, spun guiltily around, knowing that they were well caught. When they did, Prixus saw something out of the corner of his eye to the southeast, back along the ridge road. It was just a flash of sun on metal, but it was enough to catch his attention. However, when he looked more closely, the only thing he saw was the dust hanging above the ridge road, right before it dipped out of sight into a fold of ground. His initial reaction was to relax slightly, thinking that the dust he was seeing was still from the courier who was now safely inside the camp. But while Prixus would never be accused of being smart, he was experienced, another of the Romans who had managed to survive this ten year campaign, and it was that experience that told him that any dust the arrived courier had raised would have been settled by that point. So he stared, hard, at the spot where the road came back into view, knowing that it would be only a matter of heartbeats, before any rider on that road would reappear. The idea that it could have been a man on foot didn't even occur to Prixus, and his attention was now so fixed on that spot that he was barely aware that the Optio had climbed the slope up onto the rampart.

"Oh, now you're going to pretend you're doing what you should have been doing all along," the Optio snapped caustically. "But it's not going to save you a flogging."

It was only when Prixus gave no reaction to the idea of a flogging that the Optio realized it was no act, and instantly his irritation dissolved as his attention centered on the Legionary. Prixus was a scoundrel, one of those men who could magically disappear whenever there was a work detail, or conjure his way onto a sick list. But he was a hard-bitten, veteran Legionary, and one of the best fighters in the Century—his very survival a testament to that fact—so the Optio moved immediately to his side, following his man's gaze.

"What is it?" he asked quietly. "What did you see?"

Instead of answering immediately, Prixus, as he had been trained, used one of his javelins to point to the now-settling plume of dust.

"See there, Optio? I didn't see a rider or anything, but....."

"That dust couldn't be from the courier who's already here," the Optio finished, understanding the same thing as Prixus did.

For a moment they continued staring, before the Optio asked, "When did you first see whatever it was?"

"Long enough that whoever it was would be in sight by now," Prixus replied, then added, "If they were mounted, that is."

That was when something else happened, something that—while both the Optio and Prixus saw or more accurately sensed it—neither could have described it with any level of accuracy. Again, it was more the sum total of their years of experience that told them something was happening that was, at the least, noteworthy. Perhaps it was a vagary of the breeze, which in this part of the world blew from the northeast at this time of year, but for whatever reason carried a shrill cry from the south. Or maybe it was just the fleeting glimpse of an arrow that sailed through the air and in its arc crested just above the brow of the rise that was blocking their view. Whatever it was, the Optio frowned for a moment, then made a decision.

"Stay here, and keep your eyes on that spot," he snapped, giving quick orders for the rest of Prixus' section to do the same. With that, he went bounding down the rampart, heading back towards Tetarfenus.

Pullus had by this time returned his attention and his sword back to the fighting. Even as he did so, he could see with a sinking heart that the Wa were winning. It wasn't quickly, and it was at great cost, but with more than 5 men for every Legionary, they could afford to be profligate. By this point, the front rank of the Cohorts was standing just barely on the edge of the rampart, forcing the men behind them to stand lower on the ramp, making it difficult to brace their comrades. Moving back up to the front, Pullus bent down to pick up a shield, pulling it from the lifeless fingers of one of his men, a Pandyan, whose throat had a gaping hole from a single thrust into the base. His eyes stared wide at the sky, his face bearing that look of surprise Pullus had seen so many times before, and the detached part of Pullus' mind recognized the man as Shrinar, the Legionary that Balbus had caught trying to sneak the Wa beauty out of the pillaged town. Well, Pullus thought, he doesn't have to worry about Caesar stealing any more of his women!

Hefting the shield, Pullus waded back into the fighting, welcoming the freeing of his mind as it settled into the simple needs and demands of combat. For a moment he could forget the worries of command, losing himself in the most elemental of questions: can I best my enemy? Hesitating for just a moment, he spotted one of his men of the front rank take a staggering step back from the thrust of a Wa sword. Before the man could recover, Pullus stepped in, lashing out with his shield and, coming from an oblique angle as he was, struck the Wa's left shoulder. Now it was the Wa's turn to stagger, but like all of his comrades, he recovered quickly, making a low underhanded thrust across his body that Pullus, his shield still high from his blow to the Wa's shoulder, was barely able to block.

As off-balance as the Wa was, the thrust was still able to punch through Pullus' shield just above the protective metal strip at the bottom. The force of the blow pushed the bottom of Pullus' shield towards him, while tilting the top out, a position that normally would have left Pullus exposed. But turning what would normally be a threat into an opportunity was something Titus Pullus did very well, and he did so now, whipping the tilted edge of the shield straight out and catching the Wa a glancing blow just above the ear. Unfortunately for the Wa, a glancing blow by a man as strong as Titus Pullus was the same as taking the strongest shot from any other man, and the Wa dropped like a stone. Without any hesitation, Pullus stepped over the body, while keeping his shield up and ready, remembering to give a savage thrust down into the throat of the unconscious man.

His slight advance, while putting him just ahead of the front rank of his Legionaries, also took him closer to the rampart. Now there was only a lone Wa between him and the protection that the rampart would give to his unprotected side, it was to this man that Pullus turned his attention. Fortunately for Pullus—or at least so he thought at first—the Wa was armed with one of the teardrop shaped spears, the butt end hovering out over the rampart and into space. However, while this normally would mean whoever was wielding it would be restricted, this Wa quickly disabused Pullus of that notion. With an overhand grip, the Wa—who Pullus was sure was barely out of his teens, although he had learned it was almost impossible to accurately tell the age of any Wa who wasn't either a child or incredibly old—suddenly whipped the butt end of the spear at Pullus with a seeming flick of the wrist. Although the blow was blocked by his shield, there was so much force behind it that the shield slammed back into his upper shoulder and took him back a step.

Eying his opponent with a new respect, Pullus began moving the tip of his sword in a geometric pattern, trusting his instinct that this Wa was, indeed, relatively inexperienced. As he had hoped, the Wa's eyes began following the moving sword tip despite himself, giving Pullus the opportunity he had been seeking with his shield. With enviable quickness, Pullus punched out with his shield by simply extending his left arm straight out from the shoulder. The metal boss of the Roman shield was a deadly weapon in its own right, and with any other foe, the blow Pullus launched would have been devastating. But his Wa opponent, like so many of the others he had faced, had reflexes that no cat would have spurned, and they served him well now. The boss should have hit him in the right shoulder with enough force that it would have crushed whatever bone it came in contact with, but because of a combination of leaning backward and sweeping upward with his spear to absorb some of the force, the blow didn't cause nearly the damage it should have. But it was enough to snap the solid shaft of the spear like a twig, leaving it in two pieces.

Even this blow didn't seem to have the effect Pullus expected, as the Wa simply shifted his grip on each piece of the broken weapon, before making another thrust with the business end of the spear, but Pullus blocked it, too. As the Primus Pilus did so, however, the Wa swung the other piece of the spear like a club, and because Pullus had moved his shield across his body, it was out of position to block the oncoming blow. If the club end of the spear struck Pullus where the Wa had aimed, the blow would have been strong enough to stun Pullus, at the very least; but like so many of his enemies, the Wa wasn't used to fighting a man of the giant Roman's stature. Instead, the shaft struck Pullus a solid blow on the meaty part of his upper arm, and it was only because of the heavy muscles there that it didn't break the Roman's bone. It would leave another massive bruise, but that would come later. Somehow, Pullus managed to keep a hold of his shield despite the pain, but he instantly knew that his ability to use it offensively was gone for at least the next several moments.

Consequently, he made a feint with the shield by shrugging his shoulder and twisting his upper body, and as feints went, it was one of his weakest. Fortunately for Pullus, it was enough: reacting again with unbelievable speed, the Wa shifted his weight slightly to his left, at the same time leaning his upper body backward. This dropped his left hand, holding the blade of the spear, just a matter of a few inches, but that was sufficient for Pullus. The Roman delivered a high overhand thrust, stomping forward with his right foot as he did so, thereby extending the reach of his sword and putting the power of his weight behind it. Aiming at the Wa's throat, even as quick as the Wa was, his arm was just a little too low to sweep it upward quickly enough to deflect the blade from punching through his throat. Pullus felt the grate of the bone grabbing the blade as it sliced through it, forcing him to twist the blade to make sure it didn't get stuck. Over the years he had seen too many men who, in the excitement of battle, had forgotten this elementary move that all *tirones* were taught early in training, leaving them yanking the blade, desperate and defenseless in the face of a comrade of the man they had just killed. Freeing the blade and watching the Wa collapse in a heap at his feet, Pullus was able to move a pace closer to the rampart. Now that his right side was protected, he could concentrate on trying to stem the tide of barbarians, but even as he did, he could see that it was a hopeless task.

Several paces away, the Second Century of the First Cohort was in much the same straits as the First of the First, and Balbus, like Pullus was doing everything within his power to stop the advancing Wa. He wasn't as skilled as Pullus, but he was close, and while he lacked Scribonius' intellectual ability, he more than made up for it with guile and a ferocity that outmatched perhaps even that of his Primus Pilus. Now he was standing next to the last man on the right of the leading rank, the one engaged with the Wa, and Balbus' Century was in even more trouble than the First. Whether by accident or design—he would never know— the Wa had placed an average of two ladders along the length of rampart that a Century covered, whereas the Second Century had three ladders along its front. And there was a steady stream of smaller, wiry men clambering up, shouting in a guttural way that none of his men could make any sense of, whatsoever.

Although the Romans were cutting down most of the Wa who came leaping over the palisade stakes, inevitably the Romans suffered casualties as well, and in the moment that it took for a Legionary to replace the fallen man, the victorious Wa would press a step forward, standing over the body of the man he had just vanquished. Consequently, it was a grudging, hard-fought struggle, inch by inch and foot by foot, but it was one the Romans were losing. While the leading edge of the First Century was still at the very edge of the level portion of the rampart, the men of the Second Century had already been pushed even farther back. The leading edge of the Second was halfway down the dirt ramp, and strewn in front of them were the dozens of bodies of friend and foe alike that provided testament that the men of Balbus' Century weren't giving ground without making the Wa pay. It was just a case of grim mathematics, Balbus knew; he was rapidly running out of men, no matter how many Wa they took with them.

By this time in the fight, the Primus Pilus Posterior estimated that he had fewer than half the men he had started with, a Century that had been almost 30 men short of full strength already. Even accounting for Caesar's practice—ironically enough started with the 10th Legion all those years ago when he was Praetor in Hispania—of hundred man centuries, the fighting had whittled the senior Cohorts down, so that when Balbus managed to make a quick head count, there were only 34 men of his Century still left fighting. That knowledge filled Balbus with a despair unlike any he had ever faced in his entire life, let alone his career, even when his woman had died in childbirth. He was watching the destruction of what he loved more than anything else: his Century, his boys. For no matter that some of them were at least as old as he, to Balbus they would always be his boys, and his heart filled with a desperate, angry love.

"No," he snarled. "Not today. Not *this* fucking day!"

With a feral growl issuing from his throat, Quintus Balbus literally threw himself into a small clump of Wa who were just behind their engaged comrades, looking very much like they were gathering themselves to go charging into the Roman lines.

Sextus Scribonius was hurting, both within and without. He had taken a sword thrust all the way through his left forearm fairly early on in the fighting, and it was only through the intervention of the gods that it hadn't severed an artery. Nevertheless, it was extraordinarily painful, and he had only taken the time to wrap his neckerchief around the wound and then, gritting his teeth against the agony, had one of his men tie the ends as tightly as the Legionary's strength allowed. Now it was a dull, aching throb that was manageable, but the consequence was that he had lost all feeling in his hand and was unable to hold a *vitus*, let alone a heavy shield. Even so, it was the internal ache that was causing Scribonius the most trouble, and, like Balbus, he found it hard to concentrate. For just like his second-closest companion, Scribonius was watching not just his own Century, but the entire Second Cohort being destroyed, slowly but inexorably.

In terms of outright casualties, his Century was a bit better off than that of Balbus: Scribonius' last head count had yielded 42 men, but in just the bare moments since then, he had seen at least 2 more men fall, although one had crawled quickly to the rear on hands and knees. Perhaps he would be back, Scribonius thought, but the lanky Pilus Prior wasn't counting on it. As for the rest of the Cohort, Scribonius was continually being updated by runners coming from all along the Second Cohort's front, and he had been forced to have his own reserve of three Centuries enter into the rotation some time before. Since he could no longer carry a shield, he was being a bit more circumspect than Balbus, darting in to add the strength of his sword only when it was absolutely necessary or a Wa was turned away from him by one of his men. Even so, his blade was red almost to the hilt, but again, like, Balbus, he knew it wasn't going to be enough.

Nevertheless, Scribonius resisted the temptation of looking to the rear to see if the reserve Cohorts were standing ready to assist, knowing that the sight of their Pilus Prior looking for succor would in all likelihood trigger a panic. Instead, Scribonius willed himself to continue looking to the front, which was a good thing, because in another one of those fluke moments, two Legionaries who were standing side by side were struck down at almost exactly the same instant. Suddenly, there was a gaping hole in the front rank, and because of the way the bodies collapsed, they formed a barrier preventing their reliefs from stepping into their spots. Seeing this, understanding what it meant, and what had to be done occurred to Scribonius in the time it takes to blink an eye; of all the Centurions, not just in the 10th, but in the entire army, Sextus Scribonius was by far the smartest man in the ranks. In fact, it could be argued that he was second only to Caesar in the prodigiousness of his brain, but this was something Scribonius exhibited to only a very, very few people. But while it was his brain that told him what needed to be done, the impetus to do it, to leap into the void from the side of the formation where he was standing, came from the same wellspring that had sent Balbus charging headlong into a numerically superior enemy. For, like Balbus, like Pullus and like almost every other Centurion, Scribonius truly loved his men, so there was no hesitation, when, roaring his own challenge, he used his long legs to cross the distance, squeezing himself through the ranks, then ending his progress by hopping over the bodies of the two men to go crashing into the first of the Wa who had stepped into the gap.

Gnaeus Tetarfenus, Pilus Prior of the Eighth Cohort followed the duty Optio back up the ramp, where Prixus was still standing, eyes fixed to the last spot where he had seen the puzzling event farther south along the ridge.

"Seen anything?" the Optio demanded, but Prixus' only response was a shake of his head.

"So what is this extremely urgent thing you saw?" Tetarfenus, knowing the duty Optio only by reputation, since he was from the Fifth Cohort, was unable to hide his skepticism and impatience.

When asked in such a bald way, both the Optio and Prixus hesitated, exchanging sidelong glances.

Finally, the Optio cleared his throat nervously, "Well Pilus Prior, it's hard to say exactly......"

"So, you didn't see anything other than some dust?" Tetarfenus interrupted.

"Well, no. Er, I mean, not exactly," the Optio amended, but Tetarfenus had heard enough.

"Then, until you have something substantial to report, stop wasting my time," he snapped. "In case you haven't been paying attention, we're in the fight of our fucking lives!"

Without waiting for an answer, he turned on his heel to stalk back down the rampart to his Cohort. The Optio stared at his retreating back, trying to calculate how far Tetarfenus needed to go before he could curse him without being heard. Fortunately for everyone as it would turn out, Prixus, still smarting from his rebuke by the Optio and not sure if there was a flogging in his future, kept his eyes fixed on the spot where the ridge road reappeared. What caught his eye confused him at first: things looking like slender reeds that had just popped up from the ground, but topped with flowers unlike any he had ever seen, because they were a dull, silvery color. Then, one of the Wa carrying his spear turned the shaft in his hand, so that the broad side of the distinctive tear-shaped blade was facing Prixus, who expelled an explosive gasp.. Whirling about at the sound, the Optio took one step to gaze over Prixus' shoulder, his jaw dropping and all the blood rushing from his face.

"Pilus Prior!" the Optio called.

Tetarfenus faced about, ready to issue a sharp rebuke, but the look on the Optio's face stilled his tongue. Tetarfenus ran back to the rampart,, and in the few heartbeats it took him to cover the distance, any doubt about what was approaching had been removed, as the heads of the leading Wa suddenly appeared, as if by magic, climbing the slope toward the unprotected Porta Praetoria side of the camp. They were less than a mile away, and Gnaeus Tetarfenus found himself rooted to his spot for a moment, his face a mirror of that of the Optio standing next to him. Shaking his head as if he were trying to wake himself from a bad dream, the Pilus Prior snapped back to reality, and, without a word to the two men, went sprinting down from the rampart.

"Reserve Cohorts! Rally to me!" he started bellowing at the top of his lungs. "We're under attack!"

There was a ripple of movement, as men who were kneeling, their arms draped across their shields, jumped to their feet, and the air filled with a babble of questions, each of them struggling to comprehend this new reality.

"What did he say?"

"Something about an attack!"

"Huh? From where? How?"

"How the fuck should I know?"

The ensuing scramble demonstrated once again that the men of the 10th were so experienced that the move from a position of rest to standing at *intente*—at the very least to being ready to move into position—was accomplished with great speed, even if they didn't know where they were moving, while the Centurions had run to close the gap to their Pilus Prior, meeting him roughly halfway between the forum and the rampart.

"I don't know how, but those slanty-eyed *cunni* got a force behind us," Tetarfenus gasped out, his Centurions going rigid with shock.

"How many?" asked Pilus Prior Nasica.

"Enough," Tetarfenus' face was grim. "Enough to sweep us away, unless we stop them at the walls. Get the men up to the walls, immediately."

"Reserve?" asked the Hastatus Posterior of the Tenth, a Roman named Gaius Porcinus, one of the youngest Centurions in the 10th, born in Baetica Province, like Titus Pullus. While he was somewhat taller than the other Centurions, he wasn't the same height, or breadth, as Titus Pullus, but there was a similarity in facial features that confirmed the fact that Gaius Porcinus was the son of Valeria, Titus Pullus' sister, and Titus' only nephew. His position in the Centurionate was achieved despite his uncle's every attempt to dissuade his young nephew from a life in the army, although he had plucked the youngster from the ranks of the 14th Legion—when Gaius managed to enlist, despite his mother's objections—putting him in Scribonius' Second Cohort, where his best friend could keep an eye on him. However, despite Porcinus' fresh-faced appearance, he had flourished in the Legion and had earned the right to wear the transverse crest of a Centurion in Caesar's army. Now, his nephew stood among the other Centurions of the reserve Cohorts, waiting to hear their dispositions.

"We're not going to have any reserve," Tetarfenus answered quietly. "We're going to need every man on the wall. Now, I want the Eighth there," he pointed to the spot around the Porta Praetoria, "the Ninth there, and the Tenth there. Now move!"

As the officers went scrambling to their respective Centuries, Tetarfenus grabbed Porcinus' arm, stopping him.

"I need you to go to the Primus Pilus; tell him what's happening. Tell him that we haven't gotten an exact count yet, but my guess is that there's going to be at least 10,000 men trying to get over that wall. And tell him," Tetarfenus' tone became even grimmer, "that we're going to need the 12th's reserve as well, if we're going to have any chance at stopping these bastards."

Chapter 9

The only position that wasn't hard-pressed were the camps to the south of Caesar's, where Aulus Flaminius and the 30th Legion and 14th Legion, under the overall command of The Muleteer Ventidius were repulsing the Wa with relative ease and even lighter casualties. The same was true for the camp farther to the south, next to Pollio's southernmost position, where the men of the 11th and 8th were faced by a Wa force composed almost identically in numbers to that facing Flaminius. Whether the Wa commanding these forces weren't made of the same iron as the others, or their orders were simply to make a demonstration Flaminius didn't know, but he wasn't about to complain. Not only were the reserve Cohorts standing ready in the forum, but he hadn't even had to send in the relief Centuries. Walking behind the Centuries manning the ramparts, Flaminius called out encouragement to the rankers, and advice to the Centurions, so it was almost like a training exercise. Probably not surprisingly, his men were in high spirits, now that the initial tension of the assault was dispelled and the measure of the enemy was taken. Those on relief were bantering back and forth, yelling above the noise and placing wagers on how many of these barbarians they would kill when their turn came up. The few wounded were quickly dragged out of the way by their comrades, down the ramp to the waiting stretcher bearers, who placed the wounded on the planks used for that purpose, carrying them to the hospital tent.

When Flaminius moved up to the rampart to assess the strength of the Wa assault, he was surprised and delighted to see before him a ditch almost overflowing with bodies, particularly around the ladders the Wa had thrown up against the wall. Better still, he took a quick count of the remaining ranks of those warriors still trying to cross the ditch and saw that they were a half-dozen deep, at most. However, most importantly, he could see that whatever fighting spirit was in these barbarians was quickly deserting them. Even as he watched, he saw the men to the rear—directly in front of the two ranks of archers who had stopped firing now that their comrades were at the walls—begin looking over their shoulders. Flaminius, like all the Primi Pili, was one of the most experienced Legionaries in the army, and he had seen that look, starting in Gaul and stretching across the entire known world. That look signaled victory, if his men could summon just enough of their strength to make one final push. Of course, in this case making a final push didn't mean what it would in a pitched battle; Flaminius wouldn't have dreamed of ordering a pursuit. It would be enough to break the Wa against the walls, and after seeing the scene before him, he knew it wouldn't be long before they did break.

Returning to his spot behind the fighting, Flaminius called to his clerk who stood a short distance away. Taking the wax tablet the scribe held out, he incised his report to Caesar. Once finished, he was about to snap the tablet shut and hand it to the Legionary who would dash to the waiting courier, who in turn would gallop the message to Caesar and, presumably, return with one in reply. He had finished his report; there was nothing else to say, but then he stopped, bent his head down and—if truth be known—looked slightly ridiculous, as he added one more line, his tongue out of his mouth in concentration. While Flaminius knew his letters, like all Centurions, he was no scholar, so he had to think carefully about what he was writing, hence the intense focus. Finally finished, he quickly re-read it and then snapped the tablet shut, handing it to the Legionary who, without saying a word turned and began running back toward the middle of the camp. He didn't know what the message said, nor did he care. In fact, it was better that he didn't know, because if he understood that he was essentially carrying the outcome of this battle and the fate of Caesar's army, he might have collapsed on the spot from the sheer enormity of the task.

Caesar had somewhat recovered his equilibrium and was back to directing the men fighting for their lives and his, but even as he did, a part of his mind was still occupied with what he feared was happening at the camp to the north. Like the northern camp, the Wa had managed to establish a presence on the rampart, but it was a much more tenuous affair, with the deepest penetration only two men deep and then only in a half-dozen spots. Otherwise, it was a case where a Wa would leap over the parapet and down onto the rampart, fight ferociously for anywhere from a few heartbeats to several long moments, before being cut down. Unfortunately, as with Pullus' position, it was a case of mathematics, because Caesar simply couldn't afford to lose men in the way the Wa commander could, and the latter had already proved more than willing to sacrifice as many as it took to overwhelm these pale creatures. Consequently, it was with increasing helplessness that Caesar saw his men fall, some of them able to move under their own power, crawling around and through the legs of their comrades, until they were sufficiently far enough away for one of their friends to grab them by the harness and drag them the rest of the way to safety, ignoring the screams of pain as they did so. Others weren't so lucky, either having been struck a mortal wound or hurt so severely that they were immobilized; and unless one of the men still in the fight noticed this and did what they could, these unfortunates saw their lifeblood pour into a ground that was already soaked with it.

The sound of the fighting had been roaring in his ears for so long that Caesar no longer noticed it, his mind now registering it as part of the background. It was only when there was a change in the pitch of what had become a steady dull noise that Caesar was alerted to a new development in the ongoing battle. It started with a series of shouts and screams of a much higher intensity and volume, and now looking in the direction of the source of the sound, in front of Caesar's horrified eyes he saw that several dozen paces away down the rampart—where the Fifth Cohort of the defending 25th Legion was located—a cluster of perhaps a dozen Wa were now securely on the rampart. In fact, they were moving down the ramp at a run, slashing down at the unprotected backs of the men, Caesar's men, whose nerve had at last failed and who were fleeing away from the onslaught. In doing so, they not only essentially sealed their fate—since the greatest slaughter on the battlefield came when men's collective nerve and courage finally broke and they turned to run—but their flight also threatened this whole camp. The sight caused Caesar to freeze for a moment, so unaccustomed to and shocked at the sight of his men in headlong flight that it rendered him into a form that looked very much like the statues of him spread from one end of the world to the other. It was only momentary, however, as with an abrupt shake of his head, he began heading toward the breach at a dead run, pausing only long enough to point a now-drawn sword at the small group of aides and some Legionaries who had just been relieved and who were standing nearby.

"Follow me! If we don't stop this, it's over for all of us!"

And without another glance back, sure that his men were hot on his heels, a 65 year-old general rushed headlong into battle with all the fervor of a young veteran eager to win glory.

It didn't take long for Gaius Porcinus to find his uncle; Titus Pullus was always easy to spot, for a couple of reasons. The first was his size, but it was the second one that delayed Gaius from making it to his Primus Pilus' side, as the giant Centurion was still standing hard up against the palisade, forming one side of a box that was just managing to keep the Wa in that area hemmed in. But even as Gaius weaved his way through the panting men on relief, then hopped over the numerous bodies lying in heaps, despite his relative inexperience as a Centurion, he was a hardened veteran of many battles, and he took in and understood the desperate situation at a glance. The Century that Titus was assisting, although Gaius didn't recognize it, was the Fourth of the First Cohort, but what Gaius could see was that there were no more than four men in each file standing there, ready to take their turn. Although he kept moving, Gaius did take the time to look down the ramp to where the relieving Century would be waiting, and his heart started racing even more than it had been from the exertion in getting there. He hadn't thought it possible, but the Century waiting to go back into battle was even worse off than the one currently fighting, with perhaps three men per file. And now there was a new force assaulting the camp?

In the remaining time it took Gaius to reach his uncle, he came to the simple conclusion that this was going to be the day he died, along with all of his men, the Legion, and probably the whole army. Almost overwhelmed at the thought, Gaius' stride faltered for a moment, and the feeling of impending loss that swept through him threatened to bring him to his knees. Yet, none of the thoughts racing through his head had anything to do with his own life ending, but were instead focused on the tragedy faced by the families and loved ones of his men. The very thought was so intensely painful that he gasped aloud, before ruthlessly pushing it aside, spurred by the knowledge that his uncle would never let his feelings impede his ability to do his job. Finally getting to a point where he was within a few paces of Pullus, Gaius halted, knowing that distracting his uncle at that moment, when he was engaged with a Wa, could be fatal, even for a man as experienced as the

Primus Pilus was. Waiting until he saw Pullus' blade sink deeply into the Wa's side, the warrior's mouth opening into a contorted shape by the agony of the mortal wound—although he didn't let out more than a groan that was barely audible from where Porcinus was standing—when the Primus Pilus stepped backward to take a breath, only then did Gaius move to his side.

"Primus Pilus," he called out, as always careful to refer to his uncle only by his rank in front of the men, no matter the circumstances.

Pullus turned in clear surprise at the sound of his nephew's voice, the older man covered in blood—mostly that of the Wa—his eyes narrowing at not just the sight of his nephew, but also at the import of Gaius' standing there, knowing he was part of the reserve.

"What is it?" Pullus snapped, unmindful at that moment of their blood ties, seeing instead only the Hastatus Posterior of one of his Cohorts.

If Porcinus was unsettled by the reception, he didn't betray it a bit, as he saluted; then, in as few words as possible gave his report. Even so, he had to repeat the report once more, before Pullus' mind could grasp the significance of what his nephew was telling him. It was only through a supreme effort of will that Titus Pullus didn't betray the sudden anxiety—and if truth were known—the fair amount of fear that threatened his composure. Instead, he forced himself to give only a grim nod.

"Tetarfenus is in position?"

"They were moving onto the walls as I left. I'm sure that they're in place now."

Nodding again, Pullus considered.

"All right. You're dismissed. Go back and tell Tetarfenus that he must hold, no matter the cost. Although I'm sure he knows that."

Gaius waited for more, but once it was clear that his uncle had said all he was going to—in fact turning back to the fighting, moving his sword in an easy pattern of circles as he tried to keep his aching muscles loose—he remained rooted to the spot where he was standing. Sensing this, Pullus turned back to Porcinus, his expression one of irritation at the delay of getting back to slaughtering barbarians.

"Well. What is it?"

"Primus Pilus, aren't you going to release the reserves of the 12th?"

Pullus frowned, caught clearly by surprise. How had he forgotten about that, he wondered? Was his mind so overwhelmed at what was going on that he could forget such vital details? While his first instinct was to tell Gaius to go to the Primus Pilus of the 12th and relay his orders to move them over to join the rest of the 10th's reserve, for some reason the orders wouldn't come out of his mouth. Instead, he looked carefully about him, at not just the Centuries still fighting, but the men waiting in relief. When he did, he saw the same thing his nephew had, and with great reluctance, he shook his head.

"I can't spare them, Gaius," he said quietly. "Tell Tetarfenus he's going to have to do the best he can with the men he has."

Even with the maelstrom of noise and fighting, both men could only look each other in the eyes, as each of them understood what Titus Pullus was telling his nephew. There would be only three Cohorts, a few more than a thousand men, to stop what Tetarfenus was sure was ten times that number. Swallowing hard, Porcinus couldn't trust himself to speak, instead giving a curt nod before turning to go. Before he did, Titus Pullus reached out and grabbed his nephew's shoulder.

"Gaius, wait."

When Porcinus turned back to face his uncle, the older man's expression was one that would stay with Gaius for the rest of his time on earth.

"May the gods be with you, Gaius," Pullus said as softly as could be managed in the din, blinking away what looked suspiciously like tears.

"And you...Uncle," Gaius' reply almost choked in his throat, but before either of them shamed themselves Porcinus turned away, starting out at a dead run back to be with his men to face whatever fate awaited them.

Pullus stood and watched for a few moments, until Gaius disappeared between the tents, still pitched and aligned in their neat rows, forcing down the lump in his throat, until the man he had come to love as a son was no longer in sight. Drawing a deep breath, Pullus squared his shoulders, then called to his runner, crouched just out of the range of the fighting.

"Go to Primus Pilus Balbinus. Tell him I need his reserve. Now."

Without waiting to see if he was obeyed, Pullus turned his attention back to the fighting, looking for a spot that needed some help. Quickly seeing that every single spot where ladders were against the wall was being hard-pressed, he simply chose the spot nearest him, and headed back into the fighting.

Julius Caesar was no Titus Pullus as a swordsman, but he was nevertheless highly skilled. He had snatched a discarded shield lying on the ground and was leading with it as he went careening into one of the small group of Wa who had momentarily paused at the bottom of the ramp. Their hesitation was understandable; not only were they now effectively well inside the enemy camp, but it was just as shocking to these Wa seeing the pale barbarians turning to flee. That brief moment allowed Caesar to close the remaining gap, and just as the nearest Wa sensed this new danger and was turning to face it, the 65 year-old Roman slammed into him with terrific force. Advanced age or not, Caesar was still extremely fit, hardened by years of relentless trial and exposure to the elements, and, while slender in build, was all muscle and bone. It was with this force that Caesar sent the first Wa recoiling backward, who, despite keeping his feet, was doing so only with difficulty, both arms windmilling crazily as he slammed into the Wa next to him. Their legs tangled together, finally causing the first Wa to leave his feet and crash heavily into the ground. Barely breaking stride, Caesar leapt over the first Wa, counting on whoever was behind him to dispatch the man, before he could become a threat, and attempted the same maneuver with the second Wa still struggling to stay upright. This time however, the Wa managed to dodge Caesar's blow with his shield, causing the Roman general to become the one who was unbalanced. In the instant it took for him to recover, the second Wa had accomplished Caesar's own maneuver, and with a bellow in their tongue that Caesar had no need for a translator to understand, unleashed a slicing blow at waist level that would have disemboweled the Roman, if he hadn't blocked it. As it was, Caesar heard a sharp, splintering crack from his shield and knew from hearing the sound that it was now cracked and severely weakened. Despite this, he countered with his own thrust, only dimly aware that the rest of the men following him threw themselves into the Wa, and—from the sound of it—with the same abandon their general had displayed. The Wa, again proving damnably agile, simply twisted his body from the waist to allow the point of Caesar's blade to go thrusting by at abdomen level. Fortunately for Caesar, the direction in which the Wa turned also moved the Wa's blade away from Caesar, so he was unable to make a counterattack. Instead, he made a small, hopping step even farther to Caesar's left, but twisted his torso in the process, so that when both feet were on the ground, he was squared up again, while now it was Caesar's sword that was out of range. Normally, this wouldn't have concerned Caesar because his shield was between him and the Wa, but instantly he understood that this was the Wa's target. Even as the thought flashed through his mind, the Wa unleashed a hugely powerful thrust aimed directly at Caesar's shield, just to the left and a little below the boss. Exactly as Caesar feared, the Wa had targeted the weakened part of his shield, the general realizing that the crack must be visible to the Wa, although it hadn't worked all the way through. Until, that is, this last thrust and Caesar watched in horror as, in seemingly slow motion, a spidery-thin longitudinal crack made its way through the shield in both directions from where the point of the Wa's sword had punched through, leaving a beam of daylight streaming through, when he withdrew it. Despite the shield's remaining intact, Caesar knew it would only be that way for at best two more blows, and that was only if he still had Caesar's Luck. Understanding this fact, he didn't bother using his shield offensively, instead pivoting on his left foot in answer to the move of the Wa, and in doing so, exposed his unprotected side to another Wa warrior who—seeing the chance at winning eternal glory, not to mention a reward that would instantly make him a wealthy man and elevate his status—didn't hesitate to come charging in with a sword raised high above his head, lips pulled back in a ferocious, triumphant grin.

Quintus Balbus had singlehandedly stopped the dangerous incursion of Wa in his sector, and was standing now, literally covered in blood and gore. Unfortunately, not all of it belonged to the Wa; Balbus had suffered several wounds, the most serious one a puncture wound low on his side that had driven several small links of his mail armor into his body. The pain was excruciating, and Balbus knew with utmost certainty that unless he put himself under the surgeon's blade and probe and allowed him to rummage around in his insides and get those links out, he was going to certainly die in an agony that he couldn't fathom. Nevertheless, he shook off every attempt by his Optio to guide him gently away from the fighting, finally snarling that he would run the Optio through himself if he persisted in his silliness. Now, with a brief respite in the fighting, he stood, legs shaking so violently that if it weren't for a pile of bodies that he used to lean against, he was sure he would collapse. The only concession he had made for the Optio was to allow the man to use his and Balbus' neckerchief, knotted together, to make a makeshift bandage that Balbus had insisted be drawn so tightly that it made it difficult to breathe. Despite his formidable will, he couldn't keep an agonized moan escaping from his lips, as the Optio, his own face drawn and tight, pulled and tugged at the cloth. Balbus still held his sword, and noted idly that if he didn't know better, he would have sworn that he had picked up one of the heavy wooden training swords. He was finding it much harder to maintain his concentration on all that was going on and, in fact, was losing interest in it altogether. Then there was a hoarse shout over and above the other noise, and he dully turned his head to see that four Wa had managed to establish another pocket of resistance directly in front of one of the ladders. More importantly, they had managed to push outward in a rough semicircle that opened up space for more Wa to climb the ladder and join them. Shaking his head vigorously, Balbus finally resorted to slapping himself in the face with his free hand—barely registering that it was caked with blood—before rousing himself sufficiently to begin making his way toward the latest trouble spot. Despite trying, he couldn't seem to force his legs to move in more than an unsteady wobble, but he nevertheless propelled himself towards the battle.

Gaius Porcinus was on his way back to his Century, with nothing more in mind than rejoining them as quickly as possible, so that he could at least die with his men and among friends. Crossing the forum, however, he suddenly stopped. Looking around, he saw that the entire open area was covered with wounded men, some moaning in pain, others lying quietly with that vacant look that the severely injured have, as if their immediate surroundings are no longer important. And perhaps they weren't, Porcinus thought, but as he stood there, unsure why he had stopped, it came to him with utter clarity. Without thinking further, he began speaking, using what his uncle called his "command voice," a volume just below a bellow.

"I know many of you are wounded too badly," he called. "But I'm not going to lie to you. We've been surprised by another force coming from the south."

He paused for a moment as his announcement prompted a buzzing of talk, as those who were able alternately cursed, moaned, or exclaimed to the man lying next to them, seeking solace in each other in this moment of extremis, even if they knew the man only by sight or didn't speak the same tongue.

After a moment, Porcinus continued, "So I'm asking those of you who are able to lift a sword to join us. We're going to need every man we can get, because I don't have to tell you what happens, if this part of the wall is breached."

Nobody stirred. Gaius stood there, watching in growing helplessness, as he saw men looking from one man to another. Finally, at the far end of the forum, he saw a bareheaded Legionary struggle to his feet, clearly favoring one leg. Slowly bending down, he retrieved his helmet, and it was only when he strapped it on that Porcinus recognized the Quartus Hastatus Posterior, the Centurion commanding the last Century of the Fourth Cohort, a man named Vibius Metellus. Helmet on, he stood there for a moment, saying nothing, just looking down at the rest of the wounded, but even from a distance Porcinus could see the look of disdain on his face. He saw Metellus open his mouth.

"All right you lazy *cunni*! You've been lolling about whining about your scratches long enough! It's time to earn your pay, so on your feet, you bastards!"

And to Porcinus' amazement, men stirred, forcing themselves to stand more or less upright. Some of them still had their shields, which had actually been used as their makeshift stretcher in most case, but Porcinus also saw that, good Roman Legionaries that they were, they had all kept their weapons with them. His vision suddenly became cloudy, and he found his throat tightening at the sight before him, as these battered, already wounded men gathered themselves in makeshift Centuries, sorting themselves out, as they hobbled to get into some semblance of a formation. There were at least one more Centurion and perhaps a half-dozen Optios that Porcinus could see, and they took the responsibility for organizing the men. Despite the fact that Metellus technically outranked

Porcinus, he hobbled up to the younger man with obvious pain and difficulty and rendered a salute.

"What are your orders, Centurion?"

That was almost too much for Gaius to bear, but he managed to keep his composure and said in a husky voice, "I think right now you should just stand ready at the edge of the forum and wait for developments. Do you agree Hastatus Posterior Metellus?"

Even if Metellus seemed to be ceding the command to Porcinus, not only did the younger Centurion have his own Century that he was desperate to join, respect for hierarchy was so ingrained in all Legionaries that it was extremely difficult for Porcinus to even entertain being in charge, when a more senior man was present.

Metellus, lips tightened against the pain, managed to say through clenched teeth, "I agree that's the best. I'll shake out what we have in a line there," he pointed to one spot, then another to show Porcinus, "but we don't have enough men for a reserve. And Porcinus," he finished grimly, "I don't know how much fight these men have. Or me, for that matter."

"Well, hopefully we won't need you," Porcinus replied, trying to keep his tone level, as if they were discussing the weather. Before he turned to go to his Century, Metellus suddenly thrust out his hand, which, despite his surprise, Porcinus immediately took, grasping the other man's forearm in the Roman manner.

"May Fortuna bless you," Metellus with a raspy chuckle added, "And the rest of us."

"And you," was all Porcinus could think to say, then he was moving at a trot in the direction of the main gate, scanning the Centuries now lining the wall of the camp, looking for his men.

Even as he spotted the familiar sight of his *signifer*, a man almost as tall as Porcinus and one of the Parthians recruited a few years before, Porcinus heard a chorus of shouts.

"Here they come!"

Following immediately on the heels of the warning cry, as Porcinus strode up the ramp to join his men, he heard one of them utter words so familiar and comforting.

"Jupiter Optimus Maximus, protect this Legion, soldiers all!"

It was the Legionary's prayer, and as Porcinus took his spot on the rampart, hard against the palisade stakes, he immediately saw that those prayers would be desperately needed and even then, they might not be enough.

Titus Pullus had long since lost track of time. If Caesar himself had demanded it, he couldn't have given him even a rough estimate of how long the fighting had been going on. His best guess was that it had been more than a full watch since the first fusillade of arrows had sailed over the palisade, and that the battle for the rampart had been going on for two parts of that. But he also knew that it could be longer, or shorter. Only one thing he was sure of: over the entire span of his prodigious career, through almost a hundred battles and thousands of skirmishes, he had never been as fatigued as he was at that moment. It was almost impossible for him to concentrate, and it was only through his willpower, as formidable as his physical prowess, that he was able to do so at all.

Drawing closer to the battle, Pullus felt a surge of energy, welcoming it, as he selected the spot where his men seemed to need the most help, and he managed to build up enough speed to slam into the knot of men trying to kill each other with great force. Because of his fatigue, however, his aim was off and not only did he send the Wa he had aimed for reeling backward, but he also sent one of his own men, one of the Pandyans and a relatively new *tiro*, crashing directly into the man to his left. More exactly, the *tiro* fell onto the naked blade of his comrade, and while the force wasn't sufficient to drive the blade deeply into his body, it nevertheless broke through the links of his mail and penetrated about an inch. With a sharp cry of pain, the *tiro* staggered backward even further, and, because the other man hadn't been expecting what happened, he was jerked off balance, as well. The sudden absence of two men in the front of the press of fighting immediately pitted three Wa against Pullus, although the enemy he had slammed into was still staggering backward. Blades slashed from two different angles at Pullus, one of them gashing a deep trench down his sword arm, eliciting a hiss of pain from the Primus Pilus, although he managed to block the other with his shield. Fortunately the cut wasn't deep, but it felt like a trench of liquid fire had been laid in a line down his forearm. Still, he was able to wield the Gallic blade with deadly effect, as, ignoring the pain, he took advantage of a slight overextension of the Wa who had inflicted the wound. With what looked like nothing more than a flick of his wrist—but as any of his men who had faced him on the training ground could testify, contained a huge amount of power—

he chopped down with his blade into the middle of the Wa's sword forearm, severing the man's arm, as if he were slicing through a loaf of bread. Blood spurted from the stump, as the Wa stood, paralyzed, staring down in shock at his now-missing hand, lying in the dirt, the grimy fingers still clutched tightly around the hilt.

Although it would have seemed the logical thing to do to finish this Wa off, Pullus completely ignored him, knowing that he was out of action and counting on the man either bleeding to death or being finished off by another of the Romans. Instead he focused on the Wa he had barged into, who had just recovered his balance and was bringing his sword up to bear, preparing for a lunge at the big Roman. Pullus' gaze never wavered from this man as, briefly pulling his sword arm back almost a foot behind him, he launched a low, hard thrust clearly meant to disembowel. However, at the same time, despite not moving his head, he uncoiled his left arm straight out from the shoulder with the same amount of force, punching his shield's boss flush into the face of the third Wa who had raised his blade high over his head to unleash a killing blow designed to cut Pullus in half lengthwise. Because of his posture, it was impossible even for someone with the reflexes the Wa possessed to bring his arms down to at least partially block the blow, and Pullus felt a satisfying jolt travel up his arm. Accompanying the feeling was a wet, crunching sound, as the Wa's nose and cheeks were crushed. Pullus had only intended the blow to stop the Wa momentarily, but because the warrior was stepping into his own planned strike, the force of the metal boss slamming into his face was doubled. With the cartilage of his nose shoved violently backward into his brain, the Wa dropped immediately, dead before he hit the ground, although the body continued to spasm and jerk for several moments, the man's eyes staring dully up out of a face now gruesomely concave.

Meanwhile, Pullus' sword thrust was met by a sweeping parry aimed downward and out from the Wa's body, the Roman's blade sliding up the Wa's and ending by punching air to the Wa's right. Since this was taking place in the space of time between normal heartbeats, Pullus hadn't recovered his shield back to its first position, and had the Wa been armed with a shield of his own and had used it in the same manner, Pullus could have been in serious trouble. But since he had no shield, the Wa lashed out instead with that fist, in a blindingly fast punch aimed not at Pullus' face, who was anticipating the blow and was reflexively jerking his head, but for his arm, directly onto the wound he had received moments before. Lightning flashes of pain shot up Pullus' arm and for a brief, horrified instant he thought he would pass out, as his vision was shot through with what he could swear were the sparks from a disturbed fire. But while he managed to avoid that, not even he was able to keep his grasp on his blade, even with the grip that had served him so well, and the sword fell to the earth. Now he stood with only his shield, but even as formidably skilled as Pullus was with the use of the shield, he knew he was at a severe disadvantage. Risking a quick glance, he saw that every one of his men near enough to come to his aid was furiously busy with his own private battles At this point, the prudent course for Pullus was to wage a defensive fight, hoping to wear the Wa down and wait for either an opportunity to retrieve his sword—despite the ferocious pain coursing up his arm—or for one of his men to vanquish the Wa he was currently engaged with and come to his aid. But Pullus did neither.

Instead, with his shield squarely in front of him, he went charging at the Wa, who was clearly caught by surprise by the brazenness of the attack. Nonetheless, he still managed to bring his sword to bear, the point of his blade sticking directly out from his body in an attempt to keep Pullus at bay. Pullus acted as if the blade weren't there, moving his bulk behind the shield directly onto the blade, and the point pierced the wood of the shield just to the left of the boss. However, Pullus didn't stop, and, in fact, continued to push forward with all of his strength, closing the distance between himself and the smaller Wa. In doing so, the point of the sword poked more deeply through the shield, so it was inevitable that if Pullus closed the distance any further, the point would pierce his left arm, which is exactly what he did. Now the Wa was shoved back against the palisade, with no more room to retreat, and between that and the sight of this giant barbarian—covered in blood and seemingly impervious to the fact that, as he closed the last few inches, the blade of the Wa's sword was burying itself more deeply into the arm behind the shield—his eyes widened in shock and fear. Now that Pullus was within reach, with a speed that surprised the Wa, the Roman's right arm shot out, his fingers hooked in a claw as he grabbed the Wa around the throat. If the Wa had released his grip on his sword to use both hands, he might have been able to pry the giant monster's hands off his windpipe, but the simple truth was that he panicked. Consequently, he was left grabbing wildly at the Roman's wrist, trying to pry the hand choking the life from him away from his windpipe, as his lungs quickly began screaming for air. When that didn't work, he began as he had started, beating unmercifully at the wound on Pullus' arm. This time, despite the sparks flying before his eyes, Pullus ignored the horrific pain, teeth clenched, lips pulled back in a half-grin, half-grimace that was feral, grunting in time to the hammer blows of the Wa that fell on his arm over and over. Then Pullus felt, more than heard, the crunching and popping of the Wa's trachea finally collapsing under the enormous pressure, as the Wa's eyes bulged out in vain appeal, the normally golden-yellow skin now a purplish hue that under other circumstances would have reminded Pullus of a plum. Knowing that his enemy was now dead, Pullus released him to fall limply backward. Somehow still aware of what was happening, Pullus saw that this latest threat was all but contained; there were two Wa standing back to back, surrounded by Legionaries in the same way a pack of wolves surrounds the weakest animals of a herd. Carefully squatting, knowing that bending down from the waist would make him keel over, he retrieved his sword, wincing at the effort it took to grasp the hilt. Staggering a few steps away to what was effectively the rear, it was only when Pullus tried to let go of his shield and it didn't drop to the ground that he became aware that the Wa's sword was still protruding from it and that the blade had pinned the shield to his left arm. Calling to one of his men, he had the man grasp the hilt of the sword.

Gritting his teeth, Pullus told the man, "Pull it out, quickly, but do it in a straight line, so you don't do any more damage. Understand?"

The Legionary—one of the Gayans who were in effect the newest recruits, like all of his compatriots, was deathly afraid of the giant Primus Pilus, and, if the truth were known, he would have preferred to be in the front line at that moment. Still, he gave a hard gulp, then nodded his head in answer, something that Pullus would normally have rebuked him for, but said nothing.

"Ready?" Pullus hissed. "Go."

Surprising them both, the Gayan did exactly as he had been told, pulling the blade out in one smooth motion, moving in a straight line backward. A gout of blood spurted from the wound, but Pullus saw immediately that it was darker in color and not pulsing with every beat of his heart, meaning that he hadn't severed a major vessel. Letting it bleed for a moment to flush the wound out, he then bound his neckerchief around the wound. Unknown to him at that moment, he and Scribonius were virtual twins, both suffering wounds of roughly the same severity and at the same location. As he tied the last knot, with the help of the Gayan, there was another series of shouts that alerted him of another breach, so he turned to head that way, but took only one halting step before he recognized that if he didn't rest, he would indeed pass out. Despite the desperate need, Titus Pullus was, after all, a mortal man, and all men have limits. Titus Pullus had reached his. That was how the Wa finally effectively breached the western wall of the northern camp.

Julius Caesar barely had time to register the blur of motion that suddenly streaked in from behind him, as one of his men threw his body directly into the path of the charging Wa, who just then was beginning the downswing of his raised sword. The Legionary instinctively threw his arm up, but there was no shield attached, it having been shattered moments earlier; the force of the Wa's blow was so massive that the sharp blade sliced through the Legionary's forearm as if it weren't even there, continuing down onto and through the man's helmet. Although Caesar hadn't yet completely comprehended what one of his men was doing for him and the army, he did feel the warm, sticky spray of blood and brain matter, as the Wa's sword sliced through the iron helmet and the hard bone of the skull. Its momentum was finally stopped by the lower jawbone of the stricken Legionary, who remained standing for a moment, his body suddenly jerking spasmodically, as his body tried to receive signals that were no longer being sent. Without any thought, Caesar reacted to the sight by thrusting his sword into the chest of the Wa, who was still trying to wrench his sword from the Legionary's skull, and he collapsed at Caesar's feet. Only then did Caesar fully focus on the sight to his right, his eye caught by the point of the blade and a clear foot of the sword protruding from the back of the Legionary's skull.

Before he could react, however, the man collapsed straight down into a heap, his ruined face looking curiously intact, except for the bloody, straight line separating one half of his face from the other. It was extremely unsettling, even for a man like Caesar, who had seen so much violent death and destruction to apprehend what was in effect one half of a face, the eye gazing up at him with that surprised expression so many of the dead have, but the other half literally facing in the other direction. This sight rooted Caesar to the ground, until a Centurion, the Quintus Pilus Posterior of the 15th Legion, Quintus Barbatos, nudged Caesar gently. Quickly snapping back to reality, Caesar took in the situation and saw that the outbreak had been contained: the men who had followed him and still survived mopping up the handful of Wa who were now completely surrounded. Studying his general's face, albeit when he thought Caesar wasn't looking, Barbatos was distinctly unsettled by what he saw etched in the older man's face. Not only did he look tired, he looked...Barbatos thought, but couldn't come up with a word that fit, but whatever that look was, it didn't inspire confidence. Apparently sensing eyes on him, Caesar turned from his examination of the situation before him, as the last of the Wa was cut down.

Giving the Centurion a tired smile, Caesar said, "Hot work, eh, Barbatos?"

"That it is, Caesar," Barbatos agreed, feeling slightly better with his general's ice-blue eyes now looking directly into his and experiencing the same queer but pleasant sensation every person who was favored with that look of Caesar's felt.

It was as if he could see into your soul and see your darkest secrets, but accepted them with a slightly mocking, slightly humorous tilt of the head and an upturned lip that was just the hint of a smile. Barbatos saw, if not that identical expression, one close enough that he chided himself for letting his imagination run away with him. Caesar, scared? Rattled? Not likely, the Pilus Posterior silently scoffed, feeling sure that his thoughts would be read by his general.

However, Caesar only said, "This appears to be contained now, Barbatos. But I see you're running thin. I'll have Glaxus and his Century come to relieve you," naming the Hastatus Prior of the Seventh Century.

"Caesar," Barbatos replied, the worry coming back now, "the Seventh is who we relieved. They're cut up worse than we are."

This was when Barbatos realized it hadn't been his imagination, because the expression he thought he had seen earlier now came flooding back over Caesar's features, and now that he was facing his general, Barbatos recognized what he was seeing: Caesar was in doubt, and, in fact, was having a hard time deciding on the best course of action. Everything he had tried, every trick he had learned in the four decades of war that he had waged for Rome still couldn't seem to stem the tide of these Wa. And, he reminded himself, this isn't even the camp where the main assault is focused. His reserve Cohorts had already been committed; he was completely out of artillery ammunition; even as he and Barbatos stood where they had stopped this incursion, he could hear the shouts and screams that his ears told him signaled another breach of the wall. But most troubling of all was that his men had lost heart, that they had turned and run. Well, he thought grimly, I better make them understand there's nowhere to run to. And with that, he dismissed Barbatos with a curt command to continue holding his position, calling for one of the Tribunes, as he strode in the direction of the forum.

Catching up with him, the Tribune at his side first, the Parthian Bodroges, asked for orders.

"I want you to take every slave, every *medicus*, and any other man you can find and go to the forum and create a breastworks. Use the wagons, use the livestock, use anything that's solid to make a wall. This will be our final position. Do you understand?"

Even a Tribune who wasn't a Roman by birth didn't need to be told the import of this order, on every level, and it was only through a supreme will that his hand was steady as he saluted his general, and his voice was clear and strong, as he replied, "Yes Caesar. I will see to it."

"As soon as it's ready, let me know immediately," Caesar said, but turned his attention away and back to the fighting, before the Tribune could say another word.

Pivoting about, the Parthian dashed deeper into the camp, grabbing every noncombatant that he came across, as he did. Meanwhile, Caesar moved in the direction of the hardest fighting, and, like Titus Pullus, he could never remember feeling this tired. More disturbingly, the idea that this was the day that Caesar was defeated had taken root in what to that point had been rocky soil, the tendrils of doubt and despair starting to burrow their way into his psyche. For Caesar, it was the most disturbing and potentially paralyzing emotion he had ever experienced. Even so, he continued moving toward the far corner of the camp, where the Wa had managed to tear down the rampart and were now pouring through the gap at the corner, where one side of the earthen wall met another. If this is the day I am defeated, Caesar thought, naked sword in hand, then I will give these barbarian scum something to tell their grandchildren about. Without breaking stride, he scooped up a new shield, and hurried to the new breach.

"Balbus is down!"

Even from where Titus Pullus was sitting, on a macabre makeshift couch composed of the dead, he heard that cry above what had become a dull roar of fighting. As if he had been dashed with a bucket of cold water, he let out an audible gasp as he came to his feet, his overwhelming fatigue momentarily forgotten. Looking over to where the Second Century of his Cohort was fighting, Pullus couldn't immediately make any sense of what he was seeing in the mass of moving bodies. The Wa had again managed to create a presence on the rampart, this one numbering perhaps a dozen men, and what Pullus could see was that the line of Romans holding them back was only two deep. Seeing this and understanding what it meant, Pullus whirled to call up the Century that had now gone through three rotations with the Second Century, the Fourth. His initial reaction was anger, thinking that the Princeps Posterior had taken his men back into the camp for some reason, because all that was standing there was perhaps two tent section's worth of men, the Centurion among them. That anger dissolved into a twisting knot in his stomach, as he recognized the sight before him for what it was: the Fourth Century hadn't gone anywhere. This *was* the Fourth Century, fewer than twenty men. Returning his attention to the fighting, he saw that some of the men in the second line had managed to grab Balbus and drag him out of the fighting, where he was lying just a couple of paces behind the line. Pullus, fighting the fatigue, forced himself to trot over to Balbus, arriving at the same time as one of the overworked *medici*, who knelt beside the Centurion, feeling Pullus' friend's neck for any sign of life. Just as he reached Balbus, he saw Balbus' head move slightly, and a wave of relief washed through him at the sight, but when he knelt down, the feeling was short-lived. Balbus' eyes were open, and they met those of Pullus, as his friend came into view for him, and when he smiled, it was a gruesome sight, the blood bubbling and frothing at his lips, filling his mouth and dribbling down his cheek. Pullus had seen this too many times not to know that Balbus' lungs had been punctured and that his friend was beyond hope. Nevertheless, seemingly oblivious to the fact that less than a dozen paces away that ferocious fighting was still going on, Pullus reached down to clasp the free hand of Balbus, whose other one clutched vainly at the hole in his chest, where blood was oozing through his fingers in slow, rhythmic pulses, this fluid also alive with tiny, frothy bubbles.

"What have you gone and done?" Pullus asked, his voice choked and hoarse.

"I moved the wrong way," Balbus wheezed, prompting a weak chuckle from his friend. "I thought the bastard was going for a low thrust, but he caught me good and proper. I'm sorry Titus," Balbus' voice was rapidly weakening. "I let........."

"Shut your mouth," Pullus interrupted, not wanting to hear any more. "If you don't, you're on report!"

"It's been a long time since I've been in trouble," the last words were nothing but a whisper. "Titus, tell Scribonius........" but before he could finish, he took a huge, spasmodic breath, holding it for a second as his eyes widened, then with the rattle in his throat that Pullus knew all too well, Quintus Balbus died. For a moment, Pullus remained motionless, feeling his friend's hand growing cold almost instantly.

Then, he laid the hand gently on the chest and told the medicus, "Get a stretcher bearer to take the Pilus Posterior away, out of here."

The *medicus* for the briefest of moments opened his mouth to argue, intending to tell the Primus Pilus that the stretcher bearers were so overworked as it was that they barely were getting wounded men to the forum to be treated and couldn't waste time on a dead man. Then, he saw the giant Roman's face, and this man, a Parthian, quickly closed his mouth and hurried off to obey. Meanwhile, Pullus stood up and, like Caesar, took in the scene around him. As he was doing so, a huge roar from behind him and to his left suddenly erupted, causing anyone not actually fighting to cast an apprehensive glance over his own shoulder. The surprise Wa force had clearly hit the wall around the main gate. Now everything was in the hands of the gods.

The decision Aulus Flaminius made was one born of equal parts pragmatism and bravado, but it was the luckiest decision he would ever make. With the situation well in hand, with only his frontline Cohorts needed to hold the camp, Flaminius had sent a runner to his colleague in command of the other Legion occupying the camp, the 14th. The 14th's history under Caesar was spotty, to put it mildly, although despite a rough start when, because of the incompetence of the Legate commanding them in Gaul, Aulus Sabinus, they had been wiped out to a man, their performance in this current campaign now lasting a decade had partially redeemed their reputation. Nevertheless, Caesar had never fully invested this Legion with his trust again, hence their position in this camp, the one that Caesar had deemed to be the least likely to bear the brunt of the assault. The Primus Pilus of the 14th, Gnaeus Figulus, had answered Flaminius' query with the answer Flaminius had hoped for, that like his own Legion, they were under no duress. More importantly, Figulus had assured him that he essentially had committed only half his Legion to the fight. From that information and his belief not only in his men but that Caesar, or more likely Pullus, could use every spare man, Aulus Flaminius risked his career by not bothering to consult with the Legate left in charge of this camp, Caesar's quartermaster, the old muleteer Ventidius.

"Go get Pilus Prior Felix," he ordered, naming the commander of the Fifth Cohort, whose men were standing idly a short distance away from the rampart. The runner departed, as Flaminius sent another runner to request the presence of Figulus, as well. What he was about to do was a huge risk, he knew, but deep down in his old soldier's bones, he was sure that he was doing the right thing. Once both men arrived, Flaminius wasted no time.

"Since we have the situation in hand, I think we should send our reserves, including the second line Cohorts, to Caesar's camp. I'm sure he could use some help."

The relative silence for the next few moments was profound, but whether it was because they were thinking about what needed to be done to make this happen, or because they thought him mad, Flaminius didn't know.

Finally, Figulus cleared his throat, then asked, "Did you talk to Ventidius about this?"

"Yes," Flaminius said the word even before he could think about it, and he would never be able to put his finger on exactly why he did so. "He thinks it's a good idea. That's why I called you."

For the briefest moment Figulus looked disposed to argue, or even worse, go ask Ventidius himself; but for reasons that, like Flaminius, Figulus would never be able to explain, he shrugged instead.

"Who'll be in command of the detachment?"

"Felix," Flaminius answered firmly, his tone brooking no argument. Again, Figulus opened his mouth, then shut it.

For this was yet another factor in Flaminius' decision. Felix was the best Centurion in the 30th, with the possible exception of Flaminius himself, but a combination of circumstances had seen his best fighting man in charge of the Fifth Cohort only, and not in one of the frontline formations. Still, even if he had his choice of Centurions to lead what he had in mind, Flaminius would still have chosen Felix. The next few moments saw Flaminius doing most of the talking, interrupted by a question or two from the other two men; then, once finished, both Centurions returned to their respective units to make preparations.

"On your feet you lazy bastards," was how Felix put it, bawling out the order, while simultaneously kicking one of the Pandyan Legionaries who was looking a little too comfortable resting on the ground. "We've got orders, and we have to move. Fast."

As he was getting his own Cohort ready, Flaminius had sent runners to the Pili Priori of the other Cohorts that would be marching, while Figulus was essentially doing the same. Crack Legions or not, nobody could have faulted how rapidly the 12 Cohorts of Legionaries were assembled and ready to march out of the gate. Flaminius was waiting there, and, despite his strong feeling that he was doing the right thing by taking matters into his own hands, he was nevertheless extremely nervous, especially since he had been forced to lure Ventidius to the farthest corner of the camp, where a phantom incursion was taking place. When the Legate returned and saw that more than half of the army assigned to him was missing, he would be understandably furious. In fact, Flaminius didn't think it was out of the realm of possibility that the Legate would have him taken into custody on the spot. Therefore, it put Flaminius in the perverse position of actually hoping that matters were as desperate as his instinct told him, otherwise he knew that there would be no way to repair the damage done to his career. Even with all these thoughts piling on top of one another in his mind, like all of Caesar's Centurions, particularly the Pili Primi, outwardly he was extremely calm and matter-of-fact.

"March fast, Felix, but I think you should have at least a Century out in front by a stadium at least."

Felix's face, set much like that of his Primus Pilus, showed surprise.

"You don't think these *cunni* have gotten all the way up to the road do you?"

Flaminius could only shrug, but his tone was firm and confident, as he replied, "Probably not, but I'm already putting my neck on the block as it is. I don't want to compound whatever trouble I've gotten myself into by letting you stumble into an ambush."

"I won't let you down, Primus Pilus," Felix said quietly.

"I know you won't, but if I'm right, Caesar's going to need every one of you."

Gaius Porcinus and his Century were at that very moment hurling the second and last of their javelins into the mass of Wa who had reached just the other side of the ditch. Every one of them was roaring in his own tongue, and while not one of the men on that rampart understood the words, they needed no translation of intent. Unlike the other assaults, the commander of this contingent of Wa had decided that speed would be an even better weapon than a barrage of arrow fire. And while the rear ranks, composed of archers, were firing, the intensity of the firing was nowhere near the ferocity of the barrage on the western wall. While this meant that fewer men would fall from arrows, the other benefit was that the Roman's shields were still intact when the first of the Wa came scrambling up the ladders. Since Caesar had ordered that only the ditch facing the most likely avenue of attack be sown with the lilies, the only obstacles were the sharpened stakes embedded in the wall of the ditch directly underneath the rampart and palisade. And while these stakes did their job and claimed a few Wa who were either too zealous or unlucky, the numbers were akin to catching a handful of water out of a waterfall. Porcinus was in his spot at the right of his Century, roughly in the middle between the main gate and the western corner of the camp. Although the initial assault of this enemy force was focused around the main gate, it was only a matter of moments before, again like a flood of water, the Wa in the middle ranks came boiling up the ditch. Porcinus, in the instant before the screaming warriors began throwing their ladders up against the rampart, was struck by how much this was like a raging flood brought on by a sudden storm, except instead of water this torrent was composed of flesh, blood, and iron. Then the top of a ladder suddenly came into view directly to his left, in front of his men of the first tent section of his Century. Because this was the last Cohort, the Tenth, there was a higher concentration of non-Romans. The man to Gaius' left was a Pandyan named Supor, but who had earned the nickname "Olympus," because in the winter games held every year, he had been crowned the Legion champion, and had been narrowly defeated for the title of best discus thrower in the army. But he was also a good fighter, and this was the quality that Porcinus and the rest of his comrades valued now, especially since none of the men of the relief force had siege spears. This was going to be decided one way or the other by Roman swords and shields. Since Olympus was holding his own shield and had his sword in his other hand, it was up to Porcinus to try to push the ladder away. Unfortunately, while Gaius was no weakling, it took the strength of a Titus Pullus to singlehandedly thrust a ladder—now holding two or three Wa who were scrambling upward as quickly as they could—away from the rampart. Knowing this, Porcinus didn't even try, deciding in that instant to add his own sword to stop the first barbarians up the ladder. He and Olympus struck simultaneously, so that the first Wa faced a choice that sealed his fate either way. As he dodged Olympus' blade, he consequently moved right into the path of Porcinus' savage downward thrust, the tip of his blade punching right into the soft space between clavicle and shoulder blade, sending the Wa toppling backward, striking the man immediately behind him, and starting a chain reaction of falling bodies that swept the first few Wa off the ladder.

"We couldn't have done better, if we had planned it," Porcinus shouted more loudly than he needed to than if he was just talking to Olympus, but like any good leader, he knew his men needed every small victory that came their way. "If that's not a sign that the gods haven't forsaken us, I don't know what is!"

This elicited a round of cheers, but Porcinus knew, watching the men below untangling themselves, it would be short-lived. While he watched, the first men were replaced by more Wa, their yellowish faces turned up as they clambered up the rungs, eyes almost invisible and lips thinned in a snarling mien of fear, hate, and bloodlust. Within a matter of a few heartbeats, Olympus and Porcinus attempted to repeat the tactic that had worked so well, but the next Wa was either more experienced or had observed what happened to his comrade and come up with countermove of his own. Instead of trying to twist backward to avoid one of the Roman's thrusts, this Wa did the opposite, suddenly throwing his body hard up against the ladder, while the Roman blades bit into nothing but the empty air behind him. Because of his angle to the ladder, Porcinus could see the Wa, but in order to reach him with a sword thrust, he would have to lean out over the parapet, and he had seen more than enough times what happened to men who did that. To Olympus, however, it was as if the Wa disappeared from sight, and thinking that the barbarian had somehow fallen off the ladder, he made the very mistake that Gaius knew to avoid. Counting on his own quickness, the Pandyan decided to risk a peek by moving his shield a fraction, so that he could quickly lean over to make sure that the yellow bastard had indeed been dispatched.

"Olympus, no! Don't....." Gaius shouted, but it was too late.

The Wa gave a simple upward thrust that was so quick that Gaius' brain barely registered the silvery flash, and Olympus never saw what killed him, as the point of the Wa's blade pierced the spot where the throat and chin intersect, killing the Pandyan instantly. Losing Olympus so early was bad enough, but then somehow the Wa managed to let go of the ladder with his free hand to reach up and grab the slumping Legionary by the front of his harness and, using the blade still buried in his head for added leverage, jerked the dead man up and out over the rampart. Porcinus could only watch in horror as Olympus' body fell over the side, the momentum of the Wa's tug enough to avoid hitting his comrades further down the ladder. For a moment, just the briefest of moments, there was a pause, as the Wa grabbed the ladder again with his free hand, and Porcinus thought that the man immediately behind Olympus would have the time to step into the now vacated spot. But that was a vain hope: the Legionary who had been bracing the Pandyan was a Gayan, one of the newest batch of *tiros*, and while he was now a veteran by virtue of all of the fighting this campaign had seen, he was still relatively inexperienced, the sudden death and disappearance of Olympus unnerving him so much that he froze. It was only for a matter of perhaps two or three heartbeats, but in moments like this, that is an eternity. However long a time it was, it was sufficient for the Wa who created the first crisis of this portion of the battle. With an explosive thrust of his legs, this warrior cleared the palisade, and before his feet touched the earthen rampart, he delivered a devastating, slicing blow aimed at Gaius Porcinus, who had just begun moving to fill the gap left by Olympus. The blade of the Wa's sword struck Gaius on his helmet, just above the ear, making a ringing sound not unlike a gong being struck, dropping the young Centurion, who was unconscious before he hit the ground.

Titus Pullus was still reeling from the loss of his second closest friend, a man whom Titus privately considered to be his match, if not in skill, certainly in experience and in that undefinable virtue of ferocity and refusal to accept defeat. However, matters had become so precarious, the line of Legionaries holding back the Wa from flooding into the camp so thin, that he had to force himself to put his grief away, despite the difficulty. Surveying the situation, what he saw was incredibly disheartening. No matter how the day ended, the 10th Legion was finished as a fighting force. From his quick survey, Pullus' estimate was that of the men still standing, perhaps one in ten was still unwounded. The rest of the men had all suffered wounds, mostly to the extremities, although Pullus could see men with hasty bandages wrapped around their heads, with some even continuing to fight, despite parts of their faces being covered, where a Wa sword or spear had inflicted a wound. Pullus hadn't received an update from Balbinus and the 12th for a period of time that was impossible for him to calculate but if he stepped up to within a few paces of the base of the rampart, with his front line now located on the first piece of level ground, he could look down the length of the camp at what he knew to be the remnants of the Seventh Cohort of the 12th and see that the situation was much the same as with the 10th. Despite how well the men were fighting, Pullus understood that this was the moment when the Wa's overwhelming advantage in numbers would tell. His men were fighting like the heroes of Troy, and even if he died this day—a possibility that was growing in likelihood with each passing moment—this would still rank as the greatest fight the 10th had ever put up. It was just a shame that the Republic for which these men fought so bravely would never hear of what took place today, Pullus thought sadly. Even as this thought ran through his mind, he was in motion, heading towards a spot near where the 10th and 12th met, where he could see that a bulging pocket had formed, where a group of Wa had pushed the Legionaries in that area almost all the way across the cleared area next to the rampart, so that the backs of the men in support were almost up against the first row of tents. Pullus began moving toward this spot, but when he turned to call to whatever men he could muster to come with him, fewer than two dozen men were able to answer his call. That was the moment Pullus knew what he must do, and it was with a leaden ball of shame and sadness that he grabbed one of the Legionaries by the arm, the Centurion of his Fourth Century, as it turned out.

"I don't have any more tablets, or if I do, all the slaves carrying them are dead," he shouted above the growing sounds of the fighting, as the Wa began to sense that victory was near and shouted encouragement to their comrades. "So you have to remember this order to take to the courier."

"What courier?" the Centurion asked. "They're either dead or trapped here in the camp, now that those bastards have hit the main gate."

"I know that," Pullus snapped, the strain of the moment wearing on him. "But we have to get word to Caesar somehow, so I want you to go find out if Artaxades is still alive. If he's not, then you'll have to do it. But I think he's probably still alive, because he's in the last section of his Century in the Eighth, and he's our best chance. Our only chance," Pullus amended.

Normally, a Primus Pilus wouldn't concern himself with the health or whereabouts of a lowly Gregarius in one of the junior Cohorts, but this man, a Parthian, bore the distinction of being crowned the fastest runner of the longer distances in the army.

Pullus was counting on this now, as he continued, "If he's alive, tell him to carry this message to Caesar. The camp is about to fall, and I'm ordering a fighting withdrawal to the forum, then an *orbis*. I doubt that we'll survive two parts of a watch, but if we do, we have a chance that Caesar can send reinforcements to hit the Wa from behind."

"That's not much of a chance."

"I know," Pullus admitted. "But it's the only one we have. So, tell Artaxades to strip down. No armor, no helmet, nothing that can slow him down, not even a sword or dagger. Send him out the eastern gate; have him head down the slope about halfway before he turns south. Whoever their general is, he's a clever bastard, but hopefully he didn't think to put some men farther down the ridge to stop the kind of thing we're doing."

As was normal, the Centurion repeated everything back, except for the last thing Pullus said, knowing it wasn't necessary. With a curt nod, Pullus dismissed the Centurion, who immediately turned to carry out his orders. Before he took more than two steps, Pullus called to him.

"Tell Artaxades that he needs to run faster than he ever has in his life before. The 10th depends on him."

That piece of business done, Pullus continued toward the pocket, happy to see that as tired as the men accompanying him were, they hadn't hesitated and had already run to bolster their comrades. All unit cohesion was gone by this point; Centuries had become irretrievably enmeshed with each other, so it was rare that men from the same section were fighting side by side. This, however, was where the grueling and harsh training of the Legions showed, as men who had never stood in the line together still knew exactly what was expected of them. Just before Pullus took his place at their head, he called the nearest *cornicen* to him.

"Sound the signal for fighting withdrawal," he told the man, "we're falling back to the forum."

The moment Pullus was finished, the first notes of one of the most hated horn commands began sounding, and to Pullus it was clear that it was an order the men were expecting, because none of them turned to look in disbelief or anger at the idea of giving ground. Those men still fighting understood this was the correct, indeed the only decision at that moment. I think I left it too late, Pullus thought as he waded into the fighting, his already bloodied sword held in first position. He had done all he could do as a commander for the moment. Now it was time to fight.

Centurion Felix was at the head of the column sent by Flaminius, pushing the men under his command relentlessly north, towards Caesar's camp. Every few moments, the undulations of the ridgetop road afforded Felix and his men a view of the commander's position, but they were still too far away to make out particulars. They could see the cloud of dust hanging just above the ramparts, a sign of many, many feet shuffling about. What he was unable to determine was whether the fighting was still along the walls, or if the camp had been penetrated. With that acting as a spur, he unconsciously picked up the pace of his trot, becoming aware of the increased pace only a few moments later, when the sound of his gasping became so loud he couldn't block it out. Only then did he relent a bit, the sound of the rest of his men's gasping and retching soon overwhelming the sound of his own breath in his ears. Still, although he slowed, he didn't stop yet, but he recognized that he would have to do so, soon. Otherwise, he and his men would be too winded and fatigued to do anything more than vomit on those barbarians. Just a bit farther, he thought, then we'll stop, seeing ahead of him a slight slope leading to a dip in the road that would shield him and his men from view and allow them to catch their breath.

Felix tried to remember the route from the times he had traveled back and forth during the hectic time the positions were being prepared. There would be a slope of perhaps three or four stadia, then the road would be relatively level for the rest of the little more than a mile to Caesar's camp. Once they reached the top of the slope, then he would be close enough to get a good idea of what was taking place at Caesar's camp and whether or not he would be pressing on to Pullus' position.

Artaxades' breathing was harsh, but even as he picked his way as carefully as the blistering pace he was setting would allow, he still carefully lifted his feet higher than normal to avoid tripping over a rock or root. He had left the eastern gate as directed, wearing nothing but a tunic and a dagger strapped to his belt, and had headed downhill for a distance, before turning south to run along the face of the slope. The ground was extremely rough and broken, but the Centurion giving him the message to deliver hadn't spared Artaxades any detail, impressing upon him exactly how important this message was, not just to the fate of his friends in the 10th, but to the entire army. Artaxades, despite being a Parthian, had been with the Legion now for seven years, long enough for bonds to form that were as strong as any he felt towards his blood kin. In fact, after the first year, where he had woken homesick every single day, unaccustomed to the harsh strangeness of the Roman military life, he thought of his family, his mother and father, his two brothers and three sisters, with ever-decreasing frequency. The men standing on either side of him, one of them another Parthian named Gaspar, whom Artaxades now regarded as someone closer than a brother, and the man who protected his sword side, a Roman named Numerius who meant almost as much—these men had become his family.

And it was for these men and the rest of the 10th for whom Artaxades ran now, his eyes relentlessly scanning the ground just ahead, looking for a protruding rock, root, or worse, a hole in the ground that would snap his ankle. He wasn't sure how far he had to run before he could turn and climb up the slope to use the road, but after almost tripping headlong yet again, he decided it was time to risk it. Making an arcing right turn so that he didn't break stride, his breathing almost immediately started to become ragged, his lungs screaming in protest at the sudden extra burden caused by the incline. Naturally, without thinking, Artaxades eased his pace to compensate, but then the thought of Gaspar and Numerius, who were at that moment standing in the line and could even be fighting for their lives, burst unbidden into the Parthian's consciousness. Despite the pain, he resumed his previous level of exertion, and within a couple of moments, his breathing was so labored that he couldn't even hear the sound of the hobnails in his *caligae,* when they struck the rocky soil. Nevertheless, his legs kept churning, and he could see the top of the slope barely fifty paces away, so he dropped his head and began pumping his arms furiously to dash up the last part.

Just before the top, a pain in his side became so intense that, despite himself, he slowed and in slowing saved his life and gave the army a chance at survival. That slight decrease in his pace meant that he heard the shouts of men, not anything associated with fighting, but some sort of orders. At least that's what it sounded like to Artaxades, but what he did know was that it wasn't in Latin, but in the tongue of the barbarians. He heard just enough to come to a stop before his head and shoulders crested the slope, keeping him out of sight. Panting, he paused only for a moment, before turning and heading back a short distance down the slope, then turned to continue his run to the south. He wouldn't be able to take advantage of the road, not yet.

Gaius Porcinus' first sensation was a throbbing pain on the side of his head, which only intensified when he opened his eyes to the sunlight streaming down. His helmet had been pulled off by someone, he didn't know who, and without thinking he reached up to touch the spot on his head, wincing in pain as his fingers touched the matted hair, where a deep gash ran just above his ear. It was several inches long, running from just behind his ear to his temple, but gritting his teeth, he forced his fingers to probe gently for any sign of a fracture. Despite the pain, he heaved a sigh of relief as his fingers found no obvious signs that his skull was broken. Suddenly, the sunlight was blocked by a figure looming over him, and Porcinus' eyes struggled to adjust to the sudden change. Blinking, it took a couple moments for him to recognize the face of his Optio, another Parthian named Oesalces, his swarthy features showing the strain of all that was happening.

"Hastatus Posterior Porcinus! Are you all right sir?" Oesalces had to shout to be heard over the noise of the fighting, which had continued unabated while Porcinus was unconscious.

He had been dragged several paces away from the wall, just far enough to be out of danger, but the din was still almost overwhelming, and Porcinus was sure it added to his already pounding headache. In answer to Oesalces, Porcinus sat up and immediately his head began spinning so violently he was overcome with a wave of nausea. Turning his head to the side, he vomited the remains of his breakfast onto the ground next to him. Staring at the mess, Porcinus struggled to focus, but for some reason his mind was occupied with trying to determine how long ago he had ingested what was now on the ground. It was only when Oesalces put a hand on his shoulder and gave it a hard shake that his attention on that subject was broken.

"Centurion! Are you all right? Can you stand?"

Porcinus forced himself to look up at his Optio, trying to gather his thoughts and consider the answer. After what seemed like a long time, Gaius finally nodded his head, wincing as he did.

"I think so. Help me up," he told Oesalces, holding his hand out, grabbing at the outstretched hand of his Optio, who pulled him to his feet.

For a moment, he thought he would topple over, but Oesalces held his arm as his head cleared. Once he regained his equilibrium, Porcinus turned his attention to the immediate situation.

Looking at his Century, he frowned and asked, "Where's Olympus?"

Oesalces was startled by the question, but it told him that the blow to Porcinus' head was worse than he had thought.

"Olympus was killed, sir. You were standing next to him when it happened. Remember?"

Once Oesalces uttered the words, the image of Olympus' body being hurled down into the mass of Wa warriors came flooding back into Porcinus' mind, causing an involuntary shaking that made his head hurt even more.

"Yes, I remember now. Never mind. How long have I been out?"

"Not that long. We've only had a couple more men go down, one wounded, but he'll make it, and one dead."

"He'll make it, if we survive," Porcinus answered grimly.

The mention of the dead Legionary prompted the realization that he needed a helmet, since the one he had been wearing had been buckled by the blow from the Wa sword. Porcinus could see it on the ground just a couple of steps away, where it had been tossed after being removed from his head by....who? It doesn't matter, Porcinus chided himself. All that matters is getting back in the fight and leading the men. Seeing a discarded helmet lying next to the small row of bodies that had already started to form, Porcinus trotted over to it, scooping up his ruined helmet as he did. His own felt liner was, of course, no good, so the dead man's would have to suffice, and Porcinus put that on first, wincing in pain when he settled it over his injury. Quickly affixing the transverse crest to the new helmet, he stifled a groan of pain as he pulled the helmet down onto his head, tying the chin thong as tightly as he dared.

"Where's my sword?" he asked Oesalces, but his Optio answered that he didn't know, so Porcinus picked among several now scattered about, discarding ones that he could see were cracked or just didn't feel good in his hand. Settling on one, he made a few circular motions with the tip of it as a way to loosen up his arm. Then, turning to his Optio, Porcinus gave him a grim smile.

"Well Optio, let's get back in things, shall we?"

Without waiting for an answer, but knowing his Optio would be hot on his heels, Porcinus strode to the back of his Century, calling out to the men, as he shoved his way to the front.

"I'm back boys and feeling refreshed from my nap! Let's say we kill some more of these *cunni*!"

Anything else he shouted was drowned out by the added roar of the men of the Sixth Century, Tenth Cohort, as their Centurion resumed his spot at the front. They were more than ready to keep fighting.

"One...two...one...two!"

The command rang out, bellowed by Barbatos, still standing near Caesar who, despite being in overall command, let his Centurions do their job. Barbatos was calling out the numbered commands that the Legions used when staging a fighting withdrawal: at the command of "one", lash out with the shield, pushing the enemy across from you back a step, but instead of moving forward on the second command, take a step back, shield still up, sword still ready. Still, it was a step back and not forward, and all along a steadily shrinking line, the Romans in Caesar's camp moved slowly back in the direction of the forum, where every available man was working feverishly to create some sort of prepared position. Boxes, barrels, sacks of rice, anything and everything that possessed any kind of solidity and weight was dragged or carried to form a rough, circular shape slightly larger than the forum. The tents that were in the way were yanked down and dragged elsewhere, while the guy ropes holding up the large *praetorium* tent were cut and the poles removed, but only after the desks and other pieces of solid furniture were carried away to be added to the makeshift barricade. Anything and everything that could possibly be used for protection was salvaged from the entire part of the camp to the east side of the forum, still untouched by fighting.

Meanwhile, Caesar was moving rapidly about, just behind the line of fighting men, exhorting his boys to keep their discipline, listen to the count of their Centurions, and lending his sword where needed. While it wasn't the first time he had done such things, never before had Caesar put on such a virtuoso performance; not at Munda, not at Ecbatana, not even in the bitter fighting against the Pandyans on the beaches of that kingdom. It seemed he was literally everywhere, showing up in one spot to give the final sword thrust that stopped a Wa from striking down one of his men and creating a gap in the slowly retreating line. Then he would be at another point, holding onto the harness of a man who was being pressured by the weight of barbarian soldiers who were massed together, trying to buckle the Roman line by sheer weight of numbers. Calling to others, he would stay, until the man's still able comrades came to his aid, only then removing himself to move to another trouble spot. Nobody who saw Caesar in those moments wasn't inspired to fight harder than he ever had before, and despite the seemingly overwhelming numbers of swords and spears slashing and thrusting at them, the lines held.

"One...two...one...two..."

Step by step, Barbatos and the other Centurions assigned to the task along the line called out the count, and for the brief moment Caesar took to catch his breath, he was gratified to see that the ground behind the mass of Wa still pressing against the shields of his men was covered with bodies. Most of them were Wa, but there was still a disturbingly large number of men clad in the uniform of the Legions, as well.

"Caesar!" The general was disturbed from his examination to see Bodroges', face shining with perspiration, a sign that he hadn't thought himself above the manual labor of constructing the breastworks. If he survives, he may make a good officer, Caesar thought, while still listening to the report of the Parthian.

"The breastworks are finished and ready to be occupied!"

"Good," Caesar answered immediately, but while this was good news, there was one more thing that had to be done that he didn't relish in the least. "We'll be there in just a few moments. Remember that you direct the *signiferi* to make sure their spacing is enough to cover the entire wall all the way around."

The Parthian saluted, and Caesar turned back to the next task, and as exhausted and drained as he was, he still had enough energy that a sudden, leaden ball formed in his stomach. Ignoring it, he scanned the lines of men, until he saw the man for whom he was looking. Pushing his way close enough so that he could be heard, he called out to the man.

"Barbatos!"

Hearing his name, the Centurion carefully backed away from the front line, before facing his general. Seeing Caesar beckoning him to come to him, Barbatos made his way through the lines of men, but made sure to make a joke or offer a word of encouragement and a slap on a shoulder, causing Caesar an even deeper twinge of regret over what he had to do.

When Barbatos reached his side, Caesar wasted no time, speaking in a low voice, so the men nearby wouldn't hear.

"The breastworks are ready."

Barbatos' face betrayed no emotion, but he gave a brief nod that he understood, and Caesar recognized that Barbatos knew what was coming, and he said as much.

"I can tell you know what needs to be done, and I can think of no better man than you to make sure it's done well, because our survival depends on it."

"You need me to have the first line hold off these bastards long enough for the rest of you to get to the breastworks," Barbatos replied calmly.

Perhaps it was the matter-of-fact tone, the calm acceptance of a fate that meant certain death, but Caesar's vision suddenly became clouded as the tears threatened to come pouring down his face, and it was only through his supreme will that they remained unshed. Swallowing down the lump in his throat, he couldn't speak for a moment, and when he did, his voice was husky with emotion.

"Yes, that's exactly what needs to happen. And I know that I couldn't have made a better choice for the man to do it."

Now it was Barbatos who felt the swell of emotion, and for the remaining moments of his life, the pride that he felt would buoy and sustain him, giving him the strength to do what needed to be done.

"We won't let you down, Caesar," he finally managed to say.

Both men stood for just a moment, then Caesar reached out and grabbed Barbatos by the shoulder, squeezing it hard.

"May Mars, Bellona, and Fortuna bless you and the men," Caesar told Barbatos, but he received only a nod in return before Barbatos turned about, and, without another word, headed back to the fighting.

Caesar took a moment to watch him stride, sword in hand, a proud Roman meeting his fate and his destiny with head held high, and the older man was almost overcome with a wave of sadness and remorse. He had caused this, he knew. These men were here because his thirst for fame and overwhelming desire to outstrip Alexander had brought them here, to this strange land, facing these strange men. And now most, if not all of them would die. Caesar forced himself to push the feelings down, thinking now about his next step. Surveying the men, he found the man for whom he was searching, and headed directly for him, skirting behind the men who were clutching onto the harnesses of those in front of them. Now Caesar had to ensure that the sacrifice of Barbatos and the men of the front line wasn't in vain, that with their deaths they ensured that the remainder of his force was able to move behind the barricades that were waiting for them in the forum.

Centurion Felix waited impatiently as his men caught their breath and sucked greedily at their canteens. The advance Century he had sent out ahead was now standing just below the crest of the slope, staying out of sight, because once atop it, they would be within plain sight of Caesar's camp, a little more than a mile away. Despite his impatience, Felix forced himself to wait, making sure that he could see that the force he was commanding was sufficiently recovered, before they closed the remaining distance to the general's camp. None of the other Centurions commanding this hodgepodge assortment of Cohorts from two different Legions left his spot to come talk to Felix, another sign that this was an unusual development. Felix welcomed the solitude, consumed as he was with all sorts of conflicting thoughts and emotions, and, in fact, didn't blame them for avoiding him as though he had the plague. Like his Primus Pilus Flaminius, Felix felt in his bones that this was the right thing to do, but just like his commander, he was aware that if it wasn't, his career was irreparably harmed. It was true that he would be protected somewhat by following the orders of his superior, but not only had he not hesitated, he had also eagerly accepted Flaminius' judgment that Felix was the most senior of the Centurions in command of these twelve Cohorts and that, he knew, wasn't the case. Therefore, at the very least, he would be guilty of overstepping his authority, but that was more of a nagging consideration than a real fear. Instead, his mind was almost totally consumed with what would be taking place immediately after he and his men crested the slope. He was sure that he would be able to get a better idea of what was happening in Caesar's camp, but that was only half the problem. As certain as he was that he was doing the right thing, he also felt deeply that no matter how desperate Caesar's situation might be, the real key to the battle lay to the north, where the 10th and 12th could even at that moment be in their death throes and needing help desperately. Finally, he spat on the ground in a signal, to himself at least, that the time for thinking and recovering was over.

"All right! Let's go! Caesar's waiting on us!" Felix shouted, without using his *cornicen,* as he normally would, not wanting to risk alerting the enemy with the inherently loud bass sound of the horn.

He doubted they were within earshot, but they had come too far and didn't need any kind of surprises now. His command was relayed down the column, and within a matter of a few dozen heartbeats, Felix saw the Centurion of the rearmost Century wave his hand to let him know that all was ready. Giving the command to his own Century, Felix resumed the march at the normal pace, but after just a moment he immediately increased the pace back to the quick trot. Thankfully, he and the men had recovered their breath, because the grade of the slope was steeper than it looked, and very quickly Felix could feel the burning in his thighs as they pumped, moving him up the slope, followed closely by the relief force. Keeping his eye affixed on the advance guard, he saw them disappear, and he knew that the next few moments would tell him what he needed to know. If one of the advance party came sprinting back in his direction, even before they told him anything, he would understand that it meant there was a problem in Caesar's camp. The absolutely worst possibility would be that Caesar's camp was already overrun, and that the Wa had spilled out onto the road, blocking Felix and his men from helping either Caesar or the 10th. Every stride took him closer to the top, but still he didn't see any sign from the advance party, and even with the exertion, his heart was beating faster from the anticipation.

Then he was at the top of the hill, and he managed to take an extra gulp of air in relief at the sight of the leading Century, still trotting forward. As soon as the feeling of relief came, he pushed it aside, as he looked over the heads and slightly to the left of the advance party at Caesar's camp, and as much as he thought he had prepared his mind for any possibility, it still took a moment for the sight before him to register its import. Not only was there a pall of dust hanging above the camp, almost all the way to where he knew the forum was located, but there were also black tendrils of smoke drifting up into the still air. Knowing that Caesar would never intentionally order anything inside the camp burned, Felix understood that this could come only from the enemy firing up the flammable objects inside the walls. Whether it was intentional or accidental didn't concern Felix; what did was the knowledge that between the presence and location of the dust and the smoke, the walls of Caesar's camp were breached, and Caesar had in all likelihood been forced to retreat to the forum. In short, Caesar's camp was about to fall.

Artaxades was having trouble with his vision, not only because of the sweat streaming freely down into his eyes, but also because his lungs were unable to pull in air quickly enough. Finally, it was becoming more difficult to control where his eyes focused, as they seemed now to have a mind of their own, and if he didn't know better, he would swear that he was looking in two different directions, making it impossible for his brain to interpret what it was receiving from his eyes. The pain in his side that had been the cause of his remaining undiscovered by forcing him to stop before reaching the top of the ridge was back in full force, now that he had moved farther south along the slope, perhaps another mile, before he had turned back up and finished his climb to the top. He glanced back to his right, but thankfully nobody was visible, friend or enemy, and at least now he was running along the smoother surface of the road. Blessed with unnaturally long legs, Artaxades' stride was still smooth and even, despite the intense strain he was under. His breathing would have been audible a hundred paces away, and it was the only sound roaring in the Parthian's ears now, as he pushed his body harder than he ever had before.

Never in a race had he run this fast, he was sure, and the fleeting thought crossed his mind that it was a shame this event wasn't in the Legion games, because he surely would have left his competitors so far behind that men would talk about it around the fires for years to come: the day that Artaxades had flown faster than Hermes himself. This thought seemed to give him strength, and while part of him rebelled at it, his stride lengthened even further, his legs moving so fluidly and swiftly that the balls of his feet barely touched the ground. It was as if he, in fact, possessed the winged shoes of Hermes, and just the feeling of freedom, of flight and speed made the pain bearable, the ache in his side feeling as though something was about to burst in him, his lungs close to exploding—and yet it didn't matter. Artaxades, in that moment, was sure that he was touched by the gods, blessed by them, as they saw how he was pouring every bit of energy and heart into his mission to save his friends from certain disaster.

Racing down the road, as Artaxades squinted through the pain and sweat, his vision was too blurry for him to make out much more than vague shapes and colors, so when he rounded a slight curve that put him in sight of Caesar's camp, it didn't register as anything more than a darker shape against the sky. And even if his eyes had been clear, his mind was so absorbed with keeping his body moving at the same speed he had been maintaining that it was incapable of any higher thought, such as deciphering what the straight lines of that dark shape meant. But somewhere deep in his mind, a small voice whispered to Artaxades that, since there were no straight lines in nature, this was a sign of something important, and even as his feet continued in a blur of motion, drawing him ever closer to the finish, he puzzled over its significance. He covered another stadium before the answer popped into his head, seemingly out of nowhere. It was Caesar's camp, the finish line! He was almost there! Immediately following that thought was the recollection that there was a reason he had been sent on this mission, yet it wouldn't come to him. Instead, the pain was almost overwhelming, from his feet, to his thighs, to his chest; every part of him throbbing with an agony he had never before experienced. Yet, he still didn't slow down—which was a feat in itself—and even through the pain he could see that he was within the last few stadia. That meant he *had* to remember the message he was supposed to give whomever he first came into contact with, once he got to the camp.

"One...two...one...two..."

At roughly the same time, the same thing that was taking place in Caesar's camp was being done in the northern camp, but it was Pullus who was moving behind the slowly retreating men, doing the same things Caesar was doing, in much the same way. Unlike Caesar, Pullus didn't hesitate to wade into a fight when he saw that one of the men was having trouble disentangling from the Wa, as the retreating men moved backward. As fatigued as Pullus was, he still wielded his blade with a lethal economy, striking quickly and with a brutal force that brought death to even more Wa. Pullus had no idea how many of the enemy he'd slain; it was well over a hundred, but he could look over the heads of the front rank and see that the barbarians were still several rows deep. There seemed to be no end to them, and despite killing them in the thousands, they showed no sign of despair or fatigue. Still, they came on in wave after human wave, but what Pullus had seen over the course of this fight was the only thing that gave him a sliver of hope.

While the Wa who wielded the swords did so with a skill that Pullus had never encountered in an enemy before, they numbered only perhaps a quarter of the total of the assaulting force. The rest, carrying spears with the teardrop-shaped blades, varied greatly in skill levels; in fact, the majority of them were not much better than the native levies of any of the lands that Pullus and the army had marched through and conquered. The only real question, and one on which any chance of survival this day hinged upon, was how many of those sword-wielding Wa were still left. As he moved to another spot, his eyes scanned the leading ranks of the Wa, trying to determine the ratio of barbarians with swords to those with spears, but the mental energy needed for such complex operations had long since been spent. It seemed to him that every other one of the Wa who were furiously pressing against the shields of his front ranks was carrying a sword, using it to thrust, stab, or otherwise hack his way past the thin wooden wall to get at the men behind them.

One small blessing was that at this point, men had shouted themselves hoarse, so the level of noise was significantly lower than it had been a watch, or even a third of a watch, before. That didn't mean that there wasn’t still an unholy racket assaulting his ears, but compared to earlier, it was blessedly quieter. Finally giving up trying to determine the proportions of the barbarians who were waving their swords about, Pullus instead focused on the things he could control. Moving again, he half-trotted, half-stumbled behind the woefully thin line of Legionaries, only stopping when he found the man he was searching for, his best friend Scribonius. Just like Pullus, his arm was bound tightly, and he had lost sufficient feeling in his hand that he couldn't even grasp a *vitus*, let alone a shield. Also like Pullus, his face was drawn and spattered with blood and grime, a sign of the desperate fighting that had been raging for most of the day.

"Did you hear about Balbus?" Pullus winced as he blurted out the question, but truthfully, he had neither the energy nor the ability to bring up the death of their friend in a more diplomatic fashion.

Scribonius' face became even more drawn, his mouth turning down in a frown that Pullus knew from long experience was his friend's sign of real grief.

"Yes, I heard," he finally said, not looking Pullus in the eye, as he talked. "Stupid bastard."

Despite himself, Pullus let out a short, barking laugh.

"He was that," he admitted. "But I never thought......."

"Neither did I," Scribonius cut him off. "Just like I didn't think we could ever be beaten."

His mouth twisted into a bitter grimace at this last comment, and although Pullus understood and essentially agreed with his friend, he still felt compelled to put a hand on his friend's shoulder.

"We're not done yet," Pullus said with as much conviction as he could muster. "We don't know what's happening everywhere else, so for all we know Caesar's on his way with help. We just have to hold out a little longer."

Now it was Scribonius' turn to laugh, but his held no humor.

"I really hope you're right, and the gods are listening Titus. But I think we may have come to the end of our string here."

"I don't believe that," Pullus shot back, and to his real surprise, the moment he said it he realized that, while a part of him understood the gravity of the their situation, there was clearly another part of him that still held out hope.

In that moment, Pullus chose to listen to the hopeful part of his being, and he grabbed Scribonius by the shoulder, squeezing so hard it made his friend wince.

"I think we can get out of this," he insisted. "We just have to hold on a little longer. Make these bastards pay for every foot of ground they take from us. Once we get back to the forum, we're going into an *orbis*, and we're going to hold long enough for help to come. We will hold, do you understand me? We *will hold!"*

When all was said and done, Sextus Scribonius believed his Primus Pilus and friend mainly because he wanted to believe, but at that moment what mattered was that he did, so looking his friend in the eye, he gave a curt, brief nod.

"We'll do just that Titus. You have my word on it."

Pullus didn't respond and just gave his friend another squeeze of the shoulder before he moved away, searching for the rest of his Centurions to impart the same message to them that there was hope, and to instill in them the same resolve, that the 10th would not fail this day.

Felix was in agony, but not from the exertion of the run. Now that they were within a couple of stadia of Caesar's camp, it was clear that their general needed his help. From the position of the dust cloud itself, Felix could plainly see that the camp had for all intents and purposes fallen, and that his general and the men were now in the area of the forum, putting up a last defense. But it wasn't just the dust that told him this: he was close enough now that he could hear the noise of fighting even above his harsh breathing. Up ahead, his advance Century had stopped their trotting advance, coming to the quick step that they normally used when marching. Felix could see the Centurion commanding the advance party turn to look in his direction, clearly waiting for orders. Every sign pointed to the clear-cut decision that it was Caesar's camp that needed succor, recognizing that the relief force hadn't arrived too late to help. But that knowledge didn't bring Felix any sense of relief whatsoever, because of the nagging feeling that, as badly as they might be needed by Caesar, the fort defended by Pullus, Balbinus and their men was in even greater danger.

However, given what he could see at that moment, Felix had no choice but to halt at Caesar's camp. Continuing his trot, Felix and the men following him closed the distance to the main gate of Caesar's camp, and the absence of any men manning the gate was further confirmation of the desperate situation. The advance Century had come to a halt, just as Felix had instructed them, and when Felix reached them, he called a halt to the main column. He was standing within a hundred paces of the gate and was trying to decide the best way to proceed now that they had arrived. Deciding that the best thing to do was to see the situation for himself, he ordered his Century forward, giving instructions to the Centurions of the advance guard and the Centurions of the Centuries closest to the front to remain where they were and wait for his signal to proceed. Leading his Century, Felix approached the gate with a heart that hadn't stopped pounding, even after coming to a stop, so he could hear in his ears the breath coming as if he was still running, such was his tension. Tapping his *vitus* nervously against his leg as he closed the remaining few paces, the noise now was only partially muffled by the dirt walls of the camp, and the Roman was so close that he could almost make out individual voices and sounds, shouted orders, and the clash of metal on metal.

Eyes fixed on the dirt barrier of the main gate, he drew his sword without conscious thought, made aware of this only by the rasping sound of his men doing the same, following the example of their Centurion. Felix nearly jumped at the harsh noise; it also jerked his attention partially away from the gate, as he glanced back to see his Optio who, for some reason, was looking in another direction. Felix opened his mouth to reprimand his Optio for letting his attention wander, but before anything came out, the other man raised his arm to point in the direction he was looking.

"Centurion! Someone's coming! It looks like one of ours and he's running like Cerberus is about to catch him!"

Artaxades had reached a point where the only thing he was aware of was that his legs were moving, and they were moving fast. Nothing else mattered at this point, and, if the truth were known, he wouldn't have been able to articulate why he was running faster than he ever had in his life at that moment. All he knew was that the finish line was just ahead, marked by a large, dark blur in his visual field that was looming larger with every stride. Somewhere in the recesses of his mind he knew that this was Caesar's camp, and he knew that he had to deliver a message, but for the life of him, at that moment, he couldn't remember what the message was. Whatever it was, first he had to get there, and so his arms were pumping as quickly as he could move them back and forth.

His mouth had long since gone completely dry, every drop of moisture in his body sucked inwards to try to cool it down, but he felt as if he were being baked in the *panera* oven of the Legions, like a loaf of bread. Caked around his open mouth was a rime of white, chalky material, and while it was normal for him to have this substance around his mouth after a race, never had it been this thick. Now that he was within two hundred paces of the gate, he began to veer slightly off the road in an unconscious attempt to shorten the distance, before he could finally stop. Such was his level of distress and his concentration that it wasn't until he was less than fifty paces away that he heard shouts above the roaring sound in his ears, and he was so surprised that he immediately broke stride. Gone was the smooth, ground-eating lope that he had been using; instead he began stumbling, as his limbs seemed suddenly to grow minds of their own and refuse his directions to continue with the smooth motion that had gotten him to this point.

He felt as if the world was suddenly tilted on its axis and that he was in danger of sliding off, so to compensate, he began windmilling his arms in an attempt somehow to counteract the fact that his legs seemed to be sliding out from underneath him. But although he was still propelling himself forward, it was no longer at a run, but in a stumble, and in his confused state he caught just a glimpse of a face, a Roman face with a helmet wearing a transverse crest on top of it, before he went crashing into the ground. The impact drove what little breath there was from his lungs, but he barely felt the effect of the rough ground, as the tiny, protruding sharp rocks tore into his skin, carving deep gashes as he slid to a stop.

For a moment he lay motionless, then somehow found the energy to push himself over onto his back with one arm, where he lay sprawled, face to the sun. His lungs were continuing to suck in air as fast as they could, but they still couldn't keep up, and Artaxades saw a dark, hazy mist that created a circle all around the edges of his vision, so that the only place he could still see the sky was in the center. Am I dying, he wondered? He had never felt like this after any race, no matter how hard he had run, and the last mile had been an agony that he would never have believed he could have endured, until this moment on the other side, having done it. Thoughts and images were tumbling through his mind, things he hadn't thought about in years, like his home in Ctesiphon, in Parthia. His mother, hard at work as always, preparing a meal, while his sister stood next to her, learning the work of a woman. She was looking up and smiling at him, and while he couldn't hear her words, he could see that she was calling him, probably to taste his favorite dish of spiced lamb, roasted over the spit. Oh, how he would love to have some of his mother's cooking to help him recover from this last race he had run! He was so tired, never before this tired, and it still seemed next to impossible for his lungs to draw in enough breath. Even as his mind tried to puzzle out what that meant, the dark mist continued closing in, ever narrowing into a smaller and smaller circle. But now he could hear his mother calling him.

"Arta! Arta! Come here, you foolish boy! Look what your mother has made for you, even if you don't deserve it! Your father told me he caught you sneaking away to play with those boys again! How are you going to learn how to be a mason, if you do not listen to your father and do what he tells you?"

He wanted to answer her, to assure her that he no longer needed to learn his father's skill, because he had found a home in the army, but he couldn't form the words, and even if he could, his throat was so dry that what did come out of his mouth was nothing but a croaking, raspy moan. Then, the mist came on him, as a roaring sound filled his ears, which for whatever reason seemed to snap him out of his mental daze just long enough to realize that he had failed. He hadn't carried the message that would help his friends.

"He's dead," Felix said incredulously, kneeling by the side of the fallen man and searching frantically for any sign of life. "He can't be! He can't be dead!"

Felix shook the prone man, his attempts to revive him growing increasingly vigorous, as he went from shaking to slapping him across the face. Finally, in frustration and anger, Felix brought his fist down hard on the man's chest, but still nothing happened. This courier, whoever he was, was dead. Felix's Optio, a man of indeterminate origin who claimed to come from Galatia and who had joined the Legion after the first battles against the Parthians, stood watching his Centurion. Though he spoke Latin fluently, it was still with the accent of his home lands, which was one reason that many of the other men doubted his claim to be a Galatian. Hence, his nickname became Odysseus, after the perpetual wanderer of Homer's tale. Now he stepped forward and cleared his throat.

"Centurion? I don't think that's going to bring him back. The man's clearly dead."

Felix didn't answer, but he did sit back on his haunches, forearms across his knees as he gazed down at the dead man. After a moment he stood and turned to face his Optio.

"I wonder what his message was?" he asked, although he didn't really expect an answer.

Nevertheless, Odysseus replied, "Whatever it was, it was important enough for him to run himself to death."

At first, this didn't register with Felix, as he had already stood and started walking back the very short distance to the gate. When they had spotted the courier, Felix, along with his Century, had actually run past the gate to meet Artaxades, Felix being sure that this man would be carrying a message that would provide him with more clarity about his dilemma. Now, Felix was trotting toward the gate and leading his men, as he navigated through the passageway of the dirt gate. The sounds of the fighting were very loud, and he could clearly hear commands, shouts, curses, and the ringing sound of sword striking sword or some other metal surface, all of it punctuated with the deeper thudding sound, when someone blocked a thrust with his shield. But even as prepared as he thought he was, when he entered the camp at the run, he still came to a complete stop.

By the time Felix arrived, the withdrawal to the hastily prepared fortifications had just been completed, and an appallingly small number of Roman Legionaries were standing on the makeshift parapet, their shields providing more coverage, as they desperately fought the remaining Wa force. Although Felix had no way of knowing it, this assault element was composed of barely a third of the original number of these Wa, but they still outnumbered the remnants of Caesar's command. Taking this sight in, Felix stood there with his Century, unobserved by the Wa, who clearly were not expecting other Romans to show up. They were completely focused on the final destruction of these barbarians who had invaded their land, and after a short lull in ferocity and energy, they were now pouring every last bit they had left into finishing it. That, more than any other factor, made Felix's decision for him.

Turning to his Optio, he asked, "What did you say just a moment ago? About him?" He jerked his head in the direction of where Artaxades was still lying, barely cold.

"What? Oh," Odysseus thought a moment, and said, "That he ran himself to death, just like Phidippides did at the Battle of Marathon."

Felix nodded thoughtfully, then replied, "And that message was so important that it was worth dying for, I expect. Just like this one," he finished under his breath.

And with that, Felix made up his mind.

Caesar was pleased to see that, for the moment at least, the makeshift barricade was successfully holding the Wa at bay, and for the first time he could see real fatigue showing in the movements and faces of these barbarians who, until that moment, had seemed to be impervious to the normal draining of energy that came from such strenuous activity. But as tired as they were, Caesar and his men were no less so, and in many spots around the hodgepodge of items that had been used to create this wall, the fighting taking place was almost comically slow. A Wa would thrust a spear, and a Roman would either block or parry the blow in such a way that if Caesar hadn't known how deadly serious the fight was, he would have said he was watching one of the mime shows in Rome, where battles were recreated for the crowd. Of course, the other difference was that at the end of the "battle" in Rome, something funny would take place and the crowd would roar with laughter. Here, nobody was laughing, or, in fact, doing much shouting at all—such was the fatigue.

Instead, the air was filled almost entirely by just the sounds of sword on sword, or spear against shield, along with the occasional blast of a Centurion's whistle that signaled the men standing on the rampart to step aside and let their relief take over. At least, when there were enough men to relieve them, Caesar thought bitterly, as he could see that in many spots there wasn't actually a Legionary standing behind the man on the rampart. The space enclosed by the barricade was jammed full of wounded men, with barely enough room for the paths that the *medici* and remaining slaves needed to move around, ministering to the wounded. Thankfully, now that they were back behind some sort of wall, the flow of Roman wounded being carried or dragged to the forum had slowed, but every loss was one that Caesar and his men couldn't afford. In fact, Caesar thought wearily, all he had done was buy these men perhaps a watch more of life, if that. He couldn't imagine that the commanders of the other redoubts, from whom he hadn't heard a word in only the gods knew how long, were faring any better than he was, so the idea of help never entered his mind. No, Caesar's Luck had finally run out. Of this he was sure: that today would see the final battle of his career, and the beginning of the Legend of Caesar. Shaking his head, more ruefully than with any real regret, he acknowledged to himself that perhaps this time he had overreached, that finally he had come across the one place and the one people he couldn't conquer. Standing there, surrounded by the remainder of his staff, as always, Caesar stood alone, still aloof and with every bit of his *dignitas* intact. Finally, Bodroges cleared his throat, jerking Caesar out of his reverie. Somewhat surprised, Caesar turned to see the man, the Pandyan Tribune next to him, both of them bespattered with blood and the Parthian sporting a ragged bandage wrapped around his upper thigh. When did that happen? Caesar wondered with a frown, trying to recall if he had seen it happen or had been told by the Parthian and had just forgotten.

"Caesar, what are your orders, sir?" the Parthian's tone arrested Caesar's attention, the tone of it causing him an even deeper twinge, recognizing in the words that it was as much a plea for hope and encouragement as it was a request for direction. I owe these men more than this, Caesar thought with real sadness. They have performed in a manner that would make any Roman proud, no matter where they came from.

With this in mind, Caesar answered, "We continue to fight, gentlemen. That's all we can do right now. We show these barbarians that being Roman isn't just a matter of where one is born, but what one is made of. Because both of you fought like Romans today."

To the horror and embarrassment of both men, their reaction was a welling of tears and lumps in the throat that rendered both men speechless, for they had never been praised in such a manner by Caesar until this moment. Finally, the Parthian nodded, then straightened and offered a perfect salute.

Swallowing hard, he asked, "Where will my sword be of most use?"

Caesar quickly surveyed the area, then pointed to a spot.

"It looks like Valerius' Century could use some help."

Caesar pointed to another spot, addressing the Pandyan, "And Amulius needs you there."

The Pandyan offered the same salute, then dashed away, sword held high, ready to lend itself to this last phase of the fight. Sighing, Caesar watched the two younger men move into position, before drawing his own sword. Looking about, he saw another spot where there was only a single line of Legionaries, one of his men just then wrestling with a Wa who had managed to throw a leg over the barricade and was slashing at the Roman. Unlike the two younger men, Caesar had neither the energy nor the inclination to run at this point. No, he would walk to his death with the same disdain for it he had always had.

He began moving in that direction, but had to pick his way carefully among the detritus of battle, as well as taking care not to step on a wounded man. When he got to within a few paces of his destination, something happened that he was sure was a figment of his imagination, and while he faltered for a moment, he immediately resumed his progress. But before he could take more than another couple of steps, not only did it happen again, it was also accompanied by a shout from some of the men behind him. This had been happening all day and wasn't unusual, since it typically signaled some sort of trouble, but there was something decidedly different in these shouts. It was an alarm, but it sounded.....joyful? Caesar whirled around, and this time he recognized that it wasn't his imagination, as a *cornu* blasted a series of notes a third time. And that series of notes was used to send the Legions of Rome into battle!

In the northern camp, Pullus and his men didn't have the luxury of falling back to a barricade of any kind, a fact that Pullus now realized was his single greatest mistake of this entire day, a day filled with them. However, armed with that knowledge, his men were giving ground even more stubbornly than Caesar's had, so that there were still more than a hundred paces of space left between the ragged and thin rear ranks of the Roman lines and the beginning of the forum. As they continued falling back, the Wa had continuously tried to extend their own lines farther in either direction in an attempt to turn the flanks of Pullus' men. This had forced Pullus and Balbinus—who still lived and was directing the left flank of the withdrawal—to take men and send them to the edges to meet this new threat. The result was that the Roman formation was slowly bending into a semicircle, where the ends crept more closely together. Further complicating matters was the frustration the two Primi Pili felt at the sight of the reserve Cohorts that were now spread along the southern wall. In their overwhelming desire to crush the invading barbarians, by extending their own lines in an attempt to flank them, the original Wa force had turned their backs to these reserve Cohorts. Unfortunately, Tetarfenus and the Cohorts on the southern wall were obviously too heavily engaged to allow for any detachment of one or more of their Centuries to fall on the rear of the Wa.

Pullus could see that whoever was commanding the force assaulting his position at least recognized this as a possibility, because there was a small force of Wa standing at the ready facing the reserve Cohorts. And Tetarfenus was clearly aware, because the men in the rear ranks of his force were doing the same, as these two small groups kept a wary eye on each other. While Pullus was happy that at least some of these bastards were diverted to this task, he didn't think that the reduction in numbers of men assailing his woefully thin wall of shields and flesh was going to make much difference. Still, Pullus was gratified to see the same thing that Caesar had, that these Wa were finally showing some signs of tiring. And despite the fact that the men from each Century were now hopelessly entangled, the cohesion of the overall formation was still holding, and they were still giving ground only after inflicting considerable damage on these yellow-skinned savages.

Shaking himself back to the moment, Pullus blew a blast of his whistle, seeing that the men of the front line were almost collapsing from exhaustion. Along the line under his command, each Legionary dealt a savage thrust with his shield to knock whatever man was opposing him back a step, before moving quickly aside to let the man behind him take his place. Some men chose to use their swords, instead of their shields, something that Pullus normally disapproved of doing, because it robbed his men of the chance to follow up with a thrust, if the blow from the shield sufficiently staggered the opponent. At this moment, all he cared about was that it gave his men the chance to exchange places, especially now that the Wa had figured out the rhythm and pacing used by the Legions of Rome. They had learned quickly, and observing their damnable agility, Pullus had seen a number of his men fall victim to a sudden thrust or slash of a Wa who had leaped aside or backward to dodge the thrusting impact of the shield. Thankfully, his men had seen this countermove and had also adjusted, so now the Wa, when they heard the whistle blast, couldn't be sure if they would have to dodge a shield or block a sword. This time the change went smoothly, without losing a man, for which Pullus was thankful. But like Caesar, he knew that he was buying his men little more than a third or two of a watch of life and nothing more. And like his general, the idea of doing anything less never entered his mind. Titus Pullus and the men of the 10th, or at least those that remained, would never quit fighting, not until they were all dead. The idea that help would arrive was now as far from his mind as the idea of surrender. If it hadn't happened by now, it wasn't going to happen, so there was no need dwelling on it. Now all there was to do was to die well, in a manner that would make Rome proud.

Gaius Porcinus took a breath, pausing just long enough to use his neckerchief to mop his face and clear his eyes from the stinging sweat. His head still throbbed abominably, and he found it hard to concentrate, but somehow he forced himself to continue directing his Century in the fight. While there were a number of spots at which the Wa had managed to get one or two men onto the parapet, where the fighting had the fury and frantic pace that had been present during the beginning of the first Wa assault, Porcinus' Century had managed to keep the Wa from gaining a toehold anywhere along their sector. It hadn't been without cost: Porcinus' latest count had been more than a dozen men down, although he couldn't have said who was dead and who was wounded. All that mattered at this moment was that they and their swords were missing. His Optio Oesalces was still at his spot on the opposite side of the line, his sword bloodied to the hilt and suffering a gruesome slashing wound to his cheek that had cut so deep that the flap of skin was hanging down, exposing his gums through the blood and gore. Regardless of his wound, he was cutting down any barbarian who tried to scramble up the ladder placed against the wall before him.

The Wa had altered their tactics somewhat, trying to coordinate between their archers and warriors. Archers would launch as many arrows as they could, as the warriors began mounting the ladders, only stopping when the leading man's head was no more than a couple of feet below the parapet, forcing the Romans to stay behind their shields and robbing them of the ability to see how close the men on the ladders were. The instant the barrage stopped, the first Wa would scramble to close the remaining distance, most of them choosing to try to leap high above the parapet and land cleanly on the other side of the palisade stakes. As far as Porcinus could tell, this tactic was unsuccessful as often as it worked, but since the beginning of the attack, the barbarians had managed either to make or bring more ladders, so that the tactic almost didn't matter. All along the wall the enemy was popping up, some of them seeming to levitate in the air, before landing on the dirt parapet. But that wasn't a concern for Porcinus, as long as it didn't happen in his sector, and so far it hadn't.

Farther down the wall, however, it was another story. Pilus Prior Tetarfenus was at that moment furiously engaged with two

Wa standing side by side, backs pressed against the stakes, both of them armed with swords that alternately flickered out like the tongues of a two-headed serpent, one after the other, keeping Tetarfenus and the man next to him, one of the newest Gayan recruits, at bay. For the moment, it was a stalemate; the Wa couldn't push away from the stakes to make room for any more of their comrades, but neither could Tetarfenus or his Legionary penetrate the defenses of their adversaries. Even as he was furiously thrusting and slashing at the barbarian across from him, a part of Tetarfenus was forced to admire, albeit grudgingly, the enormous skill of this yellow bastard who, without a shield, was blocking every attempt by the Pilus Prior to kill him. The best Tetarfenus had done was score a partially deflected slashing cut, high up on the Wa's arm, just below the edge of his lamellar armor. Then, the Gayan, either through fatigue or carelessness, just after making a training manual-perfect punching thrust with his shield, returned to what the Romans called the first position. Except instead of the shield's being perfectly vertical, the bottom was tilted inward just a bit. Not much, but the Wa instantly saw it and took advantage. He launched a feint, seemingly aiming a low thrust at the Gayan's legs, and the young Legionary responded by dropping his shield. If his shield had been in a true first position and held vertically, it was doubtful that what happened next would have worked, but because of the outward tilt at the top, this created more of a gap than it normally would have. So, it was into this gap that the Wa, with a quickness that Tetarfenus was just now coming to understand and appreciate was a characteristic of all these warriors, made an overhand thrust that plunged directly into the left eye of the Gayan, dropping him like a stone.

Before Tetarfenus could react, the Wa, his blade still dripping the blood and brain matter from the Legionary, made an overhand slash to his left, catching the Centurion across the jaw. Fortunately for Tetarfenus, the barbarian was at the outer limit of his reach, so that it was just the tip of the sword that struck Tetarfenus. Even so, the blow had enough force not only to slice through the flesh, but also to shatter his jawbone. Tetarfenus let out a shriek of agony, reeling backward into the shield of one his men, ironically enough saving his life, as the second Wa, on seeing what happened, followed up with a vicious, disemboweling thrust of his own that hit nothing but air. In the ensuing tangle of bodies, shields, and swords on the part of the Romans, the two Wa took advantage of the confusion and stepped forward, blades flashing in front of them as they made room for more of their own comrades. In no more than the space of a couple of normal heartbeats, they were joined by two more warriors, and what had been a minor toehold now became the most dangerous incursion of the southern wall.

"Tetarfenus is down!"

Porcinus heard the shout even from his spot further down the wall, but at the moment he was too busy to give it more than a passing thought. Besides, there was nothing he could do about it, and surely the Pilus Posterior of the Eighth would step in, if he was still alive. If not, then it would have to be the Princeps Prior. Either way, he had his own problems, as a Wa had managed to get over the wall and was quickly being joined by a comrade of his own. This was also occurring farther down the line at one of the new ladders that had been placed between the two covered by his Century. Unfortunately, because of the rotations he had already ordered, the Legionaries facing these two Wa were men from the last section of the last Century of the Tenth Cohort. And while Caesar had done what he could to abolish the practice, it had been a tradition for longer than any Roman had been alive that the most inexperienced men were in the Tenth Cohort, and of the Tenth, invariably the most inept were moved to the rear of the formation, in the last two sections of men. In the case of Porcinus' Century, these last two sections were almost exclusively composed of the newest Gayan recruits, who, because they were in the Tenth had seen less action than every other man in the Legion. That was who faced the Wa at that moment, and Porcinus could only watch helplessly as his men across from the barbarians flailed away with their swords, completely forgetting to use their shields in the manner in which they had been trained. Before he could make a move to push his way to their side, he saw the flash of silvery gray as one of the Wa struck; and even over the shouting and noise, Porcinus could hear the distinctive sound of a blade solidly striking flesh. The stricken Gayan staggered backward, making a gurgling sound that told Porcinus that the wound was mortal. Just like with Tetarfenus, there was a flurry of movement as the Gayan's dead body fell backward onto the comrade who had been holding his harness, creating a gap that the Wa took immediate advantage of, his blade still flashing in a blur of motion even the most experienced Legionary would have been hard-pressed to defend. Porcinus saw another of his men fall, but this time the Legionary went to his knees, clutching his throat as blood geysered between his fingers. It was because of this event that only one more Wa managed to join his comrade, before the two dead Legionaries were jerked unceremoniously out of the way in order to allow the men behind them to step forward. Porcinus had started to wedge his body between the files of men to make his way to the trouble spot, when a shouted warning made him turn just in time to see the man he had been standing next to drop his shield, an arrow shot by an opportunistic archer protruding from his chest, as he stared down at it with a puzzled expression, just before falling backward. Even as his mind registered this, the head and torso of another barbarian appeared as the Wa leapt over the palisade to land on the rampart. Porcinus was forced to reverse his course— vainly trying to step over his fallen comrade—and head directly for the Wa, who was slashing at the Legionary facing him.

If the relief force led by Felix thought he had pushed them hard making their way to Caesar's camp, that belief was quickly dispelled by the brutal pace that he was setting now in his attempt to reach Pullus' position. Very quickly men began dropping out of their Centuries, but this didn't stop Felix, who had determined that it was better to arrive more quickly, even if it meant with somewhat fewer men. And, unlike at Caesar's camp, he was sure he didn't have the luxury of slowing the men down to allow them to catch their breath. He would, however, at least have to slow long enough to allow the trailing Centuries and Cohorts arrange themselves from the column they were in now to the standard battle line. As he ran, he tried desperately to keep his composure sufficiently to think through how he would accomplish this feat, finally coming up with an idea. The challenge now was how to accomplish it, and he slowed enough to drop to the side of his own Century, looking for his Optio.

"Optio," he gasped, and Odysseus veered from his spot at the rear of the formation, and sprinted a few paces to reach his Centurion's side.

Between gasping breaths, Felix relayed what he planned to do.

He finished with, "I need you to drop off and make sure that the Pili Priores know what's expected of them."

Felix knew that he was asking his Optio for a huge effort, one worthy of some form of decoration, if he could pull it off, but the man gave that no thought. Simply put, he knew the stakes involved and without more than panted acknowledgement, he separated from Felix, then slowed down, looking behind him for the next Century.

His task would have been daunting, even if they had remained in the same order of march when they left their camp, as Felix had prepared for a similar maneuver when they reached Caesar's camp. However, when they stopped and Felix came to his decision, he had made matters a bit more complicated for himself later. Essentially, the decision Felix made between the two choices, saving Caesar's camp, or saving the northern one, was to choose both. Detaching four Cohorts from his force, he included two from the 14th and two from the 30th, putting the most senior Centurion, the Quintus Pilus Prior of the 14th, Lucius Statius, in command. These Cohorts were left behind to come to Caesar's aid, but Felix didn't stay long enough to direct how they should be doing this, leaving it up to Statius as to the best way to go about it. It was true that Felix was now two Cohorts short of a full Legion, but as far as he was concerned, this was really the only choice he could have made. If he had taken all twelve Cohorts with him and saved the northern camp at the expense of losing the commander of the army and the only general any man in the ranks had ever followed, Felix had no doubt that he would have fallen on his sword from the shame. Whatever was waiting for him and the men with him ahead at the northern camp, eight Cohorts would have to be enough to tip the balance.

Lucius Statius had confronted the problem of how to feed four Cohorts into Caesar's camp by choosing to spread his forces out and have them enter through the main and two side gates. He knew he was violating a basic tenet of warfare in spreading his force, but although he hadn't been with Felix when he entered the camp to see the situation, he had heard the sounds of the fighting and seen the hovering dust. Understanding its import, he was making the gamble that every barbarian in the camp was gathered in more or less the same place in the center, because whoever was commanding them wouldn't risk scattering his force throughout the camp when the battle was in its final stages. If he was right, his Cohorts and those from the 30th would descend onto the unprotected rear of the barbarians, who would be completely focused on the destruction of Caesar and however many men were still left with him. The hardest part was waiting the length of time it took for one Cohort to run the length of the eastern wall, before turning to the left and running the slightly shorter distance to the Porta Principalis Sinistra, the left gate of the camp. The other Cohort from the 30th that was going to enter through the Porta Principalis Dextra didn't have quite as far to go.

Statius stood, fidgeting by tapping his *vitus* against his leg, waiting for the third and final blast of the *cornu* that would tell him it was time for him to lead the two Cohorts of the 14th through the main gate. While he was willing to separate his force, that was as far as he was going to go in throwing away his advantage, and it was imperative that this attack be coordinated as much as possible. Even so, it was extremely hard for every man in that force, knowing that with every moment that passed, more of their comrades might be dying. Statius' Cohort was lined up in a row of Centuries, one behind the other just outside the gate, all of the men in the ranks fidgeting just as much as Statius. Some were rhythmically drumming their fingers on their grounded shields, others clenching and unclenching their sword hands, and still others yawning excessively. All of their ears were attuned to the sound that came at last: the single blast of the *cornu* from the Cohort at the Porta Principalis Sinistra, followed immediately by the answering blast by the Cohort at the Porta Principalis Dextra. Without hesitation, Statius turned to snap the order to his *cornicen* to sound the call that would unleash all three forces to the attack, but the man had already begun sounding the notes for the third time.

Unsheathing his sword, Statius shouted over his shoulder, even as he was moving through the gate, "Follow me boys! Shout it out now! Let Caesar know we're coming! These *cunni* are going to regret being born! CAESAR TRIUMPHANT!"

And with that roaring call being shouted by every man, they followed Statius into the camp.

It didn't take a man as experienced as Titus Pullus was to know that the battle for the northern camp was in its final stages. Between the pressure from the original assault element—as depleted as it may have been—and the surprise attack on the eastern wall, what remained of the 10th and 12th Legions was being squeezed between two jaws by what was, in effect, a huge, bloody beast. In several spots on the eastern wall, the Wa had managed to create pockets containing a handful of warriors, most of them the type armed with swords that Pullus worried about. At the same time, the remnants of the 10th and 12th that had been defending the western wall had retreated to the edges of the forum, while the formerly open area of the forum itself was now jammed with bodies of the wounded, the *medici*, and the surviving noncombatants of both Legions. While most of the slaves had other roles during the battle—mainly serving as stretcher bearers—now that it was only a matter of dragging a man a few paces back into the center, most of them stood huddled in small groups, shaking in terror as they watched the thin wall of Legionaries slowly whittled down, one by one. Although such complex tasks were no longer within Pullus' power to perform, if he had made the calculations, he would have realized that less than a quarter of both Legions were still standing, and of those still in the fight, perhaps one man in four was unwounded. All he knew at that moment was that his Legion, his beloved 10th Legion, the eagle under which he had been marching since its formation when Gaius Julius Caesar had been a relatively unknown Praetor of a province in Hispania, was in its death throes.

He no longer harbored any hope that help would be coming, so all that remained for him and his men was to die in a manner that would finish the history and the legend of Caesar's 10th Legion Equestris, the most famous Legion of Rome, as it should end, covered in glory. This was his pervading and really only thought at this point, as he strode around the interior of his lines, which were almost, but not quite, an *orbis*. Directly across from the eastern wall there was a gap, but while it hadn't been planned that way, neither Pullus nor Balbinus, both of whom were commanding what was in effect one half of a horseshoe, saw any need to close it. Because of the presence of the relief Cohorts, whoever was left in command of the original Wa assault force was unwilling to send any troops into that space, where they would essentially have their backs to Tetarfenus' men. It was a small blessing, and Pullus wearily recognized that ultimately it wouldn't make any difference in the outcome, although it might mean just a precious few more moments, before he and the remnants of the 10th and 12th were finally overwhelmed. Moving from one trouble spot to the next, Pullus seemed to be everywhere at once, bashing aside a Wa with a borrowed shield, when the barbarian had knocked one of his men down in one spot, then suddenly, as if by magic, he was on the opposite side of the 10th's area, thrusting his sword into the face of an enemy warrior who had just done the same thing to a Legionary. Covered in blood, some of it his own, but most of it not, Pullus and his Gallic sword were all that kept the last of the 10th from collapsing, not just because of what he did, but because of the example he set in those last moments, giving his men courage and energy that every one of them thought had long since been exhausted.

For Pullus it was all a blur of motion, color, and noise, where the thousands of watches of practice at the stakes took over, as his muscles seemed to react with a mind of their own, now that his actual mind was too exhausted to give the necessary commands. Since he had enlisted, the number of days when Titus Pullus hadn't devoted at least a third of a watch to his sword work were few and far between, and the tiny corner of his mind that wasn't utterly exhausted thought of how fitting it was that here, in the final watch of the life of the 10th, all that practice should now bear its fruits. Regardless of the heroics, not just of Pullus, but also those of the other surviving Centurions and Optios, along with those of some men of the ranks like Vellusius, the pressure from the Wa was unrelenting, forcing the already compact formation into an ever smaller space. Pullus wasn't sure how it happened, but after he was forced to give the command to take yet another few, shuffling steps backward, he found to his happy surprise that standing next to him was Sextus Scribonius. His pleasure wasn't only because Scribonius was still alive, but that here, in these last moments, he and his best friend would be side by side, swords in hands.

"Well Titus, here we are," Scribonius' voice was almost gone, but he gave Pullus a tired smile.

All Pullus could think to do at that moment was to smile back.

"Yes, Sextus. Here we are."

"We gave these bastards a good show though, don't you think?"

Pullus could tell that his friend wasn't asking this lightly, the other man's face creased by an anxious frown as he waited for Pullus to answer. Even if he hadn't thought it to be true, Pullus wasn't going to give his friend any other answer.

"One they'll never forget," Pullus replied fervently. "And one they'll be telling their grandchildren about."

"It's just a shame Rome will never hear about it," Scribonius said sadly, his words striking Pullus to his core, because that thought was his own as well, and he viewed it as a tragedy even greater than the actual destruction of Caesar and his army.

For that was one thing Pullus was sure about; if he and the 10th, along with the 12th fell, he was positive that Caesar and the rest of the army would suffer the same fate. Still, there was a part of Titus Pullus that felt the need to offer his friend some solace, no matter how shaky it might have been.

"I wouldn't be so sure, Sextus. I think that word of what happened here will spread, and it might be years from now, but Rome *will* hear about what we did in this gods-forsaken place."

"I hope you're right," Scribonius replied doubtfully. Shaking his head, he finished, "But whatever happens, I'm just glad that you're here."

As emotionally spent as Pullus was, he felt his throat tighten at his friend's words, and all he could manage was a choked, "Me as well, Sextus. Me as well."

With that, there was nothing more to say, and, as it happened, something occurred that tore Pullus' attention away from the moment. A great shout arose, but from the other side of the fighting, amidst the Wa, whose ranks were now the thinnest they'd been since they first threw themselves at the walls of the Roman camp. Still, they were deeper than those of the men opposing them, and it was at the rear of these rows, where the shouts originated, so that even with his height, Pullus was forced to stand on tiptoe to see the cause of the commotion. From his vantage point, Pullus saw a rippling disturbance in the rear ranks of the Wa, men moving aside to make way for something or someone that Pullus at first couldn't see. But then, when the barbarians in the middle of the mass of men stepped aside, Pullus finally saw what it was. It took a moment for the import of what he was seeing to hit him, but when it did, it created in him a surge of emotions that was hard for him to identify. It was equal parts rage and a certain savage anticipation, along with the recognition of what it meant finally to come face-to-face with the Wa general who had so mauled his Legion. At first, all Pullus could see was the top of his helmet, on which were affixed what looked like horns, but made of some sort of metal. Gradually coming into better view, as a small group of warriors who were obviously his bodyguard—all wearing a smaller version of the same helmet and the iron lamellar armor that Pullus had determined marked their version of noblemen—shoved their comrades aside to allow the general to pass. It was only then that Pullus finally got a good look at the man. His face was mostly obscured by the sweeping cheek guards that almost met in front of the mouth, but Pullus could see that not only was he more powerfully built than almost any Wa the large Roman had seen to this point, he was also taller. Although nowhere near Pullus' own height, he nevertheless stood a full head above the other warriors in his army.

Most importantly, he held a sword in one hand, and even from where Pullus was standing, he could see its quality and the ease with which the Wa commander wielded it. While it was curved in the same way as all the other Wa blades, Pullus could see that this blade was somewhat narrower than what he assumed was normal, and the opposite, or upper edge of the sword, was clearly sharpened for several inches along its length. Still, like the rest of these barbarians, the Wa general disdained the use of a shield, and as Pullus watched him making his way forward, Pullus could see where he was headed. Like any good military man, he had divined where the two Legions met in the *orbis*, the 12th on one side and Pullus' 10th on the other. How he could tell, Pullus had no idea, but he was sure that it was no accident that this was the point to which he was headed. And Pullus immediately began moving to intercept him.

"Titus!" Scribonius called out, and although he was about to tell his friend not to go, he instantly understood that not only would his friend ignore him, but also that it was wrong and selfish for him to try to stop his friend.

As great a Legionary and Centurion Sextus Scribonius was in his own right, he also never held any illusions that Titus Pullus was, simply put, the greatest Legionary who ever marched for Rome, and that to try to prevent him from facing this barbarian would bring shame not only to Pullus, but equal shame to Scribonius for suggesting it.

"Gut that bastard!" was what Scribonius said instead, to which Pullus gave nothing more than a grim nod before moving to intercept the Wa general.

Gasping for breath, Felix tried to ignore the steadily growing ache in his side, knowing that, if he felt such pain, so did his men. But he wouldn't let that stop him, the example of Artaxades—whose name he would learn only later, when he asked—clear in his mind and spurring him on. Behind him, the sound of hobnail boots hitting the rocky road surface, clanking bits of metal hitting each other, and the panting of almost an entire Legion of men filled Felix's ears. They were a little more than a mile away from the northern camp by Felix's reckoning, but the only time he had visited the camp in the short period of time they had before the attack, he hadn't thought to memorize the details of the approach. It simply hadn't occurred to him. However, he thought he remembered that there was a dip in the ridge a little less than a mile from the camp, and that once they had traversed down into it and climbed back up, it was less than a half mile to the camp. That's what he thought, at least, but he wouldn't know if he was right until they got there. And that was what was important at that instant: getting there.

Felix didn't envy the men of the rearmost Cohorts, eating the dust raised by the thousands of running feet ahead, but over the years every man in Caesar's army had occasion to do the same. Never before had it been in such an important cause as this, but at the moment, the dust was just like any other dust that had to be choked through and endured, and Felix knew the men would. The other problem that Felix had to sort out was how to deploy the Cohorts with him, on the run and quickly enough, so that the element of surprise wasn't lost. He understood that there wasn't any way to get all eight Cohorts into a single line: not only would it take too long, there also wasn't enough room, and that wouldn't help getting into the camp. Consequently, as he ran, he made the decision to deploy the first four Cohorts in the column in a manner similar to what Statius had done at Caesar's camp, despite not knowing how Statius' attack had transpired. The one difference was that Felix wasn't willing to spare the time to send part of his force to the far, northern gate. Instead, he decided to feed at least the first four Cohorts through the two closest gates, and only then would he have one or two of the other Cohorts make their way to the northern gate.

Now that he had decided what to do, Felix realized that despite his desperate desire to get to the camp as quickly as possible, he would have to call a halt, to pass on his orders if nothing else. As he thought about it, the more he realized that in order to give this attack the best chance for success, especially since he had no idea exactly what was happening, he would have to make some quick decisions about which Cohorts would be the first into the camp. Just as he came to that determination, the road made a gentle, sweeping bend and tilted downward, and Felix recognized that this was the dip for which he had been waiting. Once he was sure, he immediately slowed down to the normal pace Cohorts used for marching, and since he had forbidden the use of any of the *cornu* once they had left Caesar's camp, there was some confusion, because each Century almost ran into the back of the preceding one as they slowed. Fortunately, there weren't any major entanglements or injuries, although a few men tripped over their own feet and went sprawling onto the rocky road. Felix wasn't aware of any of this, his mind instead absorbed with what needed to happen next. Reaching the point where the road began to slope back upward, he held up his hand to signal a halt, then stepped to the side of his Century, looking back down the long column. This was going to be the worst and most nerve-wracking time for Felix, because the signal he gave to his Cohort *signifer*, a raising and lowering of the standard three times in quick succession, had then to be relayed all the way to the last Cohort. That signal was for all the Pili Priores, the commanders of the Cohorts, to come immediately to the front, at the double. But when dealing with a formation of slightly more than 3,000 men, valuable moments inevitably pass, moments Felix was keenly aware could not afford to be lost. But to give this attack the best chance of success, he had to force himself to take the time. After what seemed like a full watch, but was probably no more than a tenth of that, the other 7 Pili Priores were standing in front of him, chests heaving, sweat streaming down their faces.

"Right on the other side of this hill, we'll be in view of the 10th's camp," Felix announced, glad that he at least had the chance to catch his breath, since he was the one talking. "And if I remember correctly, it's a little more than 3 stadia to the Porta Praetoria."

He paused for a moment, but nobody said anything, every Centurion paying close attention to him.

"We need to get into the camp the quickest way there is, and since we don't have ladders, and we didn't bring any hooks to pull the palisade down, we're going to have to go through the gates."

Now a couple of the men exchanged glances, but Felix chose to ignore the dubious looks they were giving each other.

"So I've decided that we're going to crest the hill, in a double column of Cohorts. My Cohort will be on the right, and I want the Sixth Cohort from the 14th on the left. This will give the Sixth a shorter line to the southern gate, while my Cohort heads for the eastern. Right behind me, I want the Eighth of my Legion, but I'll let you," Felix indicated one of the Centurions, a stocky, swarthy man with thick eyebrows and coarse black hair that made him look perpetually unshaved, "decide who follows the Sixth."

His name was Aulus Frontinus, and although he nodded that he understood, he didn't look particularly happy about being given the ability to choose who would support his Cohort. Again, Felix ignored Frontinus' clear misgivings, as he continued to pass on his orders.

"While the first two Cohorts are going through their gates, I want the next two Cohorts to head all the way to the northern gate. Ideally, I'd like to wait for them to get in place before we go, but I don't think we'll have the time. That is, I don't think the 10th and 12th have the time," he finished grimly. Looking about, he asked, "Are there any questions?"

"Are we all going to be in this double column?"

Felix thought a moment then shook his head.

"No, I don't think it's as important for anyone but the first two Cohorts through each gate. The rest of you can follow us in single column. But remember, the next two Cohorts are going to the northern gate. Let's decide now who it will be."

After a quick discussion, the identities of the next two Cohorts were determined, and all that was left was the disposition of the final two. Felix announced that one Cohort would follow the leading pair to the southern gate, the other to the eastern. Once that was decided, Felix dismissed the men to return to move into position.

"I hope this works," he heard one of the Pili Priores mutter to another.

"So do I," the other man replied, still moving away so that Felix could barely hear the last part. "Because if it doesn't we're all dead men, one way or the other."

It seemed to take forever for Titus Pullus to make his way across the small remaining space behind the Legionaries still fighting, littered as it was with the detritus of the battle, including several bodies. Normally Pullus would have taken the time to say a brief prayer for his men who had fallen, but at that moment all of his attention and concentration was on meeting the barbarian that he implicitly understood was the Wa general. Whether he was the overall commander and the architect of this devastating attack on the army, or just the commander of this assault force Pullus had no way of knowing, nor did he particularly care. In that moment, all that concerned him was the challenge presented by this arrogant bastard, who even then was having his bodyguard clear a path toward the front, where the fighting was taking place. Just as Pullus had feared, the Wa general was clearly aiming at the spot where the 10th and 12th met, and before Pullus got to that spot, the first of the general's bodyguards threw themselves at the thin wall of Roman shields, three abreast and swords raised high above their heads. Pullus had noticed earlier the tendency for the barbarians to attack in this manner, and it had almost always proved fatal—to the attacker. It was a simple matter for the Legionary under assault to tilt his shield up and lift it slightly above his head as he launched an underhand thrust into the Wa's completely unprotected belly.

This time, however, the three barbarians were clearly more skilled, because as Pullus watched, each warrior performed a different maneuver, but with the same result. The three Romans facing the Wa performed the exact tactic that Pullus had seen was so effective, except in every case the Romans ended up with their blades hitting nothing but air. Still, this wouldn't have alarmed Pullus, because he had noted with approval that they had all tilted and lifted their shields in anticipation for the sweeping, downward stroke that, even if it was blocked, would probably shatter their shields but still leave them untouched. However, one of the Wa's simply stopped dead in his tracks from his full run, a feat in itself that further demonstrated these warriors' extraordinary ability and reflexes. Predictably, the Legionary across from this man did what Pullus expected of him, launching a hard underhand thrust, the bloodied point tilted upward in a brutal arc aimed for the vitals of the Wa. But since the Wa wasn't there, for a fraction of time the Roman's arm was out in space, and even as Pullus' mind shouted a warning to his man, there was a flash of metal sweeping downward, as the Wa finished the stroke he had started with his upraised sword. Before Pullus, or the Legionary for that matter, could blink, the man's arm from just below the elbow down was lying on the ground as blood sprayed from the severed stump of the stricken Legionary's arm, the severed hand in the dirt now separated from his sword.

While this was taking place, the second Wa, instead of stopping, made a hopping leap in the air, slightly spreading his legs so that the thrust from his opponent went harmlessly into the space between them. This Wa, as he was coming down, shot his free hand out with a speed that Pullus had witnessed only from the cobras that some of the men kept for sporting purposes, slapping the Roman's sword hand downward, and knocking the tip of the blade into the dirt. The instant his feet touched the ground, the Wa made an elegant, downward sweeping motion with his sword, while at the same time bringing the blade across his body, so that it was now on the right, unprotected side of the Legionary's body. With his sword buried in the dirt, there was no protection from the backhand cut that struck the doomed man in the middle of the neck, because he hadn't even had the time to hunch his shoulders to protect that most vital area. At about the same time as the first Legionary's arm was severed, the second Roman's head went spinning crazily into the air, the helmet flying off in one direction, as the head went in another, spraying blood and gore all over men on both sides.

Taking all this in, Pullus' mind couldn't register the fate of the third man, although in the blur of motion and riot of noise, he was vaguely aware of a body clad in Roman armor going to its knees, right next to the headless corpse that was just tottering over to fall forward onto the ground. Then he was there, coming in from an angle into the fighting, shield up and sword held in the first position. Because the barbarians' attention was understandably focused on their immediate opponents, they were completely unprepared for the giant barbarian to come smashing into the Wa on the left, who was in the process of kicking the stricken Roman—who had just dropped his shield to clutch at his arm—out of the way. The terrific force generated by the weight and speed of Pullus sent the Wa, already off-balance, flying off his feet as if he had been hit at short range by a scorpion. Hitting the warrior at that angle, Pullus sent the first Wa careening, both legs a couple of feet off the ground, hard into the warrior to his right, just as he was stepping around the fallen, headless corpse of the second Legionary. In turn, although the Wa managed to stay upright, he still stumbled several feet to the side, hitting the third Wa, and was at that moment lifting his sword to finish his stricken opponent, who was on his knees, blood pouring down his face, blinding him from the slicing blow that had knocked his helmet off and almost scalped him. This jolt disrupted the aim of the third Wa enough that the blade, instead of cleaving the kneeling man's skull, instead went whistling harmlessly by to strike the ground next to the Roman.

Pullus, since he was prepared for the impact, not only kept his feet, but recovered more quickly, so that he took a couple of shuffling steps to close the gap between himself and his targets. Mindful that in doing so he was placing himself directly in the path of the barbarians that the general's bodyguard had shoved to the side, he pivoted slightly, so that he was facing their ranks, his sword lashing out in a sweeping arc that was designed more to keep any overeager warrior at bay than to strike a target. As he did this, he lifted his left arm high in the air, and risking a glance to the left to make sure he hit his target, brought his shield crashing down, using every bit of his strength, so that the metal edge struck the Wa he had knocked down and who was now on hands and knees, shaking his head, trying to clear it. The wooden shield—with its several layers of thin wood and glue, bolstered and reinforced by the strip of iron around the edge and the iron boss in the middle,—was a deadly weapon itself, and when brought down from the height that Pullus was capable of reaching, and with the huge amount of power the Primus Pilus could generate, the fate of the first Wa was sealed. Pullus' aim was off, however, because he had been aiming for the small gap between the enemy's helmet and armor, where the neck was exposed. Instead, the shield struck roughly in the middle of the back of the Wa's helmet, making a loud, ringing sound, much like striking a gong, except that it ended in a loud crack, as the helmet split into two parts. As the top half flew a foot away, Pullus was only vaguely aware that it contained the top of the warrior's skull and a good portion of his brains with it, as the dead man's limbs suddenly went limp, and he collapsed face first onto the ground, where a pool of blood began quickly forming.

Instead, his attention was torn between his next target, the second Wa who was also trying to regain his balance, and the fact that he had generated such force with his blow that his shield shattered into too many pieces to count, leaving him with just the handle, and a ragged remnant of the center, with the boss still affixed. He didn't have the time to either worry about it or to grab a shield from one of the fallen men, because at that moment a flurry of movement out of the corner of his eye caused him to turn back to face the rest of the Wa, just in time to see the barbarian general roughly pushing aside the remaining men of his bodyguard. As he did so, he snapped some sort of order in a low, guttural voice that to Pullus sounded very much like the growl of a dog. Nevertheless, he was clearly understood by his men, because in ragged unison they took a step backward, swords still up at what Pullus had determined was the equivalent of their first position, the swords held with two hands out in front of them. Moving quickly, Pullus dropped his ruined shield to pick up a new one from one of his men who no longer needed it. Now there was a slight pocket of space, as men were still fighting around Pullus and the Wa general. Despite not understanding the words, Pullus, and the rest of his men within earshot, clearly understood the Wa's intent: this barbarian was claiming their Primus Pilus for himself.

"Gut that *cunnus* Primus Pilus," a man shouted. "Do it for Vellusius!"

Oh, how Pullus wished that whoever called out that name had picked another, because at the moment when he needed all of his concentration, hearing the name of one of the two remaining occupants of the first tent section Titus Pullus belonged to, and knowing what it meant, caused in him a shudder of grief at the worst possible time. Vellusius? Dead? Pullus' mind reeled at the thought, just as the Wa general, displaying the speed and ferocity of all of his warriors, launched his attack.

Just moments after Caesar heard the three blasts of the *cornu*, he and his remaining men were rewarded by the sight of Legionaries streaming through the three gates, where they quickly formed up into their Century formations. Although the original plan that Statius had sketched out was to wait long enough for at least three Centuries from each of the lead Cohorts to form up and align side by side, before starting the attack, the sight of their comrades in such extremis, surrounded by what were still a few thousand barbarian warriors, quickly dispelled his best intentions. In fact, it was Statius himself who, completely forgetting his own plan, immediately led his own Century headlong into the seething mass of Wa, those in the rearmost ranks just beginning to understand the new threat and turning to face it. In the section of the Wa lines Statius had chosen, most of the warriors didn't manage to pivot, so they were either turned obliquely or still had their backs turned when the Centurion and his men slammed into their midst. Within the space of a few heartbeats, almost a dozen Wa had fallen or had been pushed backward into their comrades, who were just becoming aware of the danger. Jammed together as they were, lending their weight by leaning against the men in front of them, who were doing the same in turn, all the way up to the edge of the makeshift parapet, the Wa of the rear ranks were hampered by the man on either side, as they attempted to spin about and face the newly arrived Romans.

Statius and his men took full advantage, and very quickly, Statius' sword was wet almost to the hilt, just like the swords of most of his men. Bashing with their shields or punching the points of their swords up and out in short, gutting stabs, Statius and his men punched a huge hole in the ranks of those Wa nearest to the eastern gate, where the Romans had entered. Even as they did so, Statius heard another roar, the same cry of "Caesar Triumphant," as the men of the Second Century—or what he assumed was the Second—got organized and threw themselves into the battle. Out of the corner of his eye, Statius got a glimpse of a row of Roman helmets, slightly behind him and to his right, the sign that whoever it was had started their own attack and were now engaged. That was the only attention he could pay to the overall situation, before he was occupied by a sudden spear thrust from one of the yellow-faced warriors across from him, the man's face contorted in a mask of fear and rage as he whipped the teardrop-shaped blade upward in answer to Statius' first parry. The move surprised Statius, and he barely avoided having the edge slice upward into his lower jaw by leaning over backwards, but he still felt the disturbed wind on his cheek as the blade slashed by in a blur. Just then, the Legionary to Statius' right sidestepped a half-step to the right, aiming his own blade at the spear-wielding Wa, who was in the process of recovering the weapon in preparation to strike again. Now it was the barbarian's turn to twist desperately to the side, but over the other noises, Statius heard the man give a shout of pain as the other Roman's blade sliced through the leather lamellar armor along the Wa's ribs. In the instant it took for the Wa to withdraw, Statius could see a long red line marking where his man had scored, and it was this small gap that he aimed for in his own attack. More out of desperation than anything else, the Wa whipped his spear around in a sweeping blow that caught Statius by surprise. Even in mid-lunge, he violently twisted his torso to avoid the slashing spearhead, but he was only partially successful. Almost simultaneously, the point of Statius' sword punched into and through the ribs of the Wa, as the edge of the barbarian's spear sliced diagonally downward, starting at a spot just below Statius' left eye. Statius' head snapped back from the impact—which ironically enough saved his life, although the blade ripped through his cheek, smashed out his front teeth, and cleaved his lower jaw in two. Staggering to the side from the blow, Statius' plight was worsened by the fact that because of the awkward angle caused by his attempt to avoid the Wa's spear, he had violated the primary rule of a thrust to the ribs: keeping the blade parallel to the ground, instead of perpendicular, like his sword now was, buried in the chest cavity of the Wa. When the barbarian collapsed, the blade was lodged firmly in the man's ribs, caught in the cartilage as if it were in a vise, and Statius felt the sword ripped from his grasp, even as he himself continued falling to the ground, a gout of blood and bits of teeth preceding him. Although he was still conscious, he suddenly no longer seemed connected to what had been taking place just a heartbeat before, as if it was no longer important. The sounds were still there, ringing in his ears, and he heard someone shout his name once, then twice, but his mouth couldn't form the answer to the call. Lying partially facedown, he saw a pool of blood slowly form around his ruined mouth, and he was finding it difficult to breathe. All around him he could see feet, some of them clad in the Roman *caligae*, others wearing what appeared to be some sort of sandal but with a leather strap protruding from between the toes, which Statius found strange. They were dancing about, kicking up dirt, some of which flew into his face, further clouding his vision, but he had the presence of mind to know that the only reason he hadn't felt the thrust of a blade between his shoulder blades was that he hadn't moved and the barbarians thought him dead. Consequently, he forced himself to refrain from reaching up to wipe the dirt from his face and eyes, or to check his injuries, which he knew were serious. Only after his men pushed these bastards back would it be safe to move, so until that moment came, Statius resigned himself to lying still and suffering in silence, as the fighting continued to rage around him. He was out of the fight now, and it was up to the rest of the men of these four Cohorts to save Caesar; so as he lay there, he offered up prayers to every god he could think of to make it so.

From the gods-only-knew-where, Caesar found that he was infused with a surge of energy unlike anything he had experienced in years, if not decades. Those three blasts of the *cornu* had sent shivers up his spine, but more importantly, from that moment forward, he moved with the purpose and speed of a much younger Caesar, and the vitality was infectious. Again, he was everywhere at once, sword in hand, offering his blade if needed, but more often offering encouragement and support. His armor, the muscled cuirass that was almost as famous as the general himself, was covered in blood and bits of gore, thankfully none of it his, though he had no idea how that was possible, as many close calls as he had suffered this day. Because Caesar still disdained his helmet, his silver hair, once so blond and bright, was standing out from his head; and between that and the shine of his bald head, in the sunlight he looked very much as though he was wearing a crown touched with fire. No Legionary still alive and fighting within that makeshift barricade, no matter where he came from, was unmoved by the sight of their general who, if not one of the gods, was certainly touched and favored by them.

As he strode by, on his way to another spot where there was trouble, more than one Legionary, standing in the line holding the harness ahead of him and supporting a comrade one or more rows up who was doing the fighting, used his spare hand to touch an amulet, or finger a small statue in a pouch hanging from the neck, a statue that theoretically would see him executed, if it was discovered. This was their own idol, their own household god, and depending on who had created it, the likeness to Caesar was either remarkable, or bore only a rough resemblance to him because it had two arms, two legs and was clearly male. Either way, in those moments, as they watched their general, more men accepted the idea of his godhead than had in the previous ten years, all because of what they were sure was a miracle occurring before their very eyes. For what else could this be, but a miracle? Less than a sixth part of a watch before, there hadn't been a man among them who didn't believe that today would be the day they died, the only questions then being in what manner and how many of these yellow bastards they would take with them. But now, from three different directions came the wonderful sight of Roman Cohort- and Century standards, accompanied by shouts that at first were indistinguishable over the noise of fighting. Then, as more Centuries entered through the gates, until there were now at least two or three Cohorts spreading around the rear of the Wa attacking the forum, the men in the interior position behind the makeshift wall finally could make out the words that the attacking Legionaries were shouting, over and over.

"Caesar Triumphant! Caesar Triumphant!"

Quickly, the beleaguered defenders picked up the cry as well, and like Caesar, men who would have sworn they could no longer lift a sword suddenly found themselves infused with an energy and a reignited desire to kill these savages who thought that they could defeat the men of Caesar's army. The fact that they had come very close to doing exactly that only served to fuel the kindling rage of men who for almost an entire day had been on the defensive, forced to watch comrades, some of them friends closer than brothers, struck down all around them. Each of them, once they had time to reflect on the events of the day would come basically to the same conclusion: that they had been chosen by their gods to witness all that had taken place on this day, to confirm what some of them had been saying privately for varying lengths of time—that their general was a god in man's form.

For them, there was no other explanation for what happened that day, no matter how much the events would be dissected later, over many campfires, for many, many days, months, and years to come. First, however, was the business at hand, and it was with a savage, renewed energy that men began clamoring to take their spot at the makeshift wall, so eager now to strike out at these barbarians who suddenly didn't act and look as confident as they had just moments before. Now, it was their turn to look over their shoulders in worry at the sounds of the fighting behind them, and there wasn't a man of Caesar's left who didn't take vicious delight in the sight. For the first time in the battle, the men of the Legions found their voice, alternating between shouting what was now the rallying cry that they were convinced would sweep them to victory, and taunting those men who were still trying with desperation to claw and scramble their way up and over the barricade. Perhaps some of them still held out hope that if they could just reach that pale grubworm of a general who was striding around, acting as if he were some sort of god, and strike him down, these other pale grubworms would lose heart. Most of them were simply trying to kill the man across from them, because that was what they were supposed to do, and until someone in authority told them differently, they would continue to do so. Whatever the motivation, the men facing each other were still trying to kill each other, one side trying to keep the other side from creating a breach wide enough for more than a trickle of Wa to pour through, the other understanding that somehow what had seemed to be a sure victory was now slipping out of their grasp. Unless they could kill that grubworm with the silver hair.

With Pilus Prior Tetarfenus out of action, command of the Cohorts on the southern wall now devolved to the Pilus Posterior, Asinius Severus, who was in command for only a short time before he was struck down by a Wa sword. That meant that the Princeps Prior, commander of the Third Century, should have been in charge, but he had fallen very early in the fight for the southern wall. Consequently, Princeps Posterior Lentulus, Centurion commanding the Fourth Century, who was wounded but still in the fight, held overall command of the Cohorts defending the eastern wall. Because the wound was to his leg and although the bleeding had been staunched with a tourniquet, it crippled his ability to move and direct the other Centuries and Cohorts. Fortunately, every one of Caesar's Centurions had been hand-picked by the general, and their one common characteristic was their ability to think independently and make decisions with a minimum of direction from above. That was the only thing that stopped the incursion started in Tetarfenus' area after he fell, from becoming a full-scale breakthrough of the Roman camp, the Centurions in the immediate area seeing him fall and recognizing the danger.

Even so, by the time there was an organized response, the Wa had managed to create a bulging pocket of snarling, slashing warriors, most of them wielding the swords that Pullus had worried about. They numbered perhaps two hundred warriors, and very quickly their intentions became clear, as they began to try cutting their way along the wall in the direction of the gate. If they could seize the gateway, it would allow for the passage of the rest of their comrades much more quickly than by climbing the ladders, no matter how numerous they were. As quickly as they started, the Centurions in command of the two Centuries between these Wa and the gate understood their enemy's intent, and slightly changed the facing of some of their Legionaries. In essence, the Romans were being pushed on two fronts, from the Wa warriors still ascending the ladders along the wall, and now from this group. The Centuries arrayed between the knot of Wa inside the walls and the gate were from the Tenth Cohort, composed of a large number of Gayans, Han, and a smattering of Pandyans. Despite their relative lack of experience, just the last watch alone had made them fully blooded veterans, so they didn't hesitate when their Centurions, after a quick conference, made what were unusual dispositions. Taking the last three men from the files in support of the Legionaries fighting on the wall, they quickly moved them into a position perpendicular to their original one, with one Century hard up against the wall, and the other to the left. If viewed from above, with the wall as the vertical axis, it would have looked as if they were forming the letter "L", although not one of the men or their officers ever entertained that thought.

Instead, they were completely focused on stopping the advance of this small group of barbarians, who had been delayed just long enough for this scratch formation that wasn't in any of the manuals, created by the sacrifice of a thin, single line of Legionaries who had fought ferociously to buy time for their comrades. Now these men were lying at the feet of the advancing Wa, although the barbarians had been whittled down in numbers by these fallen men. Still, knowing the stakes and that this was their best hope, the small horde of sword-wielding barbarians didn't hesitate, throwing themselves at the first chance at the woefully thin wall of shields. Immediately the fighting was at a frenzied tempo, as both sides met with terrific force, every man snarling and spitting his hatred for the one across from him, the Roman side using their shields in the manner in which they were trained, the Wa countering with a series of sword thrusts that seemed to come from every direction, all at once. Inevitably, men on both sides fell, but in this battle within a battle, it was the Wa who could ill afford the losses.

Nevertheless, despite their best efforts, the men of the two Centuries of the Tenth Cohort found themselves taking a step backward. It was tentative, and hard-fought, but it was a step back toward the gate. Not surprisingly, this step backwards fueled the energy of the Wa, which to the men of Caesar's army already seemed inexhaustible, and their slashes, thrusts, and stabs came even more quickly, their blades flicking out in search of fleshy targets. The men of Caesar's Legions found themselves desperately hiding behind their shields, many of them to no avail, as seemingly inexorably, they continued their backward movement. Finally, the Centurion in charge of the Century nearest to the wall had the barest moment to have a glance behind him, but the moment he did, he wished he hadn't. Not more than a half-dozen paces from the last man of his Century, desperately grasping the harness of the man in front of him who at that very moment was furiously parrying a thrust from the barbarian opposite him, was the opening that was the main gate of the camp. The gate that, if the Centurion and his men lost this fight and left it unprotected, would spell the end of the men in the northern camp and the success of the surprise attack.

Titus Pullus was immediately at a disadvantage, his mind still reeling from the knowledge that an unknown Legionary had unintentionally imparted to him. Publius Vellusius—one of the two survivors of his original tent group, formed so many years ago, when then-Praetor Gaius Julius Caesar had authorized a *dilectus* for what would become the most famous and feared Legion in the entire world, Caesar's 10th Equestris—had apparently died. Even as the giant Primus Pilus tried to process this thought, the Wa general charged at the Roman, his blade slashing down in a vicious arc that Pullus barely avoided by twisting to the side. Before he could recover himself back to a proper defensive position, the Wa—his age impossible to tell because of the helmet's almost completely masking his features, except for his eyes—brought his blade back up in an almost exact reversal of his first stroke. Normally, this would have been nothing more than a quick recovery, but because the top of the barbarian's blade was sharpened for almost half its length, instead of pulling it straight back, he made an exaggerated semicircular arc with the point, the tip aimed with precision just below the brim of Pullus' helmet. His intent was clear: either by cutting a gash in the Roman's forehead, or striking across the eyes, he was trying to blind Pullus. It would have worked, if Pullus had done the natural thing by jerking his head backward, and in fact it might have been a killing blow if the Wa's sword tip had slashed his throat, but this wasn't the first time Pullus had seen this move used, albeit on other men. And what he had seen was that the best of nothing but bad choices was to drop his head to take the blow on the brow of his helmet. In fact, that was why over the years Caesar had demanded that a strip of iron be added just above the forehead, not only to reinforce that area, but also to keep blades from sliding down and into the faces of his men.

Still, it was far from an ideal defense, and despite the helmet's being at the outermost limit of the barbarian's reach, there was sufficient force behind the sword tip to make a sound much like a bell being rung, as tiny sparks shot in every direction, the Wa scoring a glancing blow. More problematically, it made similar sparks explode in front of Pullus' eyes, and he heard a gasp of surprise and pain, only dimly aware that it came from him himself. His mind had barely cleared from the news of Vellusius; now he had to shake his head to try to clear it from the blow; yet he still had the presence of mind to keep his shield up, with elbow locked tightly against his hip. It was a good thing he did, because as quickly as the Wa commander recovered his blade back to what the barbarians used as their basic offensive position, he lashed out again with his sword. In fact, the next few moments saw a flurry of thrusts and slashes, all of them from the Wa general, the man a blur of fluid, deadly motion, forcing Pullus to stay on the defensive. As frenetic as the pace of the attack was, no less spirited was Pullus' defense: all he could do during this part of the fight was to keep his shield desperately in front and to move it just enough to block each of the barbarian's attacks. Pullus knew that if he overcommitted in one direction, a man as skilled as his opponent would make him pay for the mistake with his life. Again, all of the watches spent training for times like this were what kept Pullus alive, as it seemed that his head would never clear, there still being a ringing in his ears, and his vision was slightly blurred. Regardless of his current condition, he was thankful it wasn't worse: if he had experienced double vision at that moment, he would already be a corpse. Whatever shape he was in at the moment, he also knew that he couldn't stay on the defensive for much longer, the fatigue in his shield arm growing stronger with every heartbeat. Even as his shield absorbed another blow, the thudding sound was accompanied by a high-pitched cracking sound, telling Pullus that his shield was failing, giving him even less time.

In fact, this attack by the savage opposite him seemed to Pullus to epitomize how the entire day had gone. From the outset, Caesar's army had been on the back foot, on the defensive, which was bad enough. However, up until this battle, even when Caesar and his men were forced to defend, they had still managed to dictate matters to a certain degree. But not today; all day Pullus had been running from one spot to another, always reacting to some new threat posed by these yellow-skinned men, and now in what he realized were the waning moments of his life, Pullus was being forced to dance to the tune this little bastard was calling. That realization, even more than the idea of defeat, infuriated Pullus to a degree that came as a surprise to him. Another lightning-quick thrust from the Wa struck his shield, this time to the right of the boss and lower down, but it created a crack that moved diagonally up and across his shield, two spidery lines appearing on either side of the metal. Pullus instantly recognized that with the Wa's next strike his shield would fall apart and be useless, both as a defensive and as an offensive weapon, so, not waiting, he finally made his first offensive move. Taking a step forward that was much larger than it would be for most men, thanks to his longer legs, Pullus punched out with his damaged shield. Timing it as he did, just as the Wa general was recovering from his last attack, Pullus' opponent had no chance to cleanly dodge the metal boss that Pullus had aimed right at his face, aided by the barbarian's smaller stature. All the Wa could do was, just like Pullus moments before, try to minimize the damage. While Pullus had ducked his head, the enemy general tilted his head to the side slightly, taking the blow from the giant Roman's shield on the iron cheekpiece of his helmet, instead of squarely in his face. Once more there was a gong-like sound, as the metal from Pullus' shield struck the Wa helmet, and while it wasn't a clean blow by any means, it still contained enough power behind it that it would have knocked a lesser man off his feet. But this barbarian hadn't achieved his rank just by virtue of his birth, earning his position by a combination of that and his prowess in battle. Despite the fact that it was a damaging blow, the Wa kept his feet, and more by instinct than anything else, since he carried no shield to protect him, he made an off-balance, wild swing in an attempt to keep his opponent from following up, more than with any hope of landing a solid blow.

As poorly aimed as it was, it still struck Pullus' shield, completing the destruction of the Primus Pilus' best defense, pieces of wood exploding in every direction, disintegrating so much that in the instant before he dropped it, all that Pullus was left with was the handle of the shield, even the boss falling to the ground at his feet. This paused Pullus for a fraction of a heartbeat from his advance, his sword pulled back, ready to deliver a killing blow, but it was enough. Regaining his balance, the Wa general lunged forward, both hands clutching his sword as he raised it above his head. Pullus had seen this attack more times than he could count today, and while every other time it had seemed to be made especially for the Romans' short, thrusting counterattack into the completely exposed belly of the attacker, some instinct warned him that this was what the barbarian was expecting. More importantly, it was what the Wa was hoping for, so instead, Pullus took a hopping step to his right. While this step moved Pullus' own sword farther away from his intended target, it clearly surprised his enemy, who, even as Pullus made this move, had altered his attack by letting go of the sword with his left hand, and by simply dropping his elbow back down to his side, brought his blade into position for a disemboweling horizontal stroke. Like Pullus, the Wa general had observed what these grubworms favored when faced with the overhead attack, and had expected this grubworm, giant though he may have been, to react in the same way. And indeed, if Pullus had done as many a Roman had done so often this day, taking a simple step forward while bringing his sword forward in a sweeping underhand thrust, at the very least his sword arm would have been exposed, as the Wa's blade traveled along its horizontal path. Ideally, the giant barbarian would have stepped forward far enough so that the general's blade would have bitten deeply into the man's side, but, either way, since the man had lost his shield, the fight would have been over. Instead, his blade bit into nothing more than the air, and now it was the Wa who was vulnerable, as Pullus had immediately brought his feet underneath him, keeping his sword at the first position and ready to strike.

In the time it takes to blink an eye, Pullus did just that: the tip of his sword traveling toward the Wa at a speed that the human eye could barely comprehend. In all of the thrusts he had made, in practice or in battle, over thousands upon thousands of times, Titus Pullus was sure he had never been faster than he was in that moment, on that day. And on any other day, against any other opponent, this fight would have ended right then, because Pullus was absolutely right in his belief: he had never launched a faster or more devastating attack. Against this opponent, however, while Pullus' thrust struck, it wasn't a killing blow, as it would have been with any other foe, because the Wa general desperately twisted his body to one side, moving the part of his lower torso at which Pullus had aimed a few inches. It wasn't enough to avoid being hit altogether, but instead of punching through the lamellar armor the Wa was wearing and the blade entering several inches into his abdomen, it managed only to penetrate the armor and enter perhaps an inch deep. More importantly, the Wa was moving too quickly and violently for Pullus to finish the attack in the normal manner, with either a twisting of the blade to cause more internal damage, or a strong lateral cutting move that disemboweled the victim. Therefore, while the wound was painful and caused the barbarian to expel a sharp, hissing breath of pain, it didn't inflict the damage it should have.

What it did do was put the Wa on the defensive, so sensing that it was at least his opponent's turn to stand on his back foot, Pullus wouldn't waste the opportunity. As he recovered from his thrust, he moved forward to close the gap between himself and his opponent, back to their positions an instant before. As quickly as his arm had drawn back, it lashed out again, but this thrust Pullus not only aimed higher, but he also moved his arm out from his body a bit. Normally this maneuver was discouraged, because it robbed a man of much of the force that came from using the bulk of his body; Titus Pullus was one of the few—not just in the ranks but also in the upper classes, with the possible exception of Marcus Antonius—for whom this rule didn't apply. Moving his arm out in this manner meant that his blade was heading for the Wa at a slightly different angle. With the Roman coming at him from his left, this was a moment where the lack of a shield made the Wa vulnerable, as the point of Pullus' sword seemed to unerringly seek the barbarian's throat. In answer, the only move the barbarian could perform was to whip his sword up and across his body in an attempt to knock Pullus' blade off its path. In this he was only partially successful; instead of the point of the Roman's sword piercing his throat, the Wa managed to knock the blade upward, so that it struck him just above where his helmet flared out, on the rounded portion above the ear. Between the deflection and the smooth surface of the helmet, much of the blow's force was absorbed, but the point of Pullus' sword still tore a ragged gouge in the general's helmet and sliced into the top of the man's scalp. For the first time, the Wa let out a howl of pain, as he staggered sideways, blood almost immediately starting to flow down the side of his face. Pullus felt a savage satisfaction, but he knew that his foe was still dangerous, and, determined not to give this barbarian any chance to recover, he pressed his advantage now. Taking a shuffling couple of steps forward, he closed the distance caused by the Wa's staggering retreat, his blade already back at a modified first position, angled across his body slightly more than normal to compensate for his lack of shield.

The Wa was weaving about; whether it was because he was groggy or it was by design Pullus couldn't tell, but the end result was the same: it made the man harder to hit and forced Pullus to pause. For his part, the barbarian general, while he was reeling from the blow, never took his eyes off Pullus, despite the blood streaming down his forehead and into his left eye. Neither man made a move for the span of a few heartbeats, and while they didn't notice, the warriors around them had moved their own fighting slightly farther away, making a rough circle, as the champions of the two armies continued to battle. Pullus' arm ached from the slashing wound he had received some time before, although he couldn't tell whether the pain came from the wound or the bandage being too tight. During the lull, the Wa, with his free hand, reached up and managed to rip the helmet off his head; only then did Pullus get an idea of the man's age. His hair was long, but pulled back tightly, so that it lay flat against his skull, and Pullus saw that while it was just as black as every other Wa's the Primus Pilus had seen before, it was also liberally streaked with gray. Now that the Wa was helmetless, Pullus could also partially see the man's features, although one side of his face was obscured by blood, but what Pullus could see was the same seams and lines he himself carried. This was a man who had been exposed to the elements for most of his life, and was clearly as hard as the metal of Pullus' sword. As his mind made that comparison, Pullus was thankful for that strength, once more thanking the gods for the Gallic blade that he had carried for more than two decades.

Now that Pullus could see some of the man's face, it suddenly made this fight more immediate and more personal. This was the man who had at least a hand in the destruction of Caesar's army, and, most important to Pullus, had destroyed his beloved 10th Legion, who had caused the death of one of his best friends, Balbus, and one of his longest-term comrades, Vellusius. Suddenly, Pullus felt a surge of warmth that seemed to start somewhere in his belly, uncoiling itself like a serpent, as it made its way up through his body, and he recognized it for what it was: the return of an old friend, one that he needed now more than ever. That feeling was what distracted Pullus just for the blink of an eye, but it was all the Wa needed as, clearly sensing this lapse in his opponent, he struck with blinding speed. And it was this distraction that caused Pullus to react to the barbarian's sudden strike just a fraction more slowly than normal. Either way, it sufficed to allow the point of the Wa's blade to snake past Pullus' own and, even as Pullus swept his blade up in a desperate attempt to deflect the attack, the point punched through Pullus' mail, burying itself deeply in the Roman's body.

The sight that greeted Felix was the one thing he hadn't prepared for, and it was such a surprise that even with his sense of urgency, he came to a skidding halt. He had just reached the top of the slope, so that the northern camp was now partly in sight around a slight bend in the ridgetop road. Except that the camp was almost completely obscured, not just in a haze of dust, but by the swarming bodies of men, some of them scaling ladders, while more were massed around each one, waiting their turn to ascend. For several long moments, Felix stood motionless, staring slack-jawed at the sight before him, his mind racing as it tried to assimilate this change in the situation. Finally, he whirled around, and sprinted back in the other direction, running only a few paces, before almost slamming into the first rank of his own Century who were laboring up the road behind him.

"Stop!" Felix shouted this several times, in his excitement completely forgetting that "Stop" wasn't part of the lexicon of the Roman drill manual.

Nevertheless, his words had the desired effect as his men slid and stumbled to a halt, although not without the rear ranks colliding with their comrades in front, sending several men tumbling to the ground. The air filled with shouted curses, which Felix ignored, as he moved quickly to the side of his Century so that he could have an unobstructed view of the Centuries and Cohorts following behind his. Waving his hand over his head, his fist clenched in the correct signal, he managed to stop the entire column again, but this time, instead of waiting for the Centurions to make their way to him, he began sprinting down the road, picking a spot to stop roughly halfway in the middle. More quickly this time, he was again surrounded by the Centurions of the relief column, their faces showing a combination of concern and irritation at this disruption in the plan. Quickly, Felix explained what he had just seen, ignoring the gasps and curses of the men around him.

"We're not going to be able to form up the way we'd planned," he went on. "So we're going to shake the men out here, and then we're going to have to double-time from the top of the slope. We have to hit those *cunni* as fast as we can, before they have a chance to get organized."

"Did they see you?" asked a Centurion from the 14th.

Felix shook his head.

"I don't think so."

"Don't think so?" the man from the 14th grumbled. "For all we know, they might be forming up themselves and waiting for us."

"So?" Felix shot back. "Even if they are, we're still attacking. Unless you have a better idea?"

When put that way, the other Centurion had no real response, knowing what was going to happen, no matter if the enemy were ready or not. After a moment's silence, he wilted under Felix's glare, only shaking his head in response. With that settled, Felix turned his attention back to the matter. Taking a glance around at the ground on either side of the road, he didn't like what he saw.

"There's not enough room here to get more than two Cohorts on line, so that will have to do," he said grimly. After his rebuke of their fellow Centurion, even if the others were disposed to argue, they weren't willing to do so, and taking their silence as assent, he hurried on, ever mindful that every moment that passed was a moment lost.

"Right, so it will be the Fifth, and we'll line up from there," he pointed to a spot to the left side of the road, "to over by that clump of rocks. And the Sixth of the 14th will shake out from the rocks further out that way." Pausing to stare thoughtfully in the direction he indicated, he shook his head. "Although it looks like your last Century might be squeezed by that bunch of trees. But you'll just have to make do, at least until we get up there. The rest of you will use my Cohort as the anchor on the left. We're going to aim for the corner of the camp, so that the Sixth Century will hit those bastards closest to the corner, and my Century on the other end will hit," he paused as he tried to envision the width of the formation he was going to use and how much of the eastern wall it would cover, "just this side of the Porta Praetoria. I think," he added, with a thin smile.

"Wait, your Sixth Century is going to anchor the left?" interrupted the Pilus Prior of the Seventh Cohort of the 14th. "That means you're going in a single line? With no support?"

Felix bit back the first thing that came to his mind, grudgingly accepting that it was a valid question, even if it was wasting time.

"We need to get as many swords to bear on these *cunni* as we can, as quickly as we can," Felix explained. "If we go in a single line, at least with the first two Cohorts, we should just about cover their entire line. If we went in doubled up like normal, if their commander is a quick thinker, he can get around our flanks before the rest of you get into position."

"That's a big 'if'," the other Pilus Prior said doubtfully, but before Felix could say anything more, he gave a quick shake of his head. "But I think you're right, it's the only thing to do. So what do the rest of us do?"

Felix gave a quick outline of what he thought was the best plan of attack for the trailing Cohorts, and with that settled, the Centurions hurried to their spots. With a few curses and oaths hurled at men moving a little too slowly for their tastes, the Centurions of the relief force got their Centuries into their correct spots in what Felix was sure was record time, and almost before he had mentally prepared himself, two Cohorts were arrayed in a single line, the men with their javelins ready. Taking a breath, he drew his sword and in a quick stroke downward, launched the attack of the relieving force. Starting at the run, he led his Cohort up the slope, offering up a silent prayer to the gods that he and his men were in time.

Caesar stood motionless, swaying slightly, as for the first time since in what seemed like days, he no longer needed to move from one trouble spot to the next. While he was still within the makeshift barricade, all of the men who were still able had left the protection it had offered, leaping over the barrels, carts, and boxes in pursuit of a now-fleeing enemy. The Wa attack, as furious and nearly overwhelming as any Caesar had faced, had broken suddenly, as the four Cohorts led by Statius had slammed full-force into the rear of the unsuspecting barbarian horde. In those frantic moments, before Caesar and the remainder of his army's eyes, the Wa had gone from snarling, ferocious wolves, ravening for blood, into fearful, whipped curs, suddenly worried only about their own escape and salvation. The panic had started with those barbarians armed with the spears, Caesar had noticed, but the men armed with swords very quickly found themselves isolated, and while a large number of them had chosen to go down fighting, others had soon followed their spear-wielding comrades. The Legionaries of the relief Cohorts, still relatively fresh, had pursued the fleeing Wa with a vengeance, cutting down men without any mercy. Fueled by their example, the battered survivors behind the barricade had somehow found the energy to clamber over the parapet and join in the pursuit.

Although Caesar understood their desire to avenge so many fallen comrades, he also had gained a huge amount of respect for the cunning and guile of the faceless commander who had come closer to defeating Caesar than any other man. With that in mind, he had sent Bodroges to chase down the pursuing Legionaries, ordering them to stop at the camp walls. He had no idea if the Tribune had managed to find whoever was commanding the relief force; Caesar still didn't know the identity of the commander, nor did he know that Statius had fallen. Whereas just a short time before, he had felt more vitality and energy coursing through his body than he had in many years, now it was as if the gods were demanding a repayment, with interest, for the gift they had bestowed on him, when the crisis was at its zenith. Now it was as if the gods had seen fit to add ten more years to his age, as he found it next to impossible even to lift his arms, and the only way he could move about was at a slow, decrepit shuffle. He was just thankful that he was for the most part alone; the men left behind had been wounded and were too absorbed in their own agony to notice their general hobbling about, while the slaves and *medici* were equally focused on trying to minister to those men they deemed had the best chance to survive.

Caesar's gaze traveled over the cluttered, bloody expanse of ground enclosed by the barricade, noting sadly that those few spots of ground that he could see were almost completely soaked in the blood of his men. Bodies of the dead were stacked a short distance away from the barricade, forming a rough circle that was a gruesome image of the real barricade, and Caesar was struck by the macabre thought that if the barricade itself had been taken, the men could have at least used their dead comrades as a last-ditch protection. Fortunately, it hadn't come to that, but just barely. The roaring noise of battle had subsided, as the fighting moved back in the direction of the western wall, while Caesar's men pursued the fleeing enemy; so he cocked an ear and listened for a moment, the sounds telling him that at a spot near the southwest corner of the camp, where the first breach of the wall had happened, the barbarians had either stopped running to make a stand, or been forced to do so by his men. Either way, he could tell that there was a furious fight going on, and his instinct was to head in that direction. He took no more than a couple of steps, however, before he realized that if he were to do so, it would have to be on horseback, and even then he would have to have help to mount. For all his prodigious talents, Caesar was also endowed with a huge streak of vanity, and it was a mark of pride that even now, at sixty-five, he was able to vault into the saddle without help. This time would be different; the fatigue and ache in his bones was so deep that he knew without a doubt that if he tried, he would fail. And that would be even worse than not trying, he knew, especially now.

For today had demonstrated one thing clearly. Caesar was capable of being fooled, and he also understood the day wasn't over, and while this battle here was won, if the enemy conquered the northern camp, he and his army still faced defeat. Despite his fatigue, Caesar's mind was still active, and as he stood swaying on his feet, he was thinking through the next watches. Squinting up at the sky, he saw with a sinking heart that there was still at least a watch, probably a third more than a watch, of daylight left. This meant that the barbarian commander, if his assault force to the north was successful, still might have time to move south, using the ridgetop road. And if he did, between whatever he brought with him and the remnants of the force his men were chasing even then, the four Cohorts of the relief force wouldn't be enough to stop them from completing the victory. Yes, he took some grim satisfaction in the knowledge that this would be a victory almost as costly in terms of Wa casualties as a defeat, but starting that morning, he had also seen firsthand that such considerations weren't important to the commander of the barbarian force. After all, Caesar recognized, his counterpart had ordered his men to sacrifice their lives merely to fill a ditch, just so that the rest of his men could scale the walls! That made it highly unlikely the barbarian general would care all that much how costly it was to defeat the invading army. No, Caesar thought sadly, as courageous and motivating as the repulse of the Wa from this camp was, in the overall battle—and ultimately this campaign—it changed nothing in the overall scheme. His only hope, and oh, how slim it was, would be that Pullus and Balbinus had exacted such a heavy price for the taking of their camp that, at the very least, it caused the Wa general to stop for the day to reorganize his forces. Caesar had no real idea of how these strange people conducted military matters, whether they organized their men in units similar to Legions, or whether it was just one big, massed mob of men. But he suspected that these people were at least as ordered and organized as the Romans. So, perhaps there was some hope after all.

With that thought, Caesar gave a short, bitter laugh, aimed at himself. Normally, he would pounce on that slender reed of hope, building on it, as if it instead were a foreordained fact.. And speaking truthfully, until today, he had always viewed such developments as proof of the gods' favor, so it had never occurred to him that he couldn't take full advantage of even that slight a chance. But today had shaken him to his core, since he still vividly remembered the feeling of helplessness and confusion, when he had watched the surprise attack of the Wa springing from the tents of the camp across from his, and how he had had absolutely no idea what to do. That had never happened to Caesar before—not once—and this, more than the savage fighting, more than the appalling losses inflicted on his army, had rocked him to the soles of his feet. Suddenly, he shook his head, trying to banish this train of thought from his mind, forcing himself to concentrate on the moment at hand: if not for my own *dignitas* and reputation, he thought, then for these men who fought like lions for me today. This idea snapped him from his lethargy, at least mentally, although he still couldn't summon the energy to do much more than stumble about. Instead, he started surveying the ground around him, deciding what needed to be done to prepare for a renewal of the onslaught. Quickly realizing that his northern and eastern walls were still intact, Caesar decided that he needed to concentrate as much of his force as he could spare to those two sides, but not ignore the areas on the western wall that were breached. He briefly considered the southern wall, but almost immediately discarded it as a focus of his attention, knowing that if an attack came today, the barbarian commander couldn't spare the time it would take to move all the way to the south to attack a wall that hadn't already been weakened or breached in some way. Looking about, he tried to find one of his staff, but they were all either killed, or had gone off in pursuit of the fleeing enemy, their bloodlust as aroused as that of any ranker. Ah, to be young again, he thought wryly.

He was pleased to see that at least some of the *medici* had moved beyond the barricade to tend to the men of the relief Cohorts who had fallen. Thankfully, those numbers were few, and he watched as two men gently lifted the plank used as a stretcher up and over the barricade, where two other slaves were waiting. On the plank, the wood now stained black with blood from its cargo, was a Legionary that Caesar could see was a Centurion, his helmet still on his head, so the transverse crest was visible. This was unusual in itself; normally, wounded men either yanked the helmet off, or the *medici* removed it, because it got in the way of their ministrations. Piqued by this odd sight, Caesar walked over slowly, picking a spot where he was sure they would stop and lay the injured man, since it was one of the few clear spots left. Reaching it just before the stretcher bearers, Caesar immediately saw why the *medici* hadn't removed the man's helmet. He had suffered a ghastly facial wound, and although it was extremely hard to see, because of all the blood, it looked to Caesar as though the hanging cheekguard had been mangled by the blow from a bladed weapon, and while he couldn't say for sure, he had the impression that the edges of the metal had been driven into the flesh and bone of the man's face. Even if this man survived, Caesar knew, he would be horribly scarred and—judging from the way his jawbone seemed misaligned—would either never speak again or have a horrible time of it. Because of the blood, and the way his face was already horribly swollen, Caesar didn't recognize him at first, but then, to Caesar's surprise, the man's eyes fluttered open, and his head turned slightly as he tried to look about. The effort made him groan, but Caesar had seen enough: he recognized that it was Statius, the Pilus Prior of the Fifth Cohort of the 14th Legion. Kneeling down next to the stricken man, Caesar reached out and gently placed his hand over Statius', who blinked in surprise and turned his head with some difficulty to see that it was his general. Recognizing Caesar, without thinking, Statius tried to raise his head at least, in acknowledgement of his commander, but immediately sank back with a groan of pain. Alarmed, Caesar put a hand on the Centurion's shoulder, gently but firmly pushing him back down onto the stretcher.

"Gods forgive me, Statius! I didn't mean to give you a start! Please, lie back, you've earned a rest now. You and the men of your relief force saved this camp from falling, and I just wanted to thank you for that."

Again, out of instinct and habit, Statius tried to open his ruined mouth to answer his general, but all that came out was a garbled, unintelligible half-groan, half-mumble. Caesar patted Statius again, cursing himself for causing this man more pain.

"That's all right, don't try to talk. I'm going to have my personal physician assigned to your care." Caesar's tone was reassuring, but the thought in his mind at that moment was that he would do so, provided Statius was still alive, "He should have you up and about in no time. Although you may not be as handsome as you once were."

Only Caesar could have made such a joke at that moment, and while there was a low rumble in Statius' throat that could have been a growl of anger, Caesar saw the man's eyes turn down, a sign that he appreciated the jest. Caesar thought for a moment, because as much as he didn't want to cause this poor man any more torment, he needed some information from him, since he was the only Legionary of sufficient rank nearby.

Finally, he came up with an idea and told Statius, "Statius, forgive me, but there are a few questions I must have the answers to. So while I don't want to cause you any pain, I have to ask you some things. But I think I've come up with a way you can tell me what I need to know. What I ask is that you blink once for 'yes', and twice for 'no'. Can you do that for me?"

In answer Statius blinked, one time, and Caesar began.

"I assume that if Ventidius sent you from your camp, that it's still in our hands and, in fact, wasn't hard-pressed. But do you know anything about the southernmost camp and whether it still holds?"

Statius blinked, twice. Caesar suppressed a curse, knowing that it wouldn't do any good to upset his Centurion for something that was out of his control.

Keeping his tone even, he replied, "Very well. We'll find out soon enough. So, Ventidius sent these four Cohorts to help us. Were you the commander?"

Statius' brow furrowed, and he tried to shake his head, and in his excitement forgot that he needed to blink twice just one time, instead blinking very rapidly. At first Caesar couldn't fathom what Statius was trying to tell him, and he bit his lip in a supreme effort not to show his impatience.

"Statius, I'm afraid I've confused you," he said finally, taking the blame on his own shoulders in an effort to avoid the man's becoming even more upset than he clearly was. "But let's keep this simple, neh? Were you the commander of the relief force?"

Statius blinked twice, this time stopping to ensure Caesar understood. And while his general did, he was slightly confused. He couldn't believe that Ventidius would have sent one of the front line Cohorts, the First through Fourth, to relieve Caesar. Then a possible reason dawned on him.

"Did Ventidius send Cohorts from both Legions there? The 14th and 30th?"

Giving a single blink, Statius also nodded slightly, the relief that his general understood clear in his eyes. Caesar tried to rack his tired brain, thinking about who could possibly be the commander of the relief force, if not Statius. Technically speaking, Felix, who commanded the Fifth of the 30th was the same rank as Statius, but Caesar was sure that Statius' rank predated Felix's, which would have made him senior. But not knowing where else to start, he began there.

"Was Felix named the commander of the relief force?"

Another single blink, and Caesar thought he understood, and nodded his thanks to Statius as he stood.

Speaking more to himself, Caesar said, "Well, as soon as he comes back from chasing those bastards away, I'll have to thank him."

He had turned away, but he was almost tripped as something suddenly grabbed at one of his legs. Looking down in surprise, he saw a bloody hand grabbing at his calf. Statius was trying to struggle upright, despite the attempts of the *medici* to keep him prone, his mangled visage conveying to Caesar that there was more he wanted to tell his general. Turning back to the wounded man, Caesar knelt again.

"What is it, Statius? What are you trying to tell me that's more important than your recovery?"

Again, a gurgled moan erupted from Statius' mangled mouth, the effort this time so much that it caused a spray of blood to spatter all over Caesar's legs and the hands and arms of the men holding Statius down. Normally, this would have bothered Caesar, who was nothing if not extremely clean, but he could clearly see that there was something of momentous importance Statius was trying to tell him. Statius was no less frustrated, and, in desperation, he mimed writing something so that Caesar instantly understood. Slapping his forehead, Caesar came to his feet.

"Of course! I should have thought of that instead of tormenting you!"

Feeling another slight burst of energy, Caesar moved from Statius' side, his eyes searching the ground, looking for a wax tablet. He quickly realized the difficulty of his task; not only was the ground covered, it was covered with either dead or wounded men. His secretaries, at least two of them, were dead, and he hadn't seen the other two since early in the battle, so he was forced to look about at the men attending the wounded, since many Cohort secretaries doubled as *medici* or stretcher bearers. Of course, it was extremely unlikely that any of them were still carrying the leather bag with a supply of tablets for their Centurions. But then, Caesar spotted a man with that very thing, still dangling from his waist. Calling him over, Caesar was happy to see that the man still had a tablet, and even better, still had his stylus, although it was caked in blood from where it was thrust into his belt and one of his charges had bled all over it. Returning to Statius, Caesar handed the tablet and stylus to the prone Centurion, trying to conceal his impatience as the man laboriously wrote several lines. The more he wrote, the deeper Caesar's confusion and his concern became. Finally finished, Statius offered his general the tablet, and it was only through a supreme effort of will that the older man didn't snatch it from his grasp. Caesar opened the tablet, forced to squint at the almost illegible scrawl. Well, he thought, I don't promote men to the Centurionate based on their handwriting. Very quickly that thought fled, as he deciphered what Statius had written. Trying to restrain himself, Caesar knelt again and grasped Statius by the shoulder.

"Is this all true? That Ventidius sent twelve Cohorts and that Felix is taking the other eight to the northern camp?"

When Statius gave a simple nod, for a brief, horrifying moment Caesar thought he would faint. Could it possibly be true? Was there a chance that this battle could actually be won? Immediately, Caesar began offering prayers to every deity he could think of, including all of the gods he had learned about over these last ten years, only someone with his intellect even capable of remembering them all. Now, he ran through each and every name as he beseeched them to save what was left of his army and to grant success to Felix and those eight Cohorts.

Gaius Porcinus' head still ached abominably, but strangely, he was thankful for the pain, because it kept him from thinking about how tired he was. His Century had been whittled down even more; by his last count he had half the men with which he had started the day. It had been his Century, alongside the Second Century of the Ninth Cohort, that had stood in the path of the Wa warriors trying to cut their way to the gate, and while they had stopped this threat, it had been at a great cost. Now his Century had moved back to the wall, where more than a dozen small pockets of Wa had managed to get over the wall and onto the rampart. The fighting was furious, the pace so high that Porcinus hadn't had a chance to look behind him to see how his uncle and the rest of the 10th were faring. All he knew was that the fighting was still going on, because of the noise, but more than that he couldn't say.

At that moment, all his concentration was focused on the small group of Wa, standing back to back, all of them armed with swords, their blades flashing in the sun, as they lashed out in what seemed to be a rippling pattern that prevented the Legionaries facing them from closing the distance so that they could employ their own weapons. Waiting and watching for his chance to strike, Porcinus suspected that this seemingly random pattern of first one, then another Wa, thrusting or swinging their blades at his men was anything but random, that they probably trained in this way with at least the same diligence with which the men of the Legions stood at the stakes for watch after watch. Finally, Porcinus saw what he was looking for: either out of fatigue or carelessness, the barbarian nearest to him brought his blade back lower than normal, giving the Centurion the opening he needed. With a quick, overhand thrust, the point of his sword shot past the Wa's defense to land a killing blow right between two of the man's ribs, the blade sliding deep into the chest cavity. The Wa stood still for less than a heartbeat, before vomiting blood and collapsing at Porcinus' feet. Because he had remembered the rule of keeping his blade parallel to the ground, he was able to slide it smoothly out of the man's body, and even as the barbarian lay twitching on the ground, Porcinus stepped over him, looking for another target.

From what he could tell, it looked as though for every man he lost, his Century was striking down at least four barbarians. If that held true everywhere along the wall, his hope was that this would be enough to turn back this assault to take the gate, but he had no way of knowing if that would be sufficient to stop the enemy from overwhelming him and his men. He also understood that it didn't matter, because of what was happening behind him: if his uncle and the rest of the men in the forum didn't stop these bastards, then very shortly the Cohorts along the wall would be pressed from front and rear, and it would all be over. So he concentrated on what he had some control over, and that was keeping his Century fighting and killing. It had been some time since he had a moment to take a head count, but by his best estimate, he had just a little more than half his Century still in the fight, and at least a dozen of the men still fighting bearing some sort of wound, including himself. At that moment, the front rank of his Century had managed to cut down what had been eight of the yellow-skinned savages down to four, and there was an instant's pause, when his men were forced to take a breath. Seizing the opportunity,

Porcinus raised the whistle hanging around his neck up to his lips, and blew the signal that started the process of relief. Instantly, the men who were within reach thrust their shields out, their goal to strike their opponent and send him reeling just long enough for the Legionary to take a step to the side to allow the man behind him to take his place.

When performed properly, it was like watching a well-oiled machine in operation, and this time would have been no exception, except that these Wa had seen and heard this happen often enough by now to know what to expect. One of them, a more experienced warrior, timing his move perfectly, took a step backward just as the Legionary across from him lashed out. Instead of making contact as he expected, the Legionary's shield struck nothing but air. Preparing for the jarring contact of his shield striking flesh, the Legionary naturally put his weight behind the blow to increase the impact, but when he reached the full extension of his arm and there was nothing there, he was instantly thrown off-balance. If he had been more experienced, in all likelihood he would have been able to compensate and maintain his stance and footing, but this was another Gayan of the Tenth Cohort. The result was a staggering step forward, instead of the step to the side he should have taken, a natural reaction under the circumstances, but one that spelled his doom. The warrior next to the man who had dodged the blow was waiting, and immediately his blade chopped down onto the outstretched left arm of the Gayan. In the blink of an eye, the shield, with the hand and part of the man's arm still attached clattered to the ground, and even before the stricken man could react or cry out, the first Wa struck, as well. Just that quickly, there was a gaping hole in the front line and another man lost from Porcinus' Century. The dead man's body was a natural obstacle to allow his relief to step forward, but it was no impediment to the Wa who had created this opportunity, as he used the Gayan's body as a platform. Swinging his sword in a wide arc, the very threat posed by his blade prevented the Legionaries on either side from making their own thrusts.

Seeing this, Porcinus understood the danger, but before he could move through the ranks of his men, from the opposite side of the formation his Optio Oesalces came charging in. Holding his shield high above him to allow him to move more quickly between the ranks of the Century, Oesalces gave a bellow loud enough to be heard even above the noise of the fighting as he came charging in. Hearing the challenge, the Wa standing atop the dead Gayan's body made a half-turn, and, despite himself, Porcinus marveled at how surefooted the barbarian was on such an unsteady platform. As Porcinus watched, the Wa brought his blade up and over his head, where it seemed to hover for an instant, before slashing down to come crashing down onto Oesalces' upraised shield. Porcinus saw splinters fly from the wooden surface, but his Optio seemed to absorb the blow without any effect, his own blade lashing out in a blurry flash that Porcinus could barely register. Somehow, however, the Wa was able to follow the Optio's attempt, blocking the thrust with his own blade, as had happened so often that day. The Wa immediately countered; in fact, it seemed to Porcinus that he did so as part of the same motion he made to block Oesalces. The enemy's blade seemed to follow just behind that of Oesalces, as if chasing the Roman's shorter sword back to its lair, and it was so quick that the Optio was unable to move his shield across his body in time. As Porcinus watched in helpless horror, he saw the point of the Wa's sword puncture his Optio's chain mail armor as if it weren't even there, the blade sinking in almost to the hilt. For a brief moment, Porcinus and Oesalces' eyes locked, and the Centurion saw the almost puzzled look on his Optio's face that he had seen more than once on this day, as if the stricken man couldn't quite believe what had just happened. The Wa, still balancing on the dead body, lifted one foot and placed it on Oesalces' chest and, with a brutal kick, freed his sword and knocked the Optio down at the same time.

And the other raw *tirones* of Porcinus' Century who were standing less than a couple of paces away, who could have easily struck this arrogant yellow bastard down as he freed his sword, stood frozen in place, their mouths open in shock. The Wa's comrades displayed no such timidity, however, and before any Roman could react, two of them had muscled their way into the now yawning gap created by these two deaths. Almost as quickly, the newly vacated space was filled by Wa who had been poised on the ladder for such an opportunity, and in just that amount of time, all the progress that Porcinus' men had made in stopping this threat was undone. Porcinus couldn't stifle a groan coming from his lips, a combination of grief at the loss of his Optio and frustration at this setback.

"Fight, you bastards! Fight! Quit standing there and do your fucking jobs!"

It was quite unlike Gaius Porcinus to speak so harshly to his men; his style of leadership was more like that of his Pilus Prior Scribonius than it was his uncle's, but at that moment, if his men hadn't known better, they would have sworn to Mars and Bellona that it was the voice of their Primus Pilus, the man whom they feared more than death itself. And it was exactly what they needed just then, because in response, the Legionaries facing these fresh Wa began bashing them with their shields and following up with sword thrusts. Still, Porcinus was now afraid that this was a losing battle, and, like his uncle, he started to resign himself to the inevitability of what had first come to his mind earlier, that this was his last day on earth. If so, he thought grimly, I need to get a lot more blood on my sword. Edging his way toward the fighting, he watched for an opportunity to get stuck in. As he did so, he heard something that he was sure was a trick of the wind. It wasn't the fact that a *cornu* was blowing; the horns had been doing so all day, relaying signals back and forth. It was the direction this sound was coming from, off to his right front, which was impossible, since there were no Romans out there. But then it sounded again, and this time Porcinus was sure that he wasn't hearing things, nor was there some trick of the wind. Those were Roman horns, and they were coming from behind the attacking Wa!

Time, movement, noise, everything seemed to have come to a stop to Sextus Scribonius. Helplessly he watched as the Wa general thrust his sword into the chest of his best friend and Primus Pilus of the Legion. Scribonius had become aware that something abnormal was taking place, down the line from his spot where he was fighting with his Second Cohort, and in a brief lull in the fighting, he had moved along behind his men who were still in the fight, closer to the source of whatever strange thing was taking place. That's when he had seen Titus Pullus, facing one of the barbarians in a cleared space, as the two men did their best to kill one another. Scribonius wasn't sure at what point in the fight he showed up, but he did see that for all intents and purposes the men immediately surrounding the two combatants had stopped their own private battles to watch the one between these two champions. In fact, this wasn't all that uncommon: Scribonius had witnessed such scenes personally on two separate occasions, but those fights had involved the enemy king on one occasion, and the crown prince of his people on the other. That was what gave Scribonius the idea that the barbarian Pullus was facing was of a similar status to his people, because from Scribonius' perspective, it looked very much as though it was the barbarians who had halted their attack and were content to watch the Legionaries across from them warily, while eyeing the two combatants. As far as the Romans were concerned, any respite was welcome, so they were unlikely to disrupt this lull in the fighting. Instead, just like their foes, they were watching their Primus Pilus and shouting encouragement to him as the two men fought.

Scribonius wasn't sure what he had missed, but just bare moments after he arrived at his current vantage point, he saw Pullus make his strike that smashed the barbarian's helmet, saw the blood flowing down the man's face as he staggered backward, slashing his sword wildly in an attempt to keep his foe from pressing home his advantage. But for a reason Scribonius couldn't fathom, his friend seemed to hesitate, and in that pause, he gave the Wa the chance he needed to discard his damaged helmet. Scribonius had noticed that Pullus didn't have a shield, and he was too far away to see the remnants of it on the ground, so a part of him worried that his giant friend had once more given in to his own hubris and disdained the use of a shield, since these savages didn't carry any, either. Then, as Scribonius watched in horrified disbelief, the barbarian struck, and this was the moment that seemed to freeze all existence, as the Wa's blade struck his friend and just...kept going. Even if he had been close enough, Scribonius probably wouldn't have heard the barbarian's savage shout as he made his lunge, so mesmerized was he by a sight he truly believed was impossible. Pullus' blade had swept upward, it was true, but he had started his movement too late, so that he barely altered the trajectory of the thrusting blade. However, he did alter it, and the point punched into his body less than an inch below his left clavicle. Still, there was enough force behind the thrust that the point penetrated not only the chain mail in the front, but it also continued to travel through Pullus' muscular upper chest and the bone of his shoulder blade, then punch through the mail in back to protrude a couple of inches out of Pullus' back. Scribonius let out an anguished moan, almost as if he was the one struck, and, indeed, he felt an almost physical pain watching his best friend skewered like a roasted chicken on an enemy blade.

At the exact same time, there was a huge, collective, gasping moan that was almost immediately drowned out by an exultant roar, as the respective sides either mourned or celebrated. Remarkably, the only one who seemed unaffected was Pullus, who remained standing and, in fact, just barely rocked backward when the sword entered his body. For the remainder of his time on earth, Sextus Scribonius would never be able to determine accurately just how much time elapsed during a moment that seemed to last longer than any other of his entire life. Everything seemed to be moving in extraordinarily slow motion and, despite every fiber of his being screaming at him to move, to run to his friend's aid, he couldn't seem to lift his feet or move a single muscle for that matter. Consequently, he was a mute spectator as he watched Pullus standing, the Wa general across from him, one hand still on the hilt of the sword buried in Pullus' body, his own body extended with his right foot forward, his arm straight out from his torso in what could have been a painting illustrating the perfect sword thrust. While Scribonius couldn't see Pullus' face, he could see the barbarian's—or, rather, the half that wasn't covered in blood—and he got the strong sense that the two men were staring each other in the eye. Then, Pullus' left hand moved, still seemingly very slowly, up to his chest, his hand reaching up, as if to feel the wound in his chest, maybe to see if it was real or if, like Scribonius, he didn't believe what had happened. Seeing that motion, the barbarian made his own, what Scribonius was sure was his preparatory movement to twist the blade before withdrawing it.

Yet somehow, as slowly as Pullus seemed to move, his hand still reached the Wa's blade before the barbarian could do as he planned. Pullus' hand closed around the blade, the top of his fist hard up against his mail, and that was when Scribonius saw a change in the expression of the barbarian general. The Wa smiled grimly, as if to tell Pullus that whatever he had in mind was futile, and Scribonius saw the muscles of the Wa's arm tense as he began to remove the blade. But Scribonius, better than anyone else left alive, could have told this barbarian that, while he didn't know it, he was making a vain attempt, because he, Pullus' long-time friend, knew the strength of that grip.

When they had been *tirones*, and had been trained by their first weapons instructor Aulus Vinicius, he had instructed them in the grip that every man who had been in the First Century, Second Cohort of the 10th Legion at that time, and now every man in this enlistment of the 10th Legion, was trained to use. As part of that training, Vinicius had made the recruits in his charge perform a special exercise to strengthen their sword hand. Taking a bucket of sand, each *tirone* would thrust his hand into the bucket, with fingers splayed wide apart, and bury his hand up to the wrist. Then he would contract his fingers into a fist, while it was still in the sand. Vinicius made his *tiros* perform this exercise every day for the first three months of their probationary period, but as with anything in the army, there were men who did the bare minimum. Then there was Titus Pullus, and Scribonius remembered very well that this was his first indication that this giant specimen who stood next to him in the ranks wasn't just an overgrown, heavily muscled simpleton. Not only did Pullus do twice the number of repetitions of the exercise prescribed for him, he did the exercises with his left hand, as well as with his right. When seeing him do this one day, his tentmates teased him unmercifully, but the young giant was undeterred. Unlike the others, Scribonius wasn't the kind to mock others, even when they seemed to be doing foolish things, so one night he asked Pullus why he was doing something for the hand that wasn't going to be holding his sword.

"I might not be holding a sword with my left hand," Pullus had replied, "but I'm going to be holding a shield. And I'll be damned if some filthy barbarian knocks it out of my hand. Besides," he finished with a shrug, "you never know when it might come in handy."

From that day on, Sextus had followed Titus' example and had been following his example whenever he could, ever since. That conversation was in Scribonius' mind as he watched now, with Pullus' hand clutching the blade of the Wa sword, then seeing the Wa's expression begin to change, as his level of effort to retrieve his sword increased. Pullus was still looking at the barbarian, still unmoving, his hand perfectly immobile as well, hard up against his body. Scribonius was certain that the barbarian general, knowing the eyes of all of his men were on him, at first didn't want to appear to be exerting himself, but now he gave up all pretense of ease to begin yanking at the sword with what had to be tremendous force. Yet, not only did Pullus still hold the sword, but Scribonius saw that with every jerk by the Wa, the Roman's arm barely moved—even more evidence of his friend's massive strength. Still, Scribonius knew firsthand how sharp these bastards' swords were, so Pullus' hand had to be paying a terrible price, as the Wa continued trying to remove the blade. Even as this thought came to Scribonius, he saw the first trickle of blood running down Pullus' arm from his palm.

At that same instant, he also noticed something else: Pullus' sword, which he had been holding with the point toward the ground, began moving, making very tiny circles. Scribonius felt a grim, cautious smile come to his face, having seen that small motion many, many times before, although the times he had seen it, he hadn't appreciated it very much. Just as with the exercises, which Pullus continued religiously, he never stopped training with his sword, and his most frequent sparring partner was his best friend. Not once, not ever had Scribonius beaten his friend, but he was immensely proud of the fact that on a total of four occasions over the years, he had battled his Primus Pilus to a draw. But every other time, Scribonius had been forced to take his lumps, and the only reason he did was that he knew if he could last any length of time with Pullus, he stood an excellent chance of walking away from every battle he ever fought. The times he knew he was in trouble, however, came when he saw the same thing he was seeing now: Pullus making those tiny little circles with his blade, because it meant that he was toying with his opponent, that he had taken his foe's measure and now was just going to enjoy himself. Titus Pullus wasn't a cruel man, necessarily, but he never wanted to leave any doubt in any man's mind who the best swordsman in the Roman army was.

Now, Scribonius understood, he was about to make this Wa pay, even if Pullus was mortally wounded, which was a thought Scribonius tried to banish the moment it crossed his mind. Oblivious to what was about to happen, the Wa, for the first and last time in his long career, as illustrious and admired by his own countrymen as Pullus was, let his pride get the better of him. Infuriated by this...this *grubworm,* who refused to know when he was dead, and had the effrontery to think that he couldn't even retrieve his own sword, the Wa put every bit of his strength into his effort, finally deigning to grasp the hilt with his other hand as well. As he did so, he continued staring into the giant grubworm's eyes, satisfied that at least his face was streaming sweat and was even paler than the barbarians were normally. The giant's jaws were clenched, and despite himself, the Wa general felt a surge of respect, as his foe resolutely refused to cry out. He couldn't even fathom the pain the barbarian was feeling, and the nagging thought crossed his mind that perhaps these grubworms weren't really human, but just resembled men the way some animals looked similar, but weren't the same. Finally, the giant's mouth opened after a particularly vicious jerk of the sword, and the Wa took a savage delight in the idea that at least he would force a howl of pain from this thing. Instead, he heard a string of gibberish that he was sure only his dogs would understand.

"You don't really think that you can defeat us, do you? That *you* could defeat *me*?" Pullus asked, even as he knew that the barbarian had no idea what he was saying.

But it wasn't his purpose to be understood; his goal was something else entirely. He saw the corners of his enemy's one visible eye crinkle in puzzlement, as the Wa barbarian tried to decipher what Pullus was saying, and Pullus watched, wondering if he would die, before he saw what he was looking for.

"Your mother's a whore, and I swear after I kill you that I'm going to find your family and fuck your wife, and kill your children," Pullus hissed through clenched teeth, and this time, while the Wa didn't understand his words, there was no mistaking the menace in the tone.

The Wa, wanting to make sure that this grubworm knew who had taken his life, opened his mouth to tell this arrogant barbarian his name and ancestry.

He never saw the sword. Even Scribonius, who had just divined what was about to happen, didn't see anything more than a silver blur. One instant, Pullus' sword was pointed at the dirt, still making the little circles, then the point was aimed almost skyward, glistening with blood, brain matter, and pieces of skull. Just like Pullus' left hand was still hard up against his body, now his right hand was almost pressed against the barbarian's open mouth, separated only by the handguard of the sword. The Wa general's eyes, or at least the one that Scribonius could see clearly, was opened wider than he had ever seen from any of these barbarians, such was the man's surprise and shock, the last emotions he would ever experience. That tableau was frozen into Scribonius' mind:

Pullus, still grasping the Wa sword embedded in his shoulder, his right arm straight out but slightly lowered, because of the Wa's shorter stature, and the man who Scribonius had been sure had killed his best friend dangling from his friend's sword. The Wa general's body had gone slack, and even as strong as Pullus was, the dead weight of the body dragged his arm down, but still Pullus stood for a couple of heartbeats longer, holding a dead man on his sword, and surrounded by a sudden and almost total silence.

Then, he dropped his sword arm, kicked the dead man off his blade, and, still clutching the sword, turned and took a few staggering steps, before going to his knees. Only then did the silence break, as it was now the turn of the 10th Legion to roar their defiance and exultation and the Wa to howl in despair. Accompanying the sudden sound, there was a burst of movement, as the fighting immediately resumed, but this time, it was the Romans rushing forward, throwing themselves at the Wa, who seemed to be in a collective state of shock that allowed scores of Legionaries to make their easiest kills of the entire battle. Sextus Scribonius was oblivious to all of that, and, in fact, completely forgot his duties, as he sprinted to his friend's side, who at that moment was being surrounded by his men in a protective cordon, while one of the first Legionaries to his side knelt beside his Primus Pilus. Scribonius was there an instant later, his heart pounding not from exertion, but from fear of what he would find. Pullus was still kneeling, but only because now two men, one on either side, were holding him up, while the giant Roman's head was bowed, his eyes closed.

"Titus," Scribonius gasped, as he slid to a stop and dropped to his knees, his good hand reaching out for his friend's shoulders. As he did so, he snapped at one of the other kneeling men, "What are you sitting there for? Go get a *medicus*! NOW!"

Turning his attention back to Pullus, he saw that his friend's eyes were still closed, and Scribonius was too scared to feel for a pulse. Instead, he called his friend's name again, and again. Finally, with a shaking hand, Scribonius reached up to place two fingers on his friend's neck. It was at that moment that Scribonius heard the same blast from the *cornu* that Porcinus had, with much the same reaction. However, it stayed his hand, as he looked over his shoulder, sure that he was hearing things. Then, the horn sounded again. And Titus Pullus opened his eyes.

Hardly believing their luck, Felix and the men of the two leading Cohorts managed to close to within a hundred paces at a fast trot, before they were noticed by some of the men at the rear of the Wa formation. Keeping the same pace for a handful of heartbeats more, Felix then called a halt to his men, when they were just a matter of thirty paces away.

"Prepare javelins!"

Arms along the line of Centuries swept back in a rippling motion, each hand clutching a javelin, the points tilted skyward, followed by a pause no longer than a couple of heartbeats.

"Release!"

The air filled with the missiles, but although every man still had his other javelin, Felix made the decision to forego a second volley, and even as the missiles were still in the air, he was shouting an order.

"Charge! For Caesar!"

Consequently, the Wa of the surprise attack force had almost no chance. Little more than a handful of the Wa in the rear ranks managed to form a ragged and thin line facing Felix and the two Cohorts as they slammed into the packed mass of barbarians, cutting them down without mercy. The sudden eruption of the noise of Legionaries roaring at the tops of their lungs was the first thing that alerted the Wa immediately next to the wall of this new threat, and many of them whirled around just in time to see their comrades slaughtered. Suddenly faced with the choice of trying to continue their assault on the camp or face this new and more immediate threat, almost every Wa in the attacking force, with no order to that effect having been given, turned to face the onrushing Legionaries. Roaring out their rage, the Romans very quickly cut their way deep into the tightly packed Wa, but after the initial shock, the barbarian warriors swiftly threw themselves into this fight with as much fervor as their foes. This was understandable; the least savvy of these Wa understood that, while they had no idea how it had happened, the situation had changed and they were now fighting not just for victory, but for their survival.

The overall commander of the Wa surprise assault force, wearing a helmet of the same style as the Wa who had faced Pullus—except instead of horns, he wore the white wings of a crane—was even then ascending one of the ladders, now that a significant number of his men had made it over the wall. Ironically, this gave him a better vantage point than if he had been on the ground amidst his men, so that he could see that his force still significantly outnumbered this surprise barbarian force. Therefore, he wasn't excessively worried, having been informed by one of the warriors at the top of his ladder who was able to see into the enemy camp that the original assault force surrounded the barbarians inside. His most important decision, he understood, was whether he went on ahead into the camp, or stayed here to lead the fight against the new threat. His subordinate was a capable warrior, he knew, if slightly inexperienced, and he was tempted to let him lead the fight on this side of the wall. After all, he reasoned, the greater glory was in taking the camp. That clinched his decision, and he began to climb the ladder again, directing one last glance back over his shoulder to reassure himself that he was making the right choice.

What he saw stopped him, as he stared in the direction of the ridgetop road, where it dipped out of sight. Seemingly rising up from the ground, just as he and his force had appeared some time before, was a line of even more barbarians, coming at a fast trot. Suddenly, he no longer felt quite so confident, and he recognized immediately that his place was here, on this side of the wall. In numbers and in the way the barbarians were aligned, it looked as though they had exactly the same composition of the force that was now battling his men. While he still outnumbered the barbarians, the margin wasn't nearly as wide as it had been, but even before he finished descending to the ground, he saw yet another wave of barbarians, exactly the same as the first two! Now, for the first time this Wa general was concerned. He was still confident of victory, but it appeared that it would be much harder fought. Reaching the ground, he shoved his men aside, snapping out an order for his bodyguards to accompany him, then began to push his way to what was now the front, where the fighting was happening.

The second line of Centuries discarded their javelins as they ran, their Centurions clearly seeing how entangled the lines already were, the men on both sides fighting with a ferocity that came from still being relatively fresh and not at it for the better part of two watches as had been the defenders inside the camp. One hidden benefit of the slight delay following the first line was that it gave the two Pili Priores a chance to survey the situation and see where it appeared they were most needed. As matters stood, it still looked as if there were several thousand Wa arrayed along the wall, and from a distance they looked like a giant black-and-white mass. Hemmed in on one side by the straight line of the wall and on the other bordered by a thin line, grayish-silver tinged with red, that was much, much narrower than the mass of the Wa force, the two Pili Priores instantly saw the spot where the Roman line was the thinnest. Drawing closer, the Centurion commanding the Cohort on the left veered in that direction even farther than the original path steered by Felix. He had seen that whoever was commanding the barbarians had shifted a large number of men from the rear ranks over to the Wa right, where Felix's Sixth Century was being hard-pressed. The enemy's intention was clear: by shifting men to one wing and throwing every available man at this one Century, he was attempting to turn the flank of Felix's formation.

In fact, even as the Pilus Prior, Gnaeus Labeo, watched, the last several men of Felix's Sixth Century were either cut down or pushed backward by what appeared to be Wa literally throwing themselves at the Roman lines. A gap formed, and through it poured several hundred Wa warriors, who immediately turned to fall on the now outflanked Sixth Century. Breaking out into a full run, Labeo drew his sword as he shouted for his men to follow him, and he aimed his Cohort so that the middle of his formation would come to the aid of the Sixth Century. Startled by the change in course, the Pilus Prior of the other Cohort, Publius Varrus, nonetheless kept moving his men in the original direction, seeing that the Century at the center of Felix's formation was almost as hard-pressed as the Sixth. Following behind the third line came the fourth and final pair of Cohorts, the Pilus Prior of the Cohort on the left following the same path as Labeo. But like Labeo, this Pilus Prior, Gaius Vorenus, was one of Caesar's Centurions, and what he saw was an opportunity. In his judgment, there were enough men to handle the barbarians outside the walls. He needed to get his Cohort and the other one inside the camp, and to that end, he didn't head anywhere near the eastern wall. Instead, he led his Cohort toward the southern gate, the Porta Principalis Dextra. Now his challenge was to get his men inside the camp in time to help.

None of the men, fewer than three thousand Legionaries of what had been the 10th and 12th Legion who still remained in the fight inside the camp thought it was possible that the barbarians could increase the fury of their attack, but they were being proven wrong. Ironically, it was the sounds of the Roman horns that had spurred the Wa to increase their effort to the point that it now seemed that none of the warriors used any type of technique or tactic to vanquish the invading foe across from them. Instead, the Wa were coming in what seemed to the battered, exhausted Legionaries to be waves, but instead of being made of water, these were composed of flesh, iron, and fury. Slashing and hacking, the Wa poured every last bit of their seemingly inexhaustible supply of energy into what they understood was their last chance to crush these grubworms. The death of their general had come as a great shock, but they didn't need him to tell them that time was running out. What they did need was direction, but the Wa general's subordinate officers were either dead, or too badly scattered around the perimeter of the *orbis* to issue any orders to the entire force.

Complicating matters for the Wa further, unlike the Roman Legion, the army of the Wa wasn't trained to the level their enemy was, especially when it came to unit formations and maneuvers. Consequently, the last phase of the fight became a clash of individual warriors picking out one of the Romans across from them, and hurling themselves forward. As ground down and battered as the remnants of the 10th and the 12th were, as jumbled as their Centuries had become, all the endless watches of drill were now paying off, the Legionaries continuing to fight in the manner in which they were trained. Despite their exhaustion, the harsh discipline they so often complained about to each other was what kept the woefully thin, semi-circular *orbis* intact, no man even thinking of not giving his all when it came his time to fight.

Still, as many of these barbarians as they had killed, they still outnumbered the Legions by at least a three-to-one margin, and now every single loss of a Legionary was one that couldn't be spared. Consequently, the surviving Centurions were working with lines that were at most four men deep, and that was true only in a few spots in the formation. There were places where the Roman lines had been thinned down to the point that there was only one man standing behind his comrade who was fending off the wild swings of Wa swords or spears. These were the spots where the nearest Centurion would run over and unceremoniously grab a man from those areas that were still four deep with Legionaries, shoving the last man in the line towards the trouble spot with a shouted order. They had been doing this for some time, which accounted for the hopeless confusion among Centuries and even Cohorts. Sometimes though, it had to be the Centurion himself who ran to the nearest threat, sword held high and, if he had the presence of mind to grab one from a dead Legionary as he ran, bearing a shield. Of the 120 Centurions of the 10th and 12th Legion who had started the fight that day, now more than two full watches earlier, barely more than 30 were still standing, meaning that they were spread thinly across the entire *orbis*.

One of them had taken himself out of the fight, however, and that was Scribonius, kneeling next to his friend, who was also still kneeling—no accident, as it would turn out. Pullus, though barely conscious, had realized that toppling over in any direction would do even more damage than had already been caused by the Wa general's sword, which still protruded grotesquely from both front and back of his chest. Blood continued to flow freely, but Scribonius, looking for anything on which to fasten his hopes, saw that it wasn't the bright spray that signaled a severed artery. This meant that there was still hope, at least as far as Scribonius was concerned. Seemingly oblivious to the furious fighting now just paces away in every direction, as what remained of Pullus' Century surrounded their fallen Primus Pilus, Scribonius held onto Pullus' uninjured shoulder gently but firmly, understanding the same thing that Pullus did.

"Why aren't you in the fight?" Scribonius barely heard this question from Pullus, made even more difficult, because his friend's teeth were still tightly clenched together.

"Why do you think?" the Pilus Prior asked in astonishment, although a part of his mind understood that his friend was right, that no one man, no matter his rank or status, was more important than the rest of the men still fighting.

But for the first time in his long career, Sextus Scribonius simply didn't care about his duty, such was his concern for his friend.

"The men need you, Sextus," Pullus retorted, weakly voiced but no less adamant than Scribonius.

Understanding that a continued, outright refusal would only agitate Pullus more, Scribonius tried to mollify him by saying, "All right Titus. As soon as the *medici* get here, I'll go back to the fight."

Pullus slowly raised his head to survey the scene around them, turning to look first one way, then another with almost comical slowness, and, unbidden to Scribonius' mind came the thought that in that moment his friend looked like a giant tortoise peering about for danger, before taking its next, ponderous step. Done with his inspection, Pullus turned to face Scribonius, and for the first time looked his friend in the eye. That almost unmanned the Pilus Prior, because he had never seen his giant friend with such an ashen pallor, and it was only through a supreme effort of will that he didn't let out a gasp. Scribonius' only slight ray of hope was his friend's giving him a grimace that he recognized as Pullus' attempt at a grin and he saw no blood in his mouth, the presence of which was normally a sure sign that he had suffered damage internally.

"We're surrounded, you idiot," Pullus said, "so I don't think the *medici* are coming anytime soon."

Only then did Scribonius take his eyes away from his friend and glance around, his heart sinking at the sight and knowing his friend was right.

Taking a deep breath, Scribonius closed his eyes for a moment in a brief prayer, then replied, "All right. But only if I can try to lay you on your side, understand?"

Pullus didn't answer, but then his head bobbed once in a grim acceptance of what his friend wanted to do, as he braced himself for even more pain. Standing up, Scribonius used both hands to grasp his friend, trying to shut out the groan that escaped from his friend's lips when Scribonius began tipping him over, onto his left side. Although it seemed to be the worst thing to do, both men had seen wounds like this too many times and they knew from bitter experience that if the Primus Pilus was indeed bleeding internally, the pooling of blood that would occur, as the blood was drawn to the ground. That movement of blood downward would in all likelihood collapse his lungs, and Titus Pullus would die of suffocation, before any chance of help arrived. In addition, the weight of his own body would actually close the edges of the wound around the blade and help staunch the flow of blood. However, there was a tradeoff for this benefit, and that was the excruciating pain caused by Pullus' own bulk pressing down on the damaged tissue. But it couldn't be helped, and Scribonius deafened himself to the groans and gasps as he strained to lay his friend slowly down onto the ground. Once he was as settled as Scribonius could make him, the Pilus Prior rose to go, very reluctantly.

"Are you all right there?" he asked without thinking, and although the reply was harsh, it fed the tiny, tiny flame of hope that his friend would somehow survive.

"What, are you tucking me in now?" the prone Primus Pilus growled wheezily. "How the fuck do you think I feel, you idiot?"

Despite himself, Scribonius let out a laugh, drawing his sword.

Before he turned back to the fighting, he told Pullus, "Don't worry Titus. We're going to hold these bastards off, until whoever's out there comes to help us."

"Not if you don't stop talking and get back in the fight," Pullus was, and always would be, a Primus Pilus Centurion of Caesar's 10th Legion, to his last breath.

Reaching the southern gate, Vorenus led his Century around the dirt barriers of the gate, winding around and through it, emerging into the camp, where he immediately came to a stop. This had been by design, in order to get first his Century, then his Cohort, formed up before throwing them into the fight. But even if it hadn't, the sight before him would have brought him to a halt. The camp was an utter shambles, with smoking ruins of whole rows of Legion streets put to the torch, and looking down the Via Principalis, the street that led from the side gates to the *Praetorium* and the forum, what he saw staggered him. There were heaps of bodies, and to his experienced eye, the progress of the battle was told by those corpses. Scanning the area to his left and front, while part of his vision was obscured by those few tents that were still standing, he could see how the 12th and 10th had waged a grudging, hard-fought withdrawal back to where they were now, the forum. More accurately, Vorenus could see, they were in just part of the forum, as the barbarians had managed to collapse the *orbis* of Balbinus and Pullus down to its present size. For some reason, the large tent of the *Praetorium* of the camp was still intact; Vorenus assumed that whoever was commanding these barbarians understood its purpose and had given orders for it to remain intact, to be plundered at leisure.

Oddly enough, it was the sight of this tent that fueled Vorenus' rage, brought on by the effrontery of this yellow-skinned savage to be so sure of victory. This, in turn, caused him to start lashing out fiercely at his own men, snarling at them to move even more quickly than they already were. Yet, no matter how quickly they moved—and truly, they were scrambling into their formations with a speed they had never displayed before—the gate was a bottleneck. Vorenus, and every man of his Cohort understood that time was almost as much of an enemy now as the barbarians with their swords, and those who had made it through the gate and fallen into their spot in their Century now added their voices to Vorenus', shouting at the comrades still pouring through the gate to hurry! Why were they moving as if they had all day? The result was that, while it was the most ragged Cohort formation he had ever seen, Vorenus decided it was good enough, even before the men of the last Century had finished forming up. Unlike the relieving Cohorts outside who needed to cover a wider area, Vorenus had decided on the more traditional three-Century front, although by rights he should have waited for the trailing Cohort also to arrive and place themselves side-by-side. However, he hadn't taken the time to look back to see if the last Cohort of the relieving force was, in fact, following him. Which, as it turned out, it wasn't, meaning that if Vorenus had waited for them, as the manual said he should, he would have been too late to save the men of the forum. Instead, he raised his sword, and, without waiting for his *cornicen* to blow the command, dropped it, as he simultaneously shouted the command to advance. And, as he expected, all eyes of the Cohort had been on him, so just as if they were marching in the forum, Vorenus' Cohort began the advance, heading for the rear of the as yet unsuspecting Wa.

The last Cohort, the 10th of the 14th, hadn't followed Vorenus for the same reason that Vorenus hadn't followed Labeo. Again, the Decimus Pilus Prior was one of Caesar's Centurions, although of all Caesar's Centurions, he was the only non-Roman. He was also the newest Pilus Prior in Caesar's army, having been promoted to the post just a month before this new campaign began. He was a Parthian named Pacorus, and his promotion to lead a Cohort had caused more than its share of grumbling among the other Centurions; they had barely gotten accustomed to the idea of non-Romans being Centurions, now this? Pacorus knew how his fellow Centurions felt about him, and he also felt the weight of representing not just the Parthians in the army, but all of the non-

Romans, since he was the first non-Roman Pilus Prior. Oddly enough, this was foremost in his mind as, instead of following Labeo, he led his trotting Cohort in another direction. Making a wide enough arc, so that he and his Centuries could safely skirt the lines of men of the other Cohorts now battling with barbarians outside the camp, Pacorus led his men in the direction of the Porta Principalis Sinister, the left-hand and northernmost gate of the camp.

Being a Centurion in Caesar's army meant that, as in Caesar's camp, Pacorus instantly understood the tactical situation and what would provide the most impact to the fight inside the camp. This was why he led the way to the northern gate now, although he was understandably nervous about making the right decision. Just as at the southern camp, where Statius had understood the need for coordination, Pacorus understood that at this point in the fight, the most important thing was to maximize the force he was leading, as far as its impact on the battle was concerned. If pressed, he couldn't have articulated any of this; it was more a gut instinct than anything else, but the ability to think through a problem rapidly was a trait that Caesar valued in his Centurions almost more than any other, and this was what had recommended Pacorus to him. Now, the Parthian was going to either prove or disprove Caesar's faith in his ability to pick the right man for the right job.

It didn't seem possible, but in the space of a finger width's of the sun's travel to its home in the west, the Wa general commanding the surprise attack was seeing certain victory turn into defeat with a rapidity that he would never have believed, if it wasn't happening in front of his eyes. His men were still fighting with the same reckless fury they had started with, and the general knew that the battle wasn't lost...yet. But the last warrior he had sent up the ladder to try to catch a glimpse of what was happening in the center of the camp—the ladder being the shortest route to gather information, yet also the most dangerous—had just jumped down to inform him that while the grubworms were being hard-pressed, they were still intact and holding in the center of their camp. However, because he had to take his look while dodging thrusts from grubworm swords, he was unable to tell his general the disposition or the numbers of their own troops still left, other than a very general guess. Cursing the man, the general gave him a cuff on the head for good measure, although he knew that it was impossible to expect more from the limited time his warrior had

had, without being skewered. Now he was on the fork of a dilemma; should he stop the assault on the walls and count on the men of the main assault to finish what they had started, in order to fend off the grubworm attempt to save their doomed comrades? Or, should he continue with the mission assigned to him originally and force his way up and over this wall? He would never have thought that the grubworms could have held out as long as they had to this point, and he had to believe that one more good push would crack them. Now that these new barbarians had appeared, he no longer had the luxury of doing both things at once. His hesitation had nothing to do with the idea that the men currently engaged with the newly arrived barbarians along what was now his front line would be sacrificing their lives to allow their comrades closer to the wall to continue the attack on the camp, the main goal. Every man under his command knew his duty and would willingly lay down his life without hesitation, as many had, in fact, already done, in order to fill the ditch in the original attack.

His concern was purely practical: how many men could he afford to leave behind to continue the fighting who would be a strong enough force to hold off the grubworms, as his men continued climbing the ladders? Normally a decisive man, his reputation wasn't as esteemed as that of the general who, still unbeknownst to him, lay dead in the middle of the camp; but he had been selected as second in command because his own renown was still very great. Now, however, he was in a turmoil of indecision, switching his attention from the fighting going on outside the camp to watching with an increasingly anxious eye at his men who were still trying to ascend the ladders. There would be a sudden spurt of men clambering quickly up a ladder, whenever a barbarian behind the wall was struck down and created a gap that allowed one of his men to leap onto the dirt rampart. More than once, his men had managed to carve out a pocket of space to allow their comrades to join them in their attempt to fight their way to a gate and secure it. That was the only method he had at this point of feeding enough troops into the fight and break the back of these grubworms, once and for all. However, his gods had either turned their face away from the Wa or had some design he couldn't fathom that would bring them victory, because despite several promising starts, no Wa force had managed to get to the gate.

He had briefly considered shifting a part of his force to assault the southern gate, early in the fight, but he had been so confident of victory, so sure that his men would swarm over the wall and crush these insects that it had been only a brief consideration. Now, it was too late. The new force of barbarians had hemmed them in between the walls of the camp and their pitiful wall made of swords and shields. What sort of man would cower behind a small, portable wall anyway, he scoffed? Warriors with sufficient skill had no need for such devices, but, in fact, it was the sight of these pieces of equipment that had led not just this Wa general, but the overall commander of the entire Wa army—who now lay dead inside the camp—to underestimate the potency of this force of pale, strange and hairy creatures. That, the general realized now, had been a mistake. Consequently, he was aware that although he might escape censure for this error—since the tone of the entire campaign designed to expel the grubworms from a land blessed by the gods had been set by his now-dead superior—his error in not committing a force to the southern gate wouldn't go unnoticed. That made it even more imperative, he recognized, that this camp fall, because only then would their emperor forgive him. Still torn, he remained at his spot close to the wall, a small space made for him by his bodyguards, as he tried to force himself to think. And with every heartbeat, his chances for a solution were becoming smaller and smaller. In fact, although he wouldn't become aware of it for another span of time, the moment had passed. This last Wa general, now in command of the assault force on which the entire strategy of this attack had hinged, had just managed to snatch defeat from the jaws of victory.

Looking back, Gaius Porcinus would never be able to determine accurately how much time actually elapsed from the moment the first ladders of the surprise attack had hit the wall and the point where he had had his first inkling that the reserve Cohorts were holding the eastern wall. It was all a haze of pain, fear, and an agony that can come only from watching men under your care, men that you trained to the standards befitting a Legionary of Rome, fall to the flashing blades of this yellow-skinned horde. Barely able to lift a borrowed shield, his head aching abominably, Porcinus nevertheless drove himself to half run, half stumble to wherever his sword and body were needed along his Century front.

It was a pitifully shallow Century formation, where he was down to three men standing in their files in most places, and he had determined some time before that even just glancing back at the heaps of bodies of his men that had been rolled down the ramp of the rampart—so that they were out of the way—was a bad idea. Just the sight of more than half of the Sixth Century, Tenth Cohort of the 10th Legion lying enmeshed in a tangle of limbs and torsos was enough to take what little energy he still had.

Therefore, he resolutely kept his face turned toward the fighting, both as a way to avoid the sight, and, more importantly, to rush to the next trouble spot. Along his Century's front alone stood four ladders, out of what Porcinus—when he risked a glimpse along the length of the wall—reckoned to be more than fifty that this second force had brought with them. Even through his fatigue, he knew that matters were much the same for all the other Centuries along the wall as for what he and his Century were facing, and that, like Porcinus' Century, they were being whittled down. Now that the relief had come, however, the sight of those bobbing poles, on which were affixed wooden placards declaring Century and Cohort, had infused all of them with more energy. This new threat to the barbarians' rear, coupled with the efforts of the men battling on the wall, signaled to Porcinus that the worst was perhaps over. Men were still climbing the ladders, but whenever Porcinus risked leaning out to take a quick look down into the ditch, he saw that the huddle of men gathered around the base of each one, waiting their turn to go up, was smaller.

"Boys, I know you're tired," Porcinus had long since shouted himself hoarse, his voice now resembling that of a frog in the throes of either agony or ecstasy, forcing him to bellow out his words, "but I think this is the last of it! The bastards have had their own surprise sprung on them by Caesar, and now it's up to us to finish them off!"

No cheer came at his words, but he didn't expect one, because he knew his men's voices were no less shattered than his own. Besides, they were too tired for any extraneous display of energy, so instead he got a few grim nods or muttered words, which was enough for him. Immediately after saying this, Gaius did risk a glance over his shoulder, except this time it was directed further inward to the fighting in the center of the camp. Initially, he was heartened to see that, somehow, some way, the *orbis* was still intact. It was smaller, but it was still unbroken, giving Porcinus a sliver of hope that they were going to survive. With that examination of the overall situation, he paused again to look to see if he could spot the giant figure of his uncle down in the forum. He naturally looked to where the fighting was the thickest, knowing that it was the most likely place where the Primus Pilus could be found. Yet, after several heartbeats, as he stared hard at the knots of men tangled together, bashing and slashing away, he couldn't see his uncle anywhere near where he had been the last time he checked. Granted, it had been some time before, but now his eye traveled the entire length of the 10th's part of the *orbis*, with a steadily increasing sense of worry. Still, no sight of the largest Roman of the Legion, so he turned his attention to the part of the shrinking semicircle that belonged to the 12th, and by the time he was finished, he was almost frantic. With great reluctance, Porcinus turned his attention to the row upon row of men lying so closely packed together that it was almost impossible for the remaining *medici* to reach a man in their middle. It was only after he searched each row not once, but twice, for sight of his uncle that he forced himself to look at the only other place left, the heaps of bodies that were, from where Porcinus stood, a gruesome attempt at a last-ditch rampart, as men were piled on top of one another like bloody logs, complete with flopping limbs hanging askew on either side. Despite the difficulty of discerning any features of the unfortunates who would serve as the last bastion of the *orbis*, Porcinus was sure that if he saw the body of his uncle, he would somehow recognize it. Then he shook himself, angry at the time he had just wasted; if his uncle, the Primus Pilus, was dead, his men would never make him suffer the indignity of lying among the rankers. That is when he began searching amid the clutter and debris in the desperately narrow strip between the feet of the men of the last line and where the wounded were gathered. Perhaps fifteen paces, if that, and there were shattered shields, helmets, swords, and men who had just recently fallen, but for whom there hadn't been time for the *medici* to come assess where they would be taken, jammed side-by-side, or onto the pile.

As Porcinus' eyes traveled around this ruined patch of ground, for a moment he didn't recognize the sight of a prone Roman, because the man was extremely close to the fighting, and, in fact, he was nearly completely circled by Legionaries, who appeared to be putting up a desperate and savage fight. Once Porcinus realized what he was seeing, for a brief, horrifying moment, he was sure that the earth beneath him was tilting so violently that he would slide off. There was no mistaking the size of the prone Legionary, even without the helmet lying by his side. The only small blessing for Porcinus at that moment was that he wasn't close enough to see the blade protruding from his uncle's body, but he certainly didn't know this , and now that he had discovered the location of his uncle, he stared hard at him, willing for his Primus Pilus to move—anything to show he still lived. Titus Pullus was the only Primus Pilus Porcinus had ever followed, and with the exception of a very small handful of the senior Centurions, the same was true for the entire 10th Legion. Porcinus could no more imagine a 10th without his uncle leading it than he could envision marching in an army without Caesar leading it. Now, Porcinus offered up a silent prayer to every god he could think of to will his uncle to show some sign of life, any movement, no matter how small. Yet, even after the span of several normal heartbeats, he saw no sign of life.

"Centurion! Centurion Porcinus!"

Yanked from his vigil, Porcinus' head turned, slowly and reluctantly, to where his Tesseraurius, a Pandyan named Sutra was pointing to a spot along the wall, where a small group of barbarians had managed to create another foothold. It took a moment for Porcinus to understand why it wasn't his Optio calling his attention to this new threat, but even as he began moving to where the man was pointing, he realized that Sutra was, in fact, now his Optio, because Oesalces was dead, and he was the next in line. Casting one glance back over his shoulder, he saw no change in his uncle's position on the ground, no sign that he was alive, and it was with a deep despair that Porcinus, more out of force of habit than anything else, went back into the fight. If he had just waited a fraction longer, he would have been rewarded with the sight of a "dead" man suddenly raising his arm and beckoning to someone nearby.

"Philippus! Get over here!"

Of all the commands that Titus Pullus had uttered in his career, this was undoubtedly the weakest, at least in terms of volume, and he had to repeat it twice, before his intended target became aware that someone was saying his name. Philippus was at the back of the now three-deep line, and when he turned, he was so surprised at the sight of his Primus Pilus weakly gesturing at him that he let go of the harness of the man in front of him. Realizing he was being called to come to his fallen Centurion's side, Philippus had the presence of mind to tap his comrade on the shoulder to let him know he was leaving, then hurried to kneel at Pullus' side.

"Help me up."

At first Philippus was sure he hadn't heard Pullus correctly.

"Are you deaf, as well as stupid? I said help me up!"

Startled out of his disbelief, Philippus actually started unthinkingly to comply and clasped the prone man's proffered right arm, but fortunately for both of them, he caught himself.

"Primus Pilus, if I just pull on your arm by myself, I'm more likely to kill you than help you."

Pullus was about to snap at Philippus, but through the pain he recognized that his man was right.

"Go get some help," he said grudgingly, his reluctance at admitting this weakness emphasized by the fact that he gave the order through gritted teeth.

As Philippus hurried off to grab a comrade to help, a part of Pullus chided himself. What are you thinking, you idiot? You've got a sword sticking out of you, and you're in more pain than you've ever been in your life, and that's saying something. But as racked with agony as he was, once Pullus regained consciousness, even from his admittedly limited perspective and vantage point here on the ground, he knew that the 10th still had a chance to survive. He had heard the sounds of the horns outside the camp, and between that and his slaying of the Wa general—whose corpse lay a couple of dozen paces away and was still visible amid the tangle of the legs of both sides of the combatants, Pullus understood that he was needed, now more than ever. Once he had come back to this world, he had been cautiously pleased to see that his body weight had apparently closed the wound around the sword enough, so that the bleeding had stopped, although there was still a large, dark stain on the ground around his upper body, a sign that he had lost a substantial amount of blood. He was still sure that he was going to die, but Titus Pullus had always possessed a formidable will, and it was with this will that he determined that he wasn't done just yet.

Pullus was alerted to the presence of Philippus and whoever he had brought by the sight of two sets of bare, dirty, and blood-spattered legs. Craning his head to see, the Primus Pilus saw that the first man had returned with his own close comrade, a Parthian veteran who had been in the Parthian army and who, after Phraaspa fell, had chosen to join the victors. Pullus remembered well how suspicious he had been of this man, Artabanos, but the man had long since proven himself, so after Philippus' close comrade had fallen during the invasion of Pandya, he and Artabanos had partnered up. As Pullus recalled, it had been the Pandyan campaign, where Artabanos had, moreover, saved the life of his best friend Scribonius, killing a Pandyan who had managed to get behind the Pilus Prior and was about to bury a blade into his friend's back. Artabanos had been awarded the Civic Crown for that, much to the uproar of a large segment of the army, and it had caused Caesar a number of headaches, but he had steadfastly refused to heed the cries of the Romans in the ranks, including his officers, that this was an honor reserved for citizens of Rome only. What wasn't known, by anyone in the ranks, even now, was that it had been Titus Pullus who had prevailed on Caesar to award Artabanos this decoration, which the giant Roman had never regretted doing. It wasn't just because of gratitude for who Artabanos had saved; Pullus was indeed grateful, but he had a more practical goal. While he had been just as opposed to the full integration of non-Romans into not only the ranks, but also into the customs and benefits that Roman citizenship brought, like Caesar, he had recognized that not only was it vital to keep the ranks full, but that if it was going to be done, it had to be done all the way and not in half-measures. Now it was Philippus and Artabanos who crouched on either side of him, ready to help him up.

"Primus Pilus, your bleeding has stopped. If we sit you up, it's a certainty that we'll open the wound again," Artabanos' Latin was still accented, but easily understood.

"That's my worry, not yours," Pullus growled, even as he knew that the Parthian was right.

However, he didn't have the time to explain and argue that he knew he was going to die, and that he was going to sit up, whether they helped or not. The two men exchanged a glance that Pullus saw, but didn't make any further comment about. With a grim nod to his comrade, Artabanos put his hand, as gently as he could, under Pullus' left shoulder that was pressed into the dirt. Even that slight movement caused a fresh spate of sweat to start pouring down the Roman's face, but he stifled his groan, not wanting to give any reason for the two to hesitate. With Philippus clasping the giant's forearm, the two of them still strained to bring Pullus slowly to an upright, sitting position. Even before they were finished, for a horrified instant Pullus was sure that he would faint, such was the agony, and he felt a sudden gush of warmth on his chest and back, sign that he had indeed started bleeding again. Somehow, he managed to keep his head, as he was hauled to a position where his upper torso was upright and his legs splayed out in front of him. It took a moment for the dizziness to subside to the point where Pullus was reasonably sure that he wouldn't immediately pass out. But he also knew that he was only halfway there, and his jaws were already aching from how tightly clenched his teeth were.

"All right, pull me up the rest of the way," he finally said, holding up his right arm.

While he could still wiggle the fingers of his left arm, even that slight a movement caused a paroxysm of agony that Pullus was so certain would cause him to lose consciousness that he made absolutely sure to keep his left arm as still as possible. With both men grasping his right arm, they nevertheless could barely pull their Primus Pilus to his feet, and, as painful as the last several moments had been for Pullus, this last bit made all that seem a trifle. The sounds of the fighting that he had become accustomed to suddenly seemed to take on an echoing quality, and the bright sunshine present just a heartbeat earlier suddenly fled, as if the gods had chosen to darken the sun in the way they had on a number of occasions during Pullus' lifetime: suddenly bathing the scene before his eyes in an eerie dimness. Still, neither man knew how they had managed it, but Titus Pullus was back on his two feet, weaving as if he had downed an amphora of wine, with the gruesomely odd sight of a sword protruding from both sides of his body. But he was on his feet, and, astonishing the two men even more, he took a very wobbly, tentative step forward. Almost toppling over, he nevertheless waved both men away with a snarled warning that was as close to a whimper as either man would ever hear from his leader.

"Where's my sword?" Pullus' voice was almost unrecognizable, so strained and hoarse was it, but by this point, neither man was shocked by what was happening.

Just as Caesar had done over the years, Titus Pullus was even then adding to his own legend. But after a quick search of the area around them, neither man saw Pullus' treasured Gallic blade. Thinking quickly, Philippus drew his and offered it to his Primus Pilus, hilt first. Looking down at it, Pullus actually had to try to grasp it twice, because there were two of them and he grabbed the wrong one first. But he did manage, automatically wrapping his fingers around his thumb in the unorthodox grip that was now second nature, not just to him, but also to every man of the 10th Legion, and, truth be known, a fair number of the men marching in the other Legions. Pullus, sweat streaming down his face in rivulets, began surveying the scene around him, eyes narrowed, as he looked for some point in the fighting where he thought his presence was needed. Fortunately for him, he didn't have far to look, or to travel. In a rough semicircle, the men in his immediate vicinity who had formed a protective pocket around what they thought was the corpse of their Primus Pilus were being pushed so hard that in the amount of time it had taken the two Legionaries to help Pullus to his feet, the gap that had been about a dozen paces wide was down to a little more than half that.

Nodding his head in that direction, Pullus told the two men, "Walk on either side of me, and whatever you do, don't let me fall or I'll flay the both of you."

Even with the harsh words, both men grinned; this was the Pullus they knew; feared and loved in equal measure.

"Don't worry, Primus Pilus, we won't let you down," Philippus joked, pleased to see a shadow of a grin on Pullus' face at the play on words.

Slowly, but steadily, they made their way the short distance to a spot where Pullus was just behind the worst of the fighting.

"What are you *cunni* loafing off for? Do you really need me to do everything for you?"

For a brief moment there was no reaction from the men within earshot, but it was from disbelief, more than from not hearing him, and as the supporting men turned their heads, once Pullus saw that eyes were on him, he raised his borrowed sword high above his head. Only Titus Pullus would ever know the effort and the agony that this simple gesture cost him, but to the men who saw it, it was a sight they would remember for the rest of their lives.

"Kill. These. Bastards!"

Pullus roared this, and while he might have known the price he was paying for raising the sword, he never would comprehend where the strength to bellow those words came from, but in that moment, he was the Primus Pilus of the 10th Legion his men had followed for all these years. And despite the fact that not one of them had any voice left himself, the answering roar they all gave back rang out so loudly that it echoed off the camp walls. Titus Pullus had risen from the dead; if that was possible, how could they lose?

Outside the walls, Centurion Felix was startled by what he recognized as Roman voices, shouting in a manner that told his experienced ears that something good had happened. He was too busy to pay it more than passing attention, since at that moment he was thrusting his sword into the gut of a barbarian with a spear who had overstepped and left himself open. His sword was wet the entire length, and there was enemy blood splashed almost up to his elbow, but Felix was still concerned. There were just so many of these bastards! With this latest man dispatched, Felix stepped aside, letting a man relieve him so that he could remove himself from the immediate fighting and move along the back of the formation to get a better idea of what was happening. Even farther away, the dust was thick enough to make it extremely difficult to determine exactly what was going on, so Felix had to use a combination of his ears, his experience, and the alignment of his Centuries to get an idea of the overall situation. Once in position, Felix immediately saw that his Third Century was farther back in the long line than they should have been, to the point where it looked as if their front rank was at a spot that put them about even with the fourth or fifth man in the file of the Century to their left and the third or fourth man of the Century to the right. This made a dangerous bulge in the line, and if the barbarians could push them even farther back, there would be a crack that would allow some of their warriors to squeeze through on either side to attack the rear of the adjacent Centuries. Normally, this would be an easy problem to fix: simply ordering one of the Centuries of the second line to add their weight to the beleaguered Century was usually enough to push the enemy back. But since Felix had put his Cohort into a single line to provide a wider front, there was no second line to provide help.

As Felix watched, some of the more experienced Wa warriors that were removed from the immediate fight clearly saw this and were hurrying to the same spot, throwing themselves at the Third Century and forcing them yet another step backward. Just as the Wa general on the other side, Felix was seeing what seemed to be a victory suddenly threatened. Unlike the barbarian commander, Felix didn't hesitate. Understanding that it would be impossible to reach one of the other Cohorts to find a Century that their Pilus Prior could spare—even if they weren't as hard-pressed as Felix was at that moment— instead, the Quintus Pilus Prior ran over to where his own First Century was just then pushing forward, closer to the wall.

Felix pushed his way to the man fourth from the rear on the right hand side of the formation, grabbed the man by the shoulder, and shouted, "Follow me. Pass the word down!"

Then, repeating the command for each rank behind him, without waiting to see that he was obeyed, Felix trotted back to the Third Century. Within a few heartbeats, the men he had summoned had joined him.

"Sort this out!" he pointed to the rear of the Third Century, and every man immediately began moving, not needing any further direction.

Quickly lining themselves up in their normal places in the formation, the added weight of these men, each pushing against the man in front of him had the desired effect. At first it stopped the backward slide, but after a moment Felix saw that the Third was taking a shuffling step forward, forcing the barbarians back toward the wall. Satisfied that this crisis was averted, Felix returned to his own Century, ready to finish the job.

Hearing the huge roar farther down the line, Sextus Scribonius had too much experience to let it distract him at that moment, since he was in the process of parrying the sword thrust of one of the barbarians. Countering this move, Scribonius responded with a thrust of his own, regretting for perhaps the thousandth time that his left arm was so useless that he couldn't hold a shield, knowing that it would have come in extremely handy at this moment. Finally, after a further exchange of blows, each man blocking the other with his blade, the barbarian overcommitted himself, his sword arm extending out far enough that the distance to his body was such that he couldn't bring the blade back in time to parry Scribonius' hard overhand thrust. Catching him high in the chest, the point of the Roman's sword punched through both the lamellar armor and the breastbone of the Wa, the point severing the Wa's windpipe. Knowing that twisting the blade was not only going to be difficult because of the hard bone of the chest, but that it was also unnecessary, Scribonius made a neat recovery, not bothering to wipe his blade clean, knowing that it was useless to do so.

He did take a step backward, removing himself, much as Felix did, except he intended to try to determine what the source and cause of the sudden burst of sound was. Looking in the direction from which it came, at first Scribonius was sure that he was seeing things that his mind—so overcome with grief at the death of his friend—tried to protect him from by putting this apparition in his view. In fact, Scribonius reached up and, using the grimy back of his hand, tried to clear his eyes. But when he looked again, his giant friend was still standing there. What told Scribonius it wasn't a vision was that when Pullus turned slightly, Scribonius could clearly see the sword, still jutting from his chest and back. However, the emotion that flooded through Scribonius wasn't relief or joy at the knowledge that his friend still lived. No, it was anger that instantly coursed through him in a cold wave that was as much fear as it was rage. Suddenly completely oblivious to the situation around him, Scribonius strode in Pullus' direction, his mind filled with all sorts of choice invectives. Yet when he reached his friend's side, all the things he had come up with suddenly fled, as he stared at his friend, whose bone-white face looked at him in what Scribonius knew was Pullus' amused expression, although marred by the pain he was suffering.

"What...what by Pluto's *cock* do you think you're doing?" Scribonius spluttered, causing the thin line of Pullus' grimace to twitch.

"My job?"

Pullus' voice was back to a hoarseness that belied his condition, but his attempt at humor was completely unappreciated by his friend.

"If you haven't noticed, you've got a sword sticking out of you," Scribonius shot back. "And you have Centurions to do this."

"The Legion needs me Sextus," Pullus replied, then his eyes closed for a moment and he started to tilt in one direction, except that Artabanos was there, who put a gentle but firm hand around his Primus Pilus' waist, keeping him upright.

That sight almost undid Scribonius, and his vision suddenly clouded, but he was past caring about showing this sign of weakness in front of anyone, let alone rankers. Besides, he knew they felt much the same way, from the looks on their faces as they gazed up at Pullus, their expressions showing the strain of their emotions. Scribonius imagined that they were much the same as his own feelings: a combination of pride and grief in equal measure, as they all saw the toll this was taking on their leader.

"They need you alive, Titus," Scribonius said gently, still hoping to reach his friend with reason.

Pullus made a sound that was more groan than chuckle, but he was no less adamant than his friend.

"Alive? I'm not going to survive this Sextus and we both know it. So I might as well be useful as long as I have a breath left in me."

Words aside, Scribonius recognized the tone more than anything else, and knew that there was no swaying his friend, even if he had summoned an argument that Cicero would have envied. Not trusting himself to speak, Scribonius' only response was a shake of his head. Seeing that his friend had recognized the inevitable, Pullus turned slowly about, looking at the fighting going on all around him. Over where the Third Cohort was, Pullus' eye was drawn to a small group of men, slightly detached from the rest of the *orbis*, where about a dozen barbarians had managed to penetrate.

"Help me over there," Pullus commanded the two men. As they made their way toward this threat, Pullus called over his shoulder to Scribonius, "Go back to your men, Sextus. They still need you too."

Scribonius could only stare at Pullus' back, before, with a shake of his head, he did as his Primus Pilus ordered, understanding that it was probably the last order he would ever receive from his friend.

Like everyone else, Porcinus had heard the roar, but had been too busy at that moment to take the time to determine the cause. The incursion that Sutra had brought to his attention had grown in size, and for the first time, Porcinus' Century had started giving ground, the front rank now halfway down the dirt ramp. Glancing desperately about, Porcinus saw that he and his men were on their own: everywhere within his range of vision, the rest of the reserve force was similarly engaged. Although some Centuries were still holding the wall, a number of them were in similar straits to those in which Porcinus found himself. Unlike Felix, Porcinus didn't have the luxury of rank, nor were there sufficient men left for him to get help from another Century to bolster his own lines. He and his men were further hampered by their almost overwhelming fatigue; in fact, every time Porcinus made another thrust, or parried a Wa sword, he was sure it was the last time he would have the strength to do so.

Yet, the next time he would feel his arm moving, as if it had a mind of its own, repeating the same motions he had spent so many watches perfecting on the wooden stakes. His men were in the same state, but inevitably one of them would be a trifle too slow with his shield, or he would overextend on a thrust, leaving him vulnerable to the slashing blades of a barbarian warrior. Just like with the fighting in the forum, there was a grim pile at the bottom of the dirt ramp that had steadily grown from the first moments the Wa ladders had been thrown against the eastern wall. Porcinus' hopes, suddenly buoyed by the sounds of the horns and the sight of the relief Cohorts, were starting to plummet yet again, as he watched the continued destruction of not just his own Century, but everyone along the wall. He hadn't seen Tetarfenus for perhaps a watch by this point, and could only assume that the Pilus Prior was dead or wounded so severely that he was out of action. In fact, he hadn't seen his own Pilus Prior for perhaps a third of a watch, and assumed he had suffered the same fate as Tetarfenus. At that moment, all Porcinus knew was that he was almost out of men, and the Wa weren't.

"Centurion!"

Porcinus had taken a pause, stepping back down the ramp to catch his breath, and the man calling him was a Gayan, whose knowledge of Latin had almost been exhausted with that single word. Turning wearily toward the man, wondering what in Hades could be important enough to claim his attention at this moment, he saw the Gayan pointing. However, he wasn't pointing anywhere along the wall, but back behind the fighting to the right, in the direction of the Porta Principalis Dextra. Following the man’s finger, Porcinus squinted at the flurry of movement he was seeing, and his heart suddenly threatened to seize up at the sight of men pouring through! So great was his fatigue that his initial reaction was that he was seeing his and his men's doom, so sure that the men now entering at a run had to be those yellow-skinned, black-hearted bastards. But as he stared, it slowly dawned on him that it was extremely unlikely that the Wa would have been carrying shields. Nor would they have been carrying Roman standards!

As quickly as it had come, the despair was flushed out of him by a new wave of a hope that was so overwhelming that he couldn't restrain himself from letting out a shout of joy. Their troubles were over! Somehow, what looked like a full Cohort of men was coming to their rescue, and now more men were seeing this blessed sight, their shouts of joy mingling with Porcinus' voice. Yet as quickly as it had come, Porcinus' joy fled, not as much by a new onrush of despair as it was by puzzlement, as he saw the Roman relief force streaming by, seemingly ignoring the fighting going on to their left. Recognizing what it meant, Porcinus wasted no time. Shouting over his shoulder at his acting Optio to sound the relief for a line shift, he stumbled down the rampart, hurdling the pile of corpses without a thought, intent only on intercepting the Pilus Prior of this Cohort, whom he could see at the head of his men. Shouting to get his attention, Porcinus finally caused the head of the Pilus Prior to turn, and the sight of a dark face caught the young Centurion by surprise. In his confused and exhausted state, for a brief moment Porcinus thought it might, in fact, turn out to be a barbarian trick, since this man's skin tone had a slightly gold tint to it, and although his eyes weren't the almond shape of the men they were fighting, Porcinus supposed it was possible that there were such men fighting in the Wa ranks. But then he remembered about Pacorus, the Parthian Centurion who had caused such an uproar when he was promoted to run a Cohort, and although Porcinus had only seen him at a distance, he recognized that this was whom he was looking at. Even with his fatigue and the chaos of the overall situation, Porcinus had been thoroughly trained in a manner befitting a Centurion of Rome, so he remembered to render a salute, which the Parthian returned after pausing for a moment, giving a snapped order to his Optio to continue on to the spot Pacorus had pointed out as the place where they would form for the attack on the Wa force surrounding the forum.

"By the gods, it's good to see you, sir!" Porcinus panted.

"I'm glad we could make it in time," Pacorus' Latin was extremely good, yet another reason he had come to Caesar's attention, who always had an eye out for men with a facility for languages in the same way Caesar did.

"I know you're heading for the forum," Porcinus wasted no time. "But we could sure use some help at the wall," he gestured with a thumb back over his shoulder.

Leaning slightly to the side, so that he could see more closely, Pacorus surveyed the scene for several moments, his eyes missing nothing.

Finally he replied, "Yes, I can see that you have your hands full."

Porcinus wasn't sure what he had been expecting, but this noncommittal response completely threw him for a moment. He was about to make a sharp retort, something about how arriving so late to a fight practically guaranteed that he, Porcinus, and the rest of the men at the wall would have their hands full; but unlike his uncle, Porcinus wasn't naturally a hothead. Besides, he understood that such a comment would only hurt his chances.

Instead, he tried to match Pacorus' tone, "That we do. I don't know what your orders are, but can you spare us at least a Century? Two would be better," he finished hopefully.

Pacorus gave a barking laugh at the younger Centurion's wording.

"Yes, I can imagine," he responded dryly, then it was his turn to jerk a thumb back over his own shoulder. "But I imagine that your Primus Pilus wouldn't take it kindly if one of his junior Centurions diverted part of the force that it looks like they desperately need as much as your bunch does."

"My Primus Pilus is dead," Porcinus replied softly, trying to keep his tone even and lower lip from trembling in an unseemly display in front of this foreigner, Centurion or not.

"Balbinus is dead?" Pacorus asked sharply, for such was the legend of Titus Pullus that it didn't occur to him that it might be the Primus Pilus of the 10th.

Porcinus shook his head in answer, not saying anything in response, as his vision suddenly began swimming at the sheer enormity of what he was imparting to the Pilus Prior. For a moment, Pacorus stood there, not understanding the import of the other man's mute answer. Then his face lost its color as his jaw dropped in astonishment, and the fleeting thought passed through Porcinus' mind that suddenly Pacorus didn't look so much like a Parthian.

"*Titus Pullus is dead?*" Pacorus gasped, but again, Porcinus could only answer with a simple nod of his head.

Unbidden, Pacorus' lips formed the prayer said for the dead to the gods of his people, for Titus Pullus' reputation demanded no less.

"I'm very sorry to hear that, Centurion," Pacorus finally managed to say. "But if that's as you say, then surely the need of the men in the forum is greater?"

"If we can't stop these *cunni* from getting over the wall, then it might not matter," Porcinus replied.

And that was something Pacorus couldn't argue. In fact, if he didn't offer up aid to this Centurion, whose name he hadn't asked, then his own Cohort may be faced with the sudden appearance of an enemy in their rear. It might not tip the balance back in the barbarians' favor, but it wasn't a good idea to put him and his men in a position to test that idea.

"Very well, but I can only spare you one Century."

Porcinus opened his mouth to argue, but seeing the look on the Parthian's face, shut it again, understanding that he was lucky to get that much.

"Thank you Centurion," Porcinus said instead.

While this exchange had been taking place, the men of Pacorus' Cohort had continued running past the two men, and, as luck or the gods would have it, the last Century was just approaching. Waving his hand at the Centurion at their head, Pacorus signaled him to stop his Century. The panting man ran up to Pacorus, and, like Porcinus had, rendered his salute.

"Take your Century and go with this Centurion," Pacorus directed. "You're under his command and he'll tell you what he needs."

The Centurion didn't hesitate; this had been a day of surprises and firsts, he reasoned. One more was to be expected. Porcinus thanked Pacorus again and turned to go, but then Pacorus stopped him with a question.

"Centurion, in case this all works out, who should I say helped save this day?"

"I'm Decimus Hastatus Posterior Gaius Porcinus, of the 10th Legion, Pilus Prior," Porcinus answered, prompting a frown from Pacorus.

"If I recall, Primus Pilus Pullus had a nephew by that name," Pacorus commented.

At the mention of his uncle in the past tense, Porcinus felt a stab of pain even greater than he had experienced in the moments after his recognition that his uncle was dead.

"He still does, Pilus Prior," Porcinus answered, his tone stiff with hurt and rebuke. "And he always will."

Without another word or waiting to be dismissed, Porcinus turned and began trotting away, beckoning Pacorus' Centurion to his side as he did. Pacorus watched for only a matter of a couple of heartbeats, understanding the younger man completely. Then he turned back and began running to where the five Centuries of his Cohort were arraying in a line, prepared to pounce on the barbarian rear.

It was over, the Wa general now recognized. He still wasn't sure how it had happened, but he was now sure that at the very least his attempt to breach the wall had failed, and the taste of that was bitter ash in his mouth. Now the only thing he could do was to leave those of his men who had managed to get up the ladder and over the wall and were even now fighting to their fate, and pull the rest of the men gathered at the ladders to join their comrades in the fight against this new force. At this point in the battle, if the general had been Roman, Greek, or even Han, his goal would have been to fight his way out of this predicament to preserve what remained of his force to fight another day. But this was not the Wa way. To be defeated was so shaming that no Wa with any self-respect would dare to show his face back at the capital, and no man in the rank and file would do so, either. No, what remained was only to die with as much glory as could be salvaged and to take as many of these grubworms as possible. To that end, the general now began pushing his way to the front, no longer needing to direct matters. He was determined that he would wet his sword to the hilt, and that his gods would be so impressed with the number of his kills that they would forgive him for not bringing victory to his people. It helped that he was sure that the battle itself was won; it didn't occur to him that the force assaulting the camp holding the grubworm general would fail. So, even if the strategic aim of this prong of the attack was foiled, the loss of this camp would undoubtedly send the barbarians skulking back to their ships. And no matter what happened, they had crippled the invasion force to the point where it would be impossible for them to continue.

What this Wa forgot—which could be forgiven under the circumstances—was that this attack had been an all-or-nothing proposition and that the only troops left at the capital were the personal bodyguards of the emperor and men who were too sick to fight or still recovering from wounds received from the other engagements with these grubworms. In fact, the only hope of the Wa at this point was that the mauling the Romans had received was so savage that it removed from them any thought of continuing their thrust towards the capital. To help ensure this end, the Wa general made his way to the front, standing just behind the front line, where his warriors were still slashing and thrusting at the shields of the grubworms, who, in contrast to his own men, still stood in ordered lines several men deep. As much as he despised these pale creatures, he was nevertheless admiring of the discipline and order they brought to a battle, and it was a pity that he wouldn't survive to try to adopt some of their practices for his own army. Seeing one of the grubworms with a device on his helmet that went crossways over the top—unlike that of all the rest of the barbarians, whose plumes looked like horsehair and simply hung straight down—the general drew his sword and headed directly for him, determined that this would be the first of what would be many deaths that he would bring.

It was only because of the shouted warning of one of his men that Felix turned in time to see one of the barbarians, this one wearing a helmet mounted with the wings of some white bird, come lunging at him with a screaming shout and upraised sword. Barely able to get his shield up in time, Felix just managed to block the massive blow that shook him all the way down to the soles of his *caligae*. Before he could answer, the barbarian had recovered his blade and, in seemingly one single fluid motion changed the direction and angle of his thrust, going from a high overhand downward thrust to a vicious, upward-traveling slicing swing that originated from a point beneath Felix's shield.

Somehow, Felix managed to deflect the Wa's blade with his own, so that the barbarian's blade went flashing by diagonally, across the Roman's body. This put the Wa in a vulnerable position, and again showing why the Legions of Rome valued the shield for both its defensive and offensive capabilities, Felix made a hard horizontal thrust with his left arm. The shield, its metal boss leading the way, punched out at the barbarian general, and this time it was the Wa's turn for a desperate movement, twisting his body backward, so that, while the boss struck him on his right shoulder, by his giving way, the impact was lessened. Still, it was a painful blow, and Felix was rewarded with a hissing sound exploding from the barbarian's lips, but he had no time to savor the moment, because again his enemy's blade came flashing at him, this time with the point aimed directly for his eyes. Felix performed a slight turn and dip of his head, causing the point of the Wa's blade to strike only a glancing blow high on his helmet, but it was enough to cause lights to explode behind Felix's eyes. Fighting the surge of panic at his momentary sightlessness, Felix, in turn, made an overhand thrust at the spot where he had last seen the barbarian, just before the Wa landed his blow. While it missed, having the point of a sharp blade jabbed right at you is enough to disturb even the most disciplined man, so the Wa's recoiling backward jump gave Felix enough time for his sight to clear. Just in time to move his shield to block yet another strike from his opponent, he caught the barbarian's point with the boss, making a clanging sound and striking sparks as the blade bounced harmlessly off. In much the same way that the Wa had recognized the strengths and advantages of his opponent's style of fighting, a part of Felix was no less appreciative that these yellow-skinned barbarians were exceptionally skilled, able to move with a rapidity and fluid grace that Felix wished he, and the rest of his men for that matter, possessed. Where a Roman would strike with his sword one time, in that same span of time, these barbarians seemed to be able to strike at least twice as often, if not more times; while Felix had no idea how they did it, each blow still managed to carry the same amount of force as that of the average Legionary. Only men like Titus Pullus and a handful of others could match these men in pure skill, Felix realized, but they lacked the discipline and teamwork of the Legions. He didn't even want to think of how formidable the barbarians would be if these two strengths were combined, and the detached part of Felix's mind hoped that if they survived this day, Caesar would figure out a way to train his Legions to take advantage of what the yellow bastards could do with a sword. Both men had paused to catch their breath, the Wa general glaring at his opponent, who stared at him from above the rim of his shield, eyes narrowed in concentration.

"I will gut you like a fisherman guts a fish," the Wa general taunted, completely forgetting that this grubworm wasn't civilized enough to understand language.

Felix, while he didn't understand the words, clearly comprehended the meaning, and, in answer, made a motioning gesture with his sword, inviting the barbarian to do his worst.

"You sound like a pig grunting," Felix taunted, eliciting the exact same response from the Wa.

Not understanding the words but needing no translator, the general leaped into the air with a grace that gave witness to the hundreds of watches he spent practicing maneuvers like this. The sudden movement caused Felix to react, the point of his sword suddenly striking out like a snake, but in the delay between what his eyes saw, his brain commanded, and his arm obeyed, the spot where he aimed his thrust was now empty. His right arm was now fully extended, and anticipating that this would be Felix's move, the general had already begun his downward swing, the blade of his sword arcing in what could only be described as a beautifully precise semicircle, when, in yet another one of those accidents of battle that the beneficiaries usually attribute to an act of the gods, the warrior next to the general had just taken a thrust from a Roman sword to the throat and staggered sideways, bumping into the general just as the sword was perhaps halfway in its arc of travel. While it would have made a slightly diagonal strike across Felix's forearm, severing the Pilus Prior's sword arm and probably leading to his death, instead, the general's body was jarred hard enough so that the blade turned and missed Felix's arm by no more than a hand span.

But what this also did was upset the general's stance and throw him off balance, so that in the very instant after his sword missed its target, and before he could recover himself, the Wa general was vulnerable. And Felix didn't waste the opportunity provided him. Bringing his already extended sword up in a straight line, he brought the edge of his blade up and directly into the Wa general's throat, the point tearing into the soft flesh directly underneath his chin. Although there wasn't a lot of force behind it, since his arm was already extended, it was nevertheless a damaging blow, the Wa's head snapping back in a spray of blood and exposing his throat. Felix made a leaping step forward, his arm still extended out before him, so that the point of the blade entered the Wa's body right above his Adam's apple, the Centurion stopping only when he felt the grate of the bone that supported the man's head. When he felt that resistance, he immediately moved his arm sideways, slicing through the carotid artery and most of the muscles of the neck, causing the Wa's head, weighted down by the helmet as it was, to suddenly tilt grotesquely to one side.

For a couple of heartbeats, the barbarian stood there, blood spraying in a bright arc, as his heart continued beating, his eyes registering the same shock that almost every man experiences at his own sudden death, before collapsing in a heap. There was a moment's pause, then the Romans around Felix erupted in a roar of fierce joy, knowing that their Pilus Prior had slain an important man. Immediately around the Wa general, his own men let out howls of despair, but continued their fight with even more fury than before. Unlike their leader, they hadn't thought about the larger situation; all they knew was their job, which was to obey and to die, should their commander order it. And now that their leader was down, all that was left for them to do was to continue killing, even though it meant their own certain death.

Chapter 10

The sun, which almost every man of Caesar's army would have sworn would never, ever set, was now just barely above the low horizon, and for the first time that day, the prevailing sound was silence. At least, it was silent when compared to the sound and fury of a battle that had begun not that long after dawn. In the northern camp, there was not much left, other than smoke, ruin, and a level of carnage that nobody in Caesar's army, not even those veterans of Gaul who had been at Alesia, had ever witnessed before. If one stood in the middle of the camp and just listened, he would have sworn that he heard the keening of a relentless, lonely wind. But the breeze was almost nonexistent; taking its place was the sound of thousands of wounded, on both sides, each of them speaking a universal language of suffering and pain.

Sextus Scribonius stood, as he had been standing for some time, too weary to move, or to give any orders, for that matter. He was afraid to sit down, sure that if he did, he would never be able to stand again, so instead he just...stood there. His mind was almost as empty as the rest of his body, barely able to register the sights, sounds, and smells around him. All he knew for sure was that somehow—he had no idea how—the camp hadn't fallen. Anything more complex than that, even for someone as brilliant as Scribonius, was beyond him. Everywhere around him, men were shuffling as if they were sleepwalking, most of them doing nothing more strenuous or involved than checking on fallen comrades to see if they still lived. If they found one alive, they would raise a hand and try to call for the attention of a *medicus* to come and aid the wounded man. Even this taxed them, as they shambled from one pile of bodies to another, bending over and pulling aside the barbarian bodies, using their dagger on any Wa who showed any sign of life. Scribonius watched all of this, with a detached interest that was the best effort he could muster, observing mutely as men went about their grisly business. Then, a *medicus*, his tunic completely black from all of the blood in which he had been forced to wade this day, approached him with an expression Scribonius couldn't readily interpret.

"Pilus Prior, can you come with me?" the *medicus'* accent betrayed a Pandyan heritage, if his dark skin hadn't already proclaimed it.

Scribonius found it difficult to summon interest in what this man was saying, but he forced himself to respond.

"Why? Surely you don't need me to tell you if someone's alive or dead."

The *medicus* hesitated, and something in his manner triggered a slight flicker of interest in the Pilus Prior.

"It concerns the Primus Pilus," the *medicus* replied.

"Ah," Scribonius' curiosity faded, not willing to deal with this detail, despite knowing that it was inevitable. Couldn't these bastards allow a man to grieve for his best friend for just a few moments, he wondered? "Well, I'm sure there are other men who need your help more than he does."

The *medicus'* reaction confused Scribonius, because the man hesitated again, as if there was something more than the routine requirement of deciding what to do with his friend's body.

"I doubt that," the other man replied. "He's alive, so he needs us just as much as anyone. More, probably," he added.

Scribonius stared in disbelief; he was so sure that his last conversation with Pullus would be the final time he would ever speak to his friend, his tired mind was unable to comprehend fully what it was hearing.

"He's...alive?" Scribonius gasped.

The *medicus* nodded, but his expression was grim.

"Yes, he is. I don't know how, and I don't know for how much longer, but yes, right now he's still alive. And he's asking for you."

In Caesar's camp, the general was in much the same state as his Secundus Pilus Prior of the 10th, but he had the luxury of being attended by the handful of his slaves and staff who had somehow survived. Statianus' attack, with his four Cohorts had shattered the Wa assault, although it had been at a grievous cost. Even so, these four Cohorts, along with a scratch force that Caesar had thrown together of what remained of his forces defending the barricade, numbering about a full Cohort, were pursuing the barbarians. However, Caesar had given strict orders for the pursuit not to go more than halfway down the slope, because, as shattered as this Wa force was, until he knew what the situation was in the other camps, his army was still in great danger. As exhausted as he was, Caesar's mind was still hard at work, not just directing the care for his wounded and tallying his losses, but already putting men to work at cleaning away any debris that might hinder a defense, if there was to be another assault. Most of the camp was a smoking ruin, especially the half of the camp between the western wall, where the assault had come from, and the forum. After thinking about it for a moment, Caesar had ordered that the makeshift barricade not only stay in place, but be improved. The wall was being repaired, as well, although the ditches were still filled with the bodies of the Wa who had served the same purpose as the *fascines*, the bundles of sticks Roman armies piled on top of each other to fill a ditch. Unfortunately, he couldn't spare the men or the time to toss the bodies out of the ditch, so that this would enable the Wa to cross again with no impediment, but it couldn't be helped.

Someone had found a stool, and although it was something Caesar normally wouldn't do—taking a seat while his men worked—this time he was too tired to worry about appearances. However, his men didn't begrudge their commander on this day, nor did they try to shirk the tasks he had set out for them, knowing that what they were doing was in their interests. Once the camp was secure, Caesar had sent couriers to the three camps to the south, and it was word of their status that he was awaiting now, as he gazed out at the destruction, pain, and death around him. Caesar never liked these scenes, but today it distressed him even more, because he knew that all of what he was seeing was due to his own ambitions and dreams. Granted, his men followed willingly and had been rewarded handsomely, but he wasn't blind to the fact that as wealthy as his men all were by this point, there wasn't anywhere to spend their wealth, nor was there anything to buy. They were strangers in a strange, very strange land, and it was in this moment that Caesar's doubts and fears were their strongest. What had he done, he wondered? Bringing these men so far away, only to die on this strange, mysterious island? And for what, after all? To fulfill an ambition that he knew, and had known for some time would never be fully satisfied? That no new lands traveled through and new peoples conquered would ever be enough, because he would always hunger for more? For this was Caesar's darkest secret, one that he would admit only to himself. How could he make these men, who had given so much, give even more than they had this day?

These were the dark thoughts passing through his mind, when one of the surviving Centurions—the Primus Princeps Posterior, the Centurion in charge of the Fourth Century of the First Cohort and the only Centurion surviving from the First Cohort of the 15th Legion, the first five Cohorts of which had been one of the Legions in Caesar's camp—approached him carrying a tablet. Seeing his general deep in thought, the man, Gnaeus Carbo, stood waiting for Caesar to notice him, but he showed no sign that he was even aware there was anyone nearby. Finally, Carbo cleared his throat, and only then did Caesar look up, causing Carbo's heart to lurch at the sight of his general looking older and more tired than he had ever seen him. It was as if he had suddenly aged ten years and, for the first time, looking every one of his 65 years. Still, Caesar managed a smile, grim though it may have been.

"Quite a day, eh, Carbo?"

"Quite a day," Carbo agreed, opening his mouth to say something more, then thinking better of it.

Instead, he simply offered Caesar the tablet, which his general took with a hand that Carbo pretended wasn't slightly shaking. Opening it, Caesar scanned the contents incised in the wax, the lines around his mouth deepening as he read the grim figures.

"Are these accurate?" Caesar finally asked, hoarse from the titanic effort it was taking to control his voice.

"They're...accurate, but incomplete, Caesar," Carbo finally answered, prompting a harsh laugh from Caesar that held no humor, whatsoever.

"You mean it could be worse?"

"I'm afraid so," Carbo said softly.

Without answering, Caesar suddenly bowed his head, while Carbo stood, growing more uncomfortable. Seeing his general's lips move, he realized that Caesar was saying a prayer for all of his dead men, still filling his role as Pontifex Maximus, a post he had held in absentia for almost four decades. Finally finished, Caesar looked back up at Carbo, heaving a sigh that said more to Carbo than any words.

"Thank you Carbo. That will be all for now. Go and see to your men. As of this moment, you're the Primus Pilus of the 15th Legion, so that includes taking care of the other Cohorts, as well."

Carbo wasn't sure whether it was appropriate to thank Caesar at a time like this, and even if it was, he didn't much feel like celebrating. Like any Centurion worth his salt, Carbo wanted promotion, and he knew that promotion occurred almost always because a man higher up the ladder had fallen, but as ambitious as he was, he had no desire to vault up so many rungs in this manner. Nevertheless, he had a duty to perform, so he went off to see to it, leaving Caesar behind. Not much longer after Carbo had departed, there was a shout at the eastern gate, and one of the surviving *bucinatores*—in charge of the horn that sounded signals inside the camp, such as the changing of the watch—blew the notes that signaled an approaching rider. Knowing that this was the courier returning, Caesar roused himself from his spot and began hobbling toward the gate, careful to avoid stepping on the wounded as he passed across the forum. Normally, he would have stopped to offer some words of comfort to the men lying there, but he needed to know, now, the status of the other camps.

"How are you still alive?" Scribonius blurted this out without thinking, so amazed was he at the sight of his friend, still breathing. Pullus, back on the ground and lying in his original position, managed a wan smile.

"I've been wondering the same thing," he muttered, sure that he had broken at least one of his teeth from clenching them so tightly.

The sword was still embedded in his body, the giant Roman refusing to allow the *medici* to remove it, sure that as soon as they did, he would perish. And he had matters to attend to before that happened, which was why he had called for Scribonius. His friend knelt beside him, his eyes filled with unshed tears as he looked down at Pullus; but Pullus refused to meet them, not wanting to destroy his own composure. Even now, in what he was sure were the last moments of his life, Titus Pullus was conscious of his reputation, and he was determined that he would die in a manner that he deemed befitted a Primus Pilus of Caesar's Legions. No sniveling, no complaining about the unjustness of what had happened. Titus Pullus would leave something for men to talk about around the fire for the rest of time.

"I sent for Gaius, as well," Titus said to Scribonius, and this simple statement was too much for the Pilus Prior to bear, and now he began sobbing. Pullus frowned at his friend, saying only half-jestingly, "You're making a spectacle of yourself, Sextus."

"I don't care," Scribonius shot back. "I've lost too much today. Balbus..."

His voice trailed off, but Pullus didn't need him to finish; he knew that Scribonius was going to say, "Now you." But Pullus wasn't willing to let his friend be distracted by self-pity at this moment, because Pullus was still the Primus Pilus.

"Mourn later," he said, mustering as much as was possible the hard edge he used to let his friend know that it was the Primus Pilus speaking and not Titus. "There are things I need to tell you to do. How many Centurions from the First are left?"

Scribonius' only response was a mute shake of his head.

"That's what I thought. That means you're the Primus Pilus of the 10th Legion now, so I need you to....."

Before he got any further, Scribonius cut him off.

"What 10th Legion?" he burst out, the bitterness of a loss so huge it couldn't be put into words almost threatening to choke him. "There is no 10th Legion anymore, Titus. It was destroyed today."

"No, it wasn't," Pullus snapped, and now Scribonius could see real anger in his friend's eyes, even if his voice wasn't able to convey it. "As long as there's still one man alive and under the standard, there's a 10th Legion. The Legion will never die. You understand me, Pilus Prior?"

The use of his rank informed Scribonius that, even here at the end, Titus Pullus was a Centurion of Rome. And so was he, Scribonius admitted, as bitter and galling as it was right now, for he wanted nothing more than to find some hole to crawl into and not think or feel, anything.

"Yes, Primus Pilus. I understand. And I will obey," Scribonius spoke the words he had so often uttered by rote, without thought, but understanding the import of all that they meant, most especially to his friend.

So, if he could send his best friend, his longest companion, on his way to Elysium by assuring him that the 10th Legion would carry on without him—even if Scribonius had no idea how that was possible—it was the least he could do.

"Good," Pullus muttered. "Now, you need to get the butcher's bill as soon as possible. Delegate one of the other Centurions to do it, while you take care of getting the men organized. And you need to set a watch, immediately. I doubt these bastards are going to come back, but if they do, we need to be ready."

Scribonius, now that his mind was absorbed with practical matters, had calmed down, the tears drying from his cheeks, as he thought about what needed to be done.

"I don't know if we have enough men left to cover the western wall, let alone the whole camp," Scribonius mused.

He was surprised when his friend gave a slight shake of his head.

"The relief Cohorts are still here, aren't they?" When Scribonius assured him that they were Pullus continued, "Then use them."

"But they're not from the 10th. In all honesty, I'm not sure where they're from. I think the 14th and the 30th, but I haven't paid that close attention."

"Well it's about time the 14th did something worthwhile," Pullus grunted, eliciting a chuckle from his friend, who momentarily forgot the circumstances of their talk. "But you're about to be the Primus Pilus of the 10th Legion, so you outrank any of those bastards. Pull rank if you have to. Don't worry about what Caesar thinks. For all we know, he's dead, and even if he's not, he's not going to fault you for protecting the camp!"

Even if Scribonius was disposed to argue, he saw the sense in what Pullus was saying. Before he could say anything more, however, the sound of someone approaching at a run drew both their attention away, but because of the angle, Pullus couldn't turn his head to see who it was. So, only Scribonius saw that it was Pullus' nephew, and even as the younger Centurion approached, their eyes met and Scribonius could only give a grim shake of his head. That slowed Porcinus to a sudden walk, as if he didn't want to come near enough to learn the truth firsthand. But he made his way carefully around the other wounded in a circle to approach his uncle from an angle where Pullus could see him.

"Get over here, boy," Titus called weakly, lifting his arm in a beckoning gesture for just an instant before it fell limply back onto his body.

Now it was Gaius' turn to begin crying, seeing for the first time the sword that bore mute testimony to what was happening to his uncle. Falling to his knees at his uncle's side, Porcinus dropped his head, sobbing, as Pullus did his own examination of his nephew. Seeing the caked blood around Porcinus' right ear and down the entire side of his face, Scribonius heard his friend give a sharp hiss as he caught his breath at the sight.

"What happened to you? Are you all right?" Pullus asked, and the absurdity of the question, and the fact that his uncle was asking him caused Porcinus to burst out in a laugh tinged with hysteria.

"You're lying there with a sword sticking out of you, and you're asking me, if I'm all right?" Porcinus asked, and when put that way, even Pullus had to smile, albeit faintly.

But he was not so easily thrown off the topic, and he asked Porcinus again.

"Yes, I'm fine. I got lucky," his nephew said, causing Pullus to snort in disbelief.

"It doesn't look like you're lucky."

"Well, I am. I just have a headache."

"Did you at least kill the *cunnus* who did that to you?"

Although it would have been easier just to lie and say that he had, Porcinus had never lied to his uncle, and he didn't plan on starting now.

"If I did, it was later on. I got knocked cold for a bit. But I'm fine now," he insisted.

"Well, you let the *medici* decide that. At the very least it looks like you need stitches. Now, there's something I need to tell you," Pullus turned back to business.

Unlike Scribonius, Porcinus wasn't willing to cooperate with his uncle, not if it meant acknowledging what his eyes told him to be the truth.

"There's nothing I need to know right now that can't wait until you're better."

Again, Pullus gave a snort, but he reached out with his free hand and grasped his nephew's arm. Even near death, Porcinus thought, he has a grip that feels like it will turn the bones of my arm into powder.

"Enough," Pullus said gently, more gentle than he had been with Scribonius, because, unlike with Sextus, what Pullus had to tell his nephew didn't involve official business. "You need to listen to me. In my pack, you'll find a scroll that's sealed with my ring."

Pullus was referring to the signet ring that Caesar had given his giant Primus Pilus as a gift, after Pullus had once again saved his Legion from disaster on the beaches of Pandya. The symbol on the solid gold ring was that of a dragon, which Caesar and his men had first seen depictions of in the lands of the Han.

Continuing, Pullus said, "You need to make sure that you don't open that by yourself. It needs to be witnessed by others, because it's my will."

This caused Porcinus even more grief, and he realized that he was as disturbed by his uncle's matter-of-fact tone as he was by the words themselves. Every man in the Legion had a will, and death was a constant companion to them all, but Gaius Porcinus—and, if the truth were known, Sextus Scribonius, too—never thought that Titus Pullus would ever be in a position to talk about his will. His death was simply inconceivable to both of them, and, in fact, to every man of the 10th Legion. He was indestructible, and while his body bore so many scars that they almost connected together to form a jagged, winding line like a river, none of them thought that the man had been born or the weapon forged that could defeat him.

Ignoring the effect his words were having, Pullus bore onward, telling his nephew, "In my will, not only do I leave you everything, but I adopt you as my son and heir. That means that when you return to Rome, you'll not only be eligible for equestrian status, but Caesar has also promised that he'll endorse your elevation to the Senate."

"Back to Rome?" Porcinus repeated dully, shaking his head as if trying to wake himself from a bad dream. "Back to Rome?" he repeated again. "I'm not going to see Rome again. None of us are. We're never leaving this island!"

Not even Titus Pullus could have explained where he got the strength, but, without warning, his calloused, battle-hardened hand moved with a speed that reminded both men beside him that, despite his bulk, he moved with the speed of a much, much smaller man. The sound of his open palm slapping his nephew across the face made Scribonius jump, while Porcinus' head rocked back, almost knocking him from his kneeling position onto his backside. His ear began ringing, and the side of his face felt as though it was on fire as he stared down—open-mouthed in astonishment and not a little pain—seeing in his uncle's eyes a cold fury that he had never been the recipient of, but had seen on the battlefield.

"Don't ever say that aloud again," Pullus told him, his quiet tone in odd contrast to the action he had just taken. "The only thing that keeps these men marching forward is their belief that they'll see home again. And I want you to swear to me, on Jupiter's stone, that you have every intention of trying to return to Rome. And taking back as many of the men as you can."

Porcinus didn't answer immediately, mainly because he knew that his uncle was deadly serious, and didn't take the swearing of an oath as lightly as a lot of men did. But while the thought passed through Porcinus' mind that he could offer the oath to make his uncle happy—since he wouldn't be around to see it fulfilled, making the giving of it almost academic, he dismissed the thought immediately. If he agreed, it would be because he had every intention of fulfilling his pledge to his uncle.

That's why he hesitated, before he finally said, "I swear on Jupiter's stone that I'll do everything in my power to get back to Rome."

"And to get the men back" Pullus insisted.

Porcinus heaved a sigh, adding, "And to get the men back, as well," although he had no idea how he was going to accomplish this.

With that matter settled, Pullus seemed satisfied, and the three of them were silent for some time.

"Well," Pullus finally said, "there's no need putting it off any longer. Go get one of the *medici* and let's get this over with."

Both Scribonius and Porcinus' fragile composure, brought on by the brief period of quiet, broke immediately, but this time, Pullus didn't remonstrate with either of them.

Instead, he just said quietly, "It's going to be all right, boys," over and over.

The *medicus* answered Scribonius' call, for he had been nearby, hovering about the wounded and staying within earshot, both because he knew he would be needed, but also to hear what he was sure would be his Primus Pilus' last words, for Titus Pullus was as renowned with the noncombatants of Caesar's army as he was with the men. Besides which, he was good friends with Diocles, Pullus' servant, scribe and—despite their radically different stations in life—good friend. Over his strenuous objections, Diocles and some of the other slaves had been sent down the ridge on the eastern side to wait aboard one of the ships for the outcome of the battle, and this *medicus* knew that the Greek would want to know every detail of his master's last moments on earth.

"Yes, sir?" he asked, when he reached the three Centurions.

"You need to get this thing out of me," Pullus said, without any hesitation.

Although he knew that this was coming, the *medicus* still paused for a moment, suddenly aware of the eyes of the other two men on him, eyes that were telling him that if he caused the Primus Pilus any undue suffering, there would be a reckoning with them.

Understanding this, Pullus assured him, "Don't worry about them. Just do it quickly and it'll be all right. And I'm telling you both now," he moved his head slightly, so that he could look into both men's eyes, "don't take it out on him for doing his job. Just because I might yell like a pig going to slaughter, it's not his fault."

Scribonius tried smile at his friend's attempt at humor, but he wasn't very successful, and Porcinus could only look away, mumbling his agreement. This didn't serve to soothe the *medicus'* nerves any, but he knew that he needed to perform this task. Most of the clean bandages had long since been used up, but he had been saving one, tucked inside his tunic. If the truth were known, he had been saving it for himself, since at one point during the day's battle he was sure that he was going to be struck down, as so many others had been. Now he produced it, tearing it with his teeth into two roughly equal pieces. Looking about, he reached over for a discarded balteus, the Legionary's belt, and, stripping off the decorative strips and the dagger sheath, he examined it for a moment before realizing that he would need something, in addition. This engendered a short walk, where he found yet another balteus, and he repeated the process. Both Centurions watched the man, neither of them speaking, and for the first time Pullus' own composure seemed to be slipping away.

Squeezing his nephew's knee, Pullus said, "I just want you to know how proud I am of the man you've become, and what a fine Centurion you are, Gaius."

Porcinus couldn't trust himself to respond, his head bowing again, as the tears started anew.

Turning to Scribonius, Pullus whispered, "Sextus, no man could have had a better or more loyal friend. It's been my honor to know you, and I'll pray that the gods watch over you."

Now it was Scribonius' turn to break down, the raw emotion of the moment penetrating even the hard shell of the *medicus*, who had witnessed so many scenes similar to this, on this day alone, that he should have been inured to them by now. But he was as moved as the other two men, and it was only with a great effort of will that he kept his tone level.

"Yes, well. All right then," he mumbled as he arranged the items he had gathered just so. "Best get on with it. Centurion," the *medicus* turned to Scribonius, "if you could hold his legs please. No, like that. Yes, like that. Thank you;" he motioned next to Porcinus as Scribonius tightened his grip on his friend's legs, straddling them with his own and grasping Pullus' calf with both hands. "If you would get behind him. Yes, like that. Now, hold both of his shoulders. Tightly."

Every man has his limits, and even Pullus had reached his, groaning when his nephew tightened his grip on his shoulders. Porcinus had shut his eyes, trying to focus completely on his task as the *medicus* explained to Pullus what he was going to do.

"You've undoubtedly seen this done before, Primus Pilus," he told Pullus. "So you know that I'm going to do my best to pull the blade straight out at the exact angle, as it went in. That minimizes the damage and......"

"Would you shut the fuck up and just do it, already?" Pullus muttered through clenched teeth.

The *medicus* blinked a couple of times, then nodded his head. With a hand that was shaking only slightly—which Pullus noted and thought was a good sign—he grasped the hilt of the sword. But before he made any move, he bent down so that his eye was level with the hilt and squinted down the length of the blade, trying to determine the angle. Finally satisfied, he took a deep breath, looked down at Pullus, who gave a brief nod, his jaw muscles so tightly bunched that it looked as if the Roman had been in a brawl and had a swollen face. Then, with one smooth motion that spoke to the number of times he had performed this act before, the *medicus* withdrew the sword. It happened so quickly that Scribonius, the only one of the two holding onto Pullus who was actually looking, wasn't sure that he had seen it. Just one moment the sword was there, sticking out of his friend's body, then it wasn't. As soon as the blade was removed, a gout of blood gushed from both front and back, but the *medicus* made no immediate move to staunch the flow, prompting a sharp question from Porcinus as to why he wasn't doing so.

The noncombatant shook his head in answer, but then seeing that a non-verbal response wouldn't appease either of the Centurions, he explained, "He's had that sword in him so long that the blood has pooled inside his body. If we don't let it drain out, for some reason it will turn corrupt and will end up poisoning him."

Scribonius was about to argue, but thought better of it, mainly because even as the man was talking, Scribonius could see that the flow was slowing drastically. After just a few heartbeats, it had stopped for the most part, and only then did the *medicus* move to place the bandages on either side of Pullus' chest, soaking up some of the blood. Pullus was quiet, because he had fainted when the blade was withdrawn, but when Scribonius went to revive him, he was stopped by a gentle, but firm hand.

"Let him stay out for now, Centurion," the *medicus* told him. "He's going to want to be this way for what we have to do next."

What came next was pulling off Pullus' armor, a feat made even more difficult than it normally was from an unconscious man who was nothing but dead weight, when that weight was as much as Pullus'. Even in his unconscious state, a groan escaped from the Primus Pilus' lips, when Porcinus and the *medicus*, as gently as they could, lifted his arms above his head. This also prompted a fresh rush of blood, but the *medicus* insisted that this wasn't a bad or dangerous thing. Recognizing they had no other choice but to trust the man, both Scribonius and Porcinus followed his instructions exactly. As slowly as they could, they pulled the heavy mail shirt off of Pullus, tossing it aside once they did. This forced yet another groan from the large man, and his eyes fluttered open for a bare moment before they rolled back into his head, and he lapsed back into unconsciousness. With the armor off, the padded undershirt was next, but before they removed it, the *medicus* inspected it closely.

When asked why he was doing this, he replied, "I'm trying to see if that sword made a clean cut and sliced through the mail, this undershirt, and his tunic, or if it was dull and pushed some fragments into the wound."

Neither man needed to be told what that meant: even if Pullus survived the next watch, he would be facing a long, lingering, and extremely agonizing death as his wound putrefied from the foreign material left to fester in his body. It was true that one of the more experienced physicians might be able to fish the debris out, but the wound was so close to vital organs, such as the lungs and heart, that this would only be a last resort, because in all likelihood the operation would kill him. Both Centurions had been in the army long enough to know of men who had suffered this fate, and it was something neither of them would wish on anyone, particularly someone they cared about. Finally satisfied, the *medicus* gently pulled off the undershirt, leaving just the tunic, where the process was repeated. It was only after that and after they removed the tunic that the orderly showed any sign that could be called relief, no matter how faint.

"It looks like that bastard had a very sharp sword, because, as far as I can tell, that's about the cleanest cut I've ever seen."

Neither man had realized they were holding their breath until they both suddenly expelled it in harsh bursts, causing them to chuckle a bit. Now that Pullus was stripped, the orderly gently swabbed the wound with a rag, now completely filthy and black from performing this chore for the better part of a day on other wounds. Once he was satisfied, he took the two bandages, put them back in place, then, linking the two baltea together, had Porcinus and Scribonius heave Pullus' bulk into an upright sitting position. The way Pullus' head lolled back as they did this reminded Porcinus of the newly dead, who possess a limp shapelessness that a soldier knew all too well, but he did his best to ignore that, taking comfort in the sound of his uncle's breathing, as shallow and raspy as it was. Using the two baltea, the *medicus* pulled the bandages tightly against Pullus' body, forcing one last groan from the unconscious man.

"We're done now," the orderly said, more to soothe the other two men than anything else.

Laying Pullus back gently, Porcinus asked, "Now what?"

"Now," the orderly said grimly, "we wait. It's in the hands of the gods now. But," he shook his head, "I will say this; I've never seen anyone wounded that badly who's survived this long."

"So there's hope," Scribonius interjected, to which the orderly could only shrug.

"Where there's life, there's hope. How much?" he asked, not finishing the sentence, instead giving a slight shrug. He didn't have to say anything more.

Entering Caesar's camp, Asinius Pollio's mouth hung open as he gazed about. Only when he looked to the right side of the forum did he see anything resembling a Roman camp. Except that the usually neatly ordered streets were now crammed full of men lying in row upon row, as other men, both uniformed and noncombatant, moved about, in one spot crouching next to a man to offer a drink of water, ladling it out of a bucket, while in other places a pair of men would be grabbing the legs and trunk of a Legionary who had succumbed to his wounds. Treating the now-dead man with a care that Pollio had seen so many times before, the bearers nevertheless moved swiftly, carefully stepping over the other wounded as they took the body away to... where, Pollio wondered? Even as he watched, this scene played out on every single Legion street, sometimes simultaneously. As quickly as the corpse was removed, two more orderlies would come hurrying up, using the plank stretcher to bring another wounded man from one of the areas Caesar had designated for his physicians and the *medici*, where they assessed the casualty brought before them. Although this scene wasn't all that unusual—Caesar had long since perfected the art of rapid restoration of order and treatment of casualties after battle—Pollio had never seen anything on this scale before.

That was because, he realized, nothing like this had ever happened to Caesar's army before. Pollio had since dismounted, leaving his horse behind to walk on foot, mainly because he had reached the part of the camp where everything was in such a shambles that it was impossible even to see where the Via Principalis or Via Praetoria was, let alone follow it. But the real reason he had chosen to walk—the two Tribunes he had brought with him trailing behind him, their mental state much the same as his—was that he needed time to absorb what he was seeing. Also, he had been prepared to tell Caesar in expansive terms about the hard-fought battle they had endured to hold the southernmost camp, but all the flowery phrases that he had come up with in his mind were wilting as rapidly as if they were real blooms, suddenly exposed to a desert sun. Pollio realized now that nothing he and the men of the southern camp had faced was anything close to what had evidently happened in Caesar's.

Reaching the far edge of the forum, Pollio's walk slowed even more, then came to a stop, as he stood, open-mouthed and looking in the direction of the western wall. Normally, his eye would be met with row upon row of ordered tent lines, blocks of them neatly arranged by the Cohort and Legion they belonged to, the streets between the blocks as neatly delineated as the tents. It was a sight that was always pleasing to a Roman eye, so even more than the sight of the blackened ruins of entire blocks of tents—most of them still smoking—was the lack of order that impacted Pollio most profoundly. He would never have thought that he put so much importance on seeing what were nothing more than clumps of peaked leather arranged in regular patterns, but in that moment Pollio realized just how Roman he was. Now, standing there, his eye traveled from the southern wall to the northern wall, stopping only when he spotted something out of place in what he recognized as a scene of total destruction. Usually it was the sight of a group of Legionaries, bending over one of the many heaps of bodies, where at some point part of the fight had coalesced. From his experience in reading battlefields, Pollio knew that this sudden preponderance of corpses usually signaled some event that merited an increase in the fury of the fighting, at least to the men in that area. Usually, Pollio knew, it involved something like a *signifer* of a Cohort, or even an *aquilifer* carrying the Legion eagle, either choosing or being forced to make a stand, which naturally drew the attention and effort of the enemy to take the prized symbol. Or, it could revolve around an individual who attracted the same kind of attention, usually a Centurion, Tribune, or even Legate.

Whatever the cause, while the piled bodies weren't a new sight to Pollio, the sheer number of such heaps was, and momentarily forgetting what it was he had come to do, Pollio stood in place as he surveyed the scene. The ability to read a battlefield came only with experience, but what Pollio was trying to interpret was on a scale unlike anything he had seen, hence it took him longer to make sense of it. He noted a number of spots on the western wall where the palisade stakes were missing, telling him where the barbarians had come pouring over the wall. Turning to examine the southwest corner, he understood that this was where the biggest and probably fatal breach had occurred, as not only the wooden stakes but also a great section of the turf wall had been pulled down.

As he gradually made sense of the scene, he could see that Caesar had staged a fighting withdrawal, stopping his backward movement every couple of dozen paces, where the barbarians would renew their assault on what was essentially a mobile wall composed of wood, flesh, and iron. Satisfied that he had a sense of the flow of the battle, Pollio turned and continued heading toward the forum, reaching the jumbled mass of equipment, crates, tables, and carts that had formed the makeshift barricade. He was pleased to see that Caesar had at least organized work parties to clear a path to the barricade, so that Pollio and the Tribunes didn't have to step on the bodies that literally covered the ground entirely, to the extent that the only visible dirt was this path—cordoned off by a grisly pile of dead barbarians who, Pollio noted dismally, were already beginning to stink and draw flies. It always struck him how quickly the human body started to decay after a man's death; he had heard men claim that they could smell the stench of death, even as a man's body hit the ground. While Pollio doubted this, he did know that it took less than a watch before the first scent of that sickly sweet smell reached his nostrils.

Following the gory path, he nevertheless had to clamber over the barricade, thankful that there was a ladder in place to help him. He was no longer a young man, and he was afraid that he would break something if he had been forced to climb over the barricade by hand. But it wasn't lost on him that Caesar hadn't ordered the barricade to be taken down, and he wondered if that was because Caesar had specific information, or because he was just being cautious. If it was the latter, Pollio thought, that would be a sign Caesar had been shaken much more badly than he would want to admit, and he carried this thought with him as he gazed about at the knots of men, trying to find the general. Pollio wasn't sure what he had been expecting, but he realized he shouldn't have been surprised that the space inside the barricade had been cleaned up, as much as the time allowed. There were no bodies or much debris in the form of pierced or shattered helmets, damaged shields, or spent javelins. But what there was—in abundance—were dark stains, splotches of dirt that told Pollio of fallen men, fighting to keep the barbarians out. There were many of them that it was impossible for him to make even an estimate of the casualties suffered in this last phase of the fighting. The packed dirt area of the forum, where the wounded had been dragged during the fight, was completely darkened with the blood of the fallen, to the point where the ground was uniform in color. From above it looked as though a roughly square shape of a different type of dirt had been laid over the lighter colored soil that was a feature of this ridge.

Finally, Pollio saw one of the groups of men suddenly disperse, revealing the sight of his general, who was still seated on the stool that had been brought to him some time before. Pollio made his way in that direction, noticing that the men who had been gathered with Caesar and were now heading in different directions all wore the distinctive transverse crest of the Centurion. Surely, Pollio thought with dismay, there's more than two dozen Centurions left out of the 120 that had started the day! Caesar hadn't seen Pollio yet, concentrating instead on another tablet, inscribing something in the wax with his stylus, and it was this sight, more than anything else, that brought home to Pollio exactly how costly this battle had been. As Pollio thought about it, just as he was reaching Caesar's side, he couldn't remember the last time he had seen Caesar, out in public at least, writing his own messages. In private, certainly; Pollio knew that Caesar had been keeping a journal of this entire campaign, much in the same way as he had in Gaul, but it wasn't seemly for the general commanding the army to be forced to write his own dispatches. Caesar, head bent down and concentrating on the tablet, became aware of Pollio only when the standing man's presence blocked out the last of the daylight. Obviously irritated, Caesar looked up with a frown, squinting up at whoever it was that had dared to throw a shadow over his work. At first, he didn't seem to recognize Pollio, and in the short silence Pollio had the chance to examine this man he had been following for so much of his life. Just like Carbo, what Pollio saw was a man who seemed to have aged overnight, but in Pollio's case, this was almost literally true, since it had been just the night before that Pollio had attended the last briefing Caesar had held. How much had changed in that time, Pollio thought, only partly thinking of the battle. He was about to open his mouth, when Caesar's expression changed to one of recognition, and the general waved the tablet wearily at his lieutenant.

"I was about to send you another dispatch," he said tiredly. "I hadn't heard from you and I need to know if you have any *medici* you can spare. Mine are almost exhausted; I expect them to drop any moment. Frankly, I don't know what keeps them going," he muttered.

"Because they're needed," Pollio told Caesar quietly.

This prompted a mirthless laugh.

"That they are," Caesar agreed. Then, he turned his mind to other matters, asking Pollio, "What's your status? I assume, since you're here, that your camp held?"

"Yes, it did," Pollio replied. Not knowing why exactly, he was nonetheless compelled to be frank as he told Caesar, "I was going to tell you how hard a fight it was, and how the men fought like Trojans. But now that I've seen all this," he waved a hand around him, "I realize we had it easy."

Instead of answering immediately, Caesar looked outward in the direction Pollio had indicated, but his true gaze was inward. Watching him sit there, Pollio had a thought very similar to Carbo's earlier, thinking that Caesar looked... lost. That was it, Pollio realized, for the first time, if not in this campaign but his entire life, Caesar doesn't know what to do next. And that thought scared Pollio more than anything he had seen this day.

Even after events that men are sure have never taken place under the sun before, no matter how cataclysmic or monumental, the sun still sets, ending the day on which these events occur. Such was the case on this day, a day that the fate of an army, and the destiny of a people were forever changed. Normally, the Roman army's activity ceased with the setting of the sun—save for the obligatory guard watches—while those men not on duty retired to their respective tent sections to sit with their comrades and discuss the day or pick up an argument where they had left it off the night before. Not on this night, however; there was simply too much left to do. In the northern camp, the acting Primi Pili of the 10th and 12th Legions, Sextus Scribonius and the Primus Hastatus Posterior of the 12th, Vibius Volusenus, taking the place of Balbinus who had been seriously wounded in the closing moments of the fight, had ordered that not only torches be lit, but that all flammable debris, ruined shields, broken crates, desks from the Cohort and Legion offices that still survived, all of it be placed in several piles and set alight. The resulting bonfires provided a lurid light that allowed the men to continue working on the tasks they had been assigned by their respective Centurions, much reduced in number as they may have been.

Standing together in the forum, the two Primi Pili were discussing the next steps, and they had been joined by the Centurion who had saved their camp, Felix. The short, stocky

Quintus Pilus Prior of the 30th looked as exhausted as the other two men, and in the dancing light provided by a nearby bonfire, the crevices on his otherwise young face made him look as ancient as Caesar. Diagonally across one cheek was a hastily stitched gash, and while the blood that covered the lower half of his face had been washed off, the cut itself looked black from the dried blood caked in the wound. He also had a filthy neckerchief tied high on his left shoulder, and this too was darkened from the blood from a spear thrust that had struck a glancing blow. In fact, none of the men standing there was unmarked in some way: Scribonius had undergone the agony of having the bandage covering the wound on his arm loosened, allowing the feeling to come flooding back, bringing with it a suffering that far outweighed what should have been the toll of the injury itself. But Scribonius was lucky; when the orderly carefully unwrapped the bandage, he had done so with such gentle skill that the wound hadn't reopened, allowing the *medicus* to stitch it shut, then rewrap it with a fresh bandage. It was fresh only in the sense that it was new to Scribonius. In fact, the *medicus* had removed it from a man who no longer needed it, having succumbed to other wounds of his body, but the orderly saw no need to tell this Centurion that he was essentially sporting a dead man's bandage. For his part, Scribonius was just grateful that the bleeding hadn't begun afresh, knowing that as lightheaded as he was already, it was probable he would lose consciousness if he shed any more blood. If that happened, he knew from bitter observation that it was unlikely that he would ever wake up. Therefore he wasn't in a complaining mood, and, in fact, was thankful that he had as much of his faculties as he did, because there was so much that had to be done.

Volusenus and he had sent a joint message to Caesar that, knowing their general as they did, both understood wouldn't meet his requirement for information. While this hadn't been by accident, it had been done only because neither Scribonius nor Volusenus had finished tallying the dead and separating the wounded into the categories that Caesar always required. The simple truth was that the survivors in the northern camp were so few in number and so overcome with exhaustion that they were overwhelmed. Along with the dispatch that said that the camp had held, albeit barely, added to an estimate of effective strength and the supply situation—as far as they knew it, since a great deal of the camp, like Caesar's, had been burned to the ground—they unwittingly made the exact same request Caesar had made of Pollio for more medical help. Now, standing in the forum, the two Primi Pili had been quietly discussing ideas that would help accomplish some of the things that needed to be done, when Felix joined them. Neither man spoke directly to Felix at first, mainly because there weren't words that could adequately express their gratitude. So instead, Scribonius thrust the skin he had been drinking from, and Felix took it with a lifted eyebrow, in a silent question.

"It's rice wine," Scribonius told him, laughing at the face the other man made.

Still, Felix lifted the skin in a silent thanks, before bringing it to his mouth, taking a long, deep swallow. Coughing, he handed the skin back to Scribonius with an oath, causing the other men to laugh.

"Granted, it tastes like horse piss, but it gets the job done," Scribonius said, just before taking another long pull on the skin himself.

Scribonius and Felix had already conversed a couple of times by this point, the first concerning what Pullus had directed his friend to do, which was to keep Felix from taking the relief force from the northern camp. Fortunately, Felix hadn't put up a fight at all, instantly seeing the sense.

As he put it, "Until I get a written order telling me otherwise, my last orders were to come to your aid. Flaminius didn't specify that it was only fighting."

Truth be known, Scribonius was hugely relieved at Felix's words, because he didn't relish imposing his will on others, especially a man who had saved them, the way Pullus was happy to.

"Do you think they'll come back?" Felix asked the question that was haunting every man, regardless of rank, in the northern camp that night.

Scribonius shook his head, but not in the way Felix might have liked.

"I don't know," Scribonius said. "I know if I was their general, or if it was Caesar leading them, we'd scrape up every single man we could find and march up here and finish us. And," he finished grimly, "there's nothing we could do about it."

The other two men stood digesting this for a moment, both of them knowing that what Scribonius was saying was true.

Finally, Volusenus grunted, which Scribonius was learning was his prelude to speaking. "Well, there's not much we can do about it. Worrying isn't going to help. We just need to do what we can to get the men rested up."

"As tired as they are, I doubt there's going to be much sleep tonight," Scribonius replied, as he handed the skin back to Felix, indicating that he should finish it since it was down to the dregs. Again, silence fell, as each man was absorbed in his own morose thoughts. In the quiet between them was the bond forged by shared loss, each of them thinking of close friends they had lost today. Scribonius' first thought was of Balbus, finally coming to grips with his death when he saw the Centurion's body, his scarred face looking oddly peaceful, despite the puckering hole in his chest. Immediately on the heels of that were thoughts of another friend, and it was as if Felix could read his mind, but it took him repeating his question twice before Scribonius was jerked back to the present.

"And Pullus? Is he still alive?"

Scribonius shook his head again, but just like the previous time, it wasn't meant in the way Felix took it, whose mouth was even then opening to offer his sympathies to Scribonius on the loss of a man who was a legend.

Before Felix could say what he wanted to, Scribonius murmured, "I don't know why he's not dead. But no, he's still alive. And you know what?" Scribonius' expression was one that Felix, knowing the other man only by sight and reputation, didn't recognize; but what Scribonius' face said echoed his next words, which was a message of hope. "I think he's going to survive. I don't know how, and I surely don't know why. But I think that if he hasn't died by now, I don't think he's going to."

It was Volusenus, who opened his mouth to argue, planning to point out that as strong as Pullus was, he was still mortal, and that he had seen the fight and the blow that had felled him, and that his experience told him that Scribonius' hope was a vain one. And, to Volusenus, a foolish one. But before he uttered the words he was distracted by a sound, so like the other two, he turned to see another Centurion approaching. In the light supplied by the fires, Volusenus recognized the tall, lean figure, before he got a clear glimpse of the face, and it was enough to tell him it was Pullus' nephew. Thus, while Volusenus might have been willing to tell Scribonius the harsh truth, he wasn't about to be that severe with a youngster who was blood kin to Pullus. He didn't need that kind of trouble.

"Porcinus, I thought I told you that you were supposed to stay with the Primus Pilus!"

Scribonius' sharp tone was a cover for the stab of fear he experienced when he saw his friend's nephew approach, sure that the only reason Porcinus would leave Pullus' side was that he was no longer needed. But nothing in Porcinus' attitude or expression indicated that this was the case. Instead, he had a look on his face that could best be described as bemusement, which was explained by what came out of his mouth.

"I know you did, Pilus Prior, but the Primus Pilus outranks you. And he wouldn't let me stay, no matter what I told him. In fact, he tried to throw a cup at me, and he promised that as soon as he's recovered, he'd thrash me good if I didn't go make myself useful."

For the first, and one of the only times that night, roars of laughter could be heard coming from the northern camp.

In much the same way that Scribonius couldn't fathom why the Wa didn't come finish what they had started, down in the Wa camps the survivors of their army were huddled together, wondering when the grubworms would stride down the ridge and exact vengeance. However, unlike the Romans, the Wa were even more severely crippled in the area of leadership. Whereas Caesar lived, and even if he hadn't survived, the Legates and Centurions in his army had been trained and encouraged to take the initiative and think for themselves—within limits of course—the opposite was true with the Wa. Romans liked to think they had an extremely rigid hierarchical system, and for the part of the world they came from, they did. But it was nothing like what was developing on this island nation.

Though it was difficult, there was upward mobility between the strata of classes in Roman society. Titus Pullus was an example of a man who, if he survived and ever made it back to Rome, would be not only wealthy, but would be at least in the equestrian class and, in all likelihood through Caesar's influence, a member of the Senate. This would have been unheard of in Wa society, and, in fact, there was no mechanism of government that could be compared to even the most basic components of Roman governance. There was a class of nobility that formed the warrior core of the army, followed by an extremely small group of exclusively male priests who served as a layer between the nobility and their emperor, who they believed ruled by divine right and was a god sent to them from the heavens.

The cornerstone of Wa society was unflinching obedience to the divine will of the emperor, and whatever he directed was as much a law as any of those composed by the Senate of Rome and incised on bronze tablets. The warrior and nobility classes of Wa society served as the overseers of the mass of common people, and within the boundaries of the lands which each member of the nobility claimed as their own, their word was law almost as sacrosanct as the word of the emperor himself. And of all the laws that the emperor decreed to be inviolable, the law of obedience was of the highest order. Members of the lower classes not only were not expected to think and make decisions for themselves, but they were forbidden to do so, meaning any show of independence of thought or action was practically a guarantee to draw the wrath of their lord onto the transgressor, at the very least. Or worse, onto the entire family of the offender. The survivors of the great Wa army were overwhelmingly composed of men from the lower class, while their sword-wielding superiors were almost entirely eradicated, each trying to outdo the other in acts of valor and martial ability, in order to bring glory to their family name and draw the attention of their superiors. Although this wasn't all that different an attitude than that of their Roman counterparts, the lengths to which these men went meant that they had been almost completely wiped out.

Of the perhaps three thousand Wa that were left, just two in ten of the survivors was of the upper class, and of these, almost every one of them was in the more junior subset of their class. Of third or fourth sons—lords, each of whose holding was barely more than the size of the area filled by the ridge where the camps were located—none had ever commanded more than a handful of men at a time, if that. The two generals, the commander and his immediate subordinate, lay dead in a heap of bodies up on the ridge, and scattered throughout all of the piles were the men who acted as their lieutenants. It was a situation crying out for leadership, but again, the idea of showing the initiative that would be required for one of the minor lords to take command was so foreign a concept that it didn't even occur to any of them, at least at first. Instead, they huddled in small groups, the men of the lower class, who were nothing more than fodder for the swords of the Wa's enemies, shaking with terror as they whispered to each other, as if speaking loudly would draw the attention of the grubworms on the ridge. And it was because of this atmosphere that, starting shortly after dark, in one's and two's, men began moving quietly out of the Wa camps, heading back to whatever part of the island from which they came. This exodus was confined almost completely to the spear-wielding lower class, since the small number of nobles left could have never borne the shame of skulking away, at least preferring to die with honor. As the night progressed and the numbers of men left in the camp dwindled, the nobles began their own movement, but this was to coalesce in the northernmost camp, seeking solace and companionship with their own kind.

And yet, while they didn't run as the peasants had, they were just as terrified at what the next morning would hold. The difference was that no man among them would have uttered a word about his fears, because it would have shamed him in the eyes of his peers. Instead, they swapped stories of the battle, talking in hushed tones of things they had seen the grubworms do. In fact, if there was one prevailing attitude among all of the men left behind, it was confusion. When the sun had risen on this day of battle, every one of them had held the conviction that these pale creatures would be crushed in much the same way that the farmer crushed the grubworm under his heel when he dug it out of the ground. That the Wa were superior in every way was not doubted by any of the nobles in the Wa army. However, now that the sun had set, they had discovered the reality to be far different, and it was this newfound knowledge they found so confusing. Hadn't the divine emperor himself sent this army forward at his command? How could a man who was a god himself have underestimated these pale beings so completely? Their superiors, those very, very few who were allowed to be within the presence of the emperor—and that was only after undergoing a purification ritual that rendered them worthy and protected them from bursting into flame—had relayed the words of the emperor, that this barbarian army was hardly worthy of the massive army gathered for the purpose. Now, that army was shattered, these scared teenagers all that remained. This was how the night passed in the Wa camp, until, despite their best intentions, even the nobles became so terrified that they convinced themselves that, in fact, their duty required them to make haste to the capital, to prepare for a last-ditch defense from this army of grubworms. Therefore, shortly before dawn, unknowing and, frankly, uncaring that the lower classes had departed at least two watches before, the pitifully small remnant of the nobility left of the once-mighty Wa army also left, with only slightly more dignity than their peasant comrades.

Daylight came, the sun's rays beaming down on a horrific sight, no matter what side you had fought on the day before. After grabbing perhaps a watch of sleep, Caesar was only partially recovered, still badly shaken from all that had transpired the day before. Nevertheless, he had regained enough of his composure to present himself as someone who at least approximated the general the army had followed for ten years. During the night, Caesar had shifted troops around the four camps. Agreeing with Pullus' order to Scribonius—at least by virtue of not countermanding it—to keep Felix and the eight Cohorts there at the northern camp, Caesar summoned the rest of the 14th and the 30th, ordering Ventidius to destroy the camp, before marching to meet with him. Additionally, he had sent couriers to the southern camp, where the 5th Alaudae's new Primus Pilus was left in command—because of Pollio's absence now that he was there with Caesar—ordering the new man, Marcus Macro, to send a reconnaissance in force down the slopes of the ridge far enough to determine whether or not the Wa camp was occupied, and, if it was, the size of the force. Caesar was still concerned that the barbarians might have enough strength left for one more assault of the ridge.

As always, Caesar mentally tried to put himself in the place of whoever was commanding the barbarians. Knowing so little about the Wa was one aspect of this campaign that had troubled Caesar the most, and one of his first dispatches had been down to the fleet in the bay, summoning Zhang to come to his side. Along with Zhang, Caesar had ordered that every man, no matter what status or job, also be brought to the camp, to help in the thousand tasks that still remained. Once he dispensed with his morning list of matters to be seen to, he paused to take a breath and to break his fast. Never a hearty eater, he had even less appetite this morning, but he also realized that it was likely that he would need all of his strength before the day was out, not knowing what it would bring. As he listlessly chewed on a piece of bread, washing it down with water, the *bucinator* at the gate blew the signal that a rider was approaching. Knowing that the rider couldn't have been from the fleet, Caesar also didn't think he came from the southernmost camp. That left the camps on either side, and while he had men stationed on the rampart—which was the first thing that had been repaired as soon as it was light—they hadn't reported any movement from the Wa camp out on the plain. He hoped that this boded well, but he had been fooled the day before, and there was a nagging doubt in the back of his mind that perhaps the barbarian commander had moved his men under the cover of night, taking them to the north of the ridge—where the slight gap lay that was the only passage to the ocean for miles—and from there was launching another assault, directly from the north.

He was pondering this possibility and the best way to counter it, if it indeed proved to be fact, when the rider drew up a short distance away before dismounting. Trotting over, he rendered his salute and then held out the tablet. Taking the proffered message with one hand, while wiping the crumbs of his breakfast off his other, Caesar summoned on his badly depleted supply of resolve, understanding that now, more than at any other time under his command, his men needed to see their general in his usual calm and collected state, treating every new message as if it was exactly what he was expecting.

"Where is this from?" Caesar asked the man, his heart suddenly accelerating at the man's reply that it came from the Primus Pilus in command of the northern camp.

Could this contain the message he was dreading? That the attack had been renewed, out of sight and sound of Caesar and the men in this camp? Opening it and reading the words, it took a supreme effort of will for him not to sag in visible relief, knowing that this would be just as disconcerting as any sign of distress to the men nearby. The release of tension that he felt came from two sources: one, that there was no assault taking place, and two, according to the Primus Pilus of the 10th, who had sent out a Cohort-sized patrol down the northern slope into the gap to check for the very thing Caesar was worried about, there was no sign of the enemy anywhere about. But it was more than just the content of the message that made Caesar suddenly feel better than he had in several watches. It was the barely legible signature at the bottom, that even for a Primus Pilus whose writing was barely readable under the best of circumstances, was the first sign to Caesar that perhaps there was hope.

For the last he had heard, it was extremely unlikely that he would ever lay eyes on the giant Roman whom he had come to regard with something as close to affection as a man of Caesar's status could have for a man from the ranks. Feeling a smile crawling across his face, Caesar decided that, while these tablets were constantly reused, this was one he would keep as it existed at that moment, to serve him as a reminder that even when things were seemingly at their bleakest, where there was life, there was hope. And he had been reminded of that by what amounted to nothing but chicken scratches on a wax tablet that served as the signature of Titus Pullus, who was not only alive, but apparently still giving the orders in the northern camp.

When Aulus Ventidius arrived at Caesar's camp, at the head of the rest of the two Legions of his own position, he was still undecided about whether or not he was going to pursue any action against the Primus Pilus of the 30th, Flaminius. Although he was acutely aware by this point that Flaminius had acted on his own and had even tricked Ventidius by sending him away to fend off a phantom breach so that he could organize the relief force, Ventidius was equally cognizant that the Primus Pilus' actions had undoubtedly saved the army from destruction. The Legate, who was actually 3 years older than Caesar, but like Caesar carried the vitality of a much younger man, was still fuming at the insult borne him by Flaminius. However, he was at an age at which he was honest enough with himself to know that his anger was as much about his wounded pride—that he wasn't the one allowed to take credit for making the decision to send relief to the other camps—as it was a righteous indignation that Flaminius had so flagrantly breached the chain of command.

As it turned out, the decision was made for him by Caesar, who addressed the matter, as soon as Flaminius and Ventidius were brought to him in the newly erected *praetorium*, stitched together from panels of leather from the tents of men who no longer needed shelter. It was when Caesar had been informed by his quartermaster, who had been sent down to the fleet for the battle, that even with so many tents burned to cinders, there would be enough left to create a new headquarters tent without putting any man out into the elements that Caesar understood just how devastating the day before had been to his army. He had already sent word to dispatch one of the Liburnians back to the island that had served as the supply depot, where two Legions had been left behind to provide security, with orders to commandeer any shipping they found and to bring all but two Cohorts, one from each Legion, to his current position.

Depending on what his mounted scouts told him, they, too, having been aboard ships but who were even now beginning to reconnoiter, Caesar hoped that he and the army would no longer still be here on this ridge whenever the new troops arrived. It all depended on what lay between him and the capital, but he wouldn't know that for a couple of days, at least; so, putting that matter aside, he turned his attention to the two men standing before him. Not saying anything for a moment, as was his habit, Caesar used the time to glean as much information as he could from the two men, although they were not uttering a word. This was one of Caesar's greatest talents, the ability to observe other men's body language and deducing from it much about them, and, by extension whatever matter was being discussed, before he committed himself by opening his own mouth. Sitting on his stool now, Caesar concealed his amusement at the sight before him. His Legate, who was known throughout the army as Caesar's Muleteer, since that's how he had gotten his start with Caesar in Gaul, was standing rigidly at the position of *intente*, anger radiating from every part of him. Even his eyebrows, which many of the men likened to two large caterpillars, told Caesar that the older man was still fuming, as it looked like the two caterpillars were glaring at each other eyeball to eyeball over the bridge of Ventidius' nose. Meanwhile, Flaminius was no less perfect in his posture, but while he didn't give off the same aura of rage, the sign he was giving Caesar was one of defiance, tinged with understandable anxiety. While Caesar's vision wasn't what it once was, it was still sharp enough to see the beads of sweat on the upper lip of the Primus Pilus, despite the heat of the day not warranting it. Caesar had seen this many times before, knowing it to be a sign of great anxiety, and he supposed that Flaminius had good cause to be worried. But, while

Caesar had already decided what he was going to do about this matter, he was in no hurry to let either Flaminius or Ventidius know it, even if it was for two totally different reasons.

"So Primus Pilus Flaminius, here we are," Caesar broke the silence, grimly amused at the visible start with which the Primus Pilus reacted to the sound. "It appears that you have much to answer for, if General Ventidius is to be believed, and he's never given me any reason to doubt him."

When Caesar stopped talking for a moment, Flaminius opened his mouth as if to respond, but then shut it. Caesar sighed, knowing exactly the game Flaminius was playing. The Stupid Legionary was one of the oldest tricks in the enlisted man's book, and Caesar couldn't count the number of times he had seen it played in front of him. Some of the time he didn't mind playing along, amused to see how far a man was willing to go down that path. This wasn't one of those times, however.

"Well? Explain yourself," Caesar snapped, making his irritation plain for both men to see.

Ventidius looked relieved, but whether it was because it was Flaminius drawing Caesar's ire, or the fact that he himself was escaping Caesar's wrath Caesar didn't know, nor did he particularly care.

"Yes sir," Flaminius' face reddened, but his tone was even and clipped, a professional giving his report. "Because we had the situation at our camp so well in hand, and knowing that the brunt of the assault was going to be on your camp or on the northern camp, I decided it might be prudent to send as many men as we could spare to offer their assistance. Sir."

"Yes, yes, I know that," Caesar waved an impatient hand. "But who gave you the authority to do this?"

Now the sweat that originated on his upper lip began spreading to his forehead, beading up as Flaminius was clearly growing more uncomfortable.

"Er, nobody. Sir, I assumed General Ventidius would agree, so I didn't see the need to bother him with a detail that would take more time."

Ventidius could take it no more, snorting in disbelief, the two eyebrows now actually touching as he stared down his prodigious nose at his commander.

"That's an awful lot of assuming," the Muleteer spat. "And if you were so sure that I would agree, why did you feel the need to send me off on a fool's errand?"

Caesar turned a decidedly cool gaze on Flaminius; this was a part of the story he hadn't heard.

"Yes, Flaminius. Please explain that, and perhaps for my benefit, you could explain what 'fool's errand' you sent your superior officer on?"

When put that way, even Flaminius could see why Ventidius was still upset, and his nerves, which were already on edge, were now positively vibrating. Ventidius was glaring at the Primus Pilus as well, evidently forgetting that he hadn't been given leave to alter his position of *intente*, standing with folded arms waiting for Flaminius to explain himself. Caesar was about to rebuke Ventidius, but chose to let it go. Flaminius finally spoke again, and while his reply appeared to surprise Ventidius, it didn't surprise Caesar at all.

"I have no excuse sir. I knew the risk I was taking, and I decided to let the dice fly."

Despite himself, Caesar felt a smile tugging at the corners of his mouth at Flaminius' statement, while Ventidius appeared to become even angrier, which Caesar could understand. Flaminius, you sly dog, Caesar thought, using the exact same thing I said crossing the Rubicon. Well, at least you have good taste.

"No, you don't have a good excuse. In fact, you have no excuse," Caesar agreed, making his tone hard as he stared directly into Flaminius' eyes.

For his part, Flaminius steadfastly tried to ignore the sudden shaking in his legs, hoping that it wasn't noticeable.

Caesar paused, deliberately drawing it out, before continuing, "But although I have every right to have you scourged and crucified," his words were all the more chilling, because he was so matter-of-fact and his tone so even, "neither can I forget that your actions saved this army and this campaign from total failure. For that alone I should decorate you."

For a moment, Caesar thought Ventidius would die of an apoplectic fit right on the spot, his face turning a purplish hue that Caesar had rarely seen, so he hurried on.

"But because of your flagrant disregard for the chain of command, and for issuing orders beyond the scope of your office, I've decided that the two things cancel each other out. So you will be neither censured nor commended. No disobedience will be noted in the army diary, but Ventidius will be given full credit for issuing the command that saved the army."

When Caesar was finished, he sat silently watching the two men, again amused, although for different reasons, because this time their expressions were almost identical. Neither of them looked happy, which to Caesar was his indication that his decision was fair and equal to both of them. For while everything he had said was true, Caesar did, in fact, hold Ventidius somewhat at fault, because he should have arrived at the decision himself, and sooner. And nothing Ventidius had told him, nor what he had heard from other sources gave any indication that he had been thinking along the same lines as Flaminius. But as much as Caesar faulted Ventidius, he still valued the older man and had no intention of criticizing his lack of initiative and decisiveness, either publicly or privately. No, he mused after dismissing the pair—watching them both walk away with straight backs and clenched fists, neither of them looking at the other man—this was the best way. I don't need any more problems than I already have, and the army doesn't need the distraction that would come from the spectacle of a Tribunal of a Primus Pilus, which is by rights what should happen. Content with his decision, Caesar turned his mind to other matters.

Cohorts and Legions that had been lucky enough to be in the three southern camps were bearing the brunt of the work, something that normally would have caused massive complaints among the men. However, in yet another sign that the battle the day before was unprecedented, all the bickering and griping stopped as soon as the men marched through the gate of either Caesar's or Pullus' camp. The sight of what was clearly a ferocious battle silenced every Legionary who had been inclined to let his displeasure known, and by the time they were assembled in their respective forums, it was a somber group of men waiting for orders.

As much bickering and rivalry that took place between Legions, no man in the ranks took any joy in the sight of their comrades suffering. They had shared too much, endured too much, and spent too much time together for them not to understand the ordeal the men of the two northern camps had endured. Sextus Scribonius, standing next to Volusenus, was only slightly recovered after a fitful night's rest, and had just come from checking, for perhaps the tenth time since the sun came up, on the condition of his friend. Pullus was sleeping, aided by the poppy syrup that the *medici* reserved for the most grievously wounded. When Scribonius had gone to check on Pullus the last time, he found that he was being attended to by one of the physicians that had joined Caesar's army to augment and replace the staff of physicians that had been attached to his army from the beginning of the campaign. The identity of the man, one of the Han physicians, told Scribonius that Caesar was not only aware but extremely interested in seeing the giant Roman recover. Scribonius knew there were a number of the men in the ranks who swore these Han knew sorcery, such was their skill compared to the others, particularly with the last four Greeks still alive, none of whom looked on their Han rivals with any favor. The physician, whose name Scribonius didn't know, nor could he have pronounced even if he had, was given explicit instructions by Caesar never to leave Pullus' side, and that the Primus Pilus was his one and only patient. Although Scribonius knew that it was a good sign that Pullus was still alive, he was also aware that if any foreign material, such as one of the links from his mail shirt, or the stuffing from the padded undershirt, even a thread from his tunic, was left behind in the wound, the Han physician would need to call on every bit of his skills to keep his friend alive.

The Han didn't speak Latin, and Scribonius certainly hadn't mastered their tongue, but somehow through a combination of gestures and with the help of one of the Gayans pressed into service as an orderly, Scribonius learned that the physician was cautiously optimistic. Telling the Pilus Prior that it was normally within the first day that any sign of corruption began to present itself, the Han nevertheless emphasized that Scribonius' friend wasn't out of danger. Pullus had been semi-conscious for that visit, and his head had moved slowly back and forth as he tried to follow the conversation that was going on around him. That, to Scribonius, was a better sign than anything the Han could have said. Over the years, the Pilus Prior had observed that those men who eventually succumbed to their wounds universally showed a complete lack of interest in their own care, as if they already knew the outcome. Pullus' trying, no matter how groggily, to follow the dialogue between Roman and Han had lifted Scribonius' spirits, and he had gone to find Porcinus to tell him of this development. He found him in the process of working with the two other Centurions who survived from the Tenth Cohort, reorganizing into units that were Centuries in name only. Now, just returned from his last check on Pullus, Scribonius met with the Centurions of the Cohorts that had just arrived, assigning each Century a specific work detail.

Turning to the Pilus Prior of the Second Cohort from the 5th Alaudae, Scribonius asked, "Has Caesar decided what to do with ours yet?"

There was no need for Scribonius to expand on what "ours" meant, if only because of where they were standing. Stretching out behind the two Centurions were now-neat rows of bodies, as cleaned up and made presentable by hiding the wounds that had killed each man as time and location of the wound allowed. This was a topic that was very much on the minds of the men in the ranks and of great concern to all of them. One problem caused by the polyglot composition of Caesar's current army was that that there were so many different customs for honoring the dead. Much as Rome did with religion, men in the ranks were allowed to worship their native gods and follow the customs that prescribed how the dead were honored. While there had been men killed in the ranks, it had never been on a scale like this, and with the scouts out, it was looking likely that Caesar would be moving the army, soon. What direction they would head in, either to the northwest in the direction of the capital, or back to the east and the bay where the fleet was anchored, this was the subject of much speculation, and not just with the men. The Centurions were just as interested in their next destination as the rankers, yet it had been a custom of not just Caesar's army but of the armies of Rome for at least two centuries that the army didn't move until after the dead had been honored. There was also a more practical reason; no Roman commander liked marching without every leadership spot that had been vacated by death or incapacitating wound filled, and that had yet to happen, as well. Arranging the various ceremonies was always challenging, but the sheer scope of the numbers of men who had either to be cleansed by fire, in the Roman way, or buried in the ground like the Pandyans, or even just left to rot like the

Parthians, meant that whatever was being arranged needed to be done soon. Since the Pilus Prior of the 5th had marched past Caesar's camp on the way to the northern camp where they were standing, Scribonius was hoping that the Centurion had heard something, but he replied with a simple shake of the head. Stifling a curse, knowing it wasn't the man's fault, Scribonius turned his mind back to the tasks that he could perform at that moment. His arm ached horribly, and he found it extremely painful to flex his fingers or make a fist, which of course he found himself doing over and over as a way to distract his mind from the enormity of the losses. The final butcher's bill, as the Centurions had called it, had been completed, and the 10th Legion could field barely more than a thousand men, from its strength of almost 4,000 when the battle started. Of course, some of the missing ranks would be filled by the wounded, but it was too early to tell how many it would be, and even if every man made a miraculous recovery, the Legion still would be less than half strength. From what Volusenus told Scribonius, this was about the same for the 12th. Scribonius hadn't heard the numbers for the two Legions in Caesar's camp, but given what he knew of what happened the day before, he couldn't imagine they were any better off. Even at this point, more than halfway through the day after the battle, there were still more questions than answers, for both the living and the dead.

Knowing how unpopular his decision would be, Caesar nevertheless issued it, knowing that he couldn't spare the time to properly honor the dead. Truthfully, he had been wavering about the matter. Until, that is, a courier sent by the mounted scouts he had sent northwest in the likely direction that the Wa army would take, or what remained of it, came galloping into the camp. Within moments, the situation changed dramatically, as Caesar read the message informing him that there was no sign of any sizable force between him and the army and the barbarian capital. The report went on to say that the scouts had found the trail of those Wa nobles who had decided before the sun rose that their only course of action was to return to the capital to receive further orders. Naturally, Caesar had no way of knowing any of this, but what he did know was that according to the report, this group numbered perhaps a thousand. Even as badly mauled as Caesar's army was, he had no doubt that the men could sweep aside a force as paltry as that. But in order to make that happen, they had to move, and move fast. Still shaken from his experience yesterday, Caesar was acting out of force of habit more than anything, doing and saying those things that he knew the Caesar of two days before would do, without hesitation. Perhaps, he thought, by playing the role of Caesar, I will become Caesar again. But first, he had to issue this order, and in this order Caesar sought a compromise, hoping that the men would understand. His decision was that he would honor the dead, respecting the customs of each nationality, but he would do so en masse, not individually, as was the custom. Normally, the men of the tent section the deceased belonged to would perform the ritual cleansing, gather the wood, cremate the body and gather the ashes, if he were Roman. But now there were whole tent sections laying in the forum waiting to be sent to the afterlife, and Caesar simply didn't have the luxury of time to sort out who would tend to them. Caesar, sitting in what had become his accustomed spot on the stool outside the *praetorium,* finished the order that would put this into motion, then handed it to one of the scribes that had come from the fleet.

"See that this gets to the northern camp," he directed, then turned to relay the verbal instruction to the Primi Pili standing next to him. None of the men made a comment, but as with Flaminius and Ventidius earlier, their body language communicated very clearly to Caesar what they thought about his idea.

"I know this is... unusual," Caesar decided to be direct. "But if we can get to their capital quickly, we have the chance to defeat the army there, before they're joined by other forces that might have been summoned."

For a long moment, none of the Primi Pili reacted, which puzzled Caesar more than any irritation he might have felt at the lack of a response. After an exchange of sidelong glances, the Primus Pilus of the 21st Legion, a short, stocky Campanian named Papernus cleared his throat in a signal that he was going to speak.

"Caesar, it's just that we weren't expecting this," Papernus said carefully.

Caesar instantly understood the Primus Pilus' meaning that the "this" he was referring to wasn't the funeral arrangements.

Sitting back, Caesar folded his arms, responding coolly, "Go on."

Vibius Papernus didn't lack for bravery, but at that moment he would have much preferred to face the screaming yellow-skinned bastards than looking into those ice-blue eyes of his general. Nevertheless, he plunged forward, girded by the sight of the slight nods of the other Primi Pili encouraging him to continue.

"If we move inland, we're going to be moving away from the fleet," he began, but before he could go any further, Caesar interjected.

"Yes, Papernus, that's generally how it works. The farther from the shore you go, the farther away your support is. But that's never stopped us before."

And with that, Caesar gave Papernus the opening he needed, and he immediately pounced.

"But we've never been in the shape we're in now," Papernus argued, making a sweeping gesture with an arm in the direction of where the wounded were being tended. "What are we going to do about them, for example?"

Realizing his mistake, Caesar also recognized that the retort that came to his lips would only make matters worse. Besides, he acknowledged, if only to himself, he has a point. And they have a right to know that the wounded will be cared for.

"I've sent for all but two Cohorts from the strategic reserve we left behind on the island," Caesar explained with a patience he didn't feel. "They will come here to watch over the wounded."

"But how long will that take?" Now it was another Primus Pilus who asked the question, the Centurion commanding the 14th Legion, Sextus Spurius.

"Perhaps two weeks," Caesar replied, and while the other men initially relaxed, thinking that the men would welcome a respite of that length after what they had just been through, the more observant among them were alerted by something in the way their general spoke the words.

"But, we're not going to wait for them, are we?"

Aulus Flaminius, fresh from his escape of Caesar's wrath had promised himself that he was going to keep silent, but somehow the words escaped his lips before he could stop them, and he was forced to stifle a groan as Caesar turned to glare at him.

"No, we're not," the general said after a moment, the words clipped and short because of his clenched teeth.

There was a shocked silence, before completely forgetting the proper manner in which to do these things, the Primi Pili began talking at once.

"We can't leave the wounded unprotected!"

"Caesar, the men need to rest after what they've been through!"

"If we wait for the relief to arrive, a good number of the wounded will be recovered enough to march with us."

While the others were shouting to make their complaints heard above the racket, this last comment was spoken in almost a conversational tone, but what was said more than the volume cut through the other noise. Immediately all the men became quiet, turning their eyes to Caesar, knowing him well enough to know that of all the objections, this practical one would carry the most weight. And they were rewarded by the sight of Caesar looking suddenly uncomfortable, while still managing to shoot a look at Papernus, who had asked this last question, a look of exasperation and respect in equal measure.

"That's true Papernus," Caesar acknowledged. "But that will also give the barbarians the time to muster more forces, and they would be foolish to come and try to assault us here again, when we gave them such a beating."

"But we don't know that hasn't already started," Papernus pointed out. "And they may very well already be gathering at their capital. And," he added, "we only know the approximate location of the city as it is. We could go stumbling into another army of those bastards."

"We've seen nothing that would indicate that there is a population capable of producing more than one army of the size we just defeated," Caesar said stiffly, nettled at the open skepticism that was being displayed by his most senior Centurions.

"It wouldn't have to be the same size," Carbo, the acting Primus Pilus retorted. "It wouldn't take an army the third of the size to give us more than we could handle."

Now Caesar was being confronted with yet another new emotion, just one more in a series of sensations that he'd never experienced before over the last two days. This was a feeling of desperation, as for the first time in many, many years, Julius Caesar recognized that he was losing his grip on his army.

Although the men ultimately obeyed Caesar's directive to perform the respective funerary rites en masse, they were performed in a sullen silence, the Legions letting Caesar know they were unhappy more eloquently with their muteness than with anything else they could have done. Matters between the general and his army hung on a knife's edge for the next two days, as the army stayed in place. Considering that Caesar had every intention of moving the second day after the battle, the fact that they were still in place bore testimony to his recognition that his command over the army was in jeopardy. In round after round of meetings with every Primus Pilus, it became clear to Caesar that they weren't alone; the dissension over his plan extended to most of his Legates. With the sole exception of Ventidius- whose support for Caesar had more to do with his loathing of being seen aligned with Flaminius in anything- Hirtius, Pollio, Nero, the surviving Legates, and even most of the Tribunes looked askance at Caesar's plan to continue on to the capital. Yet, neither Caesar nor any of the Primi Pili, for that matter, would ever publicly utter the word that, if it had been years earlier, Caesar would have viewed this situation as: a mutiny. But as upset as Caesar was, a part of him understood that more than any of his other armies, this one had earned the right to a larger say in their destiny than ever before. They had, after all, followed him across an entire continent, traveling farther and fighting more than any army in the history of Rome. Meeting after meeting was held, but no resolution of the dilemma came, even after Caesar's proposal to move the wounded aboard the fleet. This appeased some of the Primi Pili, but not enough to give their assurances that the men would march when the command was given. For their part, the men in the ranks knew that something was brewing, but for one of the few and only times, word of what exactly Caesar was proposing remained between those of the upper command of the Legions. In fact, the Primi Pili had decided among themselves to keep their Pili Priores in the dark, until some resolution was made. For Sextus Scribonius, this was especially difficult, because he had no desire to be in the position that he was in, leading the 10th. Not only had he never been interested in leading the Legion, he certainly didn't want to do it while his friend still lived. In fact, Pullus was showing no sign that any foreign material had been left behind in his body, and the Han physician, who still hadn't left his side, was growing more optimistic. Even so, Scribonius knew that he would be the de facto commander of the 10th for some time, and it was in this role that he found himself beset by the other Primi Pili.

"What does Pullus say about this?"

This was the question apparently on all of their minds, but Scribonius had been firm in his refusal to subject his friend to the strain that would come from essentially holding sway over the rest of the Centurions. Ironically, the part of the camp left intact had housed the 10th, so that Pullus was at least comfortable in his own quarters; although he had been the de facto commander of the northern camp, he eschewed using the more spacious quarters available in the *praetorium*, saving his personal effects from being looted. And now that Diocles was back in the camp from his exile on the ships, Scribonius knew he was in good hands. That is what freed his mind enough to leave the task of repairing the northern camp to Caesar, which by the end of the second day after the battle, had been restored to a semblance of order and was once again defensible. The reorganization of the 10th was still ongoing, Caesar delaying his decision on whether or not to fold the 10th and 12th into one Legion, understandable given the other challenges. But as Scribonius well knew, this was a matter that had to be decided before the command to march was given. Now Scribonius had just left the *praetorium*, the last meeting dismissed by a frustrated Caesar, and he had just answered Carbo's question, making him the fourth Primus Pilus to approach him.

"Primus Pilus."

Scribonius stood, stretching his muscles that had become cramped from sitting on the stool in Caesar's office, idly flexing his left hand as he did, and he didn't respond.

"Primus Pilus!"

Again, Scribonius didn't respond, but he was beginning to get irritated that whoever was being called didn't answer.

"Primus Pilus Scribonius!"

Only then did Scribonius whirl about, finally understanding that he was the man being called, still unaccustomed to his title as chief Centurion of the Legion. Standing there was one of Caesar's scribes, beckoning to him from the entrance of the *praetorium*.

"Caesar wants to speak to you," the scribe said, causing Scribonius' face to crease into a frown. What now, he wondered? Nevertheless, he followed the scribe back into the tent, where he was ushered directly into Caesar's presence. From somewhere, Scribonius assumed from the quinquereme that served as Caesar's flagship, a desk had been brought to replace the one reduced to ashes. Caesar was sitting on a corner of it, in a pose that Pullus had seen more often than he could count, but to Scribonius this wasn't something he saw often, and he wondered how to approach his general. Finally deciding to play it safe, Scribonius stopped the prescribed distance for approaching a superior officer, came to *intente* then offered a salute, which Caesar returned with a wave. This, Scribonius thought, is unlike Caesar, who always acted with impeccable military courtesy, especially when it was addressed to him by a man from the ranks. Not this time, however, and Scribonius, who was probably the only man in the army who could have matched wits with Caesar and not been found wanting, gave himself a mental warning. Be careful, he thought, he wants something. And right now, with the army in the state that it's in, there is no telling what it will be.

"Scribonius, I need your help," Caesar immediately jumping into a subject was his style, but never this quickly.

Normally he could be counted on to at least ask how Scribonius' wound was healing, or how the men were doing. But this time he came to the heart of the matter.

"You know where things stand with the army. And it's becoming clear that it's not likely that the Primi Pili are going to budge on their own."

Scribonius wasn't sure why, but he felt compelled to defend the other Centurions.

"They're just worried that we're asking too much of the men," Scribonius said quietly.

From one of the other Primi Pili Caesar would have taken this as a rebuke, but Sextus Scribonius had a manner about him that allowed him to say things in a way that avoided offending the person with whom he was conversing at the time.

"I know they are Scribonius," Caesar replied, matching Scribonius' tone.

If the truth were known, if this conversation had taken place a few days earlier, Caesar would likely have had harsher words for Scribonius, but now things were different.

"That's why I need your help," Caesar continued, "or to be more accurate, I need Pullus' help."

This caused the lift of one of Scribonius' eyebrows, and if Pullus had been present, the sight would have caused Pullus to laugh, because the giant Roman had caused that expression on his friend's face himself on several occasions.

"How can Pullus help?" Scribonius asked in genuine puzzlement.

"Because if he agrees with me, I'm sure that the other Primi Pili will fall into line."

Although Scribonius understood Caesar's logic, he didn't share his general's seeming certainty.

"That may be," Scribonius said cautiously, "but I still don't see how I can help."

"You and I are going to pay a visit to your Primus Pilus."

Titus Pullus had long since lost track of time. His best guess was that it was three days after the battle, but he could have been off by a day, or a week. He had become accustomed to the Han physician, but the sight of Diocles, hovering over him with the worry written over his face, had made Pullus happy. From what he could gather, the Han physician was telling Pullus' servant, and Scribonius every time his friend came to visit, that it was too early to make anything more than a guess. But Titus Pullus somehow knew he would live now; if he hadn't died by this point, he reasoned, the gods must have other plans for him. He was still in agony, and was so weak that he had to have help lifting his head to drink the warm soup, or whatever vile concoction the Han had brewed up. He would never admit it, but Pullus held this Han in extremely high esteem, knowing that his ministrations were almost solely responsible for Pullus' survival to this point. The wound on Pullus' chest was still draining, requiring the bandage to be changed several times a day, but while the physicians attached to the army from the other nations would have been content with just doing that, the Han performed several other steps. As gently as he could, the Han would swab out the gaping wound in Pullus' chest, but it still was an agonizing process. Finally, Pullus had suffered enough and rebelled, threatening the Han in ways that needed no interpreter. Only after a laborious process of translation did Pullus understand that the Han was doing this on purpose, to help the healing of his body from the inside out. Once he understood the purpose, Pullus submitted to the treatment, albeit with clenched teeth. Still, he was extremely weak, and most of his time was spent sleeping as his body, and the Han, did their work. He was in this dozing state when there was a commotion in the front partition of his tent, where under normal circumstances Diocles would be conducting Legion business. Now that there wasn't much of a Legion to worry about, and with his master in the state he was in, Diocles was sitting next to the Han physician. At the noise, he leaped up, face clouded with anger as he prepared to banish whoever was making the racket, pushing the leather partition aside. He didn't get any farther than that, stopping dead in his tracks at the sight before him, of the acting Primus Pilus, which wasn't unusual, accompanied by Caesar himself, which was. Gasping in surprise, Diocles leapt aside, holding the partition open so that the two men could enter into Pullus' private quarters. Caesar barely acknowledged him, but Scribonius gave him a wink as he walked by, making the Greek feel better.

"Titus," Scribonius gently shook his friend, careful not to jar him too much.

Pullus opened his eyes, irritated that he had been disturbed from a particularly pleasant dream, frowning at the sight of his friend.

"Weren't you just here?" Pullus asked.

Scribonius shook his head, saying only, "You have a visitor."

"I know. You," Pullus replied, not thinking as quickly as he normally did.

Instead of saying anything, Scribonius stepped to the side and Pullus found himself looking into the eyes of his general.

"*Salve* Pullus," Caesar began, but before he could say anything more, Pullus, responding to habits instilled over the decades he had been under the standard, instinctively tried to sit up.

The wave of pain that suddenly burst over him forced a gasp from his lips, and for a horrified moment Pullus thought he would faint. Caesar was no less disturbed, thinking that this wasn't the way he wanted to start what could be one of the most important discussions of this campaign.

Putting a hand on the giant Roman's shoulder, Caesar said, "Pullus, forgive me! I didn't mean to give you such a start! Please, lie down, rest yourself!"

Pullus did as Caesar directed, thankful for his general's command, as it let him off the hook. Closing his eyes for a moment, Pullus waited for his head to stop spinning before he spoke.

"To what do I owe the honor of your visit, Caesar?"

With other men, Caesar would have taken a more indirect approach, but as he had with Scribonius, he came right to the point. This time it was for a slightly different reason, however; he and Pullus had a bond that he didn't share with any other man from the ranks, and the presence of the Han physician at Pullus' bedside spoke more than any platitudes Caesar could mouth.

"I need your help," he repeated the words he had used with Scribonius, and Pullus became instantly alert, knowing that it had to be important.

"Anything I can do, you know I will, Caesar."

Be careful promising, before you hear what he has to say, was the thought that ran through Scribonius' mind, but wisely he said nothing. Caesar spent the next few moments explaining his plan, the problem he was facing with the army, and what he proposed to do about it.

Once Caesar was done, the silence was oppressive as Titus mulled over what his general had asked him to do. In outlook, he was somewhere in the middle between Scribonius' skepticism and Caesar's optimism. Pullus knew that he carried a great deal of influence with the other Primi Pili, but Caesar was asking a great deal—enough that not even Pullus was sure he could fulfill what Caesar was asking. However, as well as Pullus knew and understood Caesar, the same could be said, and then some, about Caesar's knowledge of the things that motivated his giant Primus Pilus. And Caesar knew that playing on Pullus' pride was the best mode of attack in this small campaign. Regardless, Caesar knew he was running a huge risk, in two ways. The first was that as proud as Pullus was of his status and reputation among his peers, it was based on a deep and profound concern for the welfare of the men in the ranks, but Caesar was gambling that this would be overshadowed by Pullus' vanity. It was the second risk that Caesar worried about more, but it was a sign of his desperation that he was willing to ask Pullus to do something that could very well kill him.

Only when Caesar had received the reports from every scouting party did he allow himself a slight breath of relief. There was no sign of an enemy presence anywhere in the area, and it was this knowledge that prompted his calling for a formation of all the army to be held at his camp, at mid-day of the fourth day after the battle. As shrunken as the army had become, now that the mounted troops had returned from the fleet, as well, there normally wouldn't have been room to fit the entire force inside one camp, but Caesar had ordered the debris from the western half of the camp cleared. It was in this space that the army now assembled, but the general further directed that the troops be arranged in such a manner that every man was facing the *praetorium*. This was only made possible because of the cleared section of half of the camp, and was unusual enough that it had the ranks buzzing with speculation on what was going to happen. From his spot as the Primus Pilus of the 10th, in their accustomed spot at the far right of the formation, Sextus Scribonius, one of the only men who knew what was about to unfold, was far from happy. He had voiced his objection to Caesar's proposal when his general had presented it to him, and it was a sign of how strongly he felt that he renewed his objection when he and Caesar went to talk to Pullus. Caesar had clearly been unhappy with Scribonius, but neither had he rebuked him, knowing as he did how fiercely loyal the Pilus Prior was to his giant friend. And while Caesar hadn't dealt with Scribonius as much as he had with Pullus, he was aware of Scribonius' intelligence, and he respected the man for that, if nothing else. After Caesar left, Scribonius had renewed his assault on the idea, bringing his formidable intellect to bear on Caesar's proposal with unassailable logic expressed in clear, descriptive terms that he hoped would resonate with Pullus. But it was to no avail and now he stood, waiting with the rest of the men, his mouth set in a grim line betraying his worry about what the next few moments would hold. Caesar had yet to appear, and while Scribonius normally admired his general's flair for the dramatic, this wasn't one of those times, as he silently cursed Caesar for delaying. Finally, there was a flurry of movement, as the flap that served as the door to the headquarters tent was thrown aside and the general strode out. As was his habit for such occasions, he was wearing his muscled cuirass and *paludamentum*, the scarlet general's cloak that Caesar wore with a verve and style that Scribonius had never seen with any other general. Although he wasn't wearing his helmet, he wasn't bareheaded, adorning himself with the oak leaves awarded to all generals who had been declared *Imperator* on the field, a feat that Caesar had accomplished an even dozen times. Unbidden, the thought leapt into Scribonius' mind that it was unlikely that the men gathered at this moment would be inclined to award Caesar for a thirteenth time. While only a handful of men were left that had been at Gergovia, and a slightly higher number at Dyrrhachium as well, none of these men had ever seen Caesar suffer as he had a few days before. As much as the horrific number of casualties, it was the shock of seeing Caesar so shaken and uncertain in his actions that had, in turn, rocked the rankers to their very core. Scribonius supposed that it was a little much to expect that the survivors of the assault on Caesar's camp wouldn't talk about what they had seen that day in the night before this assembly, when all the men had gathered in preparation for Caesar's announcement. Did the men who believed Caesar was a god still feel the same way, Scribonius wondered?

"Comrades," Scribonius was jerked from his thoughts by the sound of his general's voice, pitched high enough to carry. Still, Caesar would have to pause frequently, not only to allow his words to be relayed, but also translated for those men whose grasp of Latin still extended only to the basic commands. "I have called you here to discuss a matter of momentous importance."

That, Scribonius thought wryly, is still an understatement.

"I have heard from your Centurions that you are unhappy at the thought of continuing this campaign to its completion by advancing now to the enemy capital that lies no more than 4 days' march away. Is this true?"

Scribonius wasn't sure what kind of response Caesar expected, but what he got was, instead of a low murmur, a roar that left no doubt about not only their agreement, but the depth of their feeling about the matter. Being as close as he was, Scribonius could see the flicker of surprise flash across the face of his general, but as always he covered it quickly, his expression back to the mask that could have been one of those of his ancestors, made after their death.

Holding his hand up for silence, it was a further mark of the men's agitation that it didn't happen immediately, but seemingly unperturbed, Caesar continued, "Yes, yes. I know how you feel. And I must say that you have wounded me, deeply."

Now it was the turn of the men to show their surprise, Scribonius among them. Where was he going with this?

"Have I not always done what's best for you? Have I not always led you to victory?"

Caesar paused again to scan the faces of the men around him, reminding Scribonius that he was watching a true master in the art of manipulating men. Even when you know he's doing it to you, Scribonius thought ruefully, you have to admire him. Like now.

"But I also understand why you feel the way you do now. The battle four days ago was not my best," the fact that Caesar admitted this was astonishing in itself, and Scribonius took it as the truest sign of his desperation yet.

"But who among you has ever faced an enemy like this? A general who would waste his men in such a profligate manner that he throws them away by using them as *fascines* to fill a ditch?"

While Scribonius knew that Caesar was a consummate actor, able to convey an emotion that he wasn't feeling at the moment, Scribonius sensed that at this moment Caesar was being genuine and although the questions were obviously rhetorical, they were meant sincerely. And being fair, these were questions that, along with what happened next, dominated the conversations around the fires of the men at night. As Scribonius knew already just from listening to the conversations in the ranks, the answer was a resounding "No." None of them had seen anything like what they faced four days before, and that, Scribonius realized, was the kernel of the issue. Because it wasn't just Caesar who had been shaken, Scribonius mused as the men were shouting their answers to Caesar, it was all of us. This army has lost most of its confidence in its ability to defeat any enemy they face, and for fighting men, confidence in one's ability is the cornerstone on which everything else is built. That was why the Centurions pushed the men so hard in training, smacking them with the *vitus* and cursing their parents, to instill in them a sense of confidence that there wasn't anything out there they needed to fear when looking over their shield. This was the moment when Sextus Scribonius suddenly understood what Caesar was doing and why.

"We have never been defeated in this campaign, and we were *not* defeated the other day," Caesar continued on, oblivious to the mental wandering of one of his Centurions. "We did not yield the field! We did not run! We stood, and we prevailed!"

This prompted a roar from the men, but compared to other times it, was more muted than usual. That could be due to our reduced numbers, Scribonius thought. Now that he believed he had an understanding of where Caesar was going with this speech, he was anxious to see if his suspicions were correct.

Once the noise died down, Caesar continued, "But we suffered grievously in doing so, that I cannot deny."

Now the general's face showed a sadness that could be seen even from the rearmost ranks of the men, and Scribonius knew his grief was genuine. However, unlike most of the others, his friend Pullus for example, Scribonius understood that it wasn't for the sake of the fallen men themselves, but for the damage done to this finely tuned instrument of war that Caesar had up to this point wielded with such skill. That, Scribonius suspected, was what Caesar was mourning, but this was a thought he kept to himself, especially from Titus, who had always thought Caesar could do no wrong.

"And for that I, your general, must atone, because whether or not we've faced a foe like the one who tried to destroy us the other day, I alone am responsible for the failures. I made mistakes, and men paid for that with their lives, and I have already made many sacrifices to the gods, of all of the men, to attempt to appease them for failing you."

Now Scribonius, and every other man, for that matter, was rocked to his core. Never before had he heard Caesar admit so freely that he had erred in conducting a battle. This was truly a day of firsts, he realized. If Caesar felt compelled to admit such a failing, who knew what else was coming?

"But these... savages owe us a debt that can only be repaid in blood! They must be made to understand the folly of resisting Rome and all that she brings to these benighted islands! Never have we encountered such a strange, backward people, more in need of the good things that civilization brings than any other we have encountered. Yet, to make this even a possibility, we must continue and finish what we started!"

Seemingly as quickly as Caesar won the men over, with this last statement he lost them. And yet, Scribonius observed, Caesar didn't seem surprised at this sudden turn. Instead, Scribonius saw just the ghost of what he knew to be Caesar's smile, as if matters were going in the direction he wanted.

"I see you do not agree, comrades. I can see the doubt, there's no need for you to shout it out, so plainly is it written on your face," Caesar's voice, still pitched high, contained no hint of censure or displeasure. In fact, quite the opposite, puzzling Scribonius even further.

"Tell me, what would convince you that what I am proposing is the correct next step for this campaign? What if," Caesar snapped his fingers, making a great show to convey to the men that this was something he had just thought of, "someone from the ranks, someone you know and respect, should speak to you to soothe your fears? Would that convince you that I am in the right?"

Even knowing what was coming, Scribonius felt a pang of sympathy and not a little anger, knowing as he did that not only did Caesar not expect any of the men from the ranks to step forward, he was counting on them not to. In the game of tables, the best player wasn't the one who thought one move ahead, but who saw several moves, in combinations, that culminated in a final goal of victory. This was what was happening now; Scribonius saw the quiet looks of triumph on the part of the Centurions nearest him, as they looked about, waiting for someone that they knew wasn't coming. For once, the men and Centurions were in perfect accord and it would have been a brave but foolhardy soul who would speak out now. Poor fools, Scribonius thought, you think you've won, when in fact you're doing exactly what Caesar wanted.

"Nobody?" Caesar asked after a moment, although the answer was obvious.

With that, Caesar turned and made a gesture in the direction of the *praetorium*, and it was clear that someone had been peeping between the flaps because nobody was visible, yet despite that the leather was suddenly thrown aside. As this happened, Caesar turned back to look in Scribonius' direction, the cue that had been agreed on earlier, and without hesitation Scribonius broke from his spot in the formation and strode over to Caesar. Conscious of all eyes on him, the salute Scribonius rendered was parade-ground perfect. After it was returned, he stepped to Caesar's side as both men looked to the *praetorium*, where something was happening. Just becoming visible as they emerged were two men, each holding the end of some object, which only became identifiable when they moved in Caesar's direction. Two more men emerged, as well, and between the two sets of men they carried a litter. Scribonius heard the ripple of muttering, as the identity of the man lying on the litter was passed through the ranks, like a wave coming into shore to where Caesar and Scribonius were standing. The bearers had been selected by Caesar personally, with one simple criterion; they were the strongest of the noncombatants, because the bulk of the man they were carrying was much larger than the norm. Even without his armor, and after losing several pounds over the last few days, Titus Pullus was one of the heaviest men in the army, and the strain of carrying him showed on the sweating faces of the orderlies, who nevertheless managed to move smoothly across the forum. What had started as a low murmur increased in volume as Pullus was carried past the ranks of first the 12th, then the 10th Legion, quickly becoming a roaring avalanche of sound. While it was true that Pullus wasn't their Primus Pilus, every survivor of the 12th had seen the deeds performed by the Primus Pilus of the 10th Legion, and it was the slaying of the barbarian general that every man there would say to their dying day was the turning point of the battle.

In short, as far as these men were concerned, they owed their lives to Pullus, and in their own way they were letting him know they had seen and appreciated his action on that day. The recipient of this heartfelt outpouring looked suitably embarrassed, but nobody missed how pale the large Roman was, and how careful he was with every movement, as if a sudden gesture of recognition might cause him pain. He was propped up in a semi-sitting position, and when the orderlies bearing him in his litter reached Caesar and Scribonius, Caesar made a great show of greeting Pullus as if he was a favored son returning after a long absence. Perhaps, Scribonius thought as he watched the pair, the older general bent over the younger man sharing a private joke that made Pullus give a chuckle, even if it was weak, that's what Pullus is to Caesar. Gods know that Pullus looks to Caesar as a father, as well as a general. Now that Pullus was near to the 10th, the shouts and cheers that had started with the 12th swelled into a roaring sound that, even with the diminished numbers, was deafening and drowned out anything else Caesar said to his giant Primus Pilus. For the next few moments neither Caesar nor Pullus could do anything, as the men of the 10th showed their love and regard for their Primus Pilus. Scribonius felt his eyes begin to fill, but he was mollified by the sight of his friend in much the same condition, as tears streamed down Pullus' cheeks, so moved by this outpouring he couldn't contain himself. Finally Caesar held both arms up in a plea for silence. In doing so, he took a few steps away from Pullus and the litter, putting Pullus behind him. Scribonius was alternating his attention between Caesar and the men of the 10th, trying to give them his own sign that it was time to cease their demonstration, so he missed Pullus signaling him the first couple of times. At last sensing movement out of the corner of his eye, the acting Primus Pilus turned to see the true Primus Pilus beckoning to him, which Scribonius immediately obeyed. Reaching Pullus' side, he saw his friend say something, but the noise was still too much to make out the words, so he bent down to put his ear closer to his friend.

"Help me up."

At first, Scribonius was sure he had misheard, but then Pullus repeated the command.

"Are you mad?" Scribonius' shock was greater than his anger at the moment, although that would come. "You're too weak to stand, not to mention that it'll tear the wound open. No, I won't help you up."

The look Pullus gave Scribonius was one that he had seen his friend give before, but it had never been aimed at him until now. As close as they were, Scribonius felt a sudden weakness in his knees, feeling very much as if he was once again a new *tirone* facing his original Pilus Prior, the famous Gaius Crastinus, who had gone on to become Primus Pilus himself and who had fallen at Pharsalus. There was no hint of warmth or friendliness in Pullus' gaze, the piercing look he gave Scribonius was that of a Primus Pilus who expects his command to be obeyed. Knowing the look and understanding there would be no further debate, with a frown plastered on his face, Scribonius extended his hand. Caesar, meanwhile, was just beginning to get the silence that he had been asking for and was about to turn back to Pullus to allow him to speak from his litter, but there was a new eruption of sound, this one even louder as the men renewed their cries. This was not only louder, it was different; more guttural, primal in nature, and the sight and sound of the men seemingly disobeying him shocked Caesar. He was about to unleash his own verbal blast, displaying a temper that he used judiciously, knowing that the sight of Caesar in a rage chilled even the most stalwart of men. But then he noticed that the men of the 10th, and all the other Legions for that matter, were pointing in his direction, gesturing to the man next to them, as their shouts rose to the heavens. Completely confused now, it took Caesar another moment to realize that while the men were pointing in his direction, they weren't actually pointing at him, but at a spot behind him. Even as Caesar turned, while he wasn't sure what to expect and prepared himself, the sight before him as he completed the turn forced a shocked oath from his mouth. Standing erect, wobbling and weaving it was true, with a face as pale as a death mask and shining as if he had thrust his face into a basin of water, was Titus Pullus, Primus Pilus of the 10th Legion. One of his brawny arms was draped around Scribonius, who was clearly bearing a great deal of Pullus' weight, his own face showing the strain. Putting one foot carefully in front of the other, with Scribonius to help him, Titus Pullus took a few, halting steps away from the litter. Stopping next to Caesar, Pullus stood there as the men cheered, until finally he raised a hand. Much to Caesar's chagrin, the men fell silent almost immediately. Gathering himself, Pullus surveyed the faces of the men of the front ranks of the 10th Legion, some faces more familiar than others, but what seized Pullus' heart and racked him with even more pain were those that were missing. Normally, Publius Vellusius would have been standing in the front rank of the First Century of the Second Cohort, beaming at Pullus with a smile that had fewer teeth in almost every formation. But Vellusius, like so many others, was gone from the ranks. In Vellusius' case it wasn't all bad news; while Vellusius had fallen, he still lived, much to Pullus' relief once he was informed. However, he would never march again, because the injury he had received resulted in the loss of his left hand and part of his forearm, keeping him from carrying a shield. Pullus wasn't sure how long he could remain standing, his head already spinning violently, forcing him to grip Scribonius' shoulder so tightly it made his friend wince, despite the fact he was wearing his mail armor.

"All right you *cunni*," compared to the normal bellow that Titus Pullus could produce, this was as close to a whisper as he ever got, but the hush that had fallen over the assembled men as they strained to hear what he had to say was total. "Caesar tells me that you don't want to finish the job we started when we set foot on this fucking island. Is that true?"

Scribonius hadn't thought it possible, but it became even quieter, to the point that he heard the buzzing of the flies that were still feasting on the scraps of men that had escaped being disposed of, in either the mass graves dug for the enemy or in whatever manner the fallen Legionary's will decreed. Men who had been looking directly at Pullus now dropped their heads, unwilling to meet his eyes, and gave him the answer he was looking for.

"So it *is* true," Pullus said, softly enough that only Caesar and Scribonius heard him.

Scribonius felt his friend take a huge, deep breath.

"This isn't the 10th Legion I know!"

It wasn't a blast that Pullus would normally consider one of his best, but it was close. His tone alone cracked like a whip above the men, who began looking even more ashamed.

"This isn't the army that I know! We fought these bastards to a standstill, despite being outnumbered! And now you want to turn tail and run? NOW?"

By the time he was through, Pullus was panting as if he had run the entire length of the ridge the camp was built on, and his sweat dripped onto Scribonius. The Pilus Prior was sure that Pullus would pass out at any moment, but somehow he managed to stay upright. When it was clear that Pullus was done, at least for the moment, only then did the silence break, a low buzz as men mumbled to the comrade next to them. Still, no man was willing to look at Pullus, and he knew that before the army would move, he would have to win the 10th.

Somehow, he gathered the strength to continue, "We have never, ever run from an enemy. And I for one have no intention of starting now! If we don't finish this, even if you live for another 40 or 50 years, you will never be able to look at yourself or your comrades again!"

At the end of his strength, Titus Pullus turned, with Scribonius' help, to face his general.

"Caesar, even if it's on this litter, I'll follow you to the capital of these bastards and make them pay for all the blood of this army they've shed."

And with that, Titus Pullus was spent, his head dropping to his chest and with Scribonius' help he went back to his litter. As Scribonius laid him down, the buzzing sound grew into yet one more roar, and as near death as Pullus looked, there was the ghost of a smile on his face.

Compared to almost any other time, Caesar's army moved with nowhere near the speed to which all of the men were accustomed. This was due to one simple reason; whereas before, if it was tactically feasible, Caesar left the baggage train behind, this time he would only move as slowly as the surviving mules and wagons could move. In all truth, the pace was due to just one wagon, and one wagon only. Now that Caesar had gotten the army marching he wasn't about to turn his back on the reason and the man who was responsible for their change of heart. In a wagon that had been made as comfortable as possible, in a hammock slung between two poles built in each end of the wagon, lay Titus Pullus. Riding in the wagon with him were the Han physician and Diocles, supplied with everything that the physician had deemed might be needed to keep Pullus as comfortable as it was possible to make him. For Caesar, knowing how superstitious the men of his army were, understood what a powerful symbol the Primus Pilus was not to just the men of the 10th Legion, but to the entire army. In the immediate aftermath of Pullus' performance, the 10th had sworn their loyalty to Caesar, renewing a vow the Legion had once made before, long ago, when facing the German Ariovistus. The rest of Caesar's army at the time had been thoroughly intimidated by the reputation of the German chieftain, with the 10th Legion being the lone exception, sending a delegation of Centurions to Caesar to swear an oath that the Legion would follow him against Ariovistus, even if the rest of the army refused to leave their winter camp. Although it was true that there were very, very few men left who were part of Caesar's army on that day in Gaul, deeds such as the 10th's are part of the history and legend of the Legion that had been Caesar's favorite for many, many years and those deeds never die. They are passed along, from the hoary veteran to the new *tirone*, and not just with members of the 10th itself. While few in numbers, the men of the other Legions who had been present, a very few of them actually having been in the 10th before being transferred to another Legion when they were promoted, composed the senior leadership of the army. And they would be damned if the 10th grabbed the glory again! So it was only a matter of perhaps a watch after Pullus' performance, which had cost the Primus Pilus dearly as far as his recovery was concerned, the other Primi Pili came to Caesar, informing him that, after a discussion among themselves, they would be marching with the 10th, as well. Whereas it might have been understandable for Caesar to gloat a bit at outmaneuvering his Centurions, he was neither interested in doing so nor did he feel secure enough in his hold on the army to do as much. For their part, the Primi Pili were chagrined enough that they didn't need Caesar to remind them of his victory, and if the truth were known, the object of their ire was the man riding in the wagon. As respected as Pullus was, he was also envied by the other Primi Pili, to one degree or another, and more than one of them had grown tired of living in the giant Roman's shadow. Being outmaneuvered as they had been by a man who was half-dead, and by virtue of a performance worthy of being penned by any of those infernal Greeks that Caesar and his lot enjoyed so much, just made the draught that much more bitter. Such was Pullus' reputation, however, that not one of the Primi Pili would have been willing to utter such thoughts aloud in front of their men, or each other, for that matter. So they kept their grumbling to themselves, for the most part, although not all of them were able to keep their true thoughts from being read in their faces, something that Caesar chose to ignore. As long as the army was moving in the right direction, that was what mattered to him, even if it wasn't at the pace he normally set. Caesar knew the general location of the enemy capital; his scouts had drawn close enough to see the smoke from the fires of the inhabitants of the city, but he still had no idea of its size or composition. None of the population centers they had come across qualified being called anything more than towns and villages to that point in the campaign, but Caesar supposed that being the capital, this could change. However, he wasn't particularly concerned; this land was so mountainous that he was hard pressed to see where there was enough flat land to plant a city anywhere near the size of Rome, and certainly not Alexandria. Before that happened, however, there was an obstacle that had to be navigated, a huge freshwater lake that lay directly athwart the line of march. The lake was oriented on a roughly northeast/southwest axis, and on the western side of the lake was another ridge that ran roughly parallel to the lake. It was on the other side of that ridge that the enemy capital lay, and his scouts had only gotten to the top of the ridge before turning back. However, the lake itself presented its own challenge, because it appeared that their target was located roughly equidistant from either the northeast or southwestern end of this body of water. And from the calculations of his *exploratores*, this lake was more than 30 miles from tip to tip, and was so wide in places that the far shore couldn't be seen, only the ridge beyond. Starting their march from the northern end of the ridge the camps had been located on, it would have been shorter to skirt the lake around its northeast edge, but his scouts had informed him that there was only a narrow strip of land between this lake and another one, but that this passage was extremely hilly and rough. Not only would it have been hard to pull the wagons over this terrain, it also was good ambush country—at least that is what his scouts had told him—and while Caesar felt in his bones that the Wa army had been shattered, his confidence had been sufficiently shaken that he wasn't willing to take that risk. Although he had managed to salvage his command over the men of his army, even if it was by what some would say was a shabby trick in using his badly hurt Primus Pilus, he knew that if there was another setback, he would lose his hold for good. Therefore he was willing to take the longer, more southerly route, which would add at least a day to the march.

Making camp the first night, there was still a pall hanging over the fires of those Legions who had suffered the most, as the fire in front of every tent section was missing several men, and in some cases, there were only one or two men at most. Sextus Scribonius, acting Primus Pilus of the 10th Legion, his arm now not only bound but in a sling, walked down the streets assigned to his Legion. Men were talking, but it was in subdued tones, much the same as the last several nights, with very little of the laughter and normal banter that Scribonius realized he missed a great deal, if only because it was missing now. At that moment, Scribonius had never felt more alone; Balbus dead, Titus still recuperating, and even young Gaius Porcinus, whose company he enjoyed despite their age difference, was busy. Part of it, he realized, was also being the Primus Pilus, and for perhaps the first time Scribonius had a glimmering of how it felt for his giant friend, the burden that was on his shoulders with every waking moment. The realization that he essentially held the power of life and death over these men, all of them, in every Century and Cohort for the entire Legion, or what was left of it, gave Scribonius a true appreciation of what his friend had dealt with every day, for almost two decades. Stopping at almost every fire, Scribonius did his best to emulate his friend, joking with one man, chiding another for something, but in a teasing manner. Yet even as he did so, he felt as if he was a fraud, but fortunately none of the men took it that way. Although Scribonius didn't know it, he was held in almost as much regard and esteem as Pullus, despite the fact that their styles couldn't have been more different. Scribonius rarely raised his voice, and while he used the *vitus*, the twisted vine stick that most rankers swore was an invention made by Dis himself to torture poor Legionaries, he did so judiciously. More than anything, Scribonius was respected as a firm but fair Centurion, who never played favorites, and who could be counted on, not only in battle, but in what composed the vast majority of time, the interludes between battles. His bravery was unquestioned, and although he didn't possess the huge strength and natural skill of his friend Titus, he was still a formidable fighter in his own right, the fact he had survived as long as Titus had in the ranks bearing testimony to that.

"Pilus Pri...er, Primus Pilus," the man corrected himself, but Scribonius didn't admonish him; he was just as unaccustomed to wearing the title as the men were bestowing it, "what's the latest word on the Primus Pilus?"

Despite the fact that Scribonius had answered this question more than a dozen times by this point, his patience was a virtue he was well known for, and his answer was the same as it had been the previous times.

"The doctor says he's almost out of danger," Scribonius told the man, a Parthian whose name he couldn't remember but whose face he knew, from the Third Century, Fourth Cohort if he remembered correctly. "The wagon ride isn't helping, but he's about as comfortable as he can be made. But that doesn't mean he's still not in rough shape. Not that he thinks so," Scribonius concluded, and like the other times, the Parthian and his comrades laughed at this sign that their Primus Pullus might be wounded but was unchanged.

"Tell him we're making sacrifices every day to every god we can think of," another man called out, this one a Roman that Scribonius did know.

Even as he promised the men that he would do so, his mind was occupied with the thought that it was even easier to remember the Romans left in not just the Legion but the entire army, there were so few left. His face didn't betray him as he moved away from this fire, heading to the next one. Perhaps the strangest sight to Scribonius was the camp itself. Because there were so few men left, there had been something of a consolidation, but neither the Centurions nor Caesar had been willing to go to the extreme of combining Legions. This meant that the Legion streets that normally contained one Cohort per block, with blocks of 5 ten-man tents, one end butted against the other with the opening for each tent facing the opposite direction, were only partially filled. Since there were sections with just one, two, or three men left out of the ten, these men had been folded into other sections. Within the same Century, if possible, but always within the same Cohort, if not, but that meant there were large, vacant spots among the normally ordered rows of tents. It looked, Scribonius said, much like an old Legionary who was missing half his teeth. Finally, shortly after dark, Scribonius had spent time with every section, something that should have taken him almost a full watch more.

Only when he was finished did he stop at his tent; he refused to occupy the tent of the Primus Pilus, although it was also the office of the Legion and even now, here in the middle of only the gods knew where, Caesar insisted that the documentation that was almost as famous as the battlefield exploits of the Legions of Rome be continued. Normally, Diocles was the chief clerk of the Legion, but that work had devolved onto the shoulders of Eumenis and Agis collectively, the other two slaves belonging to Pullus. Scribonius, after a short rest, did stop at the tent to make sure that the daily report that told Caesar of the condition of the 10th on this first day would be sent to the *praetorium*. As slowly as they marched, there had been no stragglers, although some of the walking wounded had struggled a bit, but only three had been forced to resort to the wagons. With that business settled, Scribonius went to the wagon where Pullus was recovering. Normally the wagons for the army were kept in a corner of the camp, but now the wagon containing Pullus was in the forum, near the tent used by the *medici*. Since the men wounded in the battle had been transferred to the fleet, the tent now contained only those men whose condition had worsened on the march, those walking wounded who had begun running a fever or whose sutures had ripped open from the exertion of the day's march. Announcing his presence, then climbing into the back of the wagon, Scribonius wasn't surprised to see his giant friend was awake and seemed to be waiting for him.

"How are the men?" Pullus asked immediately, not bothering with any formalities with his good friend.

If Scribonius was surprised that his friend didn't ask after his own health, he didn't show it, precisely because he had expected this reaction. Before anything else, Titus Pullus was the Primus Pilus.

"About how you'd expect, I suppose," Scribonius replied, "they're still trying to adjust to so many missing faces. But," he gave Pullus a grin, "the one thing they all said was how happy they were you were slung up in here like a roasting pig and not out there bashing them over the head."

Pullus gave a very brief laugh that was quickly cut short by the stab of pain it caused, and Scribonius winced, upset that he was the one who had caused it.

"Sorry," he said quickly. "I didn't mean to make you laugh."

"Yes you did, you ungrateful bastard," Titus grunted, but his tone was as light as his discomfort allowed.

"True," Scribonius grinned. "I'm just paying you back for all the bruises you've given me over the years."

"That's the only way you could do it, with me lying here like, what did you say? A roasting pig?"

Diocles, who had been sitting unobtrusively on the bench affixed to the side of the wagon, was quietly amused and, if the truth were known, very encouraged by the sight of the two friends who seemed to pick their relationship back up where it had been, before Pullus had suffered his near-fatal wound. To the Greek, this was the best sign yet that his master and friend was on the mend and was truly out of danger. On the other side of the wagon, the Han doctor watched the interchange with bemusement, not understanding what was said but drawing the same conclusion as Diocles, whom he was beginning to respect more with each passing day. Like most Han, he hadn't thought very highly of these pale-skinned barbarians, thinking that despite their martial prowess they were by and large bereft of anything that would classify them as civilized. However, his close contact with not just the diminutive barbarian but this giant had forced him to recognize that perhaps there was more to these strange people than just the ability to wage war.

Watching the friends now, the Han couldn't help feeling a sense of pride that his skill had something to do with the scene, but the predominant feeling was one of puzzlement, because never in his long career had he successfully treated a man as grievously wounded as this giant barbarian. To the Han, this meant that there was something inside this man that refused to submit to death, and underlying his curiosity about understanding what this spirit might be, there was a nagging disquiet that made him uncomfortable. Obviously not every one of these barbarians possessed this fierce animus that refused to submit to defeat; like everyone else attached to this army, he had seen the bodies of the dead barbarians stacked like cordwood. But if just a few of these men were like this one, and the Han suspected that the man for whom he worked, the barbarian Caesar, was of the same nature as this giant, it helped to explain why they were so formidable.

However, that meant that they would be hard, if not impossible to defeat, and while the Han took the barbarian's silver and gold, he was still of the Han, and loyal to his emperor. And he had been given very explicit instructions by the emissary of the Han accompanying this army, the man Zhang, that the moment for which this physician had been introduced to Caesar and who Zhang had persuaded Caesar to hire, was rapidly approaching. But, when confronted with the evidence of the formidable power of the spirit that these barbarians possessed, the Han wasn't sure that he could carry out the orders he had been given. Naturally, as Caesar had noted with such frustration, none of these turbulent thoughts were visible as he sat there, with a slight smile on his face, watching the two barbarians bantering back and forth. None of them—Pullus, Scribonius or Diocles—had the slightest hint of what was coming.

And he had been given very explicit instructions by the emissary of the Han accompanying this army, the man Zhang, that the moment for which this physician had been introduced to Caesar and had been persuaded to hire, was rapidly approaching. But, when confronted with the evidence of the formidable power of the spirit that these barbarians possessed, the Han wasn't sure that he could carry out the orders he had been given. Naturally, as Caesar had noted with such frustration, none of these turbulent thoughts were visible as he sat there, with a slight smile on his face, watching the two barbarians bantering back and forth. None of them; Pullus, Scribonius or Diocles had the slightest hint of what was coming.

Shortly after the march resumed the next day, one of the mounted patrols came galloping back to the column, where they made immediately for the command group where Caesar was located. Finding him still there, as it was his habit to range up and down the column, talking with his men and letting them see that their general was with them, although he no longer walked the entire day as he had in his younger days, the leader of this patrol gave him news that caused him to stop the column.

"Are you sure?" Caesar demanded of the Decurion in charge of this detachment, a Parthian.

"Am I sure that it's there? Yes," the Parthian replied cautiously. "But am I sure that the bottom is sound enough for the wagons? No," he conceded. "That I am not sure of Caesar. I believe it is, but it is still not a rock bottom. The water comes up to mid-wheel, but that is only if the wagons don't sink into mud."

Caesar pursed his lips, unhappy, but understanding the Decurion's caution. The spot that the scout was talking about was almost directly west of their current position and appeared to be roughly midway between each end of the lake. Most importantly, it would cut at least two days, probably more, off their march to the base of the ridge between their position and the capital. To this point, none of the scouts had returned with news of a pass through the ridge that was suitable for taking the wagons, and from Caesar's admittedly limited experience with this rugged island, those were few and far between. That meant that it wasn't a given that fording at this spot would save time, if the only way around the ridge was to skirt it to the south, which from what he knew to this point, was the only way around if there wasn't a pass. Caesar had sent a half-dozen scouting parties out to the north, and four of them had returned, all with essentially the same story. Even if they had taken the northern route and threaded their way between these two lakes, the ridgeline that was the last obstacle appeared to continue for many, many miles in a northerly direction. Given the information he had at that point, Caesar and the army's best option appeared to be to approach either from the south, or if there was a pass on the other side of the lake to the west of their position, descend on the capital from that direction. Frankly, Caesar's hope was that there would be a pass somewhere roughly due west that would allow them to begin their assault on the capital from that direction, for the simple reason that he would be attacking from higher ground. Whenever possible, this was his favored method of attack, using the greater momentum that came from his men charging downhill. This would only work if either the outskirts of the capital, or if whatever Wa forces remained to defend it were positioned at the base of the ridge, and his scouts hadn't ventured far enough downslope to determine that. As the Decurion sat his horse, Caesar bit back a curse, not wanting to give the Decurion the belief that he had let his general down. This in itself was unusual, and was just another sign of Caesar's awareness of the tenuous hold over his army that he didn't want to upset one of his junior officers. But neither Caesar nor the Parthian had been in this position before, so both were already unsettled. Finally, Caesar made his decision.

"We're going to head for this ford. Even if it's not suitable for the wagons, it might be enough to send some of the Legions across to block any attempt by the barbarians, if they show up from the capital."

With that, the column resumed the march.

In the capital, those nobles who survived the battle had arrived the day before, and the reception they received from the palace officials had been chilly, to put it mildly. It was only through the intercession of the commander of the emperor's bodyguard that the survivors hadn't been taken into custody and executed on the spot for failing the emperor so horribly. The commander's mercy wasn't from any kinder feelings than those of the courtiers and administrators; his decision was purely practical. He commanded a thousand hand-picked men—none of whom had been part of the Wa assault—equally divided between men who wielded the teardrop-shaped spear as their weapon and those who carried a sword. The difference was that the spear carriers, while recruited from the lower classes, were men whose bravery and skill had been proven in battle, and who were rewarded by living a life that was much different than that of their counterparts in the ranks. Although they were far from pampered, unlike the common soldiers, they had no other job than this. They were never used for farming and filled their time with training, relentlessly, so their skill with the spear was equal to that of the warriors who came from the higher class. As skilled as these men were, the royal guard commander knew that he needed every body he could throw into the ranks, since the Wa had their own scouts. While they were mounted, their horses, brought over from the mainland, were more like ponies, but they were extremely sure-footed and hardy, allowing their riders to take them up and through the narrow defiles and ridges that were such an integral part of their land. And these scouts had left no doubt that as badly mauled as the grubworm army may have been, they were still headed in the direction of the capital. Understanding this, the royal guard commander was determined that he would have to be the immovable object that would stop what had been to this point the unstoppable force of these barbarians. Contrary to Caesar's belief, the manpower resources of the Wa hadn't been completely drained; the lords who ruled in the name of the emperor in the northern part of the island had yet to arrive with their own armies. But as much as the mountainous terrain hindered any force that invaded this island, it posed almost as much of a challenge to the defenders. Their only advantage lay in their intimate knowledge of every fold of ground and passes through seemingly impenetrable lines of mountains only they knew. Nevertheless, a mountain was a mountain, and men could only ascend at a certain speed, whether they knew the shortest point or not. The last messenger that had been sent to the capital from the north said that now that the lords of the north had gathered what forces they could in the time they were given, they were still a little more than a week away from reaching the capital. This made it even more imperative that the commander use every man available to him to hold the grubworms away, no matter how soiled the cowards who had chosen to retreat might be. There was a larger question for the commander to decide, and that was whether to spend what time he had on strengthening the defenses of the capital, or to sally forth and meet these barbarians on ground that favored him and the rest of the defenders. Before he could make that decision, however, he had to know from which direction the attack would come. The obvious way for any attacker without an intimate knowledge of the land would be to skirt the ridge between the lake and the capital to approach from the south. However, the commander had to prepare himself and his men for the possibility that the grubworm scouts, who were much more numerous and better mounted, would find the location of the one pass through the hills that was the most direct route, if they came across the ford at the narrow part of the lake. Because, unlike Caesar, the commander knew that not only would the bottom of the ford support the weight of even the wagons that the grubworms carried with them, but also that the pass was just wide enough to accommodate the wagons, as well. If the grubworm general, who seemed to have the luck of the demons, found that pass and used it, this would actually be preferable to the commander than if the invader were to take the southern route, because he was certain that even with as few men as he commanded, they would be able to block the pass long enough for the lords of the north to come to their aid. As desperate as their situation might be, victory was still possible; the grubworms could be crushed and the threat to the emperor ended. As of this moment, the commander determined that the best tactic was to wait.

The end of the second day of the march found Caesar's army at the narrowest part of the lake, and although there was enough light to cross, the general made the choice to keep the lake between his army and any possible attack. Just a week before, Caesar wouldn't have even considered such caution, but much had happened in the intervening time. And while his engineering officers confirmed that the mud bottom seemed to be founded on a bed of rock and was firm enough to support the wagons, that was where the good news stopped. On crossing the ford, which was almost a mile wide and was one of the longest stretches of water that either Caesar or his most veteran men had experienced, the engineers discovered that just a couple of hundred yards from the far shore, the bottom dropped significantly. Most troubling was the presence of what felt like a strong current along the bottom, and while the water would still be only about chest deep for most of the men, the footing was made treacherous by the current. Although it wasn't a swiftly flowing river where men who lost their balance might be swept away before any chance of rescue, there also seemed to be a precipitous drop in the direction the current was flowing just a few paces to the left of their direction of travel.

This negated one of Caesar's favored tactics on crossing any body of water like this, the placement of the cavalry aligned end to end to help break the forcc of the current not only upstream but downstream to catch any Legionary swept off his feet. It was an error on the part of the Parthian scout that he hadn't performed a thorough job of scouting the entire width of the ford, but it was also something that Caesar wasn't going to punish the man for, yet another difference brought on by the series of setbacks Caesar had suffered, weakening his hold on his army. Nevertheless, it caused Caesar to reconsider using the ford, but between the added challenge that would come from the deeper crossing and the fact that no passage had been found anywhere in the vicinity of the ford through the hills ahead, he deemed it prudent to turn south the next morning and skirt the lake and the ridge. This decision didn't make him happy, as it added at the very least a day and probably more before he could even lay eyes on the capital and get an idea of what kind of resistance to expect. Finally, it just rubbed Caesar the wrong way to waste precious daylight that could be spent marching. However, as it would turn out, the watches weren't wasted at all.

Because of that hidden pass through the hills, the Wa royal guard commander learned that the barbarian army was going to cross at the ford within a watch, after it was clear to his scouts that this is where they were headed. When the next scout arrived in the capital to inform him that the grubworms were stopping for the day and making one of their infernal camps that, according to the survivors of the attack days before, were as close to impregnable as it was possible for a temporary fortification to be. As loath as the commander was to take the word of men who were shamed cowards, he couldn't dismiss the possibility that they were simply being accurate, given that they had prevailed over what had been the largest army ever assembled in the history of this island. Between that possibility and the paucity of his own forces, he immediately dismissed any idea of assaulting the barbarians, especially when he learned that they were doing so on the other side of the lake. Even with the ford, and as swiftly and silently as the men of the royal guard could move, there wasn't any way that he could hope to overcome these grubworms if they were behind those ditches and ramparts.

It was ironic, the Wa thought, that even as the grubworms were doing their fortification work, so too were the Wa, as they continued working feverishly on fortifying the grounds surrounding the imperial palace. Unlike the Han, or these previously unknown barbarians, the Wa didn't have permanent fortifications, especially around the capital. The reasons for this were twofold; the first was that the very ground these people walked could suddenly begin to shake so violently that large structures were always in danger of collapse, so such things were avoided where possible. Instead, the Wa used the terrain and the land itself, taking advantage of the rugged hills and steep, narrow valleys to aid in the defense of their sacred islands. The second reason was more from accident than any design on the part of the Wa; the simple truth was that no invasion force had ever successfully penetrated this far into the interior of their lands. This was a fact in which the Wa took enormous pride - and viewed it as the surest sign of how favored they were by their gods. But now that it had happened, it had not only shaken the very foundations of their society, it had ignited a sense of urgency and concern that was now fueling what had become an operation that continued through every watch. Unlike the Romans, however, who allowed only their Legionaries to construct camps and fortifications, the warrior class of the Wa viewed such work as beneath them. Fortunately for them, every Wa peasant had been instilled with the belief that they owed their emperor not merely allegiance, but unflinching obedience. Therefore, when the call was sent out for every available laborer within a day's walk to come to the capital, the response was immediate.

Now, thousands of peasants were hard at work, under the direction of the royal guard, creating an earthen wall to surround not just the imperial palace, but also a good part of the imperial city. Critical points like the warehouses and granaries, the armory, the barracks, and every other structure considered vital to the defense of the capital were enclosed by this earthen wall. Even Caesar, the world's undisputed master at the rapid construction of fortifications, would have been impressed if he had known that what he was about to face hadn't been present just days earlier. Yet, even as formidable as these fortifications would be, the Wa guard commander wasn't willing to put all of his faith in them, and he was pondering how to come up with another stratagem that would give him the time he needed for the northern lords to come to the rescue. This was what occupied his mind, if not his attention, as he strode along the new ditch, watching the peasants throwing dirt up onto the earthen wall, while others carried stacks of wood that were going to be used to create a palisade not unlike what the

Romans used. How could he use his knowledge of the land to their advantage? Chief among his worries was that the grubworms would find the pass, and although their army was still on the other side of the lake, he had little doubt that their scouts were even now scouring the hills, looking for any passage that would accommodate their needs. Like a thorn in his mind, no matter what he was doing, a part of him worried and picked at this as he continued supervising the work. He had received the latest report that the grubworms had indeed begun making camp on the other side of the ford just moments before, and it was as he was directing one of his lieutenants on how to use a grove of trees with such heavy underbrush that it was an impenetrable barrier to their advantage that it hit him. Here, he was taking advantage of what the land offered him in creating a choke point that would force the grubworms to move in a direction he wanted. Why should he restrict himself to just around the capital? His greatest fear was that the barbarians would locate the pass, but at the same time he had hoped they would, for the same reason he was using this grove: the terrain suited his needs and would make his job easier. So, was it a bad thing that they find the pass? In fact, wasn't this preferable to an approach from the south, where the land was too wide open to stop the grubworms from moving up to where he was standing right now? He was planning and hoping for a defense of his weakest point, rather than making the enemy come to him on ground of his choosing. Excited now, the Wa commander whirled about, looking for the mounted scout who had given him the last report. Spotting him watering his horse, he barked a command to the man, who hurried to him. There was much to do, but it had to start with this man, and the royal commander wasted no time.

Caesar was engaged in a deep discussion with Aulus Hirtius, Asinius Pollio, Publius Ventidius, the Tribunes, and the Primi Pili, going over the next day's march, when a courier arrived bearing an urgent dispatch. The general and his staff were in the outer office of the *praetorium* so Caesar spotted the man immediately on his entrance, beckoning him over. Recognizing the man as one of those assigned to the Parthian Decurion, Caesar's brow furrowed, as he wondered what the Parthian could consider so important, given the duty he had been given. While not chastising the man, Caesar had decided to remove the Parthian from the role as scout, so he and his *ala* were now charged with providing a screen along the strip of land between the other side of the lake and the ridge. Caesar thought it highly unlikely that there would be a sighting of anything other than a lone scout, which is all that had been spotted for days. Still, he accepted the offered tablet, opening it and reading the contents with pursed lips. His officers stood watching, and they were all familiar enough with Caesar to know that something potentially important was contained in that message even before he opened his mouth to confirm it.

"How long ago did you leave him?" Caesar asked the messenger, who paused to think.

"Not more than a sixth part of a watch sir," the courier replied after a moment's thought.

"Which would put him how far away?" Caesar followed up.

Again the man paused, painfully aware that not only did much ride on his answer for the army as a whole, but also for his Decurion, who he knew was in trouble with the general.

"Perhaps 4 miles. No more than five."

"From here? Counting the ford?" Caesar asked, which in fact the courier hadn't factored in, thinking of the distance only as a straight line and not how much ground had to be covered.

"No sir," the man's voice carried the slightest tremor now. "Counting the ford he's five miles away."

Caesar didn't say anything more, looking back down at the tablet, deep in thought. His officers, however, couldn't contain their impatience, and it was Hirtius who broke the silence?

"Well? What is it? Or are you going to make us guess?"

If Caesar was irritated, he didn't show it in any way, instead simply answering, "It appears that we have located a pass through the mountains."

Not unexpectedly, this created a stir, as the assembled men started talking, either to or over each other as they digested this piece of information. Caesar held his hand up, and the men immediately fell silent.

"The Decurion reports that they surprised a pair of mounted scouts, and in the ensuing chase they followed them up into the hills. But instead of cornering them in one of the draws or blind valleys, they chased them all the way to the other side, where they caught up with them just on the other side of the ridge."

"So they didn't escape to raise a warning that we found a way through?" Pollio asked, all of them instantly understanding the significance of the sequence of events.

"Apparently not," Caesar replied. "But until I talk to the Decurion and see things for myself, I'm not willing to say so definitively."

"You mean you plan on going up there?" Hirtius gasped, barely getting out the words before the others voiced similar protests.

"Indeed I do," Caesar gave the men a grim smile. "Given all that's happened, I think the least I owe to this army is that I make sure before we commit ourselves. Besides," he finished, "given the Decurion's error with the width of the ford, I'll feel more comfortable seeing for myself. Although, if this pass turns out to be practicable for the wagons, he'll have more than redeemed himself."

The two scouts the royal commander had chosen gave their lives willingly, as part of the plan the Wa had devised to gain an advantage over the barbarians. Despite their ponies' being smaller, over the type of terrain they spent most of their time traveling they were superior to the larger mounts of the grubworms, and in fact they could have evaded capture fairly easily. But that wouldn't have been conducive to the illusion that the Wa commander was trying to create: that the remaining forces were waiting for an attack from the south, confident that the pass they were using would remain undiscovered. That didn't mean they surrendered or didn't put up a ferocious fight, and in fact they helped the Wa cause by taking four of the grubworms with them before they were subdued. The Parthian Decurion and his *ala* had caught the two not far from the crest of the pass on the western side, and conscious of his earlier mistake, he and his men had pushed forward almost to the base of the ridge. Taking advantage of the thick growth, they proceeded cautiously, but didn't run into any more sentry posts or pickets. This, of course, was by design, but they had no way of knowing that they were doing exactly what the Wa wanted them to do. Satisfied that the pass was not only open, but also that the road, rough-hewn as it was and little more than two grooved tracks and of a steep but navigable grade, was passable by the wagons of the army, the Parthian and his men hurried back. By his estimate the pass was about 4 miles long, so that the courier he sent immediately after subduing the two barbarian scouts should have reached Caesar by this point. Consequently, he was expecting to be met somewhere along the way back, but not by the general himself.

At the base of the ridge on the eastern side, nearest the lake, Caesar rode at the head of his mounted bodyguard and his generals. Meeting the Parthian and his *ala*, Caesar took the man's report, but he did so while continuing to ride up the narrow track. As they rode, he questioned his Decurion further about what the Parthian had seen further up the road. Riding ahead of Caesar and his officers were the men of the bodyguard and the *ala*, but again they ran into no sign of any enemy. The slopes of the hills through which the road passed were heavily forested, with thick undergrowth, something Caesar noted with concern. It was true that it would help screen his own movements, and, most importantly, the presence of the overhanging trees would help dissipate the dust, but it also meant that there could be barbarians hidden and waiting. Through the years and countless battles Caesar had developed a keen instinct for knowing when danger lurked nearby; it was that instinct, when he had actually heeded the warning of The Seer, that had saved him on that day on the Ides of March ten years before, something that even now he didn't like to think about. However, his senses at the moment didn't alert him that there might be enemy troops lying in wait, as he and the rest of his detachment continued up the pass. Reaching the summit, Caesar and the others drew up. From this spot, through the trees, he could glimpse the land, perhaps two thousand feet below and no more than two miles away. There was nothing special that he could see, just a scattering of the curious huts that these people constructed, which were unbelievably flimsy, and adjoining each hut was a plot of land, where something other than rice was clearly being grown.

Otherwise, there was no sign of enemy activity that would indicate that they were prepared for an enemy army. No fortifications blocking the road as it entered the valley, no movement of men, mounted or otherwise. Rather than quieting his fears, these absences unsettled him even further. His self-confidence, badly shaken as it had been days before, was also tempered with a deep but grudging respect for the martial skills of these people, and although all indications were that Primus Pilus

Pullus had killed the barbarian who had commanded the attack, he couldn't discount that there was one Wa left who was as able as the dead man had been. That thought wouldn't leave the back of Caesar's mind as he continued moving, now heading downslope. Going perhaps a half mile further, once again he drew up, staring out into the open valley, but saying nothing. Pollio was on one side, Hirtius on the other, but both men recognized the expression on their general's face and knew he was deep in thought, so they remained silent as well. The only sound was the whispering of the wind through the trees, and Hirtius was struck by the thought that, all things considered, this was a beautiful country in many ways. The incongruity of the peace of the scene; the horses' tails swishing away the insects that were lazily buzzing about, the movement of the trees as the breeze blew through them, the creak of saddles, stood in stark contrast to what their purpose was for being at that spot, at that moment. Finally, Caesar gave a minute shake of his head, then, without another word, turned his horse about.

"We move tonight," the Wa commander announced to his subordinates, gathered in the building that served as the headquarters for the imperial guard. "The grubworm general has taken the bait. He was seen inspecting the pass and saw what I wanted him to see, a peaceful kingdom unprepared for attack."

His words were met with grunts of approval from the small group of assembled men. Unlike the grubworm barbarians, the Wa had far fewer leaders. Essentially, there were sub-commanders of each contingent of the command; spear carriers, sword warriors, archers, and the mounted scouts who could serve as fighting cavalry, if necessary, although the commander understood if matters reached that point the battle was essentially lost. There was also one other man present, chosen by his comrades to represent the disgraced nobles who had escaped from the first battle, his presence barely tolerated by the others.

"I want all but The Chosen with me to take up positions in the pass," the commander continued, referring to the two hundred hand-picked men who were the emperor's personal bodyguard. Not only were these men formidable warriors, but their lineage and ancestry was almost as exalted as the emperor's himself, representing the most ancient families of the islands, or at least since the Wa first began taking notice of such things. "The rest of you will be with me. We move immediately."

Finished, the commander turned to attend to other matters, but one of his sub-commanders stopped him. That one of them would speak up at such a moment was unusual, but not unheard of. However, the identity of the speaker shocked everyone present into immobility, including the commander, whose face was a frozen mask of contempt.

"Is it wise to risk everything we have left on the belief that the grubworm general has taken the bait you have laid out so carefully?"

While in every other sense it was a perfectly sensible question—one that a general like Caesar wouldn't take amiss, even if it was for the chance to demonstrate his genius in explaining his decision—it was the identity of the man asking the question that created such consternation, for it was the Wa representing the disgraced nobles who asked it. As far as the commander, and the other men for that matter, was concerned, this man should have been more silent than the sparse furniture in the room. After all, a chair could creak because of the weight put upon it, but this noble and his comrades had forfeited what little right they had to question their commander by their shameful behavior at the first battle. Behavior that, from the viewpoint of the commander, had led him and his command to make what he understood was a desperate gamble in a last-ditch attempt to save not only his capital, but indeed his emperor from the ultimate humiliation. Never in their history had the Wa been defeated, and every man from the commander down to the lowest warrior was acutely aware of this fact and the fact that their ancestors were watching. Now, this...this impudent coward was questioning his orders? But as much as he wanted to roar his disgust and anger at the man, the target of his rage *was* a member of the nobility, just like he was, even if he was a minor son. So instead, he treated the other man with an icy courtesy, although everyone present could sense the barely suppressed rage.

"While I understand your concern, it is really none of your affair. You hold no office here in the capital. I won't mention that if you and your comrades had been successful, I would not be forced to make this choice in the first place. It is a gamble, but it is the right one to make. Or are you claiming otherwise?"

Even spoken quietly, there was no mistaking the rebuke, and the menacing warning in the commander's words.

The young noble's body stiffened, but his tone was even, as he replied, "No, I am not claiming otherwise. Forgive me."

For a moment the commander continued to glare at the younger man, but then gave an abrupt nod of his head. There was a rush of air as the rest of the sub-commanders let out their collective breaths, and without another word spoken the commander turned on his heel and exited the room. As the rest of the men filed out they were careful not to look at the young noble, who was the last to leave, his normally smooth features furrowed with the worry that he felt. As each man hurried off in different directions to carry out their respective tasks, the young noble did the same, but he moved more slowly as his mind raced, almost dizzied by the idea that was coming to him. His reasoning was simple; after all, he and his comrades were already disgraced? What more did they have to lose?

"We're breaking camp and moving tonight," Caesar announced to his officers after he returned from his scouting trip. As might be expected, this got the attention of the assembled men, prompting a low buzz of conversation. Caesar held up his hand to silence the talking, the men immediately falling quiet as they waited for more.

"We're also going to be moving fast, so don't have the men fill in the ditches. Take only their stakes, and they need to be told that we're going to be moving fast, even if it is dark."

For the first time in many days, there were smiles apparent among the officers of Caesar's army; this was more like the old general they knew and loved.

"As far as marching order, I want the 14th leading the way," Caesar continued. "The 30th follows, but I will leave it up to you to determine the order after that. I want the 10th and 12th marching with the baggage train."

Raising a hand again, not in a gesture to silence, but to reassure the two Primi Pili, both of them acting, he told Scribonius and Carbo, "Make sure the men know this isn't a censure of any kind. In fact, it's the opposite. The 10th in particular needs to know that they're honoring their Primus Pilus by protecting him, because we're going to be marching faster than the baggage train tonight.

And the 12th needs to know that their general understands they have suffered enough, and they deserve to rest."

Both men nodded; the truth was that neither of them had the same concern as Caesar. Their Legions were shells of their former selves, and they knew that this was one fight that the men wouldn't mind sitting out after all that they had been through.

"I expect to march in a third of a watch," Caesar finished, and while the men responsible for making this happen weren't pleased, they also knew that it wasn't impossible to do. There might be liberal use of the *vitus* across some men's backs to encourage them to move with the necessary speed, but by the gods, they would move!

"How are we going to handle the ford?" Pollio was the one who asked this question, and unintentionally triggered the great surprise.

"We're not using the ford," Caesar replied, but without saying anything else. Again, there was a buzz of conversation, the officers confused by this news. "At least, not this one."

"Not using the ford?" Hirtius blurted out. "But how are we going to reach the pass? Surely we're not going to go down to the end of the lake, then come back up again!"

"No, we're not going to do that," Caesar agreed, mouth twitching in a ghost of a smile, but again he didn't elaborate.

Thoroughly confused now, Pollio was simply the first to ask the next question.

"Then how in Hades do you expect us to take advantage of that pass and save a day's march if we don't go by the shortest route, and that's across the ford?"

"Because we're not going through the pass," Caesar said, leaning back on his desk with folded arms, waiting for the explosion to come.

He wasn't disappointed.

"What? We aren't going to use the pass? In the name of the gods, why not? You saw for yourself! It's wide open! There's nothing to stop us from stealing a day from these barbarians!"

This came from Ventidius, who up until that moment had been silent, but who was now as agitated as everyone else there. Unlike the Wa royal guard commander, Caesar was far from upset at being questioned in this manner; the truth was, he rather enjoyed it. He also knew that by explaining things to his subordinates, he usually got more cooperation and diligence in seeing his orders carried out. When men felt informed, they took ownership in ideas that weren't necessarily their own; this was one of the great secrets of Caesar's genius for command.

"Everything you say is true, Ventidius," Caesar answered calmly. "Which is why I believe that this is exactly what the barbarians want us to think. If I were their commander, I would make it appear to be what we saw today, a completely undefended pass, just inviting us to cross by the shortest way possible. I imagine that even now, their commander is giving the same orders that I'm giving. The difference is that we're going to head for two different spots. It might be longer, but from everything I've been told by the scouts, once we skirt this ridge, the way north to the capital is wide open country. And while I don't discount that there might be a sizable barbarian army left, nothing we've seen indicates that is the case. No," he concluded, "I think they have a handful of men, at least compared to what we have, and their commander is seeking to even the odds by drawing us into a trap by taking that pass. You saw the terrain. It's a perfect spot for an ambush."

When Caesar finished, there was a moment of silence, as each man digested this. What Caesar said, as almost everything he did, made eminent sense, and when presented made the officers wonder how they had missed something so obvious. Still, their concerns weren't completely assuaged, and in yet another difference between these two foes, it was the man who was by rights the least qualified to speak who raised the question.

"What do we do about them watching us?" acting Primus Pilus Scribonius asked. "We have to assume that they have men hidden up in the hills who are watching. Granted, it's a long way off especially in the dark, but they'll surely see the torches of the vanguard."

Caesar pursed his lips, telling those who knew him Scribonius had brought up something that Caesar considered important.

"You're right, Scribonius," Caesar said, his respect for this tall, rangy man who looked more like a tutor of a patrician's children than a Centurion growing even more. Thinking about it for a moment, he decided, "That means we go without torches. The moon isn't full, but it's a half-moon and there aren't many clouds. We're just going to have to move as quickly as we can."

With these instructions, they wasted no time in hurrying out of the *praetorium*, heading to their respective commands to make it so. As they did, Caesar called to one of his scribes.

"Still nothing?"

"No, master. No new couriers have arrived."

Even as he projected an air of confidence, Caesar was beset with worry. For one reason, of the two scouting parties he had sent to the north, only one had returned. This was how he had learned of the difficulties that would be posed by taking the northern route around the lake. The other one, however, had vanished without a trace, and Caesar understood that there was no good reason for this. Perhaps he hadn't destroyed the entire Wa army after all.

He supposed he shouldn't have been surprised, the royal commander thought sourly. After all, how much more shame could those young nobles bring on themselves? Still, the disappearance of more than 200 men wasn't something he was happy about, when every man who could hold a weapon was needed so desperately. He thought about ordering a search for them, but quickly dismissed the idea. There simply was no time to waste if he wanted to be in position and give his force time to put together some hasty fortifications. His plan was simple, and based on two things; the element of surprise and the Wa's intimate knowledge of the terrain. The latter would be helped by the construction of a breastworks on both sides of the road, made from fallen logs, rocks and heavy branches. But that took time, and even with their knowledge of every fold and bump in these hills, they would be working in the dark as it was. It was this knowledge that convinced the commander not to waste what little manpower he had trying to find cowards who had scurried off. Once the grubworms were crushed, then these men could be dealt with, as well as the families who had bred such traitorous dogs. Turning his mind back to more important matters, the commander surveyed the assembled troops, lined up and waiting to head out for the pass. Calling to the man he had designated to command this group until he rejoined them, he gave him the order to move. Then he called to the palace official who had been chosen to oversee the erection of the fortifications. Watching the official approach with barely disguised scorn, the commander nevertheless kept his tone polite, knowing that while the man wasn't a warrior, he still wielded influence with the emperor.

"I request that you keep the work going through the night. We're going to crush them up in the pass, but it pays to be prudent."

While couched as a request, the official knew it was anything but. His smooth features were peculiarly ageless—brought on by another reason why the Wa commander held him in disdain—and his voice added to the feeling that he was not only ageless, but sexless as well. Which, the commander thought, was as close to the truth as it was possible to get.

"Of course, Commander," the official's speech was also marked by a sibilant quality that reminded the Wa of a serpent hissing. "I know that the Chosen Ones are to be left behind to guard the emperor, but have you detached any others from your force? As you said, being prudent, it would seem to make sense to me that we should at least have a force of archers. Please forgive me, I know I am not a warrior and have little knowledge of these matters, but when it comes to protecting the divine spirit of the emperor, I must ask."

Just like the commander, the official held his counterpart in low regard, considering him to be little more than an unintelligent brute who was good with a sword and possessed a low cunning, nothing like himself and the rest of the palace eunuchs. Relieved as they were of their testicles, so too were they relieved of all the distraction and turmoil that possession of this part of the male body seemed to bring with it, allowing him and his fellow eunuchs to devote themselves to more important matters. But just like the commander, he was aware that the warrior wasn't without influence among the other officials in the service of the emperor, so his tone bordered on the deferential. For his part, the commander stiffened at the implication that his plan might fail, but he forced himself to consider what the official was saying. As much as he hated to admit it, this eunuch had a point.

"You are right. That was an oversight on my part. However, the most I can spare is 50 of the archers."

The official wasn't happy at the paltry number, but could tell that the commander wasn't going to budge. Giving the commander a bow, he made to go but was stopped by the commander, who had decided that what had been fair for him, being asked a tough question, would be fair for the eunuch.

"Since, as you point out, it is wise to be prudent, what plans have you made to remove the emperor from the capital? And, where would you take his divinity?"

Now it was the eunuch on the defensive, his normally placid expression creasing with his discomfort at being asked.

"We have... plans," he conceded grudgingly, "but I think it is premature, don't you? As you said, you will in all likelihood be successful."

Just as the eunuch had with him moments before, the commander concluded that this was all he was going to get from the eunuch, at least in the little time he had.

"I will keep you informed, if that is even necessary," the commander concluded. "I will be sending mounted couriers to keep you apprised of developments and leave it to you to make the decision."

Their business done, the two men parted, each heading to their respective duties, both men's thinking running along markedly similar lines concerning the other.

Caesar had every reason to worry about the lost scouting party. They, in fact, had been surprised and ambushed by the leading elements of the army of the north. While not as numerous as the Wa force that had attacked the camp, the 20,000 men that marched were not only fresh, they were spoiling for a fight. The Roman scouting party had been instructed to scout far to the north, and they had obeyed their instructions, so they were intercepted well north of the lake. As darkness fell and both sides continued to make their respective preparations, the northern army of the Wa was still two and part of a third day away from reaching the capital. Catching the grubworms as they had—warned by the dust of their horses so they rode straight into an ambush—they had riddled every one of them with arrows without a sword needing to be drawn. The northern lord commanding this force had issued explicit instructions that the archers aim only for the riders and not the horses. Once his scouts had described the difference between their own ponies and the mounts these grubworms rode, he had coveted one of them for his own. Arriving at the site of the ambush, he immediately saw that his scouts hadn't exaggerated; these beasts were markedly different from the mounts the Wa were accustomed to riding. His pleasure was marred by the sight of one of the animals with an arrow protruding from its hindquarter. Demanding to know who had launched the errant arrow, it was only after threatening to execute every member of the ambush party that one of them took responsibility. The man was promptly executed on the spot, even as the lord approached the animal, which was naturally skittish. Somewhat of an expert in these matters, this lord had developed a deep love for horses, and it was with considerably more sorrow than he had shown for the executed archer, that when he saw that the arrow was lodged firmly in the bone, he decided that the animal had to be destroyed.

Nevertheless, he was left with 19 of these magnificent animals, two of which were stallions and included a half-dozen mares. Immediately, he started dreaming of how he would be crossing his island ponies with these animals and how with this many new animals he could afford to mount even more of his men, and on what horses! This train of thought was what contributed to his somewhat lax attitude about finishing the day's march. The ambush had occurred with more than a watch of daylight left, but rather than keep marching, the lord decreed that they would be stopping for the day so that he could more closely inspect each animal. Most of his vassal lords were distressed with this delay, since they had been kept informed of all that had transpired to the south, and were aware that the capital and their emperor were in jeopardy. Nevertheless, the northern lord's reputation, and the recent example of what happened to those who incurred his displeasure, guaranteed that any protests would be silent, or at best muttered among themselves. As much as they knew how potentially dangerous tarrying could be, not even they could imagine how much of an impact the northern lord's decision would have.

"What in Hades are we doing now?" Titus Pullus demanded of Diocles when the unmistakable sounds of an army breaking camp roused Pullus from his nap.

As if in answer to his question, the flap that served as the door was pulled aside, and Scribonius' head appeared.

"We're on the move," he told Pullus, not bothering to climb up into the wagon. This was his first stop before he roused the 10th, and it was out of force of habit more than anything else that Scribonius' initial thought was that the normal Primus Pilus should be kept informed.

"On the move? Where to?" Pullus asked. "Are we going up through that pass that everyone is talking about? That's going to be bumpy," he grumbled.

"No, you don't need to worry about your rest being interrupted," Scribonius replied with a laugh. "Caesar is sure that it's a trap, so we're going to skirt the lake and come up from the south like we originally planned."

Pullus considered this for a moment, then gave a half-shrug, using his uninjured shoulder.

"Well, if he's not using the pass, he's got a good reason for it," he concluded. "If he thinks it's a trap, then it probably is."

While Scribonius wasn't quite as thoroughly Caesar's man as Pullus was, he did trust his general, despite the recent setback.

"My thoughts exactly. Now, if you don't mind, I have some things to attend to. You'll be moving out in a bit, so you might as well go back to sleep."

Scribonius didn't wait to hear Pullus' reply, knowing that it would be something obscene.

"There's no point in me trying to go back to sleep," Pullus told Diocles. "Besides, I'm hungry. Get me something to eat, before this thing starts bouncing and rocking all over the place and makes me spill everything."

With Diocles hurrying off to comply, Pullus lay back and listened to sounds that were as familiar to him as the sound of his own voice by this time. Shouted orders, the sounds of livestock protesting at being roused after such a short respite, the curses of the Centurions as they hurried their men, all part of the controlled chaos that was Caesar's army on the move. Even in the dark of night, the men moved with the speed and surety that comes from tasks performed thousands of times. To an outside observer, even in daylight it would appear to the untrained eye to be a combination and series of completely unrelated actions, but as Pullus knew it would be, the army was ready to march precisely a third of a watch after Caesar had uttered his order. That didn't mean the challenges were over, because without even flickering torchlight to light the way, the advance element of the army was unable to set its normal pace. Still, despite the darkness, Caesar's army moved with a speed that probably matched the rate most other armies marched at in daylight. Unfortunately for Pullus, this meant that the man driving his wagon wasn't able to see any holes or bumps in the path they were following.

"I'm glad I ate beforehand," Pullus just managed this through teeth tightly clenched from the pain caused by the jarring ride.

In the deeper darkness of the wagon, Pullus could just barely see the smile from his servant, but he felt the hand on his shoulder as Diocles did what he could to comfort his master. Creaking along, the two of them endured the bouncing and jolting as Caesar's army moved.

Crossing the river that fed from the huge lake at about two parts of a watch after midnight, the leading element of Caesar's army, particularly the two leading Legions, seemed infused with a new sense of energy and purpose. While by rights they should have been showing signs of fatigue, having had so little rest before starting out again, the effect was quite the opposite, to the point that when the Centurions called a halt, the men in the ranks let them know there was no need. Pressing on, the darker bulk that marked the end of the ridge was to their right, as they made their turn to the west. There was no talking allowed, but even if there had been, the men would have remained silent, grimly determined to finish what was for all of them the toughest campaign they had ever participated in, no matter how long they had been marching for Caesar. Moving remarkably silently for such a large body of men and animals, Caesar and his men closed inexorably on the enemy capital. From his spot leading the command group, just behind the two lead Legions, Caesar continued issuing orders to a variety of couriers, some mounted, some on foot who trotted back along the column to give their messages to a Primus Pilus marching along with his men. At the same time, the mounted scouts continued to ride parallel to the column, but out about a mile on either side, alert for any dangers. Part of their duty was to silence any possible source of warning, which meant that every lonely farmhouse they came to was surrounded, then men sent in to put the inhabitants to the sword, regardless of age or sex. Naturally, while this order was carried out, in the event that women were found, these unfortunate souls were snatched up to be used, then disposed of, their naked bodies left behind, dully glowing in the pale moonlight like a series of markers that denoted the progress of the vengeance being brought to the Wa. Any possible finer feeling about these people had been extinguished because of the battle, but not for the reasons that might seem evident.

It wasn't what the Wa had done to their comrades that unleashed the savagery in the Roman army, it was what the Wa general had done to his own men. To the soldiers' way of thinking, if their own people didn't value the lives of these yellow savages, why should men who suffered so much at their hands? The talk around the fires after the battle had ultimately made its way to this topic, and what it meant. It's not unusual for soldiers of any army to view their foes as less than human, but what was unusual was that as far as the men of Caesar's army were concerned, that feeling had been proven to be a truth by the actions of their foes themselves. Not surprisingly, this didn't bode well for any Wa the Romans came across, no matter their station in life. Civilian or soldier was no longer a distinction at all, even if it had been a faint one before. Marching through the night, not even Caesar knew what destruction he was bringing with him.

Work on the fortifications at the pass was completed to the royal commander's satisfaction about a third of a Roman watch before dawn. Only then did he allow the men to rest, knowing they would need every bit of their strength for what was about to happen. As they did so, he also found a quiet spot to sit, away from the demands and concerns of command to allow his mind to clear and prepare itself for the coming task. He was confident that he had baited the trap, and that belief extended to what would happen when the trap sprang shut. His instructions were explicit: not until the grubworm general was fully in the middle of the trap would the command be given to open fire. The initial volley from every single archer was to be aimed at the grubworm general which is why he had them concentrated along one section of the entire trap. To further ensure there would be no escape, at each end of the trap a deadfall had been created of as many logs and rocks that could be held safely by a barrier of smaller logs, rigged so that when a pair of men yanked on a rope, the debris would tumble down the steep slope to cover the road in both directions. The interval between the two deadfalls certainly wasn't wide enough to trap the grubworm's entire army, but that wasn't his goal. Very similarly to Caesar, the royal commander's respect for the grubworm commanding this army had only grown with every message, starting with the failed attempt to repulse the barbarians when they landed on the island weeks before. As distasteful as he found it to be in the presence of the cowards that fled the most recent battle, he had forced himself to do so and had plied them with questions. From them he gleaned even more information that strengthened his suspicion that, as pale and foreign as these grubworms were, the one commanding them was of a rare quality. Therefore, his conclusion was straightforward: their best and only chance of stopping the barbarian army was to cut off the head of the serpent. From what his scouts had told him about how the barbarians marched, he had tried to estimate the width between the deadfalls to be enough to trap perhaps a third part of the grubworm army. But once the trap was sprung, not only would he remove the enemy commander, he would also block the pass from being used, and the only option left to the grubworms would be to turn about and descend the pass. And he didn't intend on them doing it unmolested; however many men he had left would be harrying the grubworms all the way back toward the lake. Even if his force wasn't strong enough to finish them off, the least he would do would be to create enough turmoil that, as the barbarians reorganized, the lords of the north would arrive and then finish them off. Normally not prone to such daydreams, the commander allowed himself to think of the kinds of accolades and rewards that would come his way for saving the emperor from the ignominy of being forced to flee, a small smile on his lips as he savored the idea. All in all, it was a good plan. As long as his prey did what he expected them to do.

With the ridge bypassed, the scouts had turned north and now they returned to find Caesar. The darkness made it extremely difficult, but the Parthian Decurion managed to trot his horse down the length of the column, until he could just make out in the gloom ahead a series of darker shapes that were different from those formed by the marching men. Understanding that these different shapes, being higher off the ground as they were, had to be mounted men, the Parthian nudged his horse in that direction and was rewarded by the guttural sound of one of Caesar's German bodyguards who rode out to meet him. Giving the watchword, he was escorted back to Caesar, who greeted him with more cordiality than the day before now that the Decurion had redeemed himself.

"Caesar, we've found something that I think you would be interested in," the Decurion said after rendering his salute. "Just a few miles ahead there's another group of low hills. They're a little to the west of this big line, and in between there's a valley."

"And? Why are you telling me about this?"

The Decurion didn't need a torch or any other source of light to detect Caesar's impatience, so he answered hurriedly, "It's just that the lead element of the army should reach that spot in another third of a watch. By my estimate there's about two parts of a watch left before dawn. If the entire army can reach that spot, we'll be shielded from view by anyone on the western side of those hills." Trying to give his commander a visual picture, he added, "This valley is essentially like the space between an upside down 'V'."

"The problem with that is where the two lines of the 'V' intersect, we would be faced with hills," Caesar replied, but before he could admonish the Parthian, the other man interrupted, which would have irritated Caesar enormously except for what the man said.

"That's just it, sir. We found a notch where this smaller hill and the ridge we just went around meet. It's less than a mile, but if we're on this side of it, we're blocked from view. I can't tell much in the dark, but what I can tell you is that coming out of that notch I can see far out into the valley. In fact, I can see the capital. It looks like there's a great deal of work going on from the number of torches I counted, but it's no more than two miles from the end of the notch and whatever it is they're working on through the night."

"Probably their defenses," Caesar mused. "So either they weren't preparing a trap, or their commander is trying to make sure both possible avenues of approach are covered. But, if what you tell me is correct, and we can get the army into this small valley before dawn, we'll have disappeared from their sight. And then in the morning, we can at least go to this spot you're talking about and see what we're facing."

Temporarily forgetting that he couldn't be seen, Caesar pointed back over the Decurion's shoulder, but then he spoke.

"Very well. Go back to the front of the column, tell the 14th what you found and guide them to a spot where they will be out of sight. If the distance to the capital is as short as you say, we should be able to prepare a very nasty surprise for these savages and end this once and for all."

Pullus had given up trying to sleep, and the constant swaying of his hammock caused by the wagon's passage over the uneven ground had threatened to send the meal he had eaten back up. The

Han physician, still in his now-accustomed spot on the bench the opposite side of Diocles, had offered Pullus a concoction that Pullus knew from experience would enable him to sleep. However, he always felt wooly-headed and his tongue was thick the next day, and his instincts told him that this next day would see something momentous happening, and he had no intentions of missing it. In fact, he had a plan of his own, a very ambitious one, but also one he knew he couldn't divulge to anyone; not Scribonius, not Diocles, and certainly not to the Han physician. Speaking of Diocles, he was curled up on the floor of the wagon, sleeping just below his master whose hammock was a couple of feet above him. Pullus envied the little Greek's ability to snatch sleep whenever there was a chance and under any circumstances, but he didn't begrudge him. He understood how vigilant his servant had been and would continue to be, fussing over Pullus like a mother hen, seeing to his every need, and for that Pullus was thankful, even if he did find it a bit irritating. So, while he was in the mood to chat, he occupied himself instead with all that he had seen in this campaign, the toughest one he had ever been on in a career that was almost as legendary as that of his general. The closest he had come to dying before this had been more than 11 years before at Munda, and he had never seen a foe in all his years under the standard that so equally matched his beloved Legions, even if their methods were decidedly different. The major difference that he could see was that where the Legions had the discipline and training to fight as one unit, from which the individual parts were almost indistinguishable, these barbarians were no less disciplined and trained. The difference was in the manner in which they were trained, for Pullus had never encountered such ferocity in any other foe that he had faced. He had no idea how this level of savage skill could be trained into a warrior, but the other explanation was that this race was unlike any other he had encountered. And thanks to Caesar, Titus Pullus had met more varieties of men, in all shapes, sizes, and colors, than almost any other man alive. It was this experience that led him to reject out of hand the second alternative; Pullus simply didn't believe that there was such a race of men. No, he concluded, it must be learned, and this was what he was thinking about as he finally fell asleep.

Dawn came to the Island of Wa, as it always did, the sun rising from the east, although it was partly obscured by a layer of clouds. In the pass, the men of the royal guard had been roused, and their commander was now walking among them, making sure all was ready. The archers, the most important part of his force for the first phase of his plan, had already begun arranging their supply of arrows by sticking them point first into the ground, immediately behind each man. There were also several quivers, stuffed with missiles, the commander ordering the entire supply to be brought to the pass, minus what would be needed by the archers left in the capital. He envisioned nothing less than a rain of arrows, counting on the speed and accuracy of his archers to keep the grubworms caught in the trap pinned down and unable to squirm away. But that wasn't all; once the barbarian general and the men caught in the deadfall were eliminated, the commander was counting on the confusion and the chaos caused by the grubworms who were outside the deadfall and who turned about trying to escape to give his archers even more targets. Although he didn't hold out much hope that he could singlehandedly defeat these grubworms before the lords of the north arrived. But if he could damage them even more than he would by the removal of their general, he would do so.

Despite the enormous temptation, the commander had refrained from sending out scouts to ride in the direction of the lake, in order to watch the grubworms. Nothing could happen now to alert the barbarians that this trap was waiting for them, and as much as he trusted his scouts and their ability to stay undetected, he couldn't take the risk. That's why he sat there, growing steadily impatient and more concerned when there was no sign of any enemy activity. No sounds of movement down the road in the direction of the lake that would indicate a large number of men approaching; no sight of the mounted scouts of the grubworms making sure the way was clear. He wasn't worried about the latter; his men were all carefully concealed under layers of dead leaves and brush, and he had promised that the slightest movement, on either side of the road, would bring execution of not just the transgressing warrior, but his entire family. Shortly after dawn, he and two of his sub-commanders had walked along the track, searching for signs that might give their presence away, but even when he had walked a short distance off the roadbed and up the slope, he had been unable to detect any sign of his own men. No, he wasn't worried by the presence of the scouts, but he was worried about their absence, and it was growing with every passing moment. All around him birds were singing and small animals were going about their business in the underbrush, further proof that he and his men were well hidden, but the peace of the scene was in direct contrast to the growing turmoil within him. Where were they?

They had just managed it, the last of the wagons rumbling up to the spot the Decurion had chosen, a perfect spot to keep the army hidden away, despite the fact that he had done it in the dark. Caesar took notice of this and decided that in the last two days the Decurion had more than redeemed himself. No camp had been made; this wasn't going to be a spot they stayed in long. Only the wagons, the slaves, and all the men in supporting roles would be staying here, along with a guard, as the rest of the army traveled the mile through the notch, climbing the low hill that screened Caesar's army from detection. Speaking of the low hill, even before the sun rose, Caesar and his staff, including the Primi Pili, had made their way to a spot where they could just see down into the valley, knowing from long experience to work their way up slowly, so that from the other side of the hill only their heads would be visible. All that would be needed were the eyes, and the presence of the torches still blazing, as the Wa continued to work frantically through the night on a substantial ditch and earthen wall. In fact, the torches served to help Caesar and his staff, because they provided an almost perfect outline that gave the Romans the dimensions of the fortifications. The sight prompted one of the staff to let out a low whistle.

"I'll have to give it to them," Pollio broke the silence. "That's a pretty good-sized position. Can anyone see how high the wall is?"

"Not yet, it's still too dark," Caesar replied, but like Pollio, he too was impressed, if not at the strength, then at the size of the enclosed space. "But it looks like the walls are perhaps a mile wide and just a bit more than that long."

"That would take half the army to defend those," Aulus Flaminius made no attempt to hide his concern. "Does that mean they still have 10,000 men left to do the same?"

Flaminius wasn't the only one who was thinking this, he was just the first to voice it. In fact, the moment Caesar and his officers saw the dimensions, every one of them did the mental mathematics that yielded the same number, prompting the same question in each of their minds. It was true that none of the scouts had reported any sign that would indicate the presence of that large a group of the enemy, but it wouldn't have been the first time something like this had happened. Not lost on any of them was the rude surprise they had all received just days before, when about that many barbarian warriors had managed to hide themselves away in one of their camps before launching the surprise second attack on the northern camp.

"I suppose we'll find out shortly," was Caesar's reply, but not even he could fully suppress the concern from his voice.

The rest of the time, before the sun came up from behind them, peeking over the ridge to their right rear, was spent in total silence, each man lost in his own thoughts. However, not lost on any of them was that from the direction they would be attacking, they would have not only the element of surprise, but their enemy would also be forced to stare into the sun. More than once, Caesar had used this to great advantage and if they were lucky, or favored by the gods, they would actually be able to close part of what was now clearly no more than the two miles to the nearest part of the fortifications, before being spotted. Finally, the first rays shot down over the ridge, and any question about this venture receiving the favor of the gods was removed from the minds of the assembled Romans. The immediate comparison that came to more than one mind was that it was as if the light from the great lighthouse at Alexandria had suddenly been transported to the top of the ridge, because of the way the long wall of the western side of the new fortifications was illuminated. Going from the gloom to bright sunshine so quickly was a bit disorienting, but immediately afterward every pair of eyes, Caesar's included, had examined the wall and far corner of the fortification.

"Wall, ditch, sharpened stakes in the ditch, all the expected defenses," Caesar remarked casually. "And it doesn't look as if the ground in front of the ditch has been prepared in any way. Given the little time they've had, I seriously doubt they could have covered up any traps without leaving some kind of trace. It's hard to tell the height of the wall without any men around to provide a scale, but my guess is that the earthen part is no more than ten feet tall. And while our palisade stakes are five feet long, with one foot buried in the dirt, these people are somewhat smaller than we are, so my guess would be the palisade is about three feet or perhaps three and a half feet high. If my dimensions of the height of the wall are correct, then it looks like the wall and the rampart are perhaps ten feet wide. Which would mean," Caesar was silent for a moment as he did the calculations, once again amazing the men around him at his ability to perform such difficult mathematic calculations in his head, "that the ditch, which is clearly wider than the wall is high, is relatively shallow, let's say about six feet deep. So," he smiled thinly, amused at the looks on the faces of his staff as he wondered why they continued to be surprised at what he considered little more than a trick one played at parties to amuse the guests, "we need 15 foot ladders. I believe we have a sufficient supply of 20 foot poles?"

This question was directed to his chief engineer, Gaius Volusenus, who was also his chief exploring officer, and next to Ventidius and Caesar himself one of the oldest men on the campaign. It had been Volusenus who had sailed to Britannia and surveyed the sites that Caesar and the army had used for both landings, and had been the co-creator of the bridge over the Rhine river that was considered a marvel of the age by the men with knowledge of such things. Over the last ten years, he had continually perfected his craft and office of *praefectus fabrorum*, including the practice of harvesting saplings of a certain size and length and keeping a supply of them for use in building ladders, scaffolds and all manner of things. Ever since they had reached the eastern lands of the Pandya, and all across the vast expanse of Asia and into the Han kingdom, they had used poles from the bamboo tree, which had proven to be the best material for a number of purposes that either Volusenus or Caesar had come across. It was light but incredibly strong, and supple enough that it could bear an enormous strain by bending, but not breaking. Now there were two wagons devoted to nothing but carrying supplies of bamboo poles, in two lengths, 20 and 30 feet, and these would supply as many ladders as needed.

"We have more than enough, Caesar," Volusenus replied, his speech marred by the missing front teeth, both top and bottom, courtesy of a Pandyan club across the face, which had left him with a horribly scarred lip.

Despite the impediment, Caesar and the other officers, as well as the men who were assigned to Volusenus when he had projects that required more than brute strength and a shovel, had learned to understand him.

"Then get started on them now. I expect them to be ready in no less than a third of a watch."

Volusenus saluted and immediately turned his horse, heading back to the wagons at a canter, while the rest of the officers waited for orders. The sun had by this point fully illuminated almost the entire fortification, and now Caesar could see that the southern wall had been erected roughly in the middle of what was the southernmost neighborhood of the city. While the other villages and towns were laid out in the same neat, symmetrical pattern that was strikingly similar to that of the city of Alexandria, this was clearly the largest population center that Caesar and his army had come across. The houses along the axis of the southern wall had been torn down, and for the first time Caesar saw an advantage in the light and flimsy construction techniques that were a feature of this land. It was true he had been warned by the Han that this was a terrible and violent land, where the ground shook and tore itself apart, but since nothing like this had happened since they had landed, it was hard for Caesar to see the advantage. Although this wasn't an earthquake, he could see that their building methods definitely allowed the barbarians to construct a wall and ditch of these dimensions very rapidly, without having to worry about excessive debris. Even as this thought ran through his mind, his eye continued in a westward direction, along the southern wall, more or less following the sun's arc, as it illuminated more of the wall. Suddenly, he stiffened in his saddle, his attention caught by something that at first he thought was some sort of illusion, a trick of his eyes that was just another part of growing old. Only after squinting, then, using a trick he had learned of pulling the skin at the corner of his eye that seemed to give him a moment of the visual acuity of his youth, did he realize that what he was seeing was real.

Immediately turning to the others, he snapped, "Figulus! Flaminius! Get your men up and ready to march, now! I want them moving by the time I get back there! Now go!"

The Primi Pili of the 14th and 30th Legion both looked at each other in alarm, but it was Flaminius who spoke for both of them.

"Now, Caesar? What about the ladders? Shouldn't we wait until they're ready?"

Glancing down from his horse, Caesar suddenly realized that because of his vantage point, he was able to see something the standing Primi Pili couldn't, because of their lower elevation. Holding a hand down, it took a moment for Flaminius to realize what Caesar was doing, then grasping the older man's hand, he put a foot against the side of Caesar's horse as Caesar levered him up. The horse shifted in protest against the boot in his side, but Caesar was already pointing.

"See there? At the eastern end? They haven't finished the wall! You won't need ladders, but only if we move now!"

Without waiting for an answer, Caesar let go of Flaminius' hand and dropped the Primus Pilus to the ground, then patted the horse gently on the neck to soothe him. He didn't need to say anything more, because both Flaminius and Figulus were racing away to rouse their Legions. As they did so, Caesar continued watching, as the entire area became bathed in sunlight, and his heart soared at the sight.

"Not only have they not finished, there's not anyone to defend the walls!"

From his vantage point—higher up than down in the valley that held the capital, dawn came earlier for the waiting Wa commander, but for the first time he was beginning to be beset by true doubt. Could it possibly be that the grubworms were such late risers? Or had something gone wrong at the ford that was delaying them? Thinking this was the most likely alternative, he finally forced himself to break from his own hiding spot to move up and around the shoulder of the hill where their ambush was set, moving away from the road to the spot where his mounted scouts were waiting in a small clearing. Seeing their commander approach, the dozen warriors jumped to their feet, still holding onto the reins of their respective ponies.

Pointing to two men, he barked a summons, and they moved quickly to face him, bringing their ponies with them.

"I have a task for you," he said brusquely, "but not under any circumstances can you betray our position. If you do, the same orders that I gave to the ambushing force apply; not only will you be executed, but your families as well. Is that understood?"

Knowing there was only one answer to give, both men bowed, the customary way the Wa showed acceptance of orders, similar to the Roman salute.

"Travel partway down the road towards the lake, but before you get within view, go into the trees on the hillside. I need you to tell me what the grubworms are doing, so move as quickly as you can without being observed. Now go," he finished, and neither man hesitated, mounting their ponies with practiced ease, then with a kick to their ribs, moved the mounts past the commander back towards the road.

Walking back, the commander moved as silently as he could, intent on discovering any man who had become impatient, eager to take out his frustration and anger on someone, but he was slightly disappointed to see that no man was moving a muscle. He knew how much it must itch, lying there covered with leaves, branches and debris, but grudgingly he acknowledged that his men were showing excellent discipline. Contemplating returning to his own hiding place, he decided against it, hoping that the scouts would be returning very shortly with news that the barbarians had simply been delayed by the ford and were even now ascending the road to the pass. Instead, he sat on a rock a short distance from the road, looking down in the direction of the lake, waiting. Time passed, and with each moment his alarm increased when there was no sign of his scouts.

He was about to take matters into his own hands and commandeer a pony to go down the road, when his eye caught movement. Perhaps a half mile down a relatively straight section, the road curved out of sight, which was one of the reasons he had chosen this spot, and it was around this bend that he saw his scouts coming at a full gallop. The speed of their advance could only mean one thing, as far as the commander was concerned: the grubworms were not that far behind! Jumping to his feet, he went down onto the road as they came pounding up, pulling to a halt in a spray of dirt that splattered all over the commander's boots, something for which they would normally be punished. But these weren't normal times, and the truth was, he didn't even notice, his mind focused on only one thing.

"Well?" He demanded. "How far behind you are they?"

Before they answered the two men exchanged a glance, snapping the commander's already frayed patience.

"I don't care who it is that tells me! How far behind you are they?" he repeated.

If he had been in a different frame of mind, perhaps the commander would have been given at least a slight warning at the sight of one of the scouts swallowing hard before he spoke.

"They're not coming sir, they...."

Before he could finish, the commander lashed out, his fist catching the unfortunate messenger on the chin, whereupon he dropped to the ground, unconscious before he hit it. The second man, now petrified, held his hands up in a pleading gesture.

"No sir! You don't understand! They're not coming, because they're not there!"

The commander, who had in fact drawn his fist back, stood there for an instant, blinking in surprise.

"What do you mean, they're not there?" he asked slowly, as if trying to make sense of a deep puzzle.

"Their camp is deserted sir! They left the ditch and walls, but everything else is gone!"

"Well, where did they go?"

Now the second scout was confused and unsure of how to respond. How was he supposed to know?

"I can't be sure, sir," he answered, somehow understanding that saying he didn't know could end up being the cause for suffering a fate similar to his comrade, who was still lying at his feet unconscious. Or worse. "We only went to the point where we could see clearly that they were gone and weren't coming this direction. But I saw what looks like a trail that is taking them south along the shore of the lake."

To the south? the commander wondered. Why would they want to go to the south, when the shortest way to the capital lay before them, so invitingly open and undefended? That's when the first tendril of a doubt that would only grow into the certainty that the grubworm commander had outsmarted him began. Shaking his head, as if it would dislodge the qualms that were blossoming forth with every beat of his heart, threatening to overwhelm him, he tried to think through what was the next right move.

Finally, without saying anything he walked over and picked up the reins of the pony belonging to the downed scout. Leaping onto the horse, he gestured with his head to summon the other man to accompany him and immediately went to the gallop down the road. This was something he had to see for himself, yet one more delay and mistake on this worst of days to make such errors.

It took less than a sixth part of a watch for both the 14th and 30th Legions to traverse the low hill that blocked their view of the capital and to descend into the valley of the capital. Although the sun was now up above the ridge, the Roman army was still protected by shadows, and anyone looking in their direction from the walls of the fortifications around the capital would have had a hard time seeing the movement of men as they rapidly descended the hill to get into position. Caesar was putting them in a front, two Legions wide, much narrower than his normal practice of at least three wings, each wing composed of at least one Legion. The reason behind this was twofold: the relatively narrow width of the unfinished fortifications would be covered by both Legions, even on their standard four Cohort front, with three Centuries for each Cohort supported by a Century behind, with room to spare. Also, Caesar was more than aware of the time factor, and while he could see that there were only laborers present at that moment, a lot of them at that, he couldn't take the chance that there were at that moment defenders hurrying to plug the gaping hole in what was otherwise an unbroken line of fortifications. It was true that even that part of the fortifications that were completed wouldn't have presented much of a challenge for Caesar's veterans, but the section of perhaps a quarter mile wide that had only a partially dug ditch, hence a very low wall, was a gift from the gods that couldn't be ignored. Caesar, who had stayed at his current position higher up the hill, supposed that the laborers, who looked to number perhaps 3,000, could have been warriors, in the same manner as his army who built the fortifications and camps that protected them, but he didn't think so. In fact, he was as close to sure that this wasn't the case as it was possible, without its being confirmed as fact by his eyes. Almost with every mile east they had traveled, Caesar had seen a deeper and deeper division between classes, to the point where, by the time they reached the Han empire, it would have been unthinkable for a member of the warrior class to dirty his hands. This didn't go unnoticed by Caesar; it was something he had observed, and like with so many other things over a career that was unparalleled in the annals of history, was stored away to be dissected and studied, and from which every advantage would be taken. His treaty with the Han empire had been one of convenience; he knew that as formidable as his army was, it couldn't have overcome the Han's vast resources. Conversely, the Han emperor had recognized that with all the other troubles he was facing, he couldn't afford to take on these pale barbarians. Hence, the treaty. But both men had plans and designs that centered on this remote island that on one side only a very few knew about, and on the other, only a single man knew.

Everything rested on what happened now, for both leaders, but at the moment this wasn't one of the foremost thoughts in Caesar's prodigious mind. Instead, it was solely absorbed in the task at hand, and as he continued his observation of the scene before him, he was cautiously pleased to see that even with all the activity at the base of the hill in front of him, he couldn't see any sign of alarm on the part of the Wa. As he sat there, the rest of the army came moving up to take their positions just behind the leading Legions. While he was sure that they wouldn't be needed for what was to come, he wanted them available in the event that he was wrong. There was another reason for wanting the rest of the army present. Jerking him from his reverie, that reason announced itself with a great clattering of noise, and he turned to see a wagon, just one, lumbering up the hill from behind him. As far as Caesar was concerned, Pullus was still an important part of this army, and while it was mostly for the men of the army, part of his reason was that of all the men who marched for him, Titus Pullus deserved to see the fall of the capital more than any other single man. Watching the wagon rattle past him, only then did Caesar nudge his horse to follow it.

Chapter 11

"Hand me that."

At first Diocles wasn't sure he heard his master correctly, particularly since what Titus Pullus was pointing to was the padded undershirt that was always the first article put on before the rest of his armor.

"What for?" Diocles asked, his face screwed up in suspicion.

"Just hand it to me," Pullus demanded, fixing his stare on the diminutive Greek.

Diocles, however, was accustomed to his master's bluster, and returned the stare.

"What for?" he repeated.

"Because I need it," Pullus snapped, still holding his arm out, trying to ignore the beads of sweat that were suddenly appearing on his forehead, just from that simple effort.

For several heartbeats they were at an impasse, the slave and master glaring at each other, before Diocles, understanding that he would never overcome his master's will, heaved a sigh.

"Fine," he snapped. "But I'm not going to be the one to clean your body for the pyre."

Despite his discomfort and the tension, Pullus grinned at his slave, knowing that Diocles was being obstinate from concern and no other motive.

"Then I guess I'll have to get incinerated dirty," Pullus joked. "Although personally I never saw the need to wash up someone who's about to get burned to ash."

"You blaspheme too much," Diocles grumbled, but did so as he not only handed his master the undershirt but also rose from his spot to help Pullus.

The Han physician, who had been unable to follow the conversation, but clearly understood that some sort of disagreement was taking place, rose in alarm at the sign of Diocles' capitulation. Pointing at the proffered undershirt and the sight of Pullus struggling out of the hammock, he began speaking in a rapid-fire monologue in his tongue that, while neither of the other two men understood the words, certainly conveyed his intent.

"I don't think he's happy," Diocles said, trying to keep a straight face at the sight of the wizened old Han showing more animation in this moment than he had in all the time they had been together.

"There's a lot of that going around," Pullus grunted, but he didn't stop, until he was sitting upright on the edge of the hammock, his feet on the floor.

Sweat was now openly streaming down his face, but this was just the beginning of his travail, as with an effort of which only Pullus knew the cost, he was forced to raise his arms, so that Diocles could put on the padded undershirt. The Han, although he made no move to interfere, continued his harangue, which didn't help Pullus' frame of mind. Neither did Pullus stop his preparations, trying to brace himself for the jolting of the wagon, which was continuing to bounce along the rutted path in the wake of the Legions moving into position. As Diocles lifted, not without effort, the chain mail shirt that had been made to accommodate his master's huge chest, the rent in it repaired at Pullus' instructions, the wagon tilted downward, sign that they were descending down onto the plain. A messenger from Caesar had come shortly before dawn telling Pullus what to expect, that his wagon would be coming with the Legions on their attack to be displayed just behind the rear ranks as a symbol to the men that Titus Pullus was still with them, even if it was in spirit. What Caesar didn't realize was that this was the opportunity for which Pullus had been waiting to put his own plan into effect. As committed to this idea as he was, Pullus nevertheless experienced serious misgivings as, with tightly clenched teeth, he kept his arms above him as Diocles grunted with the effort of lifting the mail shirt over his head, before dropping it onto Pullus' shoulders. As prepared as Pullus thought he was for what was something he had done more times than he could count, the impact of the heavy mail onto his body forced a groan from between his teeth, and a fresh bout of perspiration burst forth. Now Diocles stopped, able to look his master and friend in the eyes as Pullus stayed seated on the hammock.

"Master," Diocles said softly, "Titus, you don't have to do this."

As many times as Pullus had donned his armor, in direct contrast, he could count on one hand, and have fingers left over, the number of times Diocles had used his *praenomen*, and this more than anything gave Pullus pause. For a moment he tried to meet Diocles' gaze, but found to his shame that he couldn't maintain it.

Dropping his eyes, he murmured quietly to Diocles, "I do have to do this, my friend. I have to do it for me, not for any other reason."

"Why?" Diocles burst out, his patience finally worn through. "To prove what? You've nothing left to prove, Titus! There's not a man who doubts your courage! Not Caesar! Not Scribonius! Certainly not any ranker! So what in Hades do you have left to prove, to anyone?"

"Because I'm afraid that if I don't do it now, I'll be too afraid to, once I'm healed and don't have an excuse!" Titus snapped, some of the volume for which he was famous returning and freezing both Diocles and the Han in their spots.

His words hung in the air for several moments, as the Han stood looking from Diocles to Pullus, trying to understand what was taking place and knowing it was important. The Greek's shoulders slumped, and he dropped his head, so that his face wasn't visible to either of the other two, while Pullus continued to glare at his slave, the sudden rush of blood to his face at this visceral admission of vulnerability causing the sweat on his face to gleam like tiny, pink gems.

"Master," Diocles' voice was now shaking with the emotion he was feeling, a combination of sadness, apprehension, and sympathy for the man whom he had devoted most of his adult life to serving. "I wish I had the words to convince you that, even if that were true, that if you decided that that battle was your last and that you'd never picked up a sword again, there would be no man that would fault you, especially Caesar. You saved not just the 10th, but probably the entire army that day, when you killed their general, and I'd argue that there would be no better last battle than that one. You don't owe anyone anything more than you've given."

Pullus didn't respond for several moments, and after the span of several heartbeats Diocles began to dare that perhaps he had finally summoned the right combination of words that would sway his master and friend. That hope was dashed almost as quickly as it had blossomed.

"I owe it to myself, Diocles. It would be hard to live with the shame, if my nerve fails me, but it would be impossible to live with never knowing. I know you think I have no fear, my friend. I know the men think so too, but let me let you in on a secret."

Despite himself, Diocles found himself leaning forward in anticipation, because in fact it had always been a mystery to him how his master, and his master's friends like Scribonius and Balbus, could throw themselves into battle time and time again without hesitation, even after seeing it take them one at a time, until only Scribonius and his master were left.

"I'm afraid, just like everyone, before a battle. And I'll tell you that it's gotten worse, instead of better, as I get older. I suppose it's because I've seen so much of battle that I know how much luck plays a part in it all. You can do everything right, but if someone who's on your weak side falls, or an enemy gets behind you, you're going to die. It's that simple. So every battle I fight I realize that everyone's luck runs out sometime, and I've been blessed by the gods more than anyone, except for Caesar. It just makes sense that every time I stand ready to fight, especially on this cursed island, it's likely my last time. And this last fight I was never surer of it than in any other battle I've fought. So I am afraid, Diocles, very, very afraid. But the way I get through it, and the way I plan on getting through it today is by asking myself a question. Do I control my fear, or does my fear control me? And I refuse to bow my head to anyone or anything, unless I choose to do so, no matter what it is. *That* is how I appear to be without fear, by acknowledging that it's there, but never letting it be the master of my soul." Gesturing to Diocles to help him stand erect, made difficult not just by his weakness, but also the pitching of the wagon, he finished, "And the answer to that question I ask myself has never been more important than it is today. If I can't control my fear today, then I might as well end my days here and now and be done with it."

And with that, there was nothing left to be said, and Diocles finished helping his master face the most important test of his life, the one within.

As sturdy and hardy as the ponies of the islands of Wa were, the one being ridden mercilessly by the royal guard commander was perilously close to foundering, as he forced the last bit of energy from it in his attempt to reach the ambush site. While it had helped the pony's reserves of strength that it had been galloped downhill, it had already been taxed by doing essentially the same ride with its first rider, and its muzzle was flecked with foam and its coat was gleaming from sweat as it labored the last distance back up the road to the pass. Every time the beast flagged, the commander savagely whipped its flanks, leaving bloody streaks that were as much marks of its rider's desperation and fury than anything else. The commander had gone farther down the road than his scouts had, close enough to the lake to confirm what the scout had told him: that the grubworms had not only disappeared, but had marched to the south, leaving nothing behind except a ditch and earthen wall. Going even farther to a spot where he could see as far as possible to the south, there was no sign of any marching army, not even a lingering cloud of dust, telling him that these accursed barbarians had stolen a march in the night. Wasting no more time than necessary, he had yanked his mount about to hurry back to his waiting men. Now he was just reaching the spot where the lower deadfall was located, when his mount stumbled, recovered itself to take a couple of strides more before stumbling again, this time crashing to the ground and sending its rider flying headlong. Because of the pitch of the road, the commander slammed into the ground so quickly that he didn't have time to brace himself, leading with his head and smashing into the packed dirt with tremendous force. Only his helmet saved him from instant death, but it didn't save him from being knocked unconscious. Trailing behind him, the scout that had accompanied him watched the catastrophe from the back of his mount, which was only slightly better off than the commander's pony, now-writhing and trying to struggle back to all fours. Pulling up to the prone man, he quickly dismounted and hurried to his side, kneeling down and checking for signs of life. When he determined that the commander lived, the relief he felt warred with other emotions: worry that he would somehow be blamed for the commander's mishap, but more than anything, confusion about what he should do. For, unlike their Roman counterparts, initiative and thinking for oneself weren't traits valued by the Wa, theirs a rigidly hierarchical society. Compounding this was the fact that the commander hadn't deigned to inform the lowly scout accompanying him what he intended to do, now that he had confirmed that there was no longer an army marching up this road to fall into an ambush. Consequently, the scout merely squatted by the side of the commander, doing what he could to revive the man, while the warriors concealed on both sides of the road, mindful of the dire warning the commander had issued about moving from their spot, only watched, increasing the delay of any type of Wa response to this new development.

There were no sounds of the *cornu* during the Roman advance, again by Caesar's order, as the avenging army marched toward the fortifications. From where the leading ranks had formed up to the outskirts of the city, where perhaps four blocks of houses remained before reaching the cleared area where the new wall was located, was barely a mile. The 14th and 30th—the 14th on the right and 30th to the left—had closed about half that distance, before they emerged from the shadows cast by the ridge behind them. It wasn't more than the span of a hundred heartbeats after that, when one of the laborers turned and saw what to him appeared to be some sort of apparition summoned by the demons of his world. Raising a shaking hand, he rubbed his eyes, but the vision was still there, looking to him at first like some multi-legged beast that glittered with glints of silvery gray, like the fish from the lake. Only then did he raise the alarm, but what came out was an incoherent cry that only served to stop the other laborers from their work to look at him curiously. The palace official, one of the eunuchs, assigned to this part of the wall was already in a sour mood, because he had been stuck with the onerous task of mingling with these peasants. His bad mood was exacerbated by the sharp words exchanged with the official whom the royal commander had put in charge shortly before dawn, when he had been informed that the responsibility for failure to complete this part of the fortification by the time the royal commander returned would be on his shoulders. Striding over to where the peasant was standing, his jaw hanging open and his arm outstretched to the south, he was more than ready to take out his frustrations on someone, and this peasant would fit the bill nicely. Picking up a stick lying in a pile of debris, he raised it in preparation to strike this peasant, who seemed to have been struck dumb and who stood like a statue. Of course, it was natural that his eye travel in the direction in which the man was pointing, and it took a few heartbeats for his eye to make sense of what he was seeing. In fact, his first thought was almost identical to that of the peasant, though he had no way of knowing, but he took a couple of halting steps more, before he came to a stop next to the peasant, the hand holding the stick still hovering in the air, waiting to strike. They stood side by side for another moment, both of their mouths open, and then in an instant where class distinctions meant nothing, they exchanged the same, shocked glance. But the palace eunuch, not only more educated but also more intelligent than the peasant, was the first to break the spell, as he pivoted about and went into a full sprint, heading for the unfinished wall. Showing admirable athleticism, he leapt across the point where the ditch was not fully excavated, landing on the other side without breaking stride. Only when he was on the other side did he break the silence.

"Sound the alarm! Sound the alarm! We are under attack from the south! Summon the Chosen Ones and the archers to the southeastern wall immediately!"

"Well, they know we're here," Aulus Flaminius said, watching the sudden scramble of the peasants that were now directly in their path a little more than a mile away.

That was all the attention he could pay to this development, because being on the left of the two-Legion formation meant that with the angle of attack, his Legion would reach the remaining buildings of the southern outskirts of the capital first. As flimsily constructed as these buildings were, they were still substantial enough that they could not only hide waiting warriors, they also couldn't just be knocked down by the marching men. That meant that he had to deploy his Legion into the formation they had perfected for urban combat, which broke down the normally solid line of Centuries and Cohorts into the smaller component parts, starting with the Centuries. Normally, a Century was assigned each block, but that, of course, depended on the number of dwellings or structures in each one. Flaminius saw that these blocks, as neatly arranged as they were, would require at most five sections a block, which also enabled him to further extend his coverage along the same axis as the wall running east-west, without calling the second line to move out to the west. But that took time and effort, so he called a halt, his *cornu* player sounding the order, bringing the perfectly aligned ranks of Roman Legionaries crashing to a halt as if they were one huge beast. Which, Flaminius thought, is exactly what they are right now. A huge, slavering beast that's about to devour this piddling capital city and any yellow-skinned savage stupid enough to have sought shelter behind these walls. Ordering the call for all first-line Centurions to attend to him, Flaminius took the time—as he waited for them to come running from their spots—to examine the rows of houses before him carefully. It didn't surprise him that he didn't see any signs of life whatsoever;

even if they didn't approach from this direction, he couldn't imagine any of the inhabitants staying in their homes with the fortifications being erected just a few blocks away. No, he was sure that they wouldn't find a living soul in those buildings, or any civilian ones at least. Nevertheless, he wasn't about to just have his men advance up the streets in direction of the wall, without checking every house first.

"We're going to use the front line Cohorts for moving through these streets here, before we get to the wall," Flaminius announced to his men, once they had assembled. "I want the second line ready to fold in behind the 14th; they're going to be the first through that gap in the wall, but I want us hot on their heels! The first line will rejoin us only after we're finished clearing the streets and houses."

This was an unusual order, but it was an unusual day, on an unusual island, and during an unusual campaign, so there weren't more than the normal mutterings about this change in what had by now become an established routine for assaulting fortifications. Seeing that there were no questions, Flaminius dismissed his Centurions, who went trotting back to their respective Centuries to pass the orders. As Primus Pilus, Flaminius was responsible not only for the entire Legion and every Cohort, he also still had to run his own Century; but, truthfully, most of the day-to-day business was handled by his Optio, and it was an accepted truth that the best new Centurions in the Centurionate were those that had been Optios of the First Century, First Cohort. Following closely behind them were Optios of all the Pili Priores, who faced the same problem as Flaminius, but on a smaller scale. This freed Flaminius to continue watching as the Legion next to him advanced, slightly envious that because of their position and angle, only perhaps two Centuries of the fourth Cohort to the left of the first line would encounter the houses that the 30th had to push through. As he did so, he saw movement out of the corner of his eye that was at odds with the normal deployment of a Legion. Turning, he saw that it was a lone wagon, rattling in between the space of the rear ranks of the 14th Legion and the Legions that had been designated by Caesar to be in the second Legion line.

"Pluto's cock," Flaminius muttered. "I bet that's Pullus' wagon."

"It is," his *cornicen*, who at moments like this always stood by his side, waiting for orders, confirmed. "I talked to a friend of mine in the *praetorium* who heard Caesar say he wanted the Primus Pilus' wagon to be visible to everyone as a sign that he's still with us, even if he can't stand in the line."

Flaminius gave a laugh, but there was a tinge of bitterness to it. Neither Pullus nor Flaminius would have described themselves as friends, but the men respected each other, and while Flaminius, like every other man who had reached the exalted status of Primus Pilus, had a sizable ego of his own, even he acknowledged that Titus Pullus was in a class by himself. If asked, Flaminius would have pointed to his counterpart's vast size and strength as being the primary ingredient that made Pullus the legend that he was, but that was more to soothe his vanity than that he truly believed this. Privately, Flaminius understood that there was much, much more to what made Titus Pullus the man he was and be the symbol to every man walking in the ranks—no matter what Legion's standard they marched under—of not only Rome's unconquerable spirit, but also of their own. As long as Titus Pullus lived, Flaminius knew that most of the men in the ranks held the belief that they would, as well. Flaminius knew that Caesar, perhaps better than any man alive—even Pullus himself—understood the importance of the symbol that Pullus was, over and above his actual role as a Primus Pilus of a Legion. That's why he wasn't particularly surprised to see the wagon bearing Pullus. However, he was completely unprepared for what happened next. The wagon slowed to a stop, and Flaminius was just about to turn his attention away from it when he saw a flurry of movement at the back, as the flaps moved outwards. Dismissing it as a fluke of the wind, Flaminius' eye was caught at the sight of someone jumping down, and squinting, Flaminius recognized by size, if by nothing else, that it was Pullus' Greek body slave.

"Probably has to take a piss," he said to himself, but a moment later another figure emerged, this one Flaminius identified as one of those Han physicians—Caesar's most favored, if he remembered right—and he recalled hearing that Caesar had dispatched this old man himself to stay at Pullus' bedside, further sign of Pullus' favor. Unknown to Flaminius, or any of the other actors on the Roman side, for that matter, what happened next was almost identical to what had taken place shortly before, when the peasant had spied the oncoming Legions. Standing open-mouthed, Flaminius watched as the two reached up to help a third man down out of the wagon. Normally such solicitousness from others would have brought the object of the help under a great deal of ribbing for being so decrepit, but Flaminius understood why they were being helpful when he saw that, wearing his armor and helmet, it was Titus Pullus himself who was the recipient of their aid.

"Juno's *cunnus*, what does he think he's doing?" Flaminius' tone was a mixture of amazement, resentment, and worry at the sight of Titus Pullus, who was clearly not content to play his part in providing a symbol for Caesar's army from the comfort of a wagon.

More than once, Titus Pullus was sure he was going to pass out, but every time the dizziness and nausea threatened to overwhelm him, he stopped in his tracks for a moment to close his eyes and allow his head to clear. It was only then that he would allow either Diocles or the Han to touch him, so, posted one on each side, they would grab him firmly by the arms to make sure he didn't shame himself by losing his balance and collapsing in a heap. Looking for any small victory he could find, Pullus was pleased to see that the effort it took for his head to clear cost less and less time, so that after a few fits and starts, he had reached the rear ranks of the third line of the 14th Legion. He had no intentions of joining the 14th in their assault on the fortifications; in fact, he was saving his energy, because directly behind the 14th, Caesar had placed the 10th, and once the 14th went through the breach, the 10th would be marching to the spot where he was standing. Knowing as he did that he had a finite amount of strength and endurance—especially when compared to his normal boundless founts of both—he was doing whatever he could to reduce the number of steps he would be taking. Whereas before his near-fatal wound he would have walked back and forth, around and through the ranks of his Legion—even as small it was—several times over already, he knew this wasn't possible. But for more than two decades now, whenever the 10th Legion had gone into battle, no matter what the circumstances, Titus Pullus had been there, standing next to the Legion *aquilifer* carrying the sacred Legion eagle, and he wasn't going to change that now. This had been his resolution when he had first been told by Diocles of the developments that had led to this moment. Now, he stood, shaking off the help of the two men beside him, since his head had cleared, silently waiting for the moment when the 14th would make their move forward and the 10th would move up to meet him. It was natural that some of the men of the last line of Cohorts of the 14th would turn about to see who was behind them; they weren't at *intente,* so they had the ability to turn and look around. But none of them were prepared for the sight that met their eyes, the presence of a legend most of them had seen only from a distance, or perhaps in passing in one camp or another over the years. It didn't take more than the space of several heartbeats for a buzzing sound to begin whipping through the rear ranks of the 14th, in turn causing the men of the second line to turn to see the cause of the commotion. Before long, there was a dull roar of talk, as men poked each other and pointed in Pullus' direction. The Centurions in charge of the Centuries in the proximity of Pullus were no less amazed at the sight, and in that moment forgot their duties of keeping their men quiet; but those of the second, then first line of the Legion only knew that suddenly the ranks were buzzing for no reason at all. Above the sound of the excited chatter came the enraged roaring orders of Centurions who, as mystified as they were about the cause, knew with a certainty that their immediate superiors would be voicing their own displeasure at this sign of lax discipline. It was only when one of them, in the brief pause as he tried to regain his breath, actually listened to what men were saying that he broke ranks himself to investigate and then discovered the cause for himself. Immediately running to where the standard of the Legion was located, he found the Primus Pilus of the 14th and informed him of the reason for the uproar. Stifling a curse, the Primus Pilus only sent the Centurion back to his spot in the formation, but stayed where he himself was, listening for the command to advance, which he hoped would be coming in the next moments. That was the only way all this excitement would die down, he concluded, even as he wondered what Pullus thought he was up to with this display. Behind him and his Legion, the thinned ranks of the 10th were even now marching to take their spot in the second row, with the 12th to their left. Caesar had no intention of letting these men fight; he was close to certain they wouldn't be needed, and if his suspicions were correct, the capital was unprotected and lay like a virgin, about to be ravaged. And he intended on rewarding his two most beleaguered and battered Legions with the opportunity that men in the ranks dreamed about:

the first pickings of what would undoubtedly be the wealthiest part of the wealthiest city on this benighted island. However, he was completely unprepared for what he was seeing, as he rode from the hill to take his place at the front of the formation. He first noticed the wagon's placement with approval, knowing that it was in the perfect spot to be seen by the men of the 10th, as they marched into their spot in the attack formation. Seeing the three figures standing slightly ahead and to the side of the wagon, it took a moment for Caesar to realize what in fact he was seeing, and, like the Primi Pili of the 14th and 30th, he let out a curse as he kicked his horse in the ribs to hurry to reach the trio.

"Pullus, what by all the Furies do you think you're doing?"

Caesar's tone was a mixture of anger and astonishment, but if Pullus was cowed, he showed no sign. It wasn't lost on Caesar, or the other two men how carefully he turned his body to stand facing Caesar, but only Pullus knew what it took to give the perfect salute he rendered to his general, his only accommodation to his condition being that he didn't slam his fist into the left side of his chest, as the regulations prescribed.

"My job, Caesar," Pullus replied, his voice calm and raised enough, so that both the men in the last rank of the 14th and his own men—who had just halted in their designated spot—could hear. "The 10th hasn't marched without me into any battle, and it's not about to start now."

Acutely aware that every eye was on this exchange, Caesar could only mentally salute the large Primus Pilus, because he understood in an instant that he had been outmaneuvered. Any chastisement of Pullus would be heard by the men of his Legion, and another of Caesar's rules that had served him well was that with senior officers, it was politic to praise them in public, but reprimand them in private. There were exceptions, of course: if the offending party was performing his duties in a way that endangered others, Caesar wouldn't hesitate to take whatever action he deemed necessary to correct the situation in the moment. This, unfortunately as far as he was concerned, was not one of those times, because the only one endangered was Pullus himself. Assessing the situation and deciding what to do about it in the space of a couple of heartbeats, Caesar responded first with a salute that resulted in a pandemonium of roaring cheers. Well, so much for the element of surprise, Caesar thought disgustedly, but he knew better than to admonish the men, particularly those of the 10th.

Only after the sound subsided a bit did Caesar speak, bending down to tell Pullus, "Congratulations Pullus. You've outmaneuvered me, but all I can say is, I hope you know what you're doing, because if you die, I'm going to have to punish you."

Knowing that all eyes were on the pair, Pullus made a titanic effort by throwing his head back and laughing, understanding that while the men couldn't hear what was said, they would take their cues visually. Only Caesar, Diocles, and the Han had any idea of the strain it put on Pullus, a fresh burst of perspiration beading on his forehead, even as he showed his appreciation of Caesar's wit. In other words, both men were actors playing out a scene that the men of the 10th had seen before so many battles now, the bantering between two fighting men about to face combat, and the sight of this elicited another cheer.

Using the din to cover their conversation, Caesar asked, "How far do you plan on taking this, Pullus? If there's fighting are you going to draw your sword? Are you even capable of running your Century, let alone your Cohort and your Legion?"

"Caesar, I'm perfectly capable of directing this Legion," Pullus' tone was still calm, but Caesar knew Pullus well enough to detect the undercurrent of indignant anger that was just below the surface of his words. Then he surprised Caesar by finishing, "And I can draw my sword perfectly well. Using it?"

Pullus answered his own question with a wry grin and a shrug of one shoulder, and now it was Caesar's turn to laugh. Knowing he was outflanked, the older man shook his head before he reined his horse about, calling over his shoulder, as he trotted away to the front of the formation, "I hope I see you after this is over!"

"So do I," Pullus muttered under his breath.

With Caesar gone, Pullus braced himself then performed a parade-ground about-face, looking at the front ranks of the 10th Legion. The moment he did so, the muted chatter of the men immediately stilled, as they waited for what was as much of a ritual as the banter between Caesar and Pullus: the inspection by the Primus Pilus, normally the last thing he did before they went into battle. With a monumental effort of will, Pullus did his best to keep his military bearing as he walked toward where the Third Century, First Cohort stood waiting. This was a slight variation in the routine; normally Pullus would have begun his inspection with the Third Century, Fourth Cohort, the last of the 10th Legion at the far left of the formation. But even as shrunken as the Legion was, he didn't want to take the risk of being unable to finish the ritual, knowing how important such superstitions were to soldiers. He was no less susceptible than any of the men in the ranks; like every other man, he had his own pre-battle ritual, performed in the same order, with the same tasks since his first battle in Hispania some 27 years before. As it was, he was acutely aware that he had been unable to go through this ritual the night and morning before this day, but only he knew how nervous it made him. Otherwise, his face wore the same hard expression of tough professionalism as always, even if his skin did carry a slight glaze from sweat that was uncalled for by the temperature of this morning. Stopping before the first man, the Legionary, a Parthian with slightly crossed eyes and a nose that took an abrupt turn about midway down the bridge, started to smile up at his Primus Pilus and was about to open his mouth to say something, although he didn't know what. The words never came, frozen in his throat by the expression on his Primus Pilus' face, who glared down at the man.

"What are you smiling about, idiot?" Pullus growled, then held out his hand, palm up.

Rattled as he was by this reception, the discipline instilled in him through his Centurion's *vitus* stood him in good stead as, without thinking, the Legionary reached down and drew his sword, then reversed it to hand it hilt-first to Pullus. The Parthian, somehow knowing that something much more important than a simple inspection was taking place, made sure his gaze stayed locked at a spot where the transverse crest and helmet met as Pullus ran a thumb along the edge, ignoring the quiet grunt of pain that escaped his commander's lips as he performed this simple movement. If he had dropped his gaze he would have seen that his Primus Pilus was holding the hilt of the sword at a much lower angle than was normal for him so that he didn't have to lift his left arm quite as high, but he maintained his discipline.

Handing the sword back to the Parthian, Pullus' only comment was a muttered, "You couldn't even cut bread with this."

Normally, a statement like this would be followed by some sort of punishment, but when nothing was forthcoming the

Parthian dared to drop his gaze to Pullus' face, his own expression betraying his disappointment at failing his Primus Pilus. Pullus' own mien didn't change, his face still the hard mask; but just before he sidestepped to face the man to the Parthian's right, he gave him a wink. Moving on, Pullus didn't see the relief flooding over the Parthian's face, or the grin that spread over the swarthy man's features. Man by man, Pullus performed the oft-repeated ritual, until he reached the last man from the ranks of the First Century, First Cohort, the man who stood next to him in line of battle. The identity of that Legionary, up until the battle now almost a week before, had been a tall Spaniard named Numerius, but like so many of his comrades, he was missing from the ranks. In his place was the man who normally stood fourth man down, and this mute evidence of how ravaged the 10th was shook Pullus' composure more than anything had up to that moment. Through a tremendous effort of will, he managed to complete his inspection before sidestepping to stand in front of his best friend and acting Primus Pilus.

"I hope you know what you're doing," Scribonius echoed Caesar, after rendering his salute, of course.

"I do," Pullus assured his friend. "And I'll take it from here."

For a moment Scribonius froze, sure he had misheard Pullus.

"You mean, you plan on taking your place in the assault?" he finally gasped.

"Well, I plan on leading the 10th, like I always have," Pullus responded, his mouth twisted into a grin. "Hopefully this will be a walk in the gardens, because only the gods know if I could fight off an angry Vestal Virgin at this point."

There was no other man that Pullus would admit such weakness to but Scribonius, and his friend's face showed the concern he felt, understanding that if Pullus was willing to admit even this much, he must be very worried that collapsing was a real possibility.

"What do you want me to do?" Scribonius asked him quietly. "Do you want me to march with the Second or with you?"

Pullus considered, then said, very grudgingly, "You better stay here. Just in case."

Scribonius longed to point out that if Pullus collapsed, he needed to do so before they were inside the fortifications of the capital, but he also knew how meaningless his warning would be.

Instead he merely replied, "I'll be right here."

"Good," Pullus and Scribonius exchanged a look that communicated Pullus' gratitude more than any of his words could, while Scribonius returned his own message of devotion to the man who had been his best friend for so many years.

With nothing left to say, they both turned to face the front and waited for the blast of the *cornu* to sound the order to advance. A short time later, the deep, bass note sounded that was the signal to march, and with no hesitation, Caesar's army stepped forward.

The palace official who raised the warning was on his knees, gagging from a type of exertion with which he was completely unfamiliar, or at least since the removal of his testicles as the prerequisite to join the emperor's household. His superior, on the other hand, barely noticed the other man's distress, as he snapped out a series of orders to the hastily gathered group of men. This included the sub-commander to the royal guard, who had been left in charge by his superior, the man who was responsible for the group of swordsmen known as The Chosen Ones. He had also been placed in command of the rest of the royal guard, and he listened now to the eunuch, although he hardly needed to be told where to go and what to do. Once he heard, between gasps, from the supine eunuch what was happening and from what directions the grubworms were coming, there was nothing more to be said. Yet, for some reason, the official seemed determined to emphasize the importance of protecting the emperor, as if the warrior needed to be told! Standing with his arms crossed, he drummed his fingers impatiently on one arm in a silent signal to the official that time was being wasted. Glaring at the warrior, the eunuch hurriedly finished what he was saying, and without waiting to be dismissed—an unforgivable lapse of protocol in normal times—the sub-commander trotted off, calling to the assembled warriors. Watching his retreating back, the official savored the idea of the ways in which he would take his revenge, before reluctantly turning his attention back to the other men. None of them were warriors, but these were men entrusted with what the official knew was going to be the most important task of all.

"Is The Divinity ready to be moved?" he asked the eunuch he had appointed to the task.

Bowing his head, the other man replied, "Yes, he is prepared for his departure. However," the eunuch paused, as he tried to choose his words, "The Divinity has expressed his desire that He not be moved until the last possible moment. He says that He has been in communion with His celestial Father and Mother, and that He has asked Them to intercede on His behalf. He is expecting that the barbarians will very shortly be destroyed."

The chief official froze, his mind racing with the import of what he had just been told. Not now, he thought! Of all the times for the emperor to actually believe in his own divinity, this was the worst moment, without a doubt. It was true that he and all those in service to the emperor—which technically meant every man, woman and child on these islands—accepted as fact that the emperor was a god sent to earth to rule his people, at least on the surface. And while the official had no doubt that the common people believed this with a certainty reserved for the uneducated, for more enlightened individuals like himself, particularly one who had watched The Divinity squatting and defecating, the level of belief wasn't quite as strong. And, if the truth were known—a truth that this man would never, ever utter aloud—The Divinity was something of an idiot, hardly a fitting state for a god. Now this dolt was actually trying to make a decision that could lead to real, earthly consequences. However, he *was* the emperor and his word was supreme law. But while before that word had always been carefully guided and controlled by this official, and others, he conceded, this was a decision that went directly counter to what all of his staff knew was the proper course. Nothing, absolutely nothing, could be allowed to happen to the emperor's person. Death would be horrible, but capture would be absolutely catastrophic, because it would expose what was in essence a great lie, for how could a god be captured by mortals? Especially by these...these *grubworms*? No, the emperor had no business tarrying here. The challenge, he understood, was how to get the emperor to change his mind, while thinking that it was his own idea. Without saying anything to the others awaiting orders, the chief official beckoned to the other eunuch to accompany him and strode in the direction of the imperial quarters.

It was hard to tell, but the scout estimated that the royal guard commander was unconscious for what was the sixth part of a Roman watch. Finally the man moaned, then slowly opened his eyes, but the scout, who had never left his side, noticed that they were still unfocused. After several moments, the commander turned his head, staring dully at the scout peering down into his face.

"Commander," the scout began, but before he could say another word the man suddenly rolled to his opposite side, retched a number of times, before finally vomiting.

Only after that did he seem to have any awareness, but his manner was still lethargic, as he struggled to sit upright. Helping him to sit up, the scout waited for the commander to speak, but when he said nothing, he began to tell the man what had happened. At first the scout didn't think the commander was listening, or if he was, his wits were sufficiently scrambled that he didn't understand what was being said; but when the scout mentioned how the two of them had ridden down the road to the lake, only to find the barbarian army gone, the commander's expression changed. A look of alertness came over him, as he stared at the scout for a moment, as if trying to gather his thoughts, which in fact was exactly what he was doing.

"They....weren't there," he said slowly, prompting an affirmation from the scout, who was still petrified, keenly aware of what had happened to the man whose mount the commander had appropriated.

"They had moved south," the commander continued, putting the pieces together that had been jarred apart in his head from his fall. "And they were nowhere in sight, so they must have left their camp behind in the dark. That means......"

His voice trailed off, and his eyes narrowed, as all that he had seen and deduced fell back into place.

"The capital is under attack!"

Holding out his hand to be helped up, when the scout pulled him to his feet, he took a step to steady himself, but ignored the crushing headache; there was simply too much to do.

"On your feet! We must hurry back to the city!"

Shouting this over and over, the commander ran up the length of the road in what had been, up until this moment, the site of an ambush that was going to inflict such damage on the grubworms that they wouldn't be able to do what the commander was terrified they were doing at that moment: attacking the capital. In short, he had been fooled, and now it was a race to see what could be salvaged from his error, if anything.

Flaminius' men were thorough in their searches, but as Flaminius expected, no barbarians, warriors or civilian, were found within the tiny houses. Much to the disappointment and frustration of the men, precious little in the way of loot was found, and every one of them was struck by how barely furnished these huts were. They were uniformly neat, arranged in tidy rows, each with a plot of land on which the peasants who lived there grew a variety of edible plants, but all of the enclosures that normally held animals were empty. From what Flaminius had gathered, this neighborhood, while it was inhabited by barbarians of the peasant class, housed the artisans and skilled craftsmen of the capital and their families. In every other situation of a similar nature, in every other campaign, no matter in whose lands they were, this class of peasant was usually prosperous and could be counted on to have any manner of goods and valuables of a portable nature. Not here, it seemed: yet another example of how this entire campaign had seemed to be cursed by the gods. While Flaminius wasn't much for believing in such things, he wasn't deaf and he heard the muttered conversations around the fires at night suggesting that very thing: that the gods had turned their backs on Caesar and his men. The only bone of contention, as far as Flaminius could tell, was whether it was because they were angry at Caesar, and by extension his army, for invading these islands, or if in fact these islands themselves were cursed, or in some way were territory where not even the gods dared to interfere. Shoving these thoughts aside, Flaminius returned his attention to the sounds of the *cornu* that told him that the 14th Legion was beginning their final advance into the capital. Moving quickly from among the houses so he could see, Flaminius stood and watched as the front line of the 14th, led by its Primus Pilus Figulus, suddenly rushed forward in a roughly straight line, or at least as straight as hundreds of running men could maintain.

"They didn't use their javelins," Flaminius heard a voice behind him and turned to see his Pilus Posterior, the second-highest ranking Centurion in the Legion and commander of the Second Cohort.

From the angle where they were, it was impossible to see very far past the area enclosed by the fortifications, but Flaminius didn't see any bodies or any sign that there had been any type of defense put up around the unfinished ditch.

"Probably didn't need to," Flaminius concluded. Moving to another subject, he asked, "Are the last of the buildings searched?"

"Yes, that's what I was coming to tell you."

"Good," Flaminius grunted. "Get the men back together. It's our turn to go in as soon as the 14th is finished."

With nothing else to say, the Pilus Posterior returned to his Century, while Flaminius called to his *cornicen*, telling him to sound the appropriate notes for assembly.

The partially excavated ditch and the shapeless pile of dirt behind it barely slowed the men of the 14th down as they went streaming through the gaping hole in the otherwise unbroken wall. They had been expecting at least some resistance, but the streets in both directions were deserted, the houses appearing as empty as those on the outside of the fortifications. For men who had whipped themselves into the controlled frenzy essential for combat, especially against this enemy, the lack of anything or anyone on which to focus that ferocity was extremely unsettling. Pushing several blocks in a northerly direction, Figulus finally called a halt, as much to allow the men to collect themselves as to catch their breath. Up ahead of where he was standing—on the street running parallel to the eastern wall, closest to the deserted dirt rampart—Figulus could see that this neighborhood ended and that there was some sort of cleared area, perhaps a park or large garden of some sort. It was only there that he saw any movement, and what he saw were figures, most of them clad in black, flowing robes, running toward the northwest, to what would essentially be the far corner of the fortification. Otherwise, there was still no sign of resistance, but he nevertheless admonished the men of his own Century to remain alert, a superfluous order, given how nervous the men now arriving were. As was their custom, the Legionaries had been shouting their battle cry as they went charging into the interior of the capital's fortifications, the noise fueled and strengthened by their belief that this would be the final battle and their chance to exact vengeance. But now they had fallen silent, so that the only sound was the ragged panting of men trying to catch their breaths. The noise echoed between the houses, adding to the eerie atmosphere and contributing even further to the collective case of nerves. Behind the 14th, the 30th was entering the capital, but their orders were to move to the west from the entrance into the city, arranged in a formation perpendicular to the 14th's. Ever methodical, the Roman assault on the capital continued, and in just a few moments it was the turn of the 10th Legion to enter. Unfortunately, as small an impediment as the partially excavated ditch was to healthy men, for Pullus it was a supreme challenge; but the only concession he made was to have help down into the ditch, leaning heavily on Scribonius, instead of leaping across like everyone else. Even this was almost too much to bear, but as bad as Pullus thought it was being helped down into the ditch, it was even more agony to have to be hauled up and out of it, it taking both Scribonius and a man from the ranks to help him. As much as he tried, Pullus was unable to keep a groan from escaping from him, and he stood motionless for a moment, eyes closed and swaying, rivulets of sweat pouring down his face. Scribonius, even more alarmed at this sight, opened his mouth, then shut it, knowing that it would do no good. His friend had thrown his dice and he knew that he would be wasting his breath trying to convince Pullus he had done enough.

Opening his eyes, Pullus gave a slight shake of his head, then said loudly, "I don't know why everyone's standing around, we've got work to do."

Then he turned to Scribonius and muttered quietly, "You sound the advance. If I have to yell right now I'll faint dead away."

Hesitating, Scribonius nodded, then did as Pullus asked, and the 10th, or what was left of it, made its entrance into the enemy capital.

"We wait until we see the grubworm's general," the man who had been appointed leader of the disgraced nobles told the men with him. Turning to two others, he asked for what they were sure was the hundredth time, "You're sure you know what he looks like?"

Even if either man was disposed to point out they had supplied this information more than a dozen times, the tension of the moment dispelled any impulse to do so.

"Yes," one of them replied, "and you will know him when you see him, if only because he will be surrounded by grubworms that do not look like any of the others. They have very long hair and beards, and you can smell them before you ever see them."

"How many of them are there?"

The leader turned cold eyes on the man who asked the question.

"What does it matter how many there are?" he sneered. "We know what we must do, so it could be a hundred or a thousand, it would not matter."

Glaring at the gathered men, he dared anyone to speak, but was unsurprised when none did. The group, just shy of 300 men strong, had remained hidden when the royal guard commander gathered his men to set the ambush, and they had been alerted by the shouted alarms of the officials that the grubworms were attacking the capital. Now they were waiting for the moment they had been planning for, in a way to retrieve the honor they had lost because they hadn't died with the rest of the Wa army in the battle. In much the same way that the royal guard commander had arrived at his conclusion, their reasoning was simple. Having experienced firsthand the might and power of the grubworm army, their only hope was to cut off the head of the beast that even now was entering their capital. To strengthen their resolve, they had made a solemn vow that they would either succeed, or they would die in the attempt. From their viewpoint, they were already dead, for all intents and purposes, and had brought shame to their respective families and clans. The only way to retrieve their honor, as far as they were concerned, was with this last-ditch attempt, but now that the moment was at hand, the smell of fear sweat hung rank in the air of the enclosed space as they waited. For their hiding place they had selected a temple that was the central feature of a small park to the south of the imperial residence. Normally, this temple, and the park itself were restricted to only imperial staff and the emperor himself, but these weren't normal times, and because the only protection offered from an advancing army was the presence of the few trees that had been allowed to grace the grounds and a border of low shrubbery around the boundary, it was completely deserted. However, it lay directly in the path of the army if, that is, the grubworms headed to the imperial residence took the shortest route.

The group of men were crouching, and although the temple was large by Wa standards, it was never designed to accommodate that many men, and they were all jammed together shoulder to shoulder, as their leader watched through one of the low windows facing the imperial palace. If he was right, the grubworm general would come into his vision from the right, heading across the small park to the line of buildings that marked the outer residences of the imperial residence. These buildings, while made in the same manner and style as the other structures, were of clearly better construction and materials, marking them as different from the neighborhoods ringing the imperial grounds. Beyond the first line of buildings was another, much smaller park for the private use of the emperor that was completely enclosed by buildings. Nobody other than the palace staff had even seen it, but it was rumored that there was a spring bubbling up from the ground. On the far side, directly opposite the first line of buildings, was the residence itself, and while to the Wa it was a truly impressive structure that was massively huge, to Roman eyes it was at best the size and grandeur of a villa belonging to a modestly wealthy merchant. One feature of the building style of the Wa that had struck Caesar and the rest of the Romans was that instead of building upward, they built outward. There were no multi-story buildings on the islands, and the imperial residence was no exception. Where it did differ, however, was in the height of its single story, and in the amount of space the dwelling occupied. Because it was several feet taller than the surrounding buildings, and those trees that had been allowed to grow within the imperial compound were carefully trimmed so that their height didn't exceed that of the residence, the building was plainly visible from any direction. The leader of the disgraced nobles was sure that as barbaric as these grubworms were, they were intelligent enough to understand the significance of this, and he kept his gaze fixed at the point he believed would give him the first glimpse of the enemy. He could hear the blaring of horns and recognized from the earlier battle that these belonged to the barbarians. After an interminable amount of time, with the tension growing with every breath, the leader caught movement at the very edge of his vision through the window.

A moment later, the leading rank of the grubworm army appeared, a long line of pale but terrifying creatures, dressed in a style of armor and carrying shields that, while he had heard they were carried by the barbarians of the mainland, he had never seen before. Even stranger and more unsettling was that as more and more ranks came into sight, they were all marching in unison. This was something else that was completely unknown to the Wa, who still thought of their army, or any army for that matter, as simply a collection of individual warriors who were united in a common cause. That, however, was as far as their unity went; the type of unit drilling that was such a fundamental part of the Roman army was unheard of, even on the mainland. For the space of several moments, the leader could only stare as the first line of the 14th Legion marched by, the left flank of their formation passing no more than 200 paces away from the temple. A small group of grubworms suddenly broke from the formation, trotting out to arrange in a line directly facing the temple, forcing the leader to duck his head below the window. Deprived of any chance at being alerted, in case this group of the enemy approached the temple, the leader whispered to the others to prepare themselves, causing a rush of whispering he was certain would be heard. He gave a fierce, hissed warning, and only then did the noise subside, as he watched and waited, heart pounding so loudly that he could barely hear the sounds of tramping feet. Risking a peek, his relief was palpable as he saw that the group of grubworms were still in their original spot; and even as he watched, they suddenly turned and went running after the leading ranks of the enemy, rejoining the formation. His relief was short-lived, however; before he lowered his head again, he saw that another group of grubworms—this one from the second line—came running to replace the first. Rather than risk discovery, he dropped back down, repeating the prayer to his gods that these men be content to stand there, just like the first group. After a period of time that strained the leader's patience, he slowly raised his head so that just his eyes were above the bottom of the window, and only then did he understand that the enemy was merely taking a precaution. While he watched, a group from the third line exchanged places with the men facing the temple, telling him that this had to be a standard way these barbarians did things. Then, the third line of the enemy went marching by, the sound of their feet stamping the earth, creating a rhythmic sense of foreboding in him that took a great force of will to suppress. No matter how much he tried to shove it down, the thought that kept forcing its way into his mind was that any army that worked with such precision couldn't be of this world.

The first three lines of men continued heading towards the imperial residence, and there was a brief pause, where nobody and nothing appeared in the leader's range of vision. Alternating his gaze between the backs of the marching enemy and the spot where any new forces would appear, he had the thought that this would be a good time to strike, when the grubworms had their backs to him and his men. Just when he began to think that he had seen the entirety of the force invading his capital, another line of barbarians appeared, but he instantly saw that there was something different about this group. The most obvious thing was how much smaller it was compared to the first two, looking about half the size in number. This difference puzzled him, because up to that point, the enemy army had been remarkably uniform. Not only had they all been in step, but their ranks had been almost exactly the same width, with the same number of men. Now came these grubworms, and while they were marching in step, they looked decidedly more puny in numbers. The other oddity was that, at the far end of the line, were two of the grubworms who wore distinctively different helmets, with the feathers arranged from ear to ear, unlike the plumes of the regular barbarians. From what the leader had seen, such men wearing such helmets marched by themselves, not side by side, and the sight of two such creatures together made him wonder about the meaning. But even more astonishing was the size of one of them. Although the other grubworm was almost as tall, even from the temple the leader could see that one of them was much, much broader through the chest and shoulders. Fixing his attention on this one grubworm, the leader also noticed that he didn't seem to be quite right; there was something in the way he carried himself that seemed odd to him, as if there was something wrong.

Dimly aware that the sight of this second group of men, organized in the same way as the first, even if they were smaller in number, was significant, the leader's thought process was that the grubworms must be organized by clans, like the Wa, meaning that the first group he had seen had to be one clan, followed by another. However, he had never seen any clan group that could field that many warriors, and this thought gave him great pause. He didn't know how many clans the grubworms had, but if each one could field so many warriors, was it even possible to defeat them? As daunting as the sight was, he also recognized that the only hope his people had of defeating these pale creatures was to remove their leader, meaning that he and the others crammed inside the temple were the only hope of their people. This idea filled him with a resolve that, up to this moment, had been missing, and he took a deep breath before resuming his vigil. He was greeted by the sight of the leading ranks of the first group coming to a halt, a couple of hundred paces short of the line of buildings between his position and the palace. They were undoubtedly preparing to attack the buildings, and for a brief moment the leader of this group wondered where The Chosen Ones were, hoping that they were between the grubworms and the imperial residence. The day before, he had overheard some of the palace officials discussing the removal of the emperor, and he was sure that by this time they had carried out the plan and that the emperor was somewhere safe. To think otherwise was so horrific that he found his mind couldn't even touch on that idea. And even if the emperor was safe, that didn't remove the burden he and the other disgraced nobles carried to retrieve their honor. If, at the same time, they could end the threat to their islands, to their emperor, to their very existence, the glory would be even greater, and who could truly ask for more? Therefore, even as the unwelcome thoughts assailed him, he clung to the hope that victory could still be attained and he returned his attention back to the second group. So absorbed was he in his examination of this large grubworm that he almost missed the presence of a group of men on horseback who went trotting past the first line. Reluctantly tearing his gaze away from the giant, he cast a quick glance at the mounted men, more out of habit than anything else, and was turning his attention back to the line of grubworms when he suddenly snapped his head back to examine the horsemen more closely. There were perhaps a dozen of them, and they all looked very much alike, almost indistinguishable from each other to the Wa. Except for one man, a tall, slim man who, in marked contrast to the other horsemen, was clean-shaven. It took a moment for the significance to dawn on the leader, but then his body stiffened as he recognized that there in front of him was the grubworm general!

With the 14th aligned and waiting to enter the cluster of buildings and the 10th moving into a supporting position, Caesar decided it was time to enter the capital himself with his staff and bodyguard. Jumping his horse over the unfinished ditch he, like the men who had preceded him into the capital, was jarred by the seemingly deserted and peaceful atmosphere. However, despite the capital's giving every appearance that the city was completely undefended, he was sure that the barbarians were there somewhere, waiting for the right moment to strike. Nothing that he and his army had experienced to this point in the campaign gave him any confidence they weren't there somewhere, and when they struck, it would be with the same ferocity and single-mindedness they had exhibited before. Although he was confident that both of the Legions that had entered first, the 14th moving north and the 30th moving to the west, had thoroughly swept the areas they had passed through, he was equally convinced that an assault was coming. Riding through the ranks of the 12th Legion, which had just entered the capital themselves, Caesar acknowledged the men cheering him, calling out to some of the rankers he recognized, sharing a quick exchange that exemplified his gift for connecting with his Legions. Reaching the third line of the 10th, Caesar repeated the same scene, until he reached the leading rank of the first line, only slowing down from the trot when he reached the eagle standard of the Legion.

Looking down at the sight of his Primus Pilus, face pale and drawn from the effort he was making to lead his men, Caesar's tone was a combination of concern and exasperation as he asked, "Well Pullus? Haven't you made your point yet? I think it's time for you to go back to the wagon."

"What, and miss this?" Pullus' grin was genuine, but it was also twisted from pain. "There's no place I'd rather be, Caesar. Especially not in that bouncing death trap. Now that I'm out in the fresh air walking about, I feel a lot better than if I was stuck in there."

Instead of answering Pullus, Caesar looked over at Scribonius with a raised eyebrow, but the other Centurion merely gave a shrug and slight shake of his head in reply. Receiving and understanding the message Scribonius was sending, Caesar gave a resigned sigh.

"Well," he echoed a theme that had been oft-repeated that day, "I hope you know what you're doing. Now, if you'll excuse me....."

Caesar got no farther than that, interrupted by a sudden roar of men's voices coming from the left. Caesar, Pullus and Scribonius whirled about, but the Centurions' view was blocked by the bulk of their comrades in the ranks. Only Caesar, sitting higher up as he was, could see the cause of the sound, and his eyes narrowed as he took in the situation in the span of a few heartbeats.

"It appears that we've found at least some of the barbarians," he told the two men who were looking up at him for an explanation. "And they're headed this way. Well," his tone was still conversational, "as I was about to say, if you'll excuse me, I have some matters to attend to. It appears that they're just in a different spot than I had planned." Spurring his horse, Caesar began heading in the direction of the attack, but he called over his shoulder, "Pullus, I expect you to stay put! Let your men handle this!"

And with that, he was gone, his German bodyguard galloping behind him in a desperate attempt to catch up. From the moment the barbarians first appeared up to the present, the noise level had increased, as the *cornicen* of the Fourth Cohort, the unit closest to the temple and the onrushing threat, played the notes that told everyone the enemy was attacking. Added to this were the shouted orders of the Centurions of the Fourth as they attempted to get their men turned about to face this threat. Pullus' first action was to walk several steps away from the formation to get a better idea of what was happening, and Scribonius hurried after him, his own attention torn between his duty and concern for his friend. Although the dust raised by Caesar and his bodyguard partially obscured his vision, Pullus saw enough to assess matters, and he knew that his Legion was in trouble. The onrushing barbarians were simply moving too fast for the Fourth Cohort to change their orientation to face in the right direction, although he could see that his Centurions were nevertheless trying desperately to do that very thing. Unfortunately, their actions actually made matters worse, because in the inevitable confusion of bodies and commands that was an unavoidable effect of changing their facing, the leading edge of the barbarians—all of whom Pullus could see were the dreaded sword-wielders—slammed into the Romans. Almost immediately, the scene of the fighting was obscured by dust, and the already noisy atmosphere became even louder, the air rent by the sounds of clashing metal and the short, sharp shrieks of men struck down. That was all the sign Pullus needed, and he began striding in the direction of the battle, following his general, as he had so often before.

"Pluto's cock, are you out of your mind?" Scribonius gasped, so surprised was he that he stayed frozen in place.

"They need me," was Pullus' only reply, but he didn't slow down.

Stifling a curse, Scribonius snapped an order to the men of the First, who had already come to a halt.

"Stay put until you hear the call, and keep your eyes open for more of these bastards."

The leader of the disgraced nobles was the first to slam into the grubworms, who were scrambling about in surprise, trying to meet the attack, but he was followed immediately by more than a dozen of his swifter comrades. Within the space of a few heartbeats, he and his comrades had wetted their blades, and the sheer surprise and ferocity of their assault had pushed the closest group of grubworms backward into the second group, who was little better off in turning about to meet the onslaught. As gratifying as it was to at least partially avenge the deaths of so many comrades and friends, the leader of the Wa attack was acutely aware that their goal wasn't vengeance, but the killing of the grubworm general, so even as he slashed and hacked his way through the ranks of the barbarians, he kept his eyes on the mounted man, who was galloping in his direction. The smelly long-hairs had caught up with the general, drawing their swords as they thundered towards the Wa. Little did they know that this was exactly what he was hoping for, the leader thought, ducking a half-hearted jab from a hastily drawn sword. Although he didn't counterattack himself, one of the other nobles had reached his side and with a savage, sweeping blow caught the grubworm's arm before it could be withdrawn behind the safety of their shield, severing it at mid-elbow. And with that, he went sprinting after his friend.

"Follow me," the Wa bellowed, waving his own sword in the direction of the grubworm general.

Swarming behind him, the other Wa cut down the confused Legionaries, moving with great speed, all of them heading in a rough wedge for Caesar, his bodyguards and those generals of Caesar who were accompanying him: Hirtius, Pollio and Ventidius. Behind the charging Wa, the Centurions of the Fourth Cohort were frantically trying to get their men reorganized so that they could pursue the barbarians and fall onto them from the rear. The Wa leader hadn't thought to alert some of his men to be aware of this likelihood, mainly because he understood that he would need every sword he had at his disposal to achieve their goal of killing the grubworm general. Even if only one of them was left, this was all that would be needed to bury a blade into the chest of that arrogant grubworm, who even then was drawing his own sword, as he pointed the long-hair smelly beasts around him in their direction, shouting in his gibberish. The Third Cohort, with a bit more warning, had been able to get themselves in position to offer more resistance to the charging Wa, but the impetus of the charge and the already diminished numbers of the Third—now at barely a third of its original strength—meant that they only partially slowed the Wa. Caesar's German bodyguards, arranged in a single line abreast were pushing their way through the men of the Second Cohort, heading on a collision course with the running mass of men, waving their swords above their heads as they shouted at the top of their lungs. The two forces came crashing together, and despite the disparity in numbers, the Germans were aided by the sheer bulk of their horses that sent men flying backward. Not all of them, however; just by sheer numbers, there were Wa who managed to avoid being struck by a horse, and these men went darting through the inevitable gaps between mounts that resulted when the two forces met. Although the mounted Germans did their best to maintain a tight formation, it was a practical impossibility to ensure that the rider's thighs were touching together as they were supposed to be. Aiding the Wa was their smaller size, enabling several of the leading attackers to dodge the blades of the Germans as they chopped down in a futile attempt to stop them. Still at the head of his small group, the leader kept his attention fixed on the grubworm general, who was now within a hundred paces. For a brief instant, the way was clear, with nothing between the Wa and the mounted barbarian, and he felt a fierce exultation, sure that it would be his blade who would strike the arrogant grubworm down. Behind him he heard the clashing sound of metal on metal, as more of his men joined battle with the mounted Germans. Once numbering more than 500 men, over the years and fighting, they had been whittled down to fewer than 10 percent of their original numbers, and now they were being assailed from all sides by the Wa nobles. Some of the Wa, displaying the same reckless disregard that had been a feature of the assault, threw themselves bodily at a German, using their bodies as weapons and sweeping the surprised bodyguards from their horses. In this way, more than a dozen saddles were emptied and the now riderless horses—startled by something they had never experienced before—began plunging and kicking, lashing out with hooves that didn't discriminate between friend or foe. This only added to the chaos, as the other Germans were forced to contend with the attacking Wa, the riderless horses, as well as their own mounts. It was the most confused, chaotic fight any of them had ever been in and it further helped the Wa cause, as even more warriors came flooding through the ever-thinning line of Germans. In the span of just a handful of heartbeats, the remaining Germans had been annihilated, leaving nothing but open ground between Caesar and the onrushing Wa.

What Titus Pullus was doing could only charitably be called a run, more of a half-trot, half-stumble, but to Pullus it felt as if he was at a full sprint and was as fast as he could go. The pain he felt with each step was so overwhelming that he was sure he would faint, but somehow he managed to push himself on, focusing on the maelstrom of fighting just ahead. Over the heads of the woefully thin line that was the Second Cohort, Pullus could see that the mounted force protecting Caesar was already down to no more than 20 men, all of whom were furiously engaged with the barbarian warriors that had seemingly appeared out of nowhere, flowing around each German like water. Horses were rearing in panic, exposing their bellies to the slashing Wa blades, and the almost human screams of animals in mortal pain punctuated the crashing noise of the fighting. Just as Pullus reached the rear ranks of the Second, they launched themselves into the melee, but between their reduced numbers and the confusion, their presence didn't do much to stem the charge of the Wa. It did allow Pullus to stop and catch his breath, however, but from his vantage point, he didn't think that his Second had even slowed the Wa down. Very quickly, the sheer ferocity of the barbarian assault blunted the reinforcing Cohorts and pushed the flanks backward towards each other, with Caesar and his rapidly dwindling bodyguard roughly in the middle. Even with the lack of numbers, each man in the group of disgraced nobles accounted for multiple casualties among the Romans. Still, Pullus could see that as his Centurions reasserted control, despite the mayhem and confusion this attack was close to spending itself, and while they had come close, Caesar was in little danger of being surrounded himself. Carefully turning about, Pullus raised his right arm and moved it in the circular fashion that was the signal for the men of his Century to attend to him, then clenched his fist, the further signal that this command was intended for the entire Cohort. Immediately, the Legionaries began trotting in his direction, shields raised and javelins at the ready.

"Well?" he demanded, and he almost sounded like the normal Primus Pilus. "What are you moving like a bunch of women for? Let's finish these bastards off!"

Without waiting for the roaring response, Pullus resumed moving in the direction of the fighting, now that the rear ranks of the Second Cohort had closed to meet those barbarians who had managed to penetrate past the shattered lines of their comrades. Pullus had no intention of doing any fighting; he was sure that in his condition even the rawest of warriors could defeat him. He hoped that his presence would be enough, but try as he might, he couldn't completely banish the itch he felt in his sword hand, which he always got just before a fight. In fact, over the years he had learned to rely on this sign that trouble or danger was nearby, and he found it slightly puzzling that he was feeling it now, when in his mind he was set on his course of only directing the fight. To that end, he forced himself to concentrate on what was going on around him, as the men of his Cohort caught and passed him by, adding their own swords to the fray. Caesar was still mounted, and despite his bodyguards' best efforts he had pushed his way past them to take part in the fighting, his blade slashing first on one side then the other.

Titus watched his general in consternation, muttering under his breath, "What does he think he's doing, risking himself like that?"

"As if you wouldn't be doing the same thing. In fact, you *are* doing the same thing," Scribonius had appeared at Titus' side unnoticed.

"Shut up," was Pullus' only response, never taking his eyes off Caesar.

In fact, that was probably the cause of what was about to happen; under normal circumstances there was no way that another group of armed warriors could have gotten so close unobserved.

The Wa that had been left in command of the royal guard, along with the archers detached for his use, had positioned his men in the series of outbuildings located between the palace and the small park. His plan was to wait until the last possible moment before bursting out of hiding. While he didn't think it would happen, his ideal attack would take place after the grubworms didn't search the buildings, so intent on reaching the palace that they left them for a trailing force to clear. This would enable the

Wa to fall onto these savages from the rear, but in his heart, the Wa didn't think that would happen. Unknown to him, he was in an almost identical position as was the leader of the group of disgraced nobles: peering out of a crack in the shuttered window of the building he and perhaps 30 of his men were occupying, watching the advancing grubworms. The tension had been steadily mounting, as the leading edge of the barbarians reached the far edge of the park area, and it was only through tremendous effort that he held his nerve and didn't order his force to break from hiding. However, something completely unexpected happened. From the temple burst forth the disgraced nobles; the Wa recognized the leader immediately and only then understood that they hadn't gone slinking off, but were lying in wait, just like he and his own men. Watching in astonishment for a moment, it took a small span of time for the idea to form in the Wa's head, but once it came, he didn't hesitate. Standing up, he barked orders to the waiting men to follow him outside. Using the entrance on the opposite side, so that he and his men were still screened from view by the grubworms, he called to the other warriors, spread among the rest of the buildings. Once they emerged and had assembled in a rough semicircle around him, he quickly explained the change in the situation and what he intended to do about it.

"We will approach silently, at least until one of the grubworms notices us. Until that happens, we stay together, and nobody will begin their attack until I give the command. Is that understood?"

He glared fiercely about, but the royal guards were accustomed to obeying his orders, and the archers were unlikely to go against his wishes. Satisfied, he shouldered past his men and led them around the corner of the farthest building, heading across the park. As soon as the fighting came back into his view, he saw that the nobles had succeeded in total surprise, and the impetus of their headlong rush had pushed the grubworms—who were clearly in disarray—back almost into a complete circle. He also saw that more lines of the grubworms were making their way towards the fighting, but they weren't much better organized than those barbarians who had been the first to respond. Closing at a rapid walk, understanding that a group of men running was more likely to attract attention, the Wa took in the scene before him and instinctively understood the goal of the noble force. Even from where he was, more than 300 paces away at this point, he could see that his countrymen were clearly aiming to cut their way through all the grubworms on foot to reach the group that were mounted. Fifty paces later, he could see enough details that he noticed the differences among the mounted men, spotting the ones who were clean-shaven and how they seemed to be protected by other grubworms who not only had long hair, but hair all over their face, too, reminding the Wa of some of the apes native to the northern part of the island. He didn't need to be told that one of the clean-shaven savages was the leader of these abominable grubworms who had invaded his homeland. Still refusing to break out into a run, the Wa nevertheless quickened his pace to the point where he was as close to a trot as possible. His sword was drawn, but his attention was riveted on the mounted men, understanding that the only chance for victory was located with those clean-shaven grubworms, one in particular. The Wa was cautiously relieved to see that, as of that moment, none of the grubworm infantry had noticed him and his men approaching, but knowing it couldn't last much longer, his eyes scanned the scene, looking for a sign that would tip him as to the identity of the barbarian general. It was his countrymen who gave him the answer, when he saw some of them virtually ignore the other clean-shaven grubworms to focus on one man in particular. Once his eyes fastened onto Caesar, the Wa immediately understood that this was the leader of the barbarians, his very presence informing the Wa. It was the way he rode his horse; the way he wielded his sword as it slashed down at the Wa's countrymen around him with a disdainful ease, as if this were a task that barely took his attention. Even seated on his horse, the Wa could see that he was taller than most of the other grubworms, and his hair, what there was of it, shone like spun silver in the sunlight. This must be the leader of these savages, and without saying a word, he angled slightly from his original course, not bothering to look behind him. Although a solid ring of flesh and steel was even then beginning to form around their general, the Wa was counting on the same factors the disgraced noble used to penetrate as deeply as they had up to this point. This was their last and only hope of repelling the invaders, and the Wa was counting on this knowledge fueling his royal guard warriors to unleash the savagery that would be needed to cut this arrogant grubworm down. It wasn't until they were less than 200 paces away that the Wa saw some heads turn, as the rippling motion of several hundred legs churning in their direction caught the attention of some of the grubworm infantry. The Wa now saw faces, and while they were still too far away to hear them, the Wa could tell by the pointing and sudden rush of movement that his enemy's commanders were shouting orders to meet the new threat. But, he was sure they would be too late, as he raised his sword high in the air.

"For the Emperor! For our homeland! For our ancestors!"

With this shouted exhortation, the Wa broke into a run, hearing the roaring echoes of his call behind him, as his men followed him.

"Pluto's *cock*, where did these bastards come from?" Scribonius gasped, he being the first to spot the Wa royal guard.

Whipping his head about in response to his friend's warning, Titus Pullus couldn't stifle the grunt of pain that even this little movement caused him. On seeing the Wa just then breaking into a run, whatever discomfort he felt was forgotten, as in the span of no more than a handful of heartbeats, his eyes took in what he was seeing, and determined what it meant. Risking a quick glance back ahead of him, where Caesar, his generals, and bodyguard were in the middle of a terrifyingly small knot of his Legionaries, he performed the calculations enabled by years of experience. Even going to the dead run, he saw that if he led his men in a straight line to reach what was in essence Caesar's right flank, they wouldn't have time to shake out into even a semblance of a formation capable of stopping this sudden barbarian onslaught. The only chance for his men—and by extension for Caesar—was to turn at an angle that allowed them to intercept the Wa at the dead run. Even so, it would be desperately close and his men weren't at their best in this kind of haphazard, fast-paced kind of action; but there was no other choice.

Pointing his sword at a spot perhaps 50 paces to the right of where Caesar and the rest of his men were engaged with the disgraced nobles, Pullus shouted, "Cut those bastards off! For Caesar!"

And with the same lurching, unsteady stride, he tried to break out into a run, completely heedless of the shooting pain his sudden movement caused. Before he had taken a dozen steps, Scribonius and the leading ranks of the First Cohort went sweeping past him, as if he were standing still.

"Don't worry Primus Pilus, we'll stop these *cunni*", one of the men shouted over his shoulder.

Such was Pullus' combined fatigue and level of pain that he wasn't embarrassed he wasn't at the head of his troops as they went dashing forward. Instead, he contented himself by watching as the first of his men caught up to the barbarians, just a little less than 50 paces away from Caesar and the rest of Pullus' Legionaries. Even from where he was, he felt the impact of the collision, up through his boots and into his legs. And, as usually happened, the air immediately above the lines of men became filled with an odd assortment of equipment: helmets were the most common, but there were swords or the broken parts of those blades that snapped, fragments of shields—even an occasional severed limb—tumbling in the air, mute witness to the horrific force of the impact. Unfortunately, at least from Pullus' perspective, while the Roman counterattack blunted the force of the Wa charge, it didn't stop it, and even before the Primus Pilus reached the rear ranks of his men, he saw them taking steps backward in the direction of Caesar. Legionaries were desperately grasping the harness of the man in front of them, while they dug their heels into the dirt, but it wasn't enough to stop the ferocity of the barbarian charge. Then, just when Pullus was sure they had stabilized and at least stopped their backward movement, a flurry of streaking arrows came slashing down into the ranks of his men, originating from just behind the knot of Wa warriors. Above the noise of the fighting came shouts and cries of men struck, almost all of them in the ranks immediately behind the leading edge of Romans currently engaged with the Wa. Suddenly deprived of the weight of a substantial number of men bracing them, as they fell to the ground writhing with pain, the shaft of a missile protruding from each of their bodies, the leading edge gave even more ground. Before Pullus' horrified gaze, he could only watch as his men were pushed so close to Caesar that the next volley of arrows hurtled down into the woefully thin line of the Legionaries still battling with the disgraced nobles.

It was a situation eerily similar to what Pullus had faced in the northern camp: an assault from two sides that threatened to collapse the two groups of Romans into one disorganized, confused mass. Taking this in, Pullus instinctively found himself moving, not in the direction of the men of his Cohort, but to a point nearer to where Caesar and the men of the other Cohorts were just then turning back the disgraced nobles. The Romans had withstood the worst of the original onslaught, but Pullus saw and understood that while it had been a close-run thing, the disgraced nobles' attack had reached its zenith. They were down to fewer than half their original numbers, and while they were still fighting furiously, the numbers had tipped back in the Romans' favor. At least, on their own they wouldn't be able to finish what they started, but with this new threat, the danger to Caesar wasn't over. Seeing this, Pullus kept moving towards what was at that moment an empty spot, but even before he reached it, there was a flurry of movement to his right. Glancing over, he could only watch with horror as three of the men in the rearmost rank came tumbling backward, pushed by a knot of perhaps a dozen barbarians who had managed to penetrate that deeply into the Roman formation.

Meanwhile, the supreme commander of the royal guard and the force that he had brought with him to the pass had just crested the ridge, going back in the direction of the capital. Normally a harsh commander, the Wa was mercilessly pushing his men the last hundred paces uphill, before they could begin their downhill dash back to the capital. He had sent his remaining mounted scouts galloping to the city to confirm what he was certain was happening: that the grubworms had outsmarted him and were at that very moment in the streets of the capital. While he was sure this was the most likely scene his scouts would come across, he held out a faint hope that the small force he had left behind would fight hard enough to keep the palace from falling— long enough, at least, to allow the emperor to escape. Even as his lungs felt like they were going to explode, as he ruthlessly forced his legs to pump his body the last remaining distance to the top, his mind raced through the various possibilities he and his men might face. In the worst event, the palace would be taken, and while it hadn't been constructed for defense, it was filled with rooms and passageways that would be a nightmare to clear. He reminded himself that his main goal was to prevent the capture of the emperor, and to keep the barbarians tied up long enough for the army from the north to arrive and sweep these grubworms back into the sea. It troubled him that the palace officials hadn't seen fit to let him in on the plan for evacuating the emperor, but he had to trust that they were as committed to the safety of the Divine One as he and his men were. Reaching the top, he paused only long enough to look back down the slope to see how badly strung out his men were, understanding that he had set a brutal pace. To his pride and relief, he saw that there were very few stragglers. Still, they were only halfway, although running downhill would be undoubtedly faster, so he resumed his progress, intent only on reaching the capital in time to be of some use. He understood that no matter what happened, his life was forfeit: he had failed to protect the capital, and failure wasn't tolerated among the Wa, so the least he could do was to redeem the honor of his family and ancestors with a glorious death.

Through the gap in the rear ranks of Pullus' First Cohort came perhaps a half-dozen Wa warriors, all that were left of the more than 20 men who had punched the hole in the Roman line. At their head was the leader of this force, his skill and savagery apparent, as his sword was a blur of motion, cutting and hacking down any Roman in his path. As bad as this was, Pullus was tall enough to see that behind this small group of Wa, more of the barbarian warriors, seeing the gaping hole in their enemy's ranks, began funneling themselves into the breach. Leaving a thin line of men engaging the front rank of Romans, the Wa were essentially sacrificing these men by leaving them unsupported, in a desperate gamble to join their commander and the other five of their comrades who were just then stumbling into the open patch of ground between Pullus' Cohorts and where the remnants of the disgraced nobles surrounded Caesar and his defenders. For the briefest moment, the Wa commander paused, trying to get his bearings and reacquire the sight of his target. In a frozen tableau of time, in much the same way a painter of a fresco captured a moment in a battle, Pullus saw the barbarians gathering themselves to launch a final attack on his general, now protected by only a double line of Legionaries. And he saw that in the space of open ground, perhaps 25 paces, between the barbarians and the spot where the fight around Caesar was taking place there was absolutely nothing to stop them.

Except for him. You fool, he thought bitterly, what have you gotten yourself into this time? There is no way you can stop these *cunni*. But even as this thought was flashing through his mind, his body was moving seemingly of its own volition, as his hand reached down to draw his sword. The rasping sound it made was oddly comforting, helping to focus his mind enough that he remembered to grab a shield from one of his men who was writhing on the ground, clutching his ruined arm. Pullus had the presence of mind to crouch down to grab the shield, instead of leaning over from the waist, but as his hand grasped the handle, the agony of lifting the shield was almost too much for him. Resigning himself to the idea that his remaining moments on earth would be the most painful in a life filled with them, he still didn't hesitate, bringing the shield up and locking his elbow against his waist. Crossing the remaining distance with a couple of long strides, Pullus placed himself directly in the path of the oncoming barbarians, having just enough time to pivot to face them squarely. Then the quickest of the barbarians was on him, not surprisingly the commander, his blade held high in what Pullus had recognized was their preferred method of attack. Acutely aware that in this position he had placed his back to the barbarians battling with his own men, he knew that his only hope was that they were too occupied to notice him.

Then the leading barbarian was on him, the blade sweeping down in a seeming attempt to split him in half. Having seen this method used so often before, while it had been devastatingly effective the first few times, Pullus and his men had learned the most effective counterattack was tilting the shield up above the head and parallel to the ground while performing a thrusting underhanded stab at the unprotected lower body of the enemy. But even if he could have made the violent motion needed to jerk his shield up in time to meet this blow, somehow Pullus knew that this was what his opponent wanted. Instead, Pullus made a hopping step to his right, which caused him almost as much pain as moving his shield upward. By making the step to the right, he kept his shield between himself and his enemy, who had changed the direction of his slash even as Pullus was moving, twisting his arms to change the direction from a downward to a sideways stroke. It was a vicious, powerful blow, but it was completely absorbed by Pullus' shield; and while the impact caused the Primus Pilus to grunt in pain, the only damage done was to the shield. But while Pullus had made the right move defensively, moving to his right put his sword farther away from the Wa, who at that moment was completely vulnerable to a counterblow, as his sword bounced off violently in a downward direction. That didn't mean Pullus was powerless to retaliate, so gritting his teeth in an attempt to prepare himself as much as he could, he punched out with his shield, striking the barbarian on his right shoulder.

Under normal circumstances, this would have been enough to break the Wa's shoulder, but Pullus' strength was seriously compromised from his wound, both because of the pain and the structural damage of the torn muscles from the sword thrust that had almost killed him. However, it was enough to stagger the Wa, who took a stumbling step in the opposite direction, but before Pullus could follow up, another of the warriors had reached his leader's side. This warrior launched his attack from the same overhead position, but unlike his leader made no attempt to alter the path of his slashing blow. Conditioned by the countless watches of practice, before he could even think about the possibility of being capable of doing so, Pullus' shield arm moved up of its own volition. If it was slower than his norm, it was still quick enough, although it tore a gasp of agony from his lips, though Pullus didn't know if it was from moving his arm so violently or from the impact of the blade. As much in pain as he was, Pullus still kept the presence of mind to perform the most effective counter to this overhand blow. It wasn't his most powerful, nor his best form, but it was devastatingly effective, as his blade, coming at a slightly upward angle from just below his own waist, pierced the lamellar armor of the attacking Wa as if it weren't there, and buried itself fully half its length in the man's body. Giving a savage twist to free it, Pullus withdrew his blade, just in time for the leader, now recovered, to launch his next attack. Pullus' victim gave a great, moaning cry and dropped his own weapon to clutch his stomach; but the Primus Pilus' attention had already left him, the Roman knowing that even if the wound wasn't mortal, this barbarian was out of the fight. As it happened, the natural motion created by his twisting withdrawal allowed Pullus to parry the leader's blow with his blade, instead of his shield, and while it was only marginally better, it still wasn't as agonizing as absorbing the blow through his shield and up his arm.

Even so, the only way he was able to keep his shield in its proper position was by keeping his elbow locked firmly in the bump formed by his hipbone, and he was acutely aware that he had a finite number of moves, such as his block, before his strength finally gave out. Fortunately for him, the other four Wa, seeing their leader and one of their comrades engaging the huge grubworm, had moved past where they were fighting, hurrying to come to the aid of the disgraced nobles. Pullus was only vaguely aware that to his right and rear, the men of his Cohort were falling backward from the ferocious onslaught of this group of barbarians, but he couldn't afford to take his attention away from his opponent. For a brief instant, both men paused, the flat, black eyes of the Wa seemingly devoid of expression as he examined the huge, stinking barbarian in front of him. He noticed that there seemed to be an awkwardness in the way he held the shield he carried, but he had felt the strength behind the parry the grubworm had just performed in his own attack, so he was understandably wary. By this point, despite their continued conviction that these pale foreigners were human only in the sense that they stood upright, not one of the surviving Wa took these beasts lightly. No, they had slaughtered too many of the Wa's countrymen not to be taken seriously, and he found himself still hesitating, before he made a sudden, lunging attack. Whether it was just a matter of luck, or whether somehow the pale giant had divined his thoughts and had predicted what he was about to do, the Wa would never know in the brief span of heartbeats that composed the rest of his life. Just as his blade snaked out, Pullus' own Gallic sword was in motion, moving in a chopping, downward blow aimed at a point just behind the Wa's own now extended sword. It was almost as if he had put his arm out with the express purpose of having Pullus sever it, and that is exactly what happened. Even as the Wa's mind was trying to comprehend the sight of his detached hand lying in the dirt, Pullus made another thrust that punched into the defenseless Wa, right at the base of the throat. Before the man had toppled over to fall to the ground, Pullus had recovered his blade, now dripping with blood from his two kills, and was moving in the direction of his general.

Fighting for his very life, Caesar recognized that once again his confidence had worked against him. In his zeal to give his men an example worth following, he had been foolhardy, and he could now see that his rashness had put not just him, but his entire bodyguard and the generals that had followed him in jeopardy. At first it hadn't seemed to be anything more than a skirmish, and while the barbarians who had burst from hiding had initially caught him—and everyone else on his side—by surprise, he determined that their numbers didn't pose a true threat. But they had surprised him, not only with their single-mindedness in reaching him—which he had very quickly understood was the goal of this foray—but also with their skill in besting his men and, even more alarmingly, their agility in avoiding coming to grips with his Legionaries, so that a fair number of them had managed to reach where his bodyguard had formed a line to protect their general. However, much as Pullus had determined, although the high tide of the Wa attack would come close to Caesar, they just didn't have the numbers needed to get past his Germans and reach him. That was before this new force suddenly appeared from his right. Where they had come from, and how they got so close before he became aware of them, he didn't know. Whichever way it happened, now his concern was growing very real and immediate, as he saw them slicing through what he assumed to be the First Cohort of the 10th Legion. Immediately surrounding Caesar was a thin cordon of Legionaries on foot, but only two men deep, with no more than a dozen of his Germans still mounted after that to protect him. Some of them had merely seen their mounts killed, and were now fighting on foot, but their particular style of fighting was completely unsuited for combat on foot, particularly when mixed with the Legionaries with their short, stabbing swords. His Germans favored much longer blades, which was fine on horseback, but those men on foot were constrained from the kind of wild, undisciplined slashing swing that the German warriors were so fond of, making them next to useless.

No, Caesar recognized, he was in real trouble, but that only spurred him to even greater efforts, fighting the fatigue brought on by his 65 years and the knowledge that his men, his boys, his sons, were looking to him to set the example and to let them know they still needed to fight. Because of his higher vantage point, he was able to see the remnants of the First Cohort crumble, as the new attacking force fought their way to a linkup with the remnants of the original force. Then, out of the corner of his eye, he saw movement that was just a bit different from everything else that was taking place, but he couldn't pay any attention at that moment, leaning dangerously far away from his own mount to make a downward stab over the head of one of his Legionaries who had just had his shield shattered and was vulnerable to an attack from the barbarian facing him. Instead, the barbarian found himself on the defensive as Caesar went to the farthest extent of his reach to make a stabbing attack. Despite the fact that it didn't have as much force as he would have liked, Caesar compensated for this by aiming for the barbarian's face, and was rewarded by the point of his sword plunging into one of the barbarian's eyes. Letting out a high-pitched, screeching wail, the Wa dropped his sword to clutch at the ghastly wound, as Caesar turned his gaze to what had attracted his attention. Suppressing a gasped curse, Caesar could only watch as Titus Pullus interposed himself between the onrushing Wa and himself.

"What does he think he's doing?" Caesar said this aloud, but nobody around him was paying attention, each involved with their own fight for survival.

As Caesar watched, Pullus dispatched two of the most aggressive barbarians, but Caesar could easily see that Pullus was hampered in his movements, particularly when it came to the use of his shield. Despite this handicap, from Caesar's perspective, his Primus Pilus dispatched the two barbarians with relative ease, but even before the second man fell, over Pullus' head Caesar saw even more Wa breaking through the line of Legionaries. Before he could shout an order to summon the rest of his German bodyguards, the Wa came rushing in his direction, and only Titus Pullus was there to stop them.

Facing the onrushing Wa, Titus Pullus didn't have the time to think about his predicament, or the pain that was sending shooting stabs of agony from his upper chest down into the rest of his body. Instead, he brought his shield up to the first position and braced himself for the first of the barbarians to reach him. Leading the Wa who had been the second group to break through, one of the members of the royal guard was running at full speed, his sword above his head. Instead of trying to meet the warrior head-on, Pullus instead took a step forward, while dropping to one knee at the same time. Before the Wa could react, he was faced with the choice of running into Pullus' outstretched sword, or trying to hurdle the kneeling Roman. Choosing what seemed to be the least damaging of the two courses, the Wa made a leaping attempt to jump and clear the Roman. Pullus was prepared for this, however, and as the Wa went hurtling over him, he gave a short but powerful thrust upward with his sword. It wasn't normally something he would have done, because the momentum of the barbarian's body was so great that it could have yanked his sword out of his hand. But he had done this before, and was counting on the special grip of his sword to maintain his hold. He managed to do so and was successful enough in keeping his arm rigid, so that his sword ripped through the Wa's vitals as he passed over Pullus' head, showering the Primus Pilus in blood. Knowing that even if the barbarian wasn't dead before he hit the ground that the wound was mortal, Pullus paid him no attention, standing erect as quickly as he had knelt. The next Wa had just seen one of his comrades pay for his eagerness, causing him to try to stop his own rapid progress towards the giant grubworm. But before he could come to a complete stop, he came within a sword's reach of Pullus, which was enough. With his longer reach, he was able to make a hard thrust that met the onrushing barbarian before he could react, and in the space of a half-dozen heartbeats, Pullus had ended two more of the enemy.

There wasn't any time to savor his victories, because following closely behind these Wa were even more, four in number, but they approached the Roman more cautiously, seeing how easily he had dispatched their comrades. On a grunted word from one of the barbarians, they spread out in a rough semi-circle, two of the Wa armed with spears in the center, standing side by side. Relying on the longer reach of their weapons, they alternated their attacks, in the form of jabbing thrusts that Pullus knew were designed to occupy his attention, while the other two barbarians, carrying swords, tried to circle around him, one from each side. Without waiting, Pullus moved quickly to his right, straight at the sword-wielding barbarian on that side and unleashed a hard overhand thrust designed more to check the barbarian's own attack than to strike a blow. It worked, freezing the Wa in place for just the fraction of time that Pullus needed to suddenly pivot about on his right foot, spinning his body around so that suddenly his shield side was facing the barbarian he had just feinted. Using the momentum created by the spinning of his body, Pullus continued the motion with his arm in a hugely powerful backhand slash that was delivered at just below shoulder level. The Roman had taken a huge gamble in performing this maneuver, because the spot his blade was sweeping toward was empty when he started his movement. But he had seen that one of the spear-carrying barbarians was just beginning to take a step forward into that space, and Pullus' timing and aim were perfect: the tip and first few inches of his Gallic blade connecting with the base of the barbarian's neck. There was so much force and speed behind this blow that Pullus' blade never slowed as it severed the spearman's head from his shoulders, but even before the head was finished on its upward arc, Pullus had completed the revolution to face toward the original swordsman. Taking another gamble, Pullus' sword arm punched out in a straightforward thrust, this one aimed at the spot into which he hoped the Wa was just then stepping, and once more he was rewarded by the shock traveling up his arm as the point of his blade punched into his opponent's chest. The Wa's eyes widened in shock and surprise, as he looked down at the sight of Pullus' sword protruding from his chest, before his knees gave way, and he collapsed to the ground without uttering a sound. Using the momentum of the dead man's body and the hard twist he gave to the blade, Pullus freed his sword while turning his head to watch the remaining two Wa, who seemed to be rooted to the ground in shock.

Fortunately for them, even more Wa had managed to push their way through the ranks of the First Cohort and were just then scrambling to join the two warriors. During this brief pause, Pullus became aware again of the throbbing pain in his chest, and he ached to drop his shield, if even for a moment, even though he knew he wouldn't have the chance. While he stood watching, his chest heaving as he tried to bring in huge gulps of air, the Wa exchanged a few whispered words, gesturing with their head in his direction. Then, in the same way as the first four, they arrayed themselves in a semi-circle, except this one was composed of eight Wa. Unlike the first group, it was obvious they weren't content to wait, because as soon as they were in position, the Wa in the middle, one of the survivors of the first four, barked a command. Immediately, they began moving toward Pullus, and this time he knew that he had no tricks, and in fact not much strength, left. Still, he hefted his shield into the first position, grunting from the effort, and held his sword ready, the entire length of the blade now slick and shining with blood.

"10th Equestris!!!!!"

The bellow emanated from behind Pullus' right, and even knowing the danger, he craned his head and saw perhaps a dozen of his men, with Sextus Scribonius at their head, running in his direction.

Although they had come desperately close to succeeding, the two separate attacks with the same goal were repulsed, but not after more blood was shed, as the men of both Wa attacks were slain to the last man. Caesar was safe, but at an even greater cost to the 10th Legion. By the time the leading Legions had been made aware of the threat to their general and turned about, the fighting was essentially over. It had been a short, but very sharp, action, which had savaged the ranks of not just the 10th, but also Caesar's German bodyguards, of which there were fewer than a dozen left still mounted. A handful more were still alive but had been unhorsed, forced to fight as infantry. For at least a hundred paces in every direction from where Caesar now stood, finally dismounting from his horse, were the bodies of Wa dead, interspersed with Roman dead and wounded. Perhaps a span of two hundred heartbeats had passed since the last two Wa, standing back to back, snarling their defiance to the last, had been cut down, but the efficient Roman machine was already starting to go to work. The *medici* of the 10th had already begun moving among the carnage, pulling or kicking the dead barbarians aside to uncover a Legionary that had fallen. Quickly making an assessment, the *medici* either knelt and began ministering to the wounded man, or moved on. It was not long before they were joined by the *medici* of the other Legions, who needed no orders to pitch in to help. After the shouting and sounds of battle, it was once again eerily quiet, except for the moans of those wounded who were able to voice their agony.

Titus Pullus was only dimly aware of all this, as he again found himself on his knees, his chin on his chest as he tried to stay awake and at least partially alert. What he knew was that the fighting was over and that his exertions had opened his wound again, the warm, sticky fluid leaking from under the bandage that was beneath his padded tunic and armor to run down his torso. It wasn't long before the part of his red tunic directly below his armor darkened even more, and he occupied himself with idly watching as it spread, wondering if it would stop of its own accord or if he would need to be stitched back up again. Maybe I'll just sit here and bleed to death, he thought dully, and it was a sign of his fatigue and distress that the thought wasn't all that unpleasant. While the throbbing was still present, the pain had lessened somewhat, losing its sharp edges of agony to settle back down to what he would describe as more of an ache. All around him there was activity, but just as it had happened when he suffered the original wound, kneeling beside him was his best friend Scribonius, who was watching him closely for signs that Pullus was about to lose consciousness and topple over.

"You're like a fly buzzing around a sick cow, waiting for it to die so you can start feasting," Pullus finally broke the silence, his voice once again hoarse.

"If you'd stop acting like an idiot trying to get yourself killed every time I turn my back, I wouldn't have to," Scribonius retorted.

Scanning the area, Scribonius spotted the nearest *medicus*, who was busy attending to another wounded man. Waiting until the *medicus* finished, once he stood erect, Scribonius called him over.

"You need to help me get his armor off and check his wound. It's bleeding again," Scribonius commanded, but before the *medicus* could stoop to help, Pullus waved him away with his good arm.

"No. There are men who need you more than I do. I'll be fine."

"You don't know that," Scribonius normally wouldn't have spoken to his friend in such a sharp tone, but he was worn down from a combination of the normal letdown after a fight and worry for his friend.

"Yes I do," Pullus replied calmly, nodding with his head in the general direction of his lap. "I've been watching and the bleeding's already stopped. The stain on my tunic hasn't grown for a bit."

Looking down, Scribonius examined Pullus' tunic for several heartbeats and saw that it indeed appeared that his friend's bleeding had stopped.

"Well," Scribonius grumbled, "that just means you're not going to die right now. You're still not out of danger. But," he turned to the *medicus*, "I suppose he'll be fine for the moment. Go on about your business."

The *medicus* hurriedly complied, not wanting to be near the two Centurions, who were still bickering as he went looking for more wounded.

"Shouldn't you be getting this mess sorted out?" Pullus surveyed the scene, watching as Centurions were even then grabbing men belonging to them and shoving them in the direction of the appropriate *signifer*, most of whom had arranged themselves in the beginnings of a formation of the Legion, the first step immediately after a battle now that the danger was past.

Every man was moving as quickly as he could, although some men were either limping or helping an injured comrade towards his normal spot. It was Roman efficiency at its finest, practiced and honed over thousands of such gatherings, and it was more than just the obsession with efficiency and order that drove this. It was only after the men were formed up that the Centurions could get a reasonably accurate count of casualties, although they would then have to determine which of the missing men were wounded and which were dead. Scribonius followed Pullus' gaze, and heaved a sigh.

"I suppose so. But are you sure you're going to be all right here? I don't want you falling over and opening that up again now that it's stopped bleeding."

"I'll be fine," Pullus promised. "I'll just stay here and rest."

Knowing that any further argument was futile, Scribonius relented and stood, looking about for his own Cohort, forgetting that he was still acting Primus Pilus. Once he walked away, Pullus tried to shift into a slightly more comfortable position, but quickly determined that the pain it would cause wasn't worth the effort.

"I should have had him help me," he muttered to himself.

"Help you with what?"

The sound of a new voice caused Pullus to lift his head again, but this newcomer had approached so that the sun was immediately behind him, forcing Pullus to squint to recognize the man. Although it took a moment for his eyes to adjust, he had recognized the voice, and he wondered if Caesar approaching so that he appeared to wear a blazing halo of sunrays was done on purpose. Whatever the case, Pullus thought, it was appropriate that his general would appear as a god. Maybe I *am* dying, he joked, but only to himself, not willing to share such sacrilegious thoughts, particularly with Caesar.

"Nothing, sir. Just talking to myself."

Of all the men in this army, Gaius Julius Caesar would have been the last on Pullus' list of people to ask for help. His general, however, was not so easily put off.

"I've never known you to talk to yourself just for the sake of talking. You mentioned something about having someone help you. What is it that you need, Pullus?"

Pullus knew Caesar very well, and he could tell by his general's tone that he was teasing him, something that Caesar seemed to do with annoying frequency, particularly with Pullus, because he knew how uncomfortable it made his giant Primus Pilus. While not in the same class as Caesar, or Scribonius, Pullus did have some wit, and he had long since lost count of the times he had bitten his tongue rather than make a sharp retort that would show the older Caesar that he wasn't the only one with a tongue capable of drawing blood. Later, Pullus would attribute what came out of his mouth next to the amount of pain he was in, and the almost overwhelming fatigue that kept trying to push his eyes shut.

"Well there's a first time for everything," Pullus retorted. "At least when I talk to myself I have an enjoyable conversation."

As soon as the words tumbled out, Pullus was assailed by a feeling of horror at what under any other circumstances would be an unforgivable lapse of discipline, but Caesar immediately threw back his head and began roaring with laughter. It wasn't the kind of laugh that was done out of politeness, but a deep, rumbling bout of mirth that came from his belly. This pleased Pullus, but after a moment when it didn't stop, his initial pleasure began changing to a sense of unease. Caesar was bent over at the waist, gasping for breath as the tears streamed from his eyes, and now Pullus was alarmed, if only because heads were turning in their direction. as the men stared openly at the sight of their general so discomposed. More than the attention, it was the sense that this laughter was not something normal, but seemed tinged with something other than the humor of what Pullus had said. Could it be...hysteria, Pullus wondered? Had this last surprise unhinged his general? Before he could summon the courage to open his mouth again, however, Caesar got himself under control, wiping his eyes as he caught his breath.

Finally, he said, "Pullus, that was one of the funniest things I've ever heard you say. But I'm serious. What can I help you with? It's the least I can do for the man who singlehandedly stopped these barbarians from reaching me. Granted," Caesar hurriedly added, "I probably could have handled them myself. But the fact I didn't have to is because of you."

When put that way, Pullus was hard pressed to continue to refuse, if only because of all the men in the army, he understood how hard it was for Caesar to acknowledge even the barest possibility that he couldn't have fended off this last barbarian attack. At least, Pullus hoped it was the last attack, because he wasn't sure how many more surprises of this nature Caesar's army could take.

"If you could help me get off my knees and sitting down, that would help," Pullus couldn't look Caesar in the eye as he spoke.

Nevertheless, he was greatly relieved when Caesar said, "Of course. But wouldn't you be better off lying down?"

Pullus shook his head emphatically.

"No. If you lay me down I think I'll probably pass out. This way it will be easier for me to stay awake."

He didn't have to add the reason, that he would still be in enough pain that the idea of falling asleep was impossible. Caesar knelt down, and with a fair amount of effort helped Pullus shift his position so that he was seated on the ground, with his legs splayed out in front of him. To help keep him in a semi-upright position, Caesar walked a short distance to pick up a pair of shields, which he propped together in a way that allowed Pullus to lean back against them.

"There," Caesar said lightly, "as good as if you were reclining on a couch at table."

While not exactly true, Pullus was still grateful, and thanked his general for the help.

"Pullus, I wasn't jesting," Caesar replied. "You were the only man standing between me and those barbarians. Once again you've provided me a service that can't ever be repaid. This was the least I could do."

"Well...thank you," Pullus murmured, embarrassed and extraordinarily pleased at the same time.

"Now that you're comfortable, I'm afraid I must go. I have some matters to attend to."

"Yes sir. Of course sir. So, it's over then?"

Pullus again avoided eye contact with Caesar, but this time it was because he feared the answer. Specifically, he was afraid that he would hear his general speak of more battles, that this campaign wasn't over until every warrior on this accursed island was subdued.

"I hope so, Pullus," Caesar said soberly. "In fact, if all goes according to what I have planned, I think that it will be all over and that we'll not have to fight any of these people again, before the sun sets today."

"Thank the gods for that," Pullus replied fervently. Then, his curiosity aroused, he asked, "And what plan is that, Caesar? What new trick can you pull on these savages that will convince them not to throw their lives away trying to defeat us?"

Caesar smiled down at him.

"Well, Pullus. That you will have to see for yourself. In fact, it will be happening fairly shortly, and I want you to be there to see it. So I'm going to have you collected and put in a litter. And Pullus," Caesar finished severely, his lips set in a tight line that Pullus knew was a sign that his general was deadly serious. "I expect you to be *in* that litter, not walking beside it. Am I understood?"

"Yes, Caesar," Pullus instantly responded, but Caesar wasn't about to be thrown off.

"Yes, I know that you understand. But I also expect you to obey. Am I clear?"

When Caesar was at his most terrifying wasn't when he was roaring at the top of his lungs: it was when he spoke quietly, as he did now. Pullus looked up into the glittering points of ice that were Caesar's eyes, and as sure as he was of his standing in favor with his general, he still had to swallow a hard lump. Instead of saying anything, he gave a simple nod, which Caesar returned, satisfied he had made his point. With that, Caesar spun around on his heel and walked to his horse, throwing himself into his saddle even as he started barking out orders to his generals around him. Pullus was left to observe the army reassembling itself and wonder what was going to happen next.

Whenever Caesar chose, he could stage a spectacle of such pomp and panoply that any of the most ostentatious of the Eastern monarchs he had encountered would be consumed with jealousy at the sight. Because of the time constraints, however, this wasn't one of those times. Still, the procession that rode up into the courtyard of the palace complex was awe-inspiring, if only for the formidable appearance of the grim, blood-spattered men who marched in solid ranks, each of them carrying an unsheathed sword. Contrary to their normal practice, Caesar had ordered every horn player to blow his instrument, not in a normal rhythmic marching tune, but in a seemingly random series of notes and tempos, making for a cacophony of sound that only the iron discipline of the Centurions prevented the men from shouting down in protest. After the first several ranks of marching men rode every member of the Roman army who was mounted. They, too, rode with unsheathed swords, with one exception. In the middle of the first rank of horsemen rode Caesar; but while he was still dressed in his muscled cuirass, instead of his helmet, he wore the oak crown that he had been entitled to wear ever since he had first won the award, when he was barely out of his teens. His scarlet *paludamentum* was spread carefully across the hindquarters of his horse, and adding to the spectacle, he had adorned his face with the blood-red paint that a triumphing general wore during his parade through the streets of Rome. Truly, if he had been able to procure one or had one made, he would have been riding in the *quadriga*, the chariot pulled by four white horses that was the conveyance of a triumphant general in Rome.

Instead he chose to ride the offspring of his famous horse Toes who, while blessed with the same strange malformation of the hooves, wasn't as sound a steed as his father. Consequently, Caesar rode him only on ceremonial occasions, knowing how important the symbolism of this horse, also called "Toes," was to his men. This day, he was counting on it making an impact on the barbarians as well, who were kneeling in precise rows that no Centurion in his army could find fault with; every head bowed so deeply that their foreheads were touching the ground. These were the barbarians who had been rounded up by his men of the 14th, pulled from wherever they were hiding in the outbuildings and the palace, itself. Arranged behind them were men from the 14th, glowering at the bowed backs of the savages that had caused them so much grief and loss. While it was true that these people, almost all men, were obviously not warriors, they were the only representatives of their people currently available. Even now, the rest of the army, save for the 12th and the 10th and one Cohort of the 14th, was scouring the city, searching every house, given very specific orders to kill any warrior they found, but under pain of flogging with the scourge, not to harm the civilians. Unfortunately, at least as far as his generals were concerned, this meant that of all the highest ranking officers, only Caesar was present in this procession. And while most of them suspected, none of them would utter aloud that this was no accident: every one of these men had known Caesar for decades by this point and all of them were sure, for their own reasons, that he was up to something, but not one of them was even remotely close in his guess.

Immediately behind the mounted contingent marched the men of the 10th Legion, but there was one difference—although it was one that the men had become accustomed to over the last week—and that was the presence of a litter, borne by several burly slaves and carrying one very disgruntled Primus Pilus of the Legion. Propped up on pillows, Pullus had revived somewhat, and was now interested enough to continue leaning out from behind the curtains that barred his view. Compounding his irritation, all Pullus was able to see clearly were the rumps of the horses ridden by the remaining German bodyguards at the rear of the mounted formation. However, if he leaned over a bit more and peered through their legs, he caught an occasional glimpse, more of an impression than a full sighting; so he wasn't convinced that he was seeing the kneeling Wa arrayed down each side of the courtyard, which was as large as the forum of the Roman army's camp. Craning his neck, he ignored the pain it caused him, as the litter carrying him advanced more deeply into the large open area, peering around the moving limbs to confirm his initial impression. What he had glimpsed was, indeed, what was taking place: barbarians were all kneeling down in the same fashion as they had in the town the army had taken early in the campaign. When had that been, Pullus wondered? Unlike any campaign in which he had taken part, this invasion seemed as if it had been going on for years, not weeks. Had it really been just a matter of three months since they had sailed from the Gayan Peninsula? Well, he decided, however long it had been, he was content to watch what he fervently hoped was the last act in this drama played out in front of him.

How Caesar was going to accomplish this, Pullus had no idea, because nothing he had seen in the behavior and attitudes of these people indicated to him that they wouldn't fight, perhaps to the last inhabitant of their island. Still, Caesar had seemed very confident, Pullus reflected, and if it was an acting job, it was the best he had ever seen from his general. Finally, the litter came to a halt, then was laid very gently on the ground, but not before the bearers turned it sideways, so that one open side was now facing into the courtyard. Where Caesar had chosen to come to a halt had required the leading ranks to split and countermarch in two opposite directions, making the effect appear as if a set of curtains was being drawn aside. Still somewhat hampered in his view, Pullus finally found a spot from which he could just manage to see what was going on through the crowd of horses' legs. From this vantage point he saw his general, now alone and still mounted, surrounded on three sides by a double line, one composed of Legionaries and cavalry, the other of the rows of kneeling barbarians. The barbarians were universally clad in black, their equally black hair pulled tightly against their skulls, and the ponytails that stuck up from the back of their heads reminded Pullus of rows of freshly sprouted wheat in appearance, even with the color. None of them moved, and neither did Caesar, who lifted a hand that brought the noise of the horns, which had continued to blow throughout their entire progress to this point, to a sudden silence. For the next several heartbeats, the silence was utter and complete, without even the slightest whisper of the wind, and Pullus realized he was holding his breath. Slowly exhaling, it seemed to send a silent signal to Caesar, who suddenly began speaking. Pullus turned an ear towards the sound of the voice, and although it sounded like his general's voice, what was reaching his ears was completely incomprehensible. A sudden thought flashed through Pullus: was it possible his general had become unhinged? That the crushing pressure of this campaign had finally been too much for Caesar? Though he listened intently, the sounds and grunts that were, in fact, coming from Caesar were still completely foreign to Pullus, but there was a tug at his memory, a haunting whisper of familiarity that told him he had heard sounds like this before. However, when the thought came to him, he shook it off as too absurd. Except that it wouldn't go away, no matter how hard he tried to banish it. In the span of the next few heartbeats, Pullus was forced to acknowledge that the only time and place he had heard anything similar to what Caesar was uttering was in his very recent past. In fact, with a sense of stunned certainty, Pullus finally recognized that Caesar was speaking in the language of these barbarians!

As shocked as Titus Pullus was, it was a bare fraction of the impact it had on the assembled Wa courtiers and officials, when this grubworm began speaking in a tongue they could understand. The chief official, in particular, was so surprised that he committed the unpardonable breach of lifting his head to gape in amazement, his almond eyes going almost round as he quivered in a state of shock and fear. So overwhelmed was he that it barely registered that this...this *being,* speaking as a civilized man, mispronounced a number of words. At least as they were pronounced here in the capital. If the official wasn't faced with the evidence before him, he would have said that he was being addressed by one of the farmers in the southwest part of the island. No, it was definitely coming from this entity before him, his white face hidden behind a mask of red that made him even more terrifying to behold. His astonishment ran so deeply that the official was barely paying attention to the words, but he forced his reeling mind to focus.

"...I have led this army composed of the servants of the gods from the heavens to punish the Wa for their lack of respect to myself and my fellow gods," the being continued. "And now that I have proven my divinity by conquering your people and forcing your emperor to flee for his life, I demand that you render to me the proper obedience that befits a god. Is this understood?"

This was the first question that had been posed by the being, and the official felt all eyes of the rest of his assembled countrymen turn to him to supply the answer. But what answer could he give? Like most of the men of his status, the official was more educated than the vast majority of the Wa, and like educated men everywhere, he wasn't as prone to what he viewed as the superstitions of the peasants of his country. Whereas a farmer toiling in his fields might immediately accept what this being was saying about being a god, the official liked to think that he wouldn't be fooled so easily. On the other hand, he thought, what other explanation could there be? It was undoubtedly true that this being's army was mortal, because even from where he was kneeling he could see many of the grubworms sported bandages of varying sizes. And he had seen the attack by the royal guard left behind, daring to hope that they would actually achieve their goal of striking this being down. Many men in the grubworm army had fallen, but not this one. He had been untouched, yet again. The official vaguely recalled seeing what had to be a giant, but wearing the same style of armor and helmet as the rest of the grubworms, standing between what would turn out to be the last chance of the royal guard and this being. From where else but from the heavens would such a huge, pale creature come? And who else but a god could summon him to do his bidding? These were the thoughts that flashed through the official's mind in the pause between the being speaking and when it expected an answer.

Just when the being opened his mouth, staring down at the official with eyes that seemed to be made of the deep blue, glittering ice he had seen on his pilgrimage up the sacred mountain, the official blurted out, "Yes, lord. We understand."

Even if he had thought to perform one last act of defiance, the resolution that would be needed to do something had evaporated instantly, when the eyes of the official met that of this being. As unsettling as the pale color was, the being's piercing gaze that seemed to the official capable of seeing into the depths of his very soul quelled any such impulse. The being's face betrayed no emotion whatsoever; what the official had no way of knowing was that it was precisely for that purpose that Caesar had donned the red paint of the triumphing general. He wanted his face to be as close to a mask as possible, a living representation of the statues of the gods that graced the temples of the Capitoline hill back in Rome. Still staring down at the official, Caesar could clearly see the captive's shaking body, despite the distance between them, and he resumed speaking.

"I have decided that I will reside here, until such time that I deem the Wa have returned to the way and level of worship that meets with our favor. I am the sole authority over the Wa, and any disobedience, of any kind, will be met with the harshest of punishment. These men you see before you are my duly appointed representatives. Their word is law. Is that understood?"

Knowing that he had become the representative of his people, this time the official didn't hesitate.

"Yes, lord." Swallowing hard, he added, "but..." That was all he could get out, because the being interrupted.

"But how can they enforce the law if they do not speak your tongue? That is what you were about to say."

Any lingering doubt the official had about the divinity of this being was blown away as quickly as a puff of smoke before a strong wind. How else could he have known this was what the official was going to ask?

"I will handle that. It is not your concern," Caesar continued, amused as always at the look of astonishment on a man's face when he, Caesar, simply drew an obvious conclusion.

In reality, at that moment Caesar didn't have any idea how he would accomplish endowing his men with a working knowledge of this language. However, he had more pressing concerns just now.

"Are there other forces of your army approaching?"

For an instant, the official hesitated, touched with the brief thought of lying to the being. Just as quickly as the idea came, he brutally shoved it away, his heart suddenly hammering as if he had just gone to a full sprint, sure that the being would divine his true thoughts.

"Yes, lord."

"How many?"

The official explained about the presence of the two armies, and that the royal guard commander was even then probably approaching with the rest of the force, thrown together to defend the capital. The army formed by the lords of the north, he told Caesar, was more than two days' march away.

"Select a man you can trust. I will have some of my men escort him to meet this force outside the city, before they enter. He needs to be of sufficient rank to convince the commander that he is to surrender his men and order them to immediately lay down their weapons. Is this understood?"

The official assured him that it was. Only then did he raise himself from his bowing posture to search the ranks of the palace staff. Things had happened so quickly that they weren't arranged in their normal order, but after a moment he spotted the man, also a eunuch, who was immediately below him in the hierarchy. While the official was charged with responsibility for the entire staff, his deputy ran the group of men who serviced the emperor's needs in the palace, along with carrying out the religious duties. Calling to the deputy, he began to explain what the being required of him, but the deputy quickly assured him that he had heard every word that had been spoken by the being and had assumed it would be he that would be given this task. Meanwhile, Caesar had turned and had a quiet word with his German bodyguards, and although their expressions betrayed their misgivings, like the official and deputy, they obeyed him, a half-dozen leaving their formation to wait as the deputy scurried over. His head still bowed, the deputy ran as fast as his robes allowed, but Caesar took the time to repeat his instructions to the man. Afraid to look the being in the eye, the deputy stammered that he understood what was required of him. Then, without warning, a German leaned over and, grabbing a handful of robe, unceremoniously hauled the deputy up off the ground, dropping him over the saddle in front of him. Despite the solemnity of the occasion, more than one of the others let out a snicker. Understanding how delicate the balance was of what he was trying to accomplish, Caesar snapped an order to shut their mouths, which they did. The Germans and the deputy rode away in the direction of the road leading up to the pass, down which the royal guard commander and his men were traveling at that instant. The official watched the hairy ones trotting off and wondered if they would be in time before the commander reached the vicinity of the palace, and, indeed, if his deputy would be successful in stopping him. He knew the commander as well as anyone among the staff, and it wasn't hard for him to imagine that the commander would refuse to believe the deputy and insist on coming to see for himself—with his men—prompting a shiver from the official at the thought of the terrible price they might all pay for the commander's refusal.

"Where is the man you called your emperor?"

Turning his attention back to the being, again the official's initial inclination was to prevaricate in some way, but once more, he dismissed the idea.

"He was sent away a short time ago, lord. He is heading north."

"Is he mounted?"

The official was struck by a glimmer of sudden doubt; if this being was the god he said he was, wouldn't he already know how and where one of his peers was going? After all, it was accepted as fact among the Wa that the emperor was a god himself, though housed in mortal flesh, it was true. Seeing the official's hesitation, Caesar again made an assumption, and of all the leaps of intuition he had made, he knew this was the biggest of his life. For if he guessed wrong, he could easily envision that his carefully thought out plan would fail, and he and his men would be forced to wrest this island away from the natives by the sword. And while he would admit this only to himself, Caesar wasn't sure that the men of his army were up to it. He understood better than Pullus thought how close to the end of their tethers the men of his army were, and this whole plan of his was a direct result of that knowledge.

"Now you are wondering why a god wouldn't know another of his kind, and know where he was located at any given moment," Caesar phrased this not as a question but a statement of fact, prompting another gasp from the official.

"Y-y-yes lord. That is, indeed, the thought in my head."

"The answer is that this man you call emperor is no god. He is a mortal man, just like you. He is not divine. That," Caesar hadn't planned on saying this, but decided to continue, "is one reason why I have come. To set the Wa on the right path, worshiping the true gods. Of which I am one," he finished, carefully enunciating each word in the Wa native tongue to leave no doubt.

The official was stunned by this revelation. Of course! This was why this being, this...god had come down from the heavens with his army of pale creatures. Somewhere, somehow the Wa had lost their way and had lost their connection to the divine. Thinking on it for a moment, the official recognized that they had, in fact, become complacent, taking for granted the blessings of the gods, sure that the man they called emperor was their direct connection to them. But he wasn't, because he was a mortal. As logical a conclusion as it seemed, given the new information, the official still hesitated in fully embracing this new reality.

"You will appoint another man, who will be escorted by more of my men, to follow the emp..." Caesar caught himself, "...the mortal you have wrongly deemed to be your emperor, and you will bring him back here. Then I will demonstrate to you the proof of what I am saying. Do you understand?"

"Yes, lord."

Truly, what else was there to say? A new god had come from the heavens and had assumed the mantle of leadership over the people of Wa. Only the god knew what he had planned for the official and all the other inhabitants of the island. Then, the official was struck by another thought.

"Lord?"

"Yes?"

"How do we, I mean, how do your people address you? In whose name should they pray and make sacrifices to?"

For the first time, a very faint glimmer of emotion cracked the mask of the god, as one corner of his mouth twitched upward.

"They will call me," the god answered, "Caesar."

"How do you suppose he pulled it off?"

Scribonius had just stuffed in a mouthful of rice when Pullus asked this question, causing him to stop with his spoon still hovering in the air as he considered the answer.

Frowning, he finally gave a shrug and replied, "I don't know for sure, but I can guess."

The pair of them were seated on stools in one of the small, neat houses that ringed the larger palace. It was nightfall of the day that Caesar had singlehandedly extinguished the last embers of resistance on the island. Or so they hoped.

"And?" Pullus demanded, not willing to wait for his friend to finish chewing.

Which Scribonius was sure to do before he answered, knowing it would infuriate Pullus.

"Remember that town we took?" he finally asked, after swallowing the rice. "The one where all the people were lined up waiting for us?"

Pullus remembered very well; it had been a singularly unsettling experience and he looked back at that moment as being the first time he had gotten an indication of just how different the people of this island were from every other country he had marched through.

"Yes. What of it?"

"You remember when we caught the Legionary with that girl? That very beautiful girl?"

Pullus nodded slowly, the memory coming back to him, along with the dawning of where Scribonius was headed.

"That's right," he exclaimed. "Caesar took her. I've only caught a few glimpses of her since then. I'd almost forgotten about her."

"Obviously Caesar didn't," Scribonius commented dryly. "And I'm willing to bet that he didn't use her to just scratch an itch."

Pullus considered this, but could only shake his head in bemusement.

"They must have spent full watches through the night to make him speak that tongue as well as he obviously does."

"Well, he never did sleep a lot," was Scribonius' reply. "And you know how good he is with languages."

"For all his faults, he is a genius," Pullus agreed.

He leaned back carefully, trying not to disturb the fresh bandage a *medicus* had applied. These houses were generally well built, but they were very strange, not just to Pullus, but to all the men. Because of his condition, he had been required to allow Diocles to draft some of the Legionaries to help arrange what very little in the way of furniture there was, along with unloading the contents carried by Pullus' mule. Despite all that Diocles had done, it was still a foreign setting to Pullus, but fortunately for both of them he was as close to indifferent to his surroundings as it was possible to be. For the next several moments the two friends ate in silence, each absorbed in his own thoughts. As eventful as the entire campaign had been, this day had been full of events and actions neither man had ever seen before or ever thought he would see, for that matter. After dispatching the barbarians of the palace staff to attend to their respective tasks, Caesar had announced to his army all that had transpired. His men were no less astonished than the palace official had been, even if it was for different reasons. In the immediate aftermath of Caesar's performance, for that was the only way Pullus could think to describe what had taken place, the general had trotted Toes over to Pullus' litter, also summoning the other Centurions that were part of this spectacle. In very brief but descriptive terms, Caesar explained the situation, that for a period of time he was either unwilling or unable to specify as far as its length was concerned, he would require every man in the army to render him the strictest military courtesy. It was important, he went on, to reinforce the idea of Caesar's divinity, so he would expect the men to show a deference that supported his status.

"Unless," he finished grimly, "any of you are eager to keep fighting these bastards. I, for one, am certainly not."

Even though they would undoubtedly obey, as always Caesar had understood that by providing an explanation he offered his men some ownership in the idea, and he was pleased to see that none of the Centurions seemed troubled with the idea that their general was now a god, for all intents and purposes. Of course, he thought, as he continued talking on another matter, they haven't had time to think about it yet. That next topic concerned his plans for the emperor, about whom the Centurions looked grimly amused when they learned of his fate.

"That should do it," was Pullus' comment, summing up the sentiments of the other Centurions.

And it had done the trick, just as Pullus and the others had assumed. It was late in the day when the emperor was brought back, also draped across a German's saddle in the same manner as the deputy had been transported. Unlike the deputy, the emperor had been secured by binding his hands and feet, making him look like a trussed pig being brought back from a foraging expedition. When he was half-dragged, half-carried into the center of the courtyard, Pullus hadn't been sure what to expect, but it certainly hadn't been the sight in front of him. Even for a Wa this man was small in stature, but the reason why became apparent once he was brought close enough, so that from his litter Pullus could see that he was little better than a boy. Perhaps he was a teenager, but no more than thirteen. It was hard to tell with these people; Pullus had been very close to a number of Wa and he couldn't remember seeing any heavy beards on any of them. The most he had seen were some wispy mustaches and perhaps one or two straggly beards. This boy wasn't even close to that, and what was equally clear was that he was terrified. Although his robes were of a quality Pullus had rarely seen, and only then once they had reached the lands of the Han, they were now stained as the boy lost all control of his bladder, a dark stain spreading down the front of his gown.

In stark contrast to Caesar's red mask, which his general had actually surreptitiously reapplied after his initial exchange with the barbarian in charge, this boy's face bore only the remnants of what looked like white paint. Had his face been painted in the same fashion as Caesar's, Pullus wondered? Pullus had no way of knowing that what was standing, shaking in front of his litter barely resembled the emperor, as his palace staff and his subjects saw him. Only a very small handful of the most trusted officials were allowed access to the emperor in his natural state, whereas everyone else saw the emperor only in his ceremonial attire, complete with a heavily made-up face, with the eyebrows painted on and wearing a headdress that exaggerated the boy-emperor's height. His robes were floor-length, and, in fact, trailed behind him as he walked, which was an artifice designed to hide the fact that he wore specially built shoes with soles several inches thick. In this way, every emperor, who wasn't allowed to be seen in public at all until he could reasonably approximate the height and size of a full-grown Wa, appeared before his people as a fully-grown man, even when he wasn't. Now what Pullus was seeing was the reality: a scared boy who, by accident of birth and time had been placed as the final obstacle to Caesar's achieving godhead. Despite the fact that this boy represented an enemy Pullus had come to loathe, he actually felt a twinge of regret, knowing the boy's fate. Standing off to the side, surrounded by watchful Germans, was what Pullus was told was the commander of the royal guard. It wouldn't be until the next day that Pullus would hear that the commander hadn't come easily. In fact, as the drama in the courtyard was being played out, three of Caesar's Legions had moved into position in the outskirts of the capital, positioned as a blocking force to stop the Wa that had been in the pass, led by the commander. He had refused to order them to lay down their arms, but had reluctantly agreed to be conducted into the capital under guard to witness that, in fact, a new god had arrived and was about to prove the Wa had been following a false deity, in the form of their emperor. Even from where Pullus lay in his litter, he could see the mixture of anger and confusion on the Wa's face, but unlike his feelings for the boy emperor, Pullus had no sympathy for whatever turmoil the commander might be feeling. All he cared about was that the commander saw what was about to happen and understand the meaning, and give the order to his troops, waiting a short distance from here.

Caesar had dismounted, but was standing on a rostra built from some of his men's shields, so that he still towered above the kneeling barbarians. Despite his overall hostility towards the Wa, Pullus had to acknowledge that their discipline was impressive; he couldn't imagine a Legion staying in such a position as these barbarians were still in, kneeling with bowed heads, for nearly as long as they had been doing. But these men were clearly accustomed to obeying, something that Caesar must have seen and understood how to exploit, yet another reason why Pullus considered his general to be the greatest man who ever lived, or ever would, for that matter. Caesar began speaking, but Pullus didn't even try to listen, knowing that his general was addressing the Wa. Instead, he watched the guard commander closely, trying to interpret through his facial expressions and body language the general thrust of what Caesar was saying. When the Wa's head suddenly turned from Caesar to regard the boy emperor, who was no longer bound or even restrained by the two Germans on either side, Pullus assumed that the reason for this demonstration was close to being realized. Without the Germans to hold him up, the emperor had slumped to the ground, and while he was on his knees like the others, he sat upright, his face turned up toward Caesar. Suddenly, he let out a loud wail, tearing Pullus' gaze away from the commander, and he turned to see that now tears were streaming down the boy's face. Clearly he had just learned what Caesar had planned for him, and again Pullus felt a stab of pity. It was really just his bad luck, the Primus Pilus reflected, nothing more than that.

Caesar finished speaking, then hopped down from the rostra, demonstrating a spryness that anyone who knew his age would marvel at, and Pullus also knew this was calculated. After all, he thought, gods don't age. Immediately following that was the thought that perhaps Caesar, and by extension the army, wasn't out of danger after all. Unless he planned on wearing that red paint for the rest of his time here on the island, the moment he removed it there would be no mistaking his age. He had been cunning, wearing his oak crown to hide his silver hair and bald pate, something that he usually tried to hide by growing the hair long on one side to comb it over, in a futile attempt to hide his baldness. Before his mind went off in a direction that he could do nothing but worry about, Titus forced himself to turn his attention back to the moment at hand, and was just in time to see Caesar take the hilt of a *pugio*, the Legionary dagger, offered to him by one of the Germans. Holding it aloft so that all could see it, Caesar's voice rang out, his tone hard and demanding, and while Pullus didn't understand the words, he saw the intent when the rows of kneeling barbarians, who had remained with their foreheads pressed to the hard-packed earth, lifted their heads to look at Caesar. Pullus returned his attention back to the commander, seeing the tension radiating from his body as he seemed about to leap forward. The Germans around him saw this as well, as one of them slowly drew his sword. Hearing the rasping of the blade being drawn from the scabbard, the commander looked over at the German, his face twisting into a mask of bitter but impotent anger. For a moment, Pullus was sure the commander would leap at the German, but making a great show of disdain, he returned his attention back to Caesar and the boy. By this point the boy had begun wailing non-stop, reaching his arms out in supplication in the direction of the nearest kneeling Wa, but to a man they refused to meet his gaze or even show in any way that they heard his pleas. Caesar continued talking, his voice still hard and unyielding as he slowly made one full turn with the sword still above his head. When he returned to a point where he was facing the boy, only then did he lower his voice, but when he spoke again it was in Latin, and Pullus could just catch the words.

"Hold his right arm."

Neither German hesitated, grabbing each arm, despite the boy's clearly futile attempts to keep them to his sides. Now that the boy emperor was babbling, Pullus was sure that he was incomprehensible to the other barbarians, so out of his mind with fear was he. Then, Caesar bent down, so that his face was just a matter of inches from the boy's ears, and Pullus could see his lips moving, but couldn't hear his general's voice. Whatever it was, it caused a reaction with the boy that seemed to penetrate his fog of terror, and he suddenly looked up at Caesar, an expression on his face that Pullus couldn't easily interpret. Did he look...hopeful? The boy was actually facing away from most of the kneeling Wa, directly across from where Pullus was in his litter, so very few, if any, of the palace staff saw the change in his expression. Caesar straightened up, brandished the dagger once more, and bellowing words in the Wa tongue, made a slashing motion with the blade.

Now, sitting in the small house, Pullus could only shake his head at the recent memory.

"I thought for sure he was going to cut that boy's head off."

"So did I," Scribonius agreed. "But as I thought about it, it makes sense. He was showing the barbarians that the boy was a mortal, and not a god. What better way to do it than make him bleed? It doesn't kill the boy, but it clearly demonstrates that he sheds blood like every mortal."

"Still, I'm surprised Caesar didn't kill him. It just seems that the boy is one loose end. Caesar doesn't need someone else who holds a grudge and wants to kill him."

"True," Scribonius conceded, "but you know Caesar isn't a normally vengeful man. Yes, he'll be merciless when he doesn't see any other way to get his point across. But he doesn't kill just for the sake of killing. So," Scribonius turned to another subject, "what have you heard about this 'army of the north'?"

"Just that a delegation of palace officials is being escorted by the 25th to meet them on the road."

"Did that haughty bastard go with them?"

Scribonius had no need to expand on that question; Pullus knew exactly who he was talking about.

"Yes, the royal guard commander apparently had a change of heart once he saw that boy's blood dripping into the dirt."

"I don't know," Scribonius said doubtfully, "I don't trust him."

"Neither does Caesar. That's why he gave Gundarus specific orders that if he so much looked at anyone the wrong way, his head was supposed to part company from the rest of his body. And you know Gundarus: there's nothing he loves better than lopping off someone's head," Pullus was referring to the last of the de facto officers of the German bodyguard, a man of equal height and strength with Titus Pullus himself, something that Pullus privately wasn't very happy about.

Neither man was friends with the other, but both were friendly, in that wary sort of way in which two bulls can coexist in a herd.

"And what's Caesar's longer-range plan? Any idea?" Scribonius asked Pullus, but his friend could only shake his head, not without some frustration.

Perhaps a third of a watch before, Pullus had been carried back to what he supposed would be his quarters for the time being, fresh from the latest meeting with Caesar and some of the generals who were finished with their tasks of the day. The entire army, save for the 10th and 12th, which was serving as a de facto palace guard, was spread throughout the capital. But contrary to what Pullus and the rest of the army expected, there wasn't the normal sounds of an enemy city falling to the sword. Caesar had been very specific and very demanding in his orders: if one of his men broke the peace, he would be in the unenviable position of hoping for a flogging with the scourge, because that was the lightest punishment Caesar promised to transgressors. As long as the barbarians weren't clearly members of the warrior caste, they were to be allowed an extraordinary degree of freedom. Except for one restriction: nobody was allowed to leave the capital. To that end, the entire city was ringed by Legionaries on watch, each post no more than 50 paces away from the next, making escape next to impossible, even for a skilled warrior. There was one task that Pullus knew was being performed in the night, and while it didn't trouble him unduly, it did serve to remind him of other times, when similar things had happened in Caesar's army. Small groups of men, even as Scribonius and Pullus were eating their meal, were going from house to house, searching for any member of either the group of disgraced nobles or the remnants of the royal guard that might have escaped the fighting in order to hide. These men were to be executed, on the spot, as quickly and quietly as possible. The members of the royal guard that had been waiting at the pass for a Roman army that never showed up had been disarmed, the order given by the royal guard commander, who, when faced with both the seemingly incontrovertible proof of his emperor's mortality and the complete submission of the entire royal government had bowed to the seemingly inevitable. These men, while unarmed now, were still under heavy guard, and Pullus knew that their fate had yet to be decided.

"We have another meeting in the morning, where he says he'll explain more of what's going to happen."

"Maybe he'll tell us that we can finally go home," Scribonius sighed, thinking wistfully about the idea of seeing Rome, the city of his birth, one more time.

This sentiment surprised Pullus a great deal, because normally Scribonius was the pragmatic one of the two, and for months he had opined how unlikely he thought it was that either one of them, or any member of the army, would ever see Rome again.

"Sextus, I hope you're right," Pullus replied cautiously. "But I have a feeling in my bones that Caesar isn't going anywhere."

Morning dawned quietly and the air was still—nothing like the day before when the Legions had been preparing to assault the capital. Pullus was extremely surprised that he had gotten any sleep at all, but he attributed it to the spoonful of poppy syrup that Diocles had forced down his throat. His chest throbbed with an intensity that was only slightly less than what he experienced in the days immediately after he suffered his wound, but he wasn't about to miss the briefing that Caesar had called for a third of a watch after sunrise, even if he did have to be carried there. Thinking for just a moment of eschewing the litter and walking, he immediately banished the thought, telling himself that it was only because he didn't want to draw Caesar's wrath. The total truth was that he knew he was too weak to have any confidence that he wouldn't fall flat on his face. Another concession he made to his condition, he decided, would be to wear only his tunic, a fresh one of course. It wouldn't do to show up in one either stained with blood, like the one he had on the day before, or one with bloodstains and a huge hole in the chest, like the one he had worn a little more than a week before. In fact, Pullus wasn't sure if he had more than one clean, unstained tunic, which was the one he was wearing right then. Calling Diocles, who had taken a corner of the only room of this small house for himself, using a wood and leather screen that had traveled as much of the world as its owner, Pullus began the laborious process of making himself ready for the day. Elsewhere, the Primi Pili of the Legions, the Tribunes and Legates, those who were still in the capital at any rate, were doing the same. Every man knew that today was going to be a day that was almost as momentous as the day before, and none of them wanted to miss anything. Diocles didn't answer, annoying Pullus and sending him to walk unsteadily to the corner his diminutive servant had claimed as his own. While still technically a slave, at least as far as Rome was concerned, the relationship between the Roman and the Greek had surpassed that of master and slave so far that if the truth were known, neither of them thought of the other in such terms. The only reason Diocles wasn't in possession of a manumission document announcing that he was now a freedman was the fact that this document was essentially meaningless, here on the far side of the world. It had been years since they had been anywhere where even one person spoke or read Latin—or Greek, for that matter. The Han used a system that to Pullus looked like chicken scratch, and he hadn't seen even that here in the land of the Wa, or with the Gayans on the mainland either. Muttering a curse, Pullus turned away from Diocles' empty bed, grumbling under his breath about servants out doing only the gods knew what at the crack of dawn. He had just managed to fasten his soldier's belt, essentially with one hand because his left wasn't strong enough to help. The irony wasn't lost on him that just the day before he had somehow found the strength to heft a shield, but now he couldn't hold a belt buckle in place to pull the belt through. Fortunately Diocles entered the house, announcing himself with a quick rap on the door, carrying a wooden bowl filled with still-steaming rice.

"Where have you been?" Pullus asked sourly, but Diocles was completely unfazed.

"Getting your breakfast, and you're welcome! I managed to find a piece of pork to go with it!" His tone was so cheerful that Pullus couldn't stay upset, and he was truly grateful that he had such a servant, whose first thought was for Pullus and not himself.

The fact that Pullus cultivated this type of loyalty in others, not just slaves, was something the Roman was only vaguely aware of, but put down to the idea that he always tried to be fair in his dealings and never take advantage of his position.

"What I wouldn't give for a nice, warm loaf of bread, made with wheat, and not this slop," Pullus grumbled, but that didn't stop him from consuming what Diocles was offering.

He knew he needed to keep his strength up, and as tasteless as the white, sticky grain was to his tastes, it clearly possessed whatever it was that provided the same kind of energy his beloved bread did.

"I wonder if Caesar is going to make these people start growing wheat?" Diocles was more thinking aloud than asking a question for which he expected an answer, because he missed bread no less than Pullus did.

"I don't know, but I doubt it." Pullus had become somewhat accustomed to shrugging with only one shoulder, at most. "This island is just too mountainous. Besides, what little arable land is available is already flooded. It would have to be drained for wheat to grow."

"Well, maybe you can whisper the idea into Caesar's ear!" Diocles suggested, prompting a bark of a laugh from Pullus.

"Somehow I think he's already thought about it," Pullus replied.

Just as he finished, the slaves bearing the litter arrived, and Pullus, still grumbling, walked out of the open door and settled himself in as much comfort as he could manage.

"I don't know how long I'll be gone," he told Diocles as the bearers lifted the litter and began walking with their slow, sliding gait that was designed to provide the smoothest ride possible.

And with that, Pullus departed for the palace to meet with a god.

Since this meeting was for men of Caesar's army only and was conducted in the largest room in the palace that could be sealed off, with every entryway guarded by a combined force of Caesar's Germans and Legionaries personally selected by the general, Caesar appeared in his normal state, without the paint or crown.

"As you can imagine, we have much to discuss," Caesar announced to the assembled senior officers of his army.

The only men missing at this point were the Primus Pilus of the 25th Legion, along with Aulus Ventidius and his officers who had accompanied the Legion on its mission or who were still with the fleet. Otherwise, every man in a leadership position was present, and the stools that normally graced the *praetorium* had been brought here. The only exception made was for Pullus, who under Caesar's stern eye, was perched on a couch, trying not to look embarrassed at being propped up on pillows as he reclined. Unwilling to allow the men to whisper their speculations to each other as he normally did, Caesar raised a hand for silence.

"Truly, we have no time to waste. I need to apprise you of my plans, both for the immediate future of the men of the army, and my longer-term vision for what I hope to accomplish."

What followed, over the next full watch, was staggering in its scope, ambition, and thoroughness, even for men like Pullus who had more faith in Caesar than just about any other man present. But even for Caesar, this was breathtaking, and it told Pullus, and some of the others with equally quick minds, that this was something Caesar had thought through in a very, very detailed manner. As Pullus would try to relay later that night to Diocles and Scribonius, the gist was essentially simple: Caesar had decided that for all intents and purposes, this campaign, now in its tenth year, was over. He had reached what he considered to be the end of the known world, and because of a variety of circumstances, he had decided to take full advantage of his newly found status as a god of the people of Wa and stay put.

"This will be my new island kingdom." He said this as matter-of-factly as if he were proclaiming his decision to purchase a horse. Or a mule, even. "I will rule here for the rest of my days, with your help."

Caesar didn't appear to be particularly surprised when there was a subdued uproar over this, as men protested either to the man next to them or to Caesar that they had no desire to live on this accursed island. He listened impassively for a few moments before he raised his hand again, and because the words that would come from his mouth were so important, the men fell silent immediately.

"I did not say that those of you who wish to return home may not do so," Caesar explained patiently. "However, I can't allow you to leave just yet. There is one task that I need you men to perform."

Because Pullus was on his couch, he was somewhat isolated and unable to exchange a glance or quiet word with a man sitting next to him, so he was left to observe all of this taking place.

"What is it that you need, Caesar?" Balbinus, now partially recovered from his own wounds, was finally the man who voiced the question to which everyone else wanted an answer.

"I need you to help train the warriors of Wa into being Legionaries worthy of marching for Rome."

The reaction was immediate and intense, as men jumped to their feet, shouting their protest at this idea. Again, Caesar was unmoved, and from Pullus' vantage point, a little closer to Caesar than the others, he noticed a singular lack of expression on his general's face. Normally at this point, he would either be amused or irritated, but now he seemed to feel nothing from this outburst. Perhaps he really thinks he *is* a god, Pullus mused. Over the babel of voices, one man shouted a word that at last elicited a reaction, and that word was "impossible".

"Impossible?" Caesar pounced on this word the same way a cat did a rat intent on escape. "You say that it's impossible? Will you never learn? You've been training new men in our ways for the last several years, starting with the Parthians," Caesar expressing scorn was a dish for which Pullus knew he had no taste, and he was secretly relieved to see his peers felt the same way.

Suddenly looking down at the ground, or at each other—anywhere but Caesar—what had been a riot of noise became more muted as men continued protesting, but just in a quieter tone. It was one of his generals, Asinius Pollio who had the courage to bring up the unspoken.

"Yes, Caesar. You're right that the Primi Pili and other Centurions have become very experienced at training barbarians from a variety of lands to meet our standards. But this? This is different! Because you're not just talking about training a handful of men that answered the call for volunteers, but an entire army, full of men who, at the very best, aren't happy about their lot. At the worst?"

Pollio gave an extravagant shrug, but the point wasn't lost on Caesar.

"I didn't say it wouldn't be difficult, Pollio," Caesar acknowledged. "But not impossible. As I'm sure you have observed as well, one aspect of these Wa is their absolute, unquestioning obedience to orders. Need I remind anyone what they used to fill the ditch, instead of the bundles of wood we use?"

In fact, Caesar didn't: of all the memories this campaign would be responsible for creating in the minds of the men of the Roman army, for those who saw it firsthand, the sight of men willingly leaping into the ditch fronting the camp wall was one that would live with them forever.

Continuing, Caesar said, "The key to success lies in their belief that this dramatic change has been foreordained by their gods, and their conviction that I am one of those gods."

For Pullus, there was a feeling of unreality, listening to Caesar discussing the subject of his divinity in the same tone as he would discuss the watchword for the day. It also aroused in him a sense of disquiet that he could tell, by the expressions of the other men, was shared by them. While Pullus understood Caesar's rationale, what was becoming a growing sense of worry was the extent to which Caesar believed in his own divinity. Oblivious to the thoughts that occupied his Primus Pilus' mind, Caesar carried on explaining his plans.

"But of course, there are practical problems that must be overcome, and the most immediate is the language barrier. I know that most of you don't have my facility for languages, but I believe that for our purposes none of you needs to carry on much of a conversation with any of the Wa. To that end, allow me to introduce to you the person that will be instructing you in what you will need to know, in order to issue commands and ensure that they are understood."

Caesar nodded to one of the guards posted at a door behind him, the one from which he had entered this meeting room. The German turned, opened the door and beckoned to someone outside of Pullus' view. Although Pullus knew what to expect, the sight of the beautiful young barbarian girl was still something of a shock, and for a man who hadn't seen a woman who wasn't quaking in fear or dressed in the filthy rags the peasants of this island wore, it was a welcome jolt to the system. Pullus stared at the girl, whose own eyes were downcast, not moving them from the floor immediately in front of her as she entered, her anxiety clear for all to see. Nevertheless, she obediently came to Caesar's side, who spoke a few quiet words to her that—while Pullus couldn't hear them distinctly, he could tell by the cadence and rhythm—were in her own tongue. Clearly soothed by his words, only then did she lift her head, her oval face without blemish, and despite the fact that Pullus had seen her up close once before, he still felt his breath taken away at her beauty. From where he was sitting, her almond-shaped eyes seemed to be as black as obsidian, yet for some reason, this only added to her exotic beauty.

"This is Ko," Caesar announced, "which, as far as I can tell, means 'girl', and is what every female of the Wa is called. I wasn't pleased with that name, so she now answers to 'Diana'."

Pullus, for one, didn't see anything to indicate that this beautiful creature was a huntress, but neither was he inclined to argue the point.

"Also, while I have learned her tongue, in return I have taught her ours, and I will admit that I'm not a little surprised to find out she has a facility for languages that, while it's not equal to mine," Caesar would only bend so far, especially for a woman, "is very impressive."

Turning to the girl, he gave a nod to her. In return, she gave Caesar a slight bow, then turned to face the assembled Romans. If Caesar had demanded it, the room couldn't have been more silent, as every man in the room found he was holding his breath, waiting to hear a feminine voice, each of them as hungry as Pullus for any touch of the opposite sex.

"My...name...is...Diana," the girl's voice was low-pitched and made even softer by her nerves. "As...my master," with every word, the voice of the girl known as Diana grew stronger, "has said, I have learned your words and he has commanded me to teach you the words you will need to know, so that you can train the warriors of Wa."

And with this seemingly simple introduction, Diana began the first of the steps that would cement Caesar's status as a god among the Wa.

Naturally, while the overall goal was straightforward, the details of what was required to achieve Caesar's aim were anything but—something that Pullus and the other Primi Pili had thought about on multiple occasions. There were tense moments, starting when the 25th Legion and Asinius Pollio, along with the Wa palace officials who accompanied them, met the northern army some 25 miles north of the capital. Over two days of tense negotiations, the generals leading the force from the north finally recognized what the eunuchs, members of the royal guard, and residents of the capital had already accepted, but not before the evidence in the form of the young emperor's blood were displayed to them. Only after this evidence of mortality was almost literally shoved into the face of the generals did they acquiesce. With a watchful 25th Legion following behind them, the northern army continued southward to the capital, where they were halted a mile from the outskirts and ordered to make camp. It was no coincidence that the Wa's camp was less than a half mile from where two Legions were encamped, but the Legionaries were under strict orders not to interact or interfere with the Wa, only to watch them. Meanwhile, the Legions assigned to keep order within the limits of the capital had been put to work making repairs to all damaged structures, burying the bodies of the slain Wa, and restoring order.

Truthfully, their task was made easier by the remaining civilians, motivated by the fact that word of the demonstration of the emperor's mortality had flashed through the streets and houses of the capital. Nobody still remaining was unaware that a great cataclysm had occurred in their society and that a new deity was overseeing their lives, a fact that naturally was the cause of a great deal of apprehension. Tensions were extremely high, not helped by the obvious differences, such as in language. But putting even more strain on the situation were those differences that ran even deeper than the words spoken by each side; indeed, the very way they looked at the world around them was markedly different in a number of ways. However, where it mattered, at least for Caesar's purposes, there were distinct similarities: obedience to authority, a stoic acceptance of fate as ordained by the gods, and a very rigid class system. So, despite the language barrier, the tone used by the Legionaries when barking orders to the civilians, along with the pointed gestures and occasional shoves, was clearly understood by the terrified townspeople. There was trouble in only a handful of streets, as the Legionaries conducted a thorough search that was part census and part search for weapons, or more importantly, a search for warriors who had refused to submit. To nobody's surprise, at least on the part of the Romans, there were a fair number of men such as these, but unlike the band of disgraced nobles, they hadn't managed to band together in anything more than bunches of two's and three's, and so were easily cut down when flushed out of hiding.

This wasn't accomplished without loss, and more than one man of the Legions was left to ponder the bitter irony of seeing a close friend struck down now, when supposedly all the fighting was over. While the men of the Legions were busy with their tasks around the city, in the large meeting room of the palace, quite different work was taking place, and although Pullus was still given leave to recline on a couch, propped up on pillows, he nevertheless felt like he was in school. Of course, he had never been in a school setting before, but men like Scribonius had, so he had some idea of what it was like. Regardless, Pullus was sure that nobody from his world had ever had a teacher like the one standing before this small, select group of men, all of them but Pullus sitting uncomfortably on stools. In each man's lap was a wax tablet, and standing in front of all of them was Diana, who was teaching them a series of simple commands. The method by which Caesar had learned the Wa tongue was simple, but effective, and it was in this same way that the Centurions were now being taught. Caesar had quickly determined that there was absolutely no commonality in the symbols used by either Latins or Greeks and the people of this island. That hadn't surprised him; he had assumed that if there were similarities they would be to the written language used by the Han, but soon after the girl had come into Caesar's possession, he had Zhang look at some of the symbols that she knew, few as they were, and had been told by the Han emissary that the similarities weren't enough for him to decipher. Caesar had his suspicions that Zhang wasn't telling the truth, but he had operated as if the emissary had been honest, at least on this topic. Consequently, as Caesar learned the words for objects and actions, he had written them phonetically, using the Roman alphabet.

This was what the Centurions were doing now, as Diana started with a simple series of objects that would be used by a member of the Legions, pointing to each one, saying the word as the Centurion wrote it down and repeated it. While the Centurions were in the process of learning what they would need to know to communicate with the Wa, Caesar was closeted away with the members of the palace staff. This audience required Caesar to don the red paint again, along with the oak crown, but instead of his armor, this time he wore his Senatorial toga, with the broad purple stripe. And in direct contradiction of the customs of Rome, Caesar also wore his scarlet *paludamentum*, which normally would never be worn with a toga, but with armor. The Wa didn't know that, however, and he was using every trick he knew to create a sense of majesty that bespoke his celestial heritage. At this moment, Caesar knew that the Wa feared him and his army, but he also understood that this wasn't a viable long-term strategy. He also recognized that his days of appearing in this guise were numbered, if only because he was going to run out of red paint at some point. Though Caesar was conversant in the Wa tongue, he wasn't fluent, and some of the topics that he wanted to discuss were very complex and required him to call for Diana on more than one occasion to translate, at least to the best of her ability. Slowly, very slowly, Caesar was beginning to grasp the true scope and enormity of the task he had set for himself, but his old confidence had been restored, and he had no doubt that he would succeed—provided, of course, that there were no more nasty surprises in store.

By the time a week had passed, a number of things had happened. Most importantly, the Centurions had learned enough of the Wa tongue to at least begin the training of the members of the royal guard. Additionally, Zhang, Nero, and those Legionaries left behind to recuperate on the ships of the fleet had arrived in the capital, along with wagons of supplies. Caesar had also dispatched orders to send a ship back to the first island the Romans had captured in this campaign, off the Gayan Peninsula, where the Roman supply base was located. The Cohorts that had been left behind were recalled, with instructions to bring everything with them. Zhang's arrival had precipitated the first crisis for Caesar, for the Han had been given no forewarning of what had transpired in the capital. This Caesar had done on purpose, because he was sure the Han's reaction, when faced with this surprising development, would give him more of an idea of the true purpose for the Han emperor's insistence that Zhang accompany the campaign. As it happened, Nero, Zhang and a number of other officers came riding in ahead of the men returning from the fleet, arriving just as the daily tutoring session with Diana was ending. All of the other Centurions had returned to their quarters, the plan being that the training of the Wa would start in earnest the next day. Pullus, still confined to a litter, was waiting for the slaves to arrive, grumbling to himself that Caesar was still watching him like a hawk, or he would just walk the short distance to his own house. Later he was extremely happy that the litter-bearers were late, because he would have missed something that was both entertaining and instructive.

Alerted that they had arrived and were outside the palace, Caesar ordered the sentry at the door to hold them there, until such time as he could don his regalia to meet the newly arrived men. If it had just been Nero, he wouldn't have bothered, but he wanted to make an impression on Zhang that the Han would never forget. By the time they were allowed entry, both men were an equal mix of angry and bewildered, especially Nero, for whom Pullus had little regard, happy to see the nobleman so discomfited. With Zhang, it was almost impossible to tell, his smooth, flat features seemingly perfectly made for containing any emotion within, but Pullus thought he detected a hint of agitation in the way the Han's hands clenched and unclenched. But if the pair were surprised at their initial reception, what happened next had to flabbergast them, because when they were ushered into the large meeting room, they were greeted only by the presence of Pullus, still reclining on his couch, along with the palace official standing in front of what had once been the throne of the Wa emperor, currently empty. The chief official, whose name Pullus had learned was Kiyama, was waiting for the two men at the foot of the raised dais on which the throne sat, his face as flat and emotionless as that of Zhang. Caesar had mentioned to Pullus that this Kiyama spoke Zhang's Han tongue, and Pullus could tell by the more sing-song lilt that this was what Kiyama was speaking to the Han. Whereas Zhang had managed to suppress any agitation to that point, whatever Kiyama said eroded his hold over himself, because there was no mistaking the rush of color that came to the Han's face. He immediately shot back a reply, his tone informing Pullus that Zhang wasn't just surprised, he was clearly enraged. Obviously Kiyama had dealt with moments such as this, because the eunuch appeared completely unruffled by Zhang's outburst, and although he couldn't understand the words, Pullus could pick up the same rhythms and understood that Kiyama was repeating what he had uttered a moment before. Zhang didn't reply to this, and the silence grew as both men stared at each other, while Nero stood next to Zhang, looking completely befuddled. Finally Zhang, while not breaking the silence, at least dispelled the tension somewhat by exhaling a breath, then dropping to his knees. Glaring at Kiyama for a moment, he finished the movement by leaning forward and placing his head on the wooden floor of the room, and that was when Pullus understood what Kiyama had said. Nero, staring down at the kneeling Han, made a move as if to follow suit.

"Don't," Pullus spoke up, startling everyone in the room, and only just remembered to add, "sir."

Nero looked at Pullus in obvious surprise, which for once Pullus was willing to concede was understandable and not just due to what he saw as Nero's thickness.

"I'm sure that order that Kiyama gave was meant just for Zhang, not for you," Pullus had begun to speak in Latin, but managed to switch to Greek, remembering the surprise that Zhang had pulled when he finally revealed he understood Latin.

Nero's face was a study in confusion; not just because of what Pullus had said, but that a man Nero considered to be just a shade above the barbarians infesting these islands was speaking Greek. Consequently, Pullus had to repeat himself before Nero—who at least had the presence of mind to reply in Greek—indicated that he understood, and remained standing. Only then did Kiyama turn around and head for the door just behind the throne that Pullus knew was there, although an ornately carved wooden screen shielded the doorway from view. From where Pullus was lying on his couch, he was at an oblique enough angle to see Caesar enter, bedecked in what Pullus thought of as his god costume, moving quietly around the screen and up onto the dais, settling into the throne. Since Nero hadn't been required to kneel or otherwise avert his gaze, he let out a gasp at the sight of his general, causing Zhang to raise his head surreptitiously, just enough to see what had caused Nero's outburst, meaning his own exclamation followed immediately.

"*Silete!*" Caesar thundered the word in Latin, stilling whatever else Zhang was planning to say.

Without waiting, Caesar continued, "We will conduct this interview in Latin, since I know that not only do you speak our language, but also that you've had even more time to perfect your fluency while you were with the fleet."

Caesar paused just long enough for Zhang to understand that a response was expected, and he complied with a terse, "I understand, Caesar."

"That is the last time you will address me by name," Caesar's tone was the only indication that he was being almost genial, since his painted face gave no hint as to the emotions lying beneath. "Much has happened since we were last together," he went on, which Pullus thought was one of the most understated pronouncements Caesar had ever uttered. "And the most important change, at least as far as you are concerned, is that the Wa have recognized my divinity."

Speaking in a tone that could have been used when discussing the amount of rice left in stores, Caesar made no less of an impression on Zhang who, forgetting himself for a moment, raised himself up to stare at Caesar in open astonishment.

"I did not give you leave to cease your obeisance," Caesar's tone instantly turned as icy as the winds that came howling across the great steppes of the mainland.

To Zhang's credit, he immediately dropped back down, but again Pullus could see the fury that seemed to emanate from the Han, even if he was in a position of submission.

"As I was saying, now that I am considered a god by the Wa, I have decided that the islands that are the traditional home of the Wa will be my kingdom, subject to my rule and my rule alone."

There it was, Pullus thought, out in the open for everyone to hear and understand, because he knew that there was no way Nero would keep this to himself, and the Primus Pilus suspected that this had been no accident. Of all Caesar's generals, Nero's reputation as an inveterate gossip was widely acknowledged, and Pullus knew that everything Caesar had said would be flashing through the camps of the Roman army, now spread all around the capital. The silence hung in the air for several moments before Zhang finally spoke, his voice carefully modulated.

"That is...interesting," he paused for a moment. "Forgive me, but I do not know how to address you now."

"When we're speaking Latin, you will call me Divus Julius," Caesar replied promptly, telling Pullus that this wasn't something spontaneous, that Caesar had obviously planned it.

Up to now, Caesar had made no such demands on his men, of any rank, but Pullus had a nagging thought that perhaps this would change.

"Yes...Divus Julius," Zhang continued, "but I will say that my master will be most disappointed to hear that you have such...ambitions."

"An ambition is something to which a man aspires," Caesar pointed out, "but as I have already achieved this, it is hardly an ambition. It is a fact."

"True," Zhang granted, and Pullus realized that he had never seen the Han so off-balance or hesitant.

Which, he knew, was precisely what Caesar had intended.

"But we have a saying among the Han about a man's reach not exceeding his grasp. I cannot help wondering if perhaps you have overreached?"

"And who is there to tell me that I have done so?" Caesar asked, and while his voice was pleasant, both Pullus and Nero knew their general well enough to recognize the very dangerous undertone.

"I would remind Cae...Divus Julius that he is here only because of the assistance of the Han," Zhang replied calmly, oblivious to the gasps of the other two Romans in the room. "And that he and his army are indebted to my emperor for that assistance. If he were to require repayment of all that he has given you, it would be only just and fair. But when all the food, livestock, iron ingots, and cloth are added up, they make up such a vast sum that it would be impossible for you to pay, would it not?"

"And why would I need to do that?" Caesar demanded coldly. "As I recall, your emperor was very anxious to provide all that he did as a gift. To prevent us from taking it."

Zhang's face grew even darker, but his tone remained calm.

"Be that as it may, I have always thought that Divus Julius was, of all the great men of the world, the greatest because of his honor. It would seem to me that a repayment of a debt would be a matter of honor."

"If I were you, I would be very careful when talking about matters such as honor," Caesar said this more softly than anything he had uttered to that point, which only served to add to the menace.

"Forgive me, Divus Julius," for the first time Zhang's voice betrayed a hint of strain. "But I would be remiss in my duty to my emperor if I were not to fight for his interests, would I not?"

"That you would be," Caesar agreed. "However, I fail to see what my activities here on the islands of the Wa have to do with your emperor. You have never indicated that he held any interest in the affairs of this island. In fact," Caesar reminded Zhang, "when I asked you specifically about this very thing, you assured me that your emperor would be most pleased if we pacified this land and secured its warlike people. Well, I have done that very thing. Now you are singing a different song. Can you explain why?"

Pullus tried to fight the grin creeping up his face, but couldn't manage it. Keeping his gaze on Zhang, he saw the Han emissary close his eyes briefly in what Pullus took to be Zhang's recognition that he had been outfoxed by Caesar and forced to declare openly the intentions of his emperor in regards to the island kingdom. Simply put, Zhang was outflanked and outmaneuvered, prompting Pullus' scornful thought, what were you thinking, barbarian? That you could outgeneral the greatest general in the history of the world? Haven't you seen enough?

"Only that my emperor sent me newer instructions, since we last talked about this subject. He believes that a just compensation for all the assistance he has given you would be to turn possession of the islands over to us. Of course, you would be allowed tenancy, without taxation, for as long as you choose to stay."

"Well, that is very generous of your emperor," Caesar replied dryly. "But I am curious: when exactly did these new instructions arrive?"

"After you separated from the fleet and began your march to the capital," Zhang said.

Caesar looked over at Nero, still standing slightly behind and to the side of Zhang's kneeling body. The commander of his fleet said nothing, but gave a slight shake of the head, telling Caesar that no strange vessels had been sighted, that Zhang had had no contact with anyone who could have passed such a message.

Caesar toyed with the idea of exposing this as a lie, but decided against it, saying only, "Be that as it may, you can reply to your emperor that while I have every intention of repaying his generosity, it will not be with any lands that now belong to me, by right of not only conquest, but also divinity."

"Ah," Zhang chose to change the topic slightly, "about your divinity. May I ask how that came about?"

"Oh, I am sure you will hear all about it before the sun sets. But even deities have business to attend to, and I am afraid I must cut this audience short. I will see that you are quartered comfortably, but given the...history of the relations between your people and what are now my people, I am afraid that your safety might be in jeopardy from some of my overzealous citizens. So I will make sure that your quarters are guarded against any intruders, and that you have an escort of my men wherever you go."

"That is very kind of you," Zhang actually seemed a bit more at ease, now that he and Caesar had slipped into the duplicitous language of the courtier, "but I assure you that I can take care of myself. I would hate to place an imposition on your men for such a trivial task, when they deserve a rest after their own exertions."

"It is no imposition, and I have only your best interests at heart, "Caesar assured Zhang, lying through his teeth every bit as much as the Han. "And I would not rest easy, knowing that you might be in danger."

Recognizing that this wasn't going to be negotiable, Zhang nodded his acceptance of Caesar's edict.

In one last attempt, he asked, "Will I at least be allowed to tour the capital? There are a number of sights that are quite famous to us that I would love to explore."

I bet you would, Pullus thought, but he had no reason to worry.

"Alas," Caesar said as regretfully as he could, without making it obvious he was again lying, "but the capital still hasn't been completely pacified. At least to my satisfaction. So, I'm afraid I must insist that you remain in your quarters, or go no farther than the boundaries of the imperial park. Which is very lovely."

Grimly nodding his head in understanding, Zhang waited to be given leave to rise, which Caesar granted.

Nodding his head in the direction of the door through which they entered, Caesar told Zhang, "One of my men is waiting to escort you to your quarters. I assume your baggage is following with the rest of the men from the ships?"

Zhang nodded, then walked slowly to the door, where a burly Legionary stood framed in the doorway, waiting. Nero, clearly unsure what to do, started to turn about to follow but was stopped by Caesar.

"You and I have some things still to discuss, General."

That, Pullus thought, is an understatement. Seeing through the now-open doorway that his litter bearers had arrived, Pullus rose and looked questioningly to Caesar, who nodded his dismissal as he stood up from the throne, then stepped down from the dais, hand outstretched to Nero. Only Pullus caught the fact that Zhang had glanced back over his shoulder and had seen this exchange, his mouth twisting into an angry grimace.

Much to the surprise of Pullus and that of most of the other officers of the Roman army, the training of the men of Wa progressed much more smoothly than any of them had anticipated. Naturally, there were language difficulties, particularly in the first few weeks, but the Romans were struck by the eagerness the Wa showed. More importantly, the Wa's acceptance of the radical change to their situation was something that occupied many of the dinnertime conversations in the houses of the Centurions.

"I can't even imagine how Romans would react if they were told that everything they had come to believe as fact was not only untrue, but then were also forced to suddenly recognize a completely foreign authority they had never even heard of, before it showed up," was how Pullus put it.

Scribonius considered this for a moment, chewing thoughtfully before he replied, "If it was done the way Caesar did it to these people, I can see it being possible, at least. He moved so fast, and appeared to know so much about the Wa that they were caught by complete surprise. In fact," Scribonius tossed his spoon back into his bowl as he sat back to ruminate further, "I think the worst is still to come."

"By the gods, I hope not!" Gaius Porcinus groaned. "We don't have enough men left to keep these bastards under control if they rise up again."

The trio were, as was their long practice, eating in the privacy of Pullus' quarters, but while Gaius and Scribonius were frequent guests, there was one man missing to whose absence each man was adjusting in his own way, and that was Balbus. In fact, very little had been said between Pullus and Scribonius, for that matter, about the loss of the third of what had been incredibly close companions for many years, long before Gaius joined the group. Porcinus knew the two older men missed Balbus tremendously, but didn't feel that it was his place to bring his name up; one of them would do so, in his own time.

Now, Scribonius answered Gaius' concern with a shake of his head, saying, "Actually, I don't worry about the Wa so much. Like Caesar said, they're used to obeying orders and their class system is even more rigid than ours. From what I can gather, the idea of someone being able to elevate himself from one class to another is unheard of. No," he concluded, "I think it's Zhang and the Han we have to worry about."

Pullus regarded his friend's words as he listlessly spooned another helping of rice into his bowl. His appetite had returned, but he still found it hard to muster any enthusiasm for what he consider to be the most flavorless food he had ever tasted.

Finally, he spoke up, "I think that's why Caesar is pushing us so hard to get these barba...." he corrected himself, because Caesar had been extremely explicit in his demand that his officers stop referring to the Wa as barbarians, "...these *Wa* into fighting our way as quickly as he can."

"So the fighting's not over, is it?" Gaius asked quietly.

Pullus and Scribonius exchanged a glance, the very tone of Pullus' nephew's question telling them more than the query itself.

"No, nephew," Pullus finally answered, but his voice held no censure.

"Will it ever be?" Gaius asked him, looking his uncle in the eyes, knowing that Pullus wouldn't lie to him.

Pullus felt a great weariness descend on him, becoming so overpowering that he felt the strength leave his hand, and like Scribonius had moments before, dropped the spoon back into his bowl. Returning Porcinus' gaze, he felt almost overwhelmed with the helplessness that comes from knowing that no answer he could give would provide any comfort. Hadn't they done enough? This thought shot through Pullus' mind like a lightning bolt, and while he had experienced moments of doubt before, when he tried to shake that feeling away, this time it wouldn't leave, clinging persistently in the forefront of his mind, like a spider web one walks through.

"Maybe not for Caesar," he finally answered Porcinus, the words coming slowly, as that clinging thought started to take on a more tangible form. "But it may be for us."

Scribonius, sensing there was something more underlying his friend's words, stared at Pullus intently.

"What are you saying, Titus?" he asked Pullus.

Turning to meet Scribonius' gaze, Titus didn't flinch.

"I'm saying that I think it's time I tell Caesar that we're done. It's time to go home."

The day that Titus Pullus decided to approach Caesar, almost a week after his conversation with Scribonius and Gaius, his nerves were such that it would have been impossible for him to differentiate this day from the day of the great battle on the ridge. He understood that his relationship with Caesar was about to undergo what was likely to be its severest test, and he tried to prepare mentally for what was to come. Although he tried to be optimistic, Pullus readied himself for the worst possible outcome, yet his mind refused to fully plumb the depths of how badly things could go. Part of this was due to the natural barrier that, even after so many years together, existed between a man like Caesar and someone from the ranks like Pullus, no matter how highly ranked the latter might have been. However, what fueled Pullus' uncertainty even more was his acknowledgement, if only to himself, that just in the weeks since the capital had fallen, Caesar had changed. What worried him most was how deeply that change ran in his general. Did Caesar actually believe that he had become a god? Had he finally made that last, final step onto a plane of belief in himself that cut the last threads of what tethered him to the rest of his army, or to the Wa, for that matter?

Unfortunately, Pullus thought grimly, there's only one way to find out. Frankly, he hadn't been all that surprised, when he had approached Apollodorus—who not only had survived the battle, but had also gained a shadow in the form of Kiyama, the palace eunuch—and was told that it would be several days before Caesar could see him. Despite somewhat expecting this answer, realizing that Caesar would be busier than he ever had been before, Pullus was nonetheless disappointed. One thing the Primus Pilus had grown accustomed to, but appreciated only when it was no longer the case, was having instant access to his general. Pullus couldn't even begin to count the number of times he had rushed to the *praetorium* and been ushered in immediately, sometimes even rousing his general from the few watches of sleep he got every night. Now he had to admit that it not only stung a bit to be treated as just another item of business, but it unnerved him, too.

"I think that Caesar is trying to shake you," was Scribonius' judgment, when Pullus informed him of the delay.

"Well, he's done it," Pullus shook his head. "And I can't say that it bodes well for what I'm going to ask him."

"No, it doesn't," Scribonius agreed. Giving his friend a level look that communicated even more than the words that followed, he continued, "But I can't think of anyone better to talk to Caesar about this."

As Scribonius had hoped, Pullus understood the unspoken message, that there was more at stake than Pullus' personal relationship with Caesar, and that he was going to have to be willing to sacrifice it in order to attain the larger goal.

Standing in the large chamber that both the former emperor and current occupant used to receive audiences, Pullus tried to pass the shaking of his legs off to the lingering weakness from his wound. That may have, in fact, been true, but Pullus suspected that there was another cause to this outward sign of his anxiety. He had decided, for the first time since his performance on the day the capital fell, to wear his full dress uniform, complete with *phalarae*, torqs, and arm rings. Topping it off, he was wearing the signet ring with the dragon seal Caesar had given to him, in what he hoped would be a subtle reminder of how much Caesar had favored his most faithful Primus Pilus. He had prepared himself for the tactic Caesar used with others to throw them off balance, and that was to keep them waiting past the appointed time of their meeting. What he hadn't prepared for was the length of the delay: by the time he heard the door behind the screen open, Pullus was sure that at least a third of a watch had passed. Seeing the shadow against the wall behind the screen as it moved around the carved wood, Pullus saw that there were two figures, and he had a bare instant to try to determine who it might be before the figure of Kiyama came into view. That was the last person Pullus had expected to be part of this conversation; normally it would have been Apollodorus, or one of the other scribes, in order to provide a complete transcript of the conversation that was about to take place.

Perhaps the sight of Kiyama softened the blow of what occurred next—at least as Pullus thought about it later—but it was still quite a shock when Caesar appeared. Pullus had momentarily considered that Caesar might appear in his god costume, but he quickly dismissed the idea, sure that his prior relationship with his general would preclude Caesar's need to present himself as a deity. But standing there, watching the red-faced entity, who was now wearing a floor-length, richly embroidered gown of green stitching over a deep purple background, the material Pullus had long since learned was silk, the Primus Pilus was rocked to his core. Granted, Caesar still wore his *paludamentum* over the gown, and his head wore the oak leaves that were purely Roman, yet the figure he presented was an amalgam of cultures that Pullus was sure the world had never seen before. Taking this all in, as Caesar, his red face immobile and completely devoid of anything that might give Pullus a hint of his thoughts, moved to the raised dais where the heavy chair was located. You can't see his feet moving; Pullus realized at once that this was precisely the effect Caesar was trying to create, of effortless motion that wasn't accomplished by anything as mundane as two legs. Ascending the step, Caesar placed himself on the chair, which could only be accurately described as a throne, carefully arranging his gown so that the folds were symmetrical, and, Pullus had to admit, pleasing to the eye. Once Caesar was done with this, his red mask tilted to a point where Pullus recognized that his general was gazing at him. Or was he? Pullus wondered. Caesar was certainly looking in the direction of the giant Roman, but was he really looking *at* Pullus? It was hard to tell, Pullus barely able to discern the glittering blue points that were Caesar's eyes amidst a sea of red.

"Primus Pilus Titus Pullus, it's always a pleasure to see you," the words made Pullus jump with surprise, not only at the sudden breaking of the silence, but also at the seemingly disembodied quality of his general's voice.

Unsure how to proceed, Pullus chided himself. Of course, he thought, he's going to try to keep you off-balance.

"Thank you for seeing me, Caesar," Pullus began, but was cut off by nothing more than a lifting of Caesar's finger.

"That is Divus Julius, if you please, Primus Pilus," the mask intoned.

If Caesar's goal had been to cow Titus Pullus, he had made a serious misjudgment. In fact, what Pullus experienced was a flare of anger that hadn't been quite this strong in some time.

"I'm afraid that I can't do that, Caesar," Pullus said, albeit through teeth that were tightly clenched. "If you'll remember, I knew you before you were a god. And," he finished, "if it weren't for me and the Legions, you wouldn't *be* a god."

Suddenly, the air in the chamber seemed to be charged with an energy neither man could have accurately described, while Kiyama, despite not understanding the words, knew that something potentially very, very dangerous was taking place. For a period of time none of them could measure, the Primus Pilus and the man who claimed to be a god glared at each other, neither of them backing down. Finally, it was Caesar who broke the silence.

"Very well," despite the emotionless mien the red paint gave him, Pullus knew his old general well enough to hear the seething anger underneath the soft voice. "You may call me as you've known me before, as Caesar. But Pullus," Caesar's voice dropped in tone and volume, so that Pullus could barely make out the words, "you *will* refer to me as Divus Julius in public. Or there will be...consequences. Do you understand me?"

Pullus understood very well; this was as far as his general was willing to bend, and despite his misgivings in doing so, Pullus gave his assurance that the Primus Pilus would always refer to Caesar in the manner in which he desired when in front of others. With this tension dispelled, at least for the moment, Caesar's body seemed to relax as he sat back against the high throne, intricately carved out of one of the native woods.

"So, now that this matter has been settled, what is it you wish to see me about?" Caesar asked, and while to others his tone may have seemed almost cordial, again, Pullus knew Caesar intimately enough to detect that his general was being anything but genial, that there was still a vestige of anger left over.

Despite knowing this, Pullus plunged ahead, undeterred. "I wanted to talk to you about the future."

"The future?" Caesar repeated, now making no attempt to hide his mocking attitude. "Of all things, I thought Titus Pullus never thought about the future. Your performance when the capital fell is a perfect example of that."

Despite the barb in his words, Pullus couldn't deny the truth in them. However, he refused to allow his general to put him on the defensive, no matter how hard Caesar tried.

"Maybe it's that...'performance', as you call it, that's prompted me to think about it."

"And?" Caesar's tone was still pleasant, but Pullus had known him long enough to hear the dangerous undercurrent. "What are your thoughts on the future?"

Pullus took a deep breath, but his gaze never wavered from the seated man, whose stare was equally fixed.

"That it's time to request permission from our general for those Roman citizens among us who choose to do so to be allowed to return to Rome."

Despite Caesar's thick red makeup, Pullus could see that the general was surprised by this. No, Pullus thought, he's more than surprised: he's shocked. For the span of several heartbeats, the only sound in the chamber was the raspy sound of breathing, and the detached part of Pullus' mind noticed that he wasn't the only one who sounded as if he had just run a short distance. At least he had an excuse for it; in fact, Pullus was aware that the trembling in his legs was still there, making him realize that this was the first time he had been in a vertical position, with his armor on, and for this long a time, since the day Caesar had mentioned. Feeling beads of sweat starting to form on the back of his neck, Pullus knew that it was only a matter of time before his face would be covered in a sheen of moisture.

"This is a surprise," Caesar broke the silence, his voice thick with some emotion Pullus couldn't identify.

"Why?" Pullus immediately shot back, again without thinking, a habit of his that had caused him more than his share of trouble. "Surely you didn't think that we'd continue marching forever, that we wouldn't want to go home at some point!"

"To what?" Caesar responded, no less quickly. "Don't you remember what happened the day before I left? What do you think has happened all these years since I've been gone? That Cicero and The Boni," even through the red paint Pullus could see his lip curl in contempt as he spat out the name that a small group of Roman Senators had given themselves, "wouldn't be working tirelessly these last ten years to poison the minds of the people?"

That's when Pullus realized that, somewhere during the past decade, Caesar had somehow convinced himself that his own grievances against those Romans who composed The Boni were suffered and carried equally strongly by his men, that their identities had become so intertwined that whatever Caesar felt, he was sure the men of his army felt as well. How could Pullus let Caesar know that this wasn't necessarily the case? In fact, the events and actions of The Boni were rarely, if ever, the subject of conversation around the fires. The Romans in the army had long since moved on to more immediate topics for conversation, and the most common subject that occupied the men at night were the prospects for loot, women, and a better quality of wine than the swill made from fermented rice. However, in the last few weeks that had changed, slowly but inexorably, to the thought that had previously been, by unspoken consent, forbidden. Would they ever see home again?

"Caesar," Pullus spoke slowly, trying to arrange the words in such a way that they would not only convey what he was trying to tell his general, but do it in such a way that he himself left this chamber alive. Because the conclusion that Pullus had come to in just the opening of what looked to be a long conversation was that Caesar had, putting it simply, lost his mind. Not in a way that one would associate with most madmen; he wasn't raving, he made perfect sense, but he was no less unhinged for all that if, as Pullus was sure he did, he believed that he was actually a god. "The men of this army have followed you across the known world, and there are no words that even as great an orator as you could utter that would do justice to the sacrifices and suffering they have endured at your command. Would you disagree with that statement?"

Silence stretched out between them, growing tauter and tauter, like a string on a harp, and Pullus could almost hear an imaginary note rising, as the harpist turned the tuning knob to increase the tension on the string. At some point, Pullus was sure, that string had to snap. Finally, it did, in the form of a long, slow exhalation, which was Pullus' first indication that Caesar had been holding his breath, presumably to contain an explosion. Yet, when he spoke, his voice didn't contain a trace of ire.

"No, Pullus. I would not disagree with that statement," Caesar broke the silence, and although there was no anger in his voice, Pullus knew his general well enough to detect some emotion there that he couldn't easily identify. Was it...sadness? "In fact, I think that this is perhaps the most accurate statement you've made, since we've been together. And that is a long, long time. Neh, Pullus?"

"That it is, Caesar," Pullus agreed, and then there was another silence as each man's mind moved, unbidden, through their respective pasts, touching on and treasuring in their own way specific memories of moments, when they had acted in concert, because of circumstances and common goals.

For Pullus, his mind flew back, not to the occasion of his first decoration by a then-Praetor of one of the provinces in Hispania, but when Pullus, his former best friend Vibius Domitius, and his current close comrade Sextus Scribonius had first laid eyes on Gaius Julius Caesar. Even then, Pullus liked to think he had seen something memorable in this man—older than most Praetors by a few years—although he was honest enough with himself to acknowledge that it was just as possible that he was coloring his memory with all that had transpired. Caesar, meanwhile, had been transported as well, but not that far back, to a memory that still pained him: when at Pharsalus his most favored and trusted Legion, the first one he had formed, the 10th Equestris, had refused to obey his command to follow the fleeing Pompey Magnus and the handful of men who still kept faith with the older general. It had shocked Caesar to his core, and sitting now on his throne, he could still almost taste in the back of his throat the bitter vetch of what he saw as a betrayal—except for one man, one giant Roman who, at that time was the Secundus Pilus Prior, leader of the Second Cohort, and who had shown himself willing to strike down even his best friend in support of Caesar.

That man, standing before him now, had proven his loyalty to Caesar over and above what could be expected of a man. Caesar knew this, but how could he accomplish all that he wanted to without him and the true core of his army? Despite Caesar's decision to remain, to build a kingdom here, modeled on his beloved Rome—but with the necessary modifications his native city desperately needed but that The Boni resisted with every fiber of their beings—he was Roman to his core. And although he would never admit it to anyone but himself, he needed to hear Roman voices speaking his native tongue with the accents that betrayed their origins in the Republic. This was something he had acknowledged to himself for some time, but what Caesar was just realizing was that, of all the voices, it was Pullus' he wanted to hear spoken to him in the future, as they faced whatever came their way. Another silence had descended on the two men, while Kiyama continued kneeling, eyes cast downward, but with his mind racing.

"So, you want to go home?" Caesar asked, but now his words came so softly that Pullus had to lean forward to catch them. "You want to leave me here to face whatever comes next without you, my giant friend?"

Of all the things Caesar could have said, none of them would have rocked Pullus as much as this, the first time Caesar ever uttered the word "friend" that was related in any way to himself. There had been nothing, Pullus had told himself many times over before this meeting, that Caesar could say that would shake his resolve. And Pullus now realized he had been wrong. Were they truly friends? Pullus wondered, his mind reeling at the enormity of everything this one simple word implied. For, if they were truly friends, didn't Pullus, in fact, have an obligation to stand by his friend's side to face an uncertain future? Pullus opened his mouth, but then, completely catching him by surprise came a voice, speaking as clearly and loudly as if the person owning it was in the room.

"Caesar is a patrician by birth, and a god by choice," the voice of Sextus Scribonius admonished him, "and he's not friends with anyone. He is *friendly* with you, but that's not the same thing as being a true friend. Like me. Let's go home, Titus," Scribonius' voice finished.

For the rest of his days, Titus Pullus would always wonder about the exact circumstances of that voice, but his own was steady, as he replied, "Yes, Caesar. I, and most of the other men," he added, "want to go home." In a quieter voice, Pullus finished, "It's time, Caesar. We're ready to put our swords down."

Caesar closed his eyes, leaning back against the throne as he tried to absorb Pullus' words. It had been a desperate gamble, he admitted to himself, to call Pullus a friend, but as much as Caesar respected, and in many ways admired Titus Pullus, he could never be a friend. However, it wasn't for the reasons the voice of Scribonius had whispered to Pullus. The truth was that Caesar, the man, no longer existed, and gods did not have friends, they had worshippers. Also, contrary to what Pullus, Scribonius and a large segment of the army for that matter, believed, he hadn't lost his mind or his grip on reality. Caesar knew he was mortal and he knew he would die, probably fairly soon, although he still felt the same vitality as he had for many years now. But he believed that, in order for his plans to become realized, he had to convince everyone, not just on this island, but in the whole known world, that he was truly a god. The audience he had granted to Pullus had created quite the dilemma, and his mind raced for a way out of it. Ironically enough, if Pullus had been aware of just how caught off-guard Caesar had been, he would have felt somewhat better about his general's mental state. After all, gods can't be surprised.

"I'm afraid," Caesar opened his eyes to stare down at Pullus, "that what you're asking isn't possible. At least," he allowed, "not yet."

Pullus stood immobile, his mind working as quickly as it was capable, and although he didn't have the towering intellect of his general, despite his lack of education, Titus Pullus had a first-rate mind, something that his friend Scribonius had seen in glimpses, but very few others had.

"Very well, Caesar," Pullus replied, forcing his tone to remain calm. "What I heard you say was *not* 'no', but not *now.* Is that correct?"

Caesar's eyes narrowed; he hadn't been expecting this. He had prepared himself for an outburst, knowing that Pullus had a temper that was almost as legendary within the army as his own, or more questions, as Pullus tried to stall for time. But this?

Suspicious that he was entering into a trap of some sort, despite being unable to determine what it might be, Caesar answered, "Yes, Pullus. That is correct. While I have no overall objection to the idea, I simply cannot allow the men to go home right now."

"Then, when?" Pullus pounced immediately, for this was his goal, to force Caesar to name a date that would be acceptable to those men who wanted to return to Rome.

Caesar inwardly cursed, thankful that the red paint on his face masked his expression, because Pullus would easily have seen that he had caught Caesar out.

"That," Caesar replied stiffly, "is impossible to say. You know better than most men in the army all that needs to be done, Pullus."

"I know the military aspects of your plans, but that's all," Pullus pointed out, which was the absolute truth, because Caesar hadn't uttered a word of his overall plan to anyone. "And the training of the Wa to our ways and standards of fighting has gone better than even you expected, as you said yourself."

Now Caesar was caught in a web of his own making. By keeping his ambitions to himself, he had unwittingly put Pullus in a position that gave his Primus Pilus more power, at least in this meeting, than Caesar would have liked. Pullus was well within his rights now to ask for more information, but Caesar wasn't yet willing to divulge any of that, particularly to Pullus.

"I don't believe that I could do without my Romans for at least two more years," Caesar finally answered.

Pullus gasped in shock, his face registering the disbelief that his general could have lost touch with his men to such an extent that it led him to believe they would accept another two years of marching, especially on this universally loathed island.

"Two *years*?" Pullus just barely stopped himself from asking Caesar, if he had lost his senses. "That's impossible! How many more of us will be dead in two years?"

"Nothing is impossible," Caesar retorted. "If anything has been proven during this campaign, it's that nothing is impossible."

"Then it's time you recognize that mortal men have their limits, and we've reached ours. You may be a god, Caesar, but the men aren't. And neither am I."

It would have been impossible to tell which of the two was the more shocked at Pullus' words: the man who uttered them or the man who felt them like a physical blow so much that he let out a gasp. Pullus heard the sound, but thrust down the sudden feeling of regret at his words, reminding himself why he was there. This wasn't just for him, this was for all of those men who took ship from Brundisium almost eleven years before and who, as hard-bitten as they were, now longed for home with all the fervor of a new *tirone* in the first month of training. Sitting on his throne, Caesar was at a loss for words, unable to summon any kind of argument that would blunt the sharp pang brought on by Pullus' statement that forced him to confront a truth he couldn't deny. These men, not even Pullus, Caesar recognized, burned with the same ambition and desire he himself carried with him everywhere as a blazing torch that lit his way and kept him warm. How could he expect them to? In that moment, Caesar realized that Pullus was right, and he knew what he must do.

Scribonius, Diocles and Porcinus were sitting at the table in Pullus' quarters, where the conversation could only be described as desultory, each man more occupied with his own thoughts. Understandably, these were the only three men who knew Pullus' purpose in meeting with Caesar, and the pressure of keeping this secret had worn each of them down. Picking at the few remaining grains of rice in his bowl, Scribonius tried to force his mind away from the recurring dream, or nightmare more accurately, of a warm, steaming loaf of golden brown bread, fresh from the oven, with a stoppered jug of olive oil with which to drench it. This vision had become increasingly insistent in his mind as, despite his best attempts to keep his hopes from rising, he began to dream of what it might be like to walk the streets of his city at last. Unlike Pullus, Sextus Scribonius had been born in Rome itself, and was, in fact, the son of a wealthy equestrian, but when Scribonius followed his older brother to the camp of Catiline—in an episode that would become known as the Catiline Conspiracy—he had been forced to flee for his life, when Catiline's revolt collapsed. Scribonius now understood that the collapse had been inevitable, but that didn't soften the bitter blow of the loss of his brother, who had been killed in what he also knew now had been a farce of a battle. That is what had taken Scribonius to Hispania and seen him enlist in the *dilectus* that created the 10th Legion, Caesar's 10th, and it was Caesar who was responsible for Scribonius and all of his friends and comrades being on the far side of the world. Now, a hope that had grown so faint that he had thought it was dead was flickering back to life, filling his mind with visions he had always managed to keep at bay before now.

"What's the first thing you'd do?" Porcinus broke the silence. "I mean, if..." he didn't need to finish the thought; both men knew what he was asking.

"Go to see if my father's still alive," Scribonius replied. Then, "Or go to a bakery for a fresh loaf. I haven't decided."

This prompted a laugh from the other two men, and the next interval of time was spent with the trio alternating with their own fantasies, which helped pass the time. In fact, they were so engrossed in trying to top each other, their claims for the things they would do when back home growing wilder with each of them, that when the door opened, they were unaware that Pullus had returned. For his part, he stood there, more bemused than anything else, as he listened to his three closest friends engaging in their flights of fancy.

"I'm glad you three are spending your time so wisely," the sound of his voice made them jump, and their looks of guilt—like schoolboys caught by their tutor playing dice instead of reciting their Greek—made Pullus laugh.

"Well?" Scribonius demanded, "What do you have to tell us? Or are you just going to stand there, gawking at us?"

Pullus said nothing for another moment, as much to frame his thoughts as it was to torment his friends.

Finally ready, he said, "We're going home," prompting the three other men to let out spontaneous shouts, drowning out the rest of what Pullus was saying.

All three came to their feet, Diocles and Gaius embracing first, followed by Scribonius and Gaius, each of them slapping the object of his affection on the back, as they laughed and shouted their joy. It was the youngest of them who came to his senses first, mainly because he caught a glimpse of his uncle's face, noticing that he didn't seem to be nearly as thrilled as one would expect.

"Uncle Titus? What is it?" Gaius asked, causing the other two to break their embrace to glance over at Pullus, who had yet to move farther into his quarters.

"Yes, Titus? What are we missing?" Scribonius asked, his joy evaporating as quickly as it had come.

Pullus hesitated, again at a loss for the correct way to frame what he was about to tell his friends.

"I said," he repeated, "we're going home...eventually."

Part of the bargain struck between Pullus and Caesar had been based on a simple practicality, and that was the time of year. It was already autumn, early still, but already the days started with a snap to them; moreover, according to Kiyama and Diana, snow was a common feature of winter in these lands. As Caesar pointed out, it would have been unwise for those men wishing to do so to begin their long journey back to Rome at a time when they would in all likelihood have perhaps six weeks of traveling time, before having to find a place to winter. Better to winter here, Caesar argued, with the protection of that part of the army that was staying behind, than to be stranded on the Gayan Peninsula or in the middle of Han country. That fact alone was enough to clinch the argument, but then Caesar revealed something else that, even now, facing his friends, Pullus was struggling to come to terms with and with what it meant.

"Diana is pregnant," Caesar had told Pullus, "and my physician Chung assures me that it is a male child. He will be my heir, and he will rule as a god."

Despite the paint, Pullus could see the intensity in Caesar's face, his posture radiating the tension he was feeling, as he leaned forward to gaze into Pullus' eyes.

"I need you to be here, at least for the birth," Caesar continued, and there was no mistaking the pleading tone in his voice. "I intend on conducting a ceremony at his birth that will establish him as a god and as my heir. I plan on combining some of the rituals that I have learned the Wa use on the ascension of a new emperor, along with those we use for a birth in Rome. I want the Romans in my army to be there to see it and to carry the word back to Rome of all that's happened."

"To what end?" Pullus blurted out the question, bewildered by what seemed to him to be a simple matter of a man having a son.

"So that those men and women in Rome who wish to can come to my new kingdom and start a new life," Caesar replied calmly. "I want you to carry the word back that there is a new adventure and opportunity here in the East, but that it has the elements of government and society familiar to any Roman. I plan on installing a Senate, and, over time, I want the people to be represented in the same manner as they are back home, with ten Tribunes of the Plebs."

If Pullus' head hadn't been spinning from standing longer than he had in some time already, hearing for the first time what he knew was just the bare bones of Caesar's ambition would have been more than enough.

"Who else knows about this?" Pullus asked, his voice almost a whisper.

Caesar's answer came in the form of a shrug, and for the first time he rued the idea of wearing the red paint, because this was a time he needed his face to be seen, since he knew that the combination of expression and gesture would have given Pullus the answer.

Instead, he had to answer, "Other than Diana, you're really the first I've told of my larger plan. Some of the smaller parts of it, my generals know."

When Caesar said no more after that, Pullus felt compelled to prompt his general, "And? What do they say?"

"All of my generals are of a like mind," Caesar replied, a bit stiffly, perhaps. "They're too old to try to retrace their steps, facing the gods know what, in order to go back to a city that holds nothing for them they can't have here."

So you promised them untold riches and power, Pullus thought, but kept that to himself.

"When is the babe due?" Pullus asked.

"Three months after the beginning of the new year. At least," Caesar allowed, "the new year as reckoned by my calendar. These people are still hopelessly out of step with the seasons, at least as far as I understand it."

What year was it, Pullus wondered? Not surprisingly, Caesar's mind was running along a similar vein, because he supplied the answer; At least, the old answer: the Roman answer.

"It's the year 720, as reckoned by the founding of the city, or 478, as reckoned by the founding of the Republic," Caesar said after a brief pause to do the calculations.

Both men stood for a moment, absorbing this piece of information. Was it really, they both thought at the same time? That many years? The next Ides of March that Caesar saw would mark eleven years, since that fateful day, when he had listened to the warning of the shabbily dressed seer who sat, cross-legged, at the entrance to the Forum. What was his name? Caesar wondered, but he couldn't remember. No matter, really. What did matter was that Caesar had listened, and now, here he was on the cusp of godhead. But only if he could fulfill his plans.

"Very well," Pullus finally spoke. "We'll wait until after the babe is born and the weather breaks. But," he kept his voice tight and under control, "no longer than that, Caesar. We leave as soon as spring comes."

Caesar, careful to stifle his normal reaction that came from an underling speaking to him in such a tone, also controlled his tone, as he replied, "Then it's agreed. However, I do have one other...request."

That word stuck in his throat, but Caesar didn't want to rupture this fragile agreement.

"Yes?" Pullus asked warily.

"All I ask is that I be allowed to address the men before they leave for Rome. I'd like to give them the opportunity to make up their own minds about whether they want to return back to Rome, or take what I have to offer them."

Try as he might, Titus Pullus couldn't find any real reason not to agree to that, so he did.

In the larger world of the Islands of Wa, the Centurions and Optios trained the men of the royal guard, aided by their own rudimentary understanding of the Wa tongue, but, more importantly, by the martial spirit and willingness of the Wa themselves. There were many conversations—usually with cups of rice wine in the snug little cottages that the men of Caesar's army were just coming to appreciate—the topic being not just the adaptability, but the willingness of these Wa warriors to embrace the way of the Legions. It was almost as if what they cared about was the pursuit of martial skill for its own sake, and that whether it was used against the men of Caesar's army or in aid of themselves didn't seem to matter all that much. Meanwhile, Titus Pullus slowly regained his strength, resuming his daily exercises at the stake that he had set up in the small courtyard of what he now thought of as his quarters. Naturally, in the beginning, he couldn't even approach completing the third of a watch interval he normally devoted to working with the sword. However, it wasn't his sword work that worried him the most; the damage done to his left chest had been massive, and even with the expert ministrations of the Han physician and his assistants, his range of motion was severely restricted. He could punch forward well enough, but his lateral motion was almost non-existent; however, neither Diocles nor Scribonius seemed unduly concerned, which irritated Pullus, at least until Diocles explained.

"You're done fighting," the Greek told him. "At least, you're done fighting with the Legions. We're going back to Rome in the spring, and the Wa are giving every appearance of settling down and accepting Caesar...Divus Julius'" Diocles corrected himself, "new status as god of the people."

"I may be done fighting with the Legions, but I don't think we're going to march back across the known world without someone trying something," Pullus replied, prompting Diocles to roll his eyes at his friend, not for the words, as much as for the tone, which was best described as hopeful.

"Gods, what would you do if someone didn't want to kill you?" Diocles asked, but although he meant it rhetorically, Pullus had taken it as a serious question, and the look of horror at the thought evoked a fit of laughter from Diocles, who resumed his task of mending a tunic.

Winter came, and with it Caesar's unveiling of his entire plan, although it was still confined to just his senior officers and Centurions. What shocked Pullus to his core, and Scribonius and Gaius to a lesser degree, was the number of the Primi Pili who made it clear that they had no intention of returning to Rome.

"I'm tired of marching more than I am of fighting," was what Pullus heard from Flaminius, one of the Primi Pili who made it clear that he was staying put. "Besides," he grinned, "Caesar's promised that I can have my pick of the women, and according to Diana, she's the ugly one on this island."

Pullus could only laugh, realizing that as high as some men rose, they were still rankers in their hearts, and their tastes and what was required to make them happy were very simple.

Otherwise, the most difficult part of the winter for the select group of men who had been apprised of Caesar's plans was keeping them secret from the men in the ranks. Not a day passed when some enterprising Legionary was sure he had come up with the most inventive way to ask a question that had been put forth more times than anyone could count, but to no avail. No matter how sly the man was, no matter how subtle, the Primi Pili were as tight-lipped about Caesar's vision as they had been for the most secret war plans. Most of the reason behind this was practical, and was composed of two equally important parts. The first was that the Primi Pili knew, from bitter experience, how full their collective hands would be trying to maintain order among men who, after so many years, were told that they were free to return home. Ironically, most of the trouble wouldn't come from those Romans who were given their release and chose to take it: every Centurion was under no illusion that most of the problems would stem from those Legionaries whose enlistments hadn't run their course. There was, in fact, a fair percentage of the remaining Romans whose citizenship may have derived from the city whose name they bore so proudly, but who had been born in the Roman provinces of Africa. The fact that most, if not all, of these citizens were the sons of former Legionaries themselves who had served Pompey Magnus, made them fully Roman in the eyes of the law.

But when Caesar's Legions had suffered their first casualties in his campaign against the Parthians, a *dilectus* had been conducted to fill the empty spots in the Centuries. While this had occurred almost nine years before, after two bloody years of fighting, and since all of Caesar's Legions were enlisted for a term of sixteen years, this group of Romans still had seven years of their enlistments to go. However, the second problem that worried Caesar, and the Primi Pili, was a point of law they were sure one of the brighter men from the ranks would bring up, and that was the amount of time it would take to return back to Roman territory. To the same extent that Romans revered the rule of law, they were also extremely litigious in nature, down to the lowest Gregarius; it was not uncommon for multiple watches around a fire to pass as two members of the Roman contingent argued some point of law concerning a flask of vinegar. Understanding this, the Primi Pili, in particular, wanted to avoid the prospect of a line of outraged Roman Legionaries claiming that their hard-earned rights as citizens were being trampled underfoot. This was a problem each of them was happy to pass up the chain of command, relying on Caesar to come up with a solution to this problem, before it became one that none of them could handle. Although Pullus shared the concern of the Primi Pili, the reality was that his worries were centered on just one man, his nephew. Porcinus was a special case; Pullus had become aware, through his sister, that young Gaius Porcinus had enlisted in the 14th Legion's second *dilectus*, shortly before Caesar's campaign in Parthia was set to begin.

Fortunately, at least as far as uncle and nephew were concerned, Titus Pullus had been made aware of his nephew's impulsive act, and with a fairly healthy bribe, had managed to have his young nephew transferred into the ranks of the 10th Legion. Pullus had placed young Porcinus in the First Century, Second Cohort, under the close supervision of a man whom Pullus trusted with his life, Sextus Scribonius. Gaius Porcinus wasn't blessed with all of Titus Pullus' physical gifts: he was extremely tall, but was more wiry in build than his famous uncle. More importantly, at least as far as Pullus was concerned, was that Porcinus lacked what his uncle came to think of as his gift of fury, an unquenchable rage that simmered just below the surface of his consciousness and that seemed to surface in his times of greatest need. Nevertheless, what Gaius Porcinus lacked in this dark legacy, he more than made up for in determination and the desire to at least partially emulate his legendary uncle. Titus Pullus had visited his sister when Gaius was a young boy, after the conquest of Gaul that made not only Caesar, but also his favorite Legion, the 10th Equestris, famous. From that day forward, a life on the farm, emulating his natural father, also known as Gaius Porcinus, had left the youngster dead inside. He had been captivated by his uncle, transported by the idea of great deeds and the heroism of the Legions that had been responsible for countless young men just like him to answer the siren call of adventure and glory. Unfortunately, like the Roman citizens of the African province, Porcinus hadn't served a full enlistment, but Pullus was determined to call in every debt he believed Caesar owed him, in order to ensure his nephew was allowed to come home with his uncle. The fact that by making an exception for his nephew, Pullus created a number of headaches for Caesar and the other Primi Pili didn't concern him in the slightest. As far as he was concerned, Pullus had earned the right to call on Caesar to make an exception. It never occurred to Pullus to actually ask his nephew what he wanted.

Caesar had never felt as challenged as he did during the long winter of what would be the first year of his reign over the island of Wa. There were so many matters that required his attention, and so many decisions to make that it was rare that he caught more than a full watch of sleep at night. Yet, at the same time, he hadn't felt this vital and engaged in...ever, he realized. Unlike other men, the sheer scope of the challenges he faced seemed to instill in him an energy and focus that made him feel much younger than his years. For, what Caesar thrived on, and, in fact, what gave him the purpose and desire he needed to rise from his warm bed, shared with Diana, were the myriad problems confronting him on a daily basis. Even with his "god costume", as even his closest advisers had come to call it, there was an aura of purpose and energy that seemed to emanate from within his very soul that was visible to all who knew him. As Diana's stomach swelled, so too did Caesar's efforts increase to put the mechanisms and the framework in place to ensure his presumptive heir's prosperity and future. The most vexing problem facing Caesar was how to integrate the men of the Legions, particularly those who desired to stay, with the population he was coming to think of as his people. Specifically, Caesar's focus was on the Parthians, Pandyans, and Gayans, whose enlistment didn't end for several more years, even if he did add the time it took to return to their homes; which, he had decided, he wasn't going to do, and on this point he refused to bend. Caesar had made up his mind that when he was referring to an individual Legionary's term of enlistment, the time he spent actually under the standard was what counted. He refused to be responsible or accountable for the measure of time it might take these men to return home, if they chose to do so.

Despite knowing that this would be an extremely unpopular position, he was no less adamant about it, and was prepared for the coming storm, sure to be one of the first big challenges of his reign. His secret hope was that the idea of the trek back across the vast expanse of Asia would prove so daunting that most, if not all, of the non-Romans would elect to end their days here on these islands. Every day that passed, his facility in the tongue the Wa spoke increased, while Diana, Kiyama, and a select few others became more conversant in Latin. On the heels of these developments was a deeper understanding of Wa society and the true powers on the islands. Working in Caesar's favor was that the two most powerful lords had perished in the Wa assault, leaving underage heirs in their places, both of them having been summoned to the capital, as soon as their identities were known. On their arrival, they were subjected to Caesar, in all his majesty, in the guise of the new god that had come to this island, and the two youngsters had been suitably cowed. However, when they had attempted to leave the capital, they had been barred from doing so; Caesar may have been confident that his impression was suitably powerful, but he wasn't leaving anything to chance. Caesar's assessment of the royal guard commander was that—while he might have been suitable for service in what was in effect a largely ceremonial post, at least before Caesar and his army arrived—he wasn't sufficiently qualified for Caesar to consider him seriously for any command in his army. This posed something of a dilemma; Caesar recognized that the more quickly he integrated his army, from top to bottom, the better his chances were of handing over a stable and peaceful kingdom to his heir. Never far from his thoughts, however, was Zhang, and by extension, the Han. The courtier had seemingly adjusted to this new reality, as created by Caesar, but the general held no illusions that Zhang wasn't working furiously behind the scenes to advance his own emperor's interests. For a period of weeks, Caesar seriously weighed the viability of simply executing Zhang, but something stayed his hand, although he couldn't have said what it was. Caesar's instinct told him that Zhang still had some usefulness, and this was what kept the Han emissary alive. Finally, along with the steps Caesar was taking to solidify his grasp of the island and its people, he was wrestling with the message and the requests that he sent back to Rome. Ultimately, in his bones he worried that they would have the greatest impact on whether or not Caesar's plan would be fulfilled.

"He's got his hands full, I will say that," Scribonius mumbled through a mouthful of rice, thankful that this meal also featured a substantial helping of pork. "When spring comes, he's going to have to send Legions to the other islands, and he's going to have to spread out the ones he's keeping here on the big island more. From everything I've heard it sounds like the Wa are easing into this whole idea of Caesar being a god. At least," he amended, "that's what Caesar is putting out there."

"But what about the Han?" Porcinus asked, his mouth similarly occupied with consuming the evening meal. "What do you think is going to happen with them?"

Scribonius shook his head, saying only, "I don't know, but it's a good question."

"And it's not our problem anymore."

The words themselves would have been considered something of a surprise, but the fact that it was Pullus who uttered them made them even more so. However, his tone told his companions that, in this at least, he would brook no discussion. Which was one reason Porcinus said nothing, although it wasn't the only one. The three Legionaries, plus Diocles, were gathered for what had become a tradition: the evening meal in the quarters of the Primus Pilus. Not surprisingly, there was much to discuss, especially since it seemed that every day a new piece of information came to light about Caesar's ambitions, and while these were interesting, what did trouble Pullus and his friends was the growing list of tasks their general was assigning those Romans who were returning home. Messages, which grew in number by the day, were one thing; the latest piece of information was something else entirely. Using his title as Dictator for life, Caesar was calling for a new *dilectus*, consisting of a total of three entire Legions' worth of men, one of them from Italy itself. These men were to be transported by ship to the Asian side of Our Sea, albeit by the more traditional route that didn't risk a direct crossing. They would meet with the other two Legions, drafted from the Roman provinces, and would march, this time taking the direct route across the desert, to the Red Sea. There they would be met by a fleet, some of the ships that were part of the fleet that had ferried the Legions from the first island that had served as the supply base for this campaign. Rather than crossing through the vast wastes of Parthia, as Caesar had done, they would instead hug the coast and travel by sea. By Caesar's estimate, this trip would take at least a year to complete, probably closer to two, depending on the weather. Privately, Pullus thought that this was another sign that Caesar had lost his mind, finding it hard to believe that men who had never experienced anything comparable would be willing to sign up for a sea voyage that lasted that long. Romans by and large hated the sea and anything to do with it, and while Pullus understood that by hugging the coastline, Caesar would be doing what he could to mitigate this issue, the Primus Pilus still felt Caesar was overly optimistic. However, Pullus also recognized that it wasn't his problem to solve, and it was perhaps this moment that told him he had achieved the point of separation from his general that he needed. What surprised him was that this recognition plunged Pullus into a mild depression, as he realized that when the day did come for him and the rest of the Romans who opted to return to Rome to leave, that would be the last day he would lay eyes on the man whom he had followed his entire adult life.

Pullus wasn't the only one affected in this way; in fact, a blanket of what could only be described as melancholy settled on the shoulders of the Romans in Caesar's army, matching the mantle of snow that encased the capital and the surrounding hills. While the cold wasn't as bitter as what the men experienced in Parthia, it had a bite to it that reminded men of their wounds and injuries, when they roused themselves from their cots in the morning, and a joint ached or a back was stiff. Pullus, in particular, had cause to dislike the cold, since his latest injury was still relatively new, and this only added to his misery as he hobbled about in the mornings. Diocles, after learning the hard way that making light of this wasn't the way to take his master's mind off his problems, was always ready with hot stones wrapped in cloth that he then tied around

Pullus' chest, while the Primus Pilus performed a series of exercises the Han physician had prescribed. When the physician had first demonstrated them, Pullus had refused on the grounds that they looked ridiculous, but once he broke down and incorporated them as part of his morning routine, he was forced to admit, grudgingly, that they helped his flexibility, and, most importantly, eased the pain a great deal. But first he had to get to the point where he could move freely enough to perform the exercises, and the hot stones quickly became part of the ritual that was required for him to at least play the role of the Primus Pilus of the 10th Legion. The cold weather hadn't stopped the training of the Wa, although the regimen was modified out of necessity, so that the conditioning marches and instructions on how to build a marching camp were put on hold until the weather improved. This actually played into the hands of the Centurions, who were finding that as willing as the Wa were to learn more martial skills, the lesson that seemed to be the hardest for them to grasp was the idea of working as a team. Most of the Wa still thought of themselves as individual warriors, proud of their own skills, so it was only after a series of extremely bloody mock battles between the men of the Legions—albeit the cream of their Cohorts—and the trainees that the lesson of teamwork actually took hold. For his part, Pullus was thankful that it finally seemed to have sunk in; the camps' hospitals were already almost full to overflowing with the broken bones and cracked skulls that were a feature of a Roman battle drill. Despite his overwhelming desire to do so, he had managed to keep from participating in these drills himself, but not without a stern admonishment from Scribonius, who reminded him that the march back to Rome wasn't likely to be without challenges itself. While the men were occupied with training and integration, Pullus, Scribonius, and, to a lesser extent, Porcinus were burdened with planning for the return journey, which kept them up through the watches of the night as the time drew nearer.

It was on the occasion of the advent of the new year, as reckoned by Caesar's calendar, that the general and god deemed it time to inform the men of the ranks of the opportunity to return to Rome. Originally, Caesar planned on holding the lustration ceremony, the annual ritual that re-consecrated the standards of the Legions, while asking the blessing of the gods for the upcoming campaign season. However, his Legates and Primi Pili, even those who had elected to stay, combined forces to convince Caesar that doing so would create a conflict in a number of the men who might feel that they had been tricked into swearing their sacred oath to their Legion eagle to fight another year, then be told they could go home, if they chose. Pullus wanted to believe that this was just an oversight on Caesar's part, but deep down, he felt that it was a last-ditch attempt by his general to forestall men leaving the standard. Therefore, it was announced that there would be a meeting, held in the park of the royal palace—the only place large enough to hold all of the men—and the lustration ceremony would follow immediately thereafter. Caesar had also agreed to allow those men who had chosen to leave but still wanted to participate in the ceremony to do so, although for what reason neither Pullus nor Scribonius could determine. A possible answer came from what seemed to be an unlikely source.

"I think he's hoping that some men will take the oath and then change their minds," Diocles said. "That they won't like the idea of leaving their comrades behind."

Both Pullus and Scribonius, once they heard the Greek's explanation, believed that this was the most likely answer, and it gave them a feeling of unease. One thing both men were counting on was that the returning Romans would be composed of large enough numbers to dissuade any of the petty kings and lords, whose lands the departing men would cross through, from making mischief by trying either to wipe the Romans out, or somehow to press them into serving under their standard, instead of Caesar's. Perhaps an even more important reason was the treasure the Romans would be taking back with them, in the form of the riches of the Orient. Each Centurion would have a wagonload of treasures and wealth: gems, gold, and, perhaps most surprising, the rolls of the shiny, soft, but strong material known as silk, dyed in every color the eye could comprehend, or embroidered in a variety of patterns. Though neither Pullus nor the other Centurions had gone to the lengths of the Pandyan Tribune in bedecking himself in togas made of this material, every one of them had at least one tunic made of the material that he wore on special occasions. It was light, comfortable, and—best of all—it didn't scratch the skin the way wool did. Pullus couldn't remember who had first mentioned the idea of bringing back quantities of silk, but it was one that had immediately caught hold among men of all ranks.

Because of this, there had been a steady stream of ships moving back and forth between the mainland and the islands, due to the fact that the Han were the creators of silk and that every man had more than enough gold and jewels to pay for what was delivered. At this point, Pullus had no way of knowing how big this baggage train was likely to be, so he was happy that at least he wouldn't have to carry the burden of this great secret much longer and that he would also get an idea of the logistical issues that they would be facing.

The day of the ceremony dawned bright and cold, with the kind of cloudless sky featuring a sun that seemed to have lost its warmth, prompting the men to eschew their silk finery for the heavier and warmer woolen tunics, *bracae,* and fur-lined socks. They had suffered too much to lose toes to frostbite from standing in formation, so, although it was a technical breach of regulations, the Centurions looked the other way. Pullus stood in his quarters, allowing Diocles to fuss over him, as the Greek servant pulled out an imaginary crease and brushed off a non-existent speck of dirt—this as much a ritual now as the ceremony for which Pullus was dressed in his full uniform with all his decorations. Looking into the polished brass reflecting disc, the Primus Pilus merely gave a grunt, but Diocles knew that this meant he was pleased at the sight he presented. Leaving his quarters, Pullus walked over to Scribonius'; all Centurions of the first grade had their lodgings in what had formerly been the houses of the imperial staff, although there hadn't been quite enough room for all of them. There was a neighborhood on the northern side of the palace complex that had been deemed suitable for the remainder of Caesar's officers, and now these men were walking in small groups towards the park. Scribonius emerged, and for a moment both men eyed each other critically, a habit formed by almost a full lifetime of inspections and impossible to break even now. Realizing what they were doing to each other, they both burst out laughing.

"Well? Are you ready to hear what our future holds?" Scribonius asked, with a wink.

"Of course. I'm always interested in what a god has to say," Pullus replied, without thinking, causing Scribonius to wince, as he cast a nervous glance about for any eavesdroppers.

"You and your mouth," the Pilus Prior grumbled, but Pullus was unabashed, slapping Scribonius on his shoulder, as they made their way to the park.

Pullus, and indeed, every man in the ranks of the army, was curious about how Caesar would make his appearance. Specifically, would he show up in his god costume? And Legionaries wouldn't have been worthy of that title if there wasn't spirited wagering on the matter: some men bet on their belief that, since Caesar was appearing before his army, he would do so in the guise of the general; others insisted that now that he had invested himself in his own godhead, he wouldn't dare show his face without the red paint. While they were waiting in formation, this was the overwhelming topic of conversation, becoming so spirited that Pullus finally whirled about from his spot at the head of the First Century, First Cohort of the Legion that always occupied the place of honor on the far right, to snap an order that the next man whom he heard discussing the matter was going to have a striped back. This served to reduce conversations at least to a low mumble, which Pullus was willing to allow, especially as the appointed time for Caesar to appear came and went. Although he hadn't put any thought into it at the time, as Pullus stood there taking in his surroundings, he recognized that the arrangement of the men and the direction in which they were facing was no accident. Arrayed as they were, Pullus and his men, along with the rest of the most senior Legions, were facing east, in the direction of the ridge that lay beyond the capital. Along with the time of year, this meant that the sun didn't hit the capital until relatively late in the morning, and Pullus could see the very beginnings of the corona that announced the sun was approaching the crest of the ridge. One thing marred the ordered spectacle, and it took Pullus a few moments to puzzle out what it was. His Roman mind appreciated order, and part of the physical manifestation of order, to a Roman at least, was symmetry. Specifically, the rostra that had been built for Caesar's speech—built at the far eastern edge of the park so its back was to the ridge—wasn't exactly centered, when viewed as a whole, with the formation, or the park itself. It wasn't off by much: perhaps two dozen paces to Pullus' right from what he judged to be center, but it was enough to jar Pullus' eye, and, more importantly, it made him wonder how such a detail could have slipped past Caesar. Fortunately, he didn't have long to wait to find out that it was no accident at all.

Caesar, Pullus was forced to acknowledge, hadn't lost his touch. Even as Pullus was mulling over this apparent error in the placement of the small structure from which Caesar was going to give his speech, the answer to its placement came, literally in a blinding flash of light. For the rest of his days, Pullus, Scribonius, and, frankly, every man who saw it would wonder if, after all of the contrivances and artifice Caesar had employed to advance the idea of his godhead, this wasn't indeed a true sign of his divinity. Even if it hadn't been for the placement of the rostra, its construction would have occupied Pullus' attention, because it was unlike anything he'd seen Caesar construct. Whereas the general had usually been content with simple platforms of varying sizes for all of his other speeches, with perhaps a backdrop made of whitewashed wooden planks, this was by far the most elaborate creation Pullus had seen, at least for this purpose. It looked almost exactly like one of the temples that graced the Forum in Rome, perhaps the small temple of Castor and Pollux. The only difference was that this rostra wasn't made from stone, but in every other way, it wouldn't have been out of place in any Roman forum. It had been painted a stark, dazzling white to simulate the white marble that came from the mountains of Toscana, near Carrara. The only thing that had been left natural were the wooden doors, currently closed, preventing anyone from seeing inside.

This structure hadn't been there the day before, Pullus was sure, or he would have heard talk about it, but while it was small in size, he found it hard to believe that it could have been erected overnight, even with the nights as long as they were at this time of year. What he didn't know was that this building had already been constructed earlier—or at least the pieces had been fabricated—in the interior courtyard of the palace. The night before the ceremony, those parts had been carted to their spot and erected. It wasn't the most solid building Caesar had ever overseen, but he was sure that it would fulfill its purpose. And that purpose revealed itself in a literally dazzling fashion, when, as close to simultaneously as possible, the top of the sun crested the ridge and the doors to this makeshift temple were thrown open. That's when it was revealed to Pullus, and those others who had been curious, that the position of the temple had been no accident, as a beam of pure light shot through the doors of the temple. A gasp from thousands of throats broke the silence, as every man's eyes were fastened on the doors, waiting for what came next. And what happened was...nothing. At least, not for several more moments, and it was only later that Pullus realized that, like everything else, the pause was deliberate: the full orb of the sun had risen above the ridge, visible to the men through the opened door, the light so blinding that, despite being at *intente,* men were forced to shield their eyes. Which was precisely what Caesar wanted to happen, so that as the men chattered excitedly in the aftermath, none of them was exactly sure when and how their general appeared. Pullus was aware of a brief flurry in the doorway, as the light suddenly was blocked for a brief instant; and when he squinted, he could just make out the shape of a man silhouetted by the sun, the rays of light appearing as spears from around the head and shoulders of the figure he now recognized as Caesar. Then, the moment was over, as the sun, continuing its rise in the sky reached an angle where the upper half of the temple blocked the light, leaving Caesar simply standing there. That's when something extraordinary happened: men of all ranks, Roman, Parthian, Pandya, Han, Gayan, whatever nationality they were, dropped to their knees, holding out their arms in supplication.

"*Caesar* is *a god!"*

Pullus never knew who the first to shout this was, but it didn't really matter, since the cry was immediately taken up by dozens, then hundreds, and finally thousands of voices. The din created was almost overwhelming, making it impossible for Pullus to think, and when he looked over to his left, where the Second Cohort was standing next to his, he saw Scribonius standing there, mouth open, and he knew his friend felt the same way. As far as Caesar was concerned, he seemed content to let the clamor continue for some time, just standing there, and it gave time for Pullus to examine his general more closely. This day he wasn't wearing his god costume; in fact, he was dressed only as a Roman general, albeit one celebrating a triumph, since his face was again painted red. He's getting a little too fond of that paint, Pullus grumbled to himself, although he understood its usefulness in hiding Caesar's emotions. Finally, Caesar held up his arms, and Pullus was sure that he had never heard the men fall so silent so quickly; the sudden contrast to what had been a tumult just an instant before was disconcerting, to put it mildly. It was only because of the silence that Pullus realized his ears were ringing from what had gone on a moment before, so he wasn't sure if he would hear Caesar's first words. Fortunately, this wasn't a problem, because his general's words rang out, their tone pitched higher than his normal conversational voice, clearly and easily understood.

"Comrades," he began, and Pullus was a bit surprised and felt himself relax with this first word, realizing only then he had been bracing himself to be addressed as "subjects", or "worshippers", or "my people." Caesar, oblivious to Pullus' realization, continued, "today is indeed a momentous day, for a number of reasons. Not only do we consecrate the standards of our Legions and renew the vows to the gods that all men under the standard must make, in order to procure the gods' favor, I have an announcement to make."

It was almost as though time stopped, Pullus thought, as every man in the army leaned forward slightly, waiting to hear what Caesar would say next.

"For those men who were part of the first or second *dilectus* of those Legions that I enlisted for our campaign in Gaul, or for those Legions on their first enlistment that I enrolled for our struggle with the forces of Pompey Magnus, *and who are Roman citizens*," Caesar's voice rose even higher, "you have served me faithfully and well. No men of Rome, or of any other nation, have accomplished as much in feats of arms as you have, and there is no real way I can thank you enough, or repay you in a manner that you deserve...except for this."

Here it comes, Pullus thought, glancing over at Scribonius, who answered with a raised eyebrow, before returning his attention to Caesar.

"For any man desiring to do so, I hereby release you from service, and give you my permission; no, I give you my *blessing*, to return to Rome, to be covered in the honor and glory that you so richly deserve."

There it was, out in the open, the great secret finally out. But as Pullus waited for what he had been sure would be the inevitable explosion, the silence continued for what had to be more than a dozen heartbeats.

Finally, a quiet voice, heard only because of the great silence, asked, "You mean, we can go...home?"

"Yes," Caesar answered simply.

If he added to that response, Pullus didn't know, because an absolute avalanche of sound erupted, as men—both Roman and non-Roman—shouted their joy and relief.

Naturally, the details of Caesar's announcement had to be communicated, and it was in the chaos that ensued that Pullus and the other Primi Pili realized that Caesar's desire to make the announcement after the lustration ceremony was based on more practical reasons than anything else. Even those men who weren't eligible to go home were too excited by the news to be counted on to fulfill their duties properly, and it was only after the Centurions waded in with their *viti*, striping legs and backs, that they were finally gotten in hand. At last, some semblance of order was restored, then Caesar continued speaking.

"It gladdens my heart to see how overjoyed so many of you are at this news, and I also promise that you will not return empty-handed! For men of the most senior Legions, and who were in the first *dilectus*, I bequeath to each Gregarius the sum of 15,000 sesterces..." There was another gasp of pleased surprise, not just from the men who qualified for this bonus, but for those around them, and Caesar allowed muttering for a moment, before he raised his hand again, "For those of the second *dilectus,* the sum will be 12,000, but most importantly, I am giving men the option of whether or not to take their payment in the form of gold and silver, or in the form of goods that are produced here and in the lands of the Han that you can take back with you for trade."

This, Pullus recognized, was a shrewd move on the part of Caesar, because even with the shrunken numbers, and discounting those who would opt to stay, the outlay of hard currency Caesar was talking about had to be staggering. It was true that he and his army had stripped bare the treasuries of Parthia and the Pandyan kingdom, but Pullus knew that much of that had gone to the Han for the food and necessary supplies to keep this giant beast of an army moving. This didn't take into consideration the personal wealth, in the form of booty, each man under the standard already possessed. In point of fact, Titus Pullus was a very wealthy man, and he was idly curious just how much Caesar would be paying the Centurions, particularly those of his grade. Caesar, having announced the bonuses, moved onto the next part of his speech, and this was what Pullus had been waiting for, if only to see how the men would react.

"But while I give you my leave to depart for Rome, I cannot say that it does not sadden me. All of you are as sons to me, but you Romans in our ranks, you and I have shared so very much, seen so very much, and suffered so very much."

Caesar paused for a moment, and Pullus, feeling the hard lump forming in his throat, knew that the other men were experiencing the same emotions.

"That is why I would be remiss in my duty if I did not at least make an attempt to persuade some of you to stay here, with me and the rest of your brothers. For, although they might not have been born Roman, I challenge any man under the standard to claim that the sacrifice of the men from the other nations that now fill our ranks is any less than that which we native-born Romans have suffered!"

Caesar, his red face glistening now, moved his head slowly, from left to right, as if daring a man to speak up, but, as he knew, there were no such men in the ranks of his army. As different from one another as these men may have been, by virtue of their birth, customs, and traditions, their values were identical. Strength, bravery, fortitude, and the willingness to die, if need be, to save a comrade—these were the ties that bound the men of Caesar's army together, more tightly than anything else could have.

"I see that you feel as I do. That is good," Caesar's voice was still pitched high, but it took on a quality that made it seem as though he were now just conversing with each man, and while Pullus had seen his general do this countless times, it was still a mystery to him how he managed to do so. "And it is for those brothers, whose time is not yet up, that I ask for men to stay behind. For those that do, I offer each of them not only a bonus of 5,000 sesterces, but also 20 *iugera* of prime land of their choosing and the pick of the eligible maidens of this island to take as wives."

You crafty old bastard, Pullus thought, and how do you propose to give land away if it's already occupied? Because what Pullus had seen of this island, anything that would qualify as good farm- or grazing land was already occupied, which meant that those men who stayed behind would be faced with a problem very similar in nature to that of Legionaries who had received their own 20 *iugera* back in Italia, and that was the presence of previous occupants. In Italia, those patches of land had been confiscated from men who found themselves on the wrong side of the civil war, but even before Caesar and the army had left on campaign, Pullus had heard more than one story of vicious, bloody fights that men had been forced to wage in order to claim land that by law was theirs. Moreover, one of the many things that Pullus had learned in the subsequent decade spent traveling across Asia, it was that of all the people a Legionary wanted to fight, these Wa would be last on his list. Still, he reflected, it wasn't his problem, and he turned his attention back to Caesar, who was finishing his speech.

"I know that this is a momentous decision, for each of those affected. And I do not want to rush you into making a hasty choice, so I will give you one full week to decide if you want to return to Rome, to claim the glory that you so richly deserve, or stay here and make a new life, just as glorious, perhaps, but out of sight of Rome."

By the time he was finished, the sun had risen above the top of the temple, completely illuminating the park now. Yet, Pullus could have sworn that there was still what he would have described as a glow emanating from around Caesar, almost like a cocoon, and the giant Roman found himself rooted to his spot, as the formation broke apart and men began talking excitedly, wondering yet again, if Caesar was truly a god.

Although it didn't surprise Pullus or Scribonius that there were men who opted to remain behind, what was a shock were the numbers of men who took up Caesar's offer.

"If I were eligible, I'd stay," was how Publius Vellusius, the only other surviving tentmate of Pullus and Scribonius, put it.

The fact that he wasn't eligible was due to the simple circumstance that he was now missing most of his left arm, amputated a bit above the elbow, precluding him from holding a shield.

"I'm too old to be traipsing back across the wastes of the world, just to get back to a place that I couldn't wait to get away from," he explained the night of the ceremony, invited as a guest to Pullus' quarters for the precise reason he was fulfilling now: explaining the way the rankers thought about this development. Seeing the faces of his two friends, Vellusius allowed, "Oh, don't get me wrong. I do miss Rome. Or, I miss a good, hot loaf of bread, made with wheat."

His smile, like most of his comrades, was notable for the number of teeth that were missing, although he was doing slightly better than most of the men his age. This simple statement of yearning for something so basic prompted a chuckle from his friends, if only because they felt much the same way.

In fact, Scribonius was moved to ask, "So, if you could get bread made with wheat here, would you miss Rome as much?"

Vellusius had clearly not thought of this; deep thinking was never a strength of his, so he leaned back, as the smile was replaced by a thoughtful frown.

"Why, I never thought about that, Scribonius," he rubbed his face, as he struggled with what was for him a deeply philosophical question. "But now that I think about it, no, I don't suppose I would. In fact," his smile returned, "I would have said I missed the whores, but now that I've sampled all that this side of Our Sea has to offer in that area, I can't say that I'd miss that either."

This also evoked a laugh from both of Vellusius' dinner companions, along with Diocles. However, for once, Gaius was conspicuously absent, giving his uncle the excuse that he had pressing business with his Century's paperwork that couldn't wait any longer. While somewhat unusual, it wasn't sufficiently so to give Pullus any hint that his nephew was avoiding him for some reason. The dinner conversation continued apace, as the men discussed what had been an eventful day.

"How many do you think will stay?" Pullus asked Scribonius, who considered the question, as he worked on a piece of pork gristle, silently bemoaning the pain it caused one of his back molars, knowing from experience that this was the precursor to losing it.

Finally, Scribonius swallowed and replied, "I can't think more than a third of the men will stay behind."

This aligned with Pullus' estimate; unfortunately, they were both wrong.

By the end of the week that Caesar had allowed for the men to make up their collective minds, it turned out that fully half of them had taken his offer and were choosing to stay behind. But it wasn't the number alone that rocked Pullus and Scribonius, and Diocles for that matter, it was the identity of some of them. Or, more specifically, one of them in particular, although it explained why Pullus' nephew had made himself scarce the previous few days.

"But...why?" It was the only thing Pullus could think to ask, when Porcinus, recognizing that he could put it off no longer, had finally shown up at his uncle's quarters for dinner the night before the week was up.

They were seated at the table, but the meal hadn't been served yet, as even the man responsible for overseeing the slaves who did the cooking was anxious to hear the answer and stood in the doorway that led to the kitchen area. Diocles had never seen his master and friend like this before; if forced, he would have said it was a combination of puzzlement, a touch of anger, but more than anything else, Pullus was hurt at the confirmation that Porcinus was staying behind.

"The men," Porcinus said simply. Seeing his uncle's face, he recognized he needed to be more forthcoming, "I thought I could, but I just can't leave them behind, Uncle Titus. Who'd look after them?"

Pullus' reaction was a snort, but inwardly his derision was aimed at one target: himself. You're the one who taught the boy about taking care of his men, he thought, as he tried to come up with words that would actually contradict what he had ingrained in his nephew from the first day it became clear that Porcinus possessed what it took to lead men.

"Gaius," he said, finally, the words coming slowly as he tried to form his thoughts. "I can't tell you how proud I am that you've taken all that I've tried to teach you to heart. It does my heart good to see how much you care about your men. But," he paused, letting the word hang in the air, "the Legions have been around a long time. Long before either you or I showed up, men have come and gone from the Centurionate, and I'm sure that Caesar wouldn't appoint anyone to fill your spot who he didn't feel was qualified to meet the standard you set for leading your Century."

Porcinus was unmoved; in fact, he felt the first flaring of his own anger. It sounded as though his uncle was saying that someone could do as good a job with his Century as he did, so his tone was stiff, as he responded, "That may be true Uncle. But nobody coming in will know the men like I do, and nobody coming in will have shared with them the same things that I have."

Pullus realized then that his chances of convincing his nephew to change his decision were very, very slim. However, Pullus hadn't gotten to his current position by accepting defeat at the first sign of adversity, and he prepared himself for the coming struggle to convince his nephew to change his mind. Then, a hand reached out to grab his forearm, and he looked in surprise to see that it was Scribonius, with a look on his face that he knew all too well. It was the nonverbal warning his best friend used when he was sure Pullus was about to make a mistake, and over the years, Pullus had learned that not heeding his friend was almost always to his own detriment. Looking Pullus in the eye, in the space of perhaps two or three heartbeats, Scribonius managed to communicate to Pullus that this was one battle that, even if he managed to sway his nephew, he would regret winning for the rest of his days.

It would have been impossible to say who was more surprised, then, when Pullus turned to his nephew and said, as simply as Porcinus had moments before, "I understand. And I...respect your decision." But even as the relief flooded the younger man's face, Pullus held up a cautionary hand, "I'm not saying I agree with it, but I do understand. And I suppose that you're a grown man, and you can make your own decisions. It's just..." now Pullus' voice trailed off, as a hard lump formed in his throat and the figure of his nephew began swimming in his vision.

Now Porcinus reached out, as well, but he placed his hand on top of Scribonius', still on Pullus' forearm.

"I know," he said quietly, no less affected.

The three sat in silence for some time, dinner forgotten, as Diocles came to join them.

Reflecting later, Pullus understood that the flurry of activity that filled his days from that point forward was a blessing, keeping him from dwelling on the fact that, in all likelihood, the day he and the rest of the men leaving for Rome departed, it would be the last time he would set eyes on his nephew. Consequently, he lost himself in the myriad issues that arose once the men made their decisions, and their trip home began to get organized, now that firm numbers were known. Altogether, a force of almost 2,500 men, a little less than half of a Caesarian Legion, would be leaving in the spring, and it wouldn't have been a Roman force if Pullus—who was the highest ranking Centurion in terms of seniority—hadn't immediately organized the men into Centuries and Cohorts. This wasn't done just for organizational purposes; the truth was that none of these men would have known how they were to behave if they hadn't known exactly where they were to be in the column marching home. In theory, this was a formidable force, large enough that it was unlikely any of the nations through which the Romans passed would want to expend the amount of resources, particularly in blood, it would take to subdue them. However, as Pullus and the rest of those senior Centurions who were returning knew, this was deceiving. A fair number of these men, more than a third of the total, were Legionaries who had suffered wounds grievous enough that they had been cashiered from their spot under the standard. Publius Vellusius was an example, but there were more than a hundred men who had lost a leg, and two men who had lost both. Although they had remained with the army, they had become part of the labor force that provided support for the army on campaign, the two legless men becoming wagon drivers. In fact, it was the collective problem posed by the one-legged men that vexed Pullus the most, because their mobility was so severely hampered that unless they could find seats on a wagon, they couldn't be allowed to go. This was especially true since the wagons themselves would be fully loaded with all the booty, goods, and keepsakes each man was bringing home, for, after all, what had been the point of this entire campaign if the men didn't have something tangible to show for it? But there were more crippled men than wagons, and it forced Pullus to call a meeting, where a gut-wrenching decision had to be made. Fortunately, enough men who, faced with the choice of trying to fight their similarly afflicted comrades for a spot on a wagon or staying behind, opted to remain there on the islands, saving Pullus from a potentially painful decision.

That certainly wasn't the only issue facing Pullus, but those challenges did a perfect job of preventing him from dwelling on his nephew's decision to stay behind. Supplies had to be gathered, and not just foodstuffs; although this wasn't a military expedition, the men would be carrying their arms and armor and would be making a Roman camp, on a smaller scale, every night. This meant that materials to replace turfcutting blades, axe handles, and javelin shafts had to be fashioned and loaded onto the wagons designated for that purpose. Spare shields were loaded, although not in as great a number as would be carried normally, and sheets of leather were packed for the leatherworking immunes to fashion spare caligae, when the originals inevitably wore out. In every respect,

save that of scale, what Pullus and the other returning Centurions had to supervise was identical to the conditions with which Caesar had to contend, when he was starting out. But even with all these details, the problem that occupied the largest part of their time centered on the route they would take back to Rome. The Centurions were roughly divided into two camps: those that argued for essentially a reversal of the original route that was predominately overland, across the Gayan Peninsula and through the lands of the Han, then taking ship only at a spot just east of the huge peninsula of India, after braving the thick jungles and savage tribesmen of the lands to the south of the Han. It was this last terrain that the other group of Centurions wanted to avoid at all costs, the horrors of what had been the hardest year of the campaign fresh enough in their collective minds that they were willing to confront their huge fear of the water by advocating a route that was almost entirely by sea. They wouldn't have been Roman if they hadn't insisted that the fleet follow the coastline of the vast land mass between them and home, but since this had never been done before, none of the navarchae attached to Caesar's fleet could provide anything more than a guess about the amount of time this would take. Not surprisingly, the Centurions supporting the first plan pounced on this, and wasted no time in doing what they could to whisper in the ears of those returnees that they would find themselves adrift at sea for who knew how long; months, certainly. But could it be years? And if it was the latter, what chance did they have then of seeing Rome?
This was the atmosphere in the camps that housed the men of Caesar's army in the opening months of the year, even as winter maintained its icy grip on the islands of Wa.

During this time, Pullus caught only occasional glimpses of Diana, but he could see how her belly grew, and, despite himself, he began counting the days. The midwives—whose knowledge and experience with these matters seemed to be universal, no matter what side of the world one was on—had pronounced the likely time of birth to be the first or second week of the month named for Mars. Meanwhile, as everyone waited for the birth, Pullus, Scribonius, and a number of the other Centurions who favored the second alternative route, even with their misgivings about a lengthy sea voyage, worked diligently behind the scenes to try to counterbalance the whispering campaign of those men who wanted to march overland; but even up until a month before their predicted departure, no resolution had been met. But then Caesar intervened, adding his weight to Pullus' side, and the matter was resolved. What none of the men was told, and only a few figured out on their own, was that this had as much to do with Caesar's desire to have a portion of his fleet in a position to transport the anticipated fresh Legions back to the islands than it did with taking sides. Scribonius was one of the men who deduced Caesar's reasoning, but while he told Pullus, since it aligned with their interests, neither man felt it necessary to make this known, letting men work it out themselves, if they were so disposed. It was also no surprise that, as the day drew nearer, tempers that were already sorely tested by the inevitable monotony of life in a winter camp were stretched even tauter. However, unlike in previous winters, the punishment square didn't see nearly as much activity as the misconduct of the men warranted. Caesar and his officers, were acutely cognizant of the special circumstances that surrounded this eleventh winter of all the winters the army had spent together. In what can only be described as tragedy, men who had survived the longest and most brutal campaign of any army in Rome's history were struck down, not by an enemy, but in almost every case by a close friend, when passions and grudges over past hurts flared anew, followed by a flashing blade and an agonized shout. Despite events like this being few in number and happening every winter, when compared to all the times before, these were even more tragic, because it wasn't uncommon for a man who had struck down a comrade regaining his senses and, filled with remorse, taking his own life. Yet, the days moved as slowly as they always seemed to, no matter how much the men wished it otherwise. Not helping matters was that this was an unusual winter that lingered, much like a bad cold, and, in fact, the first sign of spring didn't come from any change in the weather. Instead, it was hailed by the tiny wail of an infant being born on, of all days, the Ides of March.

Chapter 12

Numerius Ovidius stomped his feet for what he was sure was the hundredth time, yet even as he did so, he knew it didn't really help in fighting the bitter cold. It was a habit, he supposed; where he picked it up from he had no idea. What made matters worse was that he was barely a third of a watch into his shift, standing guard at the Porta Romana, or as it was more commonly called, the Ostian Gate, since it led down the road the short distance to the port of the most powerful city in the world. Ovidius hadn't held his post very long, but he had already developed a loathing for the cold. Otherwise, this new job was turning out to be interesting, at least, since it gave Ovidius the chance to see an almost endless stream of humanity in every variety imaginable, coming from and going into Rome. And, he reflected, every once in a while, something happened that could almost be described as dangerous, adding a little spice to his day. He had finally become accustomed to the uniform, which he had thought excessive, at least until the first riot in the Forum that he and the others in his Century had been called to quell. Then he had been thankful for the helmet in particular, after receiving a solid blow from a stave waved by a wide-eyed man who had been part of the mob protesting...what was it? Ovidius couldn't even remember; there had been several such demonstrations in the slightly less than a year he had been a member of the Urban Cohorts, a quasi-military organization formed by the youngster, Gaius Octavius. Almost as soon as the name came into his head, he corrected himself, even if it was in his head; he had heard stories of what happened to men who refused to call the boy by his correct title. He was Caesar now, and had been for almost six years.

That had been—what was it?—Ovidius calculated, seven years after the man he would privately always think of as the real Caesar left on his Parthian campaign. Ovidius shuddered at the memory of that time, because the turmoil of the last few months was nothing compared to the uproar that had erupted when Marcus Antonius, defying the Senate, had marched into the Temple of Vesta and demanded to be given possession of Caesar's will. His argument was understandable, even if it had no real precedent under the law Romans supposedly revered; although Ovidius, like most of the members of his class, viewed the law as something that his social betters liked to pay lip service to, when it suited their purpose. Whatever his motives, from Ovidius' viewpoint, there was an almost equal division, across all the tribes and class lines, as to whether or not Antonius was justified in his actions. The last time Caesar had been heard from in person, at least in the form of a dispatch, was after the Pandyan kingdom had been subdued, and he had set up a Roman outpost on the huge island to the east of the southern tip of India, Julia Taprobane, as it was known. After that, there were only snatches of information, a rumor brought back by one of the few Roman traders who ventured that far across the world, or a claim by some foreigner from those parts, who had it on good authority that, while titillating, couldn't be confirmed. Neither could it be disproved, but Antonius, whose patience was never in strong supply, had loudly proclaimed that sufficient time had passed to come to the reasonable conclusion that the great Caesar, Dictator for Life, was dead, and that as his Master of the Horse and second in command, Antonius himself should be elevated into that position. His decision to violate the Temple of Vesta and invite the anger of the goddess of the hearth, not to mention Jupiter Optimus Maximus, was based in a simple assumption, and one that even those who disagreed with his actions couldn't dispute, and that was that Marcus Antonius was Caesar's heir.

Even now, all these years later, Ovidius experienced the very unusual problem of having to suppress a shudder and a laugh at the same time, as he remembered all that transpired when Antonius discovered the true contents of Caesar's will. The Master of the Horse had originally planned on opening it, with much fanfare and ceremony, on the rostra in the Forum, announcing the date and time at which he would confirm what all the occupants of the city, citizen or otherwise, assumed to be fact. The first hint of trouble occurred when the appointed time arrived, with the Forum packed to the point that those who arrived early to get a spot next to the rostra found themselves crushed up against it, unable to move, but with no sign of Antonius. Time passed; not surprisingly, people became restive, as first a third of a watch, then a full watch passed. There was much clamoring and excitement threatening to burst into full-blown violence when, under escort, not Marcus Antonius, but the young man who was barely known as Gaius Octavius arrived at the Forum. To this point, his only claim to any notoriety was due to his relationship with his great-uncle, G. Julius Caesar, with whom he had served as *contubernalis,* when the great general had finished suppressing opposition from the sons of Pompey in Hispania. Ovidius hadn't been present at that moment in the Forum, but who in Rome hadn't heard what had transpired on that day? The youngster—he was barely 26 at the time—had supplied an answer, in both the immediate and in the larger sense, with his announcement that Caesar' will, which had been opened in front of a set of witnesses, had, in fact, been quite different than what Antonius, and frankly, the rest of Rome had assumed. With little more than a few strokes of a pen, Caesar had turned Rome upside down by naming Gaius Octavius as not only his primary heir, but also as the inheritor of his name. Surprising nobody, Antonius did not react well to this news, and the immediate aftermath had seen the gutters of the streets surrounding the Forum run red with so much blood, one might have thought the spring floods had arrived.

It was a time Ovidius remembered well: he had been in his teens, and, like other young men of his class, had been swept up in the swirling maelstrom as the sides supporting each man sought to establish their dominance. It had taken a few years, but there was at least now an uneasy truce; and Ovidius was proud to count himself as one of the young Caesar's men, his willingness to show his loyalty with his fists and a club having been rewarded with this post. Numerius Ovidius was now an Optio in the Urban Cohorts, and while he enjoyed the resulting rise in his status and the money that came with it, days like this made it difficult to appreciate it. Facing him was a seemingly never-ending line of people, most of them either standing next to or sitting on a multitude of carts, wagons, and every other conveyance one could imagine, all of them demanding entrance into the city. It was the job of the men of his Century, or at least the section assigned to this gate, to ensure that anyone attempting entry was doing so for legitimate purposes. No matter how important the task might be, it was mind-numbing, onerous, and thankless, but it at least afforded a curious man like Ovidius an opportunity to see and experience just how widely varied the people of Rome's vast empire were. This day, despite the cold, was shaping up to be like all of the others. Until, that is, one of his men nudged him.

"Optio, we've got a rider, coming hard!"

Torn from his reverie, Ovidius saw that, indeed, a lone rider was bypassing the line of people awaiting entrance, prompting any number of curses and threats that the rider either didn't hear or didn't care about. Pulling up in a spray of dirt, he leaped down to stride over to Ovidius, barely sketching anything that could have been called a salute, while offering the Optio a wax tablet.

"This is from the harbormaster," the messenger announced, giving Ovidius his first hint that today might not be the same old routine and boring day, after all.

Squinting, the Optio had to read the message twice, before its import even began to sink in, and he looked up at the messenger, his jaw agape.

"They're coming here?"

"It appears that way," the courier confirmed, happy that this wasn't his problem.

Looking over the messenger's shoulder, Ovidius stared back down the road, straining his eyes again, this time in an attempt to gain sight of what the message warned about.

"Go get Proculus," he snapped to the man who had alerted him of the rider's approach, naming the Centurion in charge of this Century. "He's going to want to be here for this."

If he didn't know any better, Titus Pullus would have sworn to any god imaginable that he was dreaming. This feeling had been with him for the last several days, and this sense that he was asleep and in a world where anything was possible hadn't diminished, but instead was strengthened from the moment his ship had eased itself into the wharf at Ostia. It was understandable: this was the end of a three year journey, one that Pullus had believed on more than one occasion would never be completed. Yet, here they were: Scribonius, Diocles, and even old Vellusius beside him, as the prow of his transport nosed its way into a berthing slot, where men waited to tie the ship off.

Exchanging a glance with his friend, Pullus saw that Scribonius seemed to be in a daze, so he nudged him in the ribs and said, "Well? We're not getting any younger."

Jerked from whatever private place he had been in, Scribonius looked over at Pullus, who even then was moving from the prow of the ship and heading amidships, to where the boarding plank was being lowered.

"Speak for yourself," Scribonius snorted, unconsciously echoing their old, departed friend Balbus. "I'm like a fine wine, I only get better with age."

"Then that wine better get moving, if he wants to be the toast of Rome," Pullus called over his shoulder.

Standing on the wharf was an older man, short and squat, who looked as if he would rather have been anywhere else but at that spot. He was one of the harbormaster's men, responsible for determining the identity and intent of every ship that landed here, and while this collection of ships that had rowed into the harbor wasn't—from outward appearances anyway—any different from any other merchant fleet, the sight of the men now gathered on the upper deck gave him a strong sense of disquiet. If pressed, he couldn't have given a tangible, spoken reason for his distress; the men he was eyeing were at least his age, if not older. But there was something about them that spoke of a ferocity and ability to wreak havoc that completely negated any impediments their advanced age might have conferred. Granted, they were all dressed in Roman garb, but it was a mode of dress that hadn't been fashionable for some time, and it was almost as if these men had just appeared out of an earlier age in Rome's history. Of all the men on the ship, the one that stood out the most did so not just for what he wore, but because of his size: he was easily one of the largest men the official had ever seen, and that was counting the Germans whom he had once watched battle to the death during the games. The large man was wearing a helmet that bore a transverse crest, and there was no Roman alive who didn't know what that signified; but the color was wrong, and there was something odd about his armor. Whatever it was, the official didn't have the time to think about it, because the plank was suddenly thrown down onto the wharf, and with only a moment's hesitation, the giant hopped onto it and descended onto the wharf.

"May I ask who you are, and your business here in Ostia?"

Despite his best attempts, even the official could hear the tremor in his own voice, but the other man didn't seem to notice. When the larger man spoke, the official was somewhat surprised that it was perfect Latin, even if it did carry an accent that spoke of one of the provinces.

"My name is Titus Pullus. I am," the man paused for a moment before amending, "I *was* the Primus Pilus of the 10th Equestris..."

Before he could get any further, the official let out a gasp.

"Wait. You mean...*Caesar's* 10th Equestris?"

"Is there any other?" the larger man asked dryly.

"No," the official mumbled, feeling the flush creep up from his neck. "I don't suppose there is."

"As I was saying," Pullus continued, "I'm the commander of this contingent of Roman citizens who have fulfilled their obligation of enlistment under the standard, and are returning to Rome."

For a long moment, the official didn't say anything, frozen in his spot, as his mind tried to comprehend what he was hearing. Could this be possible?

"So, you mean that Caesar is...alive?" he asked cautiously.

Despite the fact that Pullus could certainly understand why, the hesitant tone of the official's question prompted a strong reaction.

"Of course he's alive. He's...more than alive," Pullus snapped.

"More than alive?" Now the official was bewildered. "How could he be more than alive?"

It was certainly a sensible question, but Pullus wasn't willing to expand on his statement, at least not at this moment and to this man. However, realizing that he needed to provide the official with something, he produced one of the scrolls that Caesar had given to him to deliver. He didn't unroll it; instead, he merely turned it so the official could see the seal, and was rewarded by a gasp, as the other man recognized it. His reaction was immediate and dramatic, as he fell to his knees on the dock, forcing Pullus to suppress a laugh, thinking that it was an appropriate gesture, even if the man had no way of knowing it.

"That doesn't matter right now. What matters is that you recognize whose seal this is and let us go about our business."

Even if the official had been disposed to argue before, seeing the seal of a man who had been thought dead for many years removed any such inclination, and he hurriedly jotted down the pass that Pullus would need to show to the Urban Cohort at the gate.

It took the better part of the morning for the rest of Pullus' fleet to find a mooring spot. As large a port as Ostia was, it took quite a bit of maneuvering to make room for the ships carrying the returning Romans. Before the unloading process was completed, Pullus, Scribonius, and the men on the first boat had procured the necessary cartage and horses to transport the contents of the ships, that were accompanied by Pullus, Scribonius, and the other returning Primi Pili, who had rented horses to go to Rome ahead of the men. Weaving their way through the heavy traffic of the Via Ostia, none of them was in much of a mood to talk, all of them absorbed in their own thoughts to the point where any kind of conversation would have been unwelcome. Pullus was no different, his mind still trying to reconcile the fact that he and the others had, for all intents and purposes, actually achieved their goal. It had taken three years; but more than the time, it was the cost in lives that tempered any joy or pride Pullus might have felt about actually reaching Rome. Of the slightly more than 2,500 men that had left the islands of Wa just two weeks after Caesar's child, a son, was born, there were just a few more than a thousand left. However, the dire consequences predicted by those men who wanted to take the overland route, instead of the seaborne one, hadn't materialized: only three ships had been lost due to storms. Instead, it had been just the hardship of the march itself that had struck down most men: it had become commonplace for a cry to go up in the mornings, when men discovered that a tentmate had simply...given up. The toll taken by almost an entire lifetime spent out in the elements, under the harshest conditions imaginable, just proved to be too much for so many men. In fact, it had been this development that had added an extra six months to the journey, when Pullus had made the decision to stop at the island of Taprobane and recuperate at the colony there. While there, Pullus had sent a ship ahead to let the world know that Caesar lived, but as he had learned after he and the men had made the overland trek from the Red Sea to Alexandria, the ship had never arrived. That meant that the returning veterans were the first notification that Caesar lived, but it was in Alexandria where Pullus learned of the turmoil that had descended on the Roman world, and that it wasn't confined to the Italian side of Our Sea. From a still-grieving Cleopatra, Pullus was informed of the assassination of Caesarion, who had been ruling in Caesar's stead in Ecbatana. However, according to Cleopatra, the deed hadn't been committed by the most obvious suspects, the Parthians. No, she was adamant that it had been none other than the young pretender to Caesar's name, Octavian, for whom she reserved the most vicious invective that Pullus had ever heard, no matter what the source.

"He thinks because Caesar's will named him as heir, he *is* Caesar, but he could never be Caesar," she spat. "Marcus Antonius is twice the man of Octavian, but even he's not Caesar!"

Even if he had been inclined to argue, Pullus could clearly see the raging sorrow that still wracked the queen, despite its being four years since her son's death. It was from Cleopatra that he had gotten the most complete picture of the state of affairs in Rome, and it not surprisingly had increased his own tension with every league he and his men drew nearer to the city. Watch after watch he spent closeted in the captain's cabin with Scribonius and the other Primi Pili, discussing and arguing what would happen when they showed up. For a short time, they actually discussed the idea of not going any further and, in fact, turning to go back to at least Taprobane, none of them wanting to feel as though they were contributing to more strife. As quickly dismissed as this thought was, it didn't make Pullus feel any better, and now, as he rode his rented horse close enough that the walls of the city were visible, he began having second thoughts. With an effort, he shook them away, knowing that at the very least, he owed it to the men who had survived so much to let them achieve their dream of returning home. Scribonius was acutely aware of his friend's inner turmoil, but he truly didn't know the answer to the dilemma that was posed by the fact that Caesar still lived, so he held his tongue, content to provide support to his friend by his presence. Furthermore, he had his own worries; Scribonius was not only a native of the city, he had actually been born into a wealthy equestrian family, and he had no idea what kind of reception he would receive at his father's home. That is, if his father was still alive. As the party drew closer, Pullus and the others could just make out the line of carts, horseback riders and pedestrians waiting to enter the massive gate.

"That's new," Scribonius commented, but Pullus only answered with a grunt, intent on trying to determine what the new structure meant.

Finally, he asked, "You don't suppose that's just for us, do you?"

Scribonius looked over at him in surprise.

"Why would you think that?" he asked with a laugh.

Pullus shrugged, but his tone was thoughtful, as he replied, "No reason, I suppose. But," he turned to look at his friend with an intense stare, "have you ever thought that we might not be welcome?"

In fact, Scribonius hadn't, at least until his friend mentioned it. But then his formidable intellect examined the situation, and in the time it took him to form the words, he instantly understood the source of Pullus' question, and his fear.

"That," he said slowly, pitching his voice so that only Pullus could hear, "is something I haven't thought about. But I should have." His tone turned grim and he finished, "I think we need to be prepared for anything."

Pullus was torn; a part of him was proud he had actually had a thought that hadn't occurred to his friend, but he also felt a chill of dread at the idea that he might be right. Without thinking, he reached down to touch his left hip, where his Gallic sword normally hung, then remembered that for as long as anyone could remember, men weren't allowed inside Rome's walls while bearing arms. Unless, Pullus suddenly thought, they were under orders by a Consul. Or a Dictator. Without warning, he pulled the reins on his rented horse, then guided it quickly off the road, giving a quick command to the others to follow. They were clearly puzzled, but they had long since accepted Pullus' authority over this command, so they instantly obeyed him, gathering their own horses around him. As the advance party, they had loaded only one cart with their personal belongings, but for what Pullus had in mind, they were the most important pieces of gear they owned. Only Pullus had been in full uniform, but he quickly explained what he had in mind and what he wanted of them. Again, although they were startled, and more than one looked doubtful after Pullus briefly gave his reasons, none of them hesitated and quickly began to get to work.

Tiberius Proculus, the Centurion in charge of the Third Century, First Cohort of the Urban Cohorts, was beginning to think that his Optio had lost his mind. True, Ovidius had shown him the tablet containing the news that a small army was approaching, but more than enough time had passed that they should have seen some sign of these supposed invaders. Immediately after arriving, Proculus had made the decision to close the gates, which was a feat in and of itself, requiring almost every man of his Century. But now the traffic outside was piling up, and making matters worse, the people waiting to get in were becoming increasingly restive.

Looking up to the battlements for perhaps the tenth time, Proculus called up to the man standing there, watching down the road, "Well? Anything?"

And for the tenth time, the sentry could only answer with a shake of his head. As the moments passed, Centurion Proculus could almost see his career withering in front of his eyes. He had taken the precaution of sending a man, bearing the tablet from the official on the docks, to the Curia, where the small office of the commander of the Urban Cohort on guard was located, but he was beginning to understand that he had made a very big mistake. Except that it hadn't been *his* mistake. He gave a furious sidelong glance at Ovidius, who was clearly as nervous now as his Centurion, a line of sweat trickling down the side of his face despite the cold. Proculus was just about to open his mouth and begin a verbal blast at his forlorn Optio, when the silence was broken.

"Centurion! I see a group of men approaching!"

Proculus craned his neck to stare up at the sentry, but when nothing else was forthcoming, he snapped, "And? Is that all you see, you idiot? It could be some merchants from Sicilia for all you know!"

"Oh, I doubt that sir," the sentry replied, and if Proculus hadn't been so distracted, he would have probably climbed the steps to the battlement to stripe the insolent bastard just for the tone of his voice. "Because these men are all wearing armor."

Proculus and Ovidius exchanged a glance, as the Optio let out a long, slow breath, clearly relieved that he had been vindicated. While Proculus wasn't willing to go that far, he did admit, grudgingly, that his Optio had done the right thing to alert him.

"Send three sections out behind me. I'm going to see what this is all about," Proculus commanded his Optio, then, without waiting for a reply, he stepped through the smaller postern gate cut into the larger one.

Immediately, Proculus was verbally assailed by the shouts and curses of those who had been waiting to get in and hadn't thought to leave to seek entrance through another gate.

"What's taking so long? Why aren't you letting us through?"

"What, did you lose the key?"

There was some laughter at this, but Proculus ignored everyone, instead bellowing at them to clear the roadway. It appeared that some of the more stubborn people—including a man sitting on the seat of an ox-drawn cart stacked with stinking hides, who smelled almost as bad as his cargo—would refuse, but the appearance of the sections of armed men convinced them to pull away, but not without some choice invective for the men of the Urban Cohort. However, by this point Proculus was able to see what had alerted the sentry. As the crowd parted, he had a clear view down the road, and he saw a group of perhaps thirty men, all mounted, with what appeared to be one wagon following behind them. What made them noteworthy—besides this being an unusually large escort for a single conveyance—was that, as the sentry had said, these men were clearly armored and wearing helmets. Once they were within two hundred paces, Proculus noticed something else, something that made this little procession even more unusual. Not only were these men all wearing helmets, they were wearing helmets of a style which to Proculus was very familiar; in fact, he was wearing an identical one, or almost identical, on his own head. If his eyes weren't deceiving him, every one of these mounted men was a Centurion of Rome.

He was still processing this new piece of information when the group of men, now perhaps fifty paces away, drew up at the clear command of one of the leading riders, who continued riding forward. As the lone man drew closer, Proculus could see that he was extremely large, and, in fact, it was the size of the man that gave Proculus the first tickle of recognition, and he felt his heart—which had already been beating at a somewhat elevated but steady pace—begin thumping against his chest so hard that he thought he could see his leather cuirass pulsating. Could it be, he wondered in amazement, thinking back to the one time he had seen a Roman Centurion as large as this one, many, many years before? As the mounted man approached the final few paces, Proculus' mind flew back to the occasion of Caesar's four triumphs, when Proculus had been nothing more than a youngster of perhaps twenty, or so, and was heading down a path that could only lead to disaster. He had been in one of the collegia of the Aventine, the gang of roving toughs who enforced the will of their leader, a man with the lofty name of Gaius Fonteius Vulso, who ran the whores, thieves, and protection rackets in that part of the city. Young hoodlum he may have been, but Proculus was also a Roman through and through, and he took great vicarious pride in the achievements of Rome's Legions, particularly when it came to Caesar's Legions in Gaul. When, at long last, Caesar had finally celebrated his triumph for the subjugation of what was said to be three million people, Proculus and some of his friends had been sent by Vulso to secure a prime viewing spot in the Circus Maximus. That they had done, taking care not to shove aside any equestrians or, gods forbid, plebeians or patricians, so while they weren't sitting in the first three rows, they nonetheless had a prime viewing spot for the triumph. Naturally, they had been joined by Vulso and a couple of his favorite whores, with Vulso actually wearing a white toga, as if he was just like the men sitting down on the front row. This meant that most of Proculus' friends had been sent to find their own seats, their only thanks a snarled curse from Vulso. Yet, for some reason, Vulso had liked Proculus, and he had been the only one allowed to stay. From this vantage point, he had stood and cheered, like almost all the other citizens of Rome, when first Caesar—his face painted red in a style that, unknown to Proculus, would become part of his god costume—and standing in a quadriga drawn by four white horses, then the rest of the army had come marching into the vast space of the hippodrome.

Proculus had never heard anything as loud as the people were that day, and his heart had swelled with pride at the might of Rome, here on display for all of her citizens to see. Vulso, on the other hand, had been thoroughly unimpressed; in fact, sneering at the sight of aligned ranks as they trooped past his seat, calling the men of the Legions fools who wouldn't last more than a dozen heartbeats against a real man, like Felix the Thracian, Vulso's favorite gladiator of the moment. Granted, Vulso had said this in a quiet enough voice that he wouldn't be overheard; the man was many things, but he was no fool. Still, whenever Proculus thought back to that moment, he realized that this had marked the beginning of his disenchantment, not just with Vulso, but also his way of life. Not even when it was the turn of the 10th Legion—widely known to be Caesar's favorite that had earned the nickname "the Equestrians", because of an episode in which some of them had accompanied Caesar on horseback to meet with the German chieftain Ariovistus—was Vulso impressed at the sight of their Primus Pilus. He was the largest Roman Proculus had ever seen, not just in height, but also in his breadth and musculature, and the sight of Pullus had emboldened young Proculus to challenge Vulso.

"How do you think Felix would fare against that Legionary?" he had asked his boss.

"Ha! That big oaf would only last two dozen heartbeats against Felix," Vulso had laughed, but even with his bravado, Proculus could see that Vulso was as impressed by the Primus Pilus as he was.

Now, many years later, this memory somehow dislodged itself from the recesses of Proculus' mind as the large man dismounted—if that's what it could be called, since his legs were just a few inches off the ground already. Proculus barely noticed as he tried to come to terms with his recognition that he was actually seeing the same Roman Centurion he had watched all that time ago. What was his name? Proculus thought furiously, trying to come up with it as the other man approached, one hand holding a scroll.

"You're Titus Pullus, Primus Pilus of the 10th Legion," a voice blurted out, and Proculus was barely aware that it had been he himself who had uttered the words.

Pullus stopped short, as surprised to be recognized after all these years by a man he was sure he'd never seen before as Proculus was in recognizing him.

"Yes," Pullus replied, cautiously. "I am in fact Titus Pullus. But I'm not the Primus Pilus of the 10th Legion." Seeing Proculus' confusion, he added, "I *was* the Primus Pilus. Now I'm not. I'm..." as strange as it was, this was the first time Pullus had been forced to think about what his actual status was, and he was about to say, "..retired," but caught himself. Thinking furiously—he couldn't tell how much time elapsed, but hoped it wasn't an undue pause—as he said instead, "Actually, I'm on detached duty. In fact," he continued, suddenly inspired, "that's why we're here. We've been sent by Caesar to return to Rome and meet with Marcus Antonius. He still is Master of the Horse, isn't he?"

Proculus nodded in reply, but his face was still a study in confusion.

"Wait," he held a hand up, as he shook his head, as if to clear it, "I must have missed something. You said you've been sent by

Caesar? THE Caesar? Not..." he stopped, unsure of how to proceed.

Like a large number of Romans, Proculus found it very hard to think of the youngster Octavian as Caesar, although as a Centurion, he knew better than most how costly it was not to do so, and, in fact, he had never slipped up once. But now, confronted by this man Pullus, who said that the original Caesar had sent him, Proculus simply didn't know how to respond.

"No, not Gaius Octavianus," Pullus replied, thankful that he had at least learned this piece of information from Cleopatra before arriving in Rome. "Gaius Julius Caesar, my general. That Caesar. The *real* Caesar," Pullus finished, and while his tone was quiet, it was no less emphatic.

Remembering what he held in his hand, Pullus stepped forward, offering to show Proculus at least the seal on the scroll. For his part, Proculus eyed it as if it were a snake, coiled to strike, so he leaned forward cautiously just close enough so that he could see the seal.

"What does it say?" Proculus asked, but Pullus only shrugged in answer.

Then, seeing that Proculus expected more, he snapped, "I don't know. It's not for me, it's for Marcus Antonius. That's who I've come to see."

Proculus considered this, but then indicated the men behind Pullus.

"And what about them? Are they your bodyguard?"

Titus Pullus had never been known for his patience, but now his already limited supply was exhausted. It was bad enough that he was saddled with suspicions about the reception he and his men might receive, but to have this jumped-up piece of *cac*—who, despite wearing the transverse crest, looked like little more than one of the bully boys who ran around the Subura—questioning him to this extent was more than he was willing to bear.

"Do I look like I need a bodyguard?" Pullus asked, but while his tone was quiet, its menace wasn't lost on Proculus, who took a step backward. Seeing his adversary retreating, Pullus pressed his advantage. "Me and my men have just traveled across the entire world to return to Rome, because our general orders us to do so. I have specific instructions to speak to Marcus Antonius and deliver this scroll to him in person," he waved it in front of Proculus, "and I also have more than a thousand very tired, very hungry, and very angry men who have come with me. We are Roman Legionaries returning home, and I refuse to waste any more time being questioned by someone like you. So you need to open these gates and allow me and my men to pass through them to conduct our official business, or I'm not going to be responsible for the mess my friends behind me make out of you and your...guards," Pullus finished with a sneer.

Proculus had always thought of himself as a tough man, but in the presence of Titus Pullus, he suddenly recognized that he really had no true understanding of what that meant. In that instant, any thought of resistance crumbled, and all he could do was give a weak nod, before turning and walking on unsteady legs to the postern door. As he did, Pullus watched for a moment, then turned about to return to where Scribonius and the others waited, and only then did he smile.

"It looks like you made another friend," was Scribonius' only comment.

Pullus didn't say anything, just continued to smile as he remounted, and with his friend, he watched the huge gates of Rome slowly open again.

Marcus Antonius was in one of his rages, pacing back and forth in his office in what had once been Pompey's extravagant villa. As was usual, the cause of his anger was the actions of the young Roman who had become his bitter rival in the rough-and-tumble world of Roman politics. Who did that precious pretty boy think he was? To tell him, Marcus Antonius, who should be the new Consuls for the coming year! Through the red haze of his anger, the rational part of Antonius' mind was forced to acknowledge that it had been his own fault, really, for not crushing the boy Octavian the day after the old man's will was read. He was equally cognizant that those who said it was a sign of his hubris had a point, when they opined that because he had been so sure of the provisions of Caesar's will that he had magnanimously decreed the presence of numerous witnesses when it was read, there was no way Antonius could have eliminated them all. But his one consolation, bare it may have been, was that the others in the room that day were at least as shocked as he had been, if not more so. Nevertheless, that was a jug that had been broken some years before, and now he was dealing with the aftermath of his decision, although he was still unwilling to admit to anyone, but himself, that it had been a mistake. Marcus Antonius had always been ruled by his passions, but despite his knowledge that it was a fatal flaw that would probably prove to be his undoing, he found it next to impossible to control. Yet, he realized, he would have to force himself to—if not quench his rage—at a minimum put it sufficiently aside so that he could think rationally about the best course of action.

What galled Antonius the most, if the truth were known, was that the youngster's choices for Consul were extremely shrewd, and showed a foresight that probably tipped the younger noble Roman's long-range plans, if only Antonius could divine Octavian's larger intent. This had proven to be extremely frustrating, but Marcus Antonius was too proud to admit what most of Rome already knew: in a battle of wits with the young heir to Caesar, Marcus Antonius was close to being an unarmed man. Unfortunately for Antonius and his prospects for victory, that was a truth he couldn't bring himself to recognize, if only for the reason that it would shatter his own *dignitas*, and if he had learned anything from the real Caesar, it was the importance of that essentially Roman quality. Slowing his torrid pace back and forth, Antonius made a conscious effort to gather himself by taking a deep breath, before he turned to face the visibly nervous messenger. Stories of Antonius' temper were many and legendary, and more than one of them involved the fate of the poor soul who had the misfortune to deliver a missive that had driven him into one of his famous rages. Luckily for this man, today wouldn't be one of those that added to Antonius' reputation for brutality, and he was even favored with a tight, tense smile.

"Tell your master, the young Caesar," try as he might, Antonius had to push this past clenched teeth, "that his suggestions are both welcome, and they are extremely...appropriate, given the current situation."

There was no mistaking the sudden sag in the body of the poor soul whom Octavian had sent bearing this message.

"Yes, sir. I will," the man actually managed to get this out without stuttering, but if he thought he would escape without any further trauma, he quickly learned this wasn't to be the case.

Turning to leave, he was stopped by Antonius, who told him, "Wait. I want to write a reply to your master. You might as well stand there; it won't take me long."

Without waiting for a response, Antonius sat down and took a wax tablet from a pile of fresh ones on the left side of his desk. Leaning over, he frowned as he tried to form the words that would fulfill Antonius' goal of both acknowledging Octavian's wisdom in his choices, but also send a javelin of warning to the younger man that he was overstepping. Before he could put the first word down, however, he was interrupted by a knock at the door.

"Not now," he didn't have to shout for his voice to carry. But when the knock came again, this time with an insistence that told Antonius it was important, he allowed entry, but growled, "This better be good."

The slave who approached was Antonius' most senior, and was in charge of the running of the house, which gave Antonius a clue that it was, in fact, an urgent matter, at the very least. Androcles, the slave, had been in Antonius' household for more years than either of them could easily remember, so he wasn't cowed by his master's fits of temper. However, he did know that his master would consider the news that he carried worthy of interruption, no matter what he was doing. To that end, the slave wasted no time, hurrying to his master's side to whisper in his ear. For a moment, Antonius' face registered no emotion, then he turned to look at Androcles, his puzzlement easy to read.

"Say that again?"

Androcles did as he was ordered, and now Antonius did show a reaction. In fact, it was several reactions in quick succession: shock, surprise, then...worry. Somewhat surprisingly, instead of saying a word, he turned back to the tablet, seemingly finding the words that had eluded him before. Writing quickly, he finished, then gestured to the messenger, who approached warily. Holding the tablet out, Antonius gave the man a grim smile.

"Tell your master that if he knows what's good for him, he'll get here as quickly as he can. I'm sure that he will want to be here for what's about to happen."

Titus Pullus hadn't been sure what kind of reception he would receive when he showed up at Pompey's villa, which is how he would always think of it, despite the fact that Antonius had occupied it for more than a decade. In his experience, the upper classes usually made it a point to keep their social inferiors waiting, but he was fairly sure that Antonius had never been faced with a situation like this, where a man thought dead for the last several years had risen from his grave. That had been the important piece of information Pullus had learned from the Optio Ovidius, of what Pullus was informed was the new Urban Cohort, the junior officer escorting him to Pompey's villa. As they walked, Pullus' mind was whirling from the changes wrought in the city, which seemed to have been transformed in the years since he had last seen it. One thing hadn't changed: the streets were thronged with people from all the edges of the Republic, but even here there was a major change, as Pullus saw a large number of people from the lands that had been conquered by Caesar and men like Pullus. They were mostly Parthians, although Pullus spotted a few of the nut-brown, thin, and wiry people from the lands of the Pandya. He even thought he spotted a man with yellow skin and wearing brocaded silk that Pullus knew was the uniform of a Han courtier. As Ovidius led him, the Optio proved to be a wealth of information on all that had transpired, since Caesar had disappeared into the mists of the east, but the most important piece of news was that Pullus' general had been declared dead. Moreover, while Ovidius only touched on the bitter struggle that had resulted between Antonius, Octavian, and some of the other notable men of the Republic, Pullus inferred much from what Ovidius hadn't said, although until he had a chance to talk to other sources, he wouldn't know for sure if he had guessed correctly. Probably the most notable thing Ovidius told him, outside of Caesar's status of course, was the fate of Cicero, long one of Caesar's bitterest opponents in the Senate and one of the leading figures of The Boni. If Ovidius went on a little too effusively and in too gory detail about how the Master of the Horse had finally had enough of Cicero's poison pen and had ordered the execution of Cicero, having his hands nailed to the doors of the Curia, Pullus understood that the Optio was merely displaying the avidity the lower classes showed for the bloodshed of their betters.

While this didn't surprise Pullus all that much—he had long since counted Cicero as one of the walking dead because of his refusal to understand the inevitability of Caesar and what he represented what did shock him was when Ovidius casually mentioned that at the time of his execution, Cicero had been allied with Caesar's heir, but that Octavian had done nothing to stop the process. Pullus was further surprised to learn that all the transformations he had seen weren't done at the hand of Antonius, but of the young Caesar, who had somehow managed to divert the vast treasures of the Parthians that Caesar had sent back to Rome, simultaneously keeping those funds out of the hands of Antonius who, according to most accounts, planned on raising another army to crush his young rival. What Octavian—which was how Pullus thought of him and, until forced to, how he would continue to refer to him since the real Caesar was still alive—had done was brilliant and cunning, informing Pullus that Caesar's insight into the young man had been much keener than anyone would have thought. By subverting these funds, not only did Octavian deprive Antonius of the means to destroy his young rival, but he had also cemented himself as a champion of the mob of Rome by providing all these new public works, which Octavian had insisted not be created by slave labor. In one stroke, he had provided employment for thousands of otherwise idle members of the Head Count, while giving all the occupants of the city new temples, monuments, parks, fountains, and all manner of smaller edifices. The scope of what Ovidius was telling Pullus was so vast that, in the guise of needing to rest, he had Ovidius halt for a bit so that he could gather his thoughts and try to get a sense of where matters stood. It was during this pause that Ovidius had casually mentioned one other piece of information, and of all the things that he had told Pullus, the Primus Pilus instantly understood that this was the most important, and potentially most dangerous, to him and his men.

"They made Caesar a god after they declared him dead," Ovidius had told him. "They had a festival and everything, and there's a temple dedicated to him in the Forum. It's just a short way down the Capitoline from the temple of Jupiter Optimus Maximus, and it's almost as big! You should go see it, when you get a chance."

"I'll do that," Pullus had tried to keep his tone casual, although he didn't know why.

It was highly doubtful that this Optio, who from the looks of him would have hardly been good enough to be in the Tenth Cohort of the 10th, had the wits about him to take notice of what Pullus knew was a tremor in his voice. Needing an extra moment before starting out again, he bent down to fiddle with the laces of his *caligae* as his mind raced, trying to understand the import of this last piece of news. Oh Scribonius, he thought, why didn't I bring you along?

Now, standing in the vestibule of Pompey's villa, waiting for Antonius to deign to see him, Pullus was actually thankful for the delay, his mind still racing as he thought furiously about where matters stood at this point. At least a third of a watch passed before a man appeared from the direction where, Pullus assumed, Antonius was located in the vast villa, and his first indication that he had cause for worry was that the man wasn't just a slave. Dressed in a tunic, the man approaching Pullus was clearly a patrician or highly ranked plebeian, his bearing and manner oozing that disdainful authority and belief in their own superiority that members of his class seemed to be born with, and Pullus hated him instantly. The noble was younger than Pullus, but that wasn't unusual anymore. However, Pullus saw that his hair was not only carefully coiffed, but that it also gleamed with some sort of pomade; moreover, on almost every finger was a ring, although the most important one was the iron band that marked his membership in the Senate.

"Primus Pilus Pullus," the man's voice was as oily as his hair and the smile was the kind of false beacon that didn't fool Pullus in the slightest. "It is not only a huge surprise, it's an even bigger honor to meet you."

As he spoke he extended his hand, which Pullus barely hesitated to accept, grasping the man's forearm in the Roman manner and being not in the least surprised when he felt the other man's smooth, soft hand on his own.

"I'm Quintus Dellius," the noble spoke the name as if Pullus should have recognized it, but it meant nothing to the larger man. Not seeing the reaction he was expecting, Dellius' lips thinned in irritation, but his tone didn't vary as he continued, "I've been sent by the Master of the Horse to conduct you to his office."

Without waiting, Dellius broke his clasp and turned to lead Pullus through a maze of hallways, turning this way and that, all while speaking over his shoulder in a running monologue.

"I must say that your appearance is a...surprise, to say the least," Dellius told Pullus, then before Pullus could form any kind of response, continued, "which is part of the reason for the delay in meeting with you. Marcus Antonius is a busy man, as I'm sure you know, and you showing up without any warning has thrown his schedule into disarray, I can tell you."

Pullus wasn't sure, but he thought he detected a trace of rebuke in Dellius' voice, but even if he had wanted to reply, he wasn't given the chance.

"But your presence is a cause for celebration," Dellius prattled, making it sound as though it was anything but, "and Antonius wants to do you and your men justice. How many did you say you've arrived with?"

I haven't been allowed to say a word, Pullus thought, but answered, "Just over a thousand."

"And, where are they now?"

Despite the fact that Dellius took particular pains to make his voice sound casual, Pullus wasn't fooled, detecting a hint of worry. Which, Pullus allowed, was understandable, especially if matters were anywhere near what Pullus had begun to suspect.

"Oh, I imagine by this point they're all safe and sound, completely unloaded and waiting," Pullus replied, watching the back of his guide carefully.

He was disappointed when Dellius showed no overt reaction, but then they had arrived at their destination—a set of double doors—where Dellius stopped.

"Wait here," he said preemptively, and before Pullus could respond, Dellius disappeared.

This time Pullus wasn't forced to wait long, as Dellius stuck his head out of the door, motioning to Pullus.

"The Master of the Horse will see you now."

Taking a deep, but surreptitious, breath, Pullus squared his shoulders, then followed Dellius into the room. Because he had made mental preparations, he congratulated himself on maintaining an impassive demeanor when he saw that, along with Antonius and Dellius, of course, the room contained another man. Striding to the desk behind which Antonius was seated, Pullus rendered the best salute he could muster, which Antonius returned.

"Master of the Horse," Pullus' voice was steady, despite the hammering of his heart. Then, after a brief pause, he turned to the other man, who was clearly younger than Antonius. "And Gaius Octavius. I bring greetings, and orders, from Gaius Julius Caesar."

Despite not being of the same intellectual stripe as his best friend, Titus Pullus was extremely intelligent in his own right, so he wasn't at all surprised at the reception he received at the hands of Marcus Antonius and Gaius Octavian. The latter, it must be said, clearly didn't appreciate the appellation by which Pullus had greeted him, but in this Pullus wouldn't be swayed by any instinct for self-preservation. As far as Octavian, and Roman law, were concerned, the adoption of Caesar's grand-nephew had been done posthumously, but since Caesar wasn't dead, there had been no adoption in Pullus' eyes. However, what he had worked out in the time he had been kept waiting was that this knowledge, along with the orders that he carried with him, weren't likely to be looked on with any favor by either Antonius or Octavian. In fact, Pullus was forced to acknowledge that by making him wait Antonius had done him a favor by allowing him to form his thoughts more fully and to think through what had been a massive amount of information thrust into his consciousness in a short amount of time. Though the first inkling that their reception might not be all that Pullus and the others expected had occurred on the short ride from Ostia, it was only that precious third of a watch, while Pullus waited, that gave him the opportunity to fully think through the kind of problem that his presence presented not just to Antonius, but also to Octavian.

Truthfully, the threat might have been even greater to Octavian than to Antonius, particularly when coupled with what Pullus had learned in Alexandria. And, Pullus thought, it definitely makes more sense why Cleopatra had been adamant that it had been Octavian behind the murder of Caesar's and Cleopatra's son, Caesarion. If that was true, what would his reaction be to learn that, from Diana, Caesar had been given another son? Although it was true that Caesar's newest son wasn't truly Roman, because of his mother's origin, this had been the case with Caesarion, as well; but it was also the case that Caesarion had looked remarkably like his father. Pullus had no doubt that, if the people of his own class, contemptuously called the Head Count by the upper classes, had laid eyes on Caesarion, young Octavian would have been cast aside so quickly that his head would have spun. That, in itself, made it understandable why Octavian would have no reason to love Caesarion and would view him as a threat. Yet, Pullus couldn't imagine that, given the physical differences between Cleopatra and Diana, this newest heir to Caesar would provide the same kind of visual menace. The larger danger, both to Octavian and Antonius, was the fact that Caesar, in fact, still lived, so that by the time Pullus had reached that point in front of Antonius' desk, he wasn't surprised that neither man looked at all pleased at this solid piece of evidence of Caesar's existence in the form of the large Primus Pilus of the 10th Legion.

"Well, I must say that it seems to be an understatement if I were to say that I'm surprised to see you," Antonius was the first to speak, his mouth quirking into a smile, despite his underlying feelings.

"I can imagine sir," Pullus remarked, dryly. "But here I am, nonetheless."

"Yes, here you are," Antonius murmured, shooting a glance over at his young counterpart, who was even paler than normal.

It was said about Gaius Octavian that he was pretty—this wasn't meant as a compliment—and the last time Titus Pullus had laid eyes on the then youngster, when he had been a mere eighteen, he would have agreed with that assessment. Now, standing here at the age of thirty-two, Octavian's prettiness had gone, replaced by a handsomeness that Pullus was sure would be pleasing to women. But there was something cold about that handsomeness, even if at this moment there was an air of uncertainty hanging about Octavian that, at least to Pullus, was repellent. Octavian was looking at Pullus, his blue eyes giving away nothing as he examined the Primus Pilus, which for some reason Pullus found disquieting. As sure of himself as he was, Titus Pullus still felt as though he was being measured and found wanting by Octavian, but it was a feeling Pullus shook off, reminding himself that he had the force of Caesar behind him, if not his own formidable self. But Caesar was far, far away, Pullus understood, so he forgave himself for the trickle of cold sweat that ran between his shoulder blades at that moment.

"Yes, here you are," Octavian finally spoke, his voice flat and emotionless.

"And I bring this," Pullus held the scroll out, the seal still unbroken, offering it to Antonius, who looked at it as if Pullus were holding a coiled serpent, wearing an almost identical expression as Proculus had a short time before.

As well he might, Pullus thought, because while he knew much of what Caesar was ordering Antonius to do, he knew his general well enough to understand that he hadn't been told everything. It was probable that there was more than one surprise contained in this scroll, which Pullus continued holding out to

Antonius, who finally accepted it with such reluctance it almost caused Pullus to mar the moment by laughing. Once Antonius accepted the scroll, Pullus turned to the younger Roman, who was still regarding the Primus Pilus with a gaze that reminded Pullus of a lizard he had seen sometime in the past. Reaching down, he drew the second scroll from his belt, and offered it to Octavian.

"This is for you, sir," Pullus said politely, but while Antonius seemed reluctant, Octavian acted very much as though he was going to refuse outright.

Pullus' arm remained outstretched for what he was sure was more than two dozen heartbeats, before Octavian finally leaned forward and took the scroll from his fingers. While this had been going on, Antonius had broken the seal and unrolled his scroll, and had begun to read it. For Pullus, this period of time would be one of the longest of his life, as he waited for both men to read, and, more importantly, absorb, what Caesar had written. As he waited there, Pullus stood at *intente,* but employing a trick perfected long before by countless men of the ranks preceding him, he used the extent of his peripheral vision to observe both men. Antonius' face was much easier to read: first his jaw had dropped, then a rush of blood had suffused his face with a glow that was usually a precursor to something terrible happening to anyone luckless enough to have the misfortune to be within reach. Clamping his jaw shut, Antonius only occasionally glanced up at Pullus, but the Primus Pilus kept his gaze locked at a spot above Antonius' head. Although Antonius had no doubt that Pullus was watching him, at the moment he was content to maintain the fiction. Octavian, on the other hand, Pullus was finding impossible to read, his face giving nothing away, and he didn't know the younger man well enough to recognize that Octavian showed his tension by way of a nervous twitching of his foot, which began tapping a rhythm on the floor. Pullus saw that both men had reached the end of their respective scrolls, noting that Octavian had finished his much more quickly than Antonius. Whether that was due to the fact that Octavian simply read more quickly than his counterpart, or that Antonius had more to read, Pullus didn't know, but they were both done now—with the first reading, at least, although Pullus had no doubt that both men would be going over their messages with infinite care over the next several watches, or even days.

"I must say that, as usual, Caesar has been very thorough," Antonius broke the silence, his voice suddenly hoarse, as if he had been shouting for some time before this.

"He usually is," Pullus agreed.

"So he's in good health, then?" Antonius asked, again almost evoking a laugh from the Primus Pilus, if only for the plaintive quality to his voice.

"Very good health, sir," Pullus replied cheerfully, perversely happy that the news of his general's robust condition caused such obvious distress. "In fact, I'd say that he's going to outlive us all."

"Well, he *is* a god," Antonius said ruefully. "I just didn't expect him to take it so literally."

Now Pullus couldn't avoid letting a chuckle escape, horrifying himself, but Antonius seemed to like the fact that Pullus appreciated his wit.

"Where are your men now?"

Octavian's question cut through the air like a knife, and while Pullus wasn't sure whether it was the tone or the question itself, he felt a shiver of dread, while he saluted himself for his own foresight.

"They're offloaded by now, sir."

The answer was vague, deliberately so, but Octavian wasn't thrown off.

"Yes, but where are they, exactly?"

Pullus considered his answer carefully, at least in the time he was allowed, understanding that Octavian wasn't just being curious. Before he replied, Pullus tilted his head up to look at the light streaming into the high windows, judging the time.

"I would imagine by this point that they're finishing up making their camp."

Octavian's lips thinned, and Antonius made a small sound of surprise.

"Camp? What do you mean, exactly?" Octavian's tone was quiet, but Pullus was sure that he was trying to sound menacing.

And perhaps in other circumstances, Pullus would be cowed, but while he was worried, he wasn't intimidated in the slightest, not after all he'd been through.

"I had them make a camp at the first open spot outside the port, between here and there."

"When you say 'camp', what exactly are you talking about Pullus?" Antonius interjected, and he seemed no less disturbed than Octavian.

Understanding from the reaction of the two men that he had been right, Pullus tried to sound casual as he replied, "The standard camp. At least," he amended, "the way they've been doing it the last 15 years. Standard stuff, ditches and walls."

"But why?" Antonius gasped. "They're back safely in Rome! Why would they need to construct such a camp?"

"Habit, I suppose," Pullus lied. Then, he couldn't resist asking, "If I might ask, sir, what does it matter? You know they'll fill everything in, once we're given proper billets."

As he did most of the time he was put in an awkward position, Marcus Antonius chose to bluster.

"That's none of your business, Primus Pilus!" he snapped. "And I must say I take offense that whoever it was that gave this command to construct a camp as if they were in enemy territory, felt the need to do so! I assume that was you?" he demanded.

Again, Pullus wasn't intimidated, or at least not sufficiently to show it to the Master of the Horse.

"Yes sir, I did," he said evenly. "But it makes me wonder why it's such an insult. If I were a suspicious man, I'd think that you weren't happy to see us and to know that Caesar not only lives, he thrives."

Antonius glowered at Pullus, but said nothing, while Pullus didn't shift his gaze from the seated man.

"I believe it's time that we show Pullus our dice," Octavian broke the silence, although his voice was still pitched softly.

If Pullus had thought his mind was reeling before, it was nothing compared to the swirl of thoughts and worries that were flashing through his mind as he walked, on unsteady legs, back to the Porta Romana. And if he was being completely honest with himself, Pullus was surprised that he was still walking at all, under his own power and without an armed escort. Of course, that was due to the fact that he was acting as a messenger, going back to the men waiting for him, to relay an offer from the two men currently ruling Rome. Although "offer" was a kind word, he thought bitterly; yet never before was he as anxious to get back to those waiting for him, not only for the security of familiar faces, but to talk to Scribonius. Of all the times he had sought out his counsel, Pullus was sure that it wasn't needed as desperately as it was at this moment, so he used his long legs and bulk to push his way rapidly through the crowd. Reaching the gate, he barely said a word to Proculus, taking the reins of the horse held by one of the members of Proculus' Century, leaping into the saddle and turning the horse in the direction of Ostia in one motion. Immediately kicking the horse into a quick trot, Pullus didn't bother trying to guide the horse in and around the traffic heading into the city, relying on the beast's bulk to carve a path. Just a few stadia from the walls, Pullus could see, off to the left of the road out in an open field that had probably been used for grazing, the bulk of a Roman army camp. He briefly wondered what kind of fuss the owner of the field had put up, but he was sure that one of the others in his group had handled it adequately. Heading for the main gate of the camp, only when he was within hailing distance did Pullus realize, with some chagrin, that he hadn't bothered with issuing a watchword, so by the regulations he wouldn't be allowed in camp. That, he thought, was something he was willing to risk, but he was still relieved when the sentry on duty clearly recognized him and waved him forward. Slowing to a trot, he entered the camp, but before he went more than a dozen paces in the direction of the *praetorium*, he was met by the other Primi Pili, Scribonius, and some of the other Centurions.

"Well?" Scribonius asked, by unspoken consent the spokesman for the group.

"We have a lot to talk about," Pullus replied grimly, as he dismounted. "But not here. Follow me," he called, as he strode in the direction of the headquarter tent, letting one of the members of the guard take care of his horse.

What Antonius and Octavian proposed was simple, if terrible in its own right. As Pullus had surmised, the knowledge that Caesar lived wasn't something either man viewed with any pleasure. In fact, for the first time they found themselves with a common purpose. Now that both men had gotten a taste of absolute power, neither of them was willing to relinquish it, even if it was back to the man who had originally been the source of that power. That was why those men of Caesar's army who had returned, expecting accolades and reward, were instead being threatened, implicitly and explicitly.

"Our choices are simple, if limited. At least," Pullus felt compelled to add, "as far as those two bastards are concerned. We agree to get back on the ships, tonight, and sail back across Our Sea, then march at least to Parthia. Once we're there, we can do whatever we want, as long as none of us ever show our face in Roman territory. Not just Rome," Pullus emphasized, "but any Roman province."

The silence was profound, if short-lived. Then the burst of voices blared forth, deafening Pullus, who at first held up his hand for silence. When that didn't work, he relied on his more effective method.

"*Tacete!*"

As mighty a blast as it was, it still barely matched the level of noise that was coming from the other Centurions, but, thankfully, it had the desired effect. Once order was restored, Pullus continued.

"You need to hear the rest. If we refuse, both Antonius and Octavian assured me that, despite their differences, they would combine to crush us, and claim that we are deserters that have been living in Parthia, but were expelled after Caesarion's murder and the Parthian uprising that followed."

As Pullus feared, this reignited the shouts of anger and indignation, and while Pullus again used his formidable volume to restore order, he shared their anger. Not only was it a lie, it was a slur on the honor of all of the men from every rank. What made it worse, at least as far as Pullus was concerned, was that the uprising in Parthia that unsurprisingly occurred after the assassination of the young king ruling in Caesar's name had, in fact, been caused by one of the very men in the room facing Pullus that day. Pullus was sure that this hadn't been Octavian's intent, but a chain of events had followed, one after the other, that loosened the hold of Rome over the vast lands of the Parthians—a hold put in place by Caesar that gave some of the Parthian noblemen the opportunity for which they had been waiting. They hadn't been entirely successful; indeed, Pullus had been vindicated in his choice of route, because he was sure that he and the rest of the men would still be there, snapped up by a desperate Roman praetor. Still, the Parthian situation wasn't Pullus' or any of these men's concern, but it wasn't lost on Pullus that Octavian had been the man to suggest the punitive action that threatened the returning Romans.

"Let 'em try!" Pullus recognized the voice of Gnaeus Figulus, the former Primus Pilus of the 14th Legion, and his words were met with roars of approval from the rest of the men, the din lasting for a moment, before Figulus could continue. "We don't have many men, but every one of our boys, even the crippled ones, are more than a match for anything those two *cunni* can throw together!"

It helped that he was speaking to a receptive audience, Pullus in particular, who always favored the most direct approach. But he only took one glance at his friend, and seeing a familiar frown on Scribonius' face, prepared himself for this plan, such as it was, to be destroyed with clear, unassailable logic. Perhaps Pullus could be excused for heaving a sigh, before he waved for silence, then pointed to Scribonius.

"I want to hear what Scribonius has to say."

At the beginning of the long journey back to Rome, Scribonius' presence in a meeting of Primi Pili would have caused Pullus innumerable problems with his peers, if only because there was an automatic assumption by his counterparts that Pullus wanted his friend there only for political purposes. However, by this point, every man there had been present when some challenge or situation arose and it had been Scribonius whose solution had proven to be the best alternative. In many ways, the respect with which Scribonius was regarded was second only to Pullus, and if you had asked Pullus, he would have instantly offered up his friend as the man most worthy of that honor. Consequently, when Pullus now called on Scribonius, all eyes turned to him, and the men fell quiet, waiting to hear what the former Secundus Pilus Prior had to say. The man himself, although he recognized how the others viewed him, was still uncomfortable being the center of attention, which he found quite distracting. Nevertheless, he applied his mind to the situation.

"Figulus, you're certainly right in what you say," Scribonius began, but everyone knew that more was coming, "our men could cut down raw troops like wheat, and it would cost Antonius and Octavian a huge number of lives, before they could overwhelm us just with sheer numbers. But then what?"

He fell silent for a moment, as he let this sink in with the others, and each man began to cast his mind past the immediate future. Before they could arrive at their respective conclusions, however, Scribonius continued his own thoughts.

"Let's face certain facts. While it would make the two of them extremely unpopular with the mob, since most of the men we killed would be from the Head Count, what about us? Would we be viewed as being any better?"

"Of course we would! We'd just be defending ourselves! Surely no Roman would fault us for that!"

This came from Tiberius Fonteius, who was the shortest-tenured of all the Primi Pili, stepping into the shoes of Vibius Batius, the Primus Pilus of the 5th Alaudae who was slain by a freak shot from an arrow during the battle of the ridge. It had surprised Pullus, and the other Primi Pili, for that matter, that Fonteius hadn't chosen to stay behind to enjoy what was the pinnacle of a man's career, but, like Pullus, he had grown tired of watching his men die.

Scribonius regarded Fonteius for a moment, then said, "In theory, no, they wouldn't find any fault in our actions. But that's dependent on one condition, and it's a condition that I'm sure neither Antonius nor Octavian is willing to fulfill for us—Octavian in particular—and that's not spread poison in the mob's ear. Do you think that if we decide to stay and fight, they're not going to do exactly what they promise? And if we choose to make our stand here, they're going to surround us and none of us will be able to tell the citizens of Rome the truth. If we had the opportunity to state our case in the Forum, then by all means, I'd agree with you, but they're not going to give us the opportunity to do that." Looking over to Pullus, Scribonius asked, "How many Urban Cohorts are there? And one is already out there, digging in to stop us from entering the city."

"I think there are three," Pullus said reluctantly, "and yes, they're digging in. But I saw those men up close. They're not going to give us any trouble."

"But for how long?" Scribonius countered. "Isn't the 9th just two day's march away?"

"Those bastards," Figulus spat. "I doubt they're much better than these Urban Cohorts that Pullus is talking about."

This was another thing Pullus had in common with Figulus, and, in fact, with most of the men in the room. The 9th Legion had been left behind by Caesar when he embarked for Parthia for the simple reason that he didn't trust them. In the last stages of the civil war, after the defeat of Pompey, and even after Scipio was crushed at Thapsus, and the resistance to Caesar devolved onto the shoulders of the slain general's sons, the 9th had defected to them. It was a betrayal that not only stung Caesar, but the men of the 7th, 8th, and 10th, as well, because they had been collectively known as the Spanish Legions in honor of where the Legions were formed, and was something in which the men took great pride. Now, the thought that it would be the 9th they would likely have to face first was an example of a mixed blessing.

"The 9th may not be very good, but in numbers alone, they're more of a challenge than the single Cohort that's out there right now," was Scribonius' comment.

Pullus thought he was getting a glimmering of where Scribonius might be going, which prompted him to ask that very question.

"Where are you going with this, Sextus?" he asked his friend quietly.

"Well, it seems to me that whatever we do, we have to do it as soon as possible. Every watch that goes by means that Antonius and Octavian have more time to put their own plan into motion. We need to move, and move quickly. But the question is, where do we move to, and what do we do?"

It had long been a habit of Sextus Scribonius to answer a question with one or more of his own, but this was one time Pullus wasn't willing to humor his friend.

"Enough with the Socratic *cac*, Sextus," he snapped, exasperated. "Tell us what you think we should do."

Scribonius did just that, and it was a testament to the boldness and scope of his plan that for several long moments, there was a silence in the headquarters that hung over the men inside, as they digested Scribonius' proposal.

Finally breaking the silence, Pullus asked, "Unless anyone else has a better idea, I think we know what we need to do."

Nobody raised a hand. The rest of the night passed with the Centurions filling out the details of the plan put in motion by Scribonius, and by the time they were through, most of them didn't think it was worth going to the trouble of returning to their own tents for what would be about a watch's worth of sleep. Neither did any of them feel much like talking or spending time together, discussing what the morning would bring. For most of them, it was in the hands of the gods, and by this time the next day, their respective fates would be decided, one way or another.

As eventful as the day before had been, the next one dawned in a manner almost identical to the previous one: cloudless and bitter cold, although it would warm up quite a bit as the sun rose in the sky. Centurion Proculus didn't think he had ever been as tired as he was that morning, but the nervous energy that came from the unknown challenges this day promised kept him awake. The men of his Cohort were just as tired, and if Proculus was being truthful, he wasn't sure that, despite all of their labors throughout the night, they had done much good. It was true that the Via Ostia was blocked, but it wouldn't take much maneuvering for the men in that camp to bypass it. And after his meeting with Titus Pullus the day before, and seeing firsthand the hard-bitten men that comprised the Legions, he privately prayed that this was exactly what Pullus and his men would do: just go around. He had prided himself on being a hard man, until the day before, and now he just wanted to live to see another sunrise. Proculus had been summoned to meet with the Master of the Horse and the young Caesar, and it was the older man who had given him the order to begin the process of blocking off this camp from access to Rome. But it had been Octavian who had told Proculus that Pullus and his men were actually deserters, and not returning heroes, who needed to be put down like mad dogs, before their cowardice and dishonor was known to the good citizens of the city. Proculus hadn't believed a word of it; all he knew was that the two most powerful men in Rome wanted these men dead, and that it was his misfortune to be the commander of the duty Cohort.

Of course, the other two Urban Cohorts had been mobilized and arrived late in the day and were given their own tasks. One Cohort had been sent to a spot between the port and where Pullus' men were camped, constructing a barricade similar in nature to that of Proculus' Cohort. As inexperienced a tactician as Proculus may have been, he didn't think it was a smart idea to divide what force they had, understanding that their only chance lay in strength of numbers. The paving stones were too solidly embedded to dig up, so on the roadway itself, a number of wagons had been turned on their sides, then weighted down with a variety of materials. Only on the flanks of the road had ditches been dug, and it was such a ditch that Proculus was inspecting now, although he wasn't sure what he was looking at. Nevertheless, he frowned as he stared down into its depths, giving a grunt that he hoped would be sufficient to let his men know he was satisfied. Speaking of the men, they were understandably nervous, but since Proculus wasn't much better off, he provided little comfort to these men who, up until today, had been barely more than glorified guards. Now they were expected to fight and stop men who, whatever their circumstances were concerning their status, had managed to survive a campaign that had lasted thirteen years? Antonius had told him that the 9th had already been dispatched and were even now marching on Rome, so that Proculus and his men "only" had to contain Pullus' for a day, as if it was such an inconsequential order that it barely merited mention.

In the middle of the night, reinforcements had arrived, in the form of what looked like every man from the various *ludi*, the gladiator schools, of which there were three in the city or nearby enough that men could be summoned. Although Proculus thought of them as little better than rabble, he was nonetheless glad of their company, even if they were kept separate and under the eye of their guards, on the left flank of his own position; the other Cohort occupied the space to his right. The eastern sky—which at least meant that the sun would be over Proculus' shoulder—was just beginning to turn pink, when he heard a commotion behind his position in the form of shouts of challenge, followed by what he assumed was the shouted watchword. Turning away, he told his Optio Ovidius, standing next to him, to stay put as he went to find out the cause of the disturbance. He had gone perhaps a hundred paces from the makeshift breastworks when he saw in the gloom ahead a group of men striding in his direction. At their head, Proculus saw a slender figure, and with the help of the torchlight provided by the two men flanking the leader, he recognized the young Caesar, dressed in armor, with his *paludamentum* swirling behind him. Instead of closing the gap, Proculus stopped, came to *intente,* and rendered his most perfect salute, which was barely acknowledged, as Octavian swept past.

"Well?" Octavian snapped. "Is there any sign of them yet? Or are they still cowering behind their walls like the cowards they are?"

Proculus wasn't the smartest man, but he instantly understood,—both by the words and the volume with which they were spoken—that Octavian had meant this to be heard by the men manning the barricades. So, he's going through with his story, Proculus thought, as he wheeled about and hurried to catch up with his commander.

"No sir, no sign sir. We can't see much, of course, but there's been no sign of them."

"Good," Octavian's voice had dropped down to a point where he could almost be talking to himself. "The longer they stay there, the better." Having reached a spot where he had to clamber up onto the parapet that had been constructed to give the men a perch from which to fight at an advantage, he turned and beckoned to Proculus to join him, raising his voice again, as he said, "But I know your men will do their duty to protect Rome and its citizens from these scum, Centurion! And I can see that they're ready!"

Octavian clearly expected a cheer when he was finished, but when none was forthcoming, even in the pale light Proculus could see the flush of anger and embarrassment rush to the other man's face.

Nevertheless, his voice didn't change in inflection, as he continued, "But you need to know that you're not alone! Help is coming! Even now the 9th Legion is on its way and might be here by the end of the day!"

This did rouse a cheer, with what Proculus thought was an embarrassing level of enthusiasm, but in his heart he couldn't blame his men for their feelings. Like himself, he knew that none of them had joined the Urban Cohort with the prospect of facing the most veteran Legionaries that Rome had to offer, especially those that had clearly swept every enemy they met from the field. This robust answer to Octavian's words wasn't lost on the young Caesar either, Proculus could tell, because now his lip curled up in the same way that a man smelling a fresh turd might.

He said nothing, however, instead turning back to face in the direction of the camp, so that only Proculus could hear him mutter, "All we need is a day. Just...one...day."

Proculus wasn't sure what moved him to respond, but he assured Octavian, "My boys will give you that, sir. They may not be the equal of the Legions, but they're good boys, and they'll do their duty."

How he would live to regret those words. At least, for the rest of what remained of his life, which wasn't very long.

"Ready?"

Scribonius was the man who asked the question of Pullus, who didn't respond immediately. Instead, in his usual thorough fashion, he took a step to the side from his spot at the head of the column that had been formed up, squinting in the low light at the men neatly arranged in their ranks and files. Despite the fact they were parading in the normal fashion in which they started the march every single day, that was the only part that was familiar, to any of them.

"I suppose so," Pullus said finally, turning back from his inspection, "although I've never gone into battle dressed like this."

Scribonius grinned, reaching out to finger the shiny material of the tunic that Pullus had chosen.

"It *is* strange," he admitted, "but I think we look magnificent!"

"That we do," Pullus agreed. Then, with a cheerfulness that he had practiced so many times before battle, he said, "Let's not keep them waiting."

Turning to one of the three *cornu* players that still remained, Pullus nodded, and the man began blowing the notes that sounded the command to advance. While the notes were the same, the horn that normally blew them was the *bucina*, the horn that was used to sound the changes of the watch and the various other pieces of information that were required for the smooth running of the camp itself. This difference was due to the simple fact that not one *bucinator* was left, but since this had been the case for the last year of the journey home, the men were accustomed to respond, and such was the case this day. Stepping out, Titus was at the head of the column, and the air filled with the tramping sound of almost a thousand marching men. Exiting the camp, in order to reach the road, the column would have to perform an oblique turn, but in doing so, they would intersect the road less than two hundred paces from the barricade. If they made the same type of oblique turn in the opposite direction, however, they would be able to skirt the spot where the fortifications ended, waiting for more manpower to presumably extend the line to...where? Pullus wondered about that; were Antonius and Octavian planning on completely encircling Rome from his puny force? He thought that extremely unlikely. No, he was sure Scribonius was right, that the pair was buying time for a sufficiently strong force to crush Pullus and his men. And if Pullus and his men had decided to go back aboard the ships and sail away—essentially caving in to the demands of the Master of the Horse—they would have to perform what would be in effect two oblique turns to reverse their direction, but Pullus had already been informed of the presence of a barricade blocking the road into the port and knew that navigating a way around it was a practical impossibility, thanks to presence of the vast array of warehouses and shops spread on either side of the Via Ostia.

Not that this was ever a consideration; neither Pullus nor any man of the returning veterans was disposed to come all this way and not achieve his goal. Given the options, the most prudent one would have been to make the oblique turn that would take Pullus and his men to the far end of the fortifications. Now that the light was growing stronger, it was hard for Pullus to squint into it and see clearly, but he trusted his experience, which told him there was a large force of men waiting for that move. However, what Pullus saw also told him that it was unlikely that these were the Urban Cohorts facing him. Despite his low opinion of them, he couldn't imagine they would be allowed to form up in what looked like little more than a random mob of men. Gladiators, the insight flashed into his mind. Of course! These would be the only other experienced men available to the two masters of Rome on such short notice, so for a moment Pullus was tempted to deviate from his plan and head his men directly for this group of men, whom he held in such scant respect, sure that his men would make short work of them. He suppressed the thought, resisting his instinct to fight, so that when he came to the spot where he needed to make his decision, he didn't hesitate, ordering an oblique turn that pointed the column directly to the road. From a purely tactical viewpoint, this was the worst choice available to him and the men, since he would put the column in a position that made them vulnerable to attack from the mob of men on what would be their right flank. Because of the distance and the waxing light, Pullus couldn't quite make out what the far end of the fortifications looked like, but he was sure that there was another force positioned there. He was right: that was where the other Urban Cohort was located, setting up what would be a textbook pincer maneuver, as Pullus and his men presumably were to assault the barricade across the road. Antonius and Octavian would have a good chance of not just delaying, but also mauling Pullus' men so badly that it would be a case of the 9th just coming in to mop up the remnants.

However, neither Pullus, nor any of his men of any rank, had any intention of fighting his way through the barricade. This was why they were attired in a manner that would be the envy of every class of working woman, from the lowest Suburan whore to the highest paid courtesan of the sort whose wares men like Antonius would be happy to sample. While Pullus wasn't sure Scribonius' plan would work, one thing he knew down to his old soldier's bones: Rome had never seen a spectacle like this.

Numerius Ovidius was standing just a few paces away from his Centurion and the young Caesar, so he could hear every word they said, although their conversation, such as it was, echoed his own thoughts.

"What in Hades is *that*?"

It was a combination of gasp and whisper, so Ovidius couldn't determine which of the other two men uttered the words, but his eyes were no less riveted to the sight before him. It looked like...nothing he had ever seen before, Ovidius realized, and a part of him applauded the idea that he was viewing something he was sure would be an event that would live in Roman history for the ages, something he could tell his grandchildren about. Provided he survived the day, and that sobering thought arrested his momentary flight of fancy.

"I don't know exactly, but it looks like a formation of whores on parade," Octavian was trying to sound scornful—at least, that's what Ovidius thought—but he wasn't very successful.

What was true was that the marching men were clad in what looked like tunics made of some sort of material from which a glow emanated in the steadily rising sun, and because of the vast array of colors, the winking light given off was simply the most spectacular thing Ovidius had ever seen. And yet, in stark contrast was the rhythmic movement of men marching in perfect cadence with each other, looking like a multi-legged beast whose upper body was composed of rippling scales of almost a thousand colors. So enthralled by the sight, it took a moment for Ovidius to realize that, again in stark contrast to what looked like a marching festival, the formation was marked and divided by men carrying what looked like Cohort and Century standards. Despite this martial touch, when the marching column made its turn and began angling towards the road, once they came within perhaps three hundred paces, Ovidius could see that none of the men appeared to be armed. He wasn't the only one to notice.

"They're not carrying weapons," Ovidius clearly heard the surprise in his Centurion's voice. "None of them, it looks like."

"Then this will be the easiest battle you ever fought," Octavian replied curtly.

The words caused Ovidius to tear his glance away from the approaching column to stare over at the place where Proculus and Octavian were standing, and he saw the look of confusion and uncertainty on his Centurion's face.

"Sir?" Proculus' tone was hesitant, as he kept shifting his glance from the man at his side to the column, still approaching inexorably and showing no signs of slowing down to shake out in anything other than this column. "I'm not sure I understand."

"What's there to understand?" Octavian snapped, and Ovidius could see the red creeping up the back of the young Caesar's neck, disappearing into the blonde curls. "You have your orders. They haven't changed, just because these cowards are too afraid to carry weapons into battle!"

"But, they're not..." Proculus started to protest, but was stopped when Octavian turned on him.

Ovidius couldn't see Octavian's face, but whatever was in it caused Proculus, who was facing Ovidius, to turn as pale as if he were dead; and although Ovidius couldn't hear what was said, he didn't really need to, just from his Centurion's reaction. Proculus didn't answer and that apparently didn't satisfy Octavian, but all the other man could muster was an abrupt nod of his head. Understanding, after a moment that this nod was all he would get at the moment, Octavian turned his attention back to the scene before him, as did Ovidius. That's when he saw that following the column were a number of wagons, all of them obviously heavily laden because of the way they rocked ponderously back and forth over the uneven ground, before they reached the roadbed. Now that the column was a little more than a hundred paces away it stopped, brought to a crashing halt by a shouted command that was instantly repeated down the length of it. Ovidius stared at the now immobile mass of men, his attention torn between the sight before him and the scene to his left, where both Proculus and Octavian also stood, seemingly struck as immobile and dumb as the colorful formation a short distance away. This pause gave Ovidius a chance to examine the waiting men more closely; it was then that he noticed that despite his initial impression, there was some sort of order to the colorful, shiny tunics worn by the men. He quickly determined that those men he was sure were Centurions were dressed in scarlet red tunics, similar to the soldier's tunic, but of so deeper and richer a color that there was really no comparison between the two. Ovidius also noticed that while uniform in color most, if not all, of the tunics had some sort of embroidery on them, but he was too far away to make out what it was, or even if the embroidery was the same. Ovidius then saw that the men who were standing in what would have been his own spot in such a formation were also dressed in a uniform manner, but the color of their tunics were a deep, rich blue, most of them also similarly embroidered. For the men in the ranks, there didn't seem to be any pattern of wear, at least that he could determine, but his examination was cut short by the sight of a group of men detaching themselves from the column. All of them wore red tunics, and as they approached, they got close enough that Ovidius could see that, in fact, the embroidered pattern was different for every man, although many were very similar. Every man held his arms out to his sides, showing that he was obviously completely unarmed, although every man wore the Legionary's belt and carried a *vitus*. Leading them was the huge Roman who had faced down Proculus, his hands held out as well, but there as something in his bearing that would have drawn every eye towards him, even if he had not been so large and muscular.

"That's far enough," Octavian's voice was cold, but Ovidius thought he detected a tremor there. "Have you come to throw yourself on my mercy?"

"No, Gaius Octavius," Pullus answered calmly, eliciting a hiss of indrawn breath from the man he was addressing.

"That is Caesar, to you," Octavian hissed.

"You're right," Pullus answered, which Octavian clearly wasn't expecting. "You're Caesar's adopted son and heir."

Pullus paused, and like his first sight of the colorful column, Ovidius would always remember that moment. Not what was said, as much as this moment, when it seemed as though time itself had stopped, when everything was momentarily suspended; in his later imaginings, as brief as they would turn out to be, Ovidius would think that everywhere there was a Roman presence in the world, that every man, woman, and child paused their own activities, as if waiting for what would happen next.

"But he's not dead, and we're the proof of that." Before Octavian could react further, Pullus raised his voice, using the power of his lungs to bellow, "We are here to tell you that Caesar, the *real* Caesar lives! He is now a living god, in the Islands of Wa, a land far, far to the east, where the sun rises! We are the Romans of his army who have been released from our service and sent home to..."

"That's a *lie*!" Octavian's voice wasn't nearly as powerful as Pullus', so what came out was a screeching howl of rage, as he pointed a shaking finger down at the giant Roman. "He's a liar! They're deserters and they've concocted this story to prevent justice from being done! Don't listen to his lies!"

Turning to Proculus, his face was twisted with rage and fear as he grabbed Proculus by the arm with a strength born of desperation.

"What are you standing there like a statue for, you...*idiot*?" Octavian snapped. "Give the order or I will! Release your javelins and cut this lying dog down!"

Ovidius happened to be watching Proculus' face as Octavian screamed at him, and he knew his Centurion well enough to see the flicker of anger cross his face at Octavian's invective. Still, he had been given an order, and perhaps if Octavian hadn't insulted him, he would have instantly obeyed. But he didn't; he paused for a moment, and Titus Pullus, veteran of thousands of moments where the outcome rested on the edge of a blade, understood the opportunity he was given.

"Proculus," he called up to the Centurion, "you can see we're unarmed. We're not here to cause any trouble. We're here as Roman *citizens*," he emphasized the word, understanding that if Proculus was like any Roman, this made an enormous difference, "and honored veterans of years of service to Gaius Julius Caesar, whom you rightly revere as a god, asking that we be allowed to march to the Forum and make our case to the people of Rome themselves. Let them decide the truth of the matter."

"No!" Ovidius didn't think it possible, but Octavian's voice was even shriller. "They can't be allowed into the city! You have no idea what kind of trouble they're here to stir up!"

"But they're unarmed, sir," Proculus had finally found his voice, and while there was a tremor there, his anger at Octavian's slur gave him the courage he needed to look the other man in the eye. "What kind of mischief can they really make, if they're not carrying any weapons?" Proculus' voice dropped, but Ovidius could still hear what his Centurion said, "Unless they're telling the truth? Is that why this is such a problem?"

"How *dare* you?" Octavian hissed. "How dare you accuse me of lying?" Straightening his back, the young Caesar tried to reassert his self-control, for which he had been famous, up until this moment. "Very well. You're relieved of command, effective immediately. Where's your Optio?"

Spinning around, he spotted Ovidius, who in that instant profoundly regretted his curiosity and need to stand closely enough to hear.

Snapping his fingers, Octavian commanded, "Come here Optio. Let's see if you're a better Roman than this fool who's so easily swayed by a coward."

"Octavian," Pullus' voice cut through the air, stopping Ovidius in his tracks. "I just heard you call me a coward. I'm no such thing, but I think you are, and I'm willing to prove it." He had said these words relatively quietly, but now he raised his voice, so that everyone nearby could hear. "Therefore, I challenge you, Gaius Octavius, to single combat, here and now, in the style of our revered ancestors, that you may meet me in a manner befitting a member of the clan of the Julii, and as the heir of Caesar, the greatest warrior I have ever known."

Octavian's gasp of shock was audible several paces away, and Ovidius had moved to a spot where he could see the look on the man's face. While Octavian kept his head immobile, Ovidius could see his eyes darting back and forth. He looks like a trapped rat, Ovidius thought. However, Octavian remained motionless and, more importantly, silent, not answering Pullus' challenge. Finally, after what was probably more than thirty heartbeats' of time had passed, Pullus broke the silence.

"That's what I thought," he said softly.

Then, dismissing Octavian with a contemptuous shake of his head, he turned back to Proculus.

"Centurion, I'm going to have my men come and clear this barricade away. Whether you choose to obey him," he indicated Octavian with a dismissive gesture, "or allow us our rights as

Roman citizens is up to you. But I tell you this now. I give you my word as a fellow Centurion and Primus Pilus of Caesar's 10th Legion, that if you choose to obey young...*Caesar* here," it was the first and would be the penultimate time Titus Pullus ever referred to Octavian by the title he so desired, "we won't resist. You'll be able to cut us down like wheat before the scythe, and all that will be left to show that we ever existed will be these." He plucked at the shiny tunic he was wearing, thankful that it was not only a cool day, but that sweat didn't show up as easily with silk as it did wool. "They'd make fine keepsakes for your men, and I suppose that they could be viewed as your reward for obeying him."

Finished, Pullus stood there, feet apart, arms at his side, and looking up calmly at Proculus. Octavian seemed to have given up resorting to histrionics and shouts, standing there as pale as a corpse, staring down at Pullus with undisguised hatred, and, both Proculus and Ovidius recognized, with more than a little fear.

"If you let them pass, I will promise you one thing," Octavian said very softly, so that only the two men next to him could hear, "but both of you will be dead men." Surprising them both, he gave a chuckle then, laced with bitterness and loss, "And you can join me in Hades."

Numerius Ovidius never got the chance to ask Proculus what had convinced him to do as he did, but if he had, Proculus' answer probably would have surprised him. It hadn't been the insult, and it hadn't been the threat of death that spurred him to act. No, it was something much, much simpler, but for all its simplicity, every bit as powerful a motivator, and that had been when Titus Pullus had called him a "fellow Centurion". That simple act of respect and recognition of Proculus as an equal had done more to give Proculus the courage to defy the most powerful man in Rome than anything else could have. Not only did he defy him by allowing Pullus' men to pass, but he went even further by ordering his own men to jump down and assist in tearing down the barricades. Seeing the flurry of activity, the men on either flank who hadn't been able to hear the exchange between Pullus and Octavian assumed that, for whatever reason, these men were no longer a threat and were being allowed to pass. For the first time in his life, Octavian simply panicked at the sight of both Urban Cohorts streaming from their positions to help tear down the barricades, turning and fleeing back to the city, but not before snapping an order to a handful of his bodyguards, who stayed behind. With so many hands, the work went quickly, as the wagons were emptied and then set back upright before being hauled across the road. All this activity certainly didn't go unnoticed, which was another oversight of both Antonius and Octavian, because by the time the work was finished, the road was lined with people, all the way to the Porta Romana. Some had been trying to start their daily business, while others, hearing about some sort of excitement, had come to gawk, and in this they weren't disappointed by what they saw that day. With the barricade clear, the marching column of Pullus' men resumed, except that this time they had an armed escort of an Urban Cohort leading the way. It was not, however, the Cohort of Proculus, because there had been an incident that left the Cohort in complete disarray. Somehow, in the confusion of all the work being done, both the Centurion and the Optio of the Cohort had vanished. In fact, it wouldn't be for another third of a watch before their bodies were found by their frantically searching men. Having the other Cohort leading the way was no accident and had been another suggestion from Scribonius.

"If they lead the way into the city, it will be hard for anyone to stop us," was how he put it.

As it would turn out, Octavian had been so panic-stricken that he hadn't thought to order the gate to be closed, not that it would have done anything more than delay this impromptu procession. The sight of Rome's walls had instilled the veterans with a thrill of anticipation, but the Centurions did their best to keep emotions in check, as they drew closer.

"It's not over yet," was repeated down the ranks, but for Pullus the sensation was one of trying to curb a stallion that wanted its head to gallop.

His own sense of suppressed excitement, still tinged with fear of what lay ahead, made the sensation even stronger, but from outward appearances, he was the same, impassive figure of the Primus Pilus and man who had led these veterans across the world. As he had hoped, thanks to Scribonius' suggestion, the gates were wide open, and now that he could see past them, he saw that the throngs of people that had gathered outside continued inside, as well.

"Smarten it up boys, we've got an audience," he called over his shoulder.

Entering under the archway, the first thing that struck Pullus was the silence, which he found a bit disorienting. He wasn't sure what he was expecting, but he had thought that people would be chattering or shouting to the marching men, but they seemed to be...uneasy. That was it, he realized: the people watching this weren't sure what they were seeing, and that's when he got the idea.

"Boys, I think these good people would like to hear a tune, don't you?" he bellowed.

There was only a moment's hesitation, before he was answered by a roar of approval and affirmation, to which he replied, "I think there's only one song for this occasion, don't you?"

Again, he was answered positively, but there was a moment's silence, with only the crashing sound of the hobnailed *caligae* bouncing off the stone walls of the buildings. Then, a lone voice started singing, then was instantly joined by the other voices, so that before a few heartbeats had elapsed, even the sound of marching was overwhelmed by a masculine chorus, bellowing out a song. It was based on a melody that had first been heard by the people of Rome fifteen years before, on the occasion of Caesar's first triumph, for his conquest of Gaul, and it had been created by the men of the 10th. Over the years, it had been adopted by the entire army and verses had been added, as Caesar and his army marched, fought, and died their way across an entire world. On the long march back, the returning veterans had added even more verses, so that the song was now very long, filling the entire time it took to march to the Forum and then some, which caused Pullus to amend the route on the fly. But it was more than worth it, because not only did it pass the time, it told the citizens of Rome a truth that would have been denied to them. In fact, the song was so informative that the marching column formed a tail as people hurried along behind them, to hear the entire story of the wondrous things that Caesar and his men had seen and the valorous deeds they had performed in their name. In this impromptu parade, which took more than a third of a watch, any chance that Antonius and Octavian had to stop the citizens of Rome from learning the truth was shattered, and the consequences would reverberate for years to come.

By the time they reached the Forum, Pullus and the men were met by both Marcus Antonius and Gaius Octavius, who, while he had regained some of his color, still looked very close to the edge of collapse. Antonius was more composed, but it was easy to see his wariness, as he watched the formation, minus its escort of Urban Cohort, which had peeled off shortly before the formation came marching into the very heart of Rome. Both men were standing on the rostra, and once Caesar's veterans came to a halt, Pullus, Figulus, Scribonius, and the other Primi Pili, all adorned in scarlet, detached themselves from the men and came marching in their own small formation. Clutched in Pullus' sword hand opposite his *vitus* was another scroll, and the two men on the rostra glanced at each other, their thoughts running along similar tracks.

"What now?" Octavian muttered.

"I don't know, but keep your mouth shut, boy, and let the adults handle this," Antonius was a master at using just the side of his mouth so that at a distance one wouldn't know that he was speaking.

In another sign of Octavian's state of mind, he turned and shot his older colleague a poisonous glance; normally, he had too much self-possession that he would never have deigned to acknowledge Antonius' gibe. But today hadn't gone anything like what had unfolded in his mind, and it was on a pair of shaking legs that he now stood, thankful that the toga he had donned after returning to the city hid the signs of his fear. Nevertheless, he chose not to reply, instead turning back to watch the small group of men approach. The earlier atmosphere of silence had been shattered, at first by the song sung by Caesar's veterans, then by the tumult of roaring approbation that grew with every chorus, as the citizens of Rome—the despised Head Count who individually meant nothing, but collectively meant everything—had learned of all that Caesar and his brave men, Roman men, had accomplished, and learned their story in a manner that guaranteed that it would be absorbed. Verses of the ditty would be sung in the taverns, the *insulae*, and wherever Romans gathered, for many, many decades to come, and both of the men standing on the rostra knew it. What they didn't know, and what was the cause of equal fear—even if Antonius hid it better—was what the mob would do, once they learned the truth. At worst, both Antonius and Octavian understood that they might be breathing their last breaths of air, seeing their last view, and for Antonius, at least, it brought him some comfort that he would die here, in Rome, in the Forum. Now, Pullus called a halt to his

Centurions, directly in front of the rostra, where he rendered a salute, prompting the crowd, which was now packed so densely that not a paving stone was visible, to stop their shouting. It couldn't have been called quiet; there was a thrumming buzz as people continued whispering their own opinions of what was happening before them, or youngsters tugged at their father's sleeve in a demand to be lifted, so that they could see, as well.

"Marcus Antonius, Master of the Horse, I am Titus Pullus, the former Primus Pilus of the 10th Legion Equestris, of *Caesar's* Legion, and these men are under my command, at least until I discharge my last duty, and that is to convey them back to Rome." Pullus swallowed hard; this was the point where it could all go wrong. Lifting the hand with the scroll high in the air, so that it could be seen by all, he continued, "And I bring orders from the man who was Dictator for Life and who has been rightly deified here in Rome, because he has also been recognized as a god in the lands from which we departed, more than three years ago."

Pausing again, it was a good thing that he did, because now the buzzing grew into a rolling thunder of sound that wasn't quite a mob in full voice, but was still impossible to shout over. Waiting for it to die down, Pullus picked back up, "And I have come here, as a Roman citizen, freely born and invested with all the rights of a man who has fought for Rome, and I claim my right to address my fellow citizens!"

The roar resumed, quickly rising in its intensity to the point that it easily beat their previous volume, as each Roman in the crowd, both men and women—despite the fact that the latter had no such right themselves—shouted their support of Pullus' right to be heard. Standing on the rostra, both Antonius and Octavian were thinking furiously, but while the latter Roman's mind was clearly superior and capable of working much more quickly, it was the experience of a lifetime that led Antonius to draw the conclusion first that Octavian would reach a few heartbeats later. For Octavian knew that Pullus was only partially correct: a Roman citizen did have the right to be heard, but only a certain type of citizen, namely a man of property, meaning that he had to be at least an equestrian. However, while Octavian suspected quite strongly that a man like Titus Pullus had the wealth that was required to enter the equestrian class, provided he had a sponsor, he knew without a doubt that Pullus hadn't been officially entered into the rolls of Rome as such. That meant that, technically, Pullus did not, in fact, have the right to speak to the crowd. Octavian was about to open his mouth to call for silence, so that he could make this point, but his mind had continued operating, moving past the immediate victory he was sure he could gain by citing the ancient laws of Rome, and he quickly realized that the crowd assembled before him wasn't the type to be swayed by such legal niceties. In fact, they would probably view his argument as quibbling, just the sort of thing that the upper classes liked to use when doing something to take advantage of their social inferiors. From that, it didn't take much to convince Octavian that he was likely to be rent limb from limb, torn apart by a mob that he knew was equal in savagery to their ancestors, who had ripped apart the Gracchi. This was the same conclusion reached more quickly by his senior colleague, who held absolutely no illusions that a large number of people in this crowd were looking for an excuse to take out their inherent rage and frustration on a noble Roman. Pullus stood there, looking up, clearly expecting an answer, but thankfully for once, the noise of the crowd worked to the advantage of the two men standing up there, because it gave them the pause they needed to reach a mutual conclusion. Holding his hands up for silence, it took a moment, but the crowd did fall silent, waiting and watching as Antonius looked down at Pullus, a politician's smile plastered on his face.

"Titus Pullus, it is good to see you again, my giant friend! Know that I've made sacrifices every week for you and all of your comrades who, as far as we knew, disappeared into the mists at the end of the world!"

The first statement was a bald-faced lie; Antonius and Pullus had met briefly, but the 10th had never been under Antonius' command in Gaul, and after Pharsalus, Pullus had gone with Caesar and the two Cohorts of the 6th Legion, when the 10th had mutinied and been marched back to Rome in disgrace by Antonius. However, his second claim about making sacrifices was true, but only because he had viewed them as the politically wise thing to do, in order to appear to honor Caesar and the men who marched away with him.

"And of course you can address the people," Antonius continued, flashing that same false smile more widely, as he scanned the audience, turning his head so that as many people as possible could see his sincerity. He ignored the intake of breath to his right.

"Are you *mad?"* Octavian whispered, but Antonius didn't reply, at least to his colleague.

"So please, come join me on the rostra and let us know all that has transpired and what Caesar wills of us!"

Not surprisingly, this was met with approbation by the crowd, and the volume increased, as Pullus ascended the steps of the rostra and approached the two men. For a brief moment, the three of them had the cover of the crowd to conduct a quick conversation.

"*Salve* Marcus Antonius," Pullus, while no politician, understood that much of what was taking place was theater and that he had a role to play, so his manner was warm as he offered his arm to the older man first.

Antonius didn't take the offered arm; instead, he swept Pullus into a hug, as if he were in fact greeting a friend whom he hadn't seen in many years. This was met by an even larger uproar from the massed spectators at the sight of this friendship and amity. It was a good thing that they couldn't hear what Antonius whispered into Pullus' ear.

"I don't know what you're up to, you son-of-a-whore, but I swear by Dis I'll make you regret it, even if it means my death!"

Pullus, while he hadn't been prepared for the hug, had expected this kind of reception, so he was unmoved by the other man's words.

"Antonius, by the time this is over, you're going to want to kiss my feet. But I might kill you anyway, just for fun."

Breaking the embrace by mutual consent, both men smiled broadly at each other, while their eyes told a completely different story. When Pullus stepped away, however, Antonius, smile still on his face, was a mass of confusion. What did the big oaf mean by that? How could he possibly think that Antonius would be grateful? Meanwhile, Pullus came to face Octavian next, who, it must be said, was doing his best to emulate his older colleague, but without much success.

"Greetings...*Caesar*," Pullus' own smile never wavered, but there was no mistaking the dripping contempt and condescension with which he invested the name, and Octavian's smile faltered.

Regardless of his true feelings, now that Antonius had set an example, he couldn't allow himself to be seen as anything other than as warm in his greeting as the other man. Unfortunately for Octavian, while Marcus Antonius wasn't near Pullus' height, his build and musculature did match, and in definition surpassed that of the Primus Pilus. However, Octavian was neither tall nor robust, so that the sight they presented when they hugged was very much like a son greeting his father, which wasn't lost on the crowd. Even above the clamor came sounds of laughter from the nearest members of the mob, and even Pullus had to suppress a snicker.

His words contained no humor, as this time he was the man who initiated the whispered exchange:

"I notice that Proculus' Cohort wasn't the one to escort us in, and I haven't seen any sight of him. Any idea why?"

Octavian pulled away to give Pullus a cold stare, while the smile stayed.

"They disobeyed my orders, and they were punished for it. Just like you will be."

"Let me tell you something, you gutless little cocksucker," Pullus' words hit Octavian like a slap in the face, as he physically jerked and tried to take a step backward; but Pullus' hand was on his shoulder and clamping down like a vice. "You're not fit to clean the *cac* off Caesar's *caligae*, I don't care if you are his heir or not. If you ever threaten me or any of my men, I've already taken steps to make sure that you'll be identified as Caesarion's killer," Pullus was bluffing, and it was a guess on his part, but he instantly saw the truth in Octavian's eyes as the blood drained from his face and the smile completely disappeared. "So you better hope I live a long and happy life, along with all my men. Now," he clapped Octavian on the shoulder, as one comrade does to another, "listen and learn something."

Antonius had watched the exchange and was in a position to see Octavian's face, so he saw that whatever Pullus said to him had scored a telling blow. Now that, he thought, is something I'll have to find out more about. Then, Pullus turned away and stepped to the front of the rostra, flanked by Antonius and Octavian, and as Antonius had, Pullus held his hands up for silence. It wasn't lost on either man next to him that the crowd quieted down much more quickly for one of their own than they had for Antonius, and it told Antonius that he had been wise to act as he had. With the crowd suddenly silent, the transition from the tumult of noise to the quiet was quite striking, and it even caused Pullus to pause for a moment. But then he spoke, and in doing so, unleashed his other surprise.

"Actually, fellow citizens, I'm not a public speaker," Pullus began, his voice carrying as well as any Roman trained in oratory like Caesar, even if it was for an entirely different reason. With lungs like bellows, he continued, "So instead, I ask your indulgence for a moment, while I ask another man, someone who is better prepared than I am to inform you of all the momentous events that we have seen with our own eyes." Turning a bit, Pullus extended a hand to indicate one of the men in the scarlet tunics who had come with him to the foot of the rostra. "Sextus Scribonius is, or was," Pullus amended with a smile and nod to his friend in what Octavian had to acknowledge grudgingly was a nice touch, "the Secundus Pilus Prior of my own 10th Legion. While I have gained great renown, my friend Scribonius is no less accomplished as a Legionary and Centurion of Rome. And I am lucky to count him as a true friend," the rebuke to Antonius couldn't have been much clearer, and the Master of the Horse felt the blood rush to his face, "but what's most important is that he is a member of the equestrian order, of the family of the Scribonii, one of the oldest and most distinguished in Rome. I believe he is much better qualified to tell this tale of ours and bring you the greetings from Caesar."

Pullus gestured to Scribonius, who had clearly been expecting the summons and who had begun striding towards the stairs. As he did so, Pullus turned in that direction, but before he did, his eyes met those of Octavian's, and he gave him a smile that was unlike the false politician's smile all three men had been wearing. This smile was meaningful, and in that instant Octavian understood that he had been outmaneuvered. Even if he had invoked the letter of the law, this low-born oaf had been ready for this eventuality, because it was easy to prove that Scribonius was, indeed, an equestrian. For the first time, Gaius Octavius experienced the bitter taste of complete and utter defeat. As formidable as his own intellect was, he had convinced himself that he would never be overmatched, that nobody existed, with the exception of his uncle, who was as intelligent and cunning as he was; and if his uncle wasn't dead, he was still very far away. Now he was learning differently, which made it impossible to keep the smile on his face. Unaware of this inner turmoil, Scribonius mounted the rostra, and the hug he exchanged with Pullus was so clearly heartfelt that it unintentionally exposed to the watching crowd the artificiality of what had taken place between Pullus and the two leaders of Rome. Breaking the embrace, Pullus handed the scroll to Scribonius, and with a flourish that was intended to be seen by the crowd, offered Scribonius the spot on the rostra he had just vacated. As the lanky, older man took the scroll and began to unroll it, Octavian was struck by the thought that he looked more like a tutor or one of the philosophers declaiming in the Forum than one of Caesar's most senior Centurions. His examination was interrupted when Scribonius unrolled the scroll, and it took an enormous effort of will to keep his jaw from dropping; the scroll that Scribonius was supposedly going to read from was completely blank!

The plan that Sextus Scribonius had outlined was both simple and comprehensive in its scope.

"If we don't handle this the right way, we're going to have to spend the rest of our lives looking over our shoulders," was how he had put it the night before. "And that's if we live past the next couple of days, which I don't think is likely."

To that end, what he proposed was to put the minds of the two most immediate threats at ease.

"We need to let those two know that we're not a threat," he explained. "And the only way I see to do it is by giving them what they want in such a way that there's no mistaking our intent, but still honors Caesar."

"And how do we do both?" Gnaeus Macro, former Primus Pilus of the 17th Legion asked. "Caesar's orders are very clear. He's still the First Man, and he's letting them know it."

"That's true," Scribonius granted. "But let me ask you this." He paused a moment as he gathered his thoughts. "Let's say, just for the sake of this discussion, that we tell the mob that Caesar's orders are...nothing, essentially." Seeing the blank looks on the others' faces, he expanded, "By that I mean that he orders that whatever his Master of the Horse has decreed as far as the running of Rome, is in fact in accordance with his wishes."

There was a shocked silence, but it was quickly obliterated by the shouts of the other Centurions, each of them competing with the others to get his point across, so that in the space of a couple of heartbeats, it was inevitable that there was an increase in volume. Finally, Pullus' voice overrode those of his companions.

"And what about those fresh Legions that Caesar's ordered, and the fleet that's waiting for them?"

Since this was the question that most of the other Centurions had raised, they immediately fell silent, waiting for Scribonius' reply.

His face was grave, but he didn't hesitate, answering Pullus, "That's what we need to decide. Because make no mistake," he leaned forward in his chair, his voice throbbing with an intensity that was normally lacking in his speech, "there is no easy answer here. At least, not one I've been able to determine. So what we need to come to terms with is this simple question. In order to guarantee our own lives, do we need to ignore Caesar's orders?"

Ultimately, by the time Sextus Scribonius had finished supposedly reading from a blank scroll, then added his own words, he was able to guarantee the safety of the returning veterans of Caesar's army. It meant that Caesar would be waiting, in vain, for reinforcements that would never come, but after a night spent arguing until shortly before dawn, the Centurions reached the conclusion that this was their only real course of action. And as could be expected, it was Scribonius who had offered the clinching argument.

"We're here. Caesar's on the other side of the world. It will take years for him to find out we didn't obey his orders, and it would take years for him to come himself or send someone else. And while he may be a god, personally I wouldn't bet on it meaning that he won't die. We've all seen that he aged, just like all of us, and I suppose he may stop at some point. But do any of you really believe that?" When there was no answer, he continued, "And if he is a god, then does he really need our help? He'll find a way. Besides," he finished, and if the truth were known, this was what provided those doubters with the conviction he was right, "haven't we already done enough for Gaius Julius Caesar? Isn't it time we enjoy the rewards we've earned?"

However, while Scribonius had informed the people that all matters concerning the running of Rome would be left in Rome, he also confirmed that Caesar's will naming Octavian as his heir was to be considered as valid, and that, in fact, Caesar was decreeing that he and Marcus Antonius, Master of the Horse, would rule jointly and equally in Caesar's name. Pullus, standing to the side of Scribonius, knowing what was coming, had subtly shifted his position so that he could study the faces of the two men, as Scribonius revealed this part of the plan. Shock first, he saw, then surprise, followed closely by relief, but as he had suspected, it wasn't long before both men thought through the vast implications of this fictional decree. For, while it was true that it more or less rendered Pullus, Scribonius, and all of the returning veterans irrelevant, it was a solution neither man truly wanted. Pullus could almost see both men immediately begin plotting the method whereby they would wrest control from their rival, and it made Pullus' heart heavy, as he recognized that this meant that in all likelihood there would be more strife among Romans. But, he told himself, that isn't our fight. He and the survivors who had returned with him were done. Even as this thought flashed through his mind, Titus Pullus felt as if a huge burden was being lifted from his shoulders, and, turning back to watch Scribonius finishing his own oration, he felt a smile forming on his face.

Epilogue

Caesar never received the reinforcements, but the truth was that it hadn't surprised him all that much. It had been more of a hope than anything else, and since the reinforcements never showed up, the fleet that had been waiting in the Red Sea had dispersed. This, also, wasn't a huge loss. It hadn't been the entire fleet, and navies were extremely expensive propositions to maintain, so the subtraction of those ships turned out to be a net gain to his treasury. And it wasn't until a little more than seven years after Titus Pullus and the men in his care had returned to Rome, that Gaius Julius Caesar breathed his last, sometime in the night, peacefully. He had been preceded by most of his Legates; only Aulus Hirtius still lived, and he had been appointed as the official guardian of Caesar's son and heir who, even at barely ten years old, had shown to be a prodigy much in the mold of his father. In physical appearance, however, he couldn't have been more different. It was true that he had inherited his father's height, particularly when compared to the Wa, but where Caesar's hair had been like spun gold as a youth, his son's was as black as a crow's wing, and while his eyes were rounder than those of other Wa, his skin was the same golden hue. Most striking, however, was that his eyes were all Caesar: blue like the color of the deepest ice one saw in the glaciers of high mountains, and the mixture of Wa and Roman was extremely striking. The most important thing was that the native-born Wa accepted him and his divinity.

If some of the Wa had doubts about Caesar's divinity, however, they all believed at least in his infallibility, thanks to the two repulses of the Han invaders. These occurred when the Han emperor, angry at what he considered the ingratitude of the upstart Caesar, tried to take by force what he hadn't been able to gain by guile. The second defeat had been so thorough and bloody that it would convince the Han, for many generations, that the Wa were best left alone. As far as Zhang, the Han emissary, was concerned, soon after the first failed invasion he had just...disappeared one day, never to be seen or heard from again. The men of Caesar's army for the most part settled down on the islands, intermarrying and mingling with the people of Wa who, if not happy, were at least resigned to this new reality in their lives. In truth, for the average Wa peasant, nothing really changed, and the ranks of the nobility had been so ravaged in their attempt to dislodge Caesar's army, there was in fact a shortage of men of this rank. Which, not surprisingly, Caesar supplied with his Centurions. Slowly, but gradually, the two cultures merged, but in one area they stayed completely Roman, and that was in the organization and training of what were now known as the Legions of Wa, while at the same time harnessing the martial spirit and skill inherent in the people.

Titus Pullus, Sextus Scribonius, and the rest of the men who returned to Rome never marched another day under the standard, and, in fact, lived out their days as men of wealth and status of varying degrees. In the particular case of the two friends, both of them found themselves elevated into the rolls of the Senate, with both Antonius and Octavian as their sponsors, although it must be said that for whatever reason, the two pairs of men had as little to do with each other as possible. Pullus and Scribonius purchased adjoining estates in the countryside not far from Rome, and it should surprise nobody that they didn't go into Rome often. One oddity, at least as far as their neighbors were concerned, were the additions both men made to their estates, making them almost impregnable to an attack from all but the largest force, complete with a private security force that appeared to be almost completely composed of former comrades, who lived in comfortable housing on the estate. However, most Romans assumed that this was just from ingrained habit and put it down to that and thought little more about it.

Unfortunately, Titus Pullus' premonition of upcoming strife was absolutely correct. In fact, in less than a year, the relationship between the two co-rulers had degenerated to the point that Rome wasn't big enough for both of them. In a move that astonished the Roman world, the two men essentially split the huge Republic into two parts, with Marcus Antonius setting himself up as the ruler of all Roman possessions on the southern side of Our Sea. Then, within a year of installing himself as ruler of the East, word arrived in Rome that he had relocated his headquarters to Alexandria, and it wasn't even in the space of a month or two after this move that word arrived that he and Cleopatra had become a couple. Meanwhile, on the Rome side of Our Sea, despite Pullus' low opinion of the man now recognized by all—except Pullus, of course, as Caesar—not even Pullus could deny that Octavian was proving to be a wise ruler. He also proved to be a master manipulator, because while appearing to be the voice of moderation and compromise, he maneuvered his rival into a position where armed conflict was inevitable. When hostilities finally flared again, pitting Roman against Roman, it was the subject of many, many watches of speculation in the taverns, wineshops, and whorehouses on both sides of the Roman world why neither man called on Titus Pullus, Scribonius, or any of the men who would have been the most experienced and formidable men in either army. However, it should have been no surprise that, even if they had been called, no member of that most select group would have answered the call, not just because every one of these men had endured their fill of fighting. More importantly—even if it was the unknown reason—lending support to one or the other side would have ruptured the uneasy truce between the two men vying for control of Rome and the only group of men who could have made a difference over and above that provided by their sword arms. No, Pullus, Scribonius, and their comrades had fought their last battle, one that changed history and saw Caesar, the *real* Caesar, triumphant.